HIGH SOARS THE EAGLE

Hilda Petrie- Coutts

This novel is dedicated to the memory of my beloved grandson Byron Conn
who believed Scotland should become an independent country.

All the characters in this book are fictional and any similarity to any actual
person alive or dead is purely coincidental.

Chapter One

It was April 1746. The weather wet with a wind that moaned through the dark pines and trembling birch, keening around that small, white walled croft where a young woman stood at her door letting the breeze take long, red gold hair, eyes straining along the narrow path leading downwards from the hill and seeming to disappear as it girded the shores of the loch.

Would he come today—Alan, beloved husband whom she had not seen in so many weary months, torn from her side by events wholly unexpected, but charged with adventure and romance? Her lips murmured sighing plaint into the wind, as hands stretched out longingly before her.

'Alan—Alan, m'eudail—darling of my heart—where are you?' Above her head an eagle flew, talons bearing a struggling fish caught in the deep waters of Loch Dhu. She watched its flight as it soared ever upwards towards its mountain eyrie. Would that she also had wings to fly high, high above the line of mist wrapped hills, peaks still white with winter's snow, that she might take sight of her beloved.

Suppose he had fallen in battle before the English, as had many another in the latter months since the Prince had first unfurled his banner at Glenfinnan. Last August that had been, when he called all men to follow, that he might secure the throne of his Stuart forefathers from the Hanoverian George 2nd. Yes, and to disentangle Scotland from an unwanted union with the old enemy with whom they had so unwillingly been forced to become one country nigh on fifty years ago!

Charles Edward Stuart had come and at first men could not believe it. For no promised backing of French army attended him, no supply of arms—of gold, merely some few friends, as white cockade in bonnet and brandishing the claymore, his sheer charisma had drawn men to him, as many of the clans doubtful at first arose, and with banners waving came streaming towards Glenfinnan at the head of Loch Shiel, looking so fine in their tartans, reckless of the future.

Great victories the highlanders had seen at the start, first the joy of entering Edinburgh, even though the castle was held against them by the government forces, nevertheless it was with triumph that Charles Edward Stuart dined in the royal palace of Holyrood, holding gracious court there for a few weeks. Stories had come back to this far distant glen and Kieran had imagined herself dancing with the handsome adventurer for whose advent all had prayed over the long years. Not that she would really have wished to dance with any but her husband! But the Prince was said to be very fair.

At that time it seemed all was joy and light heartedness; a dream that had been coming true! Kieran sighed, and tossed wind tangled hair back from eyes grey as the low hanging clouds above her head, reflected now in the silver grey of the loch. Months ago, reports had reached them of a wonderful victory at Prestonpans, as afterwards the Prince and his advisors decided to advance into England—and took Carlisle in November, the Prince they said looking very fine as he rode his white charger though the streets to the strains of dozens of bagpipers and acclamation of his wild Highlanders.

When she had heard account of all this, Kieran had felt as though her heart would explode with pride in her countrymen's achievements. A relatively small force proceeding onwards like a scythe through corn—Manchester fell and then on to Derby. London was not much more than a hundred miles away. But word had come of two well equipped English armies advancing towards them—and false rumours of a third. Decision was made to retreat to Scotland and there consolidate.

News that the Jacobite army was once more on Scottish soil and after victory at Falkirk was now moving north, was brought to the glen by word of a wounded Stewart, whose sword arm was now useless and whose feet raw from marching with boots in shreds, had limped his way home amongst the still brown heather to collapse at his mother's door. He explained that Charles Stuart and Lord Murray were making for area between Inverness and Nairn, where they hoped to recruit more men to replace casualties and those who had deserted.

People, including Kieran, had gathered fearfully at Morag Stewart's door to question her son Rory as to the fate of loved ones over these last months. Some heard news that sent them grieving home to the small crofts, managed with courage and difficulty during the men's absence by their womenfolk. Others exchanged worried glances to learn that the second son of King George, William Duke of Cumberland, a seasoned soldier, was leading one of two well equipped armies seeking to engage the Highlanders in bloody battle.

That had been over a week ago. So now this wet April morn, Kieran Stewart experienced a deep unease sweeping throughout her being as she stood there. Why had she this presentiment of approaching disaster? Surely the weather was to blame—this incessant rain, the brooding silence of the glen.

'Guid morrow tae ye, Mistress Stewart,' came a croaking voice and coming towards her between the dripping, gold budding gorse stepped an old woman, wrapped about in a wet plaid, grey hair straggling over deep set dark eyes, wrinkled face like crunched paper, mouth missing several teeth.

'Why, greetings to you, old Maisie! Will ye not come in and take some small refreshment?' Kieran stared uneasily at the woman, who was both feared and respected by all in the glen as being endowed with the sight— an ability to see into the future. She was also possessed of medical knowledge beyond the normal, had healed some near to death and stepped in as midwife when necessary, gently guiding new life into the world. What did she here today?

'Aye—I would rest these aching limbs of mine awhile!' the old eyes swept reflectively over the lovely young girl before her. She was very fair, this Kieran Stewart who had been a Macgregor before marriage to Alan, eldest son of Malcolm Stewart, declared tacksman in his elderly father's stead, for Malcolm had been afflicted with strange memory loss and had kept to his fireside these last few years. The once proud man was now helpless as child, but still looked on with honour in the neighbourhood.

'Then come away in,' said Kieran forcing a smile and stepped back that the woman might cross her threshold. There by the peat fire sat Malcolm Stewart, a dreamy look in pale blue eyes, red rimmed from the smoke. He barely lifted his gaze from the crackling, smouldering peat as old Maisie entered and took a seat beside him.

'Grant ye guid day, Malcolm Mac Iain. How is it with you?' she inquired solicitously. He did not reply and she nodded her head broodingly.

'As well he is, as he is, perhaps young mistress,' she said to Kieran.

'What do you mean, Maisie?' But even as the question passed her lips, Kieran wished she could have bitten it back, for she feared what she was to hear. But Maisie did not reply but instead sat musing into the fire. Kieran now offered a plate of newly baked bannock, some cheese, and a glass of the fine claret saved against Alan's return to this special visitor, who looked up and smiled gravely.

'Ye are kind, young mistress,' she said, and breaking off a piece of bannock, sat eating it as she considered the girl. What she had just seen in the fire had appalled her and her heart was softened towards this young creature who had no notion of what lay so immediately ahead. But the future could not be altered anymore than the past. So she regarded the girl slowly with a stern, unblinking gaze.

'Ye should be strong in the days to come. However painful events may be, keep that deepest part of your soul inviolate. Do not seek revenge lest it destroys all.' She rose to her feet. 'I thank you for this hospitality child.

We shall not meet again, so my blessing upon ye.' She raised a hand towards Kieran and turned to the door.

'Wait! Wait, Maisie—did you see something just now? Alan—he is not dead?' she forced the words out. The old woman paused and looked at her compassionately.

'Not dead,' she replied. 'Better perhaps he were!'

The words echoed through time. Then she was gone, leaving Kieran to restrain a shudder. She turned to her father-in-law, who had not stirred at the advent of the old seer nor yet at her departure. Malcolm lived in a shadowy world of his own these days, but seemed to recognise Kieran at times, when he would turn a kindly smile on her. On other occasions he seemed to be reliving past clan conflicts and would sometimes raise his right arm as though wielding a sword. Then he would mutter fiercely to himself and continue to stare into the fire.

'Was that old Maisie I spied leaving the house,' inquired a young voice and Kieran smiled at the lad who came in, carrying a basket of peats in his strong young arms. Lachlan was her husband's twelve year old step brother, born late to Malcolm Stewart. His mother Ishbel, Malcolm's second wife had died in giving birth to her child and when his father had succumbed to dementia, had been devotedly cared for by Alan. The boy adored Kieran, who although just a few years older than himself he looked on as mixture of sister and mother.

'Lachlan! Yes it was Maisie—and I could wish she had not come!' She forced a smile at the lad, who approached the fire and bowed his head courteously to his father who had retired to an inner world where none could reach him. His gesture was ignored. It had not registered with Malcolm Stewart. The lad turned his face back towards Kieran.

'You wish she had not come--how so?'

'It's no matter. Did you meet any on the hill today?' she asked as she threw another peat on the fire. He shook his head.

'No Kieran. In this rain most keep to their homes. Wild weather it is, as though the very sky is weeping!'

'Do not say so!' she rounded on him angrily and he stepped back in surprise. Then she reached a hand out and touched his arm. 'I'm sorry, Lachlan! My mind is disturbed at the strangeness of old Maisie's words!'

'Why—what did she say to offend?'

'It was more an implication of evil to come!' She gave a small shudder.

'I should not let it worry you—she is a strange person!' He stretched a hand out, and took one of the bannocks. 'You are fine at the baking,' he said with a cheerful grin. 'Is it true old Maisie has the evil eye?'

'I think it is simply that she has the sight,' said Kieran slowly. 'She is able to see into the future beyond man's normal ken, not that she has any real evil in her—but I would not choose to cross her.'

'Did she make mention of my brother Alan?' he asked quickly.

'She said he was not dead,' replied Kieran quietly.

'Why, then surely that is matter for rejoicing, not a long face,' replied the boy, reflecting that women were difficult to read in their moods. Normally Kieran would have reproved him for his lack of courtesy. Instead her thoughts were dwelling on the old seer's words and wondering what they portended.

Suddenly the man sitting head bent at the fireside, straightened, rose to his feet. He seized a poker and started to wield it around his head like a sword, uttering the war cry of his clan! Lachlan caught at Kieran's arm and pulled her to a corner of the room. Round and round Malcolm Stewart thrust and feinted. Then as unexpectedly as it had started his action came to an abrupt end. He uttered a heart rending cry!

'Alas—Alas! Woe is me to have seen this day! The flower of Scotland's youth, lie in their bluid on cauld Drummosie moor!' Then as the two young people watched appalled, he sank back into his chair and pale eyes returned to gazing at the smouldering peat.

'What ever came over him,' whispered Lachlan. 'Surely old Maisie must have cast some strange spell on him!' The lads face had turned pale as he swung about to look appealingly at Kieran.

'Not so,' she replied slowly. 'I believe he spoke in prophecy! If I am right then I fear greatly for Alan!' Her eyes dilated as she spoke, for before her in imagination, she saw the twisted forms of countless men lying dead and dying. She drew in a deep breath and ran to the door and stared out into the relentless rain that was sluicing down. The wind was driving it from the north east and she prayed that if Alan was engaged in battle this day, then this blinding nonstop downpour would not be in his face, but at his back!

'Come awa in Kieran! Ye'll be soaked if ye stand there in the rain!' And at the sound of her young brother-in-law's voice, she managed to get a grip on herself. The eagle caught her eyes again, returning with yet another fish. Then even as she watched its progress, another larger bird swooped and their forms engaged, the fish fell and the original eagle flapped awkwardly to the heather. Was it an omen? Did the vanquished eagle represent Charles Edward Stuart—its victorious adversary the Duke of Cumberland?

'I am getting as fey as puir Malcolm,' she whispered to herself and shaking the rain from her face, went in to attend to her household duties. She glanced at the now quiet form of her father-in-law bent over in his chair staring once more into the fire, and occasionally muttering to himself.

As well it was that none of the inhabitants of that remote croft, perched high on a hillside in Appin, saw the happenings on the battlefield that black day, when a badly armed, hungry and exhausted Jacobite army, faced the fresh and well armed force of the Duke of Cumberland arrayed against them.

There was no disputing the extreme courage of the Highlanders, as due to some error of judgement they were kept stationary, facing the barrage of artillery from the opposing army for what seemed an eternity, before finally being given the order to charge. When they did so swathes of them fell to grapeshot and round shot, as they fiercely engaged the enemy!

With unimaginable bravery the clans advanced again and again across the boggy ground—rain and sleet blown into their faces by the strong north easterly wind as they tried to avoid their fallen comrades and the ground ran red with the choicest blood of the highlands.

Alan Stewart with blood running into his eyes from a head wound saw the Prince for whom they had risked all, escorted from the field by Colonel Sullivan. He at least must be kept safe for the future, and before he fell in a swoon from pain of a sword thrust to his right shoulder, Alan breathed a sigh of relief. At least Charles Edward Stuart would escape from Culloden Moor with his life and surely the gallant young prince would lead them to victory another day.

It was two days later that Alan Stewart regained consciousness and returned to a bewildering world of pain. Whatever was that heavy weight pinning him down on the cold unyielding ground, for it held him in that cramped hollow completely unable to move. He heard voices though, harsh English voices approaching and as they did so, heard the death wails of those lying wounded and helpless, being slaughtered in an orgy of killing. He realised now that he was hidden beneath the bodies of two fallen infantrymen, heard the faint scream above his head, as the wounded man had his throat cut.

'The other two are already dead, Sergeant,' grunted the red coat, wiping his blade on the muddied tartan of the wounded foe he had just dispatched. 'See there's another moving over there! Kill all without mercy said Cumberland and it's a pleasure to carry out such order!'

'Let's get on with it then! Make sure none are left alive. Any prisoners you find are to be likewise dispatched—no need to be gentle about it either!' The voices faded, but Alan did not attempt to move again for another hour. It took all his depleted strength to at last pull himself inch by painful inch, from beneath the bodies of his dead comrades. At last he rolled free, but at first did not dare to raise his head. When he did so, it was to see a solid line of red coated soldiers working their way methodically amongst the dying, and behind their progress, nothing stirred.

He waited until nightfall before cautiously making a move. The redcoats seemed to have retreated to their camp for the night. It was now or never, he realised. The sword thrust to his shoulder was a throbbing agony as was the wound on his head glanced by shot. He would have lost more blood, had the body of a dead comrade pressing heavily on his own prevented such. To begin with he crawled along, not daring to rise to his feet in case some should be keeping watch over this field of the dead. At last he risked it and stumbled between the corpses of the slain until he was clear of the battlefield.

Somehow he needed to make his way back to the west coast, many weary miles away, with the redcoats no doubt patrolling the area looking for straggling Highlanders that they might continue their orgy of killing. There was of course the possibility that the clans might regroup, but considering the scale of the defeat, the great losses his side had sustained, Alan doubted such would be the case. No—home to Kieran, his dear sweet love, with her quiet grey eyes and red gold hair that cloaked her shoulders as she welcomed him into their bed at night.

It was thought of his beloved young wife that gave him strength to go forward. He had not eaten for several days and his stomach ached for lack of food, he was nauseous and faint. Even miles from Culloden, corpses lay scattered beneath every bush and rock, and such was his hunger that Alan searched their bodies and at last found one old man, his dead face dark with blood, who had small bag of oatmeal at his belt and small iron pan. This he took and mixed with water from a racing burn that runnelled its way down the hillside. He knew as he swallowed this first food in many days, that it had saved his life, for he had felt weak unto death.

The two weeks that followed seemed a nightmare to Alan Stewart as he made his way along the south side of the Great Glen, making towards the west, continuously alert to sight of those hated red coats that bloomed like patches of some loathsome flower across the land. Nor could he guess that this was just the beginning of a process by the English to eliminate the Highlanders from their wild and beautiful home. Vermin they were contemptuously referred to by Cumberland and his military, as plans were made to destroy the clan structure that held men to their chiefs. All this was mercifully veiled from Alan whose sole thought now was to regain the security of his home and feel the arms of his beloved Kieran about him.

That sword thrust to his shoulder was source of constant pain, although the wound on his head struck by glancing bullet had almost healed. He had taken to the hills as the road through the Glen presented too great a risk of encountering a redcoat patrol. Sometimes he would freeze behind a bush of gorse, as some twenty feet below him, soldiers marched relentlessly forward to the beat of drums. What now, he wondered? Surely these

English would eventually tire and return to their comfortable homes down south?

Everywhere he came across carnage. Today he heard shots and saw a family with bundles on their backs, a man, woman and a child fall at the roadside. Surely this was sheer bloody murder, he thought aghast. And then through his head a disgraceful idea arose to be swiftly banished. Would it not perhaps have been better if Prince Charles Edward Stuart had not come to these shores, bringing such retribution on his people? But no, he thought defiantly, the bonny Prince was son of their rightful King who should have been crowned James 3rd in place of the Hanoverian usurper who sat on his throne.

A sudden shout alerted him to new danger, as his movement upon the hill was noticed by a troupe of about twenty armed redcoats, proceeding along the road below. Shots rang out and of a sudden the soldiers started up the steep hillside towards him, then as Alan made desperately to run, felt himself pulled by the foot, to slither painfully down into what he realised was the hidden entrance to a cave.

'Quiet man—haud your peace,' whispered a deep gruff voice, and he became dimly aware of a tall man wrapped about in a torn plaid, who pushed him to the extremity of the small cave, whilst replacing the concealing covering of gorse across the entrance. He turned to Alan in the darkness and placed his hand across the younger man's face. 'Quiet now—they come!' he intoned softly.

They heard panting and struggling and cursing within feet of their hideout, the sound of men calling furiously to each other that—'the rebel could not have gone far!' Then the noise faded, but still the two men remained absolutely still. For they knew that the soldiers would make return down the hill once they realised they had lost their prey. Ten minutes later, they heard the harsh, clipped English voices as the redcoats scrambled back down to the road to reform and to march onwards.

'Friend, my hearty thanks to you for your kindness,' breathed Alan now. 'May I learn the name of one to whom I am so indebted?' His companion did not answer at once, but pulled the severed gorse bush aside that he might scan the scene below him. Light diffused into the cave as Alan was now able to discern outline of the other. A tall, well built fellow, his torn plaid secured at the shoulder by a silver broach, then as the man turned, saw his features. A shock of long, dark curls framed a weather beaten, bearded face, the eyes large and well set, mouth firm, his expression grave.

'Sorley Mor Stewart of Appin—and you, my friend?' he demanded.

'Alan Stewart of Glen Ardoch,' replied the younger man. 'So we live but some twenty miles apart!' He held out his hand which was seized in a strong, confidant grip.

'Glad I am to meet you friend,' replied Sorley warmly. 'Is there any news of the Prince?'

'I have spoken to none since I dragged myself off the battlefield wounded, but lucky to escape the ministrations of the redcoats. They were systematically working across the moor, killing any wounded showing sign of life—butchery in its vilest form!' and he swore.

'Damn them to deepest Hell,' agreed Sorley Mor. 'Your shoulder is injured?' He had noted the bloodstains.

'A bayonet thrust, the man not facing me but another—caught me sideways!' It was relief to speak of the happening which he had revisited mentally many times a day.

'I heard they are trained to fight so—catch a man off guard! And your head?' inquired Sorley quietly.

'It has healed itself—a bullet skimmed it. I fell when the bayonet went through me—as I did so, saw men leading the Prince away! Happily he is safe!' he glanced at his companion. 'And you—you are hurt?'

'My thigh, a musket ball went through—luckily did not break the bone, but did much damage—then there is a slash to my sword arm!' He lifted the tartan to expose his thigh and Alan whistled in sympathy,

'How did you get this far, disabled so?'

'I caught a riderless horse—managed to mount it. Rode for some miles when a redcoat patrol appeared out of nowhere, fired on me! The horse fell. I stumbled forward, dived into a burn. They thought I'd drowned.' He looked at the younger man inquiringly. 'Does the shoulder pain you overmuch still?'

'Enough!'

'May I see it?' He smiled and added. 'I am a surgeon, Alan.'

'A surgeon—you mean a real one?' asked Alan voice surprised.

'I studied at Edinburgh years back—spent many years abroad since then,' explained Sorley Mor. 'Let me see that wound, friend.' His fingers were skilful as he tended the hurt, Alan exclaiming to see the bag of instruments and dressings the other produced. 'I kept these wrapped in oilskin in my surgeon's bag at my waist—luckily all remained dry after my dive into the burn!' he straightened up. 'That was a nasty wound—but you were lucky!'

'My grateful thanks to you, Sorley!' and he ventured to the front of the small cave and risked a look out. Yet another redcoat patrol was passing on the road below and he cursed. He pulled his head back and as he did so heard a volley of shots. He risked another glance, but the soldiers were walking briskly forward again. He looked inquiringly at Sorley Mor.

'I thought they had seen us—why the shots do you suppose? I can see no-one else on the road!'

'Do but cast your eyes to the right—below that line of rocks. What do you observe?' asked the other quietly.

'Why sheep—just a few sheep lying very still—they killed them then? But why do such a thing and then march on and leave them there?'

'Work it out, Alan! I heard them talking when I hid on the bank of the burn. The intention is to kill as many of our people as they can, drive off our beasts and kill all sheep so that hunger will prevail across the highlands!' As he looked into Sorley Mor's grim face, Alan realised the man was speaking truth and his blood ran cold at the implication. If this was to be Cumberland's policy, how far into the highlands would he proceed? Surely not as far as his own dear Glen Ardoch! Then he gave a wry laugh.

'Such may be their intention—carrying it out, prove a very different matter!' he snorted. ' Just think man, how many black cattle deck our hillsides—to collect all those a mammoth task, nor do I imagine our people would tamely allow it! Then consider how wide spread our people, small houses clustering in every glen, others in hollows on innumerable hillsides. I do not think Cumberland has enough troops to carry out such nightmare!'

'He has all the forces of the Hanoverian regime at his beck and call. I hope I am wrong in my fears, but this is tactic employed throughout history by conquering armies who seek to break the will of a people—starve them into submission!' Then Sorley Mor gave slight smile as he saw the consternation on the younger man's face. 'But come, Alan—let us worry about our immediate problem—how to get out of this cave unseen and make our way back to the west coast!'

'I cannot wait,' breathed Alan.

'You have a wife waiting for you?'

'Her name is Kieran—she is beautiful! All a man could dream of!' He glanced at Sorley Mor. 'What of you.....' he began then desisted, as he thought he detected a look of pain on the man's face.

'My wife died seventeen long years ago in giving birth to our only son. He died at my side back there at Culloden.' And the words quietly spoken, and without emotion jarred Alan to the reality of their desperate present, like immersion in the cold of a winter tarn. He said nothing, for no words would serve. Instead he placed a sympathetic hand on Sorley Mor's arm. For long minutes there was silence. Then Sorley spoke.

'When did you last eat?'

'Some small oatmeal I took from a dead man's pouch some a few days after the battle. It has been long gone.'

'Well, below us lie some randomly killed sheep! When night falls, we will attempt to drag one up here—how say you?' Alan nodded eager agreement and pulled his plaid about him to wait, for it was bitterly cold in the cave.

They found twin lambs shot at their mother's side and these the men carried up through the wet roughness of the heather. Together they skinned the lambs, and as Alan watched, Sorley dug a hole in the floor of the cave, placed the meat in this and positioning stones above, and proceeded to make a small fire over all using dead heather to make kindling with few sticks he had gathered, Half an hour later, the meat was not cooked through, but no longer raw and was tender. The juices ran from the corners of their mouths as both enjoyed their first real meal in many days.

Then they slept, blessing the heavy mist that had fallen and would obscure any slight sign of smoke from the fire. But as they slept, both men groaned in their dreams, reliving the horrors of battle as men were mercilessly mown down by musket fire and mouth of canon spraying death. When they awoke it was to peer out on a rain-swept dawn. Alan followed Sorley Mor to a small burn that gurgled its way down the hillside, swollen by rain, it waters peat brown. Both men cupped their hands and drank, then splashed their faces—straightened, looked around.

There was no sign of life yet, the redcoats probably still sleeping in tents in a nearby clearing along the road. All was quiet save for a curlew's cry.

'Well Alan, we have a choice! Either we play safe and remain hidden in our cave and risk eventual discovery—or make for home.' He looked for an answer.

'Then let's go! And may the Lord go with us!' said Alan devoutly.

'You have faith, my friend?'

'Why yes. I believe in the Lord God and his son Jesus!' and the words were spoken with conviction. Sorley Mor sighed.

'I envy you that faith, friend. Mine discarded when my wife died and now having lost the fine son to whom she gave birth, I can find no consolation in myths of the church!'

'No myths, Sorley man—but deepest truth. I pray that one day you may regain your faith,' said Alan softly. 'So come—let us go then!'

The long days and nights that followed were fraught with danger for the Jacobites. On several occasions they were glimpsed by armed patrols of redcoats as with legs scratched by gorse and briers, cut by rocks, they progressed leaping, crouching, struggling and breathless from one mountainside to the next, always keeping high above the road as shots would ring out at such elusive target, but each time they disappeared with the swiftness of deer on their native hillsides.

They had skirted Fort William and now were above the Linnhe Loch as they paused for thought. The ferry at Ballachulish was bound to be closely guarded by the military—but perhaps it might be possible to take a fishing boat at night—further along the loch? Afterwards they could never believe their good fortune that an old man, well into his seventies, who had lost both a son and a grandson at Culloden, took risk to row them over in the early hours, torches of the militia playing over the dark waters as they safely evaded peril of being shot on sight.

'I pray the good Lord be with you, my sons,' his only word to them. They whispered their thanks and immediately made for the shelter of a small wood and there spent the night.

'The Glen of Ardoch lies this way—your home some miles more I think, friend Sorley. How would you like to be my welcome guest for a while—if you have none to welcome your homecoming?'

'Members of the clan there will be there. Close family none, save an elder brother who declined to rise with all others of Clan Stewart of Appin! But he had excuse—an Episcopalian minister.' If Alan thought it strange that his friend who had lost his faith should have a brother a minister of the church, he made no comment. Then as dawn painted flame onto the waters of the loch, Alan became aware of another shade of red, streaming out along the road below them. Surely not here too!

They flattened themselves amongst the heather and slithered their way towards a screen of silver birch and scrub alder and took shelter behind a great slab of granite. No small patrol this, but some hundreds of men making determined advance, some breaking off and fanning out in different direction. All this was to compelling drumbeat and shouted orders, as the two companions stared at each other in dismay.

'Down into this ditch, Alan man' and Sorley broke a birch sapling and pulled it over their heads as almost at once they heard feet lumbering up the brae towards them, but to their relief passed by in inexorable upwards progress. As they lay there, the two men suddenly heard shouts—shots and screams coming from high above them. Women's voices keening in sorrow and outrage and they sprang to their feet and rushed upwards in the direction of a tragedy they knew lay ahead.

Panting and apprehensive they reached a grassy clearing amongst the trees, and saw three white washed, turf thatched cottages and a barn, flames bursting up through their roofs, whilst from an ancient oak nearby two men swung, the bough groaning under their weight. An old woman was screeching in eldritch fright and two younger women trying to order their skirts and torn bodices, faces shocked and white.
As they panted their way to stand beneath the tree, Alan made to cut the men down, but Sorley restrained hm.

'Wait! If they soon return and see this done, they will take further retribution against these innocents,' he said thickly. 'Let us see first what we can do for the living.' He bent down over a child laying there, a boy wearing only a plaid—and his throat was cut. One of the women pointed to another child, a girl of some ten years. She was groaning, stripped naked and there was blood on her thighs. A baby lay a few yards away and it had been spitted. Alan rushed behind a tree and vomited.

'Enough of that, man. We only have to face the seeing of it—these to endure it,' said Sorley Mor thickly, as he spoke in the Gaelic to the women in soothing voice. Gradually they quietened as he lifted the little girl in his arms and calling for water, bathed her hurts as gently as a woman.

One of the women called to Alan and pointed urgently towards one of the burning cottages. He hurried over to it and to his horror saw an elderly white haired man lying in the doorway with flames eating at his leg. He was moaning in agony.

'Grandfather is lame—cannot walk. We told the soldiers so—and they laughed—and did this,' she said in wooden tones. And Alan dragged the man out, but even as he did so, the old heart gave way and the man expired. Alan beat out the flames and choked on fresh vomit that came up into his mouth. And with the nausea came anger, fierce and all consuming. What kind of beasts were those who had done such deed. He remembered Sorley Mor's prediction based on brief overheard conversation by their enemy that such was to happen all over the highlands, and his spirit groaned.

A few hours had passed, the redcoat patrol returning to the road at a tangent. Three large and two small graves lay under the whispering birches, the oak tree bare of its human fruit, as now Alan and Sorley helped the distressed mothers with their shocked, frozen faces and the traumatised little girl up the wooded slope into a cave entered by a crevice in the rocks. Here they would stay until sure that the redcoats had left the area—then perhaps with help of neighbours build new shelters of some kind.

The men would have stayed, but Alan was filled with anxiety for the safety of his own wife and family. Now they proceeded with greater caution, for the drums of the redcoats announced their presence ahead. Somehow they had to evade capture by those who dealt death and retribution in such terrible coin. But at least the weather was improving. May had brought trembling new leaf to the trees, fresh grass springing and myriad wild flowers decking the hillsides.

Kieran stood at her doorway as she did every morning, looking hopefully along the rough pathway that led steeply downwards encircling the mysterious waters of Loch Dhu. The sun was shining, the breeze shimmering across water which glittered with a million golden sequins. Spring in all its loveliness was wakening the land to new life, yews suckling tiny lambs, one of the cows soon to calf and all felt right with the world—or would have done so, had it not been for the disturbing rumours of atrocities committed in a nearby glen by the English soldiery.

She was just about to cross the yard to collect eggs from the hen coop when she thought she saw movement down below. She felt a tremor of fear pass over her, stared, and then an explosion of joy filled her heart! It was Alan! He was safe—and at his side another. Kilting up her skirts she started to run down towards them, crying his name in sobbing breath.

'Alan! Alan, m'eudail—you are safe—safe! Thank God—oh, thank God!' Minutes later she was caught up in his arms and felt his kiss.

'Kieran, darling of my heart, how is it with you?' He looked at her face, seeing the shadows around eyes that spoke of tensions endured, as she gasped to see the barely healed scar at his temple.

'I am fine—fine, as are we all. But you—you have been wounded?' She looked up at him anxiously, her hands fondling his face. He kissed those hands and stroked her hair.

'A bayonet wound to my shoulder,' he said lightly, 'the wound healed through the medical skill of my companion. Kieran, allow me to present Sorley Mor Stewart, my good friend and surgeon, likewise wounded at Culloden!' and at his words, Kieran looked across at the tall, black haired, black bearded man wrapped about in a faded plaid, whose deep blue eyes were shining tenderly at the reunited couple. He came forward smiling.

'My greetings, Mistress Stewart! For many long miles, Alan has been extolling your beauty and now I see why! Alan man, she is indeed very fair—hair the red gold of ripening corn and eyes grey as a summer storm!' and he bowed courteously to the girl, lifting her hand to his lips.

'Why Mr Stewart, you are a poet sir,' she said blushing, then with Alan's arm about her waist the three of them climbed back up the way she had come to the welcome of the small croft that was home and love and comfort to Alan. Their voices were heard by Lachlan, but earlier returned from Loch Dhu with a fine salmon. The boy came round the side of the croft and gasped in pleasure to see his brother and hurled himself down the pathway towards them, crying out Alan's name.

'Why Lachlan—how you have grown, almost a man now,' smiled Alan as they embraced. Perhaps it was not quite true, but the lad squared his shoulders in youthful pride, pulling himself up to his full height at the words.

'The next time the Prince gathers the clans, I too will go,' he replied, eyes shining. 'Every day I practice with an old claymore I found rusted under a peat stack!'

'Then throw that weapon away, brother mine! There will be no more battles for you to involve in. The fighting over, the Prince said to be moving from one hiding place to the next, a price on his head! The redcoats are spreading out across the land, killing all who bear arms.' At his words the boy's enthusiasm wavered.

'We heard rumours—terrible things happening in Glen Lochay and even nearer. I could not believe they were true!' he said in a low voice. He looked hopefully at his brother, wishing that he would deny it. But as he looked into Alan's eyes he read the deep sorrow there, knew the rumours were true.

'Lachlan, when you see the redcoats coming, take all dear to you and hide in the heather, for these English are dead to all chivalry and honour.' The lad turned to the tall stranger at Alan's side who had just uttered these words in solemn tones.

'I will always keep my father and sister-in-law safe from these cruel men,' he said defiantly, 'As no doubt you would expect son of yours to do sir!' He saw the stranger flinch slightly and Sorley Mor frowned.

'Lachlan, this is Sorley Mor Stewart, good friend of mine, whose only young son died back there at Culloden.' His brother's words brought flush to the boy's cheeks.

'I spoke thoughtlessly, sir. Forgive me,' he said and inclined his head to the older man, who patted his shoulder with a slow smile. As they entered the house the smell of peat smoke brought back to Alan memories of all that had been normal in the so recent past, as did the sight of his father sitting staring endlessly into the fire. Malcolm Stewart hardly raised his head as his first born came in, until that was Alan came to his side and raised his hand to his lips.

'Father,' he said. 'I am home!' for a brief minute a smile crossed his father's face, a sudden opening of present darkness to allow dart of joy to penetrate his brain. But that narrow window closed and Malcolm resumed his brooding into the fire, as Alan's smile faded. Why had he expected any difference in a situation that had long existed in this way?

Kieran was busy preparing a chicken and the salmon Lachlan had caught. Tonight they would have a fine feast, but for now the men sat eating bannocks and cheese washed down by smooth claret, as Lachlan listened to his brother talking with this Sorley Mor whom he now knew to be a surgeon. He heard them mention Stewart of Ardshiel who had led Clan Appin into battle, and that the greater part of the Appin Stewarts had perished on cold Culloden Moor.

'Is it true that the Campbells fought for George of Hanover?' asked Lachlan, hanging upon every word.

'True indeed—but only what one would expect of them,' replied his brother contemptuously. 'Sadly there were others who also dishonoured their swords by taking the usurpers side! Had all of Scotland been united, nothing could have stopped us. Charles Edward Stuart would now occupy the throne as Regent for his father James.' He sighed, shook his head. Too late now to amend what had happened.

'I have it on good authority, that several high placed English Lords contacted France over a year ago, asking that they should aid a Jacobite rising to re establish the Stuarts on the throne.' It was Sorley Mor who spoke. 'It was all politics—English Tories wishing to replace the Whigs, but the plan was discovered and it came to naught.'

'Yet the French had made decision to aid us—to send troops, or so it was said. Some few came later, but not enough of them. Better perhaps the Prince had waited for French soldiers at his back before raising his standard,' said Alan quietly. 'But you can never go back in life—only forwards and the immediate future looks bleak indeed.'

'What do you mean?' asked Lachlan. 'Surely all will go back to normal after a few months—the English army return down south?'

'I fear this has been too great a shock to them,' replied Alan. 'We came within just over a hundred miles of London, which must have been great fright to their government—some say that German George was on the point of packing his bags!' He gave a wry chuckle. He gave a longing glance towards Kieran who was busy at her cooking.

'Lachlan—perhaps you could take Sorley Mor for a short walk—explore the croft? I would be alone with Kieran for a while,' he said diffidently and his friend rose with an understanding smile and nothing loth Lachlan obeyed.

There was great joy in that small bedchamber, as Alan took his wife into his arms, her sweet face flushed from her cooking, and a warmer blush suffused her cheeks as he gently laid her across the bed. Their union was one of throbbing ecstasy after their many months apart as he held her to him raising her hips to receive his seed, as they then sank back exhausted and fulfilled. His lips sought her own again.

'Kieran—my heart's darling. Perhaps we will be blessed of a son of this,' he murmured and kissed her breasts imagining precious small head of babe of theirs suckling there.

'I wish it so with all my heart,' she replied, her fingers exploring his body once more, trying to convince herself that this was real, not some midnight dream. It was at this moment that they heard a crash in the room next door, loud voices, Malcolm's shout of anger—and then a shot rang out!

Alan slid off the bed, pulled his plaid about him. He had no weapon with him, but Kieran produced a knife she ever kept beneath her pillow and wordlessly gave it to him. He took it, kissed her and pointed to the window as the door burst open to reveal a crowd of redcoats in the room beyond.

'Take that rebel,' cried their officer, pointing towards Alan—'And seize his woman!' Alan fought furiously wounding two of them with his knife then fell as they pulled him down by sheer force of numbers. Kieran looked on in horror. No time now to escape by the window, for two of them now grasped her struggling form and forced her to her knees. She felt them enter her—one after the other and the pain and shock was unbelievable. And Alan was forced to watch the raping of his wife as he swore in anguish.

When the men had expended their passion, one of them kicked Kieran contemptuously onto her side. They stood looking down on her, faces grinning. Then they turned to start eating the food she had cooked

'Fitting punishment for a rebel's whore,' smiled their officer, chewing on a chicken's wing. 'Now take this fellow outside and shoot him!' Then as Kieran cast one last despairing glance at her husband, he was dragged bound out of the house—a shot rang out.

They had gone and now. Kieran staggered painfully outside in search of Alan Stewart, beloved husband, now a sightless corpse crumpled dead beneath the rowan tree at the door. Dead like his father Malcolm, shot at his own fireside. Alan's bright spirit had fled and she tore her hair in anguish, crying curses on the ones who had done this deed.

She must find a spade, give burial to Alan, the last service she could do him in this world. She was bathing his bruised face, his blood on her hands, when she heard voices—and saw Lachlan and the man Sorley. She looked up woodenly from her task as they came running towards her.

'Oh—not dead? Kieran say it is not so,' cried the lad, staring down in horror. 'We were up high on the hill, heard shots—shouting! Saw the soldiers coming away from the croft.'

'We could never have got down here in time,' said Sorley Mor with tears in his eyes. 'Let me,' he said and took the cloth from her and continued to wipe away the bloodstains. Then he wrapped the body in the Stewart tartan and seeing the spade Kieran had brought ready, asked quietly, 'Where would you wish we lay him?'

'Beneath the rowan where he fell,' she replied. 'We were in the bedroom when they came. He had only a knife—fought like a lion. But it was to no avail, too many of them—too many, alas!' And she started to moan in the manner of women down the ages who keen for their loved ones. Lachlan placed a comforting young hand on her shoulder. It was pushed away.

'I will look after you now,' he whispered through his tears.

'Your father lies within,' she said lifting her head. 'They shot him too—a defenceless old man! No shame in them. No shame.' Lachlan turned about in horror and rushed into the house and they heard him cry out at what he saw. Later two graves lay close to the croft door, father and son resting together. Kieran had disappeared, made her way down to the loch side, where she stepped into the freezing water and started to cleanse herself of the redcoats' indecencies, sobbing as she did so.

And as she waded out into the pure water where it shelved abruptly downwards Kieran was tempted to swim out and sink like a stone, to seek her husband in the world beyond. But then self harm was a sin was it not, but in such circumstances? Then another thought came into her head. What if a child should be born to her of her husband's lovemaking? Such had been his wish she knew. But what if those others who had defiled her body had planted alien seed!

She heard her name called and turning slowly around saw Sorley Mor wading out towards her. He was holding a plaid. He held it out wordlessly and stony faced she took it. Above their heads an eagle flew, great spread of wing lifting it ever higher into its eyrie.

He stared at her bruised and swollen face, his blue eyes full of sympathy. 'Kieran—I know there is nothing I can say or do at this moment to help you. But hear this. You are my friend's widow, a friend who in our short time together became as a brother to me. My charge to care for you as best I can—as a brother would.' He looked at her steadily as she stood shivering on the bank, holding the plaid tight about her.

Her grey eyes at last met his insistent stare. She saw the honesty there in his steady dark blue glance, and strong slightly arrogant features, the wind ruffling his black curls back from his wide forehead. And she knew she could trust this stranger. He reached out a hand—and she took it and glanced around her.

'We must find Lachlan,' she said decisively. 'Alan would wish me to care for him.'

'We will do so,' he replied. 'Come!'

Chapter Two

They clambered slowly back up the steep path towards the croft that had offered such warm welcome to Alan Stewart short hours before. Now his grave held all that remained of one who had fought bravely for his Prince and his country. They glanced apprehensively around as they came, for the redcoats might always return—although there was little here now to attract them, for they had stolen all food and belongings they had found.

'At least they did not fire the house,' said Sorley Mor reflectively, 'Strange that, considering the way they are behaving across the country!'

'I could never live here again,' she said through tight lips. 'What they did to me—I could not bear to be in this place more.'

'Hush now, try not to think on it,' he replied awkwardly, although his heart bled for her sorrow at the outrage she had endured. 'Look—here comes Lachlan. He also needs help in his grief, for he is but young.' And the lad walked down to greet them, his face pale, shocked—but with new determination in his eyes.

'I have shaped two crosses to mark their graves,' he said thickly, voice roughened through tears. 'What should we do now—for those fiends may return?'

'We will see if they have left anything usable in the house, which I doubt,' replied Kieran, 'then we will make for the shielings high in the hills, where all take the cattle in the summer months. There we will find shelter.' Sorley looked as though he would remonstrate, but seeing that her mind had shifted somewhat from her sorrow thought it not the time to deflect her purpose.

They entered the house together and Kieran blenched to see the pool of blood before the fire where Malcolm had expired, turned resolutely away and cried out as she saw damage wherever her eyes fell. China smashed, all food stripped from cupboards, chairs broken, and Alan's precious books lay ripped in a pile on the floor and had been urinated on. In the bedroom pillows had been destroyed feathers covering the floor, all clothing had disappeared from the cupboard, the bed where her husband had made love to her at tilted angle, legs broken, mattress covered in something unspeakable.

She turned to the silent Highlander at her side, eyes bewildered, full of pain. 'Why? Tell me why,' she cried!

'It is so they think to break the spirit of our people,' he replied quietly. 'Their behaviour worse than that of ravening wolves—and this I fear is but the beginning of what is to follow. The English will be remorseless in their revenge!'

'Perhaps we should salvage what we can,' put in Lachlan practically. 'This bedding I will wash in the burn—we will need its warmth. That shredded tartan can perhaps be mended, serve some purpose. And see Kieran, they have left the cooking pots—these we will take!' He watched as she started to gather all together, nodded satisfaction then went out carrying the spoiled bedding in his arms.

He bent over the peaty burn, its waters gurgling over rocks and stones and thrust the evil smelling bedding into the cleansing waters of a pool. Again and again he washed away the defilement, slapping the blankets against a large slab of granite until satisfied. Then he spread all on branches of a tree to dry in the soft wind.

The livestock! He suddenly wondered what had become of the six goats and their few sheep. As to the hens, they had gone and would no doubt be making a meal for their assailants this night. But what of the cows, for they had been some distance away cropping the young grass in the meadow down by the loch—where his father's old horse would also be grazing, awaiting return of a master it would never see more. He hurried downwards towards the pasture and as he approached, realised his journey was in vain. But perhaps not so entirely, one lone shaggy coated beast emerged between the birches that bordered the field—and it was a cow soon due to calf.

He approached her calmly, calling to her as he walked. She lifted her head and lowed plaintively, then recognising his voice came slowly towards him. He whispered into her ear then having no rope to secure her, merely kept calling as she fell in behind him. Sorley saw him coming and gave a cry of approval.

'Well done, Lachlan. Now this is what I suggest. When you took me up on the hill earlier—before the redcoats came, you showed me the cave behind the waterfall which Alan had spoken me of.....' he was interrupted by the boy who turned an anguished face upon him.

'Had we not been in that cave at that time, with the sound of the rushing water blocking all other noise, we would have heard the redcoats coming, might have been able to aid Alan—my father—and Kieran!' There were tears in his eyes again. As long as he was occupied with some task he was able to put aside his grief, but it was too new, too raw and he was after all, but thirteen. Sorley Mor put an arm about the boy's shoulders.

'Listen to me, Lachlan Stewart! You are no longer a child, and although young need now to take on man's stature! Yes, we might have heard the soldiers arrive and have run down to the house—but what then? I was unarmed save for a knife and my surgeon's tools and you unable to take on armed men with guns, however bright your courage. Likely we too would now be dead—and how would that help your sister-in-law who has suffered rape and bereavement?' His fingers pressed down firmly onto Lachlan's shoulder and felt the boy relax.

'I'm sorry, Sorley Mor! You were speaking of the cave—Alan's cave!'

'I think it better place than the shielings for Kieran to take shelter, for the next few weeks at least! How say you, lad?'

'Surely none would ever find us there—but what of the cow?' the boy was thinking logically now.

'We take her up there with us—tether her nearby until she becomes accustomed to the place. But for ourselves, we will carry what possessions Kieran has collected and I think we must go soon! It is already some hours since the redcoats were here. Although I doubt they will be back again this evening let us take no chances!' Their low voices carried to Kieran, who was standing at the doorway staring with blankly ahead.

'Kieran!' the lad called.

'Why, you are back Lachlan—and with the cow in calf!' A flash of her old spirit came into her eyes. 'Well done my dear,' she said proud of his achievement and the look in his eyes was reward for her words. But what was he saying now—urging her to listen carefully?

'Kieran—time for us to go! But not to the shielings, for Sorley Mor thinks the soldiers will possibly make their way up there.'

'Then where—where do we go?' She turned her grey eyes on this stranger who had been good friend to Alan, looking at him pleadingly, 'Where to then?'

'To the cave behind the waterfall, where burn falls sheerly down across its hidden face—it is there that Lachlan took me earlier, showing me this place that Alan had mentioned as being safe haven in case of emergency!'

She nodded listlessly and gathered the large bundle of belongings onto her back, pointing out another she had prepared to Lachlan, but Sorley lifted this, whispering to Lachlan to have a care of the cow and to bring that rusted claymore and the spade and any other implements he could discover—and then they were off. Kieran did not look back.

They had not gone more than seventy yards up through the heather, when the sound of fresh shots rang out and they froze, trying to establish from whence these came—slightly further to the west it seemed. Sorley took the bundle from Kieran's back leaving her unhampered as now he managed all, climbing up swiftly before them, following the course of the foam crested Ardoch burn that noisily hurled itself down in the deep rocky channel it had cut over the many years. Kieran leapt up easily at his side with all the lithe grace of a highland woman, Lachlan keeping pace behind with the cow in tow.

They paused for a moment, hearing voices carried faintly on the wind. Those familiar shouts, more shots and the sounds of keening—more shots—then silence. And now they hurried faster, panting from exertion, ankles cut by rocks and heather roots, legs scratched by the all pervasive gorse. Above them the burn twisted in its course, until at last they saw the solid lace curtain of the falls in all its majesty, pouring down sheerly hundreds of feet, its noise deafening. To the naked eye, no sign existed of that hidden cave behind the water's fury, its spray now touched by the scarlet rays of the sinking sun.

The narrow shelf of rock that ran behind the waters turbulence was slippery and sloped downwards making it dangerous in the extreme to brave this hazardous entrance to the cave.

'I will go first,' said Lachlan boldly, leaving the shaggy cow to munch on a patch of sweet damp grass near the side of the side of the falls. 'See—it is easy, Kieran!' and to prove his words he moved fearlessly forward. He flung the sword, spade, bucket and other necessities he had been carrying into the mouth of the cave and turned to take the girl's hand. Once she was safely in, he went back and took one of the large bundles Sorley had been carrying, leaving that man to follow on his heels with the rest of their belongings.

They were safe—for now at least and Kieran breathed a deep sigh of relief. She tried to see about her in the gloom of the cave. She knew the place well, although Lachlan did not realise this, for it was here that Alan had sometimes brought her in the early days of their love. They had made a bed of heather in the far corner some twenty feet back spread with an old blanket, left it there for other occasions. Yes and on a shelf of rock above the bed had been a lamp, flint—and a jar of oil. She stood on her toes, felt about with exploring fingers. Sorley turned in surprise as a soft light now illumined the interior of their hiding place.

'Now this was something I had not looked for,' he said musingly. 'It is almost as though Alan had foreseen the need of it.' He looked at Lachlan. 'Tomorrow we will gather more heather for bedding, make this place comfortable as we're able. We will also need twigs, wood, for kindling a fire for warmth and cooking.'

'Yes and we will need something to eat!' added Lachlan. 'My stomach rumbles.'

'That is something you may have to live with for now,' replied Sorley. 'If only we had a gun there are deer on the hill—I saw them as we started out. But there again, the noise of a gun fired would bring the redcoats on us.'

'Tomorrow I will risk going down to the loch to fish,' said Lachlan calmly. 'I leave my rod there at all times in a hollow by the bank. I also know how to make snares to trap hares—can bring down a bird with my sling. We will not starve! Glad I am though that it is not winter!'

'I brought a large bag of oatmeal with me,' said Kieran now, 'Look in that bundle, Lachlan. It was in the barn—the soldiers did not see it—and if not broken in our climb, here in my apron some eggs I gathered behind the shed before we left!' Sorley looked at her admiringly. To have provided for them in this way in the midst of her grief demonstrated the metal of this woman so beloved of his friend Alan.

'I can contribute this,' he said. He produced a small bottle of brandy, offered it first to Kieran and then to Lachlan, but both refused—as he then took a sip. He sighed, and laid himself down across the entrance to the cave and wrapped himself in his plaid. Kieran blew out the lamp and lay down on her heather couch, Lachlan close by her. During the night they heard nothing above the roar of the waters that concealed their refuge—but Sorley was aware of Kieran's wild sobbing and Lachlan's own occasional soft moan. As for the man, as he tried to sleep he saw again in his dreams the terrible moment when his young son had been blown apart by the death that belched from the enemies canon.

Morning dawned, though not immediately apparent for the interior of the cave was denied all normal light. But Lachlan sensing it was time to rise, made his way along the precarious shelf of rock behind the falls and out onto the hillside. He knew it would have been wiser to discuss his plans with the others, but started downwards following the course of the burn until he was on the floor of the glen. And here nothing stirred, although several larks were already pouring out ecstatic melody upon the wing. He approached the house on cautious feet—knelt at the two newly lonely graves and holding his hand across his breast made solemn pledge.

'My father and my brother—may you rest in the peace of the just,' he said in trembling tones. 'I, Lachlan Mac Malcolm will now take my place as head of our house and tacksman—and will be revenged on those who slew you. This I solemnly swear!' Then he rose to his feet, looked across at the house that was home no more, and turned away to the left, looking carefully around, before plunging between bushes of golden gorse and sprays of gold tipped broom and fringe of graceful young birch and so continuing for a quarter of a mile.

Here it was, the clearing where the MacColls and MacMichaels lived in their small cots—and over there by the burn should be the home of Mistress Morag Stewart and near it the hut which housed the seer, old

Maisie! He sniffed, for the acrid smell of smoke filled the air and he feared what he would see. He crouched amongst the springing heather and stared. No movement anywhere—nor yet any sign of the detested uniforms of the redcoats. He started forward, approached nearer—and as he came saw shapes upon the ground and he hesitated, for he guessed what these were.

Too many there were for the boy to bury, nor had he a spade with him. The shock of seeing those he had grown up amongst lying slaughtered like cattle brought a choke to his throat—women, children—two old men and he groaned. Yes and there lay old Maisie. Kieran had told him Maisie had mentioned that they would not meet again. She had been right in this—and in her other predictions. There was no sign of Morag Stewart's newly returned soldier son Rory and Lachlan guessed the redcoats had taken him away with them.

Why do this to people so poor? Why murder them, burn their homes? They offered no possible threat to the soldiers! Cottars lived a frugal existence, cultivating their small strips of land for which they paid rent to the Laird through his factors, their small possessions of no worth to any other. Life was hard, yet the spirit of the people was strong in their loyalty to the clan and their chief, their men folk always ready to rise, steadfastly answering his call to battle with a neighbouring clan who might have lifted some of their precious animals. It was the way it had ever been in the highlands. But—what now?

Around the corpses of the slain, lay carcases of goats and sheep. Lachlan lifted one of the dead goats onto his shoulders and prepared to return back up to the cave of the waterfall. He would not go to the loch today. Fishing could wait until the morrow. He started off, panting at the weight on his back, climbing ever higher seeking the path of the Ardoch burn. As he reached it, he paused for the sound of drums came towards him on the wind. It was the redcoats announcing their inexorable progress to destroy and kill—and he swore under his breath.

'Lachlan! Where have you been? I was so worried!' cried his sister-in-law's sweet voice, as Lachlan edged his way along the slippery shelf of rock and so in to the hidden entrance of the cave. He threw the dead goat on the floor. He poured out his story to the girl in terse broken words and by the flickering light of the oil lamp saw her blanch in shock.

'All are dead there, Lachlan? All you say?' she whispered.

'All! Old Maisie among them, shot in the chest, poor creature!' he said sadly. 'I would have buried them, lacked the means to do so. I brought the goat—it will make a meal.'

'That was well thought on,' said a deep voice and Sorley Mor appeared, carrying large bundle of twigs. He had overheard Lachlan's words as now dropping his load, came towards him and placed his hands on the lad's shoulders. 'Alan said you had become a man. He was right.'

'Why—thank you, Sorley Mor. Sad I am though that it has taken events such as these to make me so.' His sorrowful words touched even Kieran's grief stricken heart, as she opened her arms and held him to her.

'Hush now, brother of mine. You will become a man such as Alan would have had great pride in,' she said simply. 'Now come, Lachlan. Sit and eat for I have made oatcakes.' He sank down at her words, aware of the warm smell of baking in the cave. He glanced around. She had already done her best to make this extraordinary cavern in the hills into a home of sorts.

'You are so calm,' he said wonderingly.

'My grief for Alan will be with me until the end of time,' she replied simply. 'When he left to join the Prince, I think then I knew in my heart that I might not see him again. At least I had the joy of his presence yesterday for those precious short hours before.....' and her voice faltered as her tears began to fall and she wiped them resolutely away with her sleeve as Lachlan looked tactfully aside, his own grief still very near the surface.

The cow had calved, a fine daughter small replica of her shaggy mother. And now there would be milk to be had, after the calf had taken its fill. Despite the never ending rain, the beast had not attempted to move away from the spot near the waterfall, where much fine new grass had shot up between the heather and gorse, as if knowing that her owners were close by.

Slowly over the next few weeks life began to take on a strange normality. Kieran was painfully recovering from her physical hurts as well as the deep shock of all that had happened. But she was young, vigorous, and had not yet attained her nineteenth birthday. Sorley Mor Stewart left the cave every day to explore the nearby glens to assess the mayhem spread there by the steadily advancing patrols of Cumberland's troops. Each day on return he was very quiet, his face grim.

'I met a man today—a Cameron,' he said. 'What I heard at his lips was not good. The greater part of his clan either dead or captured, those who escaped and managing to arrive back to their homes, finding them burnt out shells, their families dispersed high into the hills! As it is here in this glen, all cattle driven off as well as sheep and goats—houses ransacked before being put to the fire!'

'They are just plain evil, these English,' exclaimed Lachlan.

'Perhaps we should not judge an entire nation by its army,' said Sorley slowly. 'I have also heard tales of how their common soldiers are treated by their officers.' He paused, wondering whether to continue.

'What mean you,' asked Kieran curiously, coming closer.

'For even minor misdemeanours their men are given up to five hundred or a thousand lashes with the cat-o-nine tails, carried out before the assembled battalion. In their kindness, they only apply three hundred lashes at a time, the others on subsequent days, a doctor in attendance!' He shook his head. 'There, I should not have mentioned it, but perhaps it goes in some way to explain the barbarity of their treatment of our own people, their senses blunted to all humanity.'

'I care not about this,' said Kieran now. 'However brutally men have been used, surely they still know the difference between right and wrong? That it is inexcusable to murder women and children, the old——to rape!'

'It is by doing so that they think to break the spirit of the highlands,' said Sorley quietly. 'My fear is that they will achieve their object.'

'Never,' shouted Lachlan fiercely. 'I am surprised to hear you suggest such!' But Kieran placed a soothing hand on the lad's arm as she made a question.

'Where are they taking all the cattle then?'

'To Fort Augustus and I hear that men from the south—farmers from England are coming up to buy not only our beasts and I am speaking of thousands, but sheep and goats as well for sale. Huge markets held daily. They are also destroying all ploughs and harrows they find and other farming implements. They intend to starve our people as well as to burn all human habitation.' He sighed. 'We may have to make plans to leave this place,' he said.

'Glen of Ardoch is our home,' cried Lachlan angrily. 'Where else should we go? We need to be strong—theses English will go home when they think they have done their worst to us.'

'Do you think I do not understand all this? But consider Lachlan, what the future holds. In the highlands, it is our cattle that represent a clan's wealth. These English are aware of this. They would reduce us to beggary, no money to buy more cattle—and for those living in areas with few trees, how are they to get timber to rebuild. Stones we have aplenty, but roof poles are needed.'

'What else did you learn from your Cameron friend,' asked Kieran?

'Archie is a real friend indeed, a man who persuaded me to take up medicine and at his advice I completed my training in Edinburgh as physician. I speak of Dr Archibald Cameron, brother to Lochiel himself!'

'You know him—Dr Cameron,' cried Kieran in surprise. 'Alan mentioned him to me as a most wonderful man. Furthermore his reputation as fine doctor is well known to most in the region.' She stared at Sorley Mor, looking at him objectively for perhaps the first time in all the weeks since he had come into their lives, for so far she had been so absorbed in memories of the horror that had befallen her that beyond feeling an instinctive trust for him, she had not viewed him as person in his own right. He had just been there, a friend of Alan's who had become their protector.

'Tell me of yourself, Sorley,' she said now. 'You spoke of a son who died back there at Culloden—he was your only child?'

'My wife died giving birth to our babe. I was then but a young man and married just a year. I placed Luke with foster parents who brought him up with their own two sons—and months back like Luke they also fell on the field. I only knew my son for a few brief months. We met at Glenfinnan. I had been abroad for many years—lately returned to Edinburgh to practice medicine.' The staccato sentences were jerked out, obviously a trial for him to speak of personal matters.

'You never married again?' she persisted?

'It never entered my head. Medicine has been my life, that and dreams of restoring the house of Stuart to the throne of Scotland! That dream is no more. But I can only hope that my medical skills will offer future of sorts if life ever returns to something approaching normal.'

She looked into his eyes, even in this dim light their deep blue startling against his tan, his dark hair and beard needing a comb and realised that despite the slight arrogance of his expression, Sorley Mor was a handsome man. He smiled under her steady gaze and flushing she looked away.

'Perhaps you will find new happiness one day,' she said softly, 'Marry again mayhap?' There would surely be someone who would see his good qualities she thought. She hoped so, for he deserved some kindness in his life. But in no way was she interested in becoming part of his future. When it was safe for them all to be on their way again, he would disappear and she wished him well.

He looked as though he would make reply to her suggestion, but instead gave a slight smile and disappeared from the cave. Lachlan looked after him.

'He is a strange man, this Sorley Mor,' he said reflectively. 'Well educated too and sometimes when we are out together tell me tales from the days of ancient Greece. Seemingly they had warriors to match our own all those centuries ago. I wish I knew more of the world, Kieran—of what lies beyond our own mountains and glens—beyond Scotland itself.'

'Perhaps one day you will travel, but it will have to be after these English leave our land and we can start to live as ordinary human beings once more.' But when would that be? Already the heather was in bloom and the rowans starting to colour and still the atrocities continued. What if they had to remain living in this cavern until winter and the snows came early to the north. Days of blizzards there would be and the whole world white, passes blocked and without food how would they survive?

29

Kieran sighed and decided to risk going outside into the fresh August air, for she had been feeling quite nauseous of recent days. Lachlan watched as she started to the exit of the cave and making her way along that dangerous slippery edging of rock that ran behind the deafening fall of water. She had been very tense recently, her original grief and apathy replaced not by despair but an underlying anger. Whilst understanding it, nevertheless it made him feel uneasy.

Kieran clambered free of the rocks and glanced around as the scent of the heather rose sweetly to her nostrils and with the spicy smell of small alpine plants a joy after the smoky atmosphere of the cave. There contentedly munching the grass was the cow—she had named her Agnes and blessed the foresight of Lachlan in bringing her up here on that day of horror last May. She walked over to the beast and fondled the shaggy head between its long curved horns, as the calf nuzzled her.

It was delightfully warm today, and so peaceful. No sound of men or drums, only the sound of larks singing far above in the heavens and the buzzing of bees amongst the heather and cry of the curlew. Then she saw it, the eagle soaring upwards towards its eyrie, carrying something in its claws—was it a salmon? It had no doubt been fishing in Loch Dhu and thoughts of the pleasure of swimming in its tranquil waters almost made her risk a trip down to its banks, some hundreds of feet below. But caution took over.

There was a deep pool she knew of where the burn collected in a hollow, and it was only five minutes scramble from where she stood. Sheltered by rowans and birch she stood on the banks of the pool and looked around, then stripped off her skirt and blouse and stepped off the bank down into the gurgling brown water. The shock of its cold embrace made her gasp. But it was such delight to be able to wash freely. She splashed and laughed like a child.

At last she climbed out wringing the water from her hair, but would wait for the sun to dry her skin before putting her clothes back on. She stared back at the water. A cloud passed over the sun and now the water became a mirror and she looked down at its surface with surprise. Her hands went to her waist. It had thickened slightly. Perhaps the lack of exercise was responsible, but then there had also been that strange tenseness to her breasts.

'I am pregnant,' she breathed! And as she stood there, trying to absorb the shock, her first thoughts were of Alan and of their passionate lovemaking on his last fateful day on this earth. She remembered his words—'Perhaps we will be blessed by a son of this!' And her heart was full of joy. 'Oh Alan, Alan, I will bring him—or her, up to be proud of you,' she whispered. Then before her eyes as though in mockery, she saw a rash of scarlet uniforms and of one man in particular, their captain who had ordered her defilement and had been the first to instigate it. Until now she had not recollected his appearance, but now she remembered with startling clarity the cruel mouth and strange green eyes—and a limp.

'Suppose I should bear a child to that creature or other of his men,' she whispered. 'I could not stand it, would kill the child!' But then to kill a child would be murder—and not possible for one who despite all that had happened, was a Christian and believed in the Holy Son of God. 'I pray I may not be put to such a test,' she murmured and hastily dressed and started back up to the cave.

Sorley Mor had caught his breath as he watched Kieran prepare to step down into the pool. He had not meant to spy merely to watch over her—and then had been unable to look away. She was he decided unbelievably beautiful, fine shoulders, thrusting breasts, sweet curve of hip and long slim legs, her hair shining red gold in the sunlight. He stayed behind the bushes until she emerged from the pool—saw her motion as her hands encircled her waist—and guessed. She was to bear Alan a son and his heart throbbed with a tenderness of feeling which would have been hard to describe.

He had known all along since the tragic happenings on the day of Alan's return, that it was possible that she might bear a child of that occasion. Whether it would be Alan's—or another's he hardly dared to consider. He remembered the appearance of Alan Stewart, fair haired, blue eyed and as he knew bold and courageous. It was to be hoped that the child would be his, fitting memory of a man whose friendship Sorley had esteemed.

But whoever had fathered the babe which he calculated should be born late December or January, Kieran would need extra care and attention and how was he to give this in an isolated cave behind the fury of the falls? Well, no need to make decision at this time. Better to wait a few weeks then to move before the days turned colder and storms raged over the mountains. As it was the spring and summer had been unusually wet this year. But plans must be made and with the redcoats still rampaging about the countryside, hanging, raping, burning and destroying all in their path, this would be no easy task.

Briefly he considered return to Edinburgh, for there he could easily slip back into his profession of physician and hope that none would remember he had disappeared at the time of the rising. He could make a home there for Kieran and the lad—and the child to be born. But how to get there, over land would be perilous in the extreme? They could instead make for France but with all boats destroyed by the troopers, little chance to row out to one of the French ships that sometimes loomed out of the mists, in hope it was said of carrying the Prince to safety.

He bit his lip in frustration, and slipped quietly away as Kieran prepared to climb back upwards to the cave. It was still early in the day. Perhaps he would risk a journey to the coast, to see for himself what the chances were of finding a fishing boat. It was only about ten miles of a walk and he started off. Half an hour later he was skirting the far end of the shore of Loch Dhu and cursing as the midges rose from the bracken fringed banks of the water. Every so often he would pause and look around cautiously. But he saw no one—the glen seemingly empty of people. Nor was there any sound of the redcoats' guns.

'What in Heaven's name-----!' He had almost stumbled over the body of a man lying face downwards in the bracken. He bent and turned the man over—peered down at the bruised features and cried aloud in shock.

'David—brother—is that you,' he gasped? The man looked up at him unseeingly at first, then seemed to rally and focussed his eyes on Sorley.

'Sorley—you are alive! I feared you dead at Culloden!' The words were whispered between lips caked with blood.

'I got away with my life. My son died. I have been in hiding like many another. But you did not go out and as man of God this was thing understandable—so what has happened to you?'

'The soldiers came to the village. They said that as an Episcopal priest I must accordingly know the names of all who had risen for the Prince, that I should make a list for them. I refused!' The words bleakly spoken told their own tale. Sorley looked down at him with pity.

'Surely even such as they, must have had some reverence for a minister of the church!' Sorley's eyes were damp.

'They tied me to a tree—beat me,' was the quiet retort, and biting back an expletive Sorley Mor carefully lifted the shredded shirt from his brother's shoulders and lowered his breeches, and winced at what he saw. David's back was bloodstained and crisscrossed with purple welts from neck to his buttocks.

'May they rot in hell!' he snarled, but David merely sighed.

'They were just brutal men who had lost any finer feelings,' he said. 'I was lucky. Some there they hanged, others shot—some taken with them—and the women.....!'

'I can imagine,' and his hands went to the small leather bag he ever carried at his belt. Before applying the salve, he tore a piece from his shirt and dipping it in the clear waters of the loch, bathed the bruised and bloodied back of the quiet man before him.

'I am blessed in having a physician for a brother,' breathed the Rev David Stewart, painfully replacing his clothing. 'I thank you for this care of me, Sorley!'

'Where were you bound for? You are some many miles from your home,' probed Sorley Mor as he considered that he must change his earlier plans to make for the coast to seek for a boat. He could not in all conscience leave his brother alone here and in such plight.

'I just started walking—and walking. None were left alive there save three poor women raped and widowed who ran up into the hills to the shielings. Brother, it is nothing short of a miracle that we have met here as we have. What are the chances of such a thing?' His eyes, dark blue as those of his younger brother shone with a spiritual light as he reached a hand out to Sorley, who clasped him to him in a wordless embrace.

'Do you think you can walk a couple of miles, if I support you?'

'Why, yes. I feel a new strength in your presence,' replied the other and so they set off, Sorley Mor retracing his path along the shore of the loch, but walking slowly now, his arm about the cruelly used man at his side. They stopped several times and Sorley realised his brother was near fainting at times.

'When did you last eat,' he demanded now as they left the loch behind and started to ascend the hill, the sound of the Ardoch burn music in their ears.

'Three days since, if I recollect aright,' murmured David Stewart.

'Then no wonder you are so weak! Fool that I am not to have thought of it before! Here—I have a piece of bannock with me—dry, but better than nothing. Chew on it slowly.' Then they were off again, and now the sound of the falls prevented further speech. They were seen as they ascended the last twenty feet. Lachlan had been waiting crouched amongst the heather and rocks bordering the massive rush of water. He had seen two men approaching—recognised Sorley Mor—and wondered who his companion might be. In all the many weeks they had been hiding in the cave, none other had been near the place.

Now the youth rose up from his hiding place and hurried down to greet them. They moved back from the falls that they might speak and when they did had to shout above the water's turbulence.

'Sorley—glad I am that you have returned! Kieran went for a walk earlier and has been in a strange mood since her return. But you bring a friend with you?' His young eyes examined the man at Sorley's side, saw from his pallor that the man was unwell—and that despite silver that streaked his temples and the gentle look in his eyes, the stranger resembled Sorley.

'My brother—David Stewart,' introduced Sorley. 'David, this is Lachlan Mac Malcolm Stewart, whose sister is widow of Alan Stewart, a man who became a close friend after Culloden! We travelled together dodging the Redcoats bullets all along the Great Glen and found our way to his home.

But on the day of his return to his young wife, the soldiers came. Alan died fighting with naught but a dirk in his hand! To my sorrow, the lad and I were not in the house—but high up here on the hill!'

'They dishonoured my sister,' cried Lachlan, not knowing why he felt he could reveal this shameful secret to the stranger. 'Sorley brought us to the cave behind the waterfall and here we have stayed ever since!'

'My son, dreadful things are now happening all over the Highlands at the hands of the English. I feel sorrow for the great loss of your brother—and I imagine of your home.' He stared at the youth with deep sympathy.

'They killed my father too. He was locked into his own mind, a man old before his time— him they killed also! I hate them—hate them! Will destroy any Englishman who crosses my path,' cried Lachlan, fury in his eyes. The Episcopalian minister looked at him pityingly. He spoke in gentle words.

'Dear lad, you have suffered greatly. But vengeance is mine saith the Lord. It is honourable to defend yourself and your loved ones—but we also have to forgive those who despitefully use us.'

'Forgive? Who are you to say I should forgive! Perhaps if you had suffered as we have.......' He broke down into choking sobs, his shoulders shaking with his emotion. Sorley put an arm about him.

'Lachlan, my brother David is a priest of the Episcopalian church and whom they beat almost to death, because he would not reveal the names of those who left to fight for the Stuart cause!' The words, calmly spoken registered with the lad. He lifted his head and stared wonderingly at the minister.

'You are a man of God—and they used you so? And yet you say to forgive? Surely this is thing impossible!' he blurted.

'In our own strength, yes—very difficult, I agree. But with help from our gracious Saviour, all is possible.' His words seemed to float in the air, blending with the roar of the waters. Lachlan looked at him in awe. Then he knelt there in the wet heather.

'I pray you bless me, minister,' he said simply and felt the touch of the other's hand on his head. Then he rose. 'Come,' he said. 'Follow me but use great caution, for the way is slippery, dangerous!' Then with Lachlan leading and Sorley Mor guiding his brother's cautious footsteps along the hidden entrance to the cave, they negotiated the slanting shelf of rock and found themselves inside, where a surprised Kieran stared at the stranger.

Sorley introduced his brother, whose strength at that moment failed him and he slid to the rocky floor of the cave, completely exhausted and barely conscious. It was many hours later that David Stewart raised his head and found himself lying on his side on a bed of heather, under the pale light of a flickering oil lamp. A girl's sweet face bent over him, lips parting to an encouraging smile.

'You—are Kieran?' he asked quietly.

'Kieran Stewart—and you sir, are Sorley's brother I am told—and a priest of the Episcopal church?'

'My name is David.' He raised himself on an elbow and looked around. He saw Sorley and Lachlan sitting near the entrance to the cave and realised they were fashioning snares. They looked up as they heard the exchange. Sorley got to his feet.

'You slept the night away, David,' he said. 'While you slept I attended to your hurts. You did not even stir while I did so.'

'My back feels much improved—my thanks, Sorley.' The other smiled.

'I see you have met Kieran, who has made this cave a home for us during these last fraught weeks.' David's gaze returned to the fair young face above him.

'Sorley told me of your great loss, that your dear husband Alan returned to you and died defending his home.' He looked at her compassionately. Even in the dim light of the cave he could see that this Kieran Stewart was extremely beautiful, but also sensed courage and strength in her.

'Did Sorley also tell you of what the soldiers did to me?' She looked down at him broodingly. He nodded. 'I am with child,' she said now. 'It may be of my husband's making in those few hours we spent together—or then again.....!' Her voice faltered. He sat up and took her hand in his.

'My child—you have suffered terrible abuse and cruelty. But now a new little life is coming into the world, an innocent life Kieran, who will look to you for care and protection-and what every child needs—love!' He felt her withdraw her hand. She turned her head away. When she spoke, her voice was low and full of pain.

'Should the child not be my husbands, how then can I care for the product of rape? I saw the man—the captain who ordered my defilement—and who was the first to......! He limped, had green eyes and a face I will never forget. Suppose his face should stare up at me from my child's?'

'We will pray to God that you will be given the strength to deal with this, should the occasion arise. Hopefully you will bear your own dear husband's child. But from your appearance I imagine the birth to be some months away and other matters of concern at this time.' At his quiet words she nodded and seemed to regain control of herself.

'You speak wisely. I have prepared a meal. It is not much, for we are almost out of oatmeal—but I have made oatcakes, and there's milk—and some fish.'

They sat together around the small peat fire on which they cooked their meals and which gave some warmth. Any smoke that seeped out of the cave would have been unseen below, dispersed by the hurtling sheet of waters and the darkness of the rocks surrounding its concealed entrance.

'Tell me, David Stewart—how is it with the people of your village—'tis near Ballachulish I hear?' Kieran stared at the minister, this unlikely brother of Sorley Mor and so different in character. What she heard appalled, but did not surprise her, for Sorley brought back similar tales every week on return from his scouting amongst the surrounding countryside. Yes, it was terrible to hear of the hangings, shootings—rape— burning of houses. But she flinched to hear how an Episcopalian minister should have been stripped and bound to a tree and lashed with a cat of nine tails. She had seen his hurts last night, when Sorley had dealt with them, as the man had fallen into exhausted slumber.

'Is nothing sacred to these English,' she burst out. 'That they even murder babes and small children—and beat priests!'

'They follow the orders of the Duke of Cumberland—Butcher Cumberland he is now being called!' It was Sorley Mor who spoke. 'I fear that the way of life that has persisted in the Highlands for centuries, is soon coming to an end. The bond between chief and clan members is being broken. Many of our chiefs and tacksmen are now rotting in jails or on prison ships, some awaiting execution, others to be sold into slavery in the colonies. Other chiefs have taken to the hills and many others making their way where possible across the sea to Norway or France or further still.'

'So what are your own plans, brother?' asked David leaning towards him.

'I thought mayhap, that I would seek to return to Edinburgh where I own a small house, and to practice medicine there once more. Kieran and Lachlan shall accompany me. She could perhaps be said to be my housekeeper.' Sorley stared at Kieran as he spoke for this was the first time he had offered this solution and wondered how she would take it.

'What—leave the Highlands,' she said in a bleak voice. 'I think I would die away from all I love!' Her grey eyes filled with quick tears which she blinked away. 'Nor would it be fitting to live with a man unmarried.'

'We could mend the latter,' said Sorley daringly. 'We could marry! No, I do not mean that we should really be as man and wife—but in name only, to protect your reputation.'

'You are asking me to marry you?' The gaze she fixed on him was stormy.

'Yes. But not to become my wife, a formality just you understand.' He was not making a very good job of the solution he offered, was aware of it.

'But I could never marry a man I do not love—and I do not love you, Sorley Mor!' She flung the words at him defiantly and saw his head drop. She bit her lip, 'Apart from anything else, I am still grieving my husband!'

Strangely it was Lachlan who spoke now in support of Sorley Mor. He adored his lovely sister-in-law and worried for her future. Also he had become deeply attached to the strong, courageous Highlander who had taken the place in his mind of his late father and brother—for without the man's help Lachlan knew their plight would have been difficult in the extreme. He had already learned much from Sorley, who had been opening the youngster's mind to tales from the classics as well as stories of his own travels in Europe—and also helping to promote his growing interest in medicine.

'It seems to me, Kieran, that Sorley Mor honours you by offering the protection of his name!' He fixed his eyes earnestly on his sister, who frowned at his intervention.

'Speak not of those things you do not understand,' she exclaimed angrily, tossing her head and withdrawing to the back of the cave.

Sorley stared after her then with a sigh, made his way to the cave entrance and disappeared seeking the peace of the shadowed hillside outside, in which to reflect. He was followed by his brother, who negotiated the slippery shelf behind the fury of the falls with ease considering his former entrance there in near fainting condition. He placed a hand on Sorley's shoulder.

'Give her time,' said the Rev David Stewart softly. 'But your suggestion is a good one, my brother. Have patience. She has been deeply wounded by events, experienced horrors such as a mere man may not fully understand—her violation at the hands of those animals!'

'And do you think I do not realise such?' cried Sorley tormented. 'David, I offered her my name—to protect her and the child she will bear. What she does not know is that I love her!' The words burst out almost in shame. 'I said the marriage would be one in name only—although in my heart I dream that it might in time become a true marriage!'

'Well, if you truly love her, consider whether it might not be asking too much of yourself to live with her merely as a friend shall we say?'

'It is as such I have been doing since we came to the cave. I would merely continue in the same way.' His eyes were sad. 'When my wife died all those years ago, I swore I would never love again—never face such pain of parting a second time. I threw myself into my career as physician and surgeon both on the continent and back in Edinburgh. It was only when word came that Charles Edward had arrived at Glenfinnan, that I took horse to the west and joined him. A surgeon is always needed on a campaign.'

'And what of the son Shona bore you,' probed David gently. 'We often wondered in the glen, why you did not contact the boy—or other members of your clan?'

'I wanted nothing to remind me of my grief!'

'But—the child, Luke?'

'As you know, he was placed with foster parents as is not unusual in such cases where the mother dies. I met Luke at Glenfinnan—found him to be a fine son indeed. He died at my side at Culloden. Do I regret that I never knew him during his growing years—of course I do! But regret gets you nowhere, does it.' His gaze was sombre as he faced the other.

David stared curiously at this brother of his whom he had barely seen over the years. Sorley Mor was tall, big as his name suggested, with thick dark hair and beard, his intensely blue eyes shining from a face deeply tanned. He was a handsome man, and one who stood apart from the commonality of men.

'We can do little about the past—the future ours to make the best we can of—with the Lord's help!' David sighed. 'So much has happened since the Prince came among us last August. A tragic year in which hopes of a Stuart restoration have sunk into the dust, and yet what courage has been shown.'

'There may be many who wish Charles had remained over the water. Yet surely if there was a real chance to restore the Stuart monarchy he was right to pursue it. Yet I wonder if he had guessed the outcome, whether he would have decided otherwise.' The two men exchanged glances then stared down at the dark grey waters of Loch Dhu far below them. The wind was rising, shivering through the red berried rowans and pale gold of the dwarf birch that guarded the path of the burn. And it seemed as though a sigh was rising from the earth itself, a sigh of mourning for a land bereft of all that men had held dear.

'Have you news of the Prince?' asked David. Sorley grinned.

'The last I heard was that he was at Glen Moriston—aided by some who make fools of the soldiers by leaping down the hillside screaming and making swift attack and snatching food from their pack horses. Seems there is a cave, well hidden and there the Prince is safe for the present.'

'How did you hear of this—alone up here on Ben Ardoch?' the other eyed him curiously.

'Why, I do not stay in the cave all the while! Remember how I came upon you at the far end of Loch Dhu? No brother, I spend my days exploring all within a thirty mile radius, sometimes sleeping in the heather when the distance back is great. I meet—speak with those whom I can trust.' Sorley seated himself on a rock and David sank down beside him.

'So—what is to happen with Charles Edward? I take it he seeks flight back to France. We must not allow Cumberland's troops the delight of capturing him!' The priest's expression was proof of his feelings.

'This will not happen! Despite the thirty thousand pounds they offer as reward for his whereabouts, none in the Highlands have taken it up!' snorted Sorley.

'Already the help he had of Flora Macdonald who disguised him as her maid and had him rowed safely from Uist to Skye back in June is becoming legend. She is arrested you know and on a ship to be transported to London for her part in his escape. A brave woman indeed,' sighed David.

'There must be hundreds through whose hands the Prince has passed as he is taken from one place of comparative safety to another. The military are all over the land and our shores festooned with naval sloops waiting to prevent any small boat leaving the shore to transfer the Prince to whatever French vessel waits in the mist to bear him away. Only of course there is hardly a boat to be seen in all Morar, for they destroy all such that they find, even fishing boats.' Sorley shook his fist. As he did so, the sinking sun made a scarlet ribbon of the loch and the hills were touched with an angry flame.

'I am confident that he will make his escape though.' The priest made sign of the cross.

'So am I! David, yet despite my inner conviction that none would betray there have been ugly rumours—and certainly no more than rumours—of a spy amongst our own people, who would sell secrets for English gold. One of the chiefs it is said!' and Sorley spat out the words. 'If he is discovered I would not give a fig for his life!'

'Do you believe this?'

'I had it from Doctor Archie Cameron!' Sorley said and staring at him in consternation, the priest sighed appalled. He stared musingly into the dying sunset.

'No doubt it would be a Campbell—or from another of the clans who have supported the Hanoverian government,' suggested David Stewart meditatively. Sorley noticeably winced.

'It is hard to realise that some of those harrying supporters of the Stuarts and murdering and burning and raping are fellow Highlanders,' growled Sorley Mor. 'A few of the chiefs have played both sides—sent one son to fight for Charles Edward—another son for Cumberland!' He sighed in frustration. 'Had we but been united as a country...!'

'Yet when you come down to it Sorley that which should draw all men together is what does in fact divide!'

'How so,' queried Sorley.

'I mean the futile division between Catholic and Protestant! The very belief in God and his lovely Son the Lord Jesus, and the way in which men seek to worship, in their arrogance each side declaring that their form of teaching is right, this it is that causes so much heartache and violence!'

Sorley stared at his quietly spoken brother, knew that he was correct in what he said. But you could not interfere with a man's conscience—yet in God's heaven, if such a place existed, would there be one section for Catholics another for Protestants—and surely the idea was laughable?

'It gets dark. Let us get back inside,' he said shortly and as he did so, a dark cloud passed over the setting sun and rain started to splash down as they sought the comfort of the cave behind the falls.

Chapter Three

Three days had passed, days in which Kieran had kept apart from Sorley Mor as much as was possible in the close confine of the cave. He knew the reason and felt frustrated because of it. His proposal of marriage to the girl had shattered the feeling of harmony between them when she had merely looked on him as kindly protector and good friend of the husband she still deeply mourned.

But they lived in the real world, harsh and cruel as it had become, and soon for their own preservation it would be necessary to venture out of their present security behind the curtain of the waters and make for a place where they would be able to obtain food and shelter—and in his mind Sorley had now come to the conclusion that Edinburgh offered the best solution.

Had Kieran not been pregnant they might have continued in the cave despite the rigors of approaching winter, and had he but a gun shoot one of the deer occasionally glimpsed at evening like ghosts on the hill, then they could have survived. But even if he had a gun, the noise of it would have brought the enemy upon them.

September had arrived, the days getting shorter, the rain soaked summer reaching into an equally squally autumn. Sorley decided to take another trip to the coast to see whether it was still as closely guarded by the redcoat soldiers. He had heard that on the 25th July, the Duke of Cumberland had returned to London to a hero's welcome, had been replaced by a reluctant Albemarle who together with Lord Loudoun now seemed to be in overall charge.

The English were still feverishly searching for the Prince, seemingly getting clues as to his whereabouts, but as soon as they followed these up, found he had disappeared like a will of the wisp. Vigilance around the shores had lessened slightly—but still a ring of soldiers had spread outwards overlooking every inlet of the sea.

'I may be away for a few days. Do not venture from the cave until I return,' instructed Sorley.

'May I come with you,' cried Lachlan eagerly.

'No, lad—important it is that you watch over Kieran—and David for he is not too strong yet. When you go on the hill to check your snares, be extra vigilant that you are not seen. I leave all in your hands. Do not let me down!' and he exchanged a warm smile with Lachlan.

'I will not,' exclaimed the boy, disappointed not to be accompanying Sorley, but understanding the trust he had been given.

'Where are you going,' asked Kieran?

'To explore a way to get us all to Edinburgh,' he said evenly.

'I refuse to go there—will not leave the Highlands! You cannot make me!' she cried, her eyes sparkling with annoyance, but he ignored her. David already knew of his plans, they had consulted together the night before and now the priest raised a hand in blessing.

'Go with God, my brother,' he said softly. Kieran merely frowned and turned her face away and with a sigh, Sorley Mor made careful way along that narrow ridge behind the falls, where one slip would have meant death.

It was raining again, in fact had barely stopped over the many weeks. His feet crunched through the wet heather and bog myrtle, down the soggy hillside, spangled with tiny streams racing down its sides in miniature reflection of the mighty Ardoch burn. His plaid was soon soaked through but he ploughed on regardless. He was skirting Loch Dhu now, alert for any sign of the redcoats, but the heavy rain was proving a blessing, keeping the English within their camps, and making only small forays into glens already plundered, stripped bare of all that moved.

He was near the coast now and still it rained, with a heavy mist falling, thick and all enveloping. It was then he heard it—the sound of a drumbeat, marching feet. He climbed higher up the steep brae he had been traversing and knelt behind a thick clump of gorse. To his dismay he saw about thirty men pass below him, a mounted officer in the lead—and then some twenty yards behind, just discernible out of the gloom, two mounted soldiers leading a heavily laden packhorse.

He thought quickly—it would be dangerous in the extreme—but? He seized a heavy stone that came to his hand and sprang like a banshee at the nearest of the two men, striking him on the head to slip lifeless from his horse. At the movement, his companion turned his head. His shout never left his lips, for Sorley Mor's dagger found his heart and he fell with a thud. The riderless horses whinnied, snorted but did not attempt to run and the pack horse merely shuddered in relief at this unexpected delay. Some twenty yards ahead, the rest of the troop proceeded onwards, unaware of what had occurred.

They were bound to realise their loss before too long. With savage joy, Sorley divested the dead soldiers of their muskets, pistols and shot and rolled their bodies off the road into the water filled ditch below. He then released the pack horse of its burden, slicing through the retaining straps of the heavy bulging bags with his bloodied dirk. Food! Cheese and bread and other precious provisions, and brandy!

In another pack he found many small items of little value, obviously pilfered from the homes of despoiled Highlanders. But here was a woman's shawl—and in the last bag he discovered six fine linen shirts and hose and breeches. There was also a red coat with gold facings. This must be the property of the captain of the disappearing troop, the sound of their drumbeat faint echo on the air.

With a satisfied smile, Sorley hastily filled a couple of canvas bags. He took only those things of immediate use, as he clambered his way back up into the hills. He needed to move quickly. He would be a dead man if the redcoats discovered him. It was a shame that he could not spend more time exploring the situation at the coast—but the need to get these precious provisions back to those in the cave was of greater importance. Cumbered about with his acquired weaponry as well as the bags he began to tire, the old wound on his thigh an aching misery. He longed to rest awhile.

He looked for some form of shelter, but found none on that mist wrapped hillside. Then, out of the gloom he saw something—two figures propped against a face of bare rock, three children at their feet. He approached, stared. The women and the little ones were all dead, their starved faces spelling out the cause of their demise—hunger! They were also without clothing.

He swore savagely and his fury made the muscles of his neck bulge. His fears for Kieran's future of should they not escape the cave before the rigors of an approaching Highland winter intensified, their difficulties in obtaining food spelled out in terrible coin by the scene he had left behind. Once the snows came, the outlook would be bleak indeed. And so he plunged onwards and upwards through the ling and scree his thoughts centred on the lovely young woman whom he had come to love.

It was dark now. He realised he had lost all sense of direction. Better to stop and attempt some sleep, to make better progress in the morning. If he could not find his way in the thick night, neither would his eventual pursuers, seeking vengeance for those he had killed. Nor did he feel any slightest compunction for their deaths.

He lowered the baggage he carried to the ground, wrapped himself about in his heavy wet plaid, and laid his head on clump of heather as pillow. Above his head a night bird made lonely cry—an eagle perhaps?

Morning dawned. The mist had lifted slightly, turning pale shimmering gold in the thin rays of the sun. Where was he? He glanced around. Hills arose in seemingly unbroken chain, glittering with racing burns—but there in the distance he saw light glancing on a familiar sheet of water—and recognised it as Loch Dhu. He was within a couple of hours of the cave.

He broke off a piece of his stolen bread and washed it down with water from a tiny burn nearby, then took a mouthful of brandy to warm him—and collecting his booty, started off once more.

As he approached the end of the loch, he inhaled the all too familiar smell of burning, saw smoke rising. But where was it coming from? Kieran's village had been long burned—he dived for shelter in the fine leaved cover of young birch bordering the loch shore and made his way cautiously forward. As well he did so. Men were coming towards him, a dozen or more of them, red coated, disgruntled. They were driving a cow and her calf.

They passed within yards of him, so close indeed that Sorley Mor overheard their speech of the last few to march past.

'Captain is right disappointed that the wench we pleasured back in the spring had not remained in her house! That's why he determined to leave it standing!' Sorley could smell the man's sweat.

'Ah, for a return visit? I remember her. Red hair and a fine pair of hips—a good ride she gave!' The other man gave a coarse laugh. 'Well, if she's hiding nearby, then she no longer has a house! But the place looked deserted, a complete waste of time!'

'The whole area is deserted now,' growled another. 'Burn their houses, deny them their cattle and all other means of sustenance and you get no more bloody rebellion!'

'Achnacarry is burned down and Borrosdale and Ardshiel! All fine houses belonging to the rebel lords stand bare to the sky!'

'Some good booty for us lads—providing we are careful.......!' and their voices faded away. Sorley burned with a fierce anger. It was of course Kieran to whom they had referred. He thanked his foresight in insisting she move into the cave—had she been there in the croft today!

Lachlan had also seen the spume of smoke rising further down the hillside and from its direction knew it to be his family home. His face flamed scarlet. Not content with murdering Alan and his father whose graves they must have marched over, they needs come back to burn the only house standing in that whole area. Why? What cruelty obsessed these men? Did those who murdered and pillaged with such ease behave so in their own country? Surely not—for it would not be tolerated.

He started down the hillside, keeping carefully behind the cover of gorse and scrub birch and alder, until he was standing staring at all that remained of the home of Malcolm Stewart and his fathers' before him, and saw the barn and sheds were also smoking shells. The rowan sheltering the two lonely graves was scorched, its scarlet berries and leaves dried by the ferocity of the fire that had consumed all. Below it the crosses he had placed to mark the graves of his father and brother had been kicked down.

He was about to replace them, when he heard a quiet voice.

'Lachlan Stewart—why are you here instead of watching over Kieran?'

'Sorley Mor! You are returned, thanks be to God,' cried the youth brokenly. 'See what those devils have done! Why burn a house no longer inhabited? Why desecrate these graves?'

'Lachlan, I hid as they passed me down by the loch side, heard them speak. They made their return that their Captain might again violate your sister-in-law. I actually heard them say this!'

'He wanted to rape Kieran again—I can hardly believe such villainy,' exclaimed the boy. 'How right you were to insist we stay in the cave of the waters!'

'Just so,' said Sorley firmly. 'Now my young friend, are you going to help me carry this load up to the cave? Food we have now—and weapons!' As he spoke he stood back and pointed to that which he had laid at his feet. Lachlan gasped as he saw the muskets and noticed the pistols at Sorley's waist.

'Where did you get these from, Sorley Mor? Have you been fighting?'

'Not exactly—I dispatched a couple of redcoats and as they no longer had need of their belongings—or of that carried on their pack horse, I relieved them of it!' A hard smile broke over his face and Lachlan stared up at him in awe.

'A mighty warrior you are, Sorley Mor! Your name will be kept fresh among our people in song!' cried the lad ecstatically and lapsed into the Gaelic.

'Unless a Hanoverian noose encircles my head first—come then. Let us carry all safely up into the cave.'

David saw them first. He had realised that Lachlan had not returned from his snares and ventured out to look for him. Peering down, he saw the lad struggling up the hillside towards him at Sorley Mor's side, both of them heavy laden.

'There you are Lachlan—and Brother, you are safe! I have been concerned for you. There is smell of smoke in the air—and earlier I heard shouting.'

'Let us get back into the cave,' said Sorley with a faint smile, 'And there I will explain all.' He noticed that David was walking firmly now, had regained his strength. This was good. He would need it.

Kieran looked up in amazement as the men came in and threw the two heavy canvas bags down and then carefully placed the muskets against the wall of the cave.

'You are back,' she said to Sorley. Not by slightest expression would he see the anxiety that had coiled within in her during his absence.

'I am back' he agreed, 'And bringing food and a shawl for you!' He sank down on the couch of dried heather that was his and stretched his long legs before him and breathed sigh that now at last he could relax. And looking down on him, David Stewart smiled and made silent prayer of thanks to God who had brought his brother safe through the dangerous terrain he had travelled. Then he too sat and stared across at Kieran.

'My child, Sorley has told me that the soldiers returned to the glen,' he said quietly. 'They are gone now—but alas they burned your house and outbuildings.'

'What—it has gone? Alan's home destroyed like all else? It's true I could never have lived there again—the memories of what happened there too terrible. But why burn an empty house?' Her lips were trembling with sorrow and anger, as she dashed away the tears that gathered in her grey eyes. She stared down at Sorley.

'Can you tell me why?' she demanded.

'Their captain—he came back for you, Kieran! I heard his troopers laughing about it as I hid in the undergrowth at the loch shore.' He looked at her steadily, seeing the outrage in her eyes, but better so this present hurt, that she might realise the need for escape from their present situation.

'Would that I had met him that I might have killed him,' was all she said icily. She turned to her young brother-in-law. 'Lachlan—did you see any of this?'

'No Kieran. I saw smoke rising when I went out to check my traps. We have a fine hare for supper, sister.' he said placated, thinking by this to distract her hurt.

'And then?'

'Why—I went down to see where the smoke was coming from, feared it was from our home—and it was. All in flames! The soldiers had even kicked over the crosses I placed at the graves! My curse on these evil doers!' he cried, his face torn with pain.

'Mine also,' she spat. 'And then....?'

'I saw Sorley Mor. We came back together—met David just outside the cave. That is all.'

'Perhaps not all,' said Sorley of a sudden. 'Kieran, when last did you milk the cow?'

'Early this morning as always—why?' she asked anxiously.

'The redcoats were driving a cow and a calf before them,' he said quietly. It is only now that it came into my mind. Lachlan, would you check for the cow. She wanders around freely these days—but should not be far away.'

'She will come to my call,' the boy said and disappeared. Fifteen minutes later he was back, his face anguished.

'She is gone—and her calf! I looked carefully on the hill for any traces of the soldier's presence, noticed footmarks in the squelchy ground near the pool and other traces of those devils. Kieran—they must have been close to the entrance of the cave. It was nothing short of a miracle that none of us went out at that point, the roar of the waters masking noise of the soldier's presence.' He looked extremely shaken.

'So no more milk, or butter,' she said tonelessly.

'Unpack the bags, Kieran,' said Sorley tiredly. 'There is food in plenty.' And then his eyes closed as he put his head down on his arms and fell into an exhausted slumber. David looked down on him anxiously. He knew that Sorley had been pushing himself top the limits of his strength and that all their lives were in the hands of this man who bore little resemblance to the young brother of their childhood. The shy, earnest child had become a strong and passionate man of a bright courage, but sadly one who had lost his faith.

When Sorley Mor awoke some hours later, it was to find that Kieran had indeed unpacked the bulging canvas bags. Food was stacked on a rock shelf now, and an appetising stew simmered over the fire. In a far corner, the redcoat officers clothing had been thrown in a disdainful pile, whilst the girl had draped the warm, blue woollen shawl about her shoulders.

'It suits you,' he exclaimed pointing to it, as he got to his feet and stretched.

'Where did you find it?' she asked curiously.

'In the baggage of a redcoat troop, to which I helped myself when the two fellows escorting it—well fell off their horses,' he said with a wry smile. 'They would have stolen it from some poor woman whose house they ransacked.'

'I see. Are you hungry, Sorley Mor?'

'Famished,' he replied and waited as she poured stew into one of the bowls she had brought from the house all those months back. He had often wondered at the way in which her grieving mind had at that time detached itself from the brutality she had suffered, allowing forethought of their future needs to prevail over sorrow. He took the bowl and set to hungrily.

'Here is bread spread with butter you brought,' she said, 'and cheese. A shame about our cow, poor beast—but we will manage.'

'You are a good cook, Kieran,' exclaimed Lachlan approvingly as he attacked his own bowl with youthful appetite. As for David, he had lowered his head and spoken a quiet blessing on the food before joining in. When they had finished, David looked questioningly at his brother.

'Tell us of those two soldiers who—fell off their horses?' he asked.

'Perhaps it is not for a woman's ears,' he replied, glancing at Kieran.

'Speak on,' she said firmly.

47

With a shrug he did so and graphically described his killing of the two men and of helping himself to the contents of the baggage they had guarded. He went on to tell of his journey through the thick clinging mist—the shock of coming across the two women and their children dead of hunger. It was at this that Kieran cried out in horror although the account of the soldier's deaths had provoked no reaction.

'Those poor women—I grieve for them! How can it be that none around offered food?' she cried, for hospitality to the stranger was the cornerstone of highland behaviour, an unwritten code of courtesy and caring.

'Because Kieran, there are none left to do so! The glens have been stripped of their cattle, goats, sheep, chickens—and also now of their people. Those who have not been hanged or beaten to death have faced starvation unless they were able to make their way to the towns. I have spoken to others who have told me of it. It is not merely this glen of yours my dear, but the situation exists across the highlands!'

'I can confirm that from all I have heard,' exclaimed David Stewart. 'Some hardy folks have indeed taken to the high peaks, to live as we are doing in caves. But when the winter comes, survival in such places will be extremely hard.'

'Which is what I have been telling you, Kieran,' added Sorley Mor. 'This is early September. The first snows come to the mountains in October and by November the route we must take south will be almost impassable. For we will not be able to go by Wade's roads you understand—there will be soldiers right along the way.'

'They have a chain of forts right across the Great Glen,' added David, 'And also on Mull and Skye—Castle Stalker is theirs, war ships are constantly on the lookout for any sign of the French making attempt to rescue the Prince by sea.'

Sorley Mor glanced at his brother in surprise, had not realised the other had such knowledge of events. At his unspoken question, David smiled.

'People reveal much to a priest,' he said quietly,' knowing all that is heard is never revealed.'

'Proof of that lies in the way they tried unsuccessfully to beat the names of those known to you who rose for the Prince,' said Sorley respectfully. 'You would have thought that they would have shown some respect for an Episcopal minister, since the official Church of England is similar to ours. Yet here they are treated with the same scorn as Catholics.'

'Even some protestant ministers have been tortured or so I have heard, if they have shown mercy to wounded clansmen,' remarked David sadly.

'But when will all this stop? When will our land be free of these English and we have our chiefs back and our old ways,' asked Lachlan plaintively.

'Possibly never,' replied Sorley Mor. 'They intend to send hundreds maybe thousands or those who supported Charles Edward to the colonies as indentured servants—slaves in other words. The glens once empty of our people, save those who dastardly support the House of Hanover—Clan Campbell for instance, whom they will trust to carry out their orders, the empty glens then will be peopled by farmers from the south. A very different world awaits us Lachlan.'

'How do you know all this to be so—surely you are only guessing at it,' whispered Kieran whose face had gone very white as she listened to their talk.

'Kieran—I have often been away from the cave for long days at a time, have I not? On such occasions I have slipped close to the camps of the redcoats, listened to their officers discussing strategy as laid down by Cumberland and now by Albemarle. I would slither up to their tents with their sentries pacing close by.' He chuckled into his beard.

'You did this?' she looked at him in horror. 'You could have been caught, hanged!'

'Would you have missed me,' he asked curiously. Her only response was an icy glare.

'Then there are those poor men captured at Culloden and rounded up afterwards and who are now kept in the most dire of circumstances in the noisome holds of prison ships, packed together so that they can hardly turn or breathe and sitting in their own ordure,' put in David.

'This is terrible,' cried Kieran softly. 'Glad I am that Alan died a clean death, did not suffer such!'

'The prisons at Inverness and Aberdeen and Perth are as I've been told, also crammed with prisoners in like condition. Manacled, near starvation— waiting a trial which may bring merciful deliverance of the rope.'

Now at last Kieran began to realise the true plight of her country. An adventure entered into with laughter and bright courage, to replace the usurper on the British throne by the true Stuart heir to a four hundred year old dynasty, had ended in this appalling manner, Scotland never to be the same again. She pulled her hair over her face and started to moan softly as her young mind attempted to deal with such horrors.

'The Prince may yet gather men together again—the clans rise and fall upon these cruel English!' cried Lachlan now, refusing to believe the stark reality of the situation. His body trembled with emotion.

'No. Charles Edward is waiting opportunity to escape these shores,' said Sorley quietly. 'At least we may hope that they will not capture him! Too many have died for that to happen.'

'Do we know where he is hiding,' asked Lachlan through his tears.

'The less people know where he is, the better,' explained Sorley Mor. 'It is kept very secret, passing him from one set of loyal friends to another, none knowing where next he is he is to be brought. That way none can be tortured into revealing his whereabouts.' He smiled at the boy. 'Be of good heart, Lachlan Mac Malcolm. You will make a good life for yourself I know. A different life it must be. But you will survive and this is what is important now.'

'Why did you bring the clothing of the English officer here,' asked David now? 'Of what use to us are white breeches and a red coats?'

'They can be dyed black, make a disguise for you and me, David. And there are six fine white linen shirts! If we are going to make attempt to leave the cave in the next few days, we cannot afford to look too conspicuous. I wish we had a razor that we might both dispense with these beards,' he added.

'You have your skene dhu have you not,' said David. 'We will shave each other.'

'I have scissors,' said Kieran, raising her head and listening to their conversation. 'Your hair is that of a wild man, Sorley Mor. It needs must be tamed if we are to mix with the gentle folks of Edinburgh!'

At her words his face creased to a smile and relief shone from his eyes, she had agreed to his plan!

'So you have thought it over, decided? That is very courageous of you,' he said softly. 'I will do all within my power to keep you safe on the journey.'

'Then perhaps I should also accept your offer of marriage—in name only of course, if you still wish it that is. I have given much thought to the matter and as long as it is thoroughly understood that we continue as we are now—no more than friends.' The last words were faltered and her face flushed with confused emotion as she looked at him. But her eyes spoke clear and uncompromising message.

He could hardly believe it. His own eyes as he returned her glance were soft with a light she had never surprised there before.

'Kieran—I now formally ask you to do me the honour of becoming my wife and bearing my name. I promise I will respect the privacy of your person—unless and until you should decide otherwise.' And to his relief, she nodded her agreement.

'Why then, as minister of the church, perhaps you would both like me to hear you exchange your vows? We could have the ceremony here in the cave—Lachlan to be witness?' At the Rev David Stewart's suggestion, Kieran looked taken aback for a minute then almost reluctantly, whispered agreement.

'But not here in the cave,' exclaimed Sorley Mor. 'We will stand together on the hillside in this the land we love so dear. The redcoats will not return in the near future—nothing here for them now.'

'Then go outside the three of you—I will need a few minutes to myself,' said Kieran, frantically wondering what had made her agree to this unwanted marriage. At her command they took themselves out.

The mist had lifted, and the loch glittered silver below them in the evening light, a slight breeze whispering through the birch and alder cladding the sides of the burn, the roar of the waterfall deafening as always, more so as due to the constant rain, the burn was in spate.

David motioned that they should move some yards away from the falls that their voices might be heard.

'Do you Sorley Mor Stewart take this woman Kieran Stewart to your wife........?' intoned David Stewart, and Sorley affirmed it was so in a strong voice.

When it came to the question then put to her, Kieran hesitated for a long moment. What would Alan have said to her marrying again so soon after his death? Since it would be no true marriage, was it terribly wrong to take this vow before God? And suddenly she knew she had a peace about it, that Alan would have understood the circumstances in which her pledge was given.

'I do,' she replied firmly. She removed Alan's ring from her finger and gave it to Sorley. 'You will need this,' she said simply and held out her hand that he might replace it. He raised her hand to his lips and kissed it.

'I will keep all promises I have made to you, Kieran,' he said. Then David made the sign of the cross over them and said a poignant blessing— and Lachlan smiled his delight at what had happened. Now whatever the future held, the four of them were one family, Sorley Mor his brother. He had accepted the Edinburgh physician in place of his dead father and Alan, and swore in his young heart always to be loyal to him.

The four of them continued outside as the light began to fade and then retraced their steps to the cave entrance, slipping with an agility born of much practice behind the curtain of waters.

'I am married again,' thought Kieran, her heart pounding in sudden excitement. But it was no real marriage, she reassured herself. Why then did she feel this strong urge within her to feel his arms about her—to experience his kiss? And angry with herself, she walked over to her heather couch.

'I am tired,' she said tonelessly. 'I bid you goodnight—husband!'

'Sleep well—wife,' was his quiet rejoinder. He wrapped himself about in his plaid, and as he lay there in the dark, staring into the glow of their small fire, Sorley's thoughts were chaotic. He had accomplished the first half of his dream, was now married to the girl who had obsessed his mind with her wild beauty and turbulent spirit. But could the second part of his deep longing possibly come about? Would Kieran Stewart ever come voluntarily to his arms—to his bed? He sighed and at last he slept.

The following morning Lachlan was the first to rise. He made his way along the outer edge of the cave behind the waterfall, to stand looking down at the glen and the loch below, saw its waters partly masked by translucent veil of mist. All about him the mountains hid their heads amongst low hanging cloud, merging with the mist pouring its silent way down their gaunt sides. A fine drenching rain commenced to fall and there was a definite chill in the air.

'Sorley Mor has the right of it,' he breathed. 'We must start our journey soon, before the weather worsens.' But how to leave all this behind, all that despite its devastation was home to him?'

He walked across to some bushes to relieve himself raised his head and stared. Not fifteen feet away a stocky pony was grazing on the sparse grass amongst the heather. He gasped in surprise and started towards it, whispering softly as he approached. It raised its head warily, looked as though it would flee. The boy then stood still and called to it. The pony looked at him distrustfully at first, then to his delight started to move towards him. Then it halted about a yard away, whinnied and shook its mane indecisively.

A minute later he was stroking its neck, which quivered its ongoing distrust. Then at last the little beast relaxed and Lachlan bent and snatched a handful of the straggly grass and offered it. It had accepted him. He had nothing to secure it, no rope—but after a few more soothing words, he returned to the cave, where Kieran was now up and making up the fire.

'Kieran—outside! I have found us a pony!'

'You joke,' she exclaimed, but looking at his excited face, knew he spoke truth. 'Show me,' she said. But by now the men were awake and listening to their words.

Silently Sorley Mor rose to his feet and made his own way along the ledge, to stare at the rough coated pony that backed away at sight of him.

'Wait—let me,' cried Lachlan, who had followed on his heels. 'He knows me now, trusts me!' And sure enough as the boy approached the pony it neighed and allowed Lachlan to walk over and stroke it.

'You have a way with animals,' smiled Sorley. 'I wonder where it has come from.' He bent over the pony and exclaimed at a brand on its side. 'It is a beast of the Campbell's,' he said. 'I heard that Major General Mamore's men were combing the area in search of the Prince. It must have wandered away a few miles to our benefit.'

'Mamore—you speak of the great Campbell Chief,' asked Kieran, drawing close to the pony. 'Well, I am delighted that we can deprive the Clan Campbell of it, for I imagine it will prove of great help to us, in carrying our necessities.'

'For all that the powerful Campbell lord has been involved in harrying our people as fiercely as Cumberland's own men, yet he remains a highlander and is softer in his attitude than those he calls friends.' It was David Stewart who spoke.

'Perhaps you are right—for myself I would never trust any of that clan,' snorted Sorley Mor. 'We need to tether it.' He looked on approvingly as Kieran produced a rope she had fashioned out of the torn and shredded shirt David had originally arrived there in. Now he wore linen acquired by Sorley from the redcoats' stolen baggage, as did Sorley himself. As soon as Lachlan made mention of the pony, Kieran had reached for the rope and brought it to them.

'Suppose the redcoats come back to this area, see the pony—and that telltale rope,' asked David?

'I propose that we make move today,' said Sorley.

'But—where to?' asked Kieran anxiously.

'Let us return to the cave and break our fast and discuss this,' he replied and with a final pat to the carefully tethered pony they did so.

The bread and cheese and wine made a welcome change from oatmeal and now they sat looking at each other. All four of them knew that once they left the security of this cave there would be no turning back and the thought was a difficult one.

'Well, husband—what do you suggest,' inquired Kieran now and Sorley's eyes softened as she used the word. He looked around at them, and began.

'Either we can skirt Fort Augustus and at great risk, take our way along the Great Glen to the east coast and there try to find a fishing boat to take us to the port of Leith at Edinburgh, or make our way south through the mountain passes, through Rannoch and making for Stirling—and onwards. Either way there will be outposts of redcoats to avoid—both equally dangerous. A third way might be to wait by the shores of Morar in hopes of a friendly ship waiting to rescue the Prince.'

'But there are many sloops prowling there at all times, to intercept such a French vessel,' said David. 'And if we were lucky enough to board a French ship—we would then have to accept France as our destination.'

'Besides which, we have no money,' said Kieran.

'Actually we have fifty guineas,' exclaimed Sorley with a smile.

'You—have such a sum,' cried David in surprise. His brother grinned.

'When I examined the baggage belonging to the redcoat officer, I found a small leather box amongst his spare uniform and linen. In it I discovered the gold—and also some jewels, obviously stolen from some unfortunate Highland gentlewoman. He put his hand under his bedding and produced the box in question—and its contents.

'That necklace—I take it the stones are garnets,' said Kieran curiously.

'I am no expert, Kieran, but to me they look like rubies,' he said. 'And look at this gold snuffbox with the enamelled lid, it's French. I can only take it that the fine captain stole these items from one of the great houses they have so recently put to the torch after first taking anything of value.'

'I have no wish to go to France,' cried Kieran decisively. 'I have another plan. True I am again a Stewart wife—but I am of the MacGregor. I grew up in the hills near Loch Voil. Could we not make for this area, where I know my kinsmen would assist us?' Her eyes flashed with excitement as she offered this proposition.

'But Kieran, just consider how much more difficult it is for the proscribed clan MacGregor than any other, forbidden by law bear their own name even before the recent conflict.' He shook his head. 'The Campbells of Argyle, who have ever fiercely hated this clan, recently came against all the Gregorach with great force, harrying them unmercifully. I heard tell that those returning to their glens found all of their houses burned, people fleeing high into their hills to live in caves as we have been.'

'So no succour there, sister,' sighed Lachlan.

'I still say that they would help us!'

'Then may I take it that our plan is to make our way to Edinburgh?' probed Sorley Mor impatiently. She merely shrugged and as for David he waited for an outcome to the question. Sorley sighed and continued-

'If we are to travel from where we are on the far west coast, across and down to Edinburgh on the East, then we must prepare ourselves for a long and difficult journey. One of the major problems as I see it is that our worn and faded tartans instantly proclaim us for what we are—rebels as the government would have it, who never surrendered their weapons. And such they tend to shoot on sight.' David Stewart nodded at his brother's word adding,

'I have heard that those attempting to hand over their weapons at this late stage, are shot often out of hand, if so it takes an officer's fancy!'

'But we have no other clothes,' snapped Kieran aggrieved.

'I thought perhaps we might use dye on what we have,' suggested Sorley hopefully.

'And where am I supposed to find such dye? Herbs, heather, mosses can be used, lichens—but I do not know which ones!' she said finally, dashing aside his suggestion.

'Then we will take a chance as we are,' said Sorley, 'I have the redcoat's breeches and coat—but in their present form they are definitely useless. Still the shirts and hose will serve. Now Kieran, will you gather together those items we will need upon the way—pots to cook in, food and that blanket you have. Lachlan, help her. David, you and I will bring the weapons.' And he handed a musket to his brother.

'But I have never fired a gun in anger—impossible that for a man of the church,' objected David quietly.

'Let us pray that you do not have to choose between your conscience and the saving of life,' was all the response.

To Kieran as they made their way down the hillside, keeping close to the burn and cover of bushes cladding its sides, with Lachlan leading the pony which now had their belongings strapped to its sides, the whole thing seemed a dream. She could not really believe that they had left the cave and its security for all time. But as she breathed in the spicy smell of the damp heather, juniper and gorse, she realised that suddenly she felt alive again.

They were close now to the spot where her house had stood and where Alan and his father slept their last sleep. Sorley Mor would have walked past it, but Kieran uttered a low cry and ran the fifty yards to the ruins of the croft and stood staring down at the mounds that marked the two lonely graves.

'Farewell, Alan—my heart's darling,' she breathed, but found as she turned away to join the others, that the pain she experienced on leaving this dear place was mixed with a strange sense of excitement at whatever the future might hold at the side of this man of whom she really knew so little—Sorley Mor Stewart, now her husband.

He placed a comforting hand on her arm, realising what hurt the revisiting of her one time home must have caused her—but the hand was shrugged off, nor did he attempt to replace it. Time—it would take time he knew, but hoped not too long.

'Are we making towards Inverness or taking the pass through the hills of Glencoe,' asked David walking beside his brother with a spring in his step. They had rounded the length of Loch Dhu, a choice now to be made.

'Considering the danger of skirting too close to Fort William and Fort Augustus and all the many camps they will have set up on the road between, with their soldiers still spreading out among the hills, I feel the pass of Glencoe holds slightly less of a risk. We will of course keep to the hillsides, exercise great caution.' Sorley spoke decisively.

'Then Glencoe let it be,' breathed David, his own lingering unspoken thought of finding ship to France frustratingly put aside. They covered the next few miles in silence, setting their teeth against the rain that had begun to fall. And as they proceeded they were made painfully aware of the depredations carried out by the redcoats. Every so often the burnt out shells of the poor huts of those who had lived their fragile existence in the glens, told their own bitter tale. Of people and animals, no trace remained.

Kieran had been incredulous at first, could hardly believe the devastation. Apart from what had occurred to their immediate neighbours in Glen Ardoch, the horror of the killings reported by Lachlan, she had no idea of the wider picture in the Highlands, her mind full of her own troubles, her grief at Alan's death.

Now, as they clambered warily high above the unmade track road, leaping the smaller of the burns that raced down the hillsides, struggling through the wider, deeper and dangerous torrents of brown, foam tossed waters, she held her skirts high above her knees, battling the rain that stung her face and bending before the wind that funnelled through the hills, her heart numb with grief at her country's fate.

Autumn was as wet and wild as the summer just past. She had not experienced any of its constant rain over the last months, safe within their cave, nor had she had any form of exercise to speak of. Now she needed all her will power to keep pace with the men. But determination lent her strength, although her legs ached and feet felt bruised and sore.

At last, as evening was falling, Sorley Mor glanced keenly around and pointed to an outcrop of rocks.

'Up there. That is where we will spend the night,' he said and obediently they followed in his footsteps, Lachlan still leading the patient pony with their possessions. They would obtain scant protection here from the elements but tired enough to drop were almost past caring.

Lachlan unloaded the pony forgetting to tether it in his weariness. They crouched down together and ate some of the cheese and stale bread, washed down by water from a nearby swift flowing burn and a draught of the redcoats wine. It would do for now. Tomorrow they would seek a safer place to light a fire, perhaps cook and try to dry their clothes—but with the ongoing rain such would not make too much sense.

'The pony—it has gone!' exclaimed Kieran suddenly. They rose to their feet, looking around in all directions, but of the pony saw no sign. From now on they would have to carry their bags themselves. Lachlan whispered his apology that he had not taken better care of the little beast. But what good would any recriminations have been Kieran thought, and squeezed his arm understandingly. The men sighed resignedly. All then attempted to get some rest.

'Listen—down there on the road. Do you hear it?' came Sorley's harsh whisper, as Kieran made a pillow of her shawl, preparing to sleep.

'Yes,' whispered David. 'I hear sound of a horse approaching!'

It was almost dusk now and misty. Sorley Mor raised his head above the rocks to look below, straining his eyes to search for movement. Then he saw the source of the noise, a solitary rider approaching in Highland garb. Nor would any Jacobite dare ride thus fearlessly along, he realised. No, this had to be a Campbell or member of another of the other clans supporting the Hanoverians.

But why did he ride alone? Even as he watched, he saw two men break concealment on the far side of the track and prepare to hurl themselves upon the rider. Why he shouted out in warning at that moment, Sorley Mor could never comprehend afterwards when reliving the event in memory. For those who assailed the rider would have been of a clan friendly to his own. It was the instinctive reaction to protect another human being and it was stronger than blind hatred.

Alerted by Sorley's warning shout, the rider attempted to draw his sword to fend off his assailants, but within seconds was lying on the ground, as the men stripped him of weapons and valuables and made off with his horse.

'He must surely be dead—and besides which, an enemy,' reasoned Sorley Mor to David, who had witnessed all. 'Yet in all humanity, I must go down there and see if any life lingers.' And before his resolution should falter, the physician started down the steep brae to the fellow lying on the road below him. He raised the man's head, saw he was young, good looking, lace at his throat, his shirt stained with a dark spreading patch. His assailants had taken his jacket, but his trews as far as Sorley could make were of the Campbell tartan.

'If you are going to kill me—be quick about it,' a faint whisper issued between the man's lips.

'I am a physician, friend. You have received a dirk thrust to your breast. Too dark to see much at the moment, but I am going to tear a strip from your shirt to bind the wound. 'And Sorley proceeded to do so, then sat back on his heels and stared down at his patient.

'Was it you who shouted warning?' asked the young Campbell now through pale lips. 'Who are you?'

'One who should have more sense than to involve myself with a Campbell,' came the short reply.

'I will see you are well rewarded for your help! Had those damned rebels not made off with my purse....!' He looked up at Sorley painfully.

'One gentleman does not pay another for a service,' was the curt admonition, as Sorley Mor frowned down upon him.

'Yes—of course. I crave your forgiveness, sir. But at least give me your name. I may be able to offer service of some kind to you. I am Roderick Campbell, nephew to Mamore.'

'Dr Sorley Mor Stewart out of Edinburgh whence I am trying to make return,' replied the other, wondering if he was completely mad to furnish his name. Then as they stared at each other, he tried to decide what to do next. 'Well, you cannot stay here in the road. Do you think you could manage up the hill a bit, if I support you?' But before the attempt could be made, there was the unmistakeable sound of horses approaching at speed out of the mist!

They were upon Sorley Mor before he had a chance to run—nor would he have attempted to reach the rocks where the others were hiding—could not risk betraying their presence. He found himself set upon by three burly militia men, as the others shouted curses on him. A tall elderly officer who seemed to be in authority among them was stooping over the wounded man.

'Roderick lad—are you much wounded?' the officer demanded anxiously. 'What possessed you to ride off on your own?'

'A dirk wound. I was attacked by two fellows who came from nowhere. The man you hold is innocent of any harm. He is a doctor—has been caring for me,' murmured Captain Roderick Campbell. 'Have him released, I pray you.'

At his words, the elderly officer whose features Sorley Mor could barely distinguish in the misty night rapped out an order and he was instantly released.

'Your name,' demanded his interrogator?

'Dr Sorley Mor Stewart,' was the weary reply. What use to withhold his name when the young Campbell Captain could so easily provide it?

'Ah—a surgeon of the vanquished enemy force, I take it,' said the other Campbell musingly. 'I should have you sent under guard to Fort William, and then down to London to stand trial with all other Jacobites not yet surrendered.'

Sorley did not reply, merely looked straight ahead. There seemed to be little hope for his future now. But at least the others might make it to safety and he prayed they be not discovered some few twenty yards above the road.

'Mr Stewart not only dressed my wound, Uncle—he shouted warning when my assailants fell upon me. Without that warning I would undoubtedly lie dead.' Roderick Campbell was doing his best to speak in defence of the man who had so strangely attempted his rescue. And at his words Major General John Campbell of Mamore, on whose decision the lives and deaths of so many in the western highlands rested, nodded thoughtfully.

'A strange reaction from a rebel,' he said.

'I am a physician as well as one who dreamed of a Stuart King,' replied the dark eyed man who stared so fearlessly back at him. 'The battle is over. We all know this and life has to go on. I planned to return to Edinburgh to take up my practice there again.'

'Then in recompense for your help to my nephew, I will make out a pass for you to present whenever you are challenged along the way!'

Sorley Mor could hardly believe what he heard. He drew in his breath and took a great chance.

'I am travelling with my pregnant wife and two others,' he said now. 'May I ask that you make out passes for them also, Lord Mamore?' At his words the other surveyed him darkly, hands on hips as he considered his reply. Then with a smile he nodded slowly.

'It would be churlish to refuse a man with the courage to make such a request. Where are these others? But hurry man, I am in haste to get my nephew between sheets and a proper care of him.'

'On the brae above us—I will call to them,' exclaimed Sorley and at his call and beckoning hand, with distinct hesitation, his wife, brother and young Lachlan scrambled slowly down towards them, having taken the precaution of leaving their weapons concealed behind the rocks that had sheltered them.

The three halted at the side of the road, uneasy at the prospect of drawing nearer to the tall officer whom all others there seemed to hold in high respect. Mamore scowled impatiently and motioned them to stand before him. His steel dark eyes scanned one face after another, returning to that of Kieran Stewart.

'Your names,' he inquired, still holding Kieran in his glance. She had recognised the tartan and emblem in his bonnet and looked as though she would flee back onto the hill, but Sorley Mor laid a retraining hand on her arm. And still Mamore stared musingly at the young woman, examining her unusual beauty as well as the dim light permitted.

'Allow me to introduce my wife, Kieran Stewart,' said Sorley Mor courteously, 'And my brother David and my wife's young relative, Lachlan Stewart.' Then addressing them in turn, 'This is Major General John Campbell of Mamore, who of his kindness has offered to give us passes to facilitate our journey to Edinburgh!'

'Kindness and protection—from a Campbell,' snapped Kieran angrily, her breast heaving with emotion.

But Mamore's eyes had left her and turned down to look in concern at his nephew. The young man obviously in considerable pain was unable to restrain a groan. Instantly Sorley was on his knees beside him.

'You should get him to your camp, General,' he said with authority. 'The knife went deep—but must have missed the lung, for there is no bloody foam about his lips.' He tightened the bandage and looked up.

'You speak sense,' said Mamore crisply. Come then, you will accompany us!' He addressed to his men. 'We need a stretcher for Captain Roderick Campbell—and show care! Have these men and the boy mounted, bring them!' he instructed a sergeant. Resuming his seat on his own stallion, he turned and looked down at Kieran. 'Lady, you will ride with me,' he said and before she could protest, had swung her up before him on his horse.

Trying to contain her abhorrence she kept her seat with the natural grace of one used to riding, but her heart was pounding in her breast with fury at his close proximity—and concern for the future. Sensing her antagonism in the very stiffness of her posture, he spoke no word as they rode a slight smile about his lips.

Chapter Four

Kieran Stewart would long remember that ride through the gathering gloom of a September evening with the mist snaking down between the hills, masking the emergent stars She sat almost rigidly before Mamore, her heart beating with anger that she was with the Commander whose dark deeds among the Stewarts and MacDonalds and Camerons and her own MacGregors, were almost as cruel as those of the English whose cause he espoused. Why had Sorley Mor not left the Campbell Captain to lie in his blood—why get embroiled and bring them all into such imminent danger from a feared and hated foe?

They were turning off the track now and Kieran realised that they were entering a camp—were being challenged by a sentry. She saw the shape of many tents in the flaring light of torches as respectful members of the militia came hurrying forward to take Mamore's horse and she was lifted down. She looked around anxiously for Sorley and the others and it was with relief saw them coming to join her.

The four of them stood impassively and waited for what was to happen next. Within minutes a shout went out that Sorley Mor Stewart was needed in the Major General's tent and with a reassuring glanced at Kieran he followed the guard who had come seeking him. He was pushed without ceremony into one of the larger of the canvas tents, where he found himself once more in the presence of Mamore, who was looking down in concern at Roderick Campbell lying on a folding trestle couch.

'See to his needs,' instructed Mamore. 'An orderly will supply you with whatever you require for his comfort! I do not have an army surgeon with me, so will rely on you to do your best for him!'

'I need water to wash my hands—surgical dressings if you have any,' demanded Sorley Mor. 'Also may I have my wife here to assist me as nurse,' he added daringly. Mamore stared at him, nodded assent.

'Fetch the Stewart woman,' he ordered and a soldier leapt to follow his orders. The fellow hurried to the tent where the rebels were being kept secure and snapped out her name, with message that her husband required her to help in care of their Captain. She rose to her feet and followed him casting a nervous glance behind her where David and Lachlan crouched patiently on the ground, under a guard's watchful eyes.

Mamore looked up impatiently as she entered the tent where the wounded man lay.

'Help your husband, lady,' he instructed and was about to walk away, but paused and stared keenly at Kieran's face. He swore softly beneath his breath and shook his head. It was thing impossible—yet the resemblance was very real! But this was not the time to inquire into such matters, his duty called him elsewhere to hear result of work carried out by those of his men he had earlier dispatched into the hills to search out any rebels who had so far eluded their diligence.

'We found only one man worth bringing in,' explained the sergeant who now reported to Mamore. 'Others had been before us, houses burned out wherever we looked, stock driven off. There were a few corpses discovered, mainly women and children—dead of hunger,' he added, Mamore swore, but whether in pleasure or anger the sergeant was unsure.

'The man you took—his name, Sergeant?'

'Why, he says it is John MacPherson, my lord.'

'Bring him here. He may have word of Cluny MacPherson's whereabouts!' And perhaps might also have word of the Prince, he thought. There was a rumour that two ships but which might indeed be French, but showing English colours, had been seen anchored in the waters of Loch Nan Uamh. Was another rescue attempt underway for The Pretender, he worried?

'The rebel John MacPherson, General!' and the voice made him snap out of his reverie. He stared at the haggard unshaven face of the man brought before him in chains. The prisoner was wounded, blood staining the front of the brown jacket he wore over torn trews, feet bare.

'Do you know who I am,' asked Mamore?

'A Campbell chief so I am told!' returned the man quietly.

'Major General John Campbell of Mamore commanding his Majesty King George's West Highland militia—with the power of life and death you understand.' The crisp introduction seemed to have little effect upon the man who stared haughtily back at him.

'I wish to know the whereabouts of your Chief—of Cluny MacPherson. Give me this information and if it proves truthful you may be allowed to go free.' Mamore looked at him hopefully, but the prisoner merely spat on the ground before making mocking reply.

'Cluny goes where he will—free as the wind that blows and with a hundred caves in which to shelter him!'

'Indeed—and in which particular cave is Cluny now resident?' pursued Mamore ponderously.

'That only the wind and Cluny knows!' At this the militia man guarding the prisoner caught him a blow about the head.

'Do not dare to show such insolence to the General,' he snarled. But Mamore continued as though nothing untoward had occurred.

'I hear that The Pretender is about to fly the nest—to attempt return to France. Tell me where he is and you will be well rewarded with not only your life but gold as well!'

'If thirty thousand pounds has not brought you news of the Prince—and out people poor and without food or clothing or shelter due to your cruelties—how think you my Lord Mamore that your offer to me will achieve it! You insult my name!' MacPherson stared at him fearlessly. With a curse of frustration Mamore rapped out an order.

'Take him outside—and shoot him!' Minutes later there was the sound of gunshot and Kieran raised her head from the wounded Campbell officer whose wound she was helping Sorley Mor to tend.

'What could that be,' she whispered to him. Soft as her question was, the guard at the door of the tent heard it and grinned.

'Why lady—a captured MacPherson being duly dispatched as rebel,' he said, 'one less of the scum to deal with!'

She gasped at his brutal statement, but Sorley laid a restraining hand on hers and she looked down again and helped to hold the final dressing in place as Sorley secured it. With any luck the young officer should live. He sighed and straightened up.

Now with their task accomplished, Kieran glanced down at the face of their patient—stared and frowned. He was good looking, this Campbell captain, with hair the same shade as her own and for some reason looked vaguely familiar—but why? She had never come across him before, regarded all Campbells with hatred, never having met with one socially. And as she stared down at him, the Captain opened his eyes and gasped at the sight of her.

'Mother,' he murmured longingly and attempted to reach a hand up to her. It fell back again and his eyes closed once more. Sorley and Kieran glanced at each other in amazement.

'Can he be delirious—yet does not seem so,' said Sorley, placing a hand on the man's brow and finding it cool. 'He must have been dreaming—and awoke for but a minute from his dream. Many men when wounded or near the point of death call for their mothers.' He looked up at the guard standing at his patient's bedside, 'This man will live,' he said. 'Kindly inform General Campbell that such is the case!'

Mamore's anger had cooled by the time message came to his tent that the Stewart doctor had brought healing to the young relative whom he highly esteemed. He would accordingly reward him with the promised pass for himself and his party. He drew the necessary permits toward him on the portable table and stared down broodingly once he had made them out.

'The girl—so strange the resemblance to the young woman whom he remembered, not only in her colouring—red gold hair of that hue was not unusual in the West Highland clans—but her unusual storm grey eyes, the tilt of her head and her bearing, all so like to that of Catriona Campbell, mother of the his young distant cousin, whom he styled his nephew.

But Catriona had died nigh on twenty long years ago, her Campbell husband killed by the MacGregor who had also kidnapped her, stolen her away to Balquidder and forced her into an unwanted marriage. True Clan Campbell had taken revenge on this Rory MacGregor, caught and hung him, but too late to save his forced bride who had died in childbirth, never more to see the three year old son Roderick Campbell, from whose side she had been forcibly taken by the marauding villain Rory MacGregor.

He sighed. A long time ago all of this and only brought to mind by the strange resemblance between the Stewart doctor's wife and the beauteous young woman who had gone untimely to her grave. He decided to drive the riddle from his mind—yet go it would not. He stood up.

'Have the four travellers we arrested on the road given bed for tonight. In the morning, I wish to speak with the Stewart woman,' he ordered and sat deep in thought, drinking a glass of his fine brandy before eventually retiring.

Sorley Mor glanced across to where his young wife lay sleeping at one end of the army tent, while he and his brother and Lachlan kept to the far side as far as space permitted. He could only see the outline of her shape where she rested in the foetal position, heard her sigh a name into the night—and the name was that of Alan, her late husband. Would she ever sufficiently forget her love for the young man so cruelly murdered on his return from Culloden field, to engage in a new love with him? But then why should she? He was older than she was, had little to offer at this time apart from his devotion and protection.

He fell into troubled sleep. The sounding of the pipes of Clan Diarmid awakened them. Kieran sat up and tried to order her tumbled tresses, as the others arose and straightened their clothing. Sorley Mor remembered the sound of last night's gunshot as the arrested MacPherson was casually dispatched. He knew all of their own lives were still far from secure.

His thoughts flew to his patient, the Campbell captain and stooping told Kieran he would seek permission to go to him.

'How are you this morning, Captain Campbell,' he inquired as he took the man's wrist and found his pulse beat satisfactory. The guard who had escorted him to the wounded man's tent kept his fierce gaze upon the

Stewart doctor, but relaxed somewhat as he saw the smile about the young man's lips.

'Living it would seem—and recovering apart from this pain in my chest!'

'I will give you a draught to relieve it. The blade struck deep, you know.'

'Would have killed me but for your care!' He lifted his head from the pillow and stared up at Sorley Mor. 'Why did you do it—help an enemy?' he demanded.

'I saw no enemy—merely a man in need of help,' replied Sorley Mor. 'A doctor takes oath to heal all people to the best of his ability, nor to discriminate in that care!'

'Well said,' came a deep voice behind him and Sorley Mor swung about to see the Major General John Campbell of Mamore standing there, with a musing smile on his face. 'You have an unusual attitude for a rebel Stewart and it has served you well.'

'I thank you, my Lord Mamore! The Captain must refrain from activity for at least ten days to two weeks to allow deeper healing,' and he mixed a powder with water and proffered it to the young soldier. 'Drink—it will ease your hurt,' he said.

'Tell me of yourself?' Mamore demanded curiously. 'Where did you train, Doctor Stewart?'

'In Edinburgh, and when qualified returned to Appin to work among my people,' he said quietly. 'When my wife died in childbirth, I placed the child with foster parents and left to pursue my further studies abroad.'

'In France?'

'There and elsewhere—the Low Countries.'

'When did you return?'

'Three years ago and commenced a practice in Edinburgh.'

'You would have been wiser to have stayed there! Whatever possessed you to throw up your career to chase the crazy dream of a witless young Italian in his attempt to overthrow the legitimate government of this country?'

'Is it so you describe Charles Edward Stuart,' exclaimed Sorley hotly.

'Yes my friend, I speak of a Stuart Prince born of an unstable Polish mother and raised in Italy. No true Scot I assure you, the ridiculous adventure of this spoiled puppy costing the lives of hundreds upon hundreds of the people of this land. You are an intelligent man and know I speak truth.' He stared squarely at Sorley Mor who longed to smite the contemptuous smile from the Campbell's face, but caution retrained him.

'Yet thousands were prepared to lay down their lives for him,' was all he said.

'And now are left without home or hearth or any least means of sustenance. Was it all worth it, think you?' Mamore paused. 'You say your wife died some years ago. Your present wife your second then—how long have you been wed to Kieran Stewart?'

The question unexpected caught Sorley unawares. No time to fabricate an answer, nor would he have done so.

'We wed some few weeks ago,' he said.

'Yet she is with child of some months I would surmise?' He watched the doctor's colour rise.

'Kieran's husband Alan Stewart was murdered on the day of his return from Culloden,' he said clearly. 'On that same occasion she was raped by the militia who broke into their home—though not your men, Mamore.'

'You saw this?'

'No. I had left the young couple to the joy of their reunion. Her father-in-law, who suffered a disturbance of the mind, was also murdered at his fireside. I buried them—took Kieran and Alan's young stepbrother up into the hills for safety. With winter approaching, I thought to bring her to Edinburgh. I have a house there.'

'I will see you are allowed to pass on your way without hindrance. But tell me now, your brother—where does he fit into all this?'

'David is an Episcopalian priest. He did not go out with the clans, stayed in his village, a quiet man of God. Soldiers came—tried to force him to give list of those who had left the village to join the Prince. He refused to comply with their wishes—was flogged almost to death!' Sorley's voice quivered as he spoke. 'When I came across him he was in a sorry state. Nearly all in his village killed or fled into the hills—homes destroyed.'

'Well, obviously he has much to thank you for—as have the others. I will not inquire into your own activities in the uprising. If you give your word to proceed peacefully to Edinburgh, there shall be an end of it.'

Sorley Mor could hardly believe what he heard.

'You have my word, sir,' he said.

'You may return to your tent for now—and send Mistress Stewart to me.' He saw the apprehension on Sorley's face. 'Have no fear. Your wife resembles one once known to me. I merely wish to inquire details of her family,' he said, and with new worry consuming his heart, Sorley went to give Kieran the General's request, dared not do otherwise if they were to be soon on their way out of this Campbell hornet's nest.

Mamore now dismissed the soldier on guard in the tent where Roderick Campbell lay drowsing as the doctor's drug took effect. He looked down at the young man affectionately.

'So how are you really feeling, my boy?'

'Much improved, sir! I owe a debt to the doctor.' He raised his eyes to the commanding figure at his bedside. 'I had a most unusual experience last night, can only think my mind wandered somewhat. But you see—I

66

thought I saw my mother!' His grey eyes held puzzled stare. 'I only remember her slightly—but often look at her image which I wear about my neck.' And he attempted to lift the locket he wore about his neck.

'Let me,' said Mamore gently and releasing the clasp of the fine gold chain, took the locket in his hand and pressed the catch. He looked down in amazement at the painted image. He had indeed been right in his memory of this young man's mother—the unfortunate Catriona Campbell. And while he still stared down at the painting, a feminine voice was heard instructing the guard that she was bidden to wait upon the Major General.

She came in and raised expressive eyebrows in an almost haughty stare, as the two Campbell men let out exclamations of surprise.

'You sent for me, my Lord,' she said crisply.

'Yes lady—pray you be seated,' and he pushed a stool towards her and then continued to look at her in silence. As for the patient, he was looking as though he had just seen a ghost. What was wrong with them? She frowned.

'Mistress Stewart, I have just spoken at length with your husband and since none of your party would seem to offer threat to the continuing peace of this area, you are now allowed to pursue your journey to Edinburgh.' The commander paused. 'However, there are a few personal questions I would ask you to answer.'

'Very well, sir,' she replied, watching him curiously.

'First of all, I must tell you that Dr Stewart has told me of your former marriage to Alan Stewart, a tacksman of Appin?'

'That is so,' and her lip trembled.

'I deeply regret the treatment you received at the hands of His Majesty's troops—but during insurrection such unfortunately occurs. Now tell me, was your name also Stewart before your marriage to the late Alan Stewart?'

She looked at him in perplexity. What business of his was her maiden name? But Kieran was proud of her MacGregor forebears.

'I am the daughter of one Rory MacGregor, murdered by those of your clan, Lord Mamore,' she said coldly. 'I was brought up by his brother Duncan and his wife Annie, as my own mother died in giving birth to me.'

'Her name was Catriona,' said Mamore quietly.

'It was—but how could you know that?' asked Kieran in surprise.

'Because she was a Campbell—her true name Catriona Campbell and married to the father of the patient you cared for last night. Colin Campbell and Catriona had a three year old son, Roderick here. His father died at the hands of Rory Campbell. Him we hanged a few months later. We discovered that Catriona had died in childbirth—did not realise the child had survived.'

'You are telling me that I have Campbell blood in my veins, as well as of MacGregor?' She spit out the words and glared as though she would have torn his eyes out.

'No. I say that you are a true Campbell, my dear. Catriona was already three months pregnant by her husband Colin, when she was kidnapped and forced into marriage by Rory MacGregor!'

'It is not possible—not possible,' she moaned in distraction. Then her eyes strayed to the bed where the young captain lay and who had been listening as though spellbound. And as she looked at him as though pleading that he would deny it.

'Then—you are my sister,' he exclaimed now. 'It was you who leaned over my bed last night. I thought I dreamed that it was my mother. You are so like to my childhood memory of her—and to this!' He pointed to the locket which Mamore still held. The older man now held it out to her and almost unwillingly she took the small painted image and forced herself to look at it. She gasped.

'It could be me,' she whispered. 'It is true then? I am one of the hated Campbell—my whole life a lie?'

'It would seem that through no fault of your own, true details of your birth have been hidden from you! No doubt it amused the MacGregors to bring you up as one of their own. You now know the truth, my dear. What you do with this information is of course for you to decide. Roderick and I will keep this matter private until you decide otherwise.'

'My whole life lies in ruins,' she cried distractedly.

'Say rather a new chapter may be about to begin! Know that should you desire it, you will always be welcome as member of my family in Argyll. But if you prefer, for the present at least to make your way to Edinburgh with your husband, then I wish you well—but if ever you are in need or trouble, then feel assured I will assist in any way possible.'

'You have been more than kind, Lord Mamore,' she said softly, forcing out the words. 'But you must realise that I am unable to accept kinship with any of Clan Campbell.' She sensed the power in this grey haired man with his arrogant features, the almost analytical gaze he now observed her with.

'Then we will leave matters as they are for now. But never forget Kieran, you have found a brother, who like you was brought up by other than his real parents. Blood is strong—stronger than hatred as you will no doubt realise one of these days!' Mamore's eyes were kind as he looked at her. They also expressed pity that she would not be able to throw off the hatred for her true family imbued by her upbringing. As for Roderick Campbell, he tried to raise himself on his pillow to take one last look at this newly discovered sister, before she disappeared.

'Kieran—may we not at least be friends,' he said now, stretching a hand out to her. But she rejected the gesture and rose from her stool.

'If you are finished with your questions, Lord Mamore?' she said. He nodded thoughtfully and gestured she should feel free to leave. She inclined her head to both in turn and hurried from the tent, out into the falling rain and now her tears started to fall as the shock of all that had been revealed left her feeling sick and bewildered.

How could she still pretend to be MacGregor, never mind Stewart, when the ugly truth had presented itself to her thus unexpectedly? If only she could turn the clock back by half an hour—or if only they had remained in the security of the cave, then none of this shocking revelation would have afflicted her.

'Kieran—what ails you? You seem distressed!' Sorley Mor had been watching the entrance to the tent anxiously since she had gone in, wondering just what Mamore had wanted with the girl. He had not taken the Major General for a womaniser, but in the times now prevailing across the Highlands, no-one and nothing appeared sacred. He saw the tears in her eyes and went to place a hand about her shoulders. But she pushed him away—and he stared at her, hurt.

'What is wrong, Kieran? Did Mamore offend you in some way?'

'No. He did not offend me—but destroyed all my joy in life!' she sobbed.

'Then let me have a word with him,' exclaimed Sorley wrathfully, making towards the man's tent. But she laid a hand briefly on his arm.

'No! You must say nothing—nor ask any questions!'

'Why not? Something is badly wrong—what is it? Just tell me, wife!''

'If you knew, you would no longer wish to call me so!'

'What foolishness is this,' he retorted in astonishment. But she merely shook her head and stared unseeingly towards the hills that soared about them. He swore under his breath, not knowing how best to comfort her. Then he brightened as he considered that soon they would be on their way and as though to confirm this, Mamore appeared, lifting the flap of the tent and beckoning Sorley Mor toward him.

'Your passes,' he said formally, handing the documents to the doctor. 'You will note that each states 'Under the direct protection of Major General John Campbell of Mamore' and should bring you safe to Edinburgh. I will see that you are given provisions for your journey and mounts. When you arrive in Edinburgh, you will take the horses to the military barracks at the castle.'

'You have been more than generous, my Lord Mamore,' replied Sorley Mor. 'I will in future regard Campbells in a more kindly light!' he added, and wondered at the smile of amusement that curled the others lip.

'I have no doubt of that,' was all the reply.

There were many dangers encountered in their long and tiring journey over the next two weeks, challenged on numerous occasions by troops from different branches of the militia, some of whom scowled at their passes as though doubting their authenticity. But Mamore had affixed his own seal and such could not be disputed.

At last they had left the mountains behind them and reached Stirling, where Sorley Mor left Kieran at a small inn with his brother and Lachlan, whilst he went looking for a shop where he might buy clothing to improve their appearance before venturing on to Edinburgh. He was grateful for the redcoat officer's gold, and chose suitable masculine garments—then did his best to select a warm green skirt and blouse and riding cloak for Kieran, this together with shoes.

They looked at each other in astonishment as they disported their new apparel. Sorley had chosen sober lowland clothing, such as would attract little attention, his apparel similar to that he would normally have worn in his profession as doctor.

'You look very well dressed in that way,' exclaimed Sorley Mor to Kieran, and indeed so she did, appearing very attractive despite her six months pregnancy. She had washed her hair, tied back its red gold waves with a ribbon.

She ignored his compliment, lost seemingly in some mysterious world of her own. Ever since she had spoken with Mamore, he had noticed this strange change in her. At one time he had hoped that she would eventually look on him with some kindness, if not affection—but these days she was cold in her manner with him, distant also with David and Lachlan, nor would she give any explanation for this change which was hurtful to all of them.

They rode in through the city gates, having shown their passes to sentries there who inquired their business. And yet again Mamore's seal and signature opened the way for them.

'I am supposed to present these borrowed horses to the barracks,' said Sorley Mor.

'Then you may leave them with me,' said a uniformed officer who had been observing them curiously. 'I will have them delivered on your behalf,' and he signed to a fellow guard to relieve the travellers of their stout ponies, waiting first as they removed the bag with their few belongings. Now they were all four wandering through narrow streets, where houses leaned towards each other and Kieran wrinkled her nose as she inhaled air that was redolent with smells not encountered in the country.

She stared upwards towards the Castle standing high and proud on its hill. She knew that this castle had resisted capture by the Prince in his five weeks stay in Edinburgh, when he had occupied Holyrood Palace. She also knew that her beloved Alan would have walked these streets at that time and she heaved a sigh. But she would not have been Alan Stewart's wife had he known of her true parentage—that she was of the detested Clan Campbell!

'You are deep in thought, Kieran,' said David, as they waited for a rattling carriage to pass before crossing the cobbled street.

'I was remembering Alan,' she said simply.

'He would have been very proud of the courage you have shown, my dear,' said the priest kindly. 'But now a whole new life awaits you here in this fine city!'

'It smells!'

'Yes, so it does. So do many cities, I fear. Who knows—in the years to come perhaps Sorley may be able to return with you to the Highlands we all love so well.'

'I can never return!'

'Never is a long time, my dear. I truly believe that in a few years time, matters may improve, the English relax their iron grip.'

'But it will be when all our people are dead—or sent to the colonies as slave labour,' she replied angrily. He did not reply but bowed his head not wanting her to see that he thought she was right in what she surmised. They spoke no further, merely following Sorley Mor who was walking purposefully ahead, buoyed up by knowledge that he was very near his home.

He mounted the steep steps to the solid front door with its lion head knocker, beckoning them to join him as he put a key in the lock—and let them in. The hallway was dark, but a pleasant room led off to the right, dominated by heavy dark furniture, with long, blue velvet curtains at the windows. Over the fireplace there was a large oil painting—and Kieran recognised the view of the Linnhe Loch.

'That was painted by one who knew and loved it,' she said pointing to the picture. 'How I wish we were all back there!'

'With our lives in constant danger—probably facing eventual starvation in winter,' exclaimed Sorley Mor. He felt slightly aggrieved, had hoped for a happier response to his home. 'Come then—I will show you upstairs to the bedrooms.' He noticed that Kieran's face grew darker at mention of this, but she followed him up the creaking staircase with the others behind. With a polite gesture, he opened the nearest door on the upper landing.

'I have only three bedrooms. This is for you, Kieran—and this other room for you my brother. I will put in a truckle bed for Lachlan, the two of you to share—and I will take the small box room.' He had already planned the arrangement on their way here and saw Kieran give small smile of relief that she was to sleep alone. True he had promised this—but he realised sadly that she had not completely trusted his word.

Nor had Sorley Mor the slightest notion that deep in her heart Kieran felt pang of disappointment that this marriage was indeed to be in name only, the rational part of her brain knowing that even this was straining all that was right and proper. How could she in all conscience continue at his side, even as companion, when if he became aware of her true parentage, that she was of the despised and hated Clan Diarmid he would draw back from her in deepest outrage. No, she must remove herself from these three who cared for her as soon as was possible—but how to do so when she had no money, nor any knowledge of city life.

Now at last they were safe and slowly the tension of the last months started to drain away. Kieran watched as Sorley removed his clothing and personal possessions from the room that was now hers and felt uncomfortable that she had obviously displaced him.

'We must get new clothes for you,' he said to Kieran as he made to leave the room, trailing jackets, trousers and shirts.

'And how will we do so, when you have already used all of the redcoats gold?' she demanded practically, as she sank down wearily on the bed.

'I have a little with my man of business, saved from my work as physician. Enough to keep us going for a while—but I must resume my duties immediately, and hope no questions are asked about my years disappearance.' He looked at Kieran thoughtfully. 'How would you feel about assisting me as nurse?'

'But—I have no training as such!' she exclaimed.

'You would be quick to learn, and the presence of a nurse when I am examining a female patient would help to put a woman at ease.'

'I will think about it,' she replied.

'Good. I will probably ask you to commence your duties tomorrow then,' he said walking away as though all was settled, as she closed the door crossly behind him, then threw herself down on the bed to consider what best to do. How could she lead the rest of her life as a lie?

Sorley Mor left his brother David resting in exhausted slumber, as Lachlan followed him, seeking in his mind as to what he could do to help this man who had come into their lives bringing change and hope. The noise and bustle of the Edinburgh streets had been a shock to the boy, accustomed as he was to the hills and lochs and deep quiet of the Highlands. Strange and somewhat unpleasant smells had assaulted his nostrils. But with all this there was also excitement to be in the country's capital.

'Hold my hammer for a minute, Lachlan' said Sorley now, as he reattached the painted board announcing this as the residence of a doctor. He had removed it when he had left just over a year ago and made for the Highlands to join the Prince. How long ago it all seemed now. He remembered the subsequent triumphant entry of the clans into Edinburgh as a bold Cameron had headed in through the gate opened to let out a hackney carriage, followed by an irreversible surge of kilted warriors, as the pipes encouraged them on in ever greater numbers.

Most of the bewildered citizenry had slammed themselves within doors, fearful for the future, whilst those who favoured the Jacobite cause had hung out of their windows waving welcome. But the castle was held against them, an island impregnable where the forces of the crown made occasional cannon shots to discourage any of the exuberant insurgents from approaching too near.

They had only remained in Edinburgh for a brief five weeks, where Charles Edward Stuart had taken up residence in Holyrood Palace, the home of his ancestors. A spirit of caution had caused Sorley not to resume residence in his own house at this time, his quarters on the other side of the city. He wondered now as he stood back to adjust the sign, whether any would remember seeing him with others of the Appin Stewarts. But now clean shaven and his hair clubbed neatly back, he looked very different. But how to explain his absence he wondered?

Sorley handed the hammer back to Lachlan, then as the two of them stood there, he was stridently hailed by a grey haired, elderly woman who had been watching them from the doorstep of the neighbouring house.

'And is it yourself back again, Doctor Stewart,' she cried.

'Why—it is Mistress Morton is it not? I hope I see you well,' he exclaimed with a smile.

'Well enough—well enough, although these old bones of mine trouble me cruelly at night. Where will you have been then, Doctor? I do hope you were not caught up in all the unrest in those wild areas in the north?' She fixed dark eyes curiously upon him, glancing also at the youngster at his side. As he looked at her, the perfect answer occurred to Sorley.

'I went on a visit to my relatives—and found myself a wife,' he explained. 'Young Lachlan here is kin, and will be helping me about the place.' He made to go indoors again, but the woman was not to be put off so easily.

'A wife, say you—she is here with you?'

'Where else would a man's wife be? Kieran is resting after her journey, is with child,' he added. At this the woman's curiosity seemed appeased. A smile broke across her bony old face.

'Och then, but you have done well to get wed. A doctor needs a woman to care for him. I bid you good-day Doctor Stewart!' And with a wave she disappeared into her own house. As for Sorley, he breathed a sigh of relief, for Mistress Morton was a gossip who would spread the news that their doctor whom all had missed, had found himself a wife and now would hopefully settle down amongst them again.

'What now,' asked Lachlan, who had not liked the inquisitive woman who had so blatantly probed into their affairs.

'Why—you will accompany me to the pie shop. We must eat—buy other provisions for our needs.' And followed by the boy he set off down the steps, into the narrow street. Perhaps his height and a certain arrogance of bearing might have singled him out amongst the crowds, but the busy throng were intent on their own business and careful to avoid the presence of the government troops who would seize and carry off any of whom they felt suspicious.

Here the city jails, just as in Perth, Inverness and Aberdeen, were full to overflowing with Jacobite suspects, who would eventually be transferred to prison ships to exist in the most squalid and dreadful of conditions, their eventual fate execution or sent to the colonies as slave labour. All this caused the citizens of Edinburgh but slight concern, for they felt little kinship with the wild tribes of the north who had risen against the established Hanoverian monarchy.

But even in Edinburgh there were those who in their hearts held loyal to the Stuart cause. True they might not have involved themselves in the fighting, but had Charles Edward managed to regain his family's throne, they would have applauded this. As it was, in the years to come, they would secretly sing Jacobite songs and drink toasts to the Prince across the water. But like other of Edinburgh's inhabitants they were realists. If the country was ever to get back to normal, English troops depart back to their own soil then life in Scotland's capital must resume its natural tenure of trade, banking and normality.

Lachlan followed Sorley Mor as he turned off the street where stall holders cried their wares and into a narrow alleyway. They proceeded along this dark and smoke begrimed passageway until Sorley paused outside a door with peeling brown paint. He knocked—first two knocks, followed by three and then another two. At last the door was cautiously opened a crack and an elderly man peered anxiously out at his visitors. But as he recognised the doctor he flung the door open wide and quickly beckoned them in.

'Sorley Mor Stewart—what joy it is to see you safe back again! Come away in and mind that third stair, it needs repair.' They entered and followed the old man up the steep, creaking staircase and into a small, musty office, where its single dusty window let in little light, a guttering candle on his desk adding further much needed illumination.

Their host seated himself behind his desk and pointed to a couple of wooden chairs positioned against the wall. Sorley Mor and Lachlan pulled them forward and sat, as all three stared at each other in silence for a moment. Then Sorley gave a warm smile to this old friend he had not thought to meet again.

'Mr McCrombie, allow me to introduce Lachlan Stewart, a young relative of my wife Kieran----'

'What—you have taken a wife? Why, but this is great news indeed,' interrupted Mr McCrombie startled, and reached to a small side table for a bottle of whisky and glasses. 'We must drink a toast to your happiness!' He poured a generous glassful for Sorley and himself, and a small measure for Lachlan.

'To you and your wife, my boy, may your marriage be blessed!' exclaimed the elderly lawyer now, surveying Sorley with searching glance. 'Ahem—did you perhaps find your bride on a recent visit to the Highlands?'

'Yes, sir! She is a Stewart from Appin, widow of a friend I made whilst making my way from Culloden to the west coast. Alan Stewart was murdered by a band of redcoat troopers on the very day of his reunion with his young wife. They also killed his father and—were rough with Kieran.'

The lawyer caught his meaning and stared at Sorley in shock. 'So you married this lady in pity at her condition?' He fixed his sharp dark eyes on Sorley Mor's face. 'Was this wise? A marriage made in time of stress—but it says much for your kindness of spirit, my friend.'

'I did not marry Kieran Stewart out of pity—but out of admiration for her bright courage and also concern for her good name. We lived for some months in a certain cave, together with Lachlan and my brother David. The whole area was alive with Cumberland's troopers and Argyll's men.'

'What a time you have had! You should perhaps have heeded my advice and remained here in Edinburgh as respected physician. Yet had I myself been younger, who knows? You have heard the Prince has escaped to France?' he added with satisfaction.

'What—Charles Edward is safe at last? It is true, not mere rumour?' Sorley's lips broke into a smile of relief and Lachlan who had remained silent so far, gave a sudden cry of delight.

'Tearlach is safe away? The Lord be praised,' cried the lad speaking with his strong highland lilt. 'It gladdens my heart to hear it! When he comes again, he will overcome these bluidy English swine!'

'Keep your voice down, Lachlan. I have already told you that there will not be any future uprising,' said Sorley Mor firmly. 'What is needed now is a cool head that we may survive in a very different Scotland.' He saw and ignored the sudden hurt in the boy's eyes. An outburst such as he had just made in front of the wrong people would bring disaster upon the lad. He must learn.

'Are things as bad as they say in the west,' asked the lawyer, leaning forward.

'Highland society is being systematically destroyed! Any thought to have been involved with the Stuart cause are being rounded up and shot, hung or dispatched onto prison ships to await sentence. Houses are burned to the ground, women raped, no pity for the old and infirm—for children. The redcoat soldiers have driven off all the livestock, sold the cattle and sheep to those from the south, left the people to starve. I have seen them, women and little ones lying dead and unburied—dead for lack of food and shelter!'

'If what you say is correct, then this is a far worse situation than after other attempts of the Stuarts to regain Scotland's crown!' McCrombie shook his silver head in distress. 'So you are returned to Edinburgh now. And your brother, he is an Episcopalian priest is he not—he is with you?'

'David did not rise with the clan. It was against his religious principal to do so. Despite this, he was beaten almost to death by soldiers because he would not give details of those who had risen for the Prince in his village.'

'They did that—to a priest?' McCrombie was shocked. 'What will he do for the future?'

'He has thoughts of France, at least until the savagery against our people comes to an end. Yet when if ever will the highlands be the same again?' Sorley shook his head sadly. 'Those whom David ministered to are almost all dead—some escaping to starve in the hills.'

'Perhaps I could arrange passage for him on a ship out of Leith?'

'This would indeed be a great help,' exclaimed Sorley, eyes brightening.

'I wish I too could go to France,' broke in Lachlan suddenly and flushed in embarrassment as both men turned and looked at him. 'I have always wanted to travel,' he blurted out. Sorley Mor studied the youngster thoughtfully.

'But you speak no French,' he said.

'Nor did I speak any but our own Gaelic until Kieran taught me this other tongue.' Sorley looked at him in surprise. He had not considered until now, how unusual it was for a boy from a remote west coast village to converse as he did.

'Kieran also speaks French,' added Lachlan. 'She learned it when she lived there for two years—and it was there she met my brother Alan!'

'How strange she never mentioned this,' breathed Sorley in astonishment. But this item of interest could be explored at a future time.

Not now. He glanced across at Mr McCrombie who had listened to their exchange in thoughtful silence.

'Would it be possible to arrange passage for Lachlan as well?' he asked. 'I am able to cover their costs.' He put his hand in his pocket and pulled out the ruby necklace. 'I am not sure if these stones are real—if they are then this bauble must be of some worth!'

'Let me see it!' McCrombie examined the stones carefully and nodded appreciation. 'Yes—genuine rubies and nicely set. I will not inquire as to the source of these gems.'

'Nor could I tell you,' replied Sorley Mor with a tight smile.

'Precisely—these are not normal times. So, your brother David and this young man are for France then? Leave it to me, Sorley! Now—for yourself, are you in need of funds? There is still a comfortable sum placed here in your account!' They talked further and when they left McCrombie's office, the doctor's purse was substantially heavier and plans underway for the safe future of two of his guests. But he wondered uneasily how Kieran would react when told that the boy she looked on as a young brother was to take ship for France?

Chapter Five

Sorley Mor knocked on his brother's bedroom door, found him sitting on the bed, reading one of the psalms. He looked up with an inquiring smile.

'May I come in, David—there is something I must discuss with you!' David Stewart listened gravely to Sorley's news that providing he agreed to it, a passage was being arranged for him to France—and that Lachlan wished to accompany him.

'Brother, I do not know how I can ever repay you for your kindness to me in this matter and so much else. Without your help I would be dead by now. But am I right to leave Scotland at this time? Should I not remain— try to reach out to any who have survived the atrocities meted on them by the Hanoverian regime?' he face was troubled.

'David, at this moment there is nothing you can do for our people. What good to risk arrest—being sent down to London accused as an insurrectionist!'

'But I was not involved in the fighting!'

'And do you think any would stop to listen or believe this, even though such is the case. Let things settle down as they must eventually, and then return to Scotland feeling stronger and perhaps gathering other young men into the ministry!' He clasped David to him, realising as he held that frail form that his brother was worn out with stress and the sheer horror of all he had seen.

'Then I will go. As for Lachlan, I have answered many of his questions about our faith—have wondered about his future. Maybe all that is happening now is part of a greater plan.'

'I think the boy's head is full of dreams of adventure at this time. But who knows what any of our futures may hold. You will both have to exercise great caution when boarding the ship—perhaps you could be said to be a lawyer visiting a client abroad, young Lachlan your servant.' And so they sat and talked and planned and Sorley felt a great wave of relief spread though his being that this brother of his, so different in character but to whom he had become very close in recent months, was soon be in a safe environment.

'Good—so it is settled!'

'Yes brother—it is.' Then David looked at Sorley and ventured to speak of something that had been troubling him. 'But what of your own future, and that of Kieran, for I have noticed a coldness in her manner towards all of us since that encounter with Mamore at Glencoe?'

'I wish I knew what had chanced between them! I have asked her to explain—had I perhaps offended her in some way? I also sense that she fears any marital overtures I might make. But she has my promise to respect her, not to force myself upon her.' He spoke jerkily, obviously finding it difficult to discuss the situation, but at the same time glad that David had opened the subject.

'You have behaved as a true gentleman,' said David kindly, but his gaze was troubled.

'I just do not know what else I can do in the matter—except to continue to show patience and caring!' Sorley shook his head sadly.

'She has obviously been greatly traumatised by all she has been through. But it is more than that, isn't it! I care greatly for your welfare Sorley and wonder whether this marriage that is one in name only, should be allowed to continue? To be in daily contact with a woman you love, but who shows nothing but coldness towards you, is not good for your own mental state.'

'I can only live in hope that one day Kieran Stewart will return my love. If not, well I may have to settle for friendship. But that is enough of my affairs. I now have to let her know that she will soon have to part with Lachlan—and with you also!'

Kieran was not impressed by what Sorley explained about the forthcoming departure of both Lachlan and David. In fact she was deeply shocked at the news. Whilst these two remained with them in the house, she had felt secure from any worry that her husband might demand his conjugal rights, regardless of assurances to the contrary. Despite her softer feelings towards Sorley, she realised that any future relationship between them was thing impossible.

It was bad enough that he had unknowingly wed a Campbell, could only guess at his disgust should he learn the truth of her origins. Not that she could have considered him as a real husband, for she was still grieving her beloved Alan. But strangely his image was growing dimmer in her mind and she felt guilt that this was so. Why had it all happened—why, why, why?

'You will be quite safe here with Sorley Mor. He is a good man, Kieran and will look after you and the baby when born. I will come back one day. But there is nothing for me here now and a whole world waiting to be explored across the sea,' asserted Lachlan, eyes shining with excitement. 'Say that you are not disappointed in me?'

She looked at the boy sadly. He had already suffered so much, endured hardship without complaint, been brave beyond his years. She would miss him terribly, for he was the last link to her home and the past.

'You will go with my blessing, Lachlan Mac Malcolm! You have the whole of your life before you, it is right that you should live it to the full.' She forced a smile as she spoke and saw the relief on his face.

A week later there was a knock at the door and Sorley Mor was given a sealed note by hand of a messenger sent from McCrombie's office. He broke the seal and read it. 'Mr Stewart and his young friend should be prepared to board 'The Linnet' in two days time at eight hours in the evening, their passage paid.' Sorley gave the messenger small coin and sat thinking for a few minutes.

Kieran glanced across at him curiously. Minutes before, he had smiled farewell to his last patient of the day, an old man with a badly ulcerated leg. She had helped him bandage the painful limb, their heads almost touching as she bent over with him, her fingers gentle.

'The letter—what does it say?'

'It is from my man of business. David and Lachlan leave in two days time! I hardly dared to hope things could have been expedited so quickly!' he smiled his relief that David would soon be safe away. News had been received in Edinburgh of ministers of the Episcopal Church who had received the death sentence in London—and been hung. Imprisoned Catholic priests had so far not been treated in the same way—no doubt for political reasons in Europe.

So it was really going to happen. Kieran looked at him in dismay. She could hardly believe Lachlan whom she regarded as a brother, was to be torn by fate from her side in this way. David she would miss of course, he had become a friend, a good man whom she respected not only as a man of God, but as a trusty friend. She turned her head away from Sorley to hide her sudden tears.

The Rev David Stewart prayed a blessing over Sorley and Kieran before he left the house with Lachlan, carrying a small leather bag containing little more than a change of clothes for both and his battered bible, a small sum of gold in his pocket for their future needs.

'I will accompany you to Leith Docks,' said Sorley Mor. 'Give me the bag to carry, brother.'

'No—I will take it,' said Lachlan firmly, reaching out his hand. And as he looked at the youth who had attained young manhood far too soon like many another, Sorley realised that it would be Lachlan caring for David rather than the other way round. Kieran had said farewell within doors, for Sorley did not want to draw attention to the departure of the two. They were soon amongst the usual busy yet still apprehensive crowds on the streets, as carriages rattled over the cobbles, hawkers shouted their wares and red coated militiamen marched by to arrest yet another suspected of having connection to the Stuart cause.

They picked their way carefully along the wharf, avoiding bales of goods being laden onto a waiting vessel. A keen eyed redcoat sergeant paced back and forth, eyeing all who came and left. His eyes lighted on the three who quietly approached The Linnet—and challenged them.

'You there--halt! Your names and business?' he demanded. Then Sorley Mor with great aplomb proffered the passes made out for their safe passage to Edinburgh.

'You recognise the seal of Major General John Campbell of Mamore,' he said levelly. The man glanced down at the passes uncertainly.

'These are for safe entry to the city only—not to the port,' he began, but Sorley Mor scowled impatiently.

'Are you trying to interfere with the lawful progress of those under the Major General's own protection,' he snapped.

'I suppose all is well—but I still maintain the passes are only for safe passage to the city,' he mumbled perplexed. 'On you go then. You certainly do not have the look of rebels about you!' He turned away to challenge any others who might be planning escape from arrest.

'There it is,' cried Lachlan as they approached the ship.

Sorley Mor clasped David to him in a close embrace and then clapped Lachlan about the shoulders. At a shout from an impatient Captain, that the tide was on the turn, they walked firmly up the gang plank. Fifteen minutes later, the anchor was raised and the ship slowly disappeared into the mist of the October night. Sorley breathed a sigh of relief and started to retrace his steps back to his home and the problems awaiting him there.

He found that she had already retired for the night, and made his own way upstairs to his tiny box bedroom, where he prepared himself for bed and lay brooding for many hours until exhausted, at last his eyes closed and he slept.

The weeks that followed were strange and tension filled, with Kieran continuing to show a coldness of manner that was very hard to bear. But she carried out her duties as nurse with kindness and a quiet efficiency that made her popular with the patients. December came and the mother to be, walked with a more measured stride, getting heavier as her pregnancy advanced. Christmas day dawned cold and bright and today Sorley Mor intended to take a break from the many patients who now came to a doctor they trusted and whose fees were affordable.

'Kieran—see what I have bought for you,' he said now and led her into the bedroom his brother had formerly occupied. He pointed to a wooden cot on rockers, complete with bedding and a fine white shawl. 'You may wish to have the cot in your own room to start with,' he added quietly.

She looked at the cot startled. Although the birth was only a few weeks away, she had shut her mind to the actuality of what was to happen, the fear that the babe might not be her husbands, but born of rape thus causing her to reject all desire for the birth. But now she realised that she must indeed face whatever was to be.

'Why, Sorley Mor—this was a very kind thought,' she said slowly and her fingers lifted a corner of the fine woollen shawl appreciatively. 'I suppose I should start to buy clothes for the child. But Sorley, what shall I do if the babe resembles the captain who raped me?' It was of this man she thought now, rather than the several others who had violated her.

'Let us be positive, say that our baby will be that of Alan Stewart,' he replied gently.

'You say—our baby?' she probed.

'You are my wedded wife, Kieran, any child you bear will belong to both of us.' He looked at her steadily.

'But if it does not resemble Alan? I do not think I could bear to look on it if.......' her voice faltered and her grey eyes spilled sudden tears.

'Kieran, the baby to be born is innocent of any harm, will need love and protection from his parents—and we will be his parents!'

'It may be a girl!'

'So her parents then—I would love a wee lass just like you!' he said fondly. But at these words it was as though a shutter came down in her mind and she drew back from him and turned away with a frigid inclination of her head. He sighed, could only hope that once the child arrived, it would release whatever agitation had so changed her entire personality.

January brought cold and sleet to Edinburgh and fierce winds funnelling between the hills assailed those who ventured out. Sorley Mor had to contend with an outbreak of influenza leading to some of his frail elderly patients developing pneumonia. He worked ceaselessly, not only from his surgery but visiting homes at all times of day and night, was almost exhausted, his eyes darkly shadowed from lack of sleep.

He had just returned from a struggle with death at a child's bedside which he had tragically lost, and sunk down into his armchair, almost too tired to go upstairs to his bed, when he heard a cry. He raised his head and listened. It was Kieran and he guessed the cause. She was in labour. He rose, washed his face and hands and took a mouthful of brandy to sustain him.

He knocked at her door.

'Go away,' she moaned. 'I do not want you in here!' But he disregarded her words and came quietly in. She lay on her rumpled bed, face contorted as a pain caught her.

'Kieran, you will listen to what I have to say to you. I have attended more births than I can remember and you need skilled help in your labour. Now—how long have you been experiencing pains?'

'Since last night,' she hissed between clenched teeth.

'And did not tell me? Why not, in heaven's name?' he demanded.

'Oh—just go away!' But despite her rejection of him, her eyes expressed her relief that he was there.

'I am going to examine you, my dear.' He raised the quilt and suddenly she relaxed and breathed a sigh that she would no longer have to battle away alone with the birth force that held her in relentless thrall. As Sorley's hands felt her abdomen he began to wonder at what his examination suggested. It was at dawn break that he cut the cord of a baby boy, with red hair, blue eyes and a fine pair of lungs.

'He has Alan's eyes,' she cried exultantly as having washed away the birth stains, he handed her child to Kieran.

'A fine son, my dearest one,' he said. 'But now we have more work to do!' She looked at him not understanding his meaning at first. He lifted the baby from her and placed him in the waiting crib as within a short interval Kieran's contractions started again and another child took its first gulp of air. And it was a girl—a girl with green eyes and a fluff of blond hair.

She took the second child into her arms and stared down at the heart shaped face with a frown. She could see no trace of Alan on the tiny features—and those green eyes?

'Sorley—she has no look of Alan about her and her colouring favours neither of us! Is it possible for a mother to give birth to children of two different fathers?' She was staring at her small daughter with distaste.

'I do not know the answer to your question. What I do know however, is that characteristics of parents and grandparents can be displayed in a child and this will be what has happened here. She also resembles you in the shape of her little face—the chin! She is beautiful, Kieran.'

He placed the little girl next to her twin in the crib and returned to help Kieran through the last phases of the birth process, put clean sheets on the bed and removed the bucket containing the afterbirth. Next he gently bathed the young woman and made her comfortable on her pillows. Then he placed one infant at each of her breasts and heard with satisfaction, the small sucking noises that told him the babies were bonding with their mother in this most necessary and natural of ways.

He waited until the babies were satisfied and took them from her and placed them one at each end of the cot, as Kieran looked at him drowsily and gave him her first real smile since they had left Glencoe.

Then Sorley Mor almost fell into his own bed and slept for some hours.

Over the next few weeks, Kieran was touched to receive small gifts of clothing for the twins from grateful patients, who had heard news of the birth of their doctor's children. Now also expensive carriages began to draw up outside the house, as Sorley Mor's reputation as an outstanding physician began to spread beyond their immediate area. Financially matters were beginning to improve and he found he had barely enough hours in the day to treat all who came to his door.

The babies were thriving. Kieran named her son Alan after his father and her baby daughter Ishbel, which had been the name of Lachlan's mother. If Sorley vaguely hoped she might have named the boy for him, he was not surprised however that she honoured Alan Stewart's memory in this way.

Now that Kieran no longer had time to assist him in his surgery, he engaged a nurse, Effie Munro. She was a fresh faced woman of some forty years and a widow, whose only son had died at Culloden. She had a kindly manner, was attentive and efficient and soon Sorley began to rely on her to deal with routine dressings. Kieran liked her but was distant in her manner as she was with all these days.

Sometimes the young mother would see Effie staring at her with puzzled brown eyes and Kieran knew uncomfortably that the woman sensed her coldness towards Sorley Mor and wondered at it. Soon she knew she would have to make plans to leave this house and the man she had married, and who would be repulsed by her presence here if ever he discovered the truth of her family origins. No—it was heartbreaking to face the fact that the growing love and tenderness she felt towards Sorley could never by shown.

She recognised that it would be extremely difficult to earn a living to support herself and the babies. Indeed how could she work and pay some other woman to care for them, as well as affording rent and food? Would any money she could earn stretch that far? And for this reason alone she remained with Sorley—wife in name only.

It was May, the sunshine streaming in as Kieran sat in a window seat looking down at her daughter's delicate features and trying to find any slight resemblance to Alan's dear face. Again and again the worry came to haunt her that this child might be that of the green eyed Captain who had raped her, and encouraged his men to follow his example. The suspicion would not go away and now as if the babe realised her mother's rejection, she became fretful and refused to be soothed, thus causing Kieran further cause for disapproval of the tiny mite.

With little Alan Stewart it was otherwise, for he basked in his mother's love, a truly beautiful child with an engaging smile, who kicked his little legs up in his cot and crowed happily. And so Kieran continued torn by doubts of her daughter's paternity and worries for the future should she leave this house where she was treated with so much care by a husband she had come to love, but could never live with as his true wife. It was not fair to him and this troubled her, for despite her coldness he never treated her with anything but kindness and courtesy. But it could not go on this way!

Sorley Mor called to Kieran as she was setting the table for their evening meal. At first she did not look up, deep in thought.

'Kieran—wonderful news! My brother David writes that he has found many good friends in Paris, those who escaped Cumberland's deprivations. Lachlan dreams of joining one of the French regiments when older and misses home and you Kieran.' She stared at him with a faint smile, for it was relief to learn that all was well with Lachlan—and of course Sorley Mor's brother, for she had great respect for the kindly priest.

'Perhaps in a year's time we might risk a visit to Paris to see them both,' suggested Sorley. 'Hopefully by then the English will have relaxed some of their restrictions, matters may improve.'

'I certainly could not travel yet with the babies so young, not yet weaned,' was all her reply and Sorley seated himself at the table with a heavy heart. Would she ever revert to the courageous, vivacious creature that he had fallen in love with? What had caused this change in her—and if as he suspected it had something to do with that encounter with Lord Mamore, then what had been said between them? Certainly she always deflected his questions regarding the meeting. He sighed.

In many ways Kieran was behaving as a perfect wife, kind to visitors and patients alike, an excellent cook and efficient housekeeper. But all of this he would have forgone had she come willingly to his arms and his bed. No, it looked as though he would have to accept the terms of this loveless marriage as irreversible.

Now the weather was improving, Kieran carried the babies outside to the small narrow garden which boasted a few struggling bushes and a splash of spring flowers. It offered little privacy as it was overlooked by adjacent houses and those that backed onto their own. But as she stared up into the patch of blue sky above, hazed though it was by chimney smoke, Kieran found her thoughts flying back to the beauties of her former home overlooking Loch Dhu, and the exquisite scenery of the highlands.

'I must get back to my own land! I feel I shall die in this place of tall, dark buildings and smells and a people so different to my own,' she whispered rebelliously. And it seemed as though little Alan Stewart chortled his agreement from his wicker carrying basket as his small sister cooed plaintive pleasure and reached out her tiny hands to her mother.

Kieran lifted her daughter and looked at her curiously and realised perhaps for the first time just how beautiful the little girl was. Soft silver blonde curls framed the tiny face and her eyes were an astonishing shade of green beneath the finely arched brows. She remembered Sorley's words before the birth—that the child would need love and protection—was innocent of any harm. Yes, whoever the father was, this was her daughter and deserved love.

'But I have not given you the love you deserve,' she murmured, tears rushing to her eyes as her finger traced the child's chin, so like her own. 'Please forgive me, Ishbel.' And she held her daughter's soft cheek against her own and rocked her back and forth in her arms.

From that day Sorley sensed a subtle change in Kieran, who now showed as much pleasure in Ishbel as she did in Alan. He observed it with relief, for he had been worried at her former chill towards the little girl. If only she would extend her sunnier behaviour to him as well. But alas, she continued distant as ever.

It was late afternoon and Sorley Mor sighed in relief as he closed the door behind his last patient. Pouring a glass of wine he stared from the window, down at the busy street below. It was then that he noticed a tall, uniformed officer mounting the steps to the house and a minute later there was a heavy knock at the door. Sorley experienced a wave of apprehension. Could it be that someone had denounced him as a Jacobite? But in that case it would have been more likely that several soldiers would have come for him.

'I will go, doctor,' said Effie Munro. 'Bide ye there, sir.' He heard Effie explaining the surgery was now closed apart from emergencies. But a firm voice with a Highland lilt instructed her that he desired word with the doctor and would not be denied. Then, to Sorley's sense of shock, he found himself staring across his desk at the well remembered features of Captain Roderick Campbell. He rose slowly to his feet.

'Captain Campbell—I hope I see you well, sir?' he forced the words out.

'Thanks to your efforts last year, Doctor Stewart!' he replied his former patient with a smile. 'I am stationed at the castle for a few weeks and thought to discover your whereabouts that I might personally express my gratitude for your care of me.' He stared around curiously. 'Your wife is well I hope?'

'Captain Campbell, the little I was able to do for you, was more than recompensed by the helpfulness of Lord Mamore. And I would have done the same for any man,' he added frankly. 'As for my wife, she is well and delivered of twins last January.' He was amazed at the look of joy that crossed the other's face.

'Thank God that all went well with her,' said the Campbell captain softly, his grey eyes so like those of Sorley's wife holding look of surprising gentleness. 'Childbirth carries its own dangers at times I believe,' he said quickly.

'Kieran was fortunate to give birth here—not on a winter hillside, destitute and alone as with so many unfortunates now in the north,' came the frowning response. Then realising his attitude was somewhat churlish towards a man who although a hated Campbell, had sought him out to express his gratitude over the treatment of that dirk wound, he pointed to the tray on which his brandy decanter stood.

'May I offer you a drink perhaps, captain?'

'Why, yes—that would be most civil of you,' replied Roderick. He accepted the glass from Sorley Mor's hand. 'Your good health, doctor—and that of your wife Kieran,' he said.

'You remember her name?' queried Sorley in surprise.

'She helped you to save my life I believe. I remember her as an angel of mercy. May I have the pleasure of meeting her again—just briefly of course?' Roderick's eyes met the doctor's dark gaze and they held no guile. But Sorley was about to couch a refusal in as polite terms as he could devise when the door suddenly opened and Kieran herself stood there.

'Effie said you had a visitor, husband,' she said, then stared across at Roderick Campbell in shock. He was the last person she would have expected to see there and she turned as though to flee.

'Lady—please wait I pray you! I have merely come to pay my respects to your husband for his care of me last year. I know that he saved my life—and that you assisted him in this.' He scanned her lovely face searchingly. She was as beautiful as his remembered image of her—but there was a change. It was as though a shutter had come down over all the high spirited charm he had recalled.

While the two young people stared at each other, Sorley Mor realised for the first time how like they were to each other. It was not merely that they both had the same soft red gold hair and unusual storm grey eyes, but shape of the forehead and chin—their bearing. A strange coincidence of course, he assured himself, with many of the west highland clans showing the same colouring.

And now Roderick Campbell walked across to Kieran and before she knew his purpose, had lifted her hand to his lips in quick salute.

'I have already congratulated the doctor on the safe birth of your twins—and wonder if I might have a glimpse of them?' Then his back towards

Sorley Mor and lowering his voice to merest whisper, he added, 'It would delight me to see them—sister!' Conflicting emotions chased across her face. Her strongest instinct was to refuse this man who had reminded her in this way of the fact she tried so hard to deny, of her Campbell blood.

'If you would follow me then, Captain,' she turned abruptly and mounted the stairs, followed closely by the brother she had never wished to see again and by Sorley Mor, who was quite bemused by the young soldier's wish to view their small children.

If the fellow were not a Campbell and a blood enemy, then he might quite have liked the young man, he reflected. He watched as Kieran beckoned them into the nursery, where the babies were lying in their cots and cooing happily to each other. The captain drew in his breath as he viewed the little ones.

'This is Alan Stewart—and here his sister Ishbel!' explained Kieran tonelessly. For a moment the soldier just stared down at the babies and even Sorley Mor who stood in the doorway noticed the man's gentleness of expression and was slightly puzzled. But of course, the Campbell captain would rarely come into contact with small children—unless spitting them on his sword! Then he banished the thought as unworthy, for he knew instinctively that this was one Campbell who would never lift his hand against a child.

'They are beautiful,' exclaimed Roderick at last and bending a smile on Kieran. 'The boy favours you in his colouring.'

'But he has his father's blue eyes,' she put in.

'Your daughter—her eyes now—that shade of green remind me of my father's gaze. He also had hair of a silvery blonde.' And at his words Kieran coloured angrily, for she knew he was again emphasising her Campbell blood. Yet at the same time she experienced a feeling of relief that Ishbel's green eyes were no legacy of that green eyed rapist—but as it would seem, of her grandfather.

'Thank you for your interest in our children,' she said firmly,' But I am sure you have more pressing business to attend to than spending time in a children's nursery!'

'Yes—I must go. I thank you both for your kindness in receiving me and again must state my gratitude for all that you did for me at Glencoe!' He swept Kieran a bow and inclined his head to Sorley before following the doctor downstairs and taking his leave.

That night Sorley Mor sat late in his study before retiring to his lonely bed. There had been a strange sense of tension between his wife and Roderick Campbell and he realised he must discover what lay behind it. He knew and understood her hatred for all of Clan Campbell, but what afflicted his young wife went deeper than this. Yes, he thought and it also stemmed from that first meeting with Major General John Campbell of Mamore on that track road snaking through Glencoe.

Would that they had never encountered Mamore and Roderick Campbell!

Sorley Mor was in the office of his man of business, Robert McCrombie. He was not sure what had impelled him to make this evening call on one whom he considered as both friend and lawyer and banker and now accepted a glass of Madeira, as they viewed each other across McCrombie's ancient, ink stained desk. They had exchanged the usual pleasantries and the old man watched Sorley calmly, waiting to hear what had brought him here.

'Something is troubling you, my friend?' he ventured at last.

'Yes—and I am not sure whether you can assist me in the matter, or no.'

'Trouble with the authorities—shades of Culloden?'

'No. I have been extremely fortunate in that none have questioned my absence from my practice during the rising.' He frowned, wondering how to broach the problem that had brought him to this wise and trusted old man.

'Money problems, perhaps?' he suggested.

'Thankfully—no!' replied Sorley Mor.

'So—a problem within your marriage could it be,' wondered McCrombie. He saw from the doctor's suddenly lowered gaze that he had struck home in this assumption. 'I remember that you told me of how you came to marry the lady,' he said quietly. 'I believe that it was to be a marriage in name only—not an easy matter for any man!'

'Yes, you are right. It is with regard to my wife Kieran that I have come here today.' And then he described that incident during the previous autumn, when they had found themselves in the presence of the feared Major General John Campbell of Mamore, whose power was absolute in the western highlands and islands. To this man's militia countless atrocities were attributed. He explained that from the time of a private interview with Mamore, Kieran's whole personality seemed to have changed, she had shut herself off, seemed to be undergoing some inner turmoil the cause of which she was unable to divulge.

'Is it possible that the General made some threat to her,' wondered McCrombie.

'I think not. Indeed he was unbelievably kind—sympathetic towards our party. It was only with the help of the written passes he made out, stamped with his own seal that we managed to cross the country and arrive safely in Edinburgh.' Sorley shook his head.

'That was unusually good of the man,' considered McCrombie.

'Well, it is true that I was able to dress the wound of Roderick Campbell, a young relative of his—saved the fellow's life it could be said. This obviously softened his behaviour towards out party. But he demanded a private meeting with Kieran before we were permitted to leave his camp. He seemed to take a strange interest in her.'

'She is beautiful, your wife?'

'Red gold hair and unusual grey eyes—and all that a woman should be,' replied Sorley Mor. 'She is also proving a fine mother to her twin babies, born last January. And this is another strange thing. Yesterday I had a visit from Captain Roderick Campbell, ostensibly to express his gratitude for what little I was able to do for him—but he also expressed a wish to see Kieran—and when he did so, asked that he might also see little Alan and Ishbel. When he had gone, Kieran seemed very disturbed, hardly spoke.'

'So you think there is some connection between the present estrangement between you and your wife—and this young captain and Lord Mamore?'

'Yes. You know the histories of most of the prominent families in the Highlands I know it is a hobby of yours. What can you tell me of the two men I have mentioned?'

For answer, McCrombie went across to a tall chest in the corner and opened one of its drawers. He hesitated. 'Look you Sorley, this could take some time. Why not call back in a few days when I will furnish you with all I have been able to discover, though I fear it will not shed any light on your problem.' He saw the doctor to the door and slowly mounted his creaking stairs back to his office, where he sat thinking, then opened a bulging file.

Sorley Mor had previously agreed that they should employ a nursemaid to help care for the twins and so enable Kieran to visit the shops on occasion. Today she had taken up her duties, and the doctor approved of the fair haired, sweet natured young girl whose small remuneration would she explained, help to maintain an elderly grandmother. Her name was Bess Brown and to Kieran's relief seemed to have an amazing aptitude in the care of the little ones.

Now at last Kieran could venture outside and not feel uneasy at leaving the babies to the ministrations of her husband's nurse. Effie was good with the children but would have to leave them and hurry downstairs when the doctor needed her to perform her duties in his surgery. Now with Bess to care for the twins, Kieran felt she could relax for the first time since their birth.

She sauntered along the street, wrinkling her nose at the smells that assaulted her nostrils, staring at the bewigged gentlemen and well dressed women who lifted sprays of sweet smelling herbs to their noses as they walked. Were all cities as nauseous as this one she wondered?

She hesitated trying to remember the close where stall holders sold fresh fruit, and vegetables and as she did so, found herself hailed by a voice that made her look up in dismay. It was Captain Campbell and he was crossing the road towards her, avoiding a lumbering carriage as he came.

'Mistress Stewart—Kieran! Give you good morning,' he cried and swept her a bow. She inclined her head in return and made to pass on, but he laid a restraining hand on her arm.

'Kieran—please! A moment of your time, I beg,' and his grey eyes, so very like hers, smiled down at her in delight. He was extraordinarily good looking, she realised as she awarded him a cool stare.

'Unhand me if you please,' she said coldly and relaxed as he removed his fingers. 'I would have thought that your duties at the Castle would have taken up your time,' she added.

'I have resigned my commission, will leave the army at the end of the month and return home to my glen. I have had enough of soldiering,' he added quietly.

'Of killing, perhaps—murdering the innocent?' Her words stung as they were meant to and he flinched.

'In time of war unfortunate incidents occur,' he replied. 'But I can honestly state that I personally have only killed in the heat of battle, as all men of principal must do when duty so insists.'

'And what of that which happened on Culloden's battlefield in the aftermath of the fighting—the senseless, cruel slaughter of all wounded, the rounding up of men, women and children who merely had the misfortune to live in the vicinity of moor—of all that happened since then?' her eyes blazed her anger and he stepped back uncertainly.

'Kieran, I only know that my clan and others friendly to us have been in the forefront of trying to bring peace to the highlands. If we had merely hanged a few rebels as example, do you think this would have sufficed to persuade the insurgents not to rise again and so allowing the Pretender to bring more disruption to men's lives?'

'So you are attempting to rid the land of all clans loyal to the Prince? I have seen what has been done, Roderick! Whole villages burned down, women raped, children and the elderly killed or driven into the hills, people despoiled of their cattle, sheep and goats stolen and sold for Cumberland's profit—the few miserable people left alive facing starvation!' Her eyes filled with tears as she blurted out the facts and saw him lower his head in shame.

'I know—I know. It is a sad price to pay for that young upstart's folly!'

'The folly of trying to reclaim the crown that belonged to the Stuarts for centuries of time?' she snapped back defensively.

'But that same time marches on, Kieran. We are united with the English under one crown--and since the year 1707 one parliament also, a united kingdom!'

'Say rather forced into an unwanted marriage! But one day we will be free again, our country regain its independence!' As she burst out with this he glanced around uneasily, for people were stopping to stare at the beautiful young woman in such angry exchange with a captain of the highland militia.

'Hush now, you could get yourself into serious trouble if you are overheard speaking in this vein,' he admonished. 'Since we speak of marriage, how goes it with your own marriage to the doctor? I thought I sensed a possible coolness between you, when I visited.'

'How dare you to suggest such thing! I bid you good day, Captain Campbell!' Her cheeks flushed in annoyance at his perception on such brief visit to their home.

'Listen to me, sister.....' he began

'Do not call me so,' she interrupted in revulsion

'But it is what you are, Kieran—my sister, and one whom I could wish to know better. Would you not like to see the house where our parents lived and from which your mother was torn by Rory MacGregor? It is a beautiful house in a quiet glen, on the shores of a loch, with a fine river flowing nearby and set amongst woods.' His eyes were soft as he spoke of it.

'It would be a Campbell house and so accursed to me! I must go.' And she turned on her heel and almost ran off among the crowds of shoppers. He wished to pursue her, but noting the many strange glances directed at him, he straightened up and marched firmly away.

Kieran was not to know that her unexpected meeting with Roderick Campbell had been observed by her husband. With no immediate patients to see that morning, Sorley Mor had decided to follow after her and escort her to one of the new coffee houses that were springing up. He was not sure which way she had gone at first—but then saw that distinctive red gold hair on the opposite side of the cobbled street. Was it her? Yes it was—and to his dismay, she was in conversation with Captain Campbell! A pang of jealousy erupted in his breast. He hesitated, then turned about and returned to the house. He did not witness Kieran's headlong flight from the captain.

When she came into the hallway, he opened the surgery door and called to her. She was carrying a basket of fruit and vegetables and looked slightly distraught.

'Kieran—that looks heavy. Tell me, did you see anyone we know when you were out, my dear?'

'No,' she replied sharply and his heart sank at the lie.

Back in his surgery he washed and bound a nasty looking cut on the hand of a blacksmith's apprentice as Effie spoke soothingly to the lad. And so it went on, one patient after another, skin problems, disease of the lungs, a cancer of the breast and a man who had been trampled by a horse in his master's stable and was in a sorry state. The poor fellow had several cracked ribs and much bad bruising.

'That seems to be all of them, doctor,' called Effie at last and he stretched and nodded his thanks to her.

'Thank you, then I will see you tomorrow Effie,' he said kindly and smiled as she bustled off. Now his thoughts returned to Kieran and that encounter he had observed with the Campbell captain. Why had she been speaking with one she had said repulsed her as all of his clan, and then denied the meeting? It made no sense.

'Sorley, I do not know how much longer I can remain in this city,' she said that evening as they sat at their dinner. 'I miss the beauty of the west, the smell of the heather and flight of the eagle.' Her eyes were dark with emotion as she spoke. 'I needs must return to Appin!'

'But my dear, there is nothing left there now! You must surely remember all that you personally saw of the horrors committed in the area. There would be no way in which we could survive amongst all that devastation.' He spoke sadly but she seemed not to listen.

'I want to waken and hear the sound of a rushing burn at my door, larks lilting in the sky, the call of the curlew. I want it to be the way it was,' and she burst into sudden bitter tears. 'Why did all of this happen, Sorley?' she sobbed. 'Why—why, why?' she demanded.

'We all know the reasons—the rising of the clans in support of the Prince, the revenge of the English and their friends the Campbells.' As he came out with the name of this clan, Kieran gave a gasp of despair.

'Why could they not too have supported Charles Edward? What a difference it would have made!'

'You are right in this, but their chief, the great Duke of Argyll finds it to his advantage to be on friendly terms with the English, from whom he receives many benefits and much power. As you know Kieran, a clan ever follows the lead of its chief. There may indeed be those of the Campbell clan who would not have chosen to fight against the Prince. But just as with all other clan members, a man does not have the right of refusal when called out to fight in his chief's cause, to do so would be to face disgrace and be thrown out of his home.' And as he gave this explanation, Sorley Mor found himself wondering just why hundreds of men should have to rise and fight at the whim of just one man. Was it right? Would things always be this way?

He had been abroad for many years, realised then that the feudal system observed in Scotland was not necessarily right. But then their way of life had evolved over many centuries, change difficult. Yet surely that change was in a way happening now. The glens once emptied of those whose roots went back through time, who had a special connection with the soil, their spirit bound up with the land on which they walked and toiled, once they were gone and others from the more submissive south being brought in to replace them, surely this was indeed the start of a great change.

'I would rather starve in Appin than remain in this city of overcrowded dwellings and smoke and smells!' she pushed her plate away and stood up. He looked at her pityingly. How well he understood all that she was going through, but he also realised the impossibility of their returning to an area still patrolled by the military, where life was cheap indeed.

'Kieran, you are talking wildly. Nor do you only have to think of yourself now, but of little Alan and Ishbel!'

'I know, I know—but I want them to grow up smelling the wind pouring fresh and clean from the mountains—not chimney smoke!'

'Yet I am sure that in Alan Stewart's house, one would have smelt smoke from the peat fire,' he said gently. 'But of course I know what you mean. Perhaps in a few years time things may change for the better and we may risk return, but not now, Kieran. Not now!' She merely bit her lip at his words and left the table.

'Goodnight, husband,' she said and gathering up their plates went through to the kitchen, whilst he poured a glass of brandy and sat brooding into it.

Chapter Six

Sorley Mor sat again in Mr McCrombie's office and looked at the elderly lawyer expectantly. It was a week since his last visit.

'Have you any information regarding Roderick Campbell and Lord Mamore that may shed light on my wife's change of personality?' What he heard filled him with surprise and opened strange questions in his mind, as the old man began to speak.

'Captain Roderick Campbell born in 1725 is son of the late Sir Colin Campbell and his wife Catriona also deceased.' McCrombie paused and took a pinch of snuff before continuing. 'It would seem that his father was murdered by a certain Rory MacGregor, who stole his pregnant wife. She then died later in childbirth after which it is on record that Colin Campbell's kinsmen caught and hung the marauding MacGregor.'

'So—clan enmity then?' he reflected. 'No surprise of course as the MacGregors are proscribed—not allowed to use their name or tartan by law this great many years, and have long been persecuted by the Campbells. Yet they rose bravely for the Prince,' he added lightly.

But even as he spoke, his mind seized upon one salient fact. Kieran had told him that her father had been a Rory MacGregor who had been murdered by the Campbells, and that her own mother had died at her birth and she had been brought up by her father's brother Duncan and his wife Annie. Perhaps there had been more than one man named Rory MacGregor, not an unusual name—but suppose—just suppose that...?

His face expressed the sudden tension he was enduring. Could that be it? Had Kieran been informed by Mamore that she was of Campbell blood? It would explain much, he realised, especially the strange resemblance between Roderick and Kieran. But his mind shut the thought out. This was mere speculation and could have no real basis in fact. It was thing impossible that his beautiful young wife had Campbell blood in her veins, he was fabricating a nonsense! He cleared his throat.

'Have you any further information regarding Roderick Campbell,' he asked.

'Only that as his father's only son he has inherited the family estate, a fine house and lands on the banks of Loch Tay. They call the place

Glenlarig,' explained McCrombie. 'He will return to a comfortable home, unlike the burned out shells remaining to the Highland lairds who rose for the Prince—those who still live that is. Most who survived have had their properties proscribed as you know—will spend their lives in exile.' The lawyer had been watching the other closely as he spoke, knew that something he had said had deeply affected Sorley Mor. He wondered what it could have been.

'So—nothing in all this to explain Kieran's moods,' said Sorley casually. 'What of John Campbell of Mamore though?' He thrust his suspicions to the back of his mind as he continued the conversation.

'You probably know as much or more of the Major General than I do,' replied McCrombie. 'A proud, ambitious man, a fine soldier it is said, but whose reputation has been sullied by his depredations amongst those in the west and the islands, where innumerable atrocities have been committed. It was under his command that Captain Fergusson wreaked such havoc in the islands, raping, murdering, burning and killing and driving off all livestock.' McCrombie swallowed. 'What more can be said of this man?'

'Little—yet for reasons of his own, he allowed me to walk free! Other surgeons attending the Jacobite army have been executed in London!' Sorley Mor rose to his feet. 'Thank you for your help in this matter, my old friend.'

'A pleasure indeed,' was the reply. 'And how is your work going? I have heard you spoken of as an outstanding physician!'

'Perhaps my years of study here in Edinburgh and at Leiden in Holland are proving worthwhile.'

'Your wife should be proud of her husband,' and McCrombie stared after him as he heard the doctor's footsteps on the stairs, the sound of the door banging behind him. Now what had he said that had caused Sorley to give that start?

Kieran was even more withdrawn over the next few weeks, causing her husband real concern for her health. He wondered at first if it could be that strange depression that sometimes overcame new mothers, and yet knew this to be wrong—for Kieran had shown those first symptoms of withdrawal late last year following on that encounter with Mamore. He had already dismissed his first suspicion considering her parentage—that she might have Campbell blood in her veins, as too ridiculous to contemplate.

It was in August that a new blow was dealt to the highlanders. It was enacted that from that time, all forms of highland garb were now forbidden to be worn, specifying the plaid, philebeg, kilt or trews—or any other garment of tartan, all now banned. There would be imprisonment for six months on a first offence—and seven years transportation to the colonies on a second. An oath also had to be taken not to bear any arms in the future—not to possess sword, or gun or pistol or any other weapon.

When Sorley Mor heard of it he went white. What the English government were doing was to eradicate all that the highlanders held dear, stripping them of their dignity as a people—and it was obscene!

When he told Kieran of it, she gave a cry of sorrow and pulled her hair forward over her face and sat rocking back and forth in her chair.

'Our poor people—our poor people,' she moaned. 'Is there none to protect us from the cruelties of our enemies?'

'They plan to empty the highlands of those with Jacobite sympathies, to destroy the power of the chiefs, to remove all symbols of our pride.' Sorley Mor uttered a deep sigh. 'Sadly there is nothing we can do in the matter, my dearest. I fear that our land is to be despoiled of all we hold dear. The future looks bleak indeed.' He bent forward to stroke her hair, but she drew back from him. He looked at her sadly and left the room.

Kieran bit her lip as he went. She understood that her constant rejection of this kind and decent man was not behaviour to be proud of. She now knew him for a wonderful physician, with a deep compassion towards all came to him. Had only matters been otherwise, she would have joyed to come to his arms, tell him of her love and admiration of him. But it could not be and it was unfair to him to protract her stay there in Edinburgh. But what alternative did she have when the babies were so small—and certainly return to the western highlands impossible given present circumstances.

But what about France—Lachlan was there. Surely he would help her to find accommodation in Paris. True Sorley's brother, David was there too— and would be deeply shocked at her throwing off her wedding vows. But then marriage made in the duress of fear of all that had happened—was such a true marriage? But she knew that in the sight of God it was.

She drew a cape over her gown and went out to buy a few essentials for the kitchen and glanced around as she walked along the busy street. She would never have admitted that she partly hoped to see her Campbell brother again, but drew in her breath sharply as she heard him call to her from a shop doorway. Had he been waiting for her or just coincidence? This morning he was not wearing his uniform, but dressed as a gentleman of fashion in a dark blue coat with gold buttons, lace at his chin.

'Kieran,' he called. 'I hoped I might see you! Tomorrow I leave Edinburgh and return to my home on the shores of Loch Tay.' He smiled as he fell into step beside her. 'You would love it there,' he added. 'It would be a fine place for the little ones to grow up!'

'What a ridiculous suggestion,' she flared, but even as she did so, an ignoble thought came into her mind. She could never live with Sorley Mor as his wife and the idea of France just too risky when she had Alan and Ishbel to consider. But what if she did indeed accompany her blood brother to his home? It would no doubt be beautiful there, the babies would thrive—but it would mean turning her back on all she believed in, throwing in her lot with those who responsible for destroying her people.

'Perhaps it is a suggestion you might consider,' he said, his grey eyes so like her own holding brooding expression. 'We are kin, my dear. Had our mother not been taken by the MacGregors then you and I would have grown up together as loving brother and sister.'

'Roderick—your clan joined with the English who have caused so much devastation in the highlands! My husband's clan fought against yours at Culloden. How therefore can we ever be truly become members of one family!' He merely smiled persuasively.

'Kieran—here is a packet. It contains my address at Glenlarig and directions to get there, and a sum of gold that will help you on the journey should you decide to join me there in the hills that is—and where the air is fresher than in this nauseous city!' Before she could protest he placed the packet in her basket, and with a quick bow disappeared in the direction of the castle. Frustrated, she stared after him.

When she arrived home, Kieran unpacked her basket in the kitchen and ran upstairs to her bedroom, where she placed the offending packet in a drawer, covering it with a shawl. Then she sat on the end of the bed and agonised about the future.

What was she to do? Remain here with Sorley Mor in this dreadful situation where every successive day brought deeper guilt into her mind, that she was deceiving him by not admitting a truth that would make him draw back from her in disgust? How much longer could she continue in this fashion?

Then there was still the possibility of France. She spoke the language fluently, could no doubt find employment there. But what would happen to the twins if she had to leave them in the care of others? Could she perhaps persuade their new little nursemaid Bess Brown to accompany her, for she was very good with the little ones! She rose to her feet and paced back and forth distractedly.

The suggestion made by Roderick Campbell that she should bring the twins to Glenlarig, his house at Loch Tay was of course out of the question. By doing so she would be putting final barrier between herself and Sorley Mor, shutting the door on all she believed in, her love for her late husband Alan Stewart, her clan loyalty—and yet she could no longer claim to be either MacGregor or Stewart! She was in fact a member of Clan Campbell, detested for their cruelty by all in the Highlands who owed loyalty to the Stuarts.

And so she sat there, rocking back and forth, her mind in turmoil.

A knock at the bedroom door made her look up. It was Bess Brown. The little nursemaid smiled at her.

'Mistress Stewart—wee Alan has another tooth!'

'So that was why he was so fretful,' murmured Kieran, forcing her mind back to normal mundane matters. 'But should you have left them alone, Bess—now they are crawling with such vigour we must watch them very carefully!' Bess flushed at the reprimand.

'Indeed I would never leave them unattended Mistress! Effie is with them now. I only came to tell you about the new tooth!' She turned away and slipped out of the door, wondering why Kieran so rarely smiled or seemed to take a more motherly interest in her beautiful babies. But this was a good household to work in and Bess counted herself lucky to have employment when so many were on the streets, forced to beg for their bread.

Fifteen year old Bess knew only too well the conditions prevailing in the city, where tall tenement buildings were accessed by steep, narrow, dark stairs to each of their many floors, each room often housing a family, every drop of water having to be carried up those stairs and emptied together with human waste from the windows to make its way into open sewers. The smell of all this together with the stench of the Nor Loch extending before the stately castle on its soaring rock, made this city a stink hole, so described by travellers who had visited cities abroad.

Perhaps it was because conditions were so difficult that so many spent their small sustenance on drink, arriving back to their squalid homes to show violence to their womenfolk and children. Then there were the church authorities, always on the lookout for sin with greatest zeal. Many a poor young woman had been brought to sit in front of the congregation on the penitence stool if found to have been involved in fornication.

Harshness was all around. There had been that brief few weeks of idyllic hope when the bonnie Prince had arrived in the city and many had rejoiced that an unsought union with the old enemy England might now come to an end. Alas, it was not to be. Now after the devastating defeat at Culloden many of Edinburgh's young male citizens who had been attracted to the Prince's banner, had either lost their lives on the field or been taken down to London on prison ships—her brother one of these. He had been hanged.

So Bess was doing her very best to retain her employment with the doctor's household, her aged grandmother completely dependent on her small earnings.

Sorley Mor Stewart was becoming even busier these days as his fame spread. He was also now being called on by women about to give birth, who would previously have depended on the services of well meaning but ignorant, self proclaimed midwives. This often meant that he was increasingly away during night hours and accordingly seeing less of Kieran. So it was that when he arrived home in the early hours of one September morning, he fell straight into his bed to snatch a precious few hours rest.

On wakening, he pulled his bedroom curtains and smiled to see the thin early autumn sunshine. He stretched, washed and dressed and went downstairs expecting to see Kieran preparing breakfast. There was no sign of her in the kitchen and he imagined she must have slept in. Perhaps the babies had been restless during the night.

He was hungry, had eaten little over the last twenty-four hours and discovered a steak pie in the pantry. He cut a generous portion, poured a glass of ale and proceeded to break his fast. No doubt Kieran would soon open the door and make apology for her tardy appearance.

But having dispatched his breakfast, his dark eyes held an impatient gleam that his wife had still not arisen. Suppose she was unwell? At this thought he hastily mounted the stairs and knocked at her bedroom door. There was no answer. He knocked once more—then opened the door and stared about. There was no sign of Kieran. More than this, her toilet articles had disappeared from her dressing chest and a wardrobe door was ajar. He walked across, opened it. Her clothes had gone.

He stood there stupefied. Where had she gone? Why? The children—had she taken them too? He opened the nursery door and stared at the two empty cots. Now he was seriously worried. He returned to Kieran's bedroom and there on the bed he saw it—a note addressed to him.
He opened it with trembling fingers.
Dear Husband,
It is with sadness that I address you as such for the last time. A secret matter which I may not divulge has made it impossible for me to remain your wife, even in name only.

I am taking the babies with me and Bess Brown. Her grandmother died a week ago as you know. Bess no longer has any reason to remain in Edinburgh. I have enough money to start a new life and hope that you will find new happiness in the future.

There are no real words to express my gratitude to you for all your kindness. Without your unselfish help I would not have survived. You are a wonderful man Sorley Mor as well as an amazing physician. Please forgive the hurt I now give you—but it is only to prevent a greater one in time to come.
With best wishes from my heart,
Kieran
P.S. Please do not seek to find me. I am going far away.

He gave a strangled cry of grief. Whatever the secret matter was that had so disturbed her surely she could have shared it with him? Where would she go now—and with small babies?

He ran down stairs and opened the door and looked up and down the street, but only a few citizens were abroad, making their way to their places of employment. As he stood there, he heard a voice call to him. He glanced around and saw his inquisitive neighbour standing there.

'A braw guid morning tae ye, Doctor Stewart!' she called.

'Mistress Morton, I hope I see you well?' He forced the words out.

'I mustn't grumble, although my legs were that painful last night, I couldn't sleep. I lit a candle and sat at my window. I thought I heard a sound from your door and there was your wife and your maid, carrying one of your children each and getting into a hackney coach. I do hope none of your lady's folks are taken ill, that she made such unusual departure?' Her old eyes swept over him curiously.

'Yes, you have guessed aright,' he said tonelessly. 'Ah—here comes Effie,' he added as his nurse came bustling into view along the street. 'Well, I must get on. Good day to you, mistress.' Disappointed that she had been unable to glean more interesting news, the old lady closed her door.

'Ah, Effie—I am going to be taken up with business affairs this morning. Cancel any patients who are non urgent cases. You can attend to any dressings that need changing.' If she thought the doctor sounded strangely abrupt that day, Effie put it down to the lack of sleep he was getting.

'Leave it to me, doctor.'

'Yes—and my wife and the babies are away visiting for a week or two.'

'Why, the mistress spoke no word of this to me,' exclaimed Effie in surprise. 'Perhaps a break will do her good, doctor—she has not seemed herself lately. She said that she misses the hills of her former home.' She frowned. 'I hope she will be careful—the roads are still very unsafe they say!'

'She is very resourceful,' he replied carefully, trying not to allow his deep worries affect his voice. 'She has taken young Bess with her,' he added and with a forced smile at the nurse, turned and made his way up to Kieran's empty bedroom.

He sat on the bed and tried to clear his mind of the intense shock of her departure. Then he opened the drawers of her dressing chest, looking for any clue as to her whereabouts—and found none. Then he saw it, a crumpled wrapper on the floor and lifted it. It was merely addressed to Mistress Stewart—but bore a broken seal. He could not make out the crest. Who had given her this? What had it contained?

Had Kieran met some stranger who had persuaded her to leave husband and home and go off with him? Was she capable of such duplicity? Surely not, for however trying her behaviour had become of recent months, Kieran Stewart possessed a bright honesty of spirit. But how well did he really know her, this widow of the young soldier who had become his friend and companion on their joint escape from Culloden.

He thought of the worries of his brother David that he had selflessly entered into a loveless marriage, deeply caring for a woman who did not return his love. He thought of McCrombie's quiet questioning, and expressing similar opinions. Had he indeed been a fool to hope that Kieran might one day learn to return his affection for her? Well, it would seem so. But where had she gone?

His mind was in an agony of concern for her—and for the little ones he had thought of as his own. What would happen to Alan and Ishbel torn away from the security of their home?

'Where do I start looking for her,' he whispered. 'If only I had some clue as to her plans. Money! She had written that she had enough money. If so where had it come from? He had only given her modest amounts for their housekeeping. She could not have saved any appreciable sum from that! None of what had happened made sense!

She must have received a sum of money from a man, he thought. But who could it be? He thought momentarily of Captain Roderick Campbell and dismissed the idea as ridiculous. True she had met with the young soldier recently, but it was probably merely a chance meeting. But there again she had denied meeting with any she knew that day, when he had questioned her. He had put this down to her antipathy to all Campbells.

Then his absurd suspicions aroused when listening to McCrombie came back in to his mind. He remembered that McCrombie had stated that Roderick Campbell's father had been murdered by a Rory MacGregor, who had made off with the murdered man's pregnant wife. Kieran had told him that her father had been a Rory MacGregor, who had been captured by the Campbells and hung. She had not known her own mother who had died in giving birth to her.

Could this indeed be possible—that his lovely Stewart bride was in truth a member of Clan Campbell? Had she learned this matter of Mamore last year on that encounter with the Major General? The more he thought of all that had happened, the more plausible this answer must be to the riddle of her departure.

She realised that our lives could not be lived together, Campbell with Stewart. It was thing impossible—or was it? Did it truly make such difference from which clan man and woman came if they truly loved each other? Surely the only way in this world for hatred and suspicion to change, was through love—and kindness to others.

But even as these gentle thoughts diffused his distress, he felt the deeper instinctive antagonism arise in his heart towards the clan he rightly detested. How could he ever truly love Kieran now that she was no Stewart, but Campbell? And yet, surely as his wife she was now most certainly a Stewart, whatever her antecedents had been.

At that moment he made his mind up. It did not really matter who or what she had been before becoming his wife, she was his and he would never give up hope of winning her back again.

'Doctor—I'm that sorry to disturb you, but there is a man here with a broken arm—in much pain!' Effie's glance took in the empty room, which told its own story. Not just a visit away, but everything gone. The poor doctor—poor poor man,' and her heart bled for him

'I will come, Effie,' he said heavily and as he bent his head over the workman's injured limb, found that this work that he loved and in which he found fulfilment, helped to distract the mental pain he was enduring.

'There my friend. Keep the splint in position for at least three weeks. Come back and see me then.' He straightened up.

'I've little to pay you with, doctor. And I will not be able to work for a while with this.' The grey haired man looked shamefacedly down at his feet as he spoke. The doctor smiled his understanding.

'Pay me another day—when you are wealthier,' nodded Sorley Mor compassionately. Payment from his more affluent patients helped him to care for those who were struggling to survive. He turned to the young mother whose small daughter's face bore a skin rash. The day went on, but at the back of his brain the question kept arising. Where was Kieran? Where had she gone!

He went to McCrombie and told him the whole thing—and his suspicion that Kieran may have discovered that she was of Campbell origin, not MacGregor as she had been brought up to believe. That it was for this reason she had left him, distraught to find that all she had believed in was false.

'You guessed it that day when we spoke together—and I mentioned Rory MacGregor to you. Why did you not mention then that this was the name of your wife's supposed father?' He looked at Sorley Mor gently, knowing how hard this must be for this man so loyal to the Stuarts, to come to terms with.

'The logical part of my mind considered it—but my heart rejected such appalling possibility. You will say that it is no fault of hers that she is of this tainted blood. I know it and try to imagine how I would behave should she seek to return as my wife.' He swallowed, his face registering the opposing emotions chasing through his brain.

'Man—this is an intolerable situation for you to contend with! But here is a question for you which may hold the answer.' The old lawyer stared at him compassionately.

'Well?'

'Do you still love your wife Kieran?' He held Sorley Mor's dark gaze.

'I do—yes, I do,' came from the doctor's tortured lips.

'Then you must do all you can to find her and reassure her of that love. I do not say that such will be easy.' He shook his head thinking of what it asked of the solemn faced man before him.

'She is a Campbell!'

'As you say and certainly those who lead Clan Campbell are of a different breed to most other highland clans. Their behaviour is authoritarian and they prefer the new order of the Hanoverian regime. Through it they enjoy power. Perhaps change is inevitable in the north. Centuries old structures now torn down, tartan forbidden as are the pipes, the authority of the chiefs set aside. We are facing a new and very different land, Sorley my friend.'

'I am not sure where to start looking for her!'

'Let us narrow it down. Certainly she will not attempt to return to Appin or its surrounding areas—far too dangerous still, especially with the responsibility of two babies to consider.' He rose to his feet and considered a map on the wall behind him.

'What of Balquidder then—the MacGregors?'

'A possibility there, but with the clan scattered into the high hills, their homes burned to the ground, where in that whole wild area would she start looking for those she grew up amongst?'

'She mentioned that she had been cared for by a Duncan MacGregor and his wife Annie who lived by Loch Voil. At the age of fourteen she was sent to France, stayed with relatives who had fled to Paris after the 1715 rising. It was there that she later met the man she married, whom I was proud to call friend—Alan Stewart.' He sighed heavily. 'I have been over it time and again in my head—impossible to know where to start looking. I also have a duty towards my patients.'

'Perhaps she will send word to you, at least to let you know she is safe,' suggested McCrombie hopefully, trying to assuage the sorrow and despair he saw on Sorley's face.

'I miss her presence so,' the man blurted out. 'And oh how I miss little Alan and Ishbel! I lost all contact with my own son—then when we finally were reunited, saw him blown to pieces at Culloden. I now love Kieran's children as my own and fear I will never see them more.'

'That word never, is not one you will use again—where is the bright courage that has seen you through untold dangers in the past. If you are determined to find your Kieran, then you will!' declared McCrombie. He watched as Sorley Mor rose to his feet.

'Yes, you are right of course! You are a good friend, Robert McCrombie!' He leant forward and took the lawyer's hand.

'Keep in touch with me. Let me know if there is anything I can do to help!' Then as Sorley Mor made for the door and he heard his receding footsteps, McCrombie sighed. He wished he really could see some good coming out of this strange web of circumstances.

Even as Sorley Mor's thoughts were engaged on Kieran that day, so also, were hers on him.

On that fraught night when she had taken secret, guilty departure from her husband's home, Kieran Stewart's whole energies were set on making escape from the labyrinth of tall dark buildings along which the hackney cab carried her. She held baby Alan on her lap, his sister Ishbel in the arms of Bess Brown. At last they arrived at the Bell Inn to which place the written instructions of her brother Roderick Stewart had directed her. From here a public coach would take her to Stirling, but not beyond, the road north too rough.

She waited in the common room of the inn until daybreak and then took her place in the coach with Bess and the babies. It was raining as they left Edinburgh behind and she drew a deep sigh of relief as the city of spires, narrow streets and dark tenement buildings, all crowned by the castle soaring high on its rocky bulwarks disappeared in the distance.

The two babies were restless, not liking the jolting progress of the coach, perhaps also sensing their mother's anxiety. Kieran glanced at the flat scenery through which they were passing, some of it good farmland, with woods and a few fine houses, Now at last the line of the Ochils were before them as they dropped down into the town of Stirling.

'There it is, Mistress—the inn you mentioned,' cried Bess in sudden excitement, as they placed the twins in their carrying baskets and gathered their bags together.

The Golden Lion Inn, before which the coach came to a halt with a clattering of wheels and stamping of horse hooves, was they saw a substantial yellow stone building. The driver handed his reins to a groom and helped his dozen passengers step down. When he came to Kieran he glanced at the twins and looking around summoned a young lad to carry their bags in. Kieran walked to the reception desk and asked for a two bedded room.

'How long will you be staying then, mistress?' asked the portly, elderly landlord glancing at Kieran curiously.

'That depends,' replied Kieran. 'Have you a letter for me—for Mistress Kieran Stewart,' her heart was beating as she made the inquiry.

'Why—indeed I have. It was left here by a Captain Roderick Campbell who said that all expenses of a lady of your name would be undertaken by him and left a sum for that purpose.'

'My brother,' she replied and saw his face drop. He had imagined he was being party to a liaison, strange indeed to find a Stewart related to a Campbell. He glanced at the twin babies kicking and screaming in their baskets, hungry now and making their displeasure felt. The sooner he managed to get this noisy party into a room above stairs the better. He rummaged under his desk and held a sealed letter towards Kieran.

'Here you are then, lady,' he said. 'The lad will take you to your room. You can either eat in the dining hall which can be crowded or have meals brought to your room if you prefer.'

'Yes—upstairs if you please, landlord,' said Kieran with a sweet smile. 'I am much obliged to you for your courtesy.'

As both she and Bess subsided on the hard beds in that impersonal room, Kieran felt as though all that was happening was part of some strange dream. In the morning she would awake to find herself back in Sorley Mor's house, giving her breast to the little ones before descending the stairs and preparing breakfast.

But she would never again be able to refer to Sorley Mor as her husband and as the thought registered in her mind, tears began to fall. She dashed them away.

'Mistress—you are distressed. Do you wish to return to Edinburgh,' asked Bess with a worried look in her hazel eyes. The girl was confused in her mind as to why Kieran should have taken decision to leave a good husband and a fine home. For to this girl brought up in the cramped quarters of a squalid room in a tenement block, the doctor's house was a palace.

'No Bess. I will never go back. You may if you so wish. I will give you money so that you may find employment in another part of Edinburgh—for you must never tell my husband of my plans.' She fixed her tired grey gaze on the young nursemaid, who shook her head vigorously.

'I will stay with you for always—if you will have me, my lady. I love wee Alan and Ishbel!' she declared without a second thought.

'Then so you shall!' Now—there is a jug of water on that table over there and a bowl. The babies need changing before they are fed.'

Now the babies were contentedly cooing to each other, Kieran went to the window, breaking the seal on Roderick Campbell's letter and studying it by the fading evening light.

My Dearest Sister Kieran,

If you are reading this, then it means that you have had the courage to leave life with the good doctor and trust your future to those who will truly love and support you.

As soon as you receive these few words, instruct the landlord to send message to me at Glenlarig House and I will come for you. Until then bide safely at the inn. Speak to no strangers in the meanwhile. A few more days and you will be safe amongst your true family where you will be cherished. I cannot tell you what joy it will be to receive you.

Your loving brother,

Roderick Campbell

She read the words almost blankly at first, experiencing feeling of repugnance at this missive from an enemy hand. Only Roderick Campbell could no longer be regarded as an enemy. The responsibility for all that was now happening, was hers alone. There had been no reason to accept his challenge to leave Edinburgh and seek out her blood relatives in the Highlands. So thought Kieran now, staring at the letter her mind in turmoil.

She could have thrown his earlier letter and his gold into the mud, she thought. What kind of woman was she, leaving behind all that she had held dear? Was it not dishonouring of Alan Stewart's name to seek out a member of the detested Clan Diarmid?

But there again, how could she with any decency have remained in position as wife to Sorley Mor Stewart, knowing that she was of Campbell blood He would have shrunk from her had he discovered the fact, nor could she have blamed him.

'My life is in ruins,' she murmured as she stood there. Then she turned as glanced towards her children. 'But this way their future may be assured.'

The landlord listened to Kieran's instructions.

'I will send word to Captain Campbell the morn,' he said and pocketed the gold coin Kieran tendered.

Two days went by during which time Kieran's thoughts remained troubled. But now the die was cast, no turning back. It was on the third day that she heard a clattering in the courtyard below her window. She looked down and saw a tall man in highland dress dismount from his horse and calling instructions to a groom. Beneath his bonnet with its eagle feather noticed hair as red gold as her own—and knew him for her Campbell brother. He had four attendants with him, their mounts rough coated ponies, whilst his was a magnificent chestnut stallion.

And as she watched she saw a small carriage drawn by two black horses draw up beside the group. Again he called orders then turned impatiently towards the entrance to the inn.

'Bess look after the children,' faltered Kieran between lips grown stiff. 'I must go below.' She gave a swift glance at her appearance in the mirror and pushed back a stray curl, patted the folds of her green velvet gown and taking a deep breath, slipped out of the bedroom and started to descend the stairs.

She heard his voice as he stood in haughty conversation with the landlord, as a curious crowd some the worse for drink, watched the stranger in his distinctive and in many quarters much loathed tartan.

She approached the reception desk slowly and with some trepidation and stood listening as Roderick Campbell demanded where Mistress Stewart was to be found.

'I am here, Captain Campbell,' she said in a clear unemotional voice as the crowd that had gathered around the stranger parted to allow her through. He swung about and gave a cry of delight.

'Kieran—my dearest sister!' and he held his hands out to her. She came nearer, stood quietly before him. He reached for one of her hands—lifted it to his lips. As he did so there came a harsh cry from a man in the crowd.

'A curse upon my eyes that have seen this sight,' he shouted, 'That I should observe woman of the MacGregor with a thrice damned Campbell!' All voices ceased at this intervention and Kieran turned her head to see whence the voice came. A short thick set man with black hair and beard, wearing a kilt died black and sewn into trousers, pointed accusing finger at her. She recognised him. It was Malcolm Grier as he was known, the name MacGregor being proscribed, and was distant cousin to Annie MacGregor who with her late husband Duncan had brought up Kieran as their own.

'Take that man,' cried Roderick angrily, but the fellow melted away into the crowd all of whom now looked disparagingly at Kieran, murmuring to themselves, but not daring to speak their minds outwardly for fear of the four wild looking ghillies who stood in attendance on the Campbell laird and were now joined by another who had driven the carriage.

'We would eat,' instructed Roderick.

'Why, this way then sir. I have a room where you may dine in more privacy.' The landlord clapped his hands and gave orders to a nervous looking serving man, who bowed and led these unwelcome guests to the small dining room just off the main dining hall.

Her brother held a chair out for Kieran who seated herself. It all seemed like some strange dream, sitting here and forcing small pieces of meat into her mouth and washing it down with ale as he ate fastidiously while at a separate table the ghillies wolfed down their own meal.

'My maid Bess Brown is upstairs with the children,' she said quietly. 'May I ask that food is sent up for her?' The order was immediately given.

'I am delighted that you have brought little Alan and Ishbel and look forward to seeing them safe in the home in which they will grow up.' He looked at her approvingly. 'Listen Kieran—I can only make guess at how difficult matters are for you at this time. But you have made a wise decision and I promise you will never regret it.'

She forced a smile. Never regret it—she was already doing so. Would she ever forget that accusing cry from Malcolm Grier? News of what he had seen today would soon be all around Balquidder and beyond. What indeed would Annie MacGregor say, learning that her adopted daughter, who had made an approved love match with an Appin Stewart, had betrayed her heritage? But of course, Annie must be aware that Kieran was no true daughter of Clan MacGregor, but a child of the Campbells. But at least none here knew of her second marriage to another Stewart—that she had deserted the kind and honourable physician who was her husband.

'Shall we make a start, Kieran,' suggested Roderick, as he raised a napkin to his lips. 'We have many miles to cover and the roads not of the best. You should do well enough in the carriage with the bairns.

'I must first feed the babies,' said Kieran firmly. He glanced at her and took her meaning. He smiled understandingly.

'Oh—yes, of course—go then. I will bide here for you.' She felt the eyes of many upon her as she hurried up the stairs to her room.

'You have eaten, Bess?'

'Yes, mistress,' She looked expectantly at Kieran. 'Are we to leave soon?'

'As soon as I have fed and changed the children—and we must see that they are warmly wrapped for the journey!' Half an hour later, Kieran sent Bess downstairs with a message to Roderick Campbell. He knocked and entered the room and gave a cry of pleasure as he saw the twins.

'Kieran, they are beautiful,' he exclaimed and lifted Ishbel up in his arms. 'Strange that you should have named her so,' he said softly. 'It was her grandmother's name.' She looked back at him startled.

'I could not have known that,' she said.

'Kieran—you take up Alan, and I shall carry this wee one! And you,' turning now to Bess, 'will take your mistress belongings. You can manage that?' he demanded of the little nursemaid.

'Oh yes, sir' She lifted the bags obediently and followed behind as Kieran and Roderick descended the stairs carrying the children. The ghillies were waiting for them at the foot of the stairs. Roderick nodded to the landlord, their bill already paid and the party made their way outside to the stables.

The carriage swayed and bounced along the uneven unpaved road, that eventually became little more than a rough track and the motion helped the children to sleep. Hours later, Bess looked around in awe. They had left the cultivated fields behind them and were proceeding along the shores of a narrow loch, overlooked by a majestic mountain such as the city girl had never seen, forested slopes reflected in the mirrored surface of the loch. On the far side of the carriage dense woodland clad the steep brae wearing a sparse cloak of gold and bronze, the road before them carpeted with the fallen leaves of autumn.

Once there was a delay as the carriage wheels sank into a muddy ditch, and Kieran and Bess stepped out whilst Roderick's powerful clansmen hefted the vehicle clear and their journey continued. The babies became fretful and Kieran fed them, realising that they no longer seemed satisfied by what she was able to supply and worried if she was losing her milk.

Now they pulled up before a small coaching inn that seemed to be thronging with redcoat militia. Many curious glances were directed at Kieran and Bess and a few admiring comments called forth, until they saw the ice in Roderick Campbell's eyes. They were to stop here for refreshments before proceeding on to the last part of their journey. They were also to leave the rented carriage there, the women to continue on horseback. So instructed Roderick Campbell to Kieran's dismay—what of the children she agonised?

'Mistress Stewart, I have never been on a horse before—I'm much afeared of those great brutes,' whispered Bess pulling at Kieran's arm, as some twenty minutes later they left the warmth of the inn and into a frosty late afternoon. Roderick heard her.

'You Bess will ride behind Ewan Dhu,' he ordered and the girl found herself seized under the arms and swept up onto one of the garrons, where she clutched the riders waist. Satisfied Roderick Campbell now looked at his sister.

'Ivor Mac Dugal will take baby Alan up with him. No, have no fear sister—your small son will be quite safe, I promise you. Now then,' he continued, 'Wee Ishbel with Rab—so.' She stared indignantly as her babies were disposed of into the arms of two of the fierce looking ghillies and her brother gave an amused chuckle as he glanced into her smouldering grey eyes. 'My men will care for them with their lives,' he said, 'now you, Kieran, up behind me. Ah—you are a horsewoman,' as she took his hand and leapt lightly up behind him on the chestnut stallion, which snorted at this double load.

They were off, and now were passing beneath gloomy mountains that reared out of the gathering dusk. Once they were stopped by a patrol of redcoat militia. Their Sergeant exclaimed his delight at recognising Roderick.

'Captain Campbell—your servant sir!' he cried.

'I have resigned my commission. Just a private gentleman now,' replied Roderick. 'How lie matters here, Sergeant?'

'We have rounded up those few insurgents discovered—less than twenty. They melt away into the hills as soon as they see our uniforms.' The man's clipped English accent sounded strangely in Kieran's ears.

'MacGregors I suppose,' probed Roderick.

'Yes—although of course they are not allowed to use their clan name any more, most calling themselves Drummond or Grierson or Gregory. A wild heathen bunch they are and devilish difficult to catch!' The middle aged sergeant swore an oath.

'Not for nothing are the MacGregors called 'Children of the Mist,' exclaimed Kieran recklessly. 'Their blood is Royal!' she added.

'Be that as it may lady, as far as I am concerned they are scum which my men and I are ordered to eradicate from this area—so ordered by Major General John Campbell of Mamore I'm informed.' He stared reprovingly at Kieran. 'You should keep away from all such outlaws, Maam.'

'My sister will certainly have no truck with them, I assure you,' said Roderick lightly. 'Now—I am wishful to reach my destination before nightfall. It is already dusk. Good day to you Sergeant—and good luck with your mission!'

'Bad cess tae ye,' breathed Kieran silently, as they left the party of redcoats behind, the sound of their marching feet lost in the sound of horses hooves as they swept onwards. 'May the De'il fly awa wi' them!' she added as a backwards glance assured her they could be seen no more.

Strangely neither of the babies protested their thundering passage along the rough track, sleeping peacefully against the breasts of the ghillies who bore them close. As for Bess she felt nauseous and wondered desperately how much longer this journey would take. She gave a sudden gasp, as did Kieran as they heard a great roaring of waters coming just ahead.

'We are at the falls of Dochart,' explained Roderick to Kieran's inquiry. 'It's too dark to get a good view of them. The river needs to be bridged one day, no safe ford nearby. We divert here, take that track to our right.' He then called an order to one of his men, who produced his tinder box and lit a torch he had carried strapped to his horse. He held its flaring light before them now, leading the way ahead, the horses picking their way carefully between heathered banks where young birches swept against the riders faces in the gloom. Now the stars were out and a half hooped moon pooled its silvery light upon the waters of a loch along the banks of which they were now proceeding. The bulk of a high mountain soared on its opposite bank

At last Roderick called a halt. High above them dimly seen on the flanks of a wooded brae, stood a substantial house, three stories high, built in the fashion of a French chateau.

'Glenlarig House—your new home Kieran!' he announced proudly, and spurring his horse, encouraged it to clamber up the steep path leading upwards towards the stately building, closely followed by his retainers. As they approached nearer, Kieran noticed two pillars crowned by strange shaped rocks marking entrance to the driveway.

They had reached the courtyard, and men came running from the house as now Kieran listened to her own Gaelic tongue used and the music of it set her heart pounding. Until this time, Roderick had addressed her in Scots, merely throwing orders to the ghillies in their own tongue. Of a sudden, before Roderick dismounted, Kieran felt herself lifted down by a tall, white haired, distinguished looking gentleman in highland dress, and to her surprise was drawn into his arms and kissed.

'Welcome to your home, my dear child,' he said, 'I am Iain Campbell, brother-in-law to your late father Colin and foster father to your brother Roderick. He smiled at her kindly as he released her.

'I am pleased to meet you, sir,' replied Kieran awkwardly, acutely aware that she must look a mess, hair windblown and skirt bedraggled where they had splashed through swirling burns. But had she known it, she had never looked fairer, the moonlight and flaring torches touching her hair to fairy gold and gently outlining the grace of her figure.

'My children?' she exclaimed now, as Roderick came to her side, having given orders for care of his stallion and exchanged an embrace with Iain Campbell. He smiled at the worry in her voice.

'Alan and Ishbel are fine, sister! See you, here they are then!' And sure enough the two ghillies who had carried their small charges with such care now brought them to her. With a word of thanks, she took baby Alan into her arms as Bess came shyly forward and reached for Ishbel. The little party climbed up the steps and entered by one of the largest doors Kieran had seen. The house might not have been a fortified castle, but it was well seen that it would be easy to defend.

She walked diffidently into the huge hall illumined by dozens of candles in silver branches, and where in a massive fireplace logs burned brightly with a hundred sparks flying up the chimney, staring then at the tapestries on its walls and portraits which must represent Roderick's ancestors—her ancestors too she realised. She drew in a sharp breath, for it was from this place that her pregnant mother had been kidnapped by Rory MacGregor, whom she had thought to be her father!

She paused beneath one gold framed portrait that dominated the wall above the fireplace. It was of a handsome man in his forties, with a strong, slightly arrogant face, hair and beard silver blond, his eyes an unusual shade of green. She bit her lip as she looked—could this be?

'Yes, Kieran,' said Roderick now, coming to stand at her side and sensing her unspoken question. 'This is portrait of our father, who was slain by Rory MacGregor and who is grandfather to these two little ones,' his gesture indicating the twins. 'Were he alive today, it would gladden his heart to see you here and the bairns.'

'And our mother—Catriona?' she whispered, looking in vain for a precious portrait of the mother she had never known.

'Alas, I have only that small painting in the locket I wear on my breast at all times,' he said regretfully. 'But look in any mirror Kieran and there you will see one who is her double.' He slipped an arm about her shoulders. 'It will take time for you to readjust to all of this. Best now I think to take you to your chamber. Ah—here is my Aunt Lorna at last!' As he spoke, a woman approached Kieran. She was tall and slender, wealth of dark hair white streaked at the temples drawn under a lace cap, her gown of dark blue velvet with a tartan wrap about her shoulders. It was her eyes that drew Kieran to her, dark caring eyes full of sympathy.

'No need to tell me that you are Catriona's daughter! You are so amazingly like her, my dear. I am Lorna and wife to Iain Campbell whom you have already met.' She smiled at Kieran then turned her attention on the baby boy in her guest's arms. 'Why, but he is beautiful,' she said.

'His name is Alan Stewart named for his father and I am Kieran Stewart,' replied Kieran quietly. It seemed important to try to hold onto her own identity in this house full of Campbells. Then as she signed to Bess to come nearer, 'This little one is Alan's twin sister Ishbel!'

'Ishbel—it was the name of Catriona's mother,' exclaimed the lady. 'May I hold her?' she reached for the baby who was beginning to utter hungry cry of protest.

'She needs changing, Ma'am,' put in Bess.

'So does this one,' added Kieran firmly as Alan now joined in protest.

'Come then,' said Lorna. 'Follow me.' Then she picked up a candle, and as the men stared after them, led the way out of the hall by a side door and up a flight of stairs. The room into which Kieran was shown was large, with a good fire burning in the grate. Kieran stared longingly at the four poster bed, for she was exhausted. Then she noticed the two wooden cradles placed one on each side of it.

'I was told you had twins and made ready accordingly,' said Lorna with a smile. 'There is a small chamber next door for your maid—Bess is it not?'

'Yes, Ma'am,' replied Bess who felt she must be dreaming. She had never thought to see a house as splendid as this one and felt quite overwhelmed by all that was happening. But one thing was needful now—

to help Mistress Stewart with the changing and feeding of the children who were now filling the room with their screams.

'You will find a tray at your bedside so that you do not starve before joining us downstairs for supper,' said Lorna, adding sympathetically, 'You must be fairly famished after your long journey!'

'Thirsty above all,' replied Kieran gratefully.

'Well, I will leave you in peace now. I have had warm water brought in that large jug by the basin on the small marble table, and one of the maids will bring you more when you have need of it.' Then she planted a swift kiss on Kieran's cheek and bustled off.

Kieran poured a glassful of the pale amber coloured liquid she found in a silver jug on the tray, and recognised it for whisky, cream and honey mixed with spices and it was delicious and certainly revived her. She offered some to Bess, who tasted it somewhat suspiciously. Then they each applied themselves to one of the protesting children, bathed and changed them before Kieran put them to her breast.

At last peace reigned. By now Kieran was extremely weary and could not bear the thought of going downstairs to face eating a meal watched by strangers in this Campbell household. That she was indeed one of them now was a thought she dismissed time and again. She would stay here for now, but eventually seek a home of her own however poor, in her beloved Appin. But would she ever be welcome there again, after throwing in her lot with blood relatives?

She looked up at the knock on the door. It was Lorna with a maid in tow.

'This is Annie and she will be your personal maid, Kieran,' she said quietly. 'Young Bess obviously has enough to do helping with the babies.' The middle aged maid, who had accompanied her mistress, now curtsied to Kieran and busied herself emptying the basin of used water into a bucket and pouring clean water into the jug for future use. She then attended to the fire, used the poker to stir it up and added more logs.

'Thank you, Annie' said Kieran with a tired smile.

'What of your clothes, Mistress Kieran? They will need unpacking, hanging out,' suggested Annie helpfully.

'I can attend to my mistresses clothes,' put in Bess indignantly. But Lorna Campbell placed a restraining hand on the girl's arm and Bess stepped back awkwardly. She pointed to the bags that had been brought up and placed in the corner of the room. 'Well—there are the bags!'

Annie made to go over to them, but Kieran gave a cry.

'Why not leave all until morning. I would dearly love just to sleep tonight, Aunt Lorna.' Kieran looked at the older woman pleadingly and Lorna nodded understandingly.

'Then sleep you shall, my dear. I will see you in the morning then. Come then Annie! You too Bess—but you must be hungry?' she said looking at the young nursemaid's tired face.

'Not really, my lady. I'm too weary to eat,' said Bess apologetically.

'This way then, Bess!' instructed Lorna. 'You will sleep in the neighbouring chamber so that you may rise and tend to the children should they cry in the night.' She patted Bess on the back and propelled her out, leaving Kieran to undress by the fire and climb up into the wide bed with its warm quilt—where she fell asleep almost immediately.

Chapter Seven

Kieran was awakened by the sound of the pipes, and at first stared around
bewildered until memory came rushing back. She climbed out of the
comfort of that huge bed and stepped across to the window, and drew the
heavy curtains and stared below where a piper resplendent in kilt and plaid
was marching solemnly up and down in front of the house, staring up from
time to time at her window. She opened it. She did not know the air he
played, but it seemed to reverberate poignantly amongst the hills, and this
once familiar sound tore at her heart. The piper saw movement at her
window and bowed. She turned shyly away—then resolutely moved back
to survey her surroundings.

It was she saw a beautiful day, the trees wearing their dramatic autumn
colours and the loch shining bright in the sunrise, tranquil waters reflecting
snow capped mountains above. She turned away as the children awoke.
They too had heard the pipes and added their voices to the volume of
sound as Kieran hurried to their unfamiliar cots to lift and comfort them. A
knock at her door brought Bess to her assistance.

To her dismay, Kieran realised that she was indeed losing her milk, was
so informed by her protesting small son and daughter.

'Perhaps we could find the services of a wet nurse for them,' suggested
Bess. 'At not yet ten months they are still over young to wean!'

'But surely the most natural thing in the world is for a mother to be able
to put her own babes to the breast!' And Kieran burst into a flood of tears,
while at the same moment Lorna Campbell knocked and entered with the
maid Annie behind her. She stared across at the young woman in dismay
and hurried to Kieran's side.

'Hush now, my dear. What is troubling you,' she demanded gently, as
she placed something she was carrying onto the bed.

'I fear I am losing my milk—and it may be a punishment from heaven,
for coming to this place!' So wept Kieran wildly, as the tension of the last
few days took its toll.

'How old are the babes then, child?'

'They were born last January—so ten months!'

'And fine well nourished bairns they are and a credit to you! You have done well to feed two all these months. Now I will find a good wet nurse for them, which will also give you time to regain your own strength!' She put an arm about Kieran's shoulders and held her close until the girls sobs subsided. But as she drew away, Kieran felt remorse that she had allowed a Campbell to comfort her and briefly nodded as Lorna said she must leave her now as she had matters to attend to.

Annie in the meanwhile after gesture of permission from Kieran, was busily unpacking the belonging of her new mistress under Bess's disapproving eye. All her few garments were badly creased and damp and Kieran reproached herself for not attending to them last night. It was then that she noticed the garments Lorna had previously laid out on the bed. She fingered the fine lawn shift, the dark blue velvet skirt and bodice—and the tartan shawl.

'Lady, I'm bid to tell ye that these clothes were your mother's own,' said Annie quietly. 'I am thinking that they will maybe fit quite well.'

'My mother's—is it possible,' whispered Kieran, a lump in her throat. With a soft cry she gathered up a fold of the skirt and held it against her face, and now new tears began to fall for the mother she had never known. Then she straightened, splashed her face with water and brushed her hair to shining wealth of red gold and with Annie's assistance put on clothes of a quality such as she had never owned before.

'Mistress, you look so beautiful,' whispered Bess, relieved that Kieran's tears had stopped.

'Indeed she does,' agreed Annie. 'See for yourself, Mistress—juist peep in the glass!' Kieran did so, stood before the tall oak framed cheval mirror and could hardly believe the reflection she saw there was her own.

Another knock revealed Lorna Campbell back again and this time accompanied by a strong, healthy looking young woman, with a fresh complexion and dark hair and honest expression, who bobbed a respectful curtsy to Kieran.

'This is Morag Burns,' Lorna announced. 'Morag's own young son is almost two years and to be weaned. If you agree, she will act as wet nurse for wee Alan and Ishbel?' so saying she looked at Kiernan for approval, and a smile lit up her face as she noticed the girl's change of dress.

Kieran regarded the wet nurse with a doubtful glance at first, but liking what she saw, forced a smile and inclined her head to the woman who was staring down tenderly at the two hungry children.

'May I, my lady?' asked Morag and stooping took Alan up into her arms. She seated herself, unfastened her bodice and put the child to her breast, then made a gesture to Bess indicating that she should bring Ishbel to her.

Minutes later instead of the hungry cries that had filled the room, peace prevailed.

'Time now for you to break your own fast,' suggested Lorna. 'Come now and Bess shall find her breakfast in the kitchen.'

'One question first,' put in Kieran. 'These garments I wear—they truly belonged to my mother?' Her lips trembled slightly as she framed the words.

'Indeed yes, and a there is wardrobe full of others besides. When Rory MacGregor forced his way into this house and slew your father and kidnapped Catriona and she pregnant poor lamb, all of her belongings were left behind.' Lorna Campbell's voice broke slightly as she continued, 'Catriona was my sister-in-law and very dear to me. I kept all of her things in perfect order in memory of her—none allowed near them but me.'

'You did that,' exclaimed Kieran softly

'Yes, and now very strangely you are come—you of whose existence we were ignorant, until Roderick met you in Glencoe—discovered the truth! It had always been thought that Catriona's baby had perished at birth.' Lorna's own eyes sparkled with tears.' 'Come then—later you will see all.'

Much troubled in her thoughts, Kieran descended the stairs at Lorna's side, guttering candles in sconces lighting the way, for that stairway was dark, their flickering light illumining imposing portraits of another era upon the walls. Roderick stood waiting to greet her as she entered a small dining room, where a massive oil painting of a wild waterfall attracted her gaze.

'Kieran—greetings,' exclaimed Roderick lifting her hand to his lips. 'This morning we eat here, but normally in the great hall, as is my uncle's pleasure! I hope you slept well sister and found all to your liking?' Then as his eyes took in her changed appearance, he glanced in wonder at his aunt.

'I remember my mother looking so,' he murmured, as his eyes swept approvingly over his sister's apparel.

'Does the gown not suit Kieran well,' smiled Lorna happily. 'She is so like to Catriona. How blessed we are to have her safe here among us!'

'I was awakened by the pipes,' said Kieran not knowing quite what to say to either of them. 'Your piper is a fine musician. I have longed to hear the pipes again!' This at least was true.

'Why then, Angus Mac Seumas will be delighted to learn you have said so! He was our father's piper, a dear old man well on in years, but blows as well as ever.' Roderick smiled his pleasure at her words. 'After we have eaten, I will escort you around the grounds—and as the weather is fine, you might enjoy a row on the loch?'

Lorna joined them at the dark oak table as a maid bustled in, but there was no sign of her husband Iain, just the three of them there. Kieran ate with a hunger she had not realised she possessed. There was ham and cold chicken, fresh eggs and new baked bread and she dispatched all with good appetite and felt her spirits rise. She glanced around now, her eyes lighting again on that massive painting.

'What place is that?' she asked as she examined the mighty flood of waters the artist had portrayed with such amazing realism.

'Why—we were close to it last night in the dusk. Do you remember that sound of rushing water? This is of the River Dochart which together with the Lochay empties into the loch. When it is in spate it can be formidable,' explained her brother, 'Its noise like thunder!'

'I would like to see it,' she replied. 'I remember another waterfall, a cave behind it where we hid!' Her eyes were sad as she spoke, memories of Sorley Mor pricking her conscience.

'Were you in that place for long, child,' asked Lorna, leaning forward curiously and taking her hand.

'Some months—it was dark and with a great noise of waters and very cold, but safe. It was like living in a strange womb—but I was glad to leave it in the end, to walk the heather once more, hear the cry of the eagle!'

'You will hear and see many eagles here, golden eagles' said Roderick. 'They nest in the high places and fish the loch.'

'I remember watching them at that at Loch Dhu,' said Kieran in choked tones, as she rose from the table and went to stand at the window which she found looked out on a landscaped garden rising up on the hillside, for of course this room looked out at the back of the house. Roderick joined her there and looked at her compassionately.

'Kieran, you have endured much, been tossed about by fate. I can only guess how hard it is for you at this time to put aside your previous loyalties to Clan Stewart and the MacGregors who brought you up as their own. Had we only known of your existence you would have been rescued and brought here whilst still a child to bide in your rightful home!' his eyes, dark and stormy as her own grey gaze locked with hers.

'I know all that you say must be true!' she flashed at him. 'But suppose you were told at your present age, that you were no true Campbell but a Stewart—or MacGregor, how would you deal with such situation?'

He stared back at her sombrely. 'The answer to that is—well, that I do not know,' he replied. 'But I would like to think that I would be true to the blood of my fathers.'

'You at least knew our father—and our mother, even though you were but three years old when they died. I have but that portrait of Colin Campbell in the hall on which to base my knowledge of a father—and your locket showing our mother!' She spoke bitterly now, knowing that she must accept the situation in which she found herself—and was solely of her own choosing. She could not blame Roderick for her presence here. She personally had made that cruel decision to leave Sorley Mor, considerate husband and dedicated physician—how would he be feeling now she asked herself, and blushed with sudden shame.

He seemed to sense her confused feelings.

'Come Kieran. I am longing to show you around the grounds. You will need a cloak, for it is cold outside. He led her along a dark passage way, where several coats hung on a wooden stand. She found herself wrapped in a warm plaid, and then as he opened a heavy metal studded door and they walked out into the sunshine, saw it to be the green and blue tartan of the Campbells.

Suddenly she started to laugh hysterically and startled, Roderick seized her by the shoulders and gave her a shake.

'What is it? What is wrong,' he asked and sighed relief as she quietened.

'It is I that am wrong—wrong in this place. I feel a traitor to all I have known,' she whispered with poignant stare. 'I do not know how to behave, when all seems so confused.'

'You will find surrounded by those who love you, that as the days slip by past memories will start to fade, become of less importance,' he said firmly. 'Also no doubt, you are still fatigued from your journey.' He took her hand and helped her to climb the pathway cut into rock that led to the top of the garden. From here they were able to look down at the loch—and sure enough Kieran saw an eagle swoop over its waters and fly off carrying a struggling fish in its talons. Again tears filled her eyes but she dashed them away as she stared at the dense wooded area of pine, oak and birch that bordered the garden and the small burn that gurgled its way to the far left, a bridge over its waters. It was a haven of peace here.

Suddenly the peace of that place was shattered as they heard gun shots that reverberated down the loch. Kieran put her hand to her breast as her heart started to pound. Roderick saw her distress and smiled at her.

'That will be my Uncle Iain bringing down a deer for the table,' he said casually. 'He is a fine shot you know—was off early into the hills.'

'I thought it was more of the violence that destroyed all normal life in the highlands,' she whispered.

'Most of that is long over, Kieran. Of course, we still arrest any rebels who previously escaped our net. And this is done for good reason, to prevent any future rising that might still be called by the Pretender.' As he spoke, his hair blew across his face in the breeze, that red gold hair so like hers. 'We will go this way,' he said as they retraced their steps and walked past stables and barns round to the front of the house where of a sudden came wail of the pipes as their owner tuned them and brought them into play.

Kieran stood there in the driveway and listened to the wild and beautiful air the piper played. It was one she had heard Alan Stewart play and memory of her first beloved husband came rushing back.

'Alan played this to me—when we were first wed,' she said quietly.

'Our father was also very fond of it,' replied Roderick gently, 'Or so Angus tells me. Music has a way of bringing healing at times.' He paused and looked at her and said 'Tae the hairt that loves, tae the hairt that is broken, music brings solace that may not be spoken.'

'It is a quotation,' she asked wonderingly, for it seemed an unlikely rhyme for a man of war to let pass his lips.

'No, Kieran—just thought of my own. I like to write you know, had my life been otherwise would have wished to become a poet.'

'You—a poet, brother?' she cried and she almost laughed at the notion. She saw the look of hurt cross his face. 'I'm sorry—but it is not what you expect to hear from a soldier!'

'But I was not always a soldier, Kieran, only became one when duty called and am truly glad my services are no longer required as such. And accordingly I resigned my commission as soon as I was able! Some men revel in war, in killing—I do not. I dream of a time when this land of ours may be at peace and all men regard themselves as brothers.' His grey eyes stared into hers and for a moment there was a poignant silence.

'You are not what I had imagined you to be. Perhaps one day you will recite some of your poetry to me,' she said gently and stared at him with genuine interest, her mind confused that he should speak of peace and not as she had expected of killing and retribution. He inclined his head and gave her a slightly self conscious smile.

'To write poetry—well, it is a very private thing—for in it a person reveals their deepest thoughts and dreams.' He turned his head away as they heard the sound of the pipes again, and the music brought a shimmer of tears to her eyes, for once again the melody was well known to her. As the last of the grace notes faded on the wind, Kieran approached the piper. He turned his weather beaten features upon the young woman and his dark eyes beneath shaggy grey brows beamed with pleasure.

'Greetings tae ye, child of the Campbells,' he said, 'What wondrous blessing you have come among us—reunited to your kinsfolk. This is great joy to an old man,' and bowed low before her.

'Angus Mac Seumas you are a very fine piper,' she exclaimed, pushing back the red gold curls that the breeze was blowing across her face. 'Those melodies you played very special to me and I thank you.'

'They were favourites of your father of blessed memory, lady,' he replied solemnly. 'Your mother Catriona also loved to hear me play,' he added with pride.

'I never knew either of them,' she replied sadly. 'I was brought up to feel hatred for all of Clan Campbell and now must try to reconcile myself to my true identity.' At her words he looked at her with compassion.

'It is a sad thing, this hatred between clans,' he said. 'One day perhaps the great Lord God will soften men's hearts towards each other. Until then, perhaps just strive to show caring and love for those who feel it to you, my child.' He raised his hands, lungs inflated the bag of his pipes and again the music floated wildly down the glen.

'I am glad you spoke with old Angus,' exclaimed Roderick as he led her down the long driveway, across the track road and along a sandy path that led between the heather and bracken to the banks of the loch. 'He is a very loyal servant and was quite devoted to our parents I am told.' He pointed to a small boat moored at the shore. 'Would you like to go out on the water, Kieran?'

'Yes,' she cried with sudden enthusiasm at the prospect. For months she had given every waking moment into caring for her babies and now this amazing chance to be herself again, a person in her own right and not just a mother. All thoughts of Sorley Mor drifted to the back of her mind as she decided to embrace this new way of life with her previously unknown relatives.

She stepped confidently into the boat and seated herself as Roderick pushed away from the bank, and started to row with sure strokes keeping the little craft parallel with the shore. He pointed out features of interest to her as they went, a tumbling waterfall here, isolated crofts, sheep on the hillsides, a herd of black cattle in a sheltered glen, noting with pleasure the animation on her face as she relaxed, shutting out all thoughts of the past.

'Look up there—a fine stag,' whispered Roderick, nodding his head towards a steep brae high above and sure enough there stood the many antlered beast proudly surveying all he considered his kingdom. Then disappointingly the stag disappeared. Perhaps their voices had possibly alerted it to danger?

'That was wonderful,' breathed Kieran, 'A magnificent animal!'

'A braw sight,' he agreed, grey eyes shining, delighting in her pleasure. 'There is an abundance of deer on these hills and salmon and trout in the loch. You will not go hungry sister mine!' he added proudly.

He leaned back on his oars, and as he did so, a shot rang out reverberating along the hills—and Kieran looked on in shock and horror as Roderick collapsed sideways! Another shot shattered the air, this time the bullet striking the side of the boat with splintering impact. At this Kieran reacted instinctively. Seizing the oars dropped by the inert figure opposite, Kieran started to row back furiously in the direction they had come. Her immediate concern was to get as far away from their assailant as possible. Another shot rang out and this time hitting the water harmlessly behind them.

She rowed as she had never done before, straining muscles and sinews in desperate attempt to get her brother back to the safety of his home. At this time she did not know whether he was alive or dead sheer panic driving her strenuous flight from danger. At last she recognised a small bay, the one from which they had departed. Here men were crowding down onto the shore, Iain Campbell among them.

Many hands seized the boat and pulled it on shore, as a grim faced, kilted Iain Campbell helped her out, and others of his men lifted Roderick gently in their arms. They put him down on a heather bank where Kieran slipped onto her knees beside him, lifting his head onto her lap. He was not dead she saw to her infinite relief. The bullet had clipped the side of his head, its impact causing concussion. There was much blood. But he was not dead!

'Oh—thank God, thank God,' she cried and turned a tear wet face up to Iain Campbell. 'It is not serious—he will live!'

'All thanks to you, niece,' he replied gruffly, his own shocked emotion obvious in his eyes. 'Did you perchance see who fired the shot?'

'No uncle—we were talking, happy. We saw a stag and Roderick stopped rowing that we might watch. Something scared it and it disappeared. Roderick took up his oars again—and then came the shot! There was another which caught the boat—and I moved over next to Roderick and took the oars.' Her voice faltered as she explained the chain of events, and Iain Campbell nodded and gave orders that Roderick should be carried up to the house.

'Careful now,' he instructed, as he himself took Kieran's arm and led her in procession. Lorna was waiting for them at the doorway, been alerted on looking from her bedroom window by sight of their people crowding on the shore—carrying a body with them.

'Iain—tell me he is not dead?' she cried as she saw her nephew carried in.

'Not dead, merely a head wound and is returning to consciousness I think. He owes his life to Kieran,' he said proudly. 'I must go now. We must seek out the perpetrator of this deed. Both of them could have been killed!'

'How far from the house was this?' she asked in horror, as she directed those carrying her nephew to carry him gently upstairs to his bed.

'I would say about a mile down the loch,' replied Kieran, preparing to follow the wounded man, her voice trembling in delayed shock as she spoke. Lorna placed a comforting arm about her shoulders, as together they mounted the stairs. Iain Campbell waited impatiently as his nephew was placed on his bed. He saw Roderick's eyelids flutter as the young man regained consciousness and stared about him in obvious incomprehension.

'Uncle Iain?'

'Don't worry, dear lad. You have suffered a gunshot wound to your head, but it is not bad, not bad at all,' his uncle informed him. 'Your sister is safe—she saved your life! The women will care for you now!' He reached out a hand and placed it reassuringly over Roderick's own. Then he kissed his wife and turned away summoning half a dozen of his ghillies to accompany him, and to provide themselves with guns.

As she bathed the wound on her brother's head, Kieran became aware of the very real affection she had begun to feel for him, how desolate she would have been had the shot been fatal. For the first time now, she started to wonder who it was who had tried to murder Roderick Campbell—and why? It must surely have been one of those mindless attacks born of clan hatred. So many different clans had good reason to hate and fear Clan Diarmid, not least the MacDonalds, the massacre at Glencoe ever green in memory.

'Is it true—you saved my life,' whispered Roderick now, as she attached a dressing to his wound. She dropped the blood soaked cloth she had bathed him with into a basin and straightened up.

'All I actually did Roderick, was to row—row faster than I have done before in all my life,' she explained. 'The first shot hit you. There was another that imbedded itself in the boat-----and another shot missed us altogether as I rowed away!'

He raised his head and stared at her remorsefully.

'You could have been killed yourself,' he said in a low voice. 'I would never have forgiven myself had this happened. You should have been safe in my care. I am so sorry, sister mine.' He looked up at her miserably.

'Hush now, nephew,' reproved Lorna soothingly. 'The most important thing is that you are both safe, my darling. Lie still now and rest.' She bent and kissed him. He needed no further telling, but closed his eyes again and drifted into sleep. Lorna gave orders to a maid to sit and keep watch over the young man. Then she smiled reassuringly at Kieran and beckoned her to leave the room. They stole out and descended the stairs together.

'I should go to Alan and Ishbel,' exclaimed Kieran. She had never left her babies for so long before.

'I checked on them just before I heard the shouting and your return! They are playing contentedly with Bess and Morag, are juist fine. Come you now child, you need rest, peace.'

They made their way into a small parlour that Lorna had made her own. No weapons on the walls here, or stag's heads, or large imposing paintings. All was tranquil, a great bowl of autumn flowers and berries on the polished dark oak table, tapestries on the walls. They seated themselves on a worn blue velvet couch as Kieran glanced curiously about her noticing the glass fronted bookcase, an embroidery frame, and in the corner stood a harp. Lorna Campbell pointed to the instrument.

'Do you like music, child?' she asked.

'Love it. When I was living in Paris, I learned to play the violin.' As she spoke the words, Kieran realised that until now she had completely put aside all memory of that happy time with her MacGregor second cousin, to whom she had been sent by her foster parents, Duncan and Annie MacGregor. She wondered now in retrospect why they had taken decision to send her abroad. Could it have been that as she approached young womanhood they worried in case any should recognise her resemblance to her Campbell relatives?

'When were you in Paris exactly, Kieran?' Lorna leaned towards her curiously, her dark eyes studying the young girl beside her with kindly interest.

'As a girl of fourteen, I was invited to stay with relatives there. Margaret MacGregor was cousin to my foster mother Annie MacGregor and married to a Frenchman—Captain Louis Lamont. I stayed with them for two years. Towards the end of that time, I met Alan Stewart whom I married.' As she came out with Alan's name Kieran's voice faltered slightly.

'You loved him dearly, this Alan Stewart?' asked Lorna in sympathy.

'With all my heart—and will until the day I die!'

'Tell me of him?' asked Lorna gently.

'He was handsome, loving—the elder son of Malcolm Stewart, tacksman to the Stewarts of Appin. Sadly his father was afflicted by a malady of the mind, unable to recognise people or to converse with any, lost in his own troubled world of dreams.' Kieran spoke sadly as she remembered the child like old man. 'Alan should have taken his father's place, none other to do so. His father's younger son by a second marriage named Lachlan only a lad when the Prince landed on these shores.'

'And so Alan Stewart was in Paris before the uprising?' probed Lorna gently, wondering if possibly this young man had been involved in plans for a Stuart restoration.

'Yes. We met, fell in love—and were married. My relative Margaret Lamont made my wedding gown. There were guests afterwards and dancing. We moved into a small apartment, spent a wonderful few days together.' Tears gathered in her eyes as she related this.

'Memories such as this are to be treasured in time,' sighed Lorna. 'But continue with your story.' Kieran needed no second bidding. It was strange relief to be able to unburden herself to her sympathetic listener.

'Well, not long after our marriage we received the shocking news that Margaret Lamont had died of a stroke. She was only in her fifties and her husband away with his regiment. My husband and I left Paris shortly afterwards to return to his home in Appin, where young Lachlan had been struggling to care for his father who had become helpless as a child.'

'So a lot of responsibility fell on your shoulders.'

'More so when Alan left home to join those flocking to Charles Edward's banner—then like all women confronted with war I did my best. I tried to thrust worry to the back of my mind. Lachlan helped at all times. I loved the beauty of that wild glen where we lived—just a croft house on a heathered hillside overlooking a loch, but to me a magical place. I made friends with those in the village—all dead now or scattered.'

'I was fortunate that Roderick returned from the conflict unharmed—even our old piper Angus Mac Seumas, came safely home!'

'Angus Mac Seumas led your people into battle,' said Kieran flatly.

'He did. Despite his years! Men do what they think they have to do to preserve honour. Not all wish to fight however,' mused Lorna reflectively. 'I have heard that in every clan there are those who actually refuse at first to follow their chief when so called and are threatened with forfeit of their homes or worse.'

'Perhaps if women were in charge and made decisions, then there would be less wars!' exclaimed Kieran feelingly. Lorna smiled back at her.

'Now there's a thought, child! We are the practical ones but sadly too often the ones left to mourn. Men have this belligerent streak in them—it is their nature. We on the other hand are the nurturers. Our role is to build up men's confidence and also to care and console—and to bear our children.

'You have children, Lady Lorna?'

'No, my dear—years past when Iain and I were wed less than two years, I lost a son in childbirth. The doctors explained I would never bear another. When his parents died, Roderick became as a son to us both. We love him as though he were our own.'

'It was in like manner that Duncan and Annie MacGregor loved me. I do not even know where they are now—or even if they are alive,' whispered Kieran remorsefully. 'They would shun me now did they know that I have thrown in my lot with the clan they always hated.' She rose to her feet and started to pace the room in agitation. Lorna stood up and came to her side. She took the girl's hands and looked at her firmly.

'Kieran at this time your emotions are torn by all that has happened. But one day healing will come, your mind not linger more on the hurts of the past.' The girl lifted her head and stared back at her with wet eyes.

'But how do I forget that my husband and those I loved and considered as my family, were on opposing sides to you my blood relatives whom I have only recently discovered. There is a continuous conflict in my mind! I feel a traitor to everything and everyone I have known!' cried Kieran brokenly.

'But none of this is any fault of yours! You must learn to forgive others and more importantly perhaps, to forgive yourself!' She put an arm about Kieran. 'Now we will take a glass of wine together. It will restore you, for you have endured recent severe shock.'

'Perhaps, talking of past events has helped me to forget the terror of that awful moment when I thought Roderick had died of gunshot!' As she came out with the words, Kieran suddenly realised the bond she was already forming with her brother Roderick and with Lorna Campbell. She watched as Lorna walked over to a small cabinet and poured a fine French brandy wine into two crystal glasses and handed one to Kieran.

'We will drink to......!' Lorna's words died on her lips as the sound of gunfire punctuated the peace of that room.

'Whatever was that?' cried Kieran urgently.

'I doubt they must have caught those who attempted to kill Roderick and perhaps you also, my dear.' She raised her glass again. 'Drink child, and then we must go and discover what has transpired.' They hurried out of the room and along a passageway then through the splendour of the great hall and out of the door overlooking the loch. Iain Campbell came striding up the drive towards them in front of his entourage, a triumphant smile on his face.

'They are dead, those who sought to kill Roderick Campbell,' he declared reassuringly, 'Caught less than half a mile from the house!' He saw Kieran standing there, hesitated and approached her with a troubled look in his eyes.

'Kieran, I must tell you that one of the two men we caught and slew was recognised by ghillie Ewan Dhu as a man who had insulted you at an inn in Stirling. Do you know who this man might be?' he questioned.

Kieran stared up at him in shock. 'The man you mention was distant cousin of my MacGregor foster parents. If indeed we speak of the same man, then it must be Malcolm Grier! He is dead?' she asked stiff lipped.

'He is dead. He believed he had killed Roderick, boasted of it—and said he meant to kill you also, because you had made cause with Clan Campbell.' His face was grim as he told her this.

'Oh no—Roderick might have died out there on the loch for showing care of me,' she cried in dismay. 'Malcolm Grier was only the most casual acquaintance. I did not like the man but would not have wished him dead. You said there was another?'

'I believe he was servant to Grier—a man of no account.' He turned to Lorna. 'How does our nephew, wife?'

'He sleeps. This news will please him when he wakes,' she said. 'Do you think there were any others involved in the attack?' she continued anxiously, glancing protectively at Kieran.

'I doubt it. But I will have men posted around the house for the next few days and we will keep Kieran within doors until I am satisfied as to her safety,' stated her husband firmly and the glance he cast on Kieran was protective. As she studied his somewhat imperious face, Kieran realised that his eyes reminded her of Lord Mamore's as did his mouth. Could he perhaps be a distant relative of the fierce Campbell Major General?

'I do not wish to hide away,' she exclaimed now, tossing her head. 'For months I had to live in a dark cave, always in fear of discovery by the militia. Now that I am here and have accepted new way of life, I will not hide again like a hunted animal!' and her grey eyes flashed her determination.

'Well said, Kieran, like a true Campbell!' he said kindly. 'But caution may be necessary for a short while, as my men make further search of the hills. You will stay within doors!' And the words he spoke were an order.

Roderick Campbell made a quick recovery from his head wound, and the following day rose from his bed declaring he was quite himself again, but ruefully accepting Lorna's careful attentions, as she reluctantly allowed him downstairs. He managed to detach himself from her ministrations and sought sanctuary in the library, his favourite room surrounded by the books he so loved. Kieran accompanied him and looked around the shelves with interest. Here were not only volumes on Scottish history and legend, but books of Latin and Greek literature—and many well worn books of poetry.

'I wish my own education made it possible for me to understand some of these,' she said wistfully and saw his quick interest.

'Kieran, it will be my pleasure to guide you into another world, the world of the mind and imagination!' His grey eyes beneath the bandage around his head were bright with animation. Here until now there had been none to share his delight in learning.

'Where did all these books come from?' she asked.

'Some were my father's, others I bought—but many gifted to me by our relative who at times stays at Finlarig Castle. Now in his middle years, he studied at Christchurch College, Oxford, has travelled widely and held important office and is wonderful scholar. I speak of Lord Glenorchy. You will meet him one day soon. He is a fine soldier of course, but more, he has an amazing mind!'

'I have heard tell of him.' She replied non-commitally. Then in a change of subject she asked him something that puzzled her. 'Roderick—you are handsome, a wealthy landowner—so why have you not married yet? Is there no lady to whom you have given your heart?'

He looked startled at her question and frowned as he considered his reply.

'I know that one day I will be required to wed and provide a son. But the idea of marrying an heiress as is the custom for one in my position, does not appeal to me. I might have to accept a woman with protruding teeth, a sharp tongue or given to the vapours!' He spoke lightly but his words concealed a real concern. She tried not to smile at his woeful expression.

'Then why not marry for love, brother mine?' She watched his face as she artlessly posed the question.

'An excellent idea—but where do I find the girl of my dreams? Not here along the banks of Tay I think!'

'Then you must search further afield,' she declared firmly. 'Did you meet no likely lassies in Edinburgh when you were stationed there?'

'I met one girl there at a castle ball. She was beautiful as a summer butterfly and like that insect she fluttered from one man to another, sharing her smiles and languishing glances with any who invited her to dance. To look into her blue eyes was to drown in them,' he said reminiscing. 'For a flirtatious evening she was pure delight—and danced like thistledown. But she would have been hopeless as a wife!' and he snorted.

'So, that was only one lady. There will be others—and you will find the right one eventually.'

Let us not talk of such dire event yet! Tell me, how are little Alan and Ishbel?' he asked fondly.

'Lorna found a dependable wet nurse for them Morag Burns and they are thriving and seem to have settled happily here.' But as she spoke, Kieran had sudden memory of her babies' earlier home with Sorley Mor who had adored them, considered them as his own. Although she was thinking of her husband less, memories came flooding to prick her conscience from time to time whether she would or no. He saw the change on her face and recognised the conflict of emotions she still suffered.

And so the next few days passed, the bond formed between the brother and sister ever tightening, as Iain Campbell daily scoured the countryside with fifty armed ghillies at his back, seeking out any strangers in the neighbourhood and broadening his search from Breadalbane down to the

Braes of Balquidder, the stronghold of the proscribed MacGregors, Children of the Mist, who boasted their race was royal..

Others of Clan Campbell had been there before him. Over a year back they had raised to the ground all and any habitation of the MacGregors, from fine stately house on the shores of Loch Voil, to modest croft or merest hovel, all had been levelled to mere sorrow of scattered stones and low walls amongst the fading heather and gorse. The former inhabitants had in desperation taken to the hills, dwelling in caves in the high places, where they continued to eke out a living at lifting the cattle of those clans who had supported the government forces in the recent conflict.

Iain Campbell was in a foul mood, frustrated that he had found no single member of the despised MacGregors, but knowing that he was probably observed in his every movement by those he sought. Their scouts would be watching his progress from behind every large rock or clump of gorse, or stand of birch and alder. He was loathe to make return home without some tangible result of his mission and so continued his search with dogged determination.

'Spread out again,' he ordered. Then one of his men signalled to him, pointing to a gulley. Iain Campbell spurred his horse and reached for his sword as he swept towards the place. Then he stared. What he saw was a young boy of perhaps eight or nine years, who was removing a dead hare from a snare. The child became aware of the mounted man bearing down upon him and turned to flee. But Iain Campbell caught him by the shoulders and despite the lads struggles held him fast.

'Your name, lad?' he demanded.

'Grigor!' the lad spat back at him, noting with hatred the Campbell tartan.

'Where are your parents, Grigor?'

'I have none. You Campbells slew my father and my mother died of a fever!' The boy's voice shook but his eyes blazed fury at the man who held him captive.

'Then who do you live with?'

'That I will not tell you—thrice damned Campbell!'

'Oh, but you will tell me,' exclaimed Iain Campbell grimly and tightened his grip. He produced his dirk with his other hand and held it to the boy's neck. 'Speak now!' But the boy merely spat at him in scorn. The spittle missed, but anger now stained Iain's face. What the man would have done next he would never know for of a sudden a woman's voice rang out.

'Let the lad go! Great man like you frightening a child—shame on ye!' and he swung around at the voice. A middle aged woman stood there, the wind blowing her wild, silver streaked locks, as her eyes blazed contempt.

'The lad is yours, mistress?' He looked at her curiously from cold eyes.

'That is no affair of yours—Campbell!'She stood arms akimbo, a
mocking look on her worn face. Without letting go of the boy, he urged his
horse closer to the woman, realising that despite her poor clothing and
seemingly impoverished condition, she was perhaps gently born.

'Lady—I crave your name,' he continued dropping his hectoring tones.

She looked as though she would have refused, but then with a sigh she
spoke softly, and with a quiet dignity as her eyes played over him.

'I am Annie MacGregor, widow of Duncan MacGregor, but known
these days as Annie Gregory. We are denied legal right to use our own
proud name, by pernicious law!'

He stared at the woman thoughtfully. He remembered hearing that
Kieran had been fostered by a couple of this name following Catriona
Campbell's death in childbirth. Was it possible? He dismounted and smiled
at her reassuringly. She shrank back.

'Was your husband's brother one Rory MacGregor,' he asked. Anger
flooded her face as she made haughty reply.

'You should know of this, since it was members of your clan who took
and hanged him!' she flashed back.

'Then you will remember that the hanging was in retribution for his
murder of Colin Campbell, my brother-in-law and for the kidnap of his
pregnant wife Catriona!' he cried with some venom.

'Then you are.....?' she looked at him in sudden shock.

'Iain Campbell and uncle to Kieran Campbell whom you brought up to
believe she was MacGregor, hiding all knowledge of her Campbell roots
from her. Surely this was ill done!' he said reprovingly.

'How would you have dealt with new born child, Campbell,' she hissed.

'Brought her up with her brother Roderick, whom my wife and I have
cared for as our own since that time—yet lady, the fates have been kind.
Kieran is but recently restored to our family.' At his words Annie
MacGregor turned pale.

'Kieran—is living with Clan Campbell? Glad I am then my man died on
cold Drummosie Moor and did not live to hear such evil tidings! I heard
recent rumour, but did not believe it.' She leaned up against a rock almost
fainting with shock, trembling as she spoke.

'Mistress, was it from a man known as Malcolm Grier that you heard of
it?' he probed. She nodded her head and held her hand to her breast as
though to still its sudden pounding.

'Malcolm is distant cousin,' she faltered. 'He brought an unbelievable
tale that Kieran, whom we knew to be wife of Alan Stewart, was seen in
close company of a Campbell lord at Stirling!'She turned her dark eyes
upon him interrogatively. 'It was true then?'

'Kieran's husband Alan died in the aftermath of Culloden. I do not know the details. She was befriended by another Stewart, his name Sorley Mor Stewart, a physician and until recently lived in Edinburgh. She has now discovered her true family and this fellow Malcolm Grier saw Kieran with her brother Roderick.'

'Tell me that she is well then? To me she was as a daughter—but not now, not now!' she murmured in tortured tones, wringing her hands.

'Were you aware this man Grier sought to kill Kieran?'

'What is that ye say?' her dark eyes widened in horror.

'Kieran and her brother were in a boat on the loch. He fired at them, wounded Roderick and due to Kieran's courage they escaped.' He came out with the fact grimly and noted her look of shock. It was obvious that she was not party to this. 'Grier is dead—and so is his companion!' he added.

'So why are you here in Balquidder, Iain Campbell?' she asked levelly.

'To investigate planning of this attempted murder and ensure it is realised that any further such attempts will be dealt with most severely,' he said with heavy authority. She looked at him in scorn.

'Do you think those of our race are to be so berated! But I tell you this, Campbell, none will ever seek to lay a hand on Kieran. The facts you have made known to me will be passed on to our people. She will be safe from those who once loved her.' Then she lifted her skirt to her eyes to hide the tears that were starting to fall. 'Ochone, Kieran my puir lamb,' she mourned. 'Never again will I see your face!'

'Have you any message for her?' he asked curiously. Annie MacGregor shook her head decisively.

'None!' she cried. 'For from this time forward she no longer exists to Clan MacGregor,' the words burst brokenly from her lips.

He watched as the woman straightened up from the lichened rock against which she had been leaning for support, then motioned to the lad to follow her as the two of them disappeared. He looked after them sombrely. Would his warning be enough? Instinct told him that it would. He summoned his men who had kept a discreet distance away as he spoke with the woman.

'We return home.' he said. Grumbling quietly, disappointed of a fight, they nevertheless followed behind him obediently. Knowing Iain Campbell, there would be other occasions to deal with the Gregorach.

The weeks had gone by as Sorley Mor Stewart silently grieved the disappearance of his wife Kieran and babies Alan and Ishbel. All attempts to trace her, had so far failed.

The house was depressingly empty without his wife's presence, but as his practice was attracting attention ever further afield he was given little time to ponder the situation as daily he dealt with the steady influx of patients. He engaged a housekeeper. Mistress Alison Lindsey was a well built, middle aged woman remarkably quick on her feet and who attacked the housework with enthusiastic efficiency. She learned from Nurse Effie Munro that the doctor's young wife had just disappeared with his bairns, despite the poor man being so kind with her!

Mistress Lindsey shook her head on hearing this and decided she would do all within her power to see that the doctor had the comforts of good food and a well kept home! So now Sorley Mor enjoyed meals such as he had not partaken since his boyhood yet hardly remarked the fact, his spirits afflicted by concern for his missing family.

He found he was able to afford a carriage and stabled it in a nearby mews. Always as it clattered over the cobbled streets as he made his house calls to the sick, he noticed that the red coated militia were as much in evidence as ever. They marched with precision, orders given in clipped English voices as they glanced with scarcely veiled insolence at the patient citizenry attending to their lawful daily business. Would they never go home? Was Scotland always to feel itself an occupied country? Would they never be free again to run their own affairs, instead of paying lip service to a German monarch in far off London?

So he mused and found many others who agreed with his outrage. But others again were of the opinion that at least under the House of Hanover their Protestant faith was safely pursued, nor stopped to consider the plight of the Catholics and those of the Episcopal Church. Had Prince Charles Edward Stuart been brought up as a Protestant rather than a Catholic, what difference if any would this have made to his attempt to restore the Stuarts to the throne.

Out of curiosity, he visited the great Church of St Giles, listened to the black gowned minister, severely admonishing his congregation from his raised pulpit and found the service missing in that sense of kindness and holiness he had found in his brother David's ministry. Well, none of it was for him, he decided. As far as he could see, it was their differences in religion that forced men at each other's throats. Surely the One they professed to worship would not have wished or approved this state of affairs?

'That is the last of them awa, doctor,' said Nurse Effie, as the fat, elderly man with a gouty toe was helped from the consulting room by his obsequious servant. Sorley Mor smiled and stretched.

'It has been a long day, Effie.'

'That it has, sir! At least you should be able to get a good rest now!'

'I fear not, for Lady Forsythe is likely to be brought to bed of her child tonight.'

'Would you wish me to accompany you, doctor?' He shook his head with a smile and watched as she busied herself tidying all up, emptying a bin of used dressings, and placing clean covering on the examination couch. Satisfied at last that all was in readiness for the morning, she bobbed a curtsey and left. She was a treasure and he was lucky to have her services. But now he thought of the time when Kieran had helped him as nurse. His heart was sore for a sight of her.

He sighed as he went into his sitting room where Mistress Lindsey had just lit the lamps and walked over to the window. The November night was dark and misty, a fine rain was falling and people hurrying past heads down, as they made for home. It was he realised only a month to Christmas and that brought thought of last Christmas and the cot and shawl he had given Kieran in preparation for the birth.

'Where are ye now my heart's darling,' he whispered. He sank down into his favourite chair, reached for his decanter of whisky, poured a good glass of the amber coloured fluid in which he found solace and swallowed it. A knock made him look up. It was his housekeeper in white cap and apron, calling him to his dinner.

He had only taken a few mouthfuls of the tasty roast pheasant, when there was a heavy knock at the door. He scowled in protest and rose wearily to his feet.

'No, let me go, doctor! I will tell them to come back on the morrow!' declared Mistress Lindsey protectively. 'You have to eat, sir!' He hesitated and allowed her to take a candle and hurry to the door. He heard voices, and recognised a highland lilt. Then to his surprise his housekeeper ushered in an unkempt looking heavily bearded fellow in black trews and jacket, and a shapeless feathered bonnet, which he removed revealing a shock of dark curls as he saw the doctor.

'You would be the physician, Sorley Mor Stewart,' he demanded with a cultured voice at odds with his appearance.

'I am,' replied Sorley Mor. 'However I must make plain sir, that I am not prepared to see any other patients at this time of night unless it be dire emergency!' he stared back levelly at the man, who bowed politely.

'I do not seek medical attention, Doctor Stewart, but to ask a question of you. Do you know a young woman known as Kieran Stewart?' The question coming so unexpectedly caught Sorley Mor with shock.

'You speak of my wife,' he replied. 'Have you news of her?'

'Your wife, say you?' the stranger exclaimed. 'I was not told of this, only that you had been helpful to her.'

'She is my wife and mother of our children!' Well, if this was not strictly true as far as the babies were concerned, at least he had accepted them as his own. The stranger registered the information with obvious surprise.

'Then do you know that this wife of yours is now living with a family of Campbells on the shores of Loch Tay?' His gaze locked with the doctor's

'That is not possible!' gasped Sorley Mor.

'I am a MacGregor, doctor. My race is Royal—I do not lie!' His eyes slid over the doctor's dinner as he spoke and Sorley saw the hunger in his eyes.

'Perhaps you would lay another place at table, Mistress Lindsey—and then I would be alone with this gentleman,' he said and the housekeeper quietly did his bidding and retired. He watched as the stranger dispatched a heaped plateful in an amazingly short time, while he pushed his own plate back untouched.

'Now sir—your name?' asked Sorley Mor.

'Robert MacGregor—but known as Rob Gregory,' replied the man.

'Now Mr MacGregor, what is this you say of my wife?' Sorley Mor fixed anguished dark gaze upon this man who held the secret of his wife's whereabouts. The stranger hesitated, his eyes caressing the bottle of French wine upon the table. The doctor signed that he should help himself. As the wine gurgled into the glass, its sound afflicted Sorley Mor's patience, but there had to be a certain courtesy maintained between highlanders and this was now observed.

'Tae your guid health, Sorley Mor Stewart,' said the MacGregor as he downed his wine. 'Now, you were asking me of the news I bring of your lady. To make sure we speak of the same woman, may I ask you if she has hair of that golden red shade found in the highlands and eyes of a dark grey?'

'Yes, that is her appearance. Now go on man, for God's sake! She disappeared with our twin babies just a few weeks back and I have been desperately seeking news of her ever since!' There was no mistaking Sorley Mor's agitation.

'You loved her then?' The doctor's expression was answer enough. The MacGregor shook his head in sympathy. 'Are you aware that she was brought up in Balquidder by my people?'

'She told me she was of the MacGregor before marriage to her first husband, Alan Stewart. He was a friend of mine. When he was murdered by the redcoats, I took Kieran into my care, married her.'

'So that was the way of it?'

'Now you sir, how do you come into all this?'

'I am cousin to Duncan MacGregor, he died gallantly at Culloden—and who with his wife Annie fostered Kieran. It was this way. The girl's true mother was a Campbell, taken as his own by Rory MacGregor from her husband Colin Campbell and for this deed was later hanged by Clan Campbell! Catriona Campbell bore a girl child, died in giving birth. The

135

girl lived among us until she reached the age of fourteen, when Annie and Duncan decided to send her to Paris to be educated. We have not seen her since, but heard of her marriage to Alan Stewart.'

'Most of this I have learned or guessed,' replied Sorley Mor guardedly. 'We were detained on the road at Glencoe by Major General John Campbell of Mamore. As a doctor I dressed the wound of a young man he named as nephew. Mamore saw my wife—demanded speech with her. Since that meeting she was changed in her behaviour towards me. The captain whose wound I attended bore an amazing resemblance to Kieran.'

'Her brother then—Roderick Campbell,' exclaimed MacGregor. 'It is in his house she is now living, together with his uncle and aunt—Sir Iain Campbell and his wife Lorna!' he watched Sorley Mor closely as he imparted this information. Saw the shock he had inflicted.

'She met Roderick Campbell again in Edinburgh when he was stationed at the Castle, a fleeting encounter so it seemed.' Sorley Mor's face was torn with raw emotion as he tried to come to terms with what was no longer mere conjecture but irrefutable fact. His beloved Kieran truly was member of the clan he abhorred above all others, who had treated fellow highlanders with such devastating cruelty, savaging his own Appin Stewarts, not as bestial as Butcher Cumberland's vicious militia, but responsible for innumerable acts alien to normal warfare.

'How did you come to know of Kieran's present whereabouts,' he demanded now, trying to collect his thoughts.

'A member of our clan recently recognised Kieran at an inn, the Golden Lion in Stirling. She was seen embraced by a Campbell whom we now know to be Roderick Campbell. Malcolm Grier was appalled at what he saw, nor knew of the relationship between the two. He resolved to kill both if he could.'

'He did what?' snapped Sorley Mor in horror.

'As I have heard it, he took another with him, saw Kieran and this Roderick Campbell in a boat on the loch—and fired. He thought he had killed the young man, but he was only wounded. The girl escaped unharmed.'

'Well thank God for that,' cried Sorley Mor.

'Iain Campbell tracked Grier down and slew both him and the other. We heard that Grier first admitted that it was he who had fired—had gloated in the thought that he had killed Roderick Campbell.'

'I cannot feel pity for a fellow who would shoot an unarmed man and a girl! No gallantry or cause for celebration in such an act!' said Sorley Mor in choked tones. His visitor nodded agreement and continued his tale.

'Iain Campbell took a tail of his clansmen with him and came to the Braes of Balquidder, seeking blood I would think! There by chance he met with Annie MacGregor, foster mother to Kieran and who had always loved the girl as her own. It was in this way that Annie learned that Kieran had thrown in her lot with her blood relatives and accordingly not to be spoken of more within our clan. But she is safe from any harm from those who once loved her,' he said simply.

'It was good of you to bring me this news, however unpalatable!'

'Mistress Annie MacGregor was wishful to discover of any reason that might have forced Kieran to take the road she has. Iain Campbell mentioned a doctor of your name who lived in Edinburgh and had helped the girl. We had no notion that she was your wife, sir.'

'I understand.'

'What will you do in the matter,' asked Robert MacGregor.

'That I need to think on,' he replied. 'Sadly though I fear there is little I can do, now that her mind is made up. The children, little Alan and Ishbel—do you know how they fare?' he asked hopefully.

'I did not know they existed—a sad loss to you, Doctor Stewart!' was the feeling reply. He rose to his feet. 'I must go. Friends await me. If we do not meet again, then I salute a good and honourable man who has not been well used.' He swept a bow, with his old feathered bonnet, as though they had been at court and turned to the door. Sorley Mor heard his housekeeper seeing him out.

He sank back into a chair with his thoughts in turmoil. What should he do now that what he had partly guessed from his lawyer's advice had proven to be correct? His wife had turned her back on him and on their home, not just for a time to reflect on her situation—but to take up another life. How useless then the letters he had sent to France to both to his brother and to Lachlan. Both had written back that none had seen Kieran in Paris, for his hope had been that she might have gone seeking Lachlan.

'Now that I know for absolute certainty that she is a Campbell, can I continue to love her,' he whispered and then answered his own question. 'Yes! I love Kieran Stewart and will do so until my dying day. One day we will meet again and perhaps.....?

He looked up as there was a hesitant knock on the door.

'What is it, Mistress Lindsey?' he asked wearily.

'I am that sorry to disturb you again, doctor! But a messenger had come with news that Mary Lovat has gone into labour and the midwife despairing of the delivery!' She looked at him compassionately. It was obvious that the stranger who had called had brought bad news of the doctor's wife and now when he needed peace so badly, called out yet again! He called for his coat and she hurried to get it and his medical bag—and the he was gone.

Mistress Lindsey collected the dinner plates, and noticed the doctor's was almost untouched. She sighed and shook her head. Why would any wife leave so dedicated and compassionate a man.

Chapter Eight

It was December and a few days from Christmas as Kieran Stewart looked from her bedroom window down to the snowy foreshore of the loch and on to the heights of Ben Lawers, peak stroked with the flame of dawn, where it soared majestically far across the wind tossed waters. Bare mile from here but scant few weeks ago, Roderick had so nearly lost his life—and she hers!

Already though the memory had lost somewhat of its impact, for Roderick had made a quick recovery from his head wound and when not burdened with affairs of the estate was once again to be found in his library, head down as he delved hungrily into the classics. She had taken to joining him there and listened enthralled as he explained passages from the Greek. It seemed she reflected that men in those days were as cruel and aggressive in their desires as they were today.

A knock on the door made her turn back from the window as Bess appeared with two small forms who toddled across to their mother and pulled at her skirts, lifting their small faces up to be kissed and gurgling with laughter. Alan and Ishbel could both walk now although only eleven months, but were still wobbly at times and had to be watched carefully and kept well away from the stairs.

'Alan my heart's darling,' she cried softly as she lifted him and felt his soft cheek against hers as he smothered her with kisses. She set him down and lifted her small daughter, who responded with like affection, while Alan babbled away in baby talk.

She kissed Ishbel and looked at her with pride. The little girl gave promise of astonishing beauty with her silver blond hair and green eyes. Kieran remembered regretfully how she had at first rejected this child, worrying that those green eyes might have been inherited from the rapist captain. But with the portrait of her Campbell father displaying like colouring that fear had gone.

'Make sure they are kept warm, for the weather has turned extremely cold,' she instructed Bess with a smile. 'It looks as though we may have fresh snow, a few flakes already falling,' and she nodded towards the window.

'Lady Lorna suggested they be brought down to her parlour, where there is a good fire burning, warmer there than the nursery upstairs.'

'Well, if my aunt has no objection to such an invasion, then I agree,' said Kieran fondly. She had become very attached to Lorna Campbell who had shown immense understanding of Kieran's torn and conflicting loyalties. She glanced in her mirror and straightened her skirt, before following Bess, and Morag Burns who had waited outside the door, as they carried the twins down the dark staircase, illumined by its guttering candles, with Kieran following behind.

Lorna was seated at her harp as Kieran made to enter the room and she paused in wonder at the beauty and poignancy of the music dripping melancholy into the air. It was the first time that she had heard her aunt play. Lorna rose from the lovely old instrument as she heard the door open and sound of the babies chortling voices.

'Come in. Come away in,' she called and opened her arms to the babies, who scampered towards her, falling over in their haste. She picked them up and embraced them fondly.

'They are very active now,' declared Kieran. 'Bess and Morag will have a care of them,' she added fondly.

Lorna smiled and spoke softly but firmly to the little ones, who seemed to understand that they must be quiet. 'Let them play with these,' she said and produced a rag doll for Isbell and a wooden horse for Alan. 'I made the doll,' she explained, 'and the horse once belonged to your brother as a child.' Then as Bess and Morag seated themselves on a wooden settle by the fire, watching carefully over the twins, Lorna beckoned Kieran over to a small table near the harp. On it Kieran saw a violin.

'This is for you,' said Lorna. 'I had meant to keep it until next week as a Christmas gift, but then bethought me that if we should practice together, we might entertain the family at that time.'

'What a wonderful gift,' exclaimed Kieran. 'But Aunt Lorna, it's a few years since I played when I was living in Paris. I do not think I would dare try again!'

'But you shall!' responded Lorna. She watched as Kieran lifted the instrument lovingly from its case and tuned it, and then rosined the bow. She tucked the violin under her chin, raised the bow hesitantly playing a few chords—then with new confidence she attempted the wistful highland air that had been so beloved of Alan Stewart.

Lorna nodded satisfaction. 'That was good, Kieran. Shall we play it together?' and she seated herself before her harp once more. Now the initial hesitation Kieran had displayed vanished, as the music soared, floating about the room, as Bess, Morag and the twins listened in delight. The door opened and Roderick stood there. But he spoke no word of the music, his face grave. Lorna became aware of his presence and dropped her hands from the strings.

'Roderick—what is wrong?' she asked slowly.

'Angus Mac Seumas—he has been shot! He is breathing yet, the bullet in his shoulder, but at his age—I fear for his life! Kieran, I know you are skilled in medicine. Will you come?' She had already put the violin aside and calling out to Bess and Morag to have a care of the children, ran with Lorna at her side to the great hall, where the old piper had been laid on top of the long table there, surrounded by anxious, angry Campbell clansmen.

She bent over the old man and spoke to him gently.

'Angus Mac Seumas—you are going to survive this wound. Trust in me. I am going to remove that bullet.' Then she turned and called for a bowl of warm water, and bandages, and for clean cloths—and asked if any had a knife. Many blades were anxiously proffered and she selected the slimmest of these. She looked doubtfully at the stained metal. Taking it over to the great log fire, she held the blade into the flames, the heat scorching her fingers, then waited for it to cool before bending over the old piper, who had been given a large draught of whisky by his companions.

She removed the ugly piece of lead and dropped it on the floor, staunching the bleeding, then firmly placed a dressing and bandaged it in place. During all of this, Angus had not uttered the slightest groan. At last Kieran straightened up, and wiped her hands, as Roderick slipped an arm about her, crying his thanks, then gave orders for Angus to be carefully carried to his bed.

'You have a rare skill,' he said approvingly.

'I had a good teacher—you will remember him!' The words burst out and they stared at each other.

'Come, you must be tired,' was all he said shortly. But Lorna who had been standing close by had heard the girl's cry. So Kieran still had feelings for her doctor husband. She sighed as she joined Roderick in escorting his sister back to the parlour, where the girl sank down shakily in a chair.

'Can you tell me how old Angus came to be shot,' Lorna now inquired of her nephew, drawing him aside. 'And where is Iain?'

'Can you not guess? Gone to track down the deil who fired on an old man, who was merely playing his pipes!' growled Roderick feelingly.

'I hope they catch the wretch. I cannot imagine life without Angus Mac Seumas!' said Lorna quietly. 'With this new snow fallen, I imagine it should be possible to follow the villain's footprints with ease!' she added. Then she glanced sympathetically at Kieran who was staring unseeingly into the fire, as Alan and Ishbel vied noisily for their mother's attention.

'Time perhaps for them to be fed,' suggested Lorna and in response Bess and Morag immediately gathered them up and left the parlour. She then nodded to Roderick, who bowed and made for the door.

'I will let you know when there is any news,' he called as he went.

The sudden stillness was balm to Kieran's troubled spirit. Thoughts of Sorley Mor had been chasing through her brain with memories of that man's kindness and the comradeship they had shared before that fatal meeting with Mamore. Her coldness to him once she knew her real identity seared her mind. What could he have thought of her? What was he doing now—did he hate her now for abandoning him? Instinctively she knew such would not be the case, but the hurt she had inflicted must have been very hard for him to bear

'Drink this!' Lorna poured a glass of wine and held it towards Kieran, who took it automatically and raised it to her lips, drank. Loran watched and saw colour come back into the girl's face. 'You made a wonderful job of removing that bullet,' she said approvingly. 'I would that I had like skill! We used to have a surgeon who lived in this glen, but he died at Culloden.'

'He was a Campbell,' inquired Kieran?

'Yes, indeed. Keith Campbell. He is greatly missed.'

'As must be the dozen or so Jacobite surgeons arrested and sent to London, and executed,' cried Kieran. 'That any corrupt and cruel court should execute a man for bringing medical skill to heal those with terrible wounds—this is beyond my understanding.' As the hurt and angry words left her lips, she saw Lorna flinch

'What can I say to any of this, child? Always throughout history there has been fighting—great clan battles—and also wars between Scotland and England. For this reason the uniting of the crowns, the forming of one kingdom seems to me to bring hope for the future. Sadly there is much upheaval at this present time as many still fight against the idea.'

'The Stuarts have been Scotland's ruling house for centuries! Why then should we have the German house of Hanover inflicted upon us?' cried Kieran hotly.

'Partly it is a matter of religious faith. The Stuarts are Catholic and for this reason not acceptable to most of lowland Scotland where the Protestant Church of Scotland rules supreme.'

'But under Charles Edward Stuart all men would have had the right to pursue their own path to religious faith!' declared Kieran, 'Too late now for any of this I know. The clans rose for the Prince—and were defeated— a fact that cannot be reversed!' She rose to her feet and went to the window, pulled the curtain well aside. Snow was falling thick and fast now, and she thought of those poor disposed highlanders, thrown out of homes that were then burned to the ground, their stock driven off or killed. In what kind of state would any who had survived now be, over a year later?

'I know how very difficult all that has happened must be for you, Kieran. All I can say is that it is better to look to the future rather than dwell on a past that cannot be altered.'

'Well Aunt Lorna—and do you personally agree with the fiendish revenge that the English took under Butcher Cumberland—slavishly supplemented by this clan also, and as far afield as the Hebrides. I refer to the wanton destruction of people's homes, murder, killing and driving off all of all stock so that they must starve—and the unspeakable raping of women!' Her voice trembled as she uttered the last phrase. She swung about and stared at Lorna with tears in her eyes.

'Oh my dear—you must calm yourself!'

'Calm, say you? How calm would you be Aunt Lorna, had you also been raped short minutes after lying in bed in the loving embrace of a husband who had just returned safe from Drummosie moor! I was raped by an evil captain of militia and his men who burst into our croft. They took Alan outside—and........,' her voice broke on a sob. 'I buried that same dear, murdered husband and his elderly father shortly afterwards?'

'This—happened to you?' Lorna Campbell regarded her in horror. 'You never spoke of it before!' she made to approach Kieran, who held up a hand as though to fend her off. She stood still and watched the young woman with deepest pity.

'Yes—it happened to me. It was this way. Doctor Sorley Mor Stewart had befriended Alan after the battle. They arrived at Glen Ardoch together that day. Later, Sorley Mor climbed up onto the hill together with Alan's young step brother Lachlan Stewart, seeking to give us peace together. It was then that this atrocity happened—the redcoats laughed, forced me to my knees and then......!' she swallowed. 'Sorley Mor and Lachlan arrived back at the scene too late to do more than dig the two graves.' As she blurted this out Kieran felt a strange release.

Now Lorna took her into her arms and led her to the couch. She spoke no word, merely held the girl to her as she would a child. At last Kieran's trembling ceased.

'You have been carrying this terrible thing in your heart since then?'

'Sorley Mor helped me—helped Lachlan who was grieving both brother and father. We took shelter in a cave behind a waterfall for a few months. During that time, the doctor's brother David, an Episcopalian priest joined us there. He had been beaten almost to death by the redcoats because he refused to give list of those from his village who had risen for the Prince.'

'They did that to a priest?'

'You really have no idea of what has been going on?'

'I have heard tales, but perhaps disbelieved them. Go on, Kieran, if you can dear, what happened next.' she gently probed.

'David joined us there, the four of us in the cave—always the sound of those roaring waters, getting in and out on a narrow slippery shelf of rock behind the fury of the falls dangerous in the extreme. Sorley Mor offered marriage in order to protect my good name. I was pregnant of Alan's child—children as it transpired. David married us. I made stipulation that I would never sleep with my husband, be a wife in name only.'

'That must have been a hard promise for your husband to make.' She stared at Kieran musingly. 'Did he keep it?'

'He did. I started to have fond feelings towards him—but felt it would be untrue to Alan should I acknowledge them. So I was distant with Sorley Mor. Time passed and finally he came to the decision that with winter coming and food so scarce, that we would be better to risk the dangers of the journey—redcoats on all the roads, and make for Edinburgh where he had a house and practice.'

'That would have seemed to be a good plan,' said Lorna.

'It was when travelling through Glencoe and hiding above the road, that we saw two men attack an army officer. Sorley shouted warning, despite recognising him to be an enemy. He then ran down and tended the man's wound. I speak of my brother, Roderick!'

'He mentioned with deep gratitude the doctor who had saved his life.'

'Major General Mamore came upon the scene---our party taken to his camp. Sorley Mor dressed Roderick's wound, I helped. It was then that this Mamore stared hard at me. The following morning he demanded to speak with me alone—told me of my Campbell blood.'

'It must have come as a strange surprise,' breathed Lorna.

'Shock rather! Should the truth come to Sorley Mor's ears, undoubtedly it would have caused him to shrink away from me in disgust! Nor would I have blamed him. Lorna, I was pregnant, had no money and had to live in a house with a man I respected and admired, perhaps had come to love, but knew that as soon as I gave birth, the only honourable course open to me was to leave him and fend for myself. '

'Did you not think it worthwhile to tell him the truth? If he is truly the sort of man you describe, then I believe he would have accepted a situation that was none of your making.' Lorna spoke seriously as she considered the affair.

'There was more on my mind at this time than knowledge of my Campbell blood—the fear of what might result from the rape! During my pregnancy, the thought that I might not be carrying Alan's child but that of the green eyed captain who had raped me, assaulted me every single day.'

'But that was the most awful pressure!'Lorna looked aghast.

'It was Sorley Mor who delivered the babies. When the twins were born, the boy first, such relief to see Alan so like his father—but then I saw Ishbel's colouring, those green eyes, well you can guess what I thought!'

'Oh Kieran, such unnecessary worry—for she is of the same colouring as your father and such a beautiful child.'

'At first I felt myself rejecting her—she sensed it, cried a lot. Then, I truly looked at her, and knew in my heart that whoever might have been her father, she was my dear child and needed my love as much as her brother Alan.' As Kieran explained all in simple terms, Lorna looked at her and smiled.

'And now you see how unnecessary your worries were. But continue, what finally made you decide to come here—to leave Edinburgh and your husband?'

'By chance I met Roderick in the street—in his army uniform. We spoke together. On earlier occasion he had called at our house to thank Sorley Mor for his care of him when wounded, wished to see me also and the twins. Seemingly he realised the coldness I felt towards my husband. Perhaps he guessed the reason for it. We met once more and he suggested I might like to come here to his home—to bring the twins. He left a gift of money for the journey—directions. The rest you know!'

'Did you leave a letter for your husband explaining matters and your intended destination?' asked Lorna. But Kieran shook her head vigorously, slightly shamefaced.

'Merely wrote letter of farewell. I could not risk his following me here. It was better this way. I knew he might think I had gone to France to be with Lachlan or other relatives there. I had even considered doing so at one time.'

'And so now you are attempting to come to terms with your past and embrace the future. It will require a degree of courage, but I do not think you are deficient in that. Any help that I can give you—you have but to ask,' said Lorna gently

'You have already done so much!' Kieran sighed.

'Come—dry those tears. Perhaps we should go to see how Angus Mac Seumas is faring.' They rose to their feet, drawn closer now by the revelation Kieran had made, and by those unseen but strong bonds of family entwining. They ascended the stairs to the room where the old piper lay. He tried to raise his head from the pillow as the two women entered the small chamber.

'Lady Lorna—and you Kieran, child of the Campbells restored to us by fate to save an old man's life! I greet you. Once this shoulder of mine heals from an assassin's bullet, I will play the pipes again to your delight. This I promise.'

Kieran stepped forward and took one of his old hands in hers. She stroked it gently. 'I pray that day may come soon, dear Angus Mac Seumas!'

'And in the meanwhile, when you are stronger, invite you to listen to Kieran play her violin to my harp—in your own favourite tunes!' exclaimed Lorna Campbell.

'This would be joy indeed,' then his head fell back as completely exhausted now the old man closed his eyes to sleep. They stole out of the room and made their way downstairs once more. They were on the last stair when they heard a great noise of shouting from the great hall.

'I have a feeling that they have caught the man who shot Angus,' said Lorna. 'Perhaps we should not go in there.' But Kieran ignored the warning. She saw about two dozen men making circle around another who held prisoner a young man, wild eyed with black curls and beard, blood on his cheek. They parted in their midst allowing Iain Campbell to walk through. He held up his hand for silence.

'Release him.' He studied the prisoner. 'I am Iain Campbell—this house and land that of my nephew Roderick Campbell. Now you fellow—your name?' he asked with studied politeness.

'James MacPherson, son to that John MacPherson who was captured and shot by Mamore in Glencoe last year. No trial—just shot out of hand!'

'No doubt Lord Mamore had his reasons! Your chief Rory MacPherson much involved in protecting and aiding the escape of the Pretender. I grieve you loss. But does that give you reason to invade this property and shoot at a seventy year old, unarmed piper? Think you your father would have approved such deed?' He studied the arrogant young face staring fearlessly back at him. 'Have you nothing to say in your defence?'

'Would any excuse be accepted? I think not. Therefore murdering Campbell, do your worst and may you rot in hell!' and he raised his head and gave the war cry of his clan. Iain Campbell nodded, and the MacPherson dropped to the floor throat cut, as Ewan Dhu carelessly wiped his dirk on the dead man's plaid.

'He will not attempt to kill any more pipers!' he declared. 'Help me to carry away this carrion!' Willing hands assisted him amongst grim laughter, as Kieran held on to the doorframe, her face white with horror at what her eyes had just seen.

'Come away—I said you should not go in,' cried Lorna urgently. 'Justice is swiftly dealt in such cases.' She pulled at Kieran's sleeve and the girl's last glimpse was of a serving maid cloth in hand, cleaning the blood from the floor. 'At least Angus Mac Seumas will have the pleasure of knowing he is avenged,' added Lorna, as though nothing untoward had just occurred.

'That looked uncommonly like murder,' exclaimed Kieran her face white.

'Are you telling me that the MacGregors or Stewarts would have acted differently in similar circumstances? It is sad—desperately sad, child. But until men can forget this dreadful hatred between clans, such will continue.' But Kieran merely shook her head, excused herself and hurried to her room where she flung herself upon the bed. Her maid Annie came to see if she needed ought, but Kieran sent her away until morning. She did not go below stairs to eat that night, but a sympathetic Bess brought her up a tray, her expression worried.

'You saw it then, Mistress Kieran? Just a young man of good appearance, they said, who shot old Angus in retribution for the death of his own father! At least back in Edinburgh we did not have such goings on!' She shook her young head despondently. Unlike Kieran who had grown up in the highlands, where violent death on occasion was not an unusual sight, Bess had never encountered such rough justice—hangings perhaps in the Grassmarket, but that was under the law!

'They say that it was Ewan Dhu who cut the man's throat—the man who took me up on his horse during our journey here. I liked him, thought him fierce looking—but not that he would kill!' declared Bess feelingly. Kieran attempted a smile and sought to calm the young nursemaid.

'Bess, we live in a wilder part of the country, than Edinburgh! But it is a beautiful land, rich in history and legend and song. One day I pray the animosity between those who support King George and others who remain loyal to Prince Charles Edward will be at an end. Certainly the Highlands will never be the same again Bess.' Then she told the girl somewhat of recent happenings across the Highlands, Islands and the North. She spoke of the cruelty of the Hanoverian militia, the wholesale cleansing of Jacobites from the land, houses burned and all livestock killed or driven off in order to cause starvation to any survivors, people slain whether they had risen for the Prince or no. At the end of the account, Bess shook her head in shock.

'I had no idea of any of this, mistress. In the city we merely heard of battles. That you should have been caught up in it is so sad,' she added. She sighed as she removed the tray. 'But I suppose we should be safe enough here with so many men to protect us,' She closed the door. Kieran stared after her rebelliously.

'Yes, there are many to defend us here,' she whispered under her breath. 'But to defend us from all those I have looked on as friends—those I grew up amongst.' Her sleep was restless that night, her thoughts were troubled.

Annie came in to draw the curtains the following morning. She beckoned Kieran to the window where the sun streamed in making a golden glory of the snow clad hills, the loch shimmering with silver light.

'Is it not very fair, Mistress Kieran?'

'Yes—it is,' agreed the girl. No use she realised to dwell on yesterday's events. The world went on and would not change at her wishes. But she still shuddered mentally as thought of yesterday's execution flashed across her inner vision.

'I have laid out the burgundy skirt, lady, a bodice to match and a warm shawl, for it is cold when not right up against a fire.' She drew aside as Kieran washed herself, pulled on her shift and dressed in yet another of her late mother's gowns. It suited her she realised. Fashions had changed but little over the last eighteen years. The day started as normal, with Beth and Morag bringing in the children who rushed towards her on their chubby legs and pulled at her velvet skirt. She laughed and kissed them and exclaimed at the new teeth each had produced at the same time.

When she descended the stairs, she had regained her usual poise, firmly resolving to put the MacPherson's killing behind her. Lorna joined her for breakfast, explaining that the men had made an early start, Roderick and Iain overseeing clearing of snow from path and driveway and more logs being prepared for the fires below and above stairs.

'Perhaps we should go to Angus Mac Seumas and check that he is making good progress from his wound,' suggested Kieran. It was the first mention she had made of yesterday's traumatic happenings, both women studiously avoiding the subject over breakfast. Now Lorna smiled and agreed that they must make a morning visit to the old piper.

He sat up on his pillows when the door opened and his visitors entered, a smile breaking over his leathery old face as he saw Kieran.

'How are you feeling today, Angus,' she asked solicitously, while Lorna bent and plumped up the pillows.

'It is but a pinprick of a wound and I am myself again already,' he said stoutly. 'All thanks to you, Lady Kieran—and to Lady Lorna,' he added politely. He studied the girl's face as he spoke and saw the shadows around her eyes. 'I am told that he who fired at me no longer lives to try again. That Ewan Dhu dispatched him....!'

'That is so, Angus,' Lorna intervened quickly, not wanting to reopen this subject that had so distressed Kieran. 'Now we will put all memory of it behind us.'

'I must have a look at the wound—change the dressing,' explained Kieran quietly and proceeded to do so, realising with relief that there was no sign of infection—even though it must still be quite painful. 'I will come to see you again this evening—until then try to sleep—for with sleep comes healing.' She stroked his hand before leaving.

'That is one man who has given his heart to you, Kieran,' approved Lorna as they made their way to the parlour. She pointed to the harp. 'Shall we play together, my dear?' Kieran nodded and picked up the violin, tuned it and minutes later music filled the room rising faintly to the old piper's chamber, where he listened and smiled, before falling asleep.

Roderick Campbell came in through the main door stamping the snow from his feet before entering the great hall, where he glanced up at the swords arranged in shape of a circle above the door and at the magnificent antlered heads and portraits of Campbell ancestors and painted scenes of battle around its walls. He loved this place, as he had since his childhood, the huge oak table around which many visiting Campbell dignitaries had taken seat over the years. He barely glanced at that dark mark on the floor where James MacPherson had spilled his lifeblood the previous day.

The sound of music caught his ears—Aunt Lorna—and another? He slipped quietly into his Aunt's parlour and paused by the door as he saw his sister, violin tucked beneath her chin, a look of deep sadness on her lovely face as she bowed a melody not known to him. Lorna's fingers plucked the strings of her harp dripping magic into the air as they continued to play together unaware of his presence.

'That was exquisite,' he breathed, as the last quivering chord stole away. They swung about at the sound of his voice.

'Roderick!' his aunt cried, 'How long have you been there?'

'Not long enough—for that was altogether beautiful,' he murmured. 'Kieran, I did not know you were a musician.'

'I am not. Aunt Lorna is—I merely play along with her and am sadly out of practice.' Kieran looked down self consciously.

'Perhaps you could join us on your flute one day,' smiled Lorna. 'But for now nephew, we prepare a musical offering for Christmas day.'

'So my presence is not required. I understand and remove myself!' and looking slightly hurt he retreated. As he went they hid their merriment. And suddenly now Kieran felt that life went on, despite the horror of yesterday. She was part of this family of Campbells now, her loyalty to them alone.

Later as they drank a glass of wine together, Lorna asked a question.

'Kieran, yesterday we discussed your marriage to Sorley Mor Stewart and that it was no real marriage in the true sense of the word—nothing of a personal attachment between you.'

'Yes, it is true.'

'Well, you know my dear it might be possible to have this marriage annulled, if it would please you, that is? You could then marry another, a man perhaps more befitting your station.' As she came out with the suggestion, Lorna saw Kieran draw herself up in denial.

'Sorley Mor Stewart is a thoroughly decent man, and a wonderful physician who is making a name for himself in Edinburgh,' she exclaimed hotly. 'He took me to his wife, knowing my circumstances—that I had suffered rape. How many fine gentlemen would have done so in like circumstances do you suppose?' The words she uttered were brittle and her grey eyes bore a stormy expression.

'Forgive me, child. I meant only to offer good advice. You are very young still and life is long—and without a husband like to be a lonely affair.' She spoke gently knowing there was much unresolved hurt and anger in the girl's heart.

'My marriage was a true marriage, performed by a wise and honourable priest. In the sight of God I am still Sorley Mor's wife—even though we may not be together,' she burst out tossing her hair. Lorna looked at her shrewdly, knowing now for a certainty, Kieran was in fact deeply in love with her abandoned husband. But what could be done to ameliorate such a situation.

'I will not mention it again,' she murmured and pointed to a tapestry she was working on. 'Tell me do you approve the shade of this silk for the hills?'

'Blue for the shadows perhaps and this softer green.' The distraction had worked.

The days passed and now it was Christmas Eve, which to Kieran had always been a special occasion but any celebration of it despised by the Presbyterian Church which was firmly opposed to any so called popish feast days. But in her own heart she felt that the time of the birth of the little Christ Child was an event of the most immense importance, for surely the Lord Jesus was God's gift of his Son to mankind. But it seemed that there would be no marking of Christmas here, apart from their tentative rendering of music.

Kieran remembered sadly Sorley Mor's gift of that wooden cradle and fine shawl only last year and she wondered what his thoughts must be now. When she mentioned Christmas to Lorna, it was to hear that they had never celebrated it here. But Lorna went on to add that she had once spent some months with relatives in London, had seen the way in which the English decorated their houses with fir boughs and holly and red ribbons and ate goose and mince pies and rich puddings.

'I saw similar celebrations in Paris,' responded Kieran reflectively. 'Why I wonder, is there not more joy to be had here in our own land?'

'Well we more than make up for it at the New Year! We will have a great party then, child. You will enjoy it. But I know what you mean about Christmas. At least both you and I will mark it in our own private way!'

Christmas morning dawned and Kieran rose and drew the curtains. Fresh snow had fallen once more and she looked out on a white world and shivered slightly, for the bedroom fire had burned low during the night and there was ice on the windows. But the scene before her eyes was like something out of fairyland, the brilliant morning sunshine glittering diamond bright across the loch, caressing the pine trees, boughs bending under their weight of snow and stroking gold into the hills.

She glanced over her shoulder where Annie was busily adding new logs to the fire which soon gave a satisfying blaze. She made her ablutions, and dressed hastily, choosing her favourite blue gown with lace trimmed bodice. Then she stood before the crackling fire delighting in its warmth.

'I hear the cold is freezing the men's beards when they go outside, and it's icy on the paths,' mentioned Annie. 'I fear it is like to be one of those extra cold winters.'

'How lucky we are to be safe within these stout stone walls, when so many others in the highlands are living in caves on barren hillsides, their houses burned, all they once owned destroyed,' breathed Kieran softly. Annie turned her kind, bony face upon the girl and sought a suitable answer.

'Why, perhaps those who paid such sad price should not have risen against their rightful king,' she said at last, and Annie looked at her awkwardly as she spoke. As a Campbell, she knew better than to criticise in any way the doings of those who fed and clothed her, gave her employment. One did not question their orders or behaviour.

'Many of those of whom I speak were no way involved in the rising. But no words can put any of this right,' sighed Kieran. 'But my heart goes out to any without food or proper habitation in this cold and snow.'

'Bless you for your kind heart, lady!' Annie bustled about the room, smoothing the sheets as she ordered the bed. Minutes later a knock at the door brought Bess and the children. Lorna had sewn a suit of crimson velvet for Alan and Ishbel wore a blue gown that Kieran had laboured over. They looked adorable and ran towards their mother, tumbling in their haste. She caught them up and swung them around, one after the other.

'Happy Christmas, my darlings,' she whispered and kissed them fondly. As she did so, she thought of that lonely man in Edinburgh, waking to an empty house. Why did she continue to allow these memories to afflict her she sighed? She smoothed her skirt then brushed her disordered curls back from her face. Time to go down and take breakfast with Lorna she realised.

The two women ate alone as usual, the men long gone about their daily tasks, one of which was to free from snow the surrounds of the spring from which they drew the water supply, and also to renew the stock of logs and to clear the paths about the house.

Iain and Roderick with three ghillies leading a garron had gone onto the hill to shoot deer, hunger having brought the herd down to the lower slopes where the snow was less deep. But it was not an easy task plunging through snow drifts, feet sinking into unseen ditches of freezing water. But the snow also deadened noise of their approach as they carefully ensured the wind was in their faces, to avoid their scent reaching the animals.

'A good shot, Roderick—a fine stag too! Ewan Dhu—both you and Seumas take the garron and secure the carcase once the entrails are removed, then we will return home. This will need to be hung with other recent meat in the game hut.'

'We will have plenty food for the New Year when it comes,' said Roderick as he lowered his gun. 'I was thinking perhaps we should have a party, a feast for my sister Kieran.'

'An excellent idea, she is such welcome addition to the family, a fine lass! But Roderick lad is it not time that you found a wife to grace your home?' He glanced seriously at the younger man, who shook his head.

'All in guid time, Uncle Iain! I have not seen any around here who appeals to me—nor in Edinburgh during my stay there. No Uncle, I will not take a wife for mere convenience sake to beget an heir, but wait until I meet the right woman.' His grey eyes cast a steely glance at his frustrated uncle who decided this was not the time to pursue the matter. He well knew the stubborn look on Roderick's face.

Back at the house, Kieran and her aunt had finished their morning repast and retired to the privacy of the small parlour. Lorna looked up with a smile as Bess ushered in the two small shapes who hurled themselves upon her, climbing onto her lap. As she looked at their two excited faces, Lorna Campbell realised how much joy Kieran and her babies had brought into the house. Not since Roderick was a child had life been so rewarding. She gave each a marzipan sweet and they quietened.

A little later the twins sat spellbound as Lorna and their mother played a duet on harp and violin, pausing at a knock on the door as old Angus Mac Seumas appeared and asked permission to enter, and sat down in the corner to listen intently.

'That would have delighted the angels,' he declared, as Kieran lowered her bow. 'Where did you learn to play that way, Lady Kieran—surely not among those wild MacGregors?'

For a moment there was silence and he glanced from one woman to the other as he realised that he had spoken thoughtlessly of things which were no concern of his. But all at Glenlarig knew the history of this girl, child of Campbell parents her mother stolen by Rory MacGregor when pregnant by her husband Colin Campbell. Shame it was, that none knew of the little girl's survival, all believing Catriona's babe had died with her.

'I meant no disrespect,' he stumbled awkwardly. 'Certainly the MacGregors are great pipers that I will allow—and brave and good fighters!'

'My foster father Duncan MacGregor was indeed a fine piper,' she said, suddenly finding it completely natural to talk of the past. 'However it was in Paris that I learned to play the violin.'

'Shame it is that the man Duncan died at Culloden!'

'I had not heard it,' replied Kieran in a choking voice. 'Yet why should it surprise me when so many fine men fell or were murdered soon afterwards.'

'But their memory will linger on into legend,' said Angus Mac Seumas. 'There will come a time in the long years ahead, when there will be peace between the clans—but much that is deeply distressing will occur before that.' He sat quietly, his face in his hands.

'Angus has the gift of the sight,' whispered Lorna looking uneasily at the old piper. Then in a louder voice—'What can you tell us of things to come,' she inquired. At last he raised his head, his eyes deeply troubled.

'I see the great ones of this land turning against their people. Chiefs who are no longer fathers of the clan, but rapacious landlords, forcing their people to leave this land of their ancestors, to make way for sheep!' He spoke in deep ringing tones, totally unlike his usual soft lilting accents. 'I see whole glens cleared of their people, great ships bearing them away to lands afar. I pray to the Almighty that this will not occur in my own lifetime—but happen it will. It will most surely happen!' His voice faltered, stopped. He sat very still, his face torn with grief.

Lorna poured him a glass of brandy. He took it from her hand but did not drink it at first, just sat there as though in a dream. At last he roused himself, looked down at the glass in his hand and raised it to the two ladies.

'I salute two fine musicians,' he said as though nothing unusual had transpired.

'Soon perhaps, you will be able to entertain us on your pipes,' smiled Lorna trying to bring the conversation back to normality. He nodded his head.

'Indeed and Angus will be playing for you to usher in the New Year,' he exclaimed. Then he stared across at tiny Alan and Ishbel who were watching him solemnly from Bess and Morang's arms. He smiled tenderly at the little ones, but Kieran noted that as he turned to walk away there was a troubled look on his face.

'What did you make of all that?' asked Kieran now. Lorna shook her head as they seated themselves.

'I would dismiss it as mere foolishness, were it not that so many of Angus prophecies have come to pass,' she said simply. 'But the future he speaks of, if it be true will be a time of terrible hardship. But there again, can anyone really imagine the people of the Highlands being replaced by sheep? It makes little sense!' she said lightly.

Kieran stared back at her seriously. 'Well, certainly the black cattle which were our people's wealth have been removed from all but those few estates held by the Campbells and other clans who supported the Hanoverians. I tell you Lorna, thousands upon thousands of our cattle were driven to Fort Augustus and other places to be sold to lowland farmers and the English who came up to buy them at low prices. People were left to starve, sheep and goats likewise killed or sold.

'I heard something of this—but was it really on the scale you suggest? Surely you exaggerate?' Lorna protested.

'I promise you I speak the truth. Ask Iain and Roderick if you do not believe me!' flashed Kieran. Her eyes were stormy and lips trembling with emotion.

'Your word is enough,' replied Lorna slowly. 'I had no idea that retribution so called, had been carried out in such horrific manner. We heard some rumours from London that those arrested insurgents not sentenced to suffer death were to be sent to the colonies to work as indentured servants there.'

'As slaves more like!' exclaimed Kieran forcefully. 'Did you also hear I wonder that before trial, the poor men rounded up after the battle, were crowded together long months in the holds of prison ships lying in squalid conditions in their own ordure? No help given to the wounded, who died of their infected wounds, lying amongst the living until thrown overboard?' Lorna listened appalled and noted the scarlet flush on the girl's cheeks wrought of her intense anger.

'How did you come to hear such atrocities?' she questioned.

'From my husband whose lawyer heard it from those he was in contact with in London—and from a couple of pitiful men who managed to escape by feigning death. Sadly it is all true, Lorna,' cried Kieran her eyes damp.

'Then surely the British Government carries a black stain on its conscience!' exclaimed Lorna. 'All that has happened will go down in history as a period of deepest shame. Warfare is one thing, terrible things happen when men fight each other—but to treat their innocent families in such manner, forcing them to endure starvation, driving them from their homes. It sickens me to hear of it—and as for the way prisoners were treated, I am beyond words!'

As they stared at each other, movement at the door made them turn their heads. A tall, autocratic figure, kilted, wearing a sword, plaid secured with a silver broach at his shoulder stood there, fixing a brooding gaze on Kieran. She gasped as she recognised Major General John Campbell of Mamore. As she stared at him speechlessly, Lorna rose to her feet and stretched out both hands in greeting.

'John—what surprise and joy to see you,' she exclaimed as he raised her hand to his lips. 'How did you get through the snow?'

'Difficult in places I'll allow, but worth it to see you, my dear Lorna!' He turned his gaze back on Kieran. 'Added to this delight I see that we now have the missing member of the family with us at last! Greetings, Mistress Kieran Stewart—or should I now address you as Campbell?'

'Perhaps just as Kieran, my Lord Mamore,' she replied evenly.

'Well, did I not tell you that blood is stronger than hatred? It always calls to us in the end. Roderick told me you were here—and two others?' His eyes slid across the room and lighted on the twins. 'Your children, niece,' he inquired as he walked quietly across the room and bent over them.

'Their names are Alan, after his father, and his sister is named Ishbel!' said Kieran. She moved to stand protectively at the children's side.

'They are delightful,' breathed Mamore. He bent and lifted Alan in his arms. 'This boy will make a fine soldier one day,' he declared, as Alan's small fingers reached for that shining broach. He put him down and took Ishbel in his arms. He stroked her shining pale golden curls with an exploring finger. 'Her grandfather's colouring,' he murmured softly. He gave her back into Morag's caring.

'What happened to your doctor, Lady Kieran?'

At this personal question Lorna signalled to Bess and Morag to take the children back to the nursery. Mamore stared regretfully after the little ones and waited until their curious attendants had removed them, before resuming the conversation.

'Forgive me if I am direct, but what of Sorley Mor Stewart?' he demanded.

'I could no longer live with him, after you had made my true parentage known to me. He would have despised me had he become aware of the truth. I waited until the twins were born, a few months old and able to travel before making decision to leave him. I almost made for Paris—but I met Roderick in Edinburgh. He said I should come here—helped me.'

'You say Stewart would have despised you because of your Campbell blood? Are you sure of that? He struck me as a very decent man and of a different cut to the normal run of Jacobites besotted by their affection for the Pretender!' She made no reply to him and he sighed. 'Well, that you are here is matter of rejoice for your family. I imagine it was not an easy decision, but once we make a choice in life, it is good to make the best of it. I am sure you will never regret yours.'

'Some wine, John,' called Lorna and the tension of the moment passed.

'Let us drink a toast,' suggested Mamore. 'Kieran, what shall it be?'

'Why, let us drink in celebration of the birth of the little Christ Child,' she challenged. 'And also to peace in our land and an end to killing in all its forms.'

'Why not. Why not indeed,' he replied broodingly and raised his glass.

'To the future. I pray it may it be kind to all of us!' It was at this moment that the door was opened and Iain stood there.

'Lord Mamore, you are wanted. A messenger has arrived with a despatch!' the two men hurried away, as Kieran drew a sigh of relief.

Kieran did not see much of Mamore until evening, when a feast was prepared in his honour. He had brought twenty members of his regiment with him, some to be accommodated in the house others in one of the barns, but all crowded into the great hall for dinner. Many were the admiring glances that were thrown towards Kieran where she sat between Mamore and Roderick. The huge plates of roasted venison and wild turkey and beef were piped in by Angus Mac Seumas, who was determined to do the honours, despite his barely healed wound. Wine flowed freely and the air was convivial.

Apart from the serving girls, Lady Lorna and Kieran were the only two women present and both seemed to draw many eyes. The meal drew to a close. Iain Campbell stared authoritatively at his wife.

'Lorna, think you this would be good time for you to play for us? I am sure that many here have not had the opportunity to hear music, apart from the pipes?'

'But my harp is in the parlour—I am not sure...?'

'I will send for it to be brought—and Kieran's violin.' He gave an order. Space was made at the top of the hall, chair placed for Lorna in front of her harp. She bent forward and tuned it, beckoning Kieran to stand beside her. The girl did so and rosined her bow tightened the strings to a perfect pitch and looked at Lorna.

'I am not sure I can do this,' she whispered urgently.

'Pretend we are together in my parlour, none else present—now!'

'What of the carol we practiced yesterday?' Kieran suggested. As the music started there was complete stillness in the hall and the beauty of that ancient carol touched the hearts of men who had not heard it perhaps since their childhood. One of them started to sing in a fine baritone voice. Others joined him and there was sustained clapping afterwards. Then Lorna led

Kieran in a lilting Highland air that was a favourite of both women, followed by many others, the men tapping the table in time, and it was a full hour before completely exhausted they set their instruments aside.

'Goodnight, gentlemen,' said Lorna. She gave instructions for her harp to be taken back to her parlour then, putting an arm about Kieran's waist, led her firmly from the hall, ignoring cries for more.

'I am relieved the ordeal is over,' declared Kieran. 'I never thought to play in front of so many strangers.'

'You did well. I am proud of you,' smiled Lorna and kissed her. 'And you see we did celebrate the birth of the Christ Child in our music.'

'I am glad of it,' replied Kieran softly. She made her goodnight to Lorna, realising as she did so that she had become very attached to her aunt—and that Lorna looked very tired tonight. Was she perhaps unwell? No, it must just be fatigue. She fell asleep as soon as her own head touched the pillow. Lord Mamore followed Roderick into his study where they were joined by Iain Campbell. They sat comfortably over their whisky and cigars at first, then Lord Mamore cleared his throat for attention.

'I was going to speak of this tomorrow—but we never know what another day may bring. I may have to leave early. So now I have to inform you of a new order from the London Government.'

'Do you speak of the ban on tartan,' Roderick asked. 'Here in our own glen we Campbells do not adhere to such ruling.'

'For now you are safe to continue as you are and of course to carry arms, although officially it is only members of His Majesty's forces who have permission to do so.'

'What then?' Iain Campbell asked curiously.

'The Clan Chieftains have lost their jurisdiction over Pit and Gallows!'

'You joke! Why, that is to take away all authority from the Chiefs! Who then will keep the clansmen in order?' cried Iain in dismay.

'They seek to break down the clan system!' explained Mamore. 'Some of the greater of the chiefs, for instance in our clan it will be the Duke of Argyll, will receive a goodly sum on money in recompense. It will of course only apply to those Chiefs who were loyal to King George. Others of the Jacobites as you know have been proscribed. The world is changing and I am not sure it is for the better.' Mamore's arrogant face displayed obvious disapproval.

'But what happens if we catch a man murdering another?' said Roderick.

'Catch the fellow by all means—but you may not slit his throat as I am informed was done here but recently. The man must be brought to court—and hanged, all done according to the letter of the law!' informed the Major General heavily.

'An arrant waste of time,' exclaimed Iain Campbell angrily. 'What is suitable in England cannot apply to our country! We have always had authority over our clansmen, dealt with issues of law ourselves and done so justly. I defy any to say otherwise!' He got to his feet and went to stand in front of the crackling log fire, the flaming embers as hot as his temper.

'Well Iain, it is to be so no longer,' informed Mamore ponderously. 'Once a law is passed at Westminster all have to abide by it. Although some say much good may eventually come of this union with the old enemy, I can also see great change developing to this land. It may not in the long run be to our advantage!'

'Then why do we accept it?'

'Because by our allegiance to the House of Hanover, we create respect for our clan in London. They need us as peacekeepers—to watch over all with a firm hand.'

'I like it not,' declared Roderick suddenly. 'Perhaps we should ask ourselves what has actually been gained by a political marriage most Scots have little liking for.'

'Since that union became law forty years ago, there is little now any can do about the matter,' replied Mamore reprovingly. 'The coming together of the two countries supposedly opens up new markets for us I understand— even though we have seen no proof of it as yet, and with those iniquitous taxes—malt, salt, linen! But there again, as a nation we were almost bankrupt after the Darien affair, trade important.'

'Perhaps honour more so,' exclaimed Roderick. 'I fought with my clan as bravely I hope as another. I fully approved the need to put down that futile rebellion called for by Charles Edward Stuart. What I cannot accept in my heart is the cruelty that we were party to in the wake of the battle.' His grey eyes bore shuttered expression.

'Think you that any of us liked the measures we had to take?' exclaimed Mamore. 'Had we not used the utmost severity, then we would have been fighting new uprisings in the years ahead. No Roderick, the Jacobites had to be completely crushed, all places of refuge denied them, and those who would excite others to rebellion, themselves banished to the Colonies.'

'I still say the measures were excessive!' flashed Roderick

'Then you are wrong!' Mamore's dark eyes played across the handsome features of the younger man. He felt a kindly regard for Roderick son of his second cousin, whom he designated his nephew. He had been well content with the courage and initiative the young man had displayed under his command, but displeased to learn that he had recently resigned his commission. He had imagined a fine future for him in the army.

'Well, let us not spoil a happy evening by futile disagreement,' put in Iain Campbell smoothly. Mamore nodded and a smile broke across his harsh features.

'I agree and must say how much I enjoyed the music so delightfully offered by your wife Lorna and young Kieran Stewart this evening. She is a fine addition to the family—and favours her mother,' he added fondly.

'But with a mind of her own,' declared Roderick.

'My wife tells me she still has a fondness for the Stewart doctor she so unfortunately married,' explained Iain disapprovingly. 'I would have preferred that the marriage might be annulled, legally set at nought that she might make an advantageous marriage to another.'

'She tells me she was never his wife in the true meaning of the word,' said Roderick slowly. 'It was a marriage of convenience only. But certainly she admires the man—and I have good reason to be grateful to him. He saved my life!'

'Well who knows what the future may hold. The girl is determined and possessed of a fiery spirit, this much I assessed when first I met her. But given time she will see that it is in her best interest and that of her children, to become at one with her family. As for Sorley Mor Stewart, I have heard that the good doctor is making a name for himself as a fine physician in Edinburgh, his services much sought after. No doubt in time he will welcome an official end to a marriage that prevents him taking another woman to wife.'

'It should not be too difficult to achieve. A ceremony in a cave, performed by an Episcopalian priest who had not declared allegiance to the crown, no witnesses save a young boy,' mused Iain Campbell. 'We should be able to relieve her of this encumbrance.' They exchanged looks of agreement—and smiling raised their glasses.

Chapter Nine

Christmas came and went in Edinburgh without any noticeable marking of the occasion by most of its inhabitants. The austere approach to religious matters by the Presbyterian Church and the Covenant had long since closed off the minds of its adherents to any popish form of unseemly jollity and celebration—yet the desperately poor of the city tried where they could to lay their hands on alcohol with which to dull their senses to the difficulty of their lot, staggering home to their cramped overcrowded accommodation to shout and vent their frustration on wives and children.

And still the streets resounded to the pounding feet of the militia, orders of command clashing with the cries of street vendors, while sensible citizens stayed within doors avoiding the freezing cold and whistling winds that poured in from the sea. If the union of the parliaments in 1707 had been meant to usher in a more prosperous society, today forty years later there was little sign of it. Trade was difficult. The people's health in the tall, squalid tenement buildings cause for concern and one of the greatest killers remained small-pox to which children were especially vulnerable.

But the wealthy existed comfortably as always the case, their wives wore fine gowns, attended balls with their husbands and gentlemen sat in the newly opened coffee houses to meet their business associates to drink, smoke or exchange a pinch of snuff and gossip. But they too were offended by Edinburgh's smells, which even the brisk breezes sweeping between the hills did little to disperse. It was suggested that eventually a new town should be built north of that foul smelling foetid lake below the castle the Nor Loch. Plans were discussed. But it would take a lot of money—and money was scarce these days.

Sorley Mor heard talk of those plans and approved the idea as he discussed it with Mr McCrombie, his man of business.

'Do you think it will come to pass?' he inquired now, as he sat in the lawyer's office.

'Yes, I do. But even when the official plans are eventually drawn up and approved, I doubt whether anything will happen for at least the next twenty years,' said McCrombie sagely. 'Not in my lifetime, though I would dearly love to be proved wrong!'

'Money?' pondered the doctor, 'or rather the lack of it.'

'Aye—it is ever the sticking point when great schemes are suggested. But something badly needs to be done.'

'Yet I imagine it will only be the rich of the business class who will take opportunity to move into this New Town when built, those with money—which will leave the poor in like condition to that they now endure.'

'I doubt I would trouble to move myself,' McCrombie mused, 'if I should be alive when it comes to fruition that is—and offered the choice. This place has been my home as well as my place of business for the last forty years. I'm used to it!' He glanced fondly around his office by the light of the two flickering candles, for little light penetrated from the small window, the upper storeys of the tall houses on either side of the narrow alleyway, bulging inwards towards each other, leaving only small patch of sky visible above.

'I think I might compromise,' said Sorley Mor slowly. 'I would retain a surgery here in the old city where need would be far greater—but perhaps build a house in this suggested New Town!'

'You are doing well these days, Sorley Mor. Your name bruited about as a fine and trustworthy physician. Yet I discern a look of melancholy on your face. You still yearn after your wife?' probed the elderly lawyer diffidently.

'Now that I know for certain that she has thrown in her lot with her Campbell relatives, there is little I can presently do in the matter—even should I wish to,' replied Sorley Mor in a low voice. 'But yes, I do miss her presence—and that of wee Alan and Ishbel. I loved these children as my own. Now they will grow up amongst strangers whose name would have been abhorrent to him from whom they are sprung, Alan Stewart!'

'Life is not always kind, nor easy. But one day you will meet another woman, my friend, one who will deserve your love.'

'There will never be another! Kieran Stewart is my wedded wife. She has deserted me and I struggle to come to terms with it, even though I understand why. She could at least have discussed the future with me. Who knows—we might have managed to surmount the difficulty of her parentage.' He rose from his chair and paced back and forth in agitation.

'What can I say of any comfort? Only that God moves in mysterious ways. Trust in him my friend---and in the meanwhile, if there is any other help I can offer, you have only to ask.' The elderly lawyer smiled in sympathy. Sorley Mor shook his head. His dark blue eyes held a hard angry look.

'You speak of God, but I do not believe—no, despite having an Episcopal priest as a brother! There has been nothing in my life to suggest that a loving God is in control. My first wife dying in childbirth, my only son once rediscovered shot to pieces at my side by Cumberland's canon—

and now deserted by Kieran who by a cruel twist of fate turns out to be of Campbell stock.' He rose to his feet, but McCrombie held out a restraining hand.

'Tell me, Sorley Mor—do you never feel the healing hand of God with you as you tend the sick—when you bring joy to a mother's heart as you snatch her child from the jaws of death?' The old man smiled gently at the doctor, watching his face. He saw no response to his words, the other merely passing a frustrated sigh as he looked away and turned to the door.

Back at his lonely house Sorley Mor pondered all the lawyer had said of God. But how could he have faith in a mysterious, unknown being, perhaps merely a myth invented to help men face the difficulties of life. He knew that Kieran believed, as did young Lachlan despite the horrors they had both experienced. Yes, he realised, and so as a child had he! Then following the joy of his first marriage to Jean, he had suffered the shock of her death in bearing his son—at which point he had lost his faith. Why would God want to so punish a man who had made decision to devote his life into healing the sick?

He sat there musing, a glass of whisky in his hand. What was it that David had once said? That the Almighty Being who had sent his own Son into the world had allowed his cruel death in order that Jesus might open the gates to eternal life? He had also pointed out that the road a Christian must take was not always an easy one, but that God gave believers the strength to face whatever difficulties assailed them. Suddenly the thick ice he had packed around his heart cracked.

He rose to his feet and threw the contents of his glass into the fire, where it blazed up ferociously. No more—no more of this false comfort that damaged a man's liver! With a cry he fell on his knees and held his hands out imploringly before him.

'If you are real God—then hear my cry! Help me for I am eaten up with pain. Help me to believe!' How long he knelt there he was not sure, but suddenly sensed a feeling of warmth and comfort enwrapping his whole being—soul bathed in a wondrous peace never known until now. At last he rose to his feet, an expression of wonder on his face.

'Thank you, Lord,' he murmured. 'Now I know—do not quite understand, but accept that you are indeed real and altogether awesome. Forgive I pray my years of cynicism and unbelief.' And now he felt a new purpose in himself, a determination to seek reconciliation with his young wife, despite her Campbell blood. Indeed, what did such things really matter in the sight of God? This hatred between clans was a man made folly which one day must be put to rest.

He thought of what little he knew of the days of Christ upon the earth. Jesus had lived in Palestine at a time when it was subject to the iron grip of a cruel occupying Roman force, surely not so different in context to that currently experienced in his own Scotland by English occupation. But Jesus had spoken of forgiveness in all situations—even forgiving those who barbarously hammered nails into his hands and feet.

Could Sorley Mor forgive those who had killed his young son and murdered Alan Stewart and raped Kieran, whipped his brother almost to death? He decided that he might perhaps forgive through Christ—but not to forget—that would be altogether too difficult!

There was an urgent knocking at the door and he sighed. He heard his housekeeper hurry to the noisy summons. She came to him, her face grave.

'I know it is out of hours, but, it's a child, doctor! A wee lassie fell in front of a carriage and is badly hurt. Her mother is quite distraught!' She looked at him expectantly and he smiled.

'Thank you, Mistress Lindsey—I will come!' He hurried to his consulting room. The child now lying on his examination couch was he saw perhaps three years of age. Her small face white and she was unconscious. His passed his gentle hands over her, seeking possible fractures and finding none. But she had a lump rising on the side of her head and there was bad bruising to her shoulder. She was in shock.

'Is she going to die, doctor?' the young mother looked at him appealingly. He shook his head.

'No, my dear lady—she is not badly hurt, but sometimes when people experience a great shock their mind closes down for a time, as in this case. Now I want you to take her in your arms and speak soothingly to her, sing perhaps!' She looked at him in surprise, had expected some wonderful miracle of healing—but obediently scooped the little one up in to her arms and started to croon a lullaby to her. The child's eyelids fluttered and she opened her blue eyes, gazing wonderingly up at her mother.

'Mama,' she whispered. 'My head is sair.'

'My puir wee lamb!' and the mother kissed her in obvious relief.

'You had a fall, my darling.' She placed the little girl back on the couch, where Sorley Mor made a second examination which confirmed his earlier diagnosis. The child was only badly bruised, and should make a good recovery. He gave her a draught to calm her pain. Minutes later the young woman left murmuring her gratitude the more so as the doctor would accept no payment for his advice and care. As he watched them go, feeling of sudden warmth enveloped him—and he smiled.

Bed now, for tomorrow would indeed be another and different day!

New Year's Eve at Glenlarig dawned crisp and bright and extremely cold, temperatures well below zero and a fresh fall of snow overnight had fallen over surfaces already icy, rendering walking abroad treacherous. Roderick had been expecting company to arrive for the planned festivities,

163

but sadly travelling conditions seemed to have precluded this—and Mamore and his soldiers having left immediately after Christmas, only Iain and Kieran with Roderick and Lorna Campbell would be celebrating the occasion together with their large body of attendants, and some of those holding land as tenants who had managed the journey.

All were piped into the hall by Angus Mac Seumas.

There was a fine feast the like of which Kieran had never seen before, the long table almost groaning under the weight of the many dishes, salmon and trout, great joints of venison and beef, chicken and wild turkey and swan, all served with vegetables and well seasoned gravies, followed by rich fruit pudding custards and jellies, for the cooks had indeed excelled themselves. Roderick sat at the head of the table, his sister at his side, flanked Lorna and Iain. Toasts were drunk at the conclusion. Roderick rose to his feet. He raised his glass.

'I drink a toast to my beautiful, beloved and courageous sister, lately restored to the heart of her family-----Kieran Stewart Campbell!' he intoned and she blushed as around the table glasses were raised in her honour. Other toasts were made and then Iain Campbell rapped on the table for silence.

'Ladies and gentlemen—I give you his Majesty King George,' he announced. Kieran froze at his words. All around her people enthusiastically raised their glasses. As for Kieran, she passed her glass in front of a water tumbler, as she drank a silent toast to 'The King over the water' and Roderick smiled at her action.

Now the table was cleared and pulled aside and there was song and dancing. War songs of the Campbells with their famous battle cry 'Cruachan' echoed about the hall. Then the sword dance took place, the graceful footwork of the men who executed it at odds with their wild appearance and enthusiastic cries. They lifted their swords and bowed to ecstatic applause.

Then Roderick lead Kieran onto the floor as together they performed a formal reel, the first time she had danced with this brother of hers and discovered that he was a fine dancer. He bowed to her with a warm smile as she curtsied at the conclusion. They were joined by Iain and Lorna. Then the floor was packed with the entire company and despite herself Kieran joyed in the music and laughter and she closed her mind to the fact that those who celebrated the New Year were her one time enemies. Perhaps the wine had gone to her head for it had been smooth on the palette but memory of the Rising and the cruelties of its aftermath seemed to drift away. It was the present that mattered, she thought defiantly.

But waking the next morning her head throbbing, Kieran was besieged with feelings of guilt that she had so forgotten who she was, that she had wholeheartedly allowed herself to be at one with her Campbell family. What would Sorley Mor have thought of her behaviour—or his brother the Rev David Stewart—or young Lachlan?

She stared out of the window. It was snowing again, the flakes sticking to the glass driven by a relentless wind. Was it snowing like this in Edinburgh? What was Sorley Mor doing at this moment? No doubt eating a hasty breakfast she imagined, before hurrying into his consulting room. Had he thought of her last night as 1747 became 1748? Had he raised a glass to the memory of their time together? But why should he—when she had deserted him. Perhaps he had met someone else—a woman who would be kinder to him than his lawfully married wife, and she found the notion strangely upsetting. But why should he not have the chance of some real happiness at last? She turned away from the window as Annie knocked.

'Oh Sorley, I do miss you so,' she whispered, as she pulled on her fine wool stockings. 'Why has life been so cruel to us both?' She heard the sound of the pipes and guessed it would be from the hall, the weather outside too wild for the elderly piper to brave.

Later she met with Lorna in her aunt's peaceful parlour.

'You are pale, child,' said Lorna.

'I have a headache—the wine last night I fear!'

'Come, I will give you a draught to help settle that,' smiled Lorna sympathetically. 'Oh and perhaps I should mention that we have visitors today, despite the weather! A troop of militia lost their way in the snow and presented themselves at the door less than an hour ago. Roderick is entertaining their captain in the hall, his men rest in the large barn.'

'Will they be staying?' asked Kieran listlessly.

'I doubt it—unless the weather gets worse. No, Roderick does not care for the captain or so he told me quietly—a strange man with hard green eyes and a limp!'

At those words Kieran opened her eyes in shock, for the description lightly given brought grim memory to her of the officer who had instigated her rape and ordered Alan's death! But surely it could not be the same man? No—impossible. But the notion would not leave her and after exchanging some desultory remarks about the weather and last night's celebrations, she excused herself saying she was going to the children.

She hesitated outside the partially open door to the great hall. She could hear voices. She was about to ease the door further ajar, when it suddenly swung open and Roderick stood there. He gave a warm smile as he saw her and beckoned her in.

'Kieran my darling, we have a guest who lost his way in the snow—this is Captain Richard Bradshaw. Bradshaw, allow me to present my sister Lady Kieran Campbell.' He noted in surprise that Kieran went white with shock as her eyes lighted on the stranger and he frowned in perplexity. Had she met the fellow before?

'Your servant, Captain,' she said in a clear low voice and watched the man's eyes light up in admiration as he saw her. If she recognised him, then certainly he had no memory of the woman he had raped almost two years ago. For this was indeed the green eyed Captain of her many nightmares, her presentiment on hearing Lorna's description of him proving correct.

Before she guessed his purpose he had advanced on her, raising her hand to his lips.

'An honour to meet one so charming!' he exclaimed as his eyes examined her figure in her gown of burgundy velvet. 'Fate has been kind to bring such exquisite beauty to my attention—your servant, lady!' To his chagrin she snatched her hand back as though bitten by a serpent.

'I am a married woman, sir,' she said in trembling tones.

'Then that is my misfortune—but only if you should wish it to be so,' he purred. He might have said more, but Roderick suddenly intervened.

'No doubt you wish to go to your children, sister,' he said quietly and putting a steely hand on the captain's sleeve, drew him back from her proximity. He had heard tell of this fellow before, of his unpleasant exploits among women and as well as the extreme and unnecessary cruelty he had demonstrated towards any suspected of Jacobite sympathies. He had only introduced him to his sister as a matter of form as he would have done with any visitor to Glenlarig.

'Perhaps we will meet again—and may it be very soon,' exclaimed Bradshaw with a curious smile, wondering at her reaction. She made no reply, but stalked haughtily away.

An hour later the snow stopped falling and a watery sunshine gleamed between the heavy clouds. Roderick surveyed this improvement in the weather with satisfaction.

'The break in the weather makes it possible for you to continue your journey south, Captain Bradshaw. I will see that your men are well provisioned and lend you one of my men to guide you upon your way.' Noting the inflexible note in his host's voice, Bradshaw did not seek to extend his stay. He wanted to be safe on his way to the garrison at Stirling and then to Edinburgh where he would make his report. As his horse floundered its way through the snow, his men close behind him, the image of Campbell's delightful sister came to plague him. Why had she seemed slightly familiar—and why the look of revulsion she had cast upon him. Strange, and with a muffled curse he shouted at his weary troop to make better speed.

Once he was assured that Bradshaw and his troop had disappeared into the distance, Roderick sought out his sister. He found her sitting with his aunt Lorna and noticed the tear stains on her face.

'Kieran my dear, what is amiss?' he asked quietly. She merely shook her head and rose to her feet, about to seek the door. But he drew her gently to him and pulled her head down on his shoulder. 'Come—tell me what troubles you.' He ignored his aunt's gesture that he should desist. Some mystery here and he wished to uncover its source.

'You tell him, Lorna,' she cried brokenly and turned away from him and fled in more tears. He looked after her baffled. Then in exasperation he turned to Lorna.

'What is wrong with her?' he demanded.

'Sit down and I will tell you,' she replied calmly. He did so and listened silently as for the first time he heard of Kieran's rape and the murder of her husband—and that it was at the hands of the man who had just left his house.

'Had she but told me of this, he would be dead by now,' he choked. 'Of one thing you may be sure I will settle this account with him one day! I have heard tales of the vile behaviour of this man—but to learn he violated my sister is abominable and he will die for it!' His grey eyes flashed his fury and Lorna almost drew back from him in alarm.

'I suppose the only thing you can say is that he was unaware of who she was at the time—but for a man to behave like this to any woman at his mercy is an unforgiveable act in my opinion—war, or no war,' she exclaimed with spirit. He nodded and lifted her hand to his lips.

'I agree with you,' was all he said, as he stalked away.

The weeks passed, became months and suddenly spring came to Glenlarig, early snowdrops cladding the banks giving way to flirting, dancing daffodils, and every tiny burn became a raging torrent as the snows melted and the sound of rushing water assaulted the ears in every direction. Larks were lilting in the sky and gorse tight budded with gold. Only the high peaks still held their burden of snow and high above the waters of the loch an eagle soared majestically.

'I am going to be away for a week or two,' said Roderick carelessly, as they watched the two small forms well muffled against the breeze coming off the loch, as they played in the semi wild front garden at Glenlarig. At sixteen months the twins were now steady on their feet and starting to speak.

'Where are you going?' asked Kieran in surprise. He did not answer at once, staring broodingly across the shining waters now bathed in golden sunlight. 'Well where then?' she persisted.

'To Edinburgh—family business I have to attend to,' he replied at last and with that she had to be content, for he turned away and stalked back into the house.

She looked after him uncertainly. What called him to Edinburgh, she wondered? She hoped he was not to involve himself with the military again, but sensed this was not so. She had heard that Roderick had displayed extraordinary bravery in the fighting occasioned by Prince Charles Stuart's abortive attempt to regain the throne of his fathers. That he had been on the opposing side to all whom she had loved she now accepted as a fact of life, also realising that her brother was not a man of war, but one who desired peace to pursue his literary studies, whilst also endeavouring to do the best for his tenants among whom he was very popular.

Edinburgh—Sorley Mor! The two were indelibly entwined in her mind. Now as she hurried to scoop up her small daughter who had tumbled over a large stone hidden in the grass, she found her husband's image rising up before her inner vision and breathed a deep sigh.

'My hurt,' complained Ishbel but with a smile as her mother caressed her.

'There you are, my darling! Off you go now,' she brushed the little girl down as Alan came hurrying unsteadily towards her a daffodil clutched in his small hand.

'Mama—flower!' he said proudly and pushed it towards her. She bent and kissed his chubby face.

'Why, thank you, Alan,' and she tucked the yellow bloom into the front of her blue wool jacket. How Sorley Mor would have joyed in these two he had accepted as his own. Why, oh why did these memories of him continue to afflict her?

'Kieran—is anything amiss,' asked a quiet voice and Lorna came to join her as the young mother stared wistfully at her children.

'Not really—only that Roderick has just said that he intends to visit Edinburgh,' she blurted out, dashing a tear from the corner of her eye. 'That wind is sharp still,' she added defensibly knowing that Lorna had perceived the gesture.

'Ah yes, Edinburgh? You think still of your husband?' asked Lorna gently.

'I will never forget him. I try to Lorna, oh, how I try! I just feel so guilty in my treatment of a good and honourable man.' The words were torn from deep within her. Her aunt nodded understanding.

'There is always the possibility of divorce,' she suggested. 'Normally very hard to achieve but in the circumstances in which you find yourself, I feel it might be more than possible. Another marriage might bring love and fulfilment and finally put all heartache to rest!' If she thought her words might be helpful she was soon to accept that they were not. Kiernan turned on her almost fiercely, her grey eyes damp with tears.

'Lorna, crazy though it may seem, know that I dearly love my husband. I realise that I may never be able to take my proper place as his wife—but nor will I ever contemplate divorce and marriage to another! Never—never!' she stormed angrily and now she was weeping unashamedly and Lorna looked at her in dismay, for she had thought that as the months sped uneventfully by that Kieran had closed her mind to her past. She had become deeply attached to the young girl, this daughter of her own beloved sister-in-law who had been kidnapped by the MacGregor brigand, and died too soon. She now loved Kieran almost as dearly as she did Roderick.

'Forgive me if my words hurt you—they were not meant to,' was all that Lorna said quietly and Kieran reached out a repentant hand to her. It was not right to take out her frustration on this woman who had been kindness itself to her.

'I'm sorry, Aunt Lorna. But when Roderick mentioned Edinburgh it all came flooding back to me.'

'I understand—wish there was something I could do to help.'

'There is nothing anyone can do! If only there were!' Just then a cloud passed over the sun and it began to rain. At once Kieran's thoughts returned to her children. 'Ishbel—Alan, come here my darlings! Time to go in or you will get wet,' she cried, as between them Lorna and their mother led the protesting little ones back to the house.

When Kieran came down to breakfast the following morning, it was to learn that her brother had left for Edinburgh an hour earlier, not stopping to say goodbye to Lorna or his sister. She felt slightly hurt that she had been unable to wish him safe journey, admitting to herself that she would miss their daily hour together in his library where he continued to open her mind to the classics. Still, just a couple of weeks he had said!

The object of her quiet brooding was mounted and riding south attended by two of his ghillies, Ewan Dhu and Ivor Mac Dugal. The early spring sunshine cast pencils of light before them as they rode through forests of dark pine and slender silver trunked birch trembling in fine new leaf, and swaying oak, beech and alder. Catkins danced in the breeze on the willows beside the shore of Loch Lubnaig and pale primroses starred the banks. It all looked idyllic, the blue soaring mountains reflected in the quiet waters of the loch.

But Roderick's eyes stared unseeingly at the wild beauty through which they were passing, his thoughts on the man he rode to find and to kill once he had him at the end of his sword—Richard Bradshaw who had dishonoured his sister. His agent had sent word to Glenlarig that the army captain Roderick had demanded news of, had returned to Edinburgh after a spell of leave in London. He was to be found at the castle garrison.

Roderick had not hesitated when made aware of the facts by his aunt Lorna of the shame put upon his sister by Bradshaw. His honour as brother of a loved sister and his position as head of his household dictated that he must remove this carrion from the face of the earth. Yes and he would joy in the doing of it! He had heard many tales of this man's cruelties and debaucheries. Now retribution was fast coming this evil bastard's way. And so he rode and his men glanced one from the other, wondering what it was that had caused their usually calm master to so grind his teeth from time to time in unusual fury.

They were nearing the end of the long, narrow loch when Roderick's gloomy thoughts were disturbed by the noise of shouting and sound of shots—then suddenly around the bend in the road, he saw a young man speeding desperately towards them. He was clothed in a torn and faded plaid of the MacDonald tartan. He held his hands out imploringly to Roderick, then seeming to recognise the tartan of his attendants gave a shout of despair and threw himself into the loch and started to swim strongly towards its far shore.

Then even as Roderick stared at the swimmer, others now appeared on the scene, a troop of militia marching in two's along the narrow track, under the command of a foul mouthed sergeant, who let out a string of curses as he saw his prey fast disappearing, his head a dark spot in the waters.

'Fire,' he shouted, 'and don't miss that bloody rebel if you know what's good for you!' In answer to his command a volley of shots rang out—the swimmer threw up his arms and his head disappeared under the water and was seen no more. Satisfied, the sergeant now turned his attention on Roderick and his two kilted ghillies—and gasped.

'Can you beat such effrontery? More bloody rebels daring to wear their tartan against the law of the land!' He stared scathingly at Roderick Campbell, appearing slightly more uncertain as he took in the quality of his apparel. This was obviously a gentleman of some degree.

'I am Roderick Campbell, lately Captain Campbell serving under my uncle Major General John Campbell of Mamore! You should learn to recognise this tartan sergeant. It is worn by those who serve his Majesty King George as loyal servants, helping to keep peace in this land.' His grey eyes were as hard as steel.

The man looked at him sheepishly. He signalled to his men to withdraw and be at ease. Mamore's name he knew, next only in importance to the Duke of Argyll. 'An honest mistake, sir—my apologies,' he added grudgingly.

'The man you just ordered killed. What crime had he committed?' demanded Roderick, who could not get the fugitive's despairing face from memory.

'Why—you saw for yourself—he was wearing tartan! When challenged he refused to stop and be arrested. He would have got six months in jail for his offence if a first one—the second time caught wearing this banned manner of dress, deportation to His Majesty's land in the Americas.'

'Did it not occur to you that the man may have spoken only Gaelic—might not have understood your words? He would only have seen the threat of your guns!'

'Then it is his fault for speaking only such bloody heathenish language! He is dead now and so the problem no longer exists!' and the sergeant spat into the road.

'Your name, Sergeant?'

'Sergeant Martin Brownley! I was only doing my duty—I will not detain you more, sir! I wish you safe journey,' he said uneasily, as the haughty Campbell gave him one last withering, contemptuous glance and with a word to his attendants, rode on past the red coated troop, who drew sourly to the side of the road to let him freely pass.

The incident had distracted Roderick's thoughts from the man he sought to kill. Now he considered the situation his country was presently in, with all that had seemed normal through centuries of time denied by law to thousands of his fellow countrymen. No matter that many had followed their chiefs into futile battle against a regime they detested for they had done so because their loyalty to chiefs and clan had so dictated. Was it right they should they be punished by this savage removal of all they had held dear—their native dress, the pipes and their natural right to bear arms?

'It's wrong,' he snarled into the wind. 'Clan warfare there has always been, yes and unfortunate things happen in such—but what is being put into effect now by the government at Westminster is not to be endured!' But what could be done about the situation? Was the union of the parliaments impossible to unpick now—and yet one day, in the fullness of time, he sensed Scotland would become an independent land once more! Such were Roderick's thoughts as he rode.

They were now passing through the small village of Doune and there, arms pinioned to the market cross, silver head slumped forward in death, he saw an old man with sightless staring eyes. What had he done? Did it matter—yes, it did! Everywhere he looked he had seen evidence of the continuing anger of the occupying forces, men swinging from gallows along the way, the smell choking the nostrils on approach, everywhere evidence of burned out croft houses and barns. To what had this so called British justice brought this beloved land of his ancestors?

And so he rode on, deep in thought, until he saw Stirling in the distance, its castle perched high on its rocky mount and with it came recollection of why he was on this journey that would terminate in Edinburgh and revenge for a sister's dishonour.

He decided they should break their journey at Stirling that night, and made for 'The Golden Lion Inn' After a good meal and a few sullen glances from other diners, who recognised the Campbell tartan, Roderick retired to a room, Ewan Dhu and Ivor Mac Dugal keeping silent vigil before its door, wrapped in their plaids. Both they and their horses were well rested the next morning. Again Roderick insisted on an early start and was about to mount his stallion when he heard a voice hail him.

'Captain Campbell—Roderick, is that you?' He swung about and saw a fair haired, uniformed officer in Campbell tartan beckoning him. He stared back in delighted surprise,

'Why it is Major Kenneth Campbell of Kilrannoch is it not? Well met, sir!' he exclaimed with genuine pleasure. 'Are you stationed in these parts now? I have not seen you in over a year!'

'Not so surprising when you leave the army and bury yourself on the banks of the Tay,' reproved the other with a smile. 'Where are you bound for today, cousin Roderick?'

'Edinburgh!'

'Good! We will ride together. I have been on leave and visiting my estate—must now return to the castle garrison!'

'Ah—the castle!' said Roderick sombrely, his smile fading.

'You have business there, my friend?'

'You could say that. Final business with an officer there—a Captain Bradshaw!' and his lips turned up as he came out with the name.

'Richard Bradshaw, whose very name pollutes the mouth? Who is known as worse than Fergusson in his cruelties?' the other demanded curiously.

'The same!' was the growled response.

'He has offended you then, Roderick?'

'Brought hurt to one of my family. I intend to challenge him to a duel—to kill him!'

'Then you will need a second—and I will be privileged to take this part!' And the major bowed courteously as the two of them clasped hands, while the two ghillies looked curiously on from their garrons, and waited for their master's orders which were soon given as the party of four took the road to Edinburgh.

The two men chatted as they rode, the ghillies keeping some yards behind. Almost awkwardly at first, Roderick started to mention his feelings on all he had seen on the road of the atrocities still being meted out some three years after Culloden.

'I agree with you, Roderick. It's an ill business, but they say that it is the only way to break the spirit of those Highlanders who might otherwise rise up again!'

'But do you think it right, despite clan differences and the favourable position of our own clan and those who support us, that in order to implement the laws laid down by the English government in London, we must oversee and deprive our fellow countrymen of all that has made them a proud nation in the past? Why, even within our own Clan Campbell we no longer have the right of pit and gallows!' Roderick's face expressed his frustration. 'All authority of chiefs and lairds eroded.'

'I agree with you! But times are changing my friend, and I fear Scotland will never more continue as in past generations. I have even heard, and suggestion only at this stage, that eventually it may be politic to remove the remaining poor crofters and cottars from the land, their rents providing insufficient for the pockets of the lairds—replace men with sheep!' He glanced across at Roderick as he came out with this. He saw a look of new disgust pass over the other's face as that young man pulled up his stallion to snorting halt as the major hastily did likewise. They stared at each other.

'Kenneth, the thought is horrific! Not only that but physically impossible for them to enforce. After all, you cannot dispose of thousands of people. No, it is unbelievable.'

'I hope you are right—but I heard mention of plans of enforced emigration—hundreds of families from complete villages to be sent to Canada, America and Australia! Right now this is but suggestion being discussed—yet already sequestered lands of those lairds who took part in the uprising and who have been proscribed and are either in prison or have escaped overseas—these lands are being distributed among those who have no loyalty to the people. They are wishful to rent out or sell great tracts of land to southern sheep farmers.'

'Would that we had never agreed to the Union,' ground out Roderick his face dark with anger. 'I pray that one day our country may resume its independence!'

'If that is ever to come to pass in the many years ahead, then there must be eventual end to this hatred between clans—yes, and religious toleration!' Kenneth Campbell urged his horse forward and they were off again. Roderick lowered his head in agreement.

'It is sad indeed that religious hatred should cause so many wars,' said Roderick, as they rode on together. 'Surely if there is indeed a God, and I truly believe that there is, then he must be appalled at the treatment we mete out to those who do not worship in one particular way or another.'

'Yes and may he be with our people in the years ahead if all that is predicted comes about!' added Major Kenneth Campbell. 'I fear for Scotland!'

They passed an oncoming company of red coated militia marching behind a mounted officer who saluted them, noting the major's uniform. The sprawling shape of Edinburgh was coming into view on its many hills.

'Have you somewhere to stay,' inquired the major as they cantered along the Canongate. 'If not, would you care to share my quarters in the castle garrison?'

'That is kind of you, Kenneth. When last here, I was in uniform myself,' replied Roderick as they picked their way carefully between carriages and pedestrians.

'Any thoughts of rejoining your regiment?' he asked.

'None! My business is only to settle matters with Bradshaw!'

'Ah, yes! You will challenge him of course! I think you should be aware that he is expert with both sword and pistol,' he added.

'That will avail him nothing,' replied Roderick grimly, ignoring his friend's concerned expression. As they rode on there was a brief glimpse of a tall, dark haired man, in an elegant black coat, climbing out of his carriage, with distinctive doctor's bag in his hand. Brief as that sighting was, Roderick recognised Sorley Mor Stewart and his thoughts returned to Kieran and all that his aunt had told him of his sister's continuing love for the husband she had deserted—and knew that the fault of their parting was in part his. But he comforted himself with the fact she had already decided to leave the man before his intervention, he had merely made the decision easier to implement.

But deep down he acknowledged that he had really liked the Stewart doctor and knew that he owed him his life, had repaid him badly he thought uncomfortably.

Roderick Campbell was warmly welcomed by past friends, as he entered the Castle garrison at Kenneth Campbell's side. For a while it seemed as though he had never been away. He remembered the comradeship he had shared, those he had fought beside. Then thoughts of Glenlarig returned and he knew his decision had been right. The army life was truly not for him.

But where was Captain Richard Bradshaw? He saw no sign of the man. Eventually he made casual inquiry as together with Kenneth and four other officers now off duty, they made their way out for an evening's visit to a hostelry, where they might relax for an hour or two.

'Bradshaw,' exclaimed one man. 'We do not drink in his company, Campbell! When not on duty he is usually to be found at 'The Stag and Hind' a sleazy tavern run by a landlady with a bevy of willing barmaids—

if you catch my meaning. It's on the Grassmarket.' Roderick nodded as though not really interested, but an hour later both he and Kenneth Campbell excused themselves and left.

They found 'The Stag and Hind' without much trouble. It was dark inside, the smoky interior lit by only a few guttering candles, whose light illumined scantily dressed women bending over drinkers who were leaning back in their seats to fondle them and singing bawdy songs in drunken voices. Among them Kenneth Campbell spied the fellow they sought and nudged Roderick.

'There, by that pillar—see him, with that young red haired girl on his lap! They say he likes women of this hair colouring!' Kenneth Campbell was astonished at the ire his words brought up in the younger man's demeanour. For in rejoinder Roderick came out with a string of curses completely at odds with his usual courtesy. Before the major could restrain him, he had marched across to Bradshaw and wrenched the fellow from his chair, as with his girl they fell to sprawl inelegantly on the floor. Instantly the singing and laughter subsided. Men straightened up in their seats, and swung around to stare at the instigator of this commotion, nor recognising Roderick, glanced away again—mere drunken incident.

As for Captain Richard Bradshaw, he lumbered up to his feet, held onto the table to help sustain his balance and stood staring angrily at the man who had dared to interfere in his dalliance. He was drunk, but not sufficiently to block recognition of the man who glared at him from angry storm dark grey eyes.

'Captain Roderick Campbell is it not? I presume you to be drunk, sir— otherwise I would demand an apology for your behaviour,' he said slowly, wondering what had caused his recent host on the banks of the Tay, to cause such offence. 'You caused me to fall sir—and the lady!'

'The floor is the right place for such as you, sir! No place is too low for such scum!'

'You seek to insult me sir!'

'Then obviously, as man of honour you have but one recourse, sir!' exclaimed Roderick, sweeping off his hat and bowing.

Bradshaw stared at him doubtfully. He would prefer not to engage with this particular Campbell if possible, for he was known to be close kin to Lord Mamore. But the incident had been observed by many in the hostelry and if he did not react by issuing a challenge, would lose all face among his peers.

'You have offended me, Campbell! I will meet you tomorrow at dawn, on the brae beneath the castle walls, behind the tall screen of trees— pistols, sir!' He dusted his coat down languidly.

'I thank you, sir. Major Kenneth Campbell will be my second.'

'And Lieutenant Harry Blount mine! All must be done with discretion for all our sakes. Duelling officially forbidden as you will know,' he added in a low voice. They bowed to each other and then the two Campbells haughtily left, with Bradshaw staring after them bemused and wondering what real reason had occasioned the young man's ire.

Sleep came slowly on leaden wings to Roderick Campbell that night. Now for the first time, he realised the seriousness of what lay before him. Despite his recent display of outward calm and composure, he knew that the following sunrise might be his last. And so he tossed and turned and muttered small prayers for the morrow.

At six of the clock Kenneth Campbell roused him from eventual fitful sleep. Together they quietly left the castle walls beneath a fine drenching rain. Roderick allowed his friend to lead the way on the wet grass beneath the Castle's bulwarks. They reached the spot Bradshaw had proposed and found the man approaching from the opposite direction with another.

None of it seemed quite real to Roderick as the two seconds gravely asked their principals if they wished to retract their words in any way. It was to be at twenty paces. Both men's pistols were examined. Lieutenant Blount said he would call it as no other was present. Suddenly Roderick's mind sharply focussed on the present as the paces were numbered. He cocked his pistol.

At the call to 'Fire' he swung around, his foot slipping on the wet ground. The movement saved his life! His own bullet caught Bradshaw just below the heart and he fell. Roderick too staggered, a pistol shot lodged in his shoulder. Major Kenneth ran to him.

'You are wounded, man?'

'My shoulder—not fatally I think! What of Bradshaw?'

'Look for yourself—either dead or dying!' He pointed without pity to the man who lay sprawled upon the grass, and being ineffectually tended by Blount. The young lieutenant called desperately to Major Campbell, asking for help and advice. Roderick accompanied Kenneth Campbell across to the supine figure of the rapist he had made good his promise to dispose of. As he stared down at the man, who was obviously at the point of death, he saw Bradshaw open his eyes and stare at him questioningly.

'Why,' he murmured. 'Tell me why?'

'Do you remember a young woman with red hair whom you raped at the Glen of Ardoch in Appin in the spring of 46—you and your men? You killed her husband and father-in-law!'

'Red hair,' murmured Bradshaw, trying to dredge up the memory. 'And if I do—what then?'

'She was my sister! I am avenged,' said Roderick in a voice rough with emotion.

'Ah—the lovely, proud Lady Kieran Campbell—she is the same? Is it a fact? What a joke—a damnable joke! She had a fine pair of hips!' The dying man raised his head, attempted to laugh, but blood rose up from his lungs into his mouth and he choked on that laugh, the last sound he made in this world.

'I fear he is dead,' exclaimed the lieutenant, his young face strained. 'What shall I do with him?'He stared at the major seeking advice.

'Leave him there! None saw us arrive. His death will no doubt cause inquiry, but a man such as he had many enemies. Besides, if you are worried, then there are those who for a few coins will throw the carcase into the Nor Loch!'

'I know two who will do it from sheer pleasure,' added Roderick. 'My men followed us here. See they stand behind those trees.' He summoned them, gave orders. The two ghillies laughed and nodded.

'It shall be done, Laird,' said Ewan Dhu. 'We will first just remove any items the gentleman will not be needing—in the next world!'

'We would not wish to see him unreasonably encumbered,' added his companion also in the Gaelic.

'You must get that wound attended to.' exclaimed the major as Roderick swayed slightly. 'But we will need a doctor with discretion.'

'I know just such a one,' replied Roderick. 'I will make my own way to him. You two gentlemen return to the garrison. Go quickly before your absence is noted. As for me, as I am a mere visitor, none will question my coming and going.' The two officers glanced at each other and nodded acquiescence.

'Are you sure you can make it as far as a physician on your own,' demanded Kenneth Campbell doubtfully.

'Quite sure. Now go!' He watched as they hurried away. He gave directions to his two ghillies as to where they should seek him next after they had disposed of the body. They repeated the address and bowed. They would seek their master at the house of a physician named Sorley Mor Stewart.

Roderick could never clearly recollect his arrival at the house of Sorley Mor Stewart. He remembered making his way down from the castle precincts and signalling to two men with a sedan chair awaiting hire. At his call they came forward and stared at him coldly, noticing his sash of the Campbell tartan. Nevertheless they accepted his demand to be set down at the house of the physician. Their voices he realised held the soft west highland lilt, as not far from fainting with the pain of his wound he sat slumped against the side of the sedan chair suspended between its two poles, the jolting of the men's stride exacerbating the sickening agony in his shoulder.

He handed them their due. He received no helping hand as he struggled up the steps to the house, but heard their voices uttering curses in Gaelic, as they stalked away.

Sorley Mor was just finishing his breakfast as his housekeeper hurried to open the door to whoever was knocking so persistently. A fine gentleman was standing there in apparent near fainting condition. She called urgently for the nurse who was busy preparing all for the day ahead.

'Mistress Munro—Effie, I need your help!' she called and Effie was at her side almost immediately. The nurse stared at the well dressed, red haired young man, whose face was as white as chalk and whom Mistress Alison Lindsey was supporting and gasped as she helped to bring him within doors.

'Why—it is Captain Campbell,' she exclaimed, remembering his visit of the previous year. 'Let us get him lying down on the couch in the surgery and I will fetch doctor!' But there was no need, for hearing the commotion disturbing his morning thus early and realising it must herald an emergency of some kind, Sorley Mor pushed away his plate and rose to his feet. He was just in time to hear Effie mention the patient's name and for a moment he froze. Then he walked slowly towards the examination couch where Effie was trying to remove Roderick Campbell's coat—saw the blood soaking the front of his shirt and gave swift orders to Effie as he bent over the man.

He understood at once that the wound pulsing blood was caused by a bullet, and he prepared to remove it, speed essential. Roderick restrained the cry that rose in his throat at the pain he endured, heard the sound of something clinking into a metal dish held by the nurse and lost consciousness. Sorley Mor nodded his satisfaction as he glanced at the small piece of lead and bent over again as he thoroughly cleansed and then bound the wound. Roderick would survive and hopefully there would be no infection!

It was a few hours later that two men presented themselves at the doctor's door clad in the Campbell tartan. Mistress Lindsey looked slightly distrustfully at these rough looking characters who demanded to speak with the doctor—and to see their master.

'And who might your master be?' she inquired.

'The Laird of Glenlarig—Captain Roderick Campbell,' was the haughty reply.

'Come into the hall and bide there until I find the doctor,' she instructed them and hurried to get him. Dr Sorley Mor Stewart approached his two visitors curiously. He recognised their tartan and guessed them to be young Roderick Campbell's retainers. The ghillies who were muttering together fell silent as Sorley Mor Stewart strode towards them, examining his visitors with frowning gaze.

'You are retainers of Captain Roderick Campbell?' he inquired.

'We are, Sir—and you will be Doctor Stewart?' asked Ewan Dhu with forced courtesy. 'We come seeking the young laird. He gave orders we should find him here!'

'Then come—follow me,' said Sorley Mor. He led them into his comfortable living room, where a good fire was burning. Lying on a couch and covered by a warm woollen shawl, they saw Roderick Campbell. He was sleeping, his breathing even, face still pale but with slightest hint of colour in his cheeks.

'I have removed the bullet,' informed Sorley Mor. 'His wound is clean, but he will have lost much blood on his way here—is weak. I suggest he remain with me for a couple of days!' They stared at each other uncertainly. 'I take it that the Captain was involved in a duel?' surmised Sorley Mor.

'That is so, doctor. He defended the honour of his sister. The offender is no more!' At these words the doctor surveyed them shocked surprise.

'His sister, say you?'

'Indeed yes, sir—the Lady Kieran Campbell,' explained Ewan Dhu patiently. 'The man Bradshaw visited the Laird, and I imagine must have offended the Lady Kieran in some way at that time. All I know is that when Bradshaw lay dying of the Laird's bullet, I heard mention of the Lady's name.'

'He will offend her no more,' added Iain Mac Dugal. 'We did throw his carcase in the Nor Loch!'

'Ah, yes—I see,' replied Sorley Mor trying his best to respond naturally. 'Tell me, what like was this man Bradshaw?' he asked.

Ewan Dhu scratched his cheek reflectively as he considered. 'Hard green eyes, sour expression—and walked with a limp!' he explained. 'I heard say he had an evil reputation with women folk—and cruel beyond the normal when dealing with rebels in the uprising.' He looked at the doctor curiously. 'Is it that you have met the man, sir?' But Sorley Mor shook his head.

'No. But from your description, I would say he is no loss to the world!' He could hardly restrain a look of deepest satisfaction spreading across his features, for almost without doubt, the dead man must have been the fiend who had raped his wife and encouraged his men to do likewise. 'Perhaps you would care for a dram,' he added to those who had brought this most amazing news. He walked over to a cabinet and produced glasses and a bottle of whisky. The men glanced at each other. This man was a despised

Stewart—but was obviously a fine physician and known to the Laird. Yes, it was permissible to drink with him.

They had departed, told to return in two days time, when they could escort Roderick Campbell back to his home on the shores of Loch Tay.

Two hours later the wounded man stirred on the couch and opened puzzled grey eyes to stare about him. He raised his head and glanced slowly around the room, saw someone reclining in a comfortable chair by the fire, legs extended before him. He recognised Sorley Mor and uttered a cry of relief.

'Doctor Stewart—is that you?' He realised his voice was no more than a whisper. But it reached Sorley Mor who turned his head, smiled slightly and rose to his feet.

'Captain Campbell, you are awake, sir! How is your shoulder?'

'It is a little painful—but not bad as it was before! Look, I remember climbing the steps to your front door, doctor—but no more after that!'

Sorley Mor bent over him. 'I will not disturb the dressing—no need. I removed the bullet successfully. The wound is clean, should heal well. Incidentally, your men came for you and are to return in two days time, when hopefully you should be able to leave here—but not to undertake anything strenuous.' Sorley Mor stared down into his patient's eyes that were of the same storm dark grey as his wife Kieran's, brother and sister so alike in feature and colouring he realised as he regarded the young man with thoughtful gaze.

'May I extend my gratitude to you then doctor,' replied Roderick quietly. 'For the second time I owe you my life. Nor had I any right to come to your door!' And he looked uncomfortably at Sorley Mor, acutely aware of all that had happened since last he was in this house—and that mere weeks after that occasion he had persuaded his sister Kieran to leave her physician husband and make her home with her Campbell relatives.

'How is my wife?' inquired Sorley Mor in even tones.

'You know then?'

'Of course,' ground out the other. 'So how is Kieran Stewart—and our children?'

'They are well. The twins are walking now and Kieran has settled well into our late parent's home—where she herself should have been born had it not been for Rory MacGregor's cruel kidnap of our mother Catriona. But how did you learn of her whereabouts, doctor?' Roderick looked at him uncertainly.

'One who knew her came to my house with the information just recently. But I had already come to the conclusion that she had thrown in her lot with those of her own clan—with the Campbells!' His face expressed his pain.

They regarded each other in silence for a minute. Then Roderick spoke.

'How did you know she was of Campbell blood?' he asked. 'How did you find out?'

'I began to realise that something was wrong between us after her meeting with Lord Mamore! She changed—was cold and very unhappy. At first I thought it reaction to all she had endured after the Rising. But it went deeper. Perhaps if she had discussed it with me, we could have come to an understanding!' he added sadly.

My aunt and uncle love her as though she was their own daughter—and to me she is very precious,' said Roderick quietly.

'Is she happy—truly happy?'

'I do not know how to answer you. She is charming to all who meet her and a wonderful mother to the twins and on several occasions has used her nursing skills to good effect! She spends part of each day studying the classics with me, has a thirst for knowledge. But happy?' he pondered, 'How do you judge the inner state of another person—even one you love?' The young man spoke earnestly and without prevarication.

'That is answer enough,' replied Sorley Mor. 'Now rest, Captain Campbell, for with sleep comes healing!' His patient needed no second bidding, closed his eyes and drifted into slumber.

The next morning found Sorley Mor up earlier than usual, to check on a patient who was also his brother-in-law. Thought of the relationship came to him as he walked downstairs and entered his living room where Roderick was rousing himself from sleep. He noticed that his housekeeper had already attended to the fire and drawn the curtains.

'Good morning,' he said as Roderick attempted to get up, uttering a slight groan instantly bitten back. 'How is the shoulder today?'

'Better, I thank you—but stiff,' replied Roderick ruefully. 'Perhaps I should leave today----'

'No! I suggest you remain here, Captain Campbell, until your men come for you tomorrow. Now I shall be busy with my patients for most of the day, but you should be comfortable enough in here and my housekeeper will attend your needs. There are books which may interest you since you are a scholar—not all are medical books,' and he indicated his tall overflowing bookcase.

Roderick smiled awkwardly. Now that his wound had been successfully tended, he felt ill at ease in the house of a man to whom he had brought much hurt. But despite the confusion of his thoughts, Roderick Campbell recognised an inexplicable impulse to try to know the doctor better, for he found himself strangely drawn to Sorley Mor.

'You address me as captain—but I no longer bear that title. I have left the army, was no more a professional soldier than I suspect were you, merely fulfilling what I considered to be my duty!'

'What is your point?' inquired the doctor.

'Why—that perhaps we might actually try to be friends?' Roderick steeled himself for a rebuff. It did not come. Instead, Sorley Mor walked over to the window and stared down into the street below. Most of those who walked there, scurrying about their business, would doubtless pay lip service to German George and the government at Westminster. Others who had shown the courage to support the Stuart cause, the ancient royal house of Scotland, would be quietly seeking political oblivion, and hoping their exploits in the Rising would not come to light. But could he condemn them, he who had himself quietly taken up his chosen profession once more without any pointing a finger at him as a Jacobite? Life went on!

But some things do not alter, he thought. The hatred between Stewart and Campbell went deep—deep! And now he had to recognise that in order to reach out to the young wife he loved, he must put aside this hatred and recognise it for what it was an ignoble blight of the mind that had assailed the lives of successive generations. And now his wife's brother was suggesting—friendship between them?

He turned and cast a thoughtful look at the younger man. 'We will speak later—this evening,' he said and bowed before leaving the room. Roderick looked after him.

There was a knock and Mistress Lindsey came in together with Nurse Effie. The young man allowed them to wash his face and hands and to dress, for he found himself in one of the doctor's nightshirts. He exchanged it now for one of his host's white shirts, his own as the women informed him fit only to be thrown away, being much stained with blood.

Breakfast followed and after eating he felt much stronger. Alone now in the doctor's sitting room he decided to examine Sorley Mor's large bookcase and was astonished at what he found there—volumes of Greek mythology and Roman history—Caesar, Tacitus, Suetonius. He shook his head in amazement. On another shelf he saw Plato and Aristotle, unbelievable that a mere physician should have acquired taste for such knowledge. Books also there were aplenty on medical matters—surgery. These interested him but little, but there, projecting between two works on Scottish history he came across a notebook. He took it, hesitated and then opened it. Poetry, hand written—was it of the doctor's own composition? He knew he should not read it, for such was a very private matter, but curiosity overcame his scruples.

He sat reading the contents of that notebook for over an hour and when he carefully replaced it knew a deep discomfort at having uncovered

Sorley Mor's deepest feelings, his love for Kieran, despair at her departure, but also the humanity he displayed in all that he wrote of his fellow human beings. Pain too he had found in those words, pain at the death of his first wife, pain at the death of his young son blown apart by Cumberland's cannon, revulsion, shock and burning anger at the treatment meted out to the rebels by the victorious Hanoverian forces. Then strangely, sense of peace was expressed in the most recent poem, set apart by the difference of its content. It spoke of God, of belief in his Son, the Christ and of Sorley Mor's leap of faith—the inner peace it brought.

'Would that I could claim to an equal belief,' murmured Roderick slowly. This Sorley Mor was a far more complex character than he had previously assumed. The hours slipped by and Roderick found himself delving into the Iliad, the volume describing Achilles terrible anger against Hector—and as he read became acutely aware of a similar unreasoning fury and bloodlust that had recently been show in the Highlands to that evinced by the mythological hero. He also realised that Sorley Mor's own thoughts must follow equally analytical pattern as like Roderick he delved into tales of ancient man and his beliefs, and understood that human nature had not changed overmuch through passing millennia.

Not until late in the evening did he see his host again, although throughout the day Mistress Lindsey had attended to his wants, when for the most part he had rested on the couch, his wound still troubling him, but finding reading a distraction. He lifted his head when he saw the housekeeper setting the table for two and guessed the doctor would come soon. With the fire crackling its warmth and the lamps providing a soft light, the room was a tranquil place. He would miss it when he left on the morrow and wondered how he would endure the jolting journey back to Glenlarig on the back of his spirited stallion.

'How are you feeling tonight?' asked a quiet voice and Roderick looked up from the book, had not seen the doctor enter the room.

'Much better I thank you sir!' Roderick rose to his feet.

'Then perhaps you would care to join me at table. Mistress Lindsey is ready to serve the evening meal—a fowl in rich gravy with vegetables and a fruit pudding to follow she says!' The smile he cast at his visitor was not forced and Roderick rose and took a seat opposite Sorley Mor.

'Some wine?'

'Thank you—why this is very good!' as Roderick savoured the cool French wine on his palette. Little passed between them bar the courtesies during the meal, but when the housekeeper had cleared the table and left the room, Sorley Mor indicated the two armchairs set by the fire. Then as each watched the other over a glass of brandy, Sorley Mor ventured a question.

'Roderick, according to your retainers, you received your wound in a duel—a man called Bradshaw one of them said? He was of the opinion that the fellow had offended Kieran?'

'It was he who raped her, Sorley! He actually admitted the fact as he lay dying of my pistol shot—laughed as he expired!' Roderick's face stiffened with anger as he spoke. 'Had I but been aware of the facts earlier, he would not have fouled the earth so long!'

'Would that I could have got my own hands on the de'il,' snarled Sorley Mor, eyes darkening with fury.

'Well, he's dead now! My cousin Kenneth Campbell acted as my second—a young lieutenant Blount performed that function for Bradshaw. None else observed the duel beyond Ewan Dhu and Ivor Mac Dugal. They were to dispose of the body in the Nor Loch.'

'They informed me 'twas done. Whatever our political differences, I will always hold you in high regard for this action! I have heard Bradshaw was meant to be an excellent shot—you were lucky to escape with merely hurt to your shoulder. Ah yes,' he added, 'I will change the dressing later.' They sat and regarded each other in silence broken only by the staccato ticking of the handsome wall clock. At last Sorley Mor spoke again.

'The situation we find ourselves in at this time is unusual to say the least. You are in part responsible for my wife Kieran having abandoned me, leaving her home here! I should hate you for your part in this as well as despising the name you bear. Yet at the same time I acknowledge you as my brother-in-law and against all normal instinct I find I like you well! Earlier you spoke of friendship between us. I now offer you this hand of mine as friend, Roderick Campbell!'

'I take it with great appreciation, Sorley Mor Stewart!' they clasped hands and stared solemnly at each other. Then Sorley Mor chuckled.

'What is it?'

'Why—I was just wondering what Kieran would say could she see us!'

'I think she would be very happy.'

'But what now? I love my wife. If she has decided that our separation must continue for all time, then I have to accept the situation. But a small flame of hope refuses to be extinguished.' The doctor spoke calmly, quietly, watching Roderick as he spoke.

'My Aunt Lorna says that Kieran loves you still,' Roderick ventured at last, deciding only complete honesty would serve here.

'That she loves me?' Sorley Mor stared back at him in shock. 'But she has never shown anything but complete indifference to me on a personal level!' He was about to put another question to Roderick when there was a tap at the door.

'What is it, Mistress Lindsey,' he said, trying to hide irritation at the interruption.

'I'm sorry to bother you, doctor—but a message has come that Mistress Coulter is in labour two days now and the midwife despairing of bringing forth a living child!' She realised as she glanced from one to the other that the news coming at this time was not welcome. Sorley Mor rose to his feet. 'I'll get your coat doctor!' she placated and bustled away.

It was late when Sorley Mor returned home again, just before daybreak in fact. He had struggled hard on that delivery, the child lying back to back with the mother, causing much pain. But a healthy boy now nestled in the exhausted woman's arms. The small face showed some bruising but this would soon pass. He gave instructions for his patient's care to the midwife, before leaving and eventually walking slowly up the steps to his home.

The following morning after a bare three hours sleep, he made careful examination of Roderick's shoulder and sighing satisfaction, found the wound showed no sign of infection. He straightened and looked down at his patient.

'I suggest you spend another week under my roof before attempting the journey back to Glenlarig.'

'But will that not be great inconvenience to you,' responded Roderick but a look of relief was apparent in his eyes.

'If you are able to mount the stairs, then there is a bedroom where you will sleep more comfortably than on the couch—but use this room as you will in the daytime.' And so it was decided and when Roderick's two stern faced ghillies arrived to wait upon their master, they were instructed to come back in a week's time and given money for the further stabling of the horses and for their keep at the inn where they were staying.

Back at the Castle barracks questions were raised about the absence of Captain Bradshaw. None seemed to have any idea of his whereabouts, for Kenneth Campbell and Lieutenant Blount said not a word. It was a mystery. The colonel was displeased. Bradshaw would be disciplined on his return.

Mistress Lindsey was much intrigued to learn from Nurse Effie that the doctor's guest was in fact brother to the missing Mistress of the house who had deserted her husband so inexplicably. Well, he seemed a pleasant enough young man, she thought, taking any extra work he occasioned in her stride. She noticed the doctor was walking about with an extra spring in his stride and was even heard to whistle a highland air as he went about his duties.

One thought was lifting the deep sadness from Sorley Mor's mind, the fact that Roderick Campbell had stated that Kieran loved the husband she had deserted.

Chapter Ten

During the week that followed, Stewart and Campbell reached out to each other their love of literature and ancient mythology proving bond between them, and their discussions on occasion lasted into the early hours. They spoke also of recent happenings. One evening Sorley Mor was to learn of the close brush with death Roderick and Kieran had experienced on the loch, the abortive attempt on their lives by the man Grier.

'Kieran saved my life that day,' explained Roderick. 'When I lay unconscious in the boat wounded by a gunshot to the head, she rowed us to safety—tended my hurt, as on a later occasion she also cared for our elderly piper who was attacked when he played his music outside our house as was his habit.' And he went into details of the two incidents as Sorley Mor began to have some idea of the dangers to be encountered in the seemingly secure surroundings of Glenlarig.

'Kieran ever had a cool head in emergency,' exclaimed Sorley Mor. 'When I consider the hardships she endured in our cave in Appin, and the dangers we encountered travelling through mountain passes on our road here, I feel nothing but the deepest respect for her courage—as well as my heartfelt love for her.' His eyes were damp as he remembered their adventures and her warmth of manner before that encounter with Mamore. If only the Major General had not told Kieran of her Campbell blood, how different life would have been!

'So what now,' asked Roderick posing the question that was also in the doctor's mind, 'My men come tomorrow with my horse to escort me home—make return to Glenlarig! What are your own plans for the future, Sorley Mor?'

'My work is here!'

'But your heart is with Kieran is it not? Do you intend merely to let matters slide?'

'What would you have me do?'

'Tell her of your love! Let her know that it is stronger than any problems concerning family or clan. If you do not do this, you will regret it for the rest of your life!' His grey eyes held the doctor's dark gaze with relentless intensity. What Sorley Mor would have answered was not to be known, for at that moment there was a determined knocking at the front door. Another late patient, the doctor surmised, and rose to his feet. As he did so they heard voices—his housekeeper knocked and stood there with a visitor at her side.

With gasp of surprise, Sorley Mor stared almost unbelievingly at the young man who bowed, then threw himself into his embrace. It was Lachlan Stewart! Eighteen months earlier, as stripling of thirteen years, he had taken ship to France with Sorley Mor's brother David. Now in the spring of 1748 he had filled out, grown taller and at fifteen already of a man's stature. He detached himself from Sorley now and looked around. Sorley pointed to a chair.

'Come—sit down Lachlan! Mistress Lindsey, this young man is relative of mine. He will be staying here, Are you hungry lad, for we are soon to eat!' But Lachlan had now noticed the other man in the room, looked at him hard and recognised Captain Roderick Campbell—stared at him aghast.

'I remember you,' he spat out. 'You are nephew to Mamore—a Campbell!'

'Correct,' admitted Roderick civilly. 'My name is Roderick Campbell. I am also the brother of Kieran Stewart Campbell—and Sorley Mor's brother-in-law and a guest in his house!' As these words penetrated the young man's mind, he stared open mouthed at Sorley Mor, his face expressing his confusion. None of what he heard made any sense to him.

'Come—sit, Lachlan. I will explain all,' said the doctor quietly. It took almost half an hour before the youth accepted as fact all he was told. During that time, the housekeeper came to see if they were ready to eat, but at a signal from her employer quietly withdrew. At last Lachlan made to rise to his feet.

'I do not think I should be here,' he said with youthful dignity. 'I came to give you news, Sorley Mor—sad news I fear. When I have spoken of it, I will take my leave.'

'What news is this,' cried Sorley Mor, and then instinctively—'Is it David? Something is wrong with my brother David?' Lachlan did not immediately reply and he looked at the shuttered expression on the young man's face in sudden dread. 'Tell me,' he demanded, standing and looking down at Lachlan.

'No easy way to say this. Your brother David is dead! He died two weeks ago of pneumonia.' He looked at Sorley Mor in compassion. 'He wrote a letter to you before he died. I have brought it with me—and his bible. He wished you to have it.'

Sorley Mor uttered a cry of anguish. David had been his only living blood relative. They had become very close during their time together in that cave of the waters. He had thought when David had taken ship to

France that the gentle man of God would recover his strength in a land he knew, and where he would no longer have to face danger of arrest. Now to hear of his death was a blow that struck deep.

'Was a doctor called,' he choked the question out. 'Was he given due care?'

'I stayed with him until the end. We prayed together. A physician did his best for him, but you know David Stewart never really recovered from the beating he endured at Appin from enemy soldiers who lashed him almost to death. He had not the strength to endure his illness.' Lachlan looked at Sorley Mor in pity. 'I miss him, always will,' he said. 'He became as a father to me.'

'You say he sent a letter?'

'Here, in my pocket.' He withdrew it slowly and handed the crumpled paper to Sorley Mor, who walked over to the fireplace to read it in silence. When he raised his head and turned to face Roderick and Lachlan there were tears in his eyes.

'I grieve the best of men, the dearest of brothers,' he said. He turned his gaze on Lachlan. 'Do you know what he wrote?' The young man shook his head.

'The letter was sealed, as you will have noticed,' replied Lachlan. He looked towards the door obviously wishing to leave, but Sorley Mor placed a strong grip on his arm.

'You should hear this! He writes that the time has to come when there will be no more hatred between clans and that all men should work together for the common weal of our beloved Scotland. I agree with this sentiment!' He stared from one to other of those who stared at him. 'It may be hard for most in our land at this time to sink differences, to forgive cruelty endured. But it has to come about and perhaps should start here—in this room, between the three of us!'

'David was a sick man when he wrote those words!' exploded Lachlan heatedly. 'Besides which, as a priest he was bound to forgive! But I will never forgive those who killed my brother and my father!' As he spoke vision of the bodies of the slain appeared before his eyes. He stared fiercely at Roderick Campbell, as though daring him to say anything to the contrary. 'Those who raped my sister-in-law, Kieran were animals! I will be revenged upon them one day!'

Then Roderick spoke to the youth, fixing his eyes on Lachlan's flushed face.

'I want you to listen to me! The man who vilely assaulted my sister Kieran—is dead of my hand! I am under Sorley Mor's roof because I came to him for help—was wounded in the duel which removed Bradshaw from this world!' His grey eyes held the youth's angry stare, as at last Lachlan swallowed and tried to restrain his emotion as Roderick's words penetrated his mind.

'You did this? You killed that rapist officer?' He fixed puzzled eyes on Roderick.

'Yes and with no slightest remorse. He was a disgrace to his uniform, with a record of cruelty not to be endured,' responded Roderick.

'Then for this, though a Campbell, you have my respect and gratitude.' The words were forced out grudgingly, but meant nevertheless. He jerked a bow to which Roderick responded.

'As you now understand Lachlan Stewart, my sister Kieran is presently living in my house,' said Roderick. 'Should you wish to visit her there you will be welcome—as indeed will Sorley Mor.' Lachlan was about to blurt out a flat refusal, but merely shook his head. It was at that moment that Mistress Lindsey knocked and insisted that if she did not now serve their dinner, then all would be spoiled. It was a mutton stew with dumplings, followed by a steamed fruit pudding and cream. They ate in comparative silence, each locked in their own thoughts. Roderick made compliment on the meal and rose.

'You will wish to speak together in private,' he said understandingly. 'I will retire to my chamber.' As the door closed behind him, Lachlan looked after him with a frown.

'You have actually accepted this Campbell as a friend,' he asked accusingly.

'Well—it was not easy at first, as you may guess! But even before I received this letter of my brother David, I had already come to painful conclusion that if ever this land of ours is to progress from hatred passed down from one generation to another—then each one of us has to make decision to put an end to such senseless hostility.'

'You speak of the impossible!'

'No, Lachlan. True certain of our clans chose to support the house of Hanover rather than our own Stuart dynasty—fought against their own people. The hurt of it will affect generations to come, unless we look calmly at what we would indeed have the future be.'

'What do you mean, Sorley Mor?'

'I mean that what all those in our land should work towards must be the future independence of our country from England! Nor are those South of the border the only ones we have to beware of—but those rapacious landlords who plan to rid their lands of those who have lived there for centuries of time—and replace them with sheep!'

'What is this?'

'So far it is merely a plan talked about by some lairds who have taken over properties of highland chieftains proscribed for their part in the rising!

They need money to keep up a certain style such as they have observed amongst the English aristocracy. Sheep will provide the money for this. This clearance of people may not come about in our lifetime—but come it will!'

'But what would they do with the crofters who live in these lands?' demanded Lachlan urgently.

'It has come to my ears that they plan to send them to lands overseas—to Canada, America and Australia!' Sorley Mor held the young man's bewildered gaze with sympathy. 'So you see, Lachlan—the old clan feuds will be as nothing to what this uncertain future may bring to our people.'

'I just cannot believe it,' said Lachlan, his voice shaking. 'Perhaps it is just idle talk. After all, despite the depredations, think how many thousands of people live across the highlands and islands? It would be impossible to remove all these!'

'Well, as I said, it may not happen in our lifetime, lad—but I fear it will indeed come to pass. So in the meanwhile, should we not instead of perpetuating hatred, despite the horrors we have all undergone—look to the future, try to leave past ills behind.'

'But you saw what the devastation wrought in the highlands by the English and those clans such as the Campbells who support them. Our people shot down like dogs, whether involved in the rising or not—forced starving into the high places for refuge, their beasts and sheep stolen by the thousands and sold for profit, their houses destroyed, even the poorest dwellings raised to the ground, put to the torch!' Lachlan's eyes burned with anger as he continued, 'Women and their children wandering naked in the hills in winter to starve to death! How then can you expect any who have endured all this to merely turn the other cheek?'

'I think you heard that last phrase of my brother David! Words that are those of the Christ himself—impossible words to observe in our own strength, but possible through His I think.' Sorley Mor smiled at the young man with compassion. He recognised the hatred that fell from Lachlan's lips, for similar phrases had been uttered by him on many occasions.

'I must go!'

'Go where?' inquired Sorley Mor.

'I do not know—I will find work of some kind. Before I leave though, there is matter of the bible. Wait till I find it in my bag!' He delved into the canvas bag that obviously held all his small possessions and when he straightened, held the battered leather bound book towards the doctor. 'David wished you to have it,' he said simply.

As the doctor accepted the bible, tears misted his eyes once more. He remembered the times he had seen David reading from it—had used it when he had married Sorley Mor to Kieran during their time together in the cave of the waters. So many memories! He also recalled Kieran's own love for Lachlan as for a younger brother and knew he could not permit the youth to go wandering off into the Edinburgh night, where a chance word spoken against the English government might result in his arrest by the militia who still patrolled the streets.

'You will sleep here on my couch for the night,' he said firmly. 'Roderick Campbell leaves tomorrow and you may then take his room. My housekeeper Mistress Lindsey, whom you have met, will provide you with a pillow and blankets—nay, not a word!' There was relief in Lachlan's eyes that the decision had been taken out of his hands. He had indeed worried as to where he would go.

'Thank you,' he said awkwardly. 'Perhaps there is something I can do in return to help you, Sorley Mor?'

'We will talk of it in the morning. Rest now!' and Sorley Mor left the room and obviously gave orders to the housekeeper, for she bustled back in with the bedding and gave Lachlan an encouraging smile. He fell asleep as soon as his head touched the pillow, exhausted by the trauma of David's death and the journey from France and all he had heard since he arrived in the doctor's house.

Roderick had departed with his two wild looking clansmen and Sorley Mor though relieved to see him go, knew he would miss their conversations, for despite himself he had come to have a strange affection for the young Campbell. He remembered Roderick's last words to him before mounting his stallion.

'If you truly love my sister—then let her know it!'

Lachlan had stood at his side as the Campbell landowner clattered off along the cobbled street, closely followed by his men on their garrons. He looked at Sorley Mor uncertainly.

'You treated this man as a friend?' the words were part accusation part question.

'He is Kieran's blood brother,' replied the doctor shortly, staring as a redcoat troop appeared around a corner and were now marching along the street. 'Come, I must get back to my work, my patients await me. As for you, make yourself comfortable in the bedroom Roderick occupied.' The youth nodded obedience and found Mistress Lindsey already putting clean linen on the bed. It was the same room that he had shared with David during their stay with the doctor eighteen months before and when Kieran had slept in the neighbouring chamber. He knew that there were another two floors above this one, where the rooms remained unfurnished, unused. Sorley Mor had been gifted this dwelling a few years before the 45 in the will of a rich patient he had treated.

He did not see Sorley Mor until evening, longed to get away from the house of one he had esteemed as a patriot and man of courage, who now associated with those who were friends to the House of Hanover. He had thought long on all that Sorley Mor had said about the future and dire events that might come to pass. But he was young, his thoughts solely of the present and coloured by his despair at all that had befallen his beloved highlands.

As for Kieran, he thought he would never be able to forgive her for deserting Sorley Mor. Difficult though it would have been to have overlooked her Campbell blood—yet she had been fostered by the MacGregors and raised as their own and twice a Stewart bride. How could she just have turned her back on all that? So ran his thoughts as he waited for Sorley to finish with his last patient to wearily enter his sitting room and slump into his chair by the fire.

'I have decided to return to France—enlist in one of the French King's regiments,' he declared as Sorley asked whether he had any plans for the future.

'Indeed? Would you rather kill men then, than heal them? I was going to suggest that you spend two years assisting me here—then university at Leiden! You have a good head on your shoulders, studying should come easily to you with diligent application!' He smiled at Lachlan's heated young face, knew the hurt the youth had endured at the loss of David—and what he could only have thought of as Kieran's flagrant disloyalty in making home with her Campbell relatives. To Lachlan there was only black and white, nothing between.

'You would make me into a physician?' Lachlan stared at him in astonishment.

'There are worse careers!'

'But I know nothing of medicine, have no leaning towards it!' Lachlan was bewildered at the suggestion. But as he encountered Sorley Mor's steady gaze he began to consider the doctor's words. Was his only real choice a decision either to kill or to heal? Did he in fact really desire either as a way of life?

'There is something else I would prefer to do—but know it to be impossible. When I was in Paris, I watched artists at their work—bought paper and attempted a few poor sketches. David encouraged me in this. But I realised I could never make a living at it and so the only alternative—the army!' He looked at Sorley Mor defiantly. The doctor nodded musingly.

'You do not have to make your mind up now. All I will say is that it takes many years to become a successful artist—but I imagine it can be an interesting pastime. Is it perhaps that you seek to recapture in sketch or painting the wild places that still pluck at your heart?' He saw from the expression on Lachlan's face that he had guessed rightly.

'I miss Appin—miss Glen Ardoch! I feel as though I have a deep wound in my chest, one that will never heal. In France I tried to put the hurt behind me, but in the quiet of the night it always afflicts my dreams.' He was speaking from the heart now, trying to make this man whom he had revered as brave and loyal Jacobite but now sunk into the anonymity of a pedantic physician, understand his distress.

'Lachlan, after the disaster that was Culloden, we have to put dreams of a Stuart revival from us—begin to shape a new future. Those who remain rooted in the past, will not succeed in ought but bringing retribution on their heads—and what good will that do them? Instead all sensible men must plan and put themselves in position where they can reshape the future of our land.'

'Are you saying that we must accept the House of Hanover and all it stands for?

'At this time I would say there is no option. But one day Scotland will be free again. It may take many years, centuries perhaps. But freedom is a vibrant flame that forever burns in men's hearts. Sometimes the flame may flutter, seem to dim—but always it will burn brightly up again. Believe this—accept it—and let go of the past!' His dark blue eyes held Lachlan's troubled gaze.

'Think on it, Lachlan,' he said.

Sorley Mor's patients became accustomed to seeing a serious young man standing at their doctor's side, as he examined their bodies and prescribed for their ailments. Seemingly the youth was a medical student. Certainly he had a quiet and sympathetic manner which endeared him to most. Nurse Effie Munro took Lachlan under her wing, the presence of the young man helping to assuage the hidden hurt in her heart for loss of her only young son who had died at Culloden and Lachlan took comfort from her motherliness.

The welcome sunshine of late May warmed the old stone of Edinburgh's overcrowded houses, all seeming to struggle upwards seeking the thin sunlight their very proximity precluded. But that same sunshine intensified the nauseous smells of stinking open sewers and noxious waste of the Nor Loch. Plans were now being put forward once again for the desired New Town to be built, whereby those of wealth and some standing might escape the confines of the present city.

Sorley Mor paid a visit to his old friend and lawyer Mr McCrombie. The old man was suffering stiffness in his limbs which his enforced sedentary life style did not help. He fixed his inquisitive eyes on the physician, noting the same underlying sadness in his friend's gaze.

'So, you are to make a doctor out of young Lachlan Stewart? I remember the boy well, a fiery young Jacobite with a tongue that might bring him into trouble unless curbed. How old is he now?' He leaned forward in genuine interest.

'Fifteen years—nearing sixteen and would perhaps be considered over young to take on as a student, save that all he has been through has matured him beyond the normal. He was all for joining the army of King Louis as many other of our young men have done. But he is worth more than that. He has a keen mind.'

'And I suppose he reminds you of Kieran Stewart? It came to my ears that you entertained Captain Roderick Campbell at your house a few weeks ago?'

'How did you come to learn of that?' wondered Sorley Mor in amazement.

'Nothing happens in Edinburgh that goes unnoticed. Always remember that. I also heard that a certain Captain Bradshaw disappeared from his posting at the Castle at much the same time. A mystery it would seem!' he watched Sorley Mor's face but the younger man merely looked back blankly at him.

'I never met the fellow,' was all he said. 'I heard he was of ill repute.'

'Was—not is? You fancy him dead perhaps?'

'I know not and care less! Members of the occupying force are of no interest to me,' he replied firmly.

'But of course not—yet you entertained a Campbell under your roof?' he probed. 'Did Roderick Campbell bring you word of your wife Kieran?'

'He did and she is well, as are the babies—wee Alan and Ishbel are walking now it seems!' he said despondently, 'Would that I could see them.'

'Then why not make visit to Glenlarig?' The old man leaned forward and regarded the doctor compassionately. 'Who knows, she may be hoping for some sign from you that you still love her.'

'Even if I wanted to, I could not possibly leave my patients without a doctor.'

'Yet they managed well enough when you followed Charles Edward!'

'That was before I came to have such pressure of patients from beyond my immediate area. Even my nights rarely pass without a call on my time.'

'Then why not consider taking a partner? Find a well qualified man you could put your trust in! Then you could take a few weeks away to visit Kieran!'

'I could never do that. Listen my old friend, I have a dream that in the years ahead, once Lachlan has studied at university that he may return and work with me, eventually take over the practice when I retire. This is my tentative plan.'

'A good plan indeed—if it should work. But to put all your hopes in a lad not yet sixteen and who may not have the staying power to succeed—well, just consider your own future happiness. You must meet with Kieran, seek reconciliation of your marriage—or for both your sakes, put an end to it! Take a partner on, even if only for a few months so that you can make journey north—find answers!'

Sorley Mor did consider McCrombie's advice. He certainly could do with help and it would be many years before Lachlan would be of any real use. His plans for the young man would take many years to materialise and also depend on the youth's own diligence in study. But where would he find a physician not sunk in the maze of past discredited ancient beliefs, but with a mind open to new knowledge? For Sorley Mor realised that medicine was at a crossroads, so much yet to be discovered as man started to unlock the mystery of the human body and its functions.

There were so many questions. What actually caused disease and how was it passed from one sufferer to another? By physical contact in many cases, yes—but exactly how? Then again, why when a wound had been carefully tended and appeared healthy should infection set in and sometimes death follow? Why—why-----why? He had a suspicion that lack of cleanliness played a part.

And the greatest question of all. Why was there as yet no satisfactory way of relieving the pain of surgery beyond the debatable practice of making the sufferer drunk? It was with this last concern in mind that he agreed to accompany Lachlan who was curious to observe an operation to visit Surgeon's Hall, where patients endured surgery with proceedings open to the view of students and the general public.

As they pushed their way to the front of the chattering crowd who surrounded the platform on which the surgeon was about to commence work, Lachlan almost changed his mind about wanting to be there. He stared at the paunchy little man who stood bowing to all with self importance, before signalling that those who held the patient's arms and legs should be ready to control him. Then he bent over the leg of the middle-aged man who lay before him, whose face was working with terror. What followed would remain starkly in the youth's mind for years to come!

The surgeon had worked with incredible speed, using knife and saw and depriving his patient of a limb crushed beyond repair by a load that had fallen from a crane and crushed his leg. The man's screams were terrible to hear, but the medical students who observed the case were for the most part hardened to hearing such sounds and watched the surgeon his hands red with gore, wipe his scalpel on his filthy apron as he bowed in satisfaction to the plaudits of his audience.

'I am surprised the man survived the operation—thought the pain would have killed him,' ventured Lachlan shakily as they made their way out of the theatre.

'Because of the pain to the patient, speed is essential in such surgery. There is always much loss of blood. He lives for now—but there is possible danger of gangrene setting in later!' explained Sorley Mor.

'That place was like an abattoir,' exclaimed Lachlan. 'I am certain now that I do not wish to become a surgeon, just a good physician!' They were almost free of the crowd when Sorley Mor was accosted by a tall man who looked to be in his thirties. He had an open expression, fair hair and shaggy eyebrows over eyes of a greenish hazel. But what marked his face out was a scar that ran from the right side of his forehead to the corner of his mouth. He was almost as tall as Sorley Mor.

'Is that you, Dr Stewart?' He placed a hand on Sorley's arm to detain him. 'Do you remember me? We met Falkirk back in 46!' He had uttered the words quietly, not wishing to be overheard. 'Grant,' he said, 'William Grant—a fellow surgeon!' Sorley Mor stared at him and drew in his breath sharply. He had heard this man had been arrested in the aftermath of Culloden and forced into prison ship like countless others destined for London, either to die in the confines of the stinking hull of infection or starvation, or be put on trial as a traitor. Yet here he was in Edinburgh.

'Yes—I know you,' said Sorley Mor hastily. 'I suggest that you accompany me together with my young relative Lachlan Stewart here, back to my home where we may talk privately.' The three of them walked away from the Hall of Surgery. They took a hackney carriage and Sorley Mor breathed a sigh of relief as he walked up the steps to his house. This man Grant was the first he had met in Edinburgh apart from McCrombie, who knew that he had taken part in the rising.

He introduced him to Mistress Lindsey as a fellow doctor and said the man would be his guest at dinner that night. Lachlan was then instructed to help Nurse Effie with any dressings that needed to be changed, only to call him if really needed that afternoon. Now his guest faced him in an armchair as they drank a toast to other days in fine whisky malt.

'So I was right! You were taken aboard a prison ship! Now tell me—how did you escape the clutches of devils that held you on such ghastly vessel, for I have heard of the frightful conditions prevailing on such?'

'I was originally forced onto the 'Jean' out of Leith—then transferred to the 'Pamela' at Tilbury. After many months crammed into a hold, in state of near starvation, being fed the foulest of stinking offal and all of us lying in our own ordure—it was then in despair I pretended death! I was lying between two corpses. The jailors released my fetters—put a heated iron to my heel to make sure! How I managed to control my pain at the agony of it I do not know. But they were satisfied, and I was thrown overboard with the other two like so much carrion!'

'So—into the Thames then,' questioned Sorley Mor as he listened in horror. 'You must have been so weakened by lack of food, no exercise—how did you manage to survive in the river?'

'I almost drowned, found myself blacking out and almost welcomed forthcoming death. But something sprang up in my mind, the memory of my home in Glen Moriston, a refusal to give in having survived thus long. I half swam half drifted to be cast up on the muddy shore, coughing and choking—I fainted.' His hazel eyes widened as he told of his sufferings.

'What happened next,' inquired Sorley Mor.

'A fisher girl found me! She turned me on my side, helped force the water out of my lungs, took me into her boat and rowed downstream to small inlet where she and her elderly father had a wooden shack. Why they risked their own lives to save mine I shall never understand. I was given some of her father's old clothes, for I was naked save for a loin cloth. All aboard the Pamela had been in like condition.'

'What a brave lass,' breathed Sorley Mor.

'I will never forget her! Tall for a girl, big boned, a red weather beaten face and a slow smile—she said her name was Beth. Well I found work in a brewery in Kent, gradually made my way back north taking any work I could find in the towns I passed through. I arrived in Edinburgh two weeks ago. It was with thoughts of taking up my profession again that I visited the hall of surgery today, met you.'

'So as far as the authorities are concerned, you are dead,' exclaimed Sorley Mor in satisfaction as his mind pondered a future plan for this fellow physician.

'I have changed my name—no longer William Grant but call myself John Patterson!'

'Where are you living?'

'In a cheap boarding house behind the Grassmarket—I must find work soon, the little I have earned doing menial tasks is all but gone,' he confessed.

'Do you wish to resume your work as doctor of medicine—or is surgery your preferred option?'

'Like all doctors and surgeons who flocked to the Princes banner, I performed rough surgery at that time, anything necessary to save lives! But I am qualified as a physician, it is what I am! Having observed that exhibition today only confirmed my resolve. But to set up as a physician in Edinburgh, I will need to display my credentials. And how can I do so? I qualified in Paris, spent further studies in Holland—but under my real name of Grant. I dare not set up in this name in case it should be recognised!' His face bore a despondent look.

'How would you like to work here with me, John Patterson?' He knew as he made the suggestion that it was the right one. He had instinctively taken to this highlander from Glen Moriston and after all the man had endured it seemed like fate that they had been brought together that day. His dark blue questing eyes held his guest's gaze as he waited for an answer.

'You really mean it?' New hope blazed in the other's eyes.

'I do. I cannot afford to pay you a great salary at this time, but the practice grows bigger by the month and I need help! How say you—John?' The other man looked as though he could hardly believe what he heard. To be offered this chance by a man he barely knew, was too amazing for words. In fact all he managed to murmur was but the one word.

'Thank you!' he choked out, as his eyes said so much more. He held out his hand which Sorley Mor took in a firm clasp. 'Dr Stewart, you will never regret this day, I promise you!'

'Well, for the now you will sleep on my couch, but I have other rooms above stairs so far unfurnished—I will have one prepared for you over the next few days. Do you need to return to your lodgings to collect any belongings?'

'Merely an old suit of clothes—and a battered bible!' the man replied. 'It was given me by the fisher lass. I always keep it by me for her sake.'

'You can retrieve these on the morrow.' It was at this juncture that Lachlan knocked and entered the room, saying the last patient to have dressings changed had been attended to by Nurse Effie.

'Ah, Lachlan! Let me introduce my new partner who will be living and working here—Dr John Patterson!' exclaimed Sorley Mor smilingly The youth looked at the shabbily dressed newcomer in astonishment. Had wondered why Sorley Mor had invited him home. A slight feeling of resentment arose in his breast that another was to work alongside the doctor, to be immediately dispelled as Patterson smiled at him and offered his hand.

'I hear that you are embarking on those years of study necessary to become a physician! If I can help you in any way Lachlan, be assured I will!'

'Why, thank you Dr Patterson. I know I have much to learn,' he replied, deciding that he liked the man.

A week later, Patterson was already showing his mettle as a physician as Sorley Mor began to relax in the knowledge that his new partner was a good diagnostician as well as having the ability to put his patients at their ease and blessed the chance meeting that had brought their friendship about. He had provided money for John Patterson to buy new clothes and had set about furnishing the rooms on the second floor of his house one of which now served as his partner's bedroom, the adjoining room as a small sitting room.

Although he would have trusted Lachlan with his life, Sorley Mor had not made him aware of Patterson's real identity, for even a small slip of the tongue might have brought danger not only to the former William Grant, but also to any aiding him. Nor had Lachlan questioned why a physician should have presented himself to them in such impoverished condition. For all over Scotland men of previous substance were suffering for their political beliefs. One merely accepted that such was the case.

Mistress Lindsey was also much taken with the new doctor, glad to see that Sorley Mor was walking with a lighter step, enjoying the camaraderie between them, as for Nurse Effie, she said the handsome Dr Patterson was a real charmer. Now night visits were shared between the doctors. All was going well.

Towards the end of June, Sorley Mor began to make tentative plans to take two weeks away from Edinburgh, in the reassuring knowledge that he could leave his practice in the safe hands of John Patterson. He took the man into his confidence regarding the situation in which his wife Kieran had left him and was now living with Campbell relatives on the shores of Loch Tay.

'My friend, I feel for you in such situation,' exclaimed Patterson compassionately. 'I believe you have to see her, discover if there is any likelihood that you may be reconciled—if you can personally come to terms with her Campbell blood! You know people are more than extensions of their forebears. Love can overcome all such problems!' His hazel green eyes examined Sorley Mor thoughtfully. 'See if you can bring her back here—and the children,' he suggested.

After giving careful instructions to Patterson and Lachlan, the doctor began his journey to distant Glenlarig. The die was cast. What would be would be! He left Edinburgh behind and decided to break his journey with an overnight stay in Stirling.

The next morning the sun beat down on his head as Sorley Mor Stewart mounted on a sturdy chestnut mare, saddlebags containing not only change of clothes, but a small medical bag in case of emergency, left the town of Stirling behind him as he took the road to Callander and Strathyre. All was uneventful despite being twice halted to give account of his identity to despondent troops of militia, who were frustrated at not finding any supposed rebels to arrest.

Sorley Mor's appearance, the fact that he was an Edinburgh physician and on his way to visit with a prominent Campbell family resulted in only a few desultory questions. But he drew a sigh of relief each time he was allowed to pass.

The first encounter with a redcoat patrol occurred while proceeding along the shores of narrow Loch Lubnaig, where the summer wind was ruffling the waters beneath the shadow of Ben Ledi. The second as he drew level with the track that led off the road in the direction of Balquidder and Loch Voil above which in their mountain fastnesses the proscribed MacGregors now lived in hidden caves and stealthily lifted the cattle of those who supported King George.

He stopped briefly at the Kingshouse Hotel for a meal where he received suspicious glances from the landlord, before travelling on towards the village of Lochearnhead. The place seemed deserted. As he glanced sadly about him Sorley Mor noticed an absence of people, but saw the usual pathetic ruins of burned cottages and barns, a few sheep scattered over the hillsides. He was riding higher into the hills now through a narrow pass where to the left hand side of the rough road the land fell away down into a deep glen where a burn raced in its course.

Again he saw just a few sheep—no people. His mood grew blacker as he rode. Whilst living in Edinburgh, it had been all too easy to forget what had actually happened to the highlands and its people. But how beautiful it was, the first sprigs of bell heather gleaming red between the bracken, small burns racing down the hillsides like silver lace, the sky a brilliant blue dotted with puffs of white cloud. A fine stag surveyed him from the top of a brae before disappearing into a cleft in the hillside below which boulders had fallen onto the floor of the glen as though thrown by a mighty hand.

This was not his own dear Appin, but was very fair he thought. There was a slight chill in the air now and he realised evening was almost upon him. But at this time of the year it remained light until quite late. The sinking sun threw a rosy haze over everything, before the clouds turned red, purple and magenta and the hills stood out darkly against the burning sky. He wondered how much further Glenlarig was. He hoped to find it before nightfall. He knew it was on the shores of Loch Tay and that to reach the loch he had to turn right once he reached a point where the River Dochart exploded into spectacular falls.

The track ran alongside the river, with no sound of fierce rushing water. Then at last he was almost at the cataract. Now, on this quiet summer evening it did not seem to be too impressive, but imagined that when in spate it might be formidable.

'Halt! Who are you man! Give an account of your presence here,' cried a sudden guttural voice and an armed highlander, sword in hand stood across his path. His horse shied and Sorley Mor fought to restrain the beast. He was almost too startled to reply at first, then drawing himself up glared authoritatively at the man.

'My name Dr Sorley Mor Stewart and I am seeking the house of Captain Roderick Campbell,' he replied haughtily. To his surprise the man sheathed his sword and gave a shout of welcome.

'Is it yourself then Doctor Stewart? Do you not remember me—Ewan Dhu! We met when you were caring for the laird in your house in Edinburgh. Mind you removed that pistol shot from his shoulder?' The man smiled at him. A kindness was never forgotten in the highlands. The doctor was welcome here and he beckoned Sorley Mor to follow him as he trotted before him at a quick, tireless jog.

The pathway they took through scrub birch and heather soon brought them close to the head of a broad sheet of water, stretching between mountains and hills as far as the eye could see, disappearing into the far distance. Ewan Dhu explained that this was Loch Tay, fed here at its head by the confluence of two fine rivers, the Dochart and the Lochay. He lapsed into the Gaelic now and Sorley Mor replied in kind.

A pheasant flew up from a clump of heather with a great whirring of wings as they passed and the slim shape of a weasel darted across their path. The sun had long sunk now and Sorley Mor could see little in the misty gloaming, it being past ten at night. Of a sudden another man appeared, leaping down from the bank above them, blade in hand. But Ewan Dhu held up his hand.

'Put away your skene dhu, Ivor—I bring a friend of the Lairds with me. You will mind the Edinburgh doctor—Sorley Mor Stewart?' His fierce looking, dark visaged friend stared and his bearded lips broke into a smile.

'You are welcome here, doctor,' he cried in soft sibilant tones and fell into step with Ewan Dhu as they started off again.

'We are there,' explained Ewan proudly, as glancing to his left Sorley Mor saw the shape of a great house soaring high on the hillside above them. They started to climb the steep brae towards the Campbell mansion proceeding between massive gates their pillars surmounted by strangely shaped stones and followed the driveway upwards arriving in a wide courtyard. Sorely Mor dismounted wearily and glanced around as men started to pour from the side of the house and surrounded him. A word from Ewan Dhu satisfied them and they fell in at the stranger's side as he was ushered up the steps of Glenlarig House, when the massive door opened to reveal a tall, somewhat dour looking silver haired gentleman dressed in velvet and tartan, who stared curiously at Sorley Mor.

'Good evening, sir. I am Sir Iain Campbell. May I know the name of my visitor,' he inquired courteously, as he examined the tall dark haired, blue eyed man who stood so imperiously before him.

'Dr Sorley Mor Stewart. I come seeking Roderick Campbell—and my wife Kieran Stewart!' he replied and saw the sudden shock in the other's eyes.

'You are welcome, sir,' Iain Campbell managed. 'Had you sent word of your visit, I would have arranged for you to be met, conducted here.'

'I had a welcome escort here—Ewan Dhu and his friend who visited my house in Edinburgh back in the springtime, when I was able to be of service to Captain Campbell.'

'My nephew spoke of your kindness and hospitality at that time. We must now extend similar courtesy to you, doctor.' He beckoned him into the great hall, where Sorley Mor cast a quick glance around at its splendour. He had guessed that Roderick Campbell was comfortably housed, but had not realised it was such as this.

'Come, be seated. A place here by the fire,' and Iain led him to a chair by the huge fireplace and took a seat facing him, 'A drink, sir?' He signalled to a serving man who immediately brought whisky to both men.

'Your good health, Doctor Stewart,' said his host.

'And yours—Iain Campbell,' and as his lips touched the crystal goblet, Sorley Mor was surprised the words did not stick in his throat. If any had told him that few years after Culloden, he would one day drink a toast with a Campbell, he would have thought them crazed. He realised that the older man was examining him curiously above his glass.

'I have sent word to my nephew to join us,' said Iain Campbell easily. 'As for Kieran, it might possibly be better if we do not disturb her tonight as she has already retired. We will talk after you have eaten, for you must be hungry after your journey.' He saw the sudden displeasure in Sorley Mor's eyes that he would not see Kieran directly, a look which turned to acceptance.

'It is certainly some hours since I have eaten,' replied Sorley Mor and heard his host give order to one of his servants. Shortly afterwards a young maid came in with a tray which she placed on the long, massive oak table. She bobbed a curtsey to Sorley Mor as he rose at Iain's gesture and seated himself and gratefully set to. The venison stew hastily reheated was delicious and there was fresh baked bread. As he pushed his plate aside, he realised how much better he felt after the meal.

He turned in his seat to thank Iain Campbell, but found the man had disappeared. He rose and glanced around at the portraits adorning the walls. One in particular caught his eye, that of a handsome man in his middle years. His hair and beard were silver blond and his eyes a vivid green—the same green as those of Kieran's baby daughter Ishbel.

'My father—and Kieran's,' said a well remembered voice and Roderick Campbell who had quietly entered the hall now strode over to grasp his hands. 'Welcome, my friend,' he said, real warmth in his voice. 'I had hoped that you would accept my invitation to come one day!'

'Roderick, how are you,' and he smiled his pleasure at seeing him again. 'Yes, I have finally made the journey here. Your uncle received me.'

'He told me you had arrived, thought we might like to talk alone together! Tomorrow you will meet Iain's wife, my Aunt Lorna—and see Kieran of course.'

'How is she?'

'As far as health goes she is well—still an underlying sadness perhaps, yet taking happiness in the children. They are growing fast!' His eyes examined Sorley Mor, noting his lace cravat and that his dark blue riding suit was of good material, his hair well cut. He presented a far different picture to the ragged highlander who had saved Roderick's life on the track through Glencoe. Only the steady gaze remained the same and the sense of both power and kindness you felt in the man.

'Does she ever mention me?'

'She asked after you on my return home following the duel, and when you had removed Bradshaw's bullet from my shoulder! She wanted to know how you looked—had you spoken of her during my stay with you.'

'So she still thinks of me a little? '

'More than a little I would say! You will have much to talk of on the morrow.' He smiled encouragingly at Sorley Mor. 'I will also show you around this place when you have rested. Come with me now and I will take you to your room.'

Sorley Mor stared out of the window into the summer night. The moon was pooling soft light across the still waters of the loch, the hills darkly silhouetted against a starry sky. He climbed into the welcome of the soft bed and blew out the candle on his bedside table—and fell asleep wondering what the next day would bring.

He woke early as was his custom. He saw that his bags had been brought up and placed beside his bed. Good, he could have a change of linen. Then he heard it the sound of the pipes, clear and exultant upon the air! His heart gladdened as he listened, the melody a favourite of his. Now that the pipes were forbidden by law, it was so good to hear them again— though played by a Campbell. He looked below from his window and saw the elderly kilted musician, grey head thrown back, who completed his offering with an amazing cascade of grace notes, a fine piper indeed!

He washed, dressed, stared in the mirror as he settled his cravat and wondered whether he should remain in his room until called or make his own way downstairs. As he debated the point there was a knock at the door and Roderick presented himself, dressed in black velvet jacket over his kilt, red hair tied back in a black bow at the nape of his neck.

'Good morning, Sorley Mor. I trust you slept well,' the young man inquired, with a smile. Nor did he really need to ask the question for the doctor was looking rested a determined glint in his dark brooding eyes.

'Yes, I thank you Roderick! The most comfortable bed ever I lay in.'

'Yours for as long as you will, for I am glad indeed you are here,' was the warm and courteous reply.

'Kieran?'

'She will be overseeing the dressing of the little Alan and Ishbel at this time, has not yet been informed of your visit.'

'Why not?' exclaimed Sorley Mor.

'Lorna thought to speak of it when Kieran brings the children downstairs. So shall we make our way below for breakfast now?' Back again in the great hall Sorley Mor ate hastily as he dined alone with Roderick and the doctor wondered what had happened to Iain Campbell. Then at last the door opened and Iain appeared accompanied by a lovely woman in her middle years—and behind them came Kieran. For a moment Sorley Mor could only stare as his heart started to pound with emotion as they walked into the hall laughing and talking.

He rose to his feet. It was obvious that neither Iain nor his wife had prepared Kieran for his presence, for as her eyes lighted on him, she went white with shock and uttered a cry and held onto the back of one of the tall dining chairs to steady herself.

'Kieran dear, we have a guest,' said Roderick gently, 'When Sorley Mor treated me with such kindness a few months ago, I invited him to pay us a visit at Glenlarig!' His dark grey eyes so like his sisters watched her face, saw the confusion there—and something else.

'You are very welcome here, Dr Stewart,' said Lorna in the silence that followed. 'I am Lorna Campbell, Iain's wife. My husband tells me that you arrived late last night. Had I known of it I would have welcomed you at that time, but now please know that we will do all possible to make your stay here comfortable and happy.'

'Your servant lady,' said Sorley Mor and bowed. Then his eyes sped across to Kieran. She seemed to be rallying after the shock of seeing him.

'Come Iain—Roderick. I suggest we leave Kieran and Dr Stewart to talk together for a while. We will be in my drawing room when you want us, Kieran!' said Lorna, and with that she firmly took her reluctant husband's arm, as followed by Roderick, they left the couple together. As for Sorley Mor, he could not take his eyes off Kieran. She was looking wonderful in a dark blue velvet gown with sash of Campbell tartan. He realised just how beautiful she was, her red gold hair falling in soft curls on her shoulders, lips trembling with emotion, grey eyes sparkling with tears.

'Kieran—my darling one, I can hardly believe that I am really seeing you!' he whispered softly.

'Why—do I seem a ghost,' she said lightly.

'Say a vision of loveliness rather! You are looking very well, dearest wife,' and his eyes caressed her.

'Do not call me so! We are nothing to each other now, Sorley Mor Stewart! Nor can we be since I know myself for Campbell and living now with my kinsfolk.' The words were defiantly spoken, yet there was a look of yearning in her eyes that pulled at his heartstrings.

'Whatever you may call yourself, wherever you may choose to stay, you are still my beloved wife Kieran Stewart!'

'But I am not Stewart but Campbell!' she blurted out. And as the words lashed between them, the man knew he had to make a decision. He had to accept her for one who was of Campbell blood but yet the dearest woman in the whole world to him.

He walked towards her, closed the gap between them, and while she frantically endeavoured to shrink back he reached for her, his strong hands drawing her firmly into his embrace. Then in his arms for the first time since their marriage by that cave of the waters, Kieran felt the kiss of this man she had thought lost to her pressing down on her lips as her mouth yielded its sweetness to him, and she returned his kisses with an ardour she had not known she possessed.

'I love you Kieran! The past does not matter, nor does difference of clan or circumstance!' he exclaimed huskily

'But can you truly forgive me for deserting you without a word?' she whispered, not quite believing it possible. She pulled back staring up, studying his face.

'My love, I cannot pretend that the hurt has not been hard to endure, and our time apart heavy as lead, but I came to realise that you had acted in despair as you acknowledged the truth of your birth, nor thought to share the matter with me. No doubt you feared rejection.' There was pain in his dark blue gaze as he exposed his hurt to her.

'I did—oh, I did! How could I have continued living with you pretending to be other than I was! You were worth more than being my dupe in this. Then there was the strange situation we had created for ourselves, living together but apart. It was not natural.' She blurted the words out in a faltering voice.

'No mo chridhe, it was most unnatural. I so badly wanted to speak of my love for you—but I had to hold to my promise made at the time of our marriage, when I agreed it should be in name only.'

'I was grieving Alan's death!' she cried.

'I knew it, honoured you for it. A fine man whom I was privileged to call my friend!' he said gently.

'You have behaved wonderfully well in all this,' she said, breaking away from him and walking over to the fire, staring down into its blaze. He followed her there and took her hands, forcing her to face him. She did not pull away, but hesitated, knowing that only honesty would serve now. Trembling slightly she began to explain.

'Sorley, back there in the cave of the waters, I knew that love for you was welling up in my heart, but thrust it down, feeling it disloyal to Alan's memory!' The words once out were a release. 'I felt that you had feelings for me too, but for the same reason refused to acknowledge it to be so. I do not know what would have happened had Mamore not crossed our path at Glencoe!' There were tears in her eyes now. He lifted one of her hands to his lips.

'My beloved Kieran, we have both been foolish in denying our love. Yes, it was shock to realise you were of Campbell blood, but you also have the spirit of a MacGregor and the fine courage of a Stewart! Men and women are far more than merely members of one particular clan as I now realise. What is of more importance is that we are all Scots, this dear land our home. One day I pray that it may be free of English dominion and that we may break away from this unwanted union!'

'How I agree on that!' she exclaimed. 'Oh Sorley, what time we have wasted away from each other!' Then she was in his arms again, and as he held her hard against him she could feel his passion rising and gasped at her own arousal.

It was at that moment that there was a knock at the door and two small forms ran across towards their mother, with a young maid behind and trying to restrain them. Then they paused uncertainly to see a strange man with her—a man whom she was kissing. But perhaps some slight memory of who this was stirred. Sorley Mor drew in his breath as he saw them.

'Mama—mama!' they cried. 'Want you to play with us!' they looked up solemnly, at their mother's companion.

'Come here my darlings!' cried Kieran huskily. She knelt and pulled them into her arms, kissing them repeatedly. Then she straightened. 'Come and greet your father!' she said. They looked up uncertainly at the tall man smiling down at them so tenderly. Ishbel reacted first. She walked up to Sorley Mor and pulled at his coat.

'What is—father?' she inquired innocently.

'Ishbel, how you have grown,' he breathed. He lifted her up in his arms, pushing the silver blond locks back from her forehead as he stared into those unusual green eyes, beautiful eyes, which had been of so much concern to Kieran at her birth.

'Your father little sweetheart, is a man who loves your mother and both of you in a very special way, will always love and protect you. When you are older you will understand such things.' He kissed her and put her down and turned to the little boy who was subjecting him to a frowning stare.

'Where you come from, man,' the child lisped. 'I not have father!' Looking down on him Sorley Mor realised how like Alan Stewart his little blue eyed son was, a fine boy and already showing an independent spirit, while his red hair was of Kieran's hue, his dimpled chin hers also.

'I am from Edinburgh and the house where once you lived when you were but a baby Alan! I am a doctor. I look after people you when they are sick or hurt themselves! My name is Sorley Mor Stewart! I am your mother's husband.' How much of this the young child understood was debateable he knew, but had always tended to speak to little ones with the same consideration he displayed to adults.

'Uncle Roddy look after us,' replied the child.

'Now I do so,' exclaimed Sorley Mor and without more ado, scooped him up into his arms and tossed him up and down until despite himself the little boy relaxed and began to shout with laughter.

'More! More,' he entreated, as Ishbel tugged at this interesting newcomer's jacket demanding his attention. He put Alan down and lifted Ishbel once more for a kiss. Then Kieran called to the young maid who had kept awkwardly to the back of the hall during this reunion, her hazel eyes troubled.

'Bess—come and take the children to the nursery!' she instructed. At her words Sorley Mor turned his head and stared at the girl, recognising this was the same Bess Brown whom he had employed to help care for his children. He knew she had accompanied Kieran when she had taken her precipitate departure, had not realised the girl was still with her.

'Bess, I hope I see you well,' was all he said, no word of condemnation for her complicity in his wife's desertion. She smiled back at him in relief and dropped a curtsey.

'I am very well, Doctor and so pleased to see you and the mistress together again,' she blurted, as she took each protesting child by the hand. Sorley Mor and Kieran watched them go. Then he took his wife into his arms once more, only to hear another knock at the door, which opened as Iain, Lorna and Roderick appeared and Kieran blushed as their eyes took in the rumpled appearance of her dress and her flushed face. Sir Iain Campbell tried to disguise the annoyance in his eyes. He had not anticipated this, had thought the ill matched couple might be persuaded to make final legal separation. When Lorna had suggested they send in the twins, it had been merely a courtesy to their visitor.

But if Iain looked annoyed at the turn of events, it was otherwise with Roderick. He walked towards the couple, his hands outstretched.

'Am I aright in thinking that you are reconciled,' he demanded with a glad smile.

'Oh Roderick dear—yes it is so!' cried Kieran. 'We have both acknowledged our stupidity in not revealing our true feelings for one another—my worries at what Sorley Mor's reaction would be to learn of my Campbell blood!' At her words, Roderick took her into his arms and kissed her, then shook Sorley Mor by the hand.

'Is this not all well done,' he exclaimed, turning to his uncle and aunt.

'I knew that in her heart Kieran was missing her husband,' Lorna said gently, as she approached and smiled at the couple. 'But I simply could not face the fact that we might lose one who has become as a daughter to me!'

'You are going back to Edinburgh,' demanded Iain stiffly, hand on hip. 'Will you not miss the very different lifestyle you enjoy here, Kieran?' His eyes studied her, willing her to consider the practicalities such a move would entail.

'We have not yet talked of the future,' said Sorley Mor firmly, 'but of course it will be a future shared together with our children!' Iain Campbell nodded. It was a setback to his plans, but perhaps Kieran would be amenable to advice.

'Do you as a doctor consider Edinburgh to be a very healthy spot in which to bring up small children,' he asked Sorley Mor, watching Kieran as he spoke, and saw a troubled expression cross her face.

'There is much discussion underway, plans to build a new city with fine houses, leafy walkways and squares, the Nor Loch to be drained,' explained the doctor. 'It may take a few years for it will be a major work that will change the face of Edinburgh forever.' His face expressed his own enthusiasm for the idea and Kieran smiled at the prospect. Here on the shores of the loch it was easy to forget the foul smells of ancient Edinburgh, but now memory of the stench came flooding back. It was certainly not a good place for children, although thousands existed there.

'Iain, there is no reason to make immediate plans for the future when these two have only just started to talk of it,' placated Lorna.

'Husband, perhaps you would like to walk down to the loch with me,' suggested Kieran now, not wishing to have others drawing up their future. Roderick made to accompany them, but Sorley Mor made quiet whisper that they would be alone and Roderick nodded understandingly. He watched them from the steps as they left the house and wandered off down the drive. He nodded instruction to Ewan Dhu who would undoubtedly keep close eye on them for there were always those who might offer harm to Clan Diarmid.

They were walking along the shores of the loch now, watching the waves gently lapping the shore, as the wild flowers of summer sweetened the air with their fragrance and far above their heads an eagle soared, then swooped low over the loch. When it rose from the surface of the waters, its claws bore a struggling fish.

'It reminds me of Loch Dhu and the home I still miss,' said Kieran low voiced as they stopped and faced each other. 'So much has happened in our lives over the last two years. And I am a little fearful, not sure what the future holds now that—that...' her voice faltered.

'Now that we have expressed our love for each other you would say, Kieran darling?' he said gently. 'I cannot guarantee the road ahead will be smooth only that my love will be there to sustain you in all the years to come!' He drew her into his arms and the kiss they exchanged was one of rising passion. He glanced around, then taking her hand, helped her to scramble up a small brae where wild orchids thrust their tiny pink and purple spires amidst the grass and bees visited the bell heather. He took off his jacket and tossed it on the grass and they sank down together in an embrace born of their desire for each other.

Her fingers helped his to undo her tight fitting bodice and she cried out as his lips found and caressed her hardening nipples, as later he raised her velvet skirts and she opened her thighs to receive him. And as she felt him enter her for the first time, Kieran gasped. Their climax left them throbbing still with the ecstasy of a love long denied and now fulfilled.

'My heart's darling—that was so wonderful,' he murmured as his lips sought hers again before he rolled on his side, lifted her head onto his shoulder and stroked her tumbled red gold hair. 'I will never forget this wonderful hour when first we consummated our love. And just think Kieran, this is just the beginning of our real marriage, which will be one of deepest love that nothing will ever alter!' His dark blue eyes were full of tenderness.

'I love you, Sorley Mor,' she whispered softly.

Later, much later they tidied their clothing and rose to their feet. Sorley Mor thought he heard a sound above his head. He climbed higher on the brae and looked around, saw nothing—but then the sound of gunshot shattered the peace of that place—once—twice, and the larks ceased their song! One of the bullets missed his head by inches! The second wherever it went was followed by a scream of pain from above him on the hill. Sorley Mor sank to the ground and crawled back to where Kieran was sheltering behind a heather bank.

'Are you hurt,' she cried in distress, her face white with shock.

'No, but the bullet came unpleasantly close. Now who would wish me dead do you suppose?'

'May be it was someone who hates Campbells and considered you to be one!' she faltered. The thought that she might have lost him, filled her first with shock and then a growing anger.

'We need to take shelter—over there, those rocks down by the shore—see them. Come Kieran, bend low and run!' He took her hand but as they started to run they heard someone hailing them to stop.

'Doctor Stewart, wait—wait you there. It's Ewan Dhu! I am coming down!' Minutes later the heavily bearded ghillie was beside them. Sorley Mor regarded him suspiciously, but there was that in the man's eyes that made him relax.

'Doctor—you are unhurt?' cried the man, examining Sorley Mor anxiously. As the doctor nodded his head in the affirmative, Ewan Dhu spread his hands out in distress as he sank down beside them.

'Laird Roderick—told me to keep watch over you and the lady. I saw a man rise from the heather, a gun in his hands. As you were standing there he raised the gun, and shot even as I fired at him. But oh to my sorrow, I find that I have killed Fingal Beag one of Sir Iain's stalkers!' His face expressed his agitation at what he had done.

'But why would Fingal Beag have wanted to harm my husband,' cried Kieran, white to the lips. 'I know the man! I have often seen him talking with Uncle Iain. It makes no sense unless he simply did not recognise Sorley Mor?' But there was doubt in her eyes as she said this. As they had left for their walk, this man Fingal had been standing at the door. Suddenly she felt very cold—and frightened.

'I have no understanding of the matter either lady! I did not know who it was I fired at, only that it was one who sought to kill the doctor—and Laird Roderick had placed both of you under my protection. How to explain what has happened to Sir Iain?' He shook his head in agitation. 'But at least you are unharmed, sir,' he added.

'That was more by accident than by design I think,' replied Sorley Mor shortly, but feeling sympathy for the distress of Ewan Dhu who had undoubtedly saved his life. 'I will be with you when you explain the happening to Sir Iain Campbell. The dead man his you say?'

'Yes, and more than just his favourite stalker doctor—his own son born to Nan MacNab, but out of wedlock see you.' he explained in agitation.

'His son? I did not know of this,' cried Kieran in surprise. She thought of the many times she had seen Fingal Beag, a small wiry man with heavy brows and sneering lips. But never had she heard mention that Iain had fathered him. Did Lorna know of this she wondered now, remembering that Lorna was childless. What heartache if she did, and were there more of Iain Campbell's unofficial children scattered around? And she realised her thoughts of her white haired, dignified uncle were suffering a change.

'Come Kieran, I think we should return to the house,' said Sorley Mor, glancing around doubtfully, his one thought to keep Kieran safe from harm. If one man had shown such murderous intent, could there be others similarly engaged?

It was then that they heard shouts as people started to run down the brae towards them, demanding to know what the shots had betokened. Within minutes they were surrounded by Roderick and an assortment of workers who had dropped everything when hearing gunfire.

'Kieran—you are unharmed, thank God,' exclaimed her brother. 'I feared the worst!'

'I was the target, not Kieran. The assailant lies dead at the hand of Ewan Dhu who saved my life! The assailant was I understand Fingal Beag?' Sorley Mor studied his brother-in-law's face as he gave this information saw only shock and bewilderment in Roderick's eyes.

'But that makes no sense!' cried the young man in distress. 'Why would Fingal attempt to kill a guest of mine? He was of a mean, aggressive spirit perhaps, but had all his wits about him!' He turned to Ewan Dhu and the two of them fell into the Gaelic as he questioned the ghillie. He learned a little more than Sorley Mor had told him, confirmation that the doctor had indeed been the intended target.

'Where does the body lie,' he inquired. Ewan Dhu pointed behind him. 'Go then, take two others with you and carry him back to the house—no, to one of the barns I think best.'

'I fear the anger of Iain Campbell,' said Ewan Dhu as he called two men to assist him. 'But I had your orders to keep the doctor and Lady Kieran safe!'

'Leave my uncle to me to deal with,' said Roderick coldly. An unpleasant thought had entered his mind concerning the possible motive for Fingal Beag's attempt on the doctor's life. Surely it was thing impossible though? 'Come,' he said and the little party clambered their way back up the brae.

Kieran entered the great hall between her husband and her brother. Aunt Lorna watching from a window had seen a body carried round to the back of the house, and now stared at them in concern.

'What has happened? I heard shots—what evil has occurred?'

'Fingal Beag lies dead by the hand of Ewan Dhu, who killed him in my defence after the man's bullet missed me by a hair's breadth,' explained Sorley Mor. 'Ewan saved my life. A second bullet would undoubtedly have killed me.'

'But then, surely Fingal must have shot at you by mistake, thought you an intruder,' she exclaimed in horror. It was Roderick who answered her.

'No. When I questioned Ewan Dhu, he told me he had run to Fingal as he lay dying. With his last breath the man asked him if he had been successful in killing the Stewart doctor! There is no doubt whatsoever that Sorley Mor was his intended victim!'

'But why—why would Fingal have acted so?' She sank down on a chair in obvious distress.

'We owe a debt of gratitude to Ewan Dhu that our good name was not tarnished by such act,' said a cold voice. They swung around. Sir Iain Campbell stood there, his face frozen with what—shock—anger? His eyes bore an inscrutable expression.

'You have heard, uncle? Fingal attempted to murder Sorley Mor. It was only by the grace of God that Ewan Dhu prevented this. The question being, why this man of yours should wish to kill the doctor who is known to be our esteemed guest?' Roderick walked across to his uncle and asked the question face to face

'Perhaps he had been drinking,' said Iain Campbell contemptuously. 'Since he is dead we are unable to inquire his motive!'

'I do not believe Fingal would have dared to behave so—unless ordered!'

'What are you suggesting, Roderick?' Iain Campbell's tones were cold as ice, a small muscle at the corner of his mouth twitching. The younger man drew in his breath, uncertain how to continue. He had as good as accused his much loved uncle of conniving at murder.

'Stop it, both of you!' Lorna had risen to her feet and pushed between the two angry men. 'Shame on you, Roderick, for making such suggestion,' she cried. 'Even though Fingal admitted his intention was to kill the doctor that is no excuse for supposing Iain had any involvement with such a crime!' Then as Sorley Mor and Kieran watched in silence, the two Campbell men nodded to each other in grudging close of the matter. Iain stormed away.

Chapter Eleven

Some hours had passed since such traumatic events had put so abrupt an end to delight in consummation of their love in that grassy hollow decked with orchids, thyme and bright heather clumps. But the horror of what had happened afterwards could not destroy the now openly acknowledged deep love Sorley Mor and Kieran felt for each other. If anything, the sudden danger had only made them closer as Kieran now resolved to leave Glenlarig.

'Are you sure, my dearest heart,' inquired Sorley Mor as Kieran walked with him in the garden at the back of the mansion. 'Will you not miss all of this?' They had left the house not wanting to be overheard.

'Countless other women bring up their children in a city—we too will manage!' she replied with spirit. 'Nor would I wish to remain here with the uncertainty of why any should seek to kill you, my darling.'

'It certainly was a strange happening,' he said slowly. 'I know that Roderick suspects your uncle of involvement, but shudder to believe it to be so. Do you suppose he dislikes me sufficiently to attempt my life?'

'I know he wanted me to seek an annulment of our marriage. He planned I should make a new marriage to suitably wealthy landowner. He spoke of several such, one a friend of Roderick's—a Major Kenneth Campbell! I told both Iain and Lorna that nothing would ever persuade me to seek divorce, our marriage a true one even if we could not be not together.'

'You said that? Kieran, I am so proud of you.' His eyes were soft.

'I realise he is not best pleased to see you here! But Roderick is delighted! He has become very fond of you, my dear—speaks of your joint interest in poetry and the classics!'

'I never thought to have a Campbell as a friend, but your brother is a fine young man and I like him well despite myself!' His dark eyes watched her face as he asked, 'Will you miss Roderick over much do you suppose?'

Kieran bowed her head in thought then smiled. 'Of course I will miss him. But he can always visit us in Edinburgh,' she said practically. 'After all, he is our children's uncle!'

As though by tacit consent, the couple refrained from speaking again of Fingal Beag's abortive murder attempt. Nevertheless the grim possibility pricked away in the doctor's mind that that Iain Campbell had wanted him killed! Certainly the sooner he could get Kieran and their children safe away, the better! He resolved to speak alone with Roderick, to make plans.

Iain Campbell was absent from dinner that night, with no word as to his whereabouts, the conversation around the table subdued, Roderick appearing thoughtful his eyes stern, although Lorna presented a calm, smiling face to the couple who had endured such shock that day.

'What are your plans for the future, Sorley? I hope you may stay with us longer,' she probed as they rose from the table. He looked into her eyes, read the honesty there and knew that this gracious woman had no part in whatever her husband might have planned. Kieran had told him of her love for Lorna who had become dear as a mother to her.

'Lady Lorna, my plans are to return soon to Edinburgh, with my wife and children. We have spent almost a year apart. Kieran I know will always be grateful to you for the love and kindness which has been shown her. But recent circumstances reinforce the wisdom of leaving on the morrow.' He saw her face drop, and a deep sadness fill her eyes. But she nodded her head.

'I feared you might take this decision—understand the reason. Are you quite sure this is right for you and the children though, Kieran?' she appealed, turning to the girl, but seeing the new happiness shining out of Kieran's eyes was all the reply necessary.

'I will miss you most terribly, Lorna. But Sorley Mor and I have now truly become man and wife,' she explained blushing. 'We will make our future in Edinburgh, where I will assist my husband in his work,' adding thoughtfully 'and our children receive a good education there when older!' Her steadfast voice expressed her determination and Lorna sighed—then smiled.

'Perhaps you would wish to share your wife's chamber tonight, Sorley Mor,' she said softly. 'I am so happy for you both. I hope you will eventually feel you may bring wee Alan and Ishbel back to see me!' There was a wistful tone in her voice and Kieran put her arms around her.

'I will never forget you Aunt Lorna! Nor could I bear it if I thought we would not meet again. You have helped to bring healing to my heart—told me of the mother I never knew and of my father.' Lorna folded the girl to her.

'Go now with your husband, child,' she whispered, and smiled as Sorley Mor bowed to her and lifted her hand to his lips in salute. Roderick who had been watching the exchange now came forward asking a word with Sorley who hesitated, but knew that he must talk with the young man.

'I heard you saying you are to leave tomorrow? It saddens me that you have decided so, but after today's incident I suppose it was inevitable. I will get to the truth of it before I am done.' His voice expressed his indignation at what had occurred. 'Sad recompense for a man who twice saved my life, that his own should have been threatened whilst my guest!'

'Roderick, you have been kindness itself. I will go tomorrow, but hope we may meet again soon. I have furnished the spare rooms in the upper part of my house—you will rest comfortably whenever you have a mind to come!'

'Friend Sorley, I will ride with you tomorrow and provide an escort of my men. Perhaps we cannot be too careful as things are!' he said no more and the two men grasped hands.

Lorna went to her bedchamber, where her maid helped her out of her gown. She sat before the dressing table brushing her long dark hair, white streaked at the temples and proceeded to plait it before retiring. She dismissed her maid and knelt beside her bed, her head bowed in prayer.

'Father of all, I pray your blessing and protection on my beloved niece Kieran and her babes and the husband with whom she is now one. I am fearful for the future—so much that is unexplained...' Her whispering lips became still as the door opened and Iain Campbell stood there, swaying as he clutched onto the doorframe. He stared to where his wife knelt at the side of the huge ornate curtained bed.

'Get up,' he said thickly. 'I want to talk to you!' He lurched across to her and taking her hands pulled her to her feet.

'You are hurting me, Iain! You're drunk! I would sleep alone tonight!' she cried, wrenching free of him and surveying him indignantly.

'Perhaps you are forgetting who gives the orders in this house,' he exclaimed thickly, grabbing her by the shoulders and pushing her roughly down onto the bed.

'It is not you, Iain—but our nephew Roderick who gives orders here! This is his house! Nor would he be best pleased to see you treat me so!' She spoke coldly and stared up at him without fear.

'Roderick—this foolish boy who will not wed and produce an heir for Glenlarig! And now when we have two healthy children of the family bloodline, we are to risk Kieran taking them away with that sawbones she married? Is this what you want, wife?' The words were stuttered out between lips made clumsy by the whisky he had consumed.

'Was this why you ordered Fingal to shoot Sorley Mor Stewart?' she demanded. He made no answer but stared at her guiltily.

'I see you don't deny it! You wanted to make sure her children remained here—that was it? It seems to me fitting retribution for such cowardly act that your own son should have died in the attempt!' It was the first time she had acknowledged that she knew of Fingal's parentage. It had never been mentioned between them before.

'So you knew all along about Fingal?'

'I did to my sorrow—also that he must have been conceived at much the same time as the son I lost at birth! How do you think it has made me feel, Iain? I also know there are others of your begetting amongst the villagers.'

'Well, had you been capable of giving me sons, I might not have gone elsewhere.' Then the anger died from his eyes and he opened his hands to her. 'This Glenlarig is all in all to me! Surely you can understand that?'

She looked at him, this man she had married and shared her bed with for over thirty years. He was handsome, yes, with his tall well muscled figure, fine head of silver white hair and dignified expression, but beneath assumption of gentlemanly behaviour there lurked a darker side that she had glimpsed only on odd occasions, as today.

She had always sensed to her sorrow, that she could not really trust him. Knew it was her own position as sister to the late Sir Colin Campbell and guardian of his young son Roderick that had given him status here as her husband and joint carer of the boy and the estate. With Roderick now a man grown, Iain was finding it difficult to step back. There was no doubt that he loved Roderick, but refused to accept that the days of his own authority had passed.

'How could you wish to kill the doctor who twice saved our nephew's life?' she demanded.

'I think you forget that had it not been for Mamore's kindness, he would have been dispatched down to London and hanged as traitor with all other scum who rose against King George!' he sneered. She merely shook her head appalled at his behaviour.

'They leave tomorrow,' she said quietly. 'I only pray that they never learn the truth of what happened here!'

'Fingal's dead—no one else knew of my orders. An end to this, Lorna, I am fatigued.' He sank down on the bed, rolled over and within minutes was snoring. His wife looked down on him distastefully, unbottoned his jacket, pulled off his boots and threw a coverlet over him, then moved to a deep armchair by the fire where she spent the night. She knew she would never feel respect for him again.

In the bedchamber she was sharing with her husband for the first time, Kieran gasped in his embrace as he brought her to a quivering ecstasy, and she cried out her voice blending with the soft playful night wind that moaned about the house, 'I love you—oh how I love you!' And knowing that she was ready, he plunged deep within her and in that moment of shared passion their child was conceived.

He took her again that night, gently and slowly and afterwards they fell asleep in each other's arms. He wakened a few hours later, hearing movement outside their door—voices, then all was still. He crept towards the door, opened it a few inches. Ewan Dhu lay stretched across the threshold keeping vigil there, a sword at his side. He raised his head.

'Go back to your bed doctor—sleep soundly,' was all he said. And Sorley Mor returned to lie beside a sleeping Kieran, his thoughts troubled, and at last falling into fitful sleep.

The following morning they both rose early as Kieran gathered clothes from wardrobe and chest. She was determined to take her mother's gowns with her, but leave more recent gifts of fine clothing behind. In Edinburgh they would be starting again and she knew that Sorley Mor would provide all that both she and their little ones needed.

Bess knocked at the door and was surprised to see Ewan Dhu making his way along the passageway. He was not usually to be found in this part of the house. His eyes met the girls admiringly and she blushed. Roderick had already informed Bess that she would be leaving with her mistress and her family today, returning to Edinburgh. She would miss the comfortable lifestyle of this place but not the wild scenery which she secretly found slightly forbidding, those high mountains a barrier to all she had accepted as normal in the past. She would also miss Ewan Dhu.

But young Bess was a practical soul and welcomed the fact that Kieran was returning to Sorley Mor as his wife.

'Good morning, Bess,' cried Kieran as she looked up from the garments she was folding ready for packing. 'There is much to do!'

'It's true then, Mistress Kieran—we are returning to Edinburgh?' asked the young maid with an inquiring smile.

'Yes—and I need you to gather up the children's clothes ready for our departure! Annie will help you. Oh and I must speak to Morag Burns before we leave, see she is rewarded for her devotion as wet nurse to the twins.'

As for Sorley Mor, he made his way downstairs to seek out Roderick to discuss how best they could make the long journey back to the city with two small toddlers, Kieran, Bess and such baggage as they would need.

'I have it all arranged, friend Sorley!' Roderick greeted him in the great hall, drawing him to a window seat where they might talk unheard by any that entered. And indeed there seemed much bustle about the place, doors opening and closing just off the hall, clatter and noise of horses neighing in the courtyard just beyond.

'I found Ewan Dhu on guard outside the bedroom last night,' said Sorley seeking explanation from his host. 'You considered this necessary?'

'I would prefer to talk of it once we are away from Glenlarig,' replied Roderick quietly. 'In the meanwhile, we will breakfast as soon as both you and Kieran are ready. Ah, here comes my aunt!' He rose to his feet and walked over to Lorna who presented herself looking pale, eyes reddened, but outwardly serene.

'Good morning dearest,' he said as he kissed her. 'Where is Iain? I have not seen him today!' His grey eyes were anxious as he spoke. She stroked the folds of her black skirt before replying.

'He is sleeping still—drank too much last night I fear. We have to talk, Roderick.' Her voice was low and trembled slightly.

'We will, but not now, Aunt Lorna! Let us help Sorley Mor and Kieran prepare for their journey. It is best they leave soon I think.' He spoke firmly and she nodded her agreement as Sorley Mor now drew nearer and greeted her. They exchanged a few words together and he looked at her gently understanding her distress, tears quite obviously close to her eyes at the prospect of losing Kieran and the little ones.

When Kieran entered the room they all stared at her, for she was a different creature, her eyes sparkling with enthusiasm at the prospect of returning to Edinburgh at the side of the man she could now openly declare a much loved husband.

Servants brought their early repast to the table, with Roderick bidding them to eat well in preparation for the long ride ahead. Kieran could never really remember the details of that last morning of her year long stay at Glenlarig, as their belongings were fastened in panniers to the sides of two strong ponies and Ewan Dhu and Ivor Mac Dugal each took one of the twins securely before them on their garrons and as Roderick, Sorley Mor and Kieran mounted their own horses and turned to give one last wave to Lorna Campbell and the two dozen men and women of the household who had come out to watch their departure.

As they reached the end of the drive and passed between the pillars of its gateway, a lone figure stepped out in front of them pipes in hand and bowed. Then Angus Mac Seumas with tears in his old eyes played one of the most beautiful and haunting laments Kieran had ever heard. She bent low in her saddle as the last note died away and beckoned him to her. Her lips brushed against his face.

'I will miss you, dear Angus Mac Seumas! You are surely the finest piper ever I heard. God bless you old friend.'

Tumultuous thoughts flowed through her mind as they rode along leaving the loch behind and glimpsing the rushing falls of Dochart before turning along the track road that led south towards Lochearnhead, Strathyre and Callander and on to Stirling where they would spend the night. Was she really doing the right thing in leaving all this beauty behind and depriving little Alan and Ishbel of life in one of the most affluent and important families in the land?

Then Sorley Mor reached over and touched her arm reassuringly as they rode together, as though he guessed her thoughts.

'My love, we will return to the highlands one day,' he murmured. 'This I promise you!' She nodded, thrusting back the ignoble tears that pricked behind her eyes. 'I know how much you are giving up—understand. But I also have faith that the future will be good!' He watched her face as she jogged beside him saw the confidence with which she straightened her shoulders and knew he had nothing to fear.

Kieran Stewart was as strong as burnished steel.

They made several stops along the way, had brought refreshments with them. They were on the shores of Loch Lubnaig now, the small village of Strathyre left behind. Kieran disappeared behind some bushes to relieve herself. It gave opportunity for Sorley Mor to have words with Roderick.

'You were to tell me why you thought it necessary to install Ewan Dhu outside my door last night?' he probed. They had drawn apart from the two ghillies who now led the horses down to loch to drink. Roderick hesitated as though not wishing to speak of the matter.

'None knew you were to spend the night in Kieran's chamber save only Lorna and myself. I watched my uncle stagger drunk up the stairs towards the bedroom he shares with Lorna and I followed in case he should fall or cause distress to my aunt.' He paused.

'Go on, man!'

'Well, it was then I noticed one of Iain's fellows, a friend of Fingal's making his way towards the bedroom you'd previously occupied. I thought it strange! No cause for him to be there.

'Did you ask his business?'

'Yes. I challenged him. He muttered something about an errand for Sir Iain. I sent him away with orders he should not dare be seen in that part of the house again. I was going to demand an explanation from Iain—but it was late, the man drunk. Instead, I alerted Ewan Dhu to keep watch over you during the night.' He shrugged his shoulders. 'It could all have been an innocent mistake, but after Final's attack on you I was taking no chances!' Roderick's face expressed his concern at all that had happened.

'Why would your uncle wish me harm?'

'I think because he is attached to Kieran and the babes. He is aggrieved that I have so far avoided marriage—not produced the necessary heir to Glenlarig. If I should die childless, then the estate would probably go to my nearest male relative. That would be my friend and cousin Kenneth Campbell—unless of course Kieran's wee Alan as grandson to my late father Colin Campbell should be available as the next rightful heir!'

'The child to be under his control!' ground out Sorley Mor as understanding of the puzzle dawned.

'Exactly!' agreed Roderick. 'But wheesht now, here comes Kieran—best not to burden her with any of this.' Shortly afterwards they were on the road again. An armed redcoat troop came marching along towards them. They were ordered to halt. But a quick examination of the riders and their status allowed them to proceed again, as the militia who had enjoyed their brief rest were ordered on once more.

On the road to Stirling with nightfall approaching, they were challenged one last time by another redcoat troop. Their Captain recognised Roderick Campbell and the two exchanged greetings.

'Where are you bound, Captain Redpath?' inquired Roderick.

'The Braes of Balquidder—to search through the labyrinth of caves for any of Clan MacGregor—or whatever they now call themselves! All those hills, job a nightmare!' the man snorted.

'But it is over two years since our decisive victory at Culloden,' exclaimed Roderick in assumed surprise. 'Why then after this time do you still hunt down poor highlanders who have already lost all they possessed?'

'My orders are not to give up until all involved in any way whatsoever with the late rebellion should be arrested—brought to justice. I must say it is becoming daily more difficult to find any stray rebels.' He sighed. 'I will be glad when we may leave this miserable country and return home to England!' He noticed Roderick's expression, 'Oh, but with respect for such as you who enjoy living here, Campbell!' he placated.

'But I suppose most of Charles Edward's closest advisors, and those Clan Chieftains who have not applied to the King for pardon, must all now be safe abroad.' Roderick calmed his stallion which was pawing the ground anxious to be away, as indeed was he.

'We believe Cluny still to be living in a secret cave in the region of Ben Alder, have searched there in vain. Then there is Archibald Cameron said to have escaped with the Pretender, but whom some say they have seen back in the hills again. Nothing definite—but!' and he shrugged.

'Would that be Dr Archibald Campbell,' asked Sorley Mor, not wishing to draw attention to himself but intensely interested in this particular individual. The Captain turned and stared at him. 'You know Archie Cameron,' he demanded?

'I have heard his name that is all—was merely curious. Living and working in Edinburgh, most of these names mean little. But I have heard that this particular Jacobite is said to be a most honourable man.' His expression was inscrutable. The officer laughed contemptuously.

'And will be hanged as high as others of the brood when caught!'

After exchange of a few more words they prepared to continue their journey, as the captain fetched Kieran a slight bow. You did not often come across a woman as fair as this travelling the roads. The doctor was a lucky man.

Half an hour later they saw Stirling castle appear silhouetted against an evening sky where a few stars were already visible. They clattered into the courtyard of The Golden Lion, as Kieran experienced a pang of memory, for it was here in the inn that she had met with her brother Roderick when turning her back on Sorley Mor and her home last year—so strange to return here again.

Kieran was above stairs settling the twins in a bedroom with Bess adjacent to that she would share later with her husband.

Sorley and Roderick were enjoying a quiet drink together in an alcove of the busy dining room. Even late in the evening this place thronged with travellers. Sorley Mor sensed the other was tense and put a question to him.

'Roderick would you rather leave us to finish the journey on our own tomorrow,' he asked. The younger man did not deny it, his face troubled.

'I am partly tempted to do so, for my men will have a care of you on the road to Edinburgh. I need to see my aunt urgently,' said the young Campbell in slightly anxious tones. 'She wanted to speak to me before we left, but I felt it more important to see you safely on your way.'

'Well then?' encouraged Sorley Mor.

'But she would never forgive me if I did not see you safe all the way,' he admitted with smile. 'And certainly she is always able to manage my uncle when he falls into one of his black moods.'

'They appeared a loving couple when I met them,' said Sorley. Roderick nodded.

'I have always admired Iain for his undoubted courage. He has taken the place of a father to me and I believe he loves Lorna, but I also know he has not always been faithful to her. She has seemed unaware of his casual relationships with women of the village—or perhaps too proud to believe the rumours. She is a wonderful woman you know.'

'I believe Kieran will miss her—and you also. I hope you will visit us when time allows?' And the doctor meant his words.

'I will, my friend!' Nor could either of them have guessed the circumstances of their next meeting.

The following morning saw them set off on the last forty miles to Edinburgh. Little Alan and Ishbel had behaved very well throughout the first day of the journey enjoying the novelty of riding with the two ghillies they liked and knew well. But today they were slightly fretful, possibly sore from the jolting Bess suggested. It was early afternoon when the tired party rode into those familiar cobbled streets after first submitting to questions by guards at the city gate. Kieran wrinkled her nose at the smells she had thought left behind for all time—but would get used to them again.

The horses came to snorting halt outside Sorley Mor's residence as the door opened and Mrs Lindsey and Effie stood there to greet the doctor back from his travels—and looked in amazement to see the beautiful young woman and two small children the doctor lifted down from the care of the wild looking mounted highlanders. The housekeeper had never seen Kieran before, but did not need Effie's quiet words to realise this was Sorley Mor's wife.

Then boxes and bags were being carried up the steps to the interest of neighbours who came out of their steps to observe the sight.

'Roderick, how can I thank you? But come in—and Ewan Dhu and Ivor Mac Dugal too, as soon as the horses are stabled.'

'No, my friend—we ride back to the north now, will make Stirling before nightfall and Glenlarig tomorrow! You understand my reasons?' The two men clasped each other in a warm embrace, as Kieran tried to make her brother change his mind, but he was adamant.

'No, my dearest sister, I would love to stay—but Lorna needs me back at Glenlarig. I must go. But we will meet again soon I promise!' He kissed her and, swung the twins up for a swift embrace and then mounted and minutes later Roderick and his ghillies had disappeared from view.

Kieran drew a deep breath as the door closed behind them and she followed Sorley Mor into that well remembered sitting room where the twins were already scrambling up onto the couch and staring around curiously. His own heart was full as he drew her into his arms and kissed her.

'Welcome home, mo chridhe,' he said, 'heart of my heart!'

'It looks different,' she said slowly. 'I like it.' The heavy blue curtains were the same, the tall bookcase overflowing with yet more volumes old and new, but carpet that was new and the sheepskin rug by the fire, and a fine new glossy leaved plant stood on a small table at the window and there were comfortable cushions on the two couches. She remembered the fine painting of the Linnhe Loch above the mantelpiece. She blinked sudden tears away. This was her home, her own real home and now she had to take over the reins again.

'I must speak with Mistress Lindsey. She must be wondering about me—I suppose she knew of our separation?' She had remembered the slight look of disapproval in the housekeeper's eyes when she had first seen Kieran, but immediately transformed into a welcoming smile.

'You will like her, my dearest!' said Sorley Mor quickly. 'She is a wonderful cook and has kept this place in fine order. I think we will retain her services for you will have plenty to do with the children.' She nodded her approval.

'Of course we must keep her. Now as young Bess will have a care for the twins most of the time, it will leave me free to assist you with your patients—if that is what you would like,' she added. He kissed her.

'It is what I would dearly like,' he said. 'Now let me show you what I have done to our bedroom and nursery.'

'I think that Bess should first attend to the twins, make them comfortable after their long journey!' and she picked up Ishbel who was looking fretful. 'Then they must be fed!'

'Of course—where is the girl?' He called her name and she hurried into the room and stood looking shyly at the doctor. 'Bess, the babies need changing,' he instructed. 'I think their belongings are in that bag. Later all must be unpacked. Where is Mistress Lindsey?' As though hearing him the housekeeper appeared at the door.

'Perhaps you could help me carry these bags upstairs to the bedrooms.' He suggested, as Kieran handed Ishbel over to Bess, with little Alan also clamouring for attention. Between the three of them the bags and boxes were soon deposited in the bedroom and Kieran drew a breath of surprise. The original bed she had occupied had gone, replaced by a fine large four poster bed, comfortable rugs on the floor. She pointed to it.

'You were sure you would persuade me to return then, husband?' she observed curiously. He returned her steady glance.

'I was. I have spent these last few weeks preparing the place for you.'

'Oh, Sorley Mor—I would not have minded if all had been as I left it, save of course I approve of this,' and blushing she pointed to the bed.

'Tonight we will try its comfort together,' he said pointedly. 'Listen my darling, there is something I have to tell you. There are two others in this house of ours now! One is a doctor whom I have taken as partner, a fine physician who fought on the right side in the rising, by name John Patterson. His rooms are upstairs, the rest of the house now furnished!'

She sank down on the bed digesting the news in surprise. But surely it could only be a good thing that her husband had help. She remembered the countless times she had seen him leave the house late at night when called to some emergency or to deliver a babe the midwives had despaired of.

'I look forward to meeting this Dr Patterson,' she said. 'Where is he now?'

'He is in the surgery,' cried a laughing voice, 'But I am here!' And swinging about in shock, Kieran saw Lachlan standing there in the doorway. In a moment he was in her arms. Then she held him back from her, staring at one who was now already on the brink of young manhood. He was taller, had filled out.

'Lachlan! Surely my eyes deceive me? I thought you in France!'

'I was there until David's death...' he began soberly. He saw by the way she blanched at his words that Kieran had been unaware that David had died. He glanced apologetically at Sorley Mor. 'I am sorry,' he said. 'I thought you would have told her.' Sorley Mor held up a hand to soothe his distress.

'I was going to do so quietly tonight,' he replied. 'Lachlan is making his home with us now, my dear. He is to study medicine at university in a few years time. Until then he is my apprentice and assistant to John Patterson.'

'Lachlan, I could not be happier to have you back,' she said, 'But oh how sad I am to learn of David's death! How did it come about?' He told her. Kieran's tears fell, as she realised she would never again meet with the kindly man of God who had been her loved and respected brother-in-law.

'He left his bible to Sorley Mor, made me promise to deliver it, which caused my return here. I will miss him until my dying day,' he added simply. 'Kieran, I am so happy you are back with Sorley Mor. Where are your babies?'

'With Bess, next door in the nursery, and no longer babes,' she exclaimed. 'Come Lachlan!' They found the young nursemaid sitting in a rocking chair placed between two small beds and singing to Alan and Ishbel who were dropping off to sleep after a meal and tired after the excitement of their long morning ride here.

'They were exhausted, Mistress Kieran,' she said, as Lachlan stooped over them and smiled his delight as he stared at the red haired boy and the silky blond curls of his small sister.

'This is a wonderful day,' he breathed.

They slipped quietly out of the room and made their way downstairs, Kieran trying to take in all that had happened in this house since that night last August when she had slipped away at midnight with Bess and the babes to leave the man to whom she could not reveal her true feelings. But memory all that long year of loneliness and sorrow just passed, only enhanced her present happiness.

'I will do my best to make you a good wife,' she said now, looking softly into his dark blue eyes, as they held hands before the window and then stared down at the street below, his arm about her waist.

There was a knock at the door and Mistress Lindsey inquired if they were ready for a meal to be served. The steak pie with vegetables and rich gravy was very tasty, as was the apple dumpling that followed and Kieran acknowledged that the housekeeper was a fine cook.

She sought her out in the kitchen. Mistress Lindsey looked at her with apprehension, wondering if the doctor's errant young wife, now returned, was about to terminate her own employment here in a position she loved.

'We have not yet had time to talk, Mistress Lindsey,' Kieran said pleasantly. 'I just want you to know that my husband and I hope you will continue here with us for many years to come! You must show me how you make your pastry,' she added with a smile. And at that moment Alison Lindsey took the young mistress of the house into her heart. Whatever had caused her to leave the doctor would remain a mystery. All that mattered was that she was here now, and they would get along fine together.

Later Kieran met John Patterson, as that man tired from treating a seemingly ceaseless stream of patients closed the surgery door leaving Effie to tidy up. She had told him that Sorley Mor had returned and brought his family with him and Patterson rejoiced that it was so. Kieran decided that she liked him as soon as they spoke together and his hazel eyes expressed his admiration of Sorley's wife who was certainly one of the fairest young women he had ever met. He sensed the courage and integrity in her, knew that Sorley Mor was indeed blessed in her return.

The men had been talking long of medical matters, discussing patients and at last Kieran tried to hide a yawn, the tiredness she had been fighting all evening making her yearn for bed. She rose to her feet and asked to be excused. They looked at each other a little guiltily.

'I will join you soon, my darling,' said Sorley Mor fondly. Glancing at her he realised she was probably exhausted after what had been an amazing but no doubt tiring day for his wife. She had done so well. There had also been the emotional trauma of saying goodbye to Lorna Campbell whom she loved as well as her brother Roderick.

'Go with her now,' whispered John Patterson with a smile. 'We will talk again tomorrow, my friend, when you can tell me of the conditions you observed in the Highlands. I am just so happy at the outcome of your journey north!' Sorley Mor smiled, rose and followed Kieran.

Roderick Campbell broke his journey at Stirling. He took rooms for himself and his men and arranged stabling for their horses and the two pack ponies. He retired early to his bed, leaving his ghillies to drink and take a hand at cards. But sleep did not come easily that night, as Roderick wrestled with the problem of how to speak with his uncle, who had made such dastardly attempt to kill Sorley Mor, this Stewart doctor who had unaccountably become most treasured friend.

The situation was delicate. Iain Campbell had acted as father figure to Roderick since his early childhood. He had always respected the man for his courage and undoubted ability to manage the estate, keeping all in order. But since leaving his regiment, Roderick had begun to regard his uncle with growing concern. He realised that Iain for all his courtesy towards him, always seeming to defer to him on management of Glenlarig, nevertheless often attempted to countermand Roderick's own orders when possible.

Since spending that week in Sorley Mor's house recovering from his duelling injury, and following their talks together that he had started to question all he had previously taken so much for granted. That for instance Iain like most of the other clan chiefs would hand out summary justice to all who offended him. Now though, the power of pit and gallows had been forfeited, ordered so by the authorities in London, justice to be decided in the courts. This he realised was certainly a better way to proceed. Providing of course that in such courts sentences were not agreed before the trial had begun—justice tailored to fit the wishes of those holding power.

Everything had been changing fast since Charles Edward rode off Culloden field in despair and Cumberland had taken such terrible retribution on the Jacobite clans who had risen—and on those innocent of any involvement in the rising. Scotland had to be subdued so that never again would she dare to question the sovereignty of King George and the house of Hanover. Roderick was painfully aware of the cruelties perpetrated all over the highlands by his own clan and others who had stood with them against the ill judged attempt of Charles Edward Stuart to regain the British crown for his father James, who had fate swung in the opposite direction, would now have been their rightful king.

But what had Scotland become now? A land where many of its great houses had been raised to the ground, its finest sons hunted down like animals, some sent abroad as slaves to the colonies—a land where even the meanest hovels had been destroyed, thousands of cattle seized and sold, the poor driven into the bleak mercy of the hills in winter, denied food and shelter, women routinely raped and even children slaughtered. Was this a Scotland he wanted for the future? But what could be done to reverse all this? And so he tossed and turned and found no solution to his concerns.

If only Scotland had not entered into that disastrous union with England in 1707—sold as had been later revealed, by a handful of corrupt Scottish noblemen for bribe of English gold and against the wishes of the people! One day perhaps his land would become independent again. Then and then only could the hurts of the past be put to rest, men strive to help each other, those in authority seek to better the conditions of those poorer. Perhaps it would not come in his lifetime, but come inevitably it must! At last he slept.

The remainder of their journey back to Glenlarig was uneventful and his heart warmed to see the loch rippling in the evening light. Then at last his home came into view. As he dismounted and let a groom lead his stallion away, he glanced towards the door which opened as his Aunt Lorna stood there arms stretched wide in welcome.

He ran up the steps and embraced her, swinging her in his arms.

'Aunt Lorna—all went well on the journey, Kieran, Sorley and the children safe back in their home,' he reassured her. She forced a smile.

'I am glad. I am trying to come to terms with the fact that Edinburgh is now home to Kieran rather than Glenlarig. But oh how glad I am that she is happy in her husband's love!' They went indoors and Roderick glanced around. Wondering why Iain had not been there to greet him.

'Where is Iain?'

'He rode off into the hills with some of the men just after you had left. He has not been back since then.'

'Did he say where he was going?' She shook her head.

'No. He was in a strange, distant mood. Roderick, I am concerned for the future. That night when he came drunk to bed, he actually admitted that he had ordered the killing of Sorley Mor!' She gave a shudder.

'My dear, I guessed it was so. Fingal would never have attempted to murder Kieran's husband without definite orders.' He looked at her gently. 'You knew of course that Fingal.....?'

'Was Iain's son? Yes, my dear. I have known it this many years. I think part of his present anger is at Fingal's death at the hand of Ewan Dhu, and I fear for the man. He may attempt to kill Ewan Dhu in retribution and I know how highly you esteem him!' Roderick's face darkened at her words.

'I do not think he would dare,' he said quietly. 'When he returns, my uncle and I have much to discuss for the future.' Then he looked objectively at Lorna, saw how tired she looked. It was also obvious she had recently been weeping. 'You are missing Kieran and her little rascals,' he said understandingly.

'So much,' she sighed. 'She had become as a daughter to me. Angus Mac Seumas is sadly missing her too—his piping all laments this morning!' She looked at Roderick fondly. Perhaps he would marry one day and beget children who would fill this house with laughter once again and the idea cheered her.

'You must be hungry,' and she clapped her hands and ordered a meal prepared for the laird. He set to with enjoyment, then his hunger assuaged, decided to retire. He knew he needed time to think.

Next day as he descended the stairs he heard the sound of Lorna's harp and smiled as the beautiful chords vibrated softly from her open door. He greeted her and saw she looked almost her normal self again, serene and confident and wearing a favourite gown of burgundy velvet.

'You look very elegant this morning, Aunt Lorna!' he admired.

'Word has come that Lord Mamore intends to visit. I have ordered rooms prepared, in case he brings some of his officers with him. His men can of course be accommodated in the barns.'

'Mamore—I wonder what he wants,' said Roderick. 'Is there any word of Iain?' She sighed and shook her head.

'No! Perhaps he needed time away to come to terms with Fingal's death, although I never saw sign of any special affection between them.'

'Try not to worry about the situation. Now that Kieran and the twins are away he will just have to accept the inevitable, and life will settle down as normal once more,' he comforted.

He breakfasted then proceeded to question those men of the estate whom Iain Campbell had not taken with him. None of them had any idea where he had gone, or were not saying. Frustrated he realised patience was needed now. He made his way down to the shores of the loch. A fine rain had started to fall, not really the weather to take his boat out. He stared out across the loch to the mass of Ben Lawers towering over its far banks. As he did so, he wondered about all the years ahead.

Would it be enough for him merely to enjoy all this beauty? Certainly here in this Campbell stronghold where there was peace and life was comfortable he should be happy. But how could he be content knowing that most neighbouring areas had been denuded of people, so much that had made the myriad glens and hillsides a happy contented place destroyed. Yes there were fine cattle and sheep decking these hillsides— but what of the ravaged districts where people had lost all that made life worth living?

What was the matter with him, he thought? He could certainly not reverse any of what had happened, but if he could perhaps help to restore normality to even a few of those who had suffered, then surely this would be small and worthwhile achievement.

His musings were interrupted by a shout. He turned his head, and saw Ewan Dhu struggling to restrain a woman who brought up her knee and caught him a disabling hurt. Immediately he hurried up the brae towards the woman who now turned to flee.

'Not so fast,' he cried and caught at her poor gown which ripped in his hands, exposing shapely thigh. 'Wait now. You have nothing to fear here!'

'I fear no man,' she replied haughtily. 'Unhand me at once!' adding angrily, 'you have torn my skirt, de'il tak ye. '

'If I release you, will you stand still and tell me who you are and what brings you to my land?' he demanded. She stared at him and seemed reassured at what she saw. She nodded grudging agreement. But as he stepped back noted she stood poised to flee. His eyes played over her curiously. He saw a proud, beautiful countenance, surrounded by snarled glossy black curls, wealth of hair reaching almost to her trim waist. The eyes that watched him so distrustfully were a dark violet, her nose short and straight, full lipped mouth wide above a cleft chin. He looked regretfully at her torn skirt of some brownish material.

'I apologise for tearing your skirt. But what do you here and assaulting one of my men?' he demanded, glancing with sympathy at Ewan Dhu who was holding himself in pain.

'He laid hands on me!'

'I asked her business, sir. Tried to make her wait that I might bring her to you—but she became a wild cat!' Ewan Dhu stared at the girl. 'I meant the lady no harm,' he added with dignity.

'Well, I am Roderick Campbell of Glenlarig! I ask again, what is your business here?' He watched her carefully knowing she might try to escape once more.

'I seek one Kieran Stewart, though now bearing the accursed name of Campbell,' she snapped.

'Kieran is my sister. Why do you seek her?' he asked in amazement.

'My father Robert MacGregor—or Rob Gregory the name he is forced to go by these days, sent me to speak with Kieran.' she said in quieter tones.

'But why?' he demanded in perplexity.

'Because he thought she should know that Annie MacGregor, the woman who brought her up, is now dead. She wanted a last message brought to Kieran Stewart—her last wishes.' The girl's voice was sad. 'Annie was my second cousin,' she said.

'I am sorry to hear your news,' replied Roderick courteously. 'May I now inquire your own name?' She hesitated shrugged.

'I am Sheena MacGregor—or Gregory! My race is Royal,' she said proudly.

'Well Mistress Sheena, I cannot help you in your quest for Kieran. She has left Glenlarig and returned to Edinburgh with her physician husband Sorley Mor Stewart and their little ones. I accompanied her there and returned here only yesterday.' He looked at her in sympathy.

Her face was troubled. 'I cannot go to Edinburgh,' she said. 'I must return to my father and ask him what we should do in the matter.' She made as though to flee once more.

'No, wait! First of all I want you to come to the house and let my aunt see if we cannot sort your torn skirt and offer some hospitality.'

'What—eat in a Campbell household?' Her violet eyes flashed contempt at the suggestion.

'Well, I would suggest we eat in the garden if you despise the idea of my house, but in this rain! Come, be sensible and I promise to have you put safe on your way when you desire.' He was beginning to lose patience with the girl, could have sent her off there and then, but there was something in her that strangely attracted him.

'I suppose I could do with a drink of water,' she said, ignoring the expanse of the loch just below them. He took her arm and before she could protest, guided her up the brae. She hesitated as the house came into sight, rising majestically above them. Then she shrugged.

Lorna Campbell looked from her efforts to make all in readiness in the great hall for her expected military guests and stared up in surprise at the bedraggled, bare footed young woman at her nephew's side.

'Why Roderick, you bring a visitor,' she asked politely.

'Aunt Lorna, this is Mistress Sheena—er Gregory. She has come with a message for Kieran and I have explained that my sister is no longer here with us. She has torn her dress. I wondered if one of the maids could perhaps repair it?' he suggested. Lorna stared at the woefully shabby clothes the girl wore. That skirt looked as though it would fall apart if any attempted to sew it. She also noticed that the wearer was astonishingly beautiful and carried herself with pride. Why was Roderick attempting to help such a one? She considered the name-Gregory? Of course, one of the names that those of Clan MacGregor now used, the name MacGregor proscribed!'

'Do you know my niece Kieran, Mistress MacGregor?' she asked.

'I did a few years back, when we younger,' said Sheena warily. 'Our paths do not cross now that...!' she was going to add that Kieran had shocked the clan by uniting herself with the detested Campbells. But Lorna took her meaning and sighed. This blind hatred between clans frustrating and as inevitable it seemed as time. She glanced at Roderick for guidance. He pulled a chair aside at the end of the table

'Come, seat yourself, and I will send for refreshments,' he said. She hesitated, about to refuse, then grudgingly sank onto the chair he held for her, pulling her poor skirt together, trying to cover her bare thigh. Lorna saw her embarrassment and resolved to do something to help the girl, but knew she would have to show utmost discretion.

It was obvious from the speed with which Sheena dispatched the cold breast of chicken and fresh baked bread that she had been very hungry. Roderick poured her a glass of wine and lifted glass of his own towards her.

'To your good health, Sheena MacGregor!' he said pleasantly. She raised her own glass of dark red wine to her lips, drank. 'Now, if you care to reveal the message you have brought for my sister Kieran, I will see that it reaches her in Edinburgh.' But she shook her head.

'A message from one on their deathbed is sacred matter, not to be divulged to any but the one for whom it is intended.' He realised that

Sheena was no longer speaking aggressively, but unlikely to be persuaded into revealing the message.

'Then what do you suggest?'

'That I return to my father, ask his advice!'

'If that is what you wish. But may I suggest that you stay here tonight? It is already late in the afternoon, Balquidder many miles away. To attempt such long journey on foot with night coming is foolhardy.' He glanced at Lorna. 'We can put a room at Mistress MacGregor's disposal, aunt?'

'Certainly that is possible—but do you think it wise given the visitors we are expecting and who may possibly arrive tonight—Lord Mamore?' He caught her meaning and frowned. As for Sheena, she had heard the name of the feared Campbell Major General and her face showed alarm.

'Ah yes, Mamore,' brooded Roderick, 'I had almost forgotten! You are right.' He turned to the girl. 'Those whose coming we await are less friendly to your people than my aunt and I. Therefore you may either choose to stay hidden in a chamber above stairs or if you prefer, be on your way with Ewan Dhu to protect you?'

'I will leave—leave now. And I will go alone. Nor do I believe the man you mentioned, this Ewan Dhu, would enjoy my company!' And as he remembered the earlier scene when Sheena had brought up her knee to engage with a sensitive part of that man's anatomy to such painful affect, he tried to restrain a smile.

'But you cannot go with your skirt in that condition. Come with me,' said Lorna firmly and the girl rose and hesitantly followed her out of the hall. She mounted the stairs, averting her head from sight of portraits of Campbell ancestors adorning the walls and seen by candles flickering light. How she hated all those of this name she thought wildly.

'This was Kieran's room,' explained Lorna as she led her in. She walked over to a massive oak wardrobe, opened the door and pointed to an array of garments hanging there. 'My niece left many of her clothes behind. I know she would wish me to do this small courtesy to a friend of hers—I ask you to accept whatever you select. Oh, in this chest you will find shifts, stockings.' Before Sheena could refuse, she left her alone in the bedchamber, closing the door behind her.

Sheena was going to call after her, say that she wanted nothing from any in this place—but hesitated as she looked down on her badly ripped skirt and forced herself to be practical. At that moment there was a knock at the door. A maid entered, and deposited a jug of warm water beside the china washing bowl on a marble topped table. She inclined her head politely to this unknown visitor and hurriedly left the room.

Shortly afterwards, Sheena stood looking at her reflection in the tall, cheval mirror. She gasped. It was as though a total stranger was reflected there. She had chosen one of the plainest of Kieran's gowns in dark blue wool. She smoothed its folds. It fitted her perfectly. But her hair spoiled the effect. She looked around and saw a comb lying on the dressing table possibly discarded there as two of its teeth were broken. It was hard work dealing with the snarls in her tangled locks. But at last it was done, and her mahogany dark hair fell in smooth shining waves below her shoulders.

She opened the door and hesitated there. At the sound of the door opening Lorna appeared from her own chamber and stared in amazement at the girl.

'Why Sheena, you are of a size with Kieran as I thought!' She looked approvingly at the transformation until her eyes strayed down to the girl's stockinged feet. 'Oh—wait, stay there!' Minute later she was back holding black buckled shoes. 'Try these, my dear!'

Roderick looked up as he heard their voices. His face expressed bewilderment as he took in Sheena's altered appearance. Why, the girl was actually quite beautiful. As he looked into those long lashed slightly apprehensive violet eyes he drew in his breath slowly. Such change was incredible and now he felt a definite reluctance to allow her to return to her home in the hills above Loch Voil. She dropped a small curtsey to him.

'If you have finished staring at me Roderick Campbell!' she exclaimed. He dropped his eyes awkwardly, seeking words to persuade her to stay. It was now that one of his men ran into the hall without knocking.

'Laird Roderick—Mamore comes! He is at the falls now. I rode fast to let you know as I was bid.' The man was panting. 'A party of some twenty to thirty men I would say!'

'Thank you, Keith. Let those in the kitchen know to prepare,' he instructed. He turned to Lorna hearing her utter gasp of dismay.

'It's Sheena! She ran out of the hall at the moment she heard Mamore was coming.' They hurried to the front door and stood on the steps, glancing in both directions. Of Sheena MacGregor there was no sign. Roderick cursed softly. But there was no time to waste now. But nevertheless he called for Ewan Dhu, who came and stood looking at Roderick expectantly.

'You will mind the young woman, Sheena MacGregor?' he said taking the man on one side.

'That I do, sir!' he replied feelingly.

'She heard Mamore is on his way and ran out of the house in panic—and I have no time now to seek for her. I ask you to find her and escort her safely back to her father at Balquidder. Try to avoid being seen by Mamore!' he ordered. Ewan Dhu nodded his head.

'Leave it to me, Laird! I hope her temper may have cooled in the meanwhile,' he added feelingly. And he was off and Roderick sighed relief.

Lorna looked at him anxiously. 'Where is she?'

'I have sent Ewan Dhu after her. He will take her safely home,' he told his aunt. 'Now wherever can Iain be? Mamore will find it strange that he is not here to help receive him!' He bit his lip in exasperation.

High up on the brae above the pathway that girded the loch, Sheena MacGregor was leaping along like a young deer. She had dispensed with shoes and stockings, carrying them in her hand that they might not spoil in her flight. She heard her name called and froze. Then she saw him, the man who had tried to detain her earlier and whom she had kneed. No time to hide for he had seen her and was at her side in a few loping strides.

'Have no fear, lady,' he said, not attempting to lay hands on her. 'Laird Roderick sent me to you. I am to keep you safe on your way.' His dark eyes studied her judging her mood.

'I have no need of you! I found my own way here—will find it back alone!' she said stiffly.

'Quick—down low in the heather!' he cried. 'They come, the Lord Mamore and his men!' She needed no second bidding as together they prostrated themselves behind a bank of prickly gorse. She raised her head slightly and peered down below, and saw a tall, autocratic figure in black velvet jacket and tartan trews, his plaid secured by a large silver broach, riding a magnificent black stallion, flanked by two who seemed to be officers, in front of his troop of armed militia.

Sheena watched them go, and her eyes shone with hatred as the last of the soldiers marching in twos disappeared from view in the direction of Glenlarig House. She spat contemptuously into the heather.

'Let us go,' she cried and after a cautious look around, Ewan rose and made to help her to her feet. She ignored the hand he stretched down to her and leapt up. She set off at a quick pace, the man matching his stride to hers. On they went and on, and now it was almost night, the pale stars swinging above their heads as they jogged silently together. Through Glen Ogle and past Lochearnhead and on skirting woodland, keeping to the right of the track in case any stray members of the militia might be patrolling.

'There, the turning for Balquidder,' cried Sheena breaking silence. 'I can manage the rest by myself. You should go!' She glanced over her shoulder at the man, but he held up a warning hand.

'Down, lassie!' he hissed. 'I hear the sound of horses approaching.' Immediately she bent low behind the shelter of a rock. She expected Ewan Dhu to follow her example, but instead he was standing and looking towards the mounted party of men who were almost upon them. He raised his hand and shouted and the riders pulled up their horses.

'It is Ewan Dhu,' he shouted. 'Lord Mamore is at Glenlarig.....!' But even as he shouted the information, the leader of the party, a handsome silver haired man, raised his gun and trained it on the figure waving to him from the bank above the road. Then as Sheena watched in horror from behind the rocky overhang, a shot rang out, its sound vibrating through the hills and she saw Ewan Dhu throw up his hands and fall, rolling over and over to lie on the roadside below.

With a shout of command, she saw the silver haired figure signal to his followers to proceed once more, not giving the slightest heed to the man who lay by the roadside.

'Are ye dead,' she whispered as she ran to the still figure of this man of a hated clan but who had befriended her. He did not move. She put her finger to his throat and felt a slight pulse. There was life still. What should she do, by herself there alone? She opened his shirt saw the bullet had lodged in his left shoulder, so the heart was not damaged. She could also feel a huge bruise on the side of his head. He must have sustained this in his fall down to the road. The moon was up and she could see dimly by its light. She was only a few miles from her home now, the temptation to leave the Campbell there to his fate. She got to her feet then looked back. Somehow she could not do it.

She tore strips from her new white shift, and made a pad, and tied it into position to stop further bleeding. Puffing and gasping she dragged the man up the steep slope and settled him in a small grassy hollow behind some young whispering birch. There he could lie unseen until she could bring help. She heard the sound of water. There must be a burn nearby and followed its babbling voice until she found it, dipped the remaining strip of linen into its flow and returned to bathe Ewan Dhu's face. He gave a slight groan and she lifted her head in triumph.

'You will live,' she told him. She stared down into what she could see of his dark bearded face in the pale moonlight. He opened his eyes and stared up at her in bewilderment. Then a spasm crossed his gaunt features and he tried to speak.

'It was Sir Iain Campbell. He that is uncle to the young laird,' he whispered, his face betraying his shock.

'They were Campbells and known to you—from Glenlarig is it?' She looked at him in amazement. 'Why would your own people seek to murder you?'

'Lassie, I killed Iain's son Fingal.' His voice was faint.

'You did that—but why?' None of it made sense. He tried to speak again, mumbled something about this Fingal attempting to shoot Sorley Mor Stewart, who was under his protection. Then he closed his eyes exhausted.

'I will go to my father—bring help for you,' she promised. She was not sure whether or not he heard her words. Then straightening up she sped away into the night.

Chapter Twelve

Major General John Campbell of Mamore stretched back in his chair and smiled across at Lorna. The meal he had just enjoyed had been excellent, the wine a fine French Bordeaux cool and delicious on the palette.

'My compliments to a wonderful hostess,' he said raising his glass to her. His two young officers did likewise. 'But tell me, when do you expect your husband back?' He thought she flinched slightly at the question.

'He rode off without saying where he was bound,' she replied in a quiet voice. 'He had been much distressed at Kieran's decision to return to Edinburgh with her husband!'

'I wondered at her absence,' he said questioningly. 'I had thought she was upstairs with her children. So, she is reconciled to her physician husband? Well, I am not altogether surprised.'

'Sorley Mor visited us here at my invitation,' stated Roderick. 'They have now become truly man and wife,' he said. 'We miss my sister but it was good to see her happiness as they settled their differences. I will call on them when next I am in Edinburgh!'

'The doctor was here then? For a Stewart he is an exceptional man, far thinking and with a fine mind.' He played with his glass reflectively. 'So our plans for finding a new husband Kieran have come to naught. Yet I am strangely glad at her decision.'

'I will never forget the happiness she brought into this house,' said Lorna lifting gentle gaze to Mamore.

'But you miss the little ones no doubt,' he replied. 'Well Roderick, it is up to you now to find a suitable bride and provide heirs for Glenlarig, some fine babes for Lorna to kiss.' He glanced affectionately at the young man he referred to as his nephew. Roderick however made no reply. Mamore tried again.

'Have you still found no young woman to grace your bed and board?' he inquired and Roderick coloured with annoyance at his persistence. He was about to seek suitable words to distract Mamore, when the door opened and Iain Campbell stood there, dishevelled from riding—and as they observed from his lurching feet, also extremely drunk. He focussed his eyes on Mamore.

'Greetings, Lord Mamore,' he cried thickly. 'Glad I am to see you. But what brings you to my door? Do you seek help to run down any of Clan MacPherson, or any thrice damned MacGregors?' Lorna rose to her feet.

'Come Iain, you must be tired from your journey. Perhaps you would like to rest for a while.' She attempted to direct him out of the door and towards the stairs, but he pushed her roughly away. She stumbled almost fell, her hands reaching for the table to steady herself. Roderick muttered a curse and sprang to his feet.

'Uncle Iain, you are drunk!' he cried.

'What's that you say, nephew—drunk? Maybe I have taken a dram or two to celebrate dealing with a few MacGregors whilst you have been taking your slothful ease here. What of it? Am I not master of my own house accepting criticism from no man—or woman?' He stared pointedly at Lorna and then glanced scornfully around all in the hall. Roderick drew in his breath indignantly about to respond, but Mamore forestalled him.

'Iain Campbell, it is obvious that you are indeed drunk, otherwise I would call you to account for your conduct towards your wife and discourtesy to Roderick—who is in fact master of Glenlarig, not you!' Mamore's icy tones seemed to trigger caution in Iain's mind. He stared into the smouldering gaze of one who was second in position only to the great Argyll himself.

'Your pardon, I will retire,' he announced. Roderick whispered to one of his men to help his uncle to one of the spare bedrooms. Lorna made to follow, but Roderick placed a restraining hand on her arm.

'No aunt. He is in a strange mood. Better I think to wait until he falls asleep. You should put a bolt on your door tonight.' She nodded agreement.

'Is he often like this,' inquired Mamore in concern.

'No. But he can be unpredictable at times, more especially of late. I will speak of it later.' He glanced towards Lorna and Mamore inclined his head in understanding. As for Mamore's two officers, tired at the end of the day's travelling through difficult terrain and comfortably replete after a splendid meal, they had taken scant interest in the senior member of their host's household who seemingly had been deep in his cups. However the conversation lapsed somewhat after the unpleasant episode.

'Can we persuade you to play your harp?' asked Mamore of Lorna.

'Would you forgive me if instead we were to call on Angus Mac Seumas to entertain you on his pipes? I have a slight headache and if you will forgive me would like to retire. Roderick will have a care of you,' she added with a smile. Her nephew raised his head in alarm thinking of Iain's aggressive behaviour.

'Do not concern yourself. I shall rest on the couch in my drawing room,' she whispered to Roderick on seeing his look of concern. 'I will probably stay there overnight!' He nodded his relief and within a short time the sound of the pipes echoed through the house, the old piper demonstrating his mastery of his beloved instrument to the applause of the soldiers.

Then Roderick made quiet suggestion to Mamore who nodded and rose to his feet. His men were told to remain in the hall to enjoy the pipes and then to retire at will officers in the bedrooms allocated to them, others to bed down in the barns. He followed Roderick into his study.

'A different atmosphere here tonight than that we enjoyed last Christmas,' he said quietly, as he seated himself across from Roderick, staring at him interrogatively.

'Yes,' replied Roderick pensively staring at the birch logs crackling in the fire. Although it was summer, the night had been cold. 'I regret that uncalled for incident earlier.' He glanced at Mamore.

'You wish to explain Iain's behaviour?'

'He is extremely angry at the death of his bastard son, Fingal Beag.'

'How and when did this occur,' asked Mamore. Roderick hesitated. Was it right to expose a family matter to the autocratic soldier who was watching him with such analytical gaze. But Mamore was chief of his clan, just and honourable and could be relied on to be discreet.

Roderick told what led up to Fingal's death at the hand of his own most trusted man, Ewan Dhu, explaining that he had entrusted the safety of his sister and Sorley Mor Stewart to his care when they expressed a wish to walk down to the loch to enjoy some privacy. Mamore listened intently.

'You are telling me that Fingal Beag fired upon the doctor not by accident, but by intent to kill him—and that this was on the instruction of Iain Campbell?' Mamore regarded Roderick in shock and his face darkened. 'To give orders to kill a guest in your house, never mind related to us by marriage—this is an altogether deplorable matter!'

'We would none of us have known the reason behind the planned murder, had not Ewan Dhu gone to the succour of the man he had shot, found it to be Fingal—and heard Fingal's question before expiring as to whether he had in fact killed the doctor!' Roderick's eyes betrayed his own fury at the attempted murder.

'But are we sure that Iain actually ordered the killing?' probed Mamore.

'He admitted such to Lorna before passing out drunk in their chamber that same night. The following morning Sorley Mor and Kieran and the bairns set out for Edinburgh. I escorted them together with two of my men. Saw them safe to the doctor's house, made immediate return here.'

'I find all of this most distressing,' responded Mamore frowningly. 'Did Iain give any reason for his behaviour?'

'Seemingly he wanted to retain Kieran and her children here in case I should die without issue. Little Alan would be in direct descent in such case. With Sorley Mor dead he could have persuaded Kieran to stay!'

'And do you tell me it was for that he was prepared to kill Stewart?'

'I know that the future of the estate means much to my uncle. More than that, he is used to being in charge here.' Roderick shook his head broodingly. 'When I enlisted and was away those two years he imagined himself laird. Since my return he has given lip service to my wishes, but then reversed them. Do not mistake me however. I have always respected and had much affection for Iain. But sometimes I wonder if perhaps he is not in his right mind these days. I fear for Lorna.'

'I will speak to him on the morrow before I leave. As for your sister and Sorley Mor, I will call upon them when I am next in Edinburgh.' The men went on to discuss other matters, whether there had been any fresh disturbance in this area. Mamore made a mental note to inquire exactly what Iain Campbell had been up to with his wild talk of dealing with some of the proscribed MacGregors.

The following morning just after daybreak, Roderick was awakened by sound in the courtyard below. He opened his window and called down, inquiring the reason for the noise. It was his piper, Angus Mac Seumas who called an answer to him.

'You should come down Sir Roderick. A child came with a strange message and ran off before I could stop him. He was just a young laddie. He spoke of Ewan Dhu!' At the old man's words Roderick uttered an exclamation of dismay. He had sent Sheena MacGregor off in Ewan Dhu's care. Had any disaster befallen the girl? He dressed hurriedly and within minutes was out in the courtyard, confronting the old piper.

'So tell me Angus—what message did the lad bring?'

'He said an ill thing and not to be believed! He told me that young Mistress Gregory had sent him. That Ewan Dhu was shot last night—by Iain Campbell, and in deliberate act!' He forced the words out distastefully, for surely they were unbelievable.

'Did he say if Ewan is dead?'

'He lives—is being cared for by the young woman and her family. She thought you should know!' As the old man studied Roderick's face, he drew in his breath sharply. He realised that Roderick believed the tale. Of course, Laird Iain was much disturbed by the shooting of Fingal Beag by Ewan Dhu. Had he then taken revenge for that death? But all knew Ewan Dhu had merely been protecting Lady Kieran and her doctor husband!'

'Which way did the child go?' inquired Roderick, his face pale with anger.

'He set off as though the de'il were after him. He could be anywhere by now! I was by myself out here, laird and I am not fleet on my feet these days!' he explained. Roderick forced a smile at the old man.

'You have done well to tell me of this. Keep the matter to yourself for now. Not a word to any!'

'I will be silent as the grave itself,' declared Angus Mac Seumas. He waited until Roderick was within doors once more before raising his pipes and the sound of them lilted through the glen.

Lorna had also risen early. She tidied her appearance wondering what the day would bring when her husband rose from his drunken slumber. She had remained in her small drawing room, preferring to rest on the couch rather than risking a visit to her bedchamber should he have awoken during the night.

'Roderick—what brings you down at this early hour?' she asked. He slipped an arm about her and spoke in a low voice. She listened in dismay as he explained the message Sheena had sent by the hand of a young boy.

'Do you believe this?'

''Sadly I do, Aunt Lorna! According to what the lad told Angus Mac Seumas, Sheena had watched Ewan waving to Iain. There was no mistaking that Iain recognised him. He shot him in cold blood—luckily missed his heart. Then Iain rode off with his men. So they would have observed the whole thing. I must speak with them.'

'Oh Roderick, dear heart! You have had Ewan Dhu with you since you were but children together. He is devoted to you and all know it. What possessed Iain to act so? Oh—it would be because of Fingal?'

'Sheena and her family are caring for Ewan.'

'I hope they are safe then, for when Iain came in last night he was boasting about dealing with the MacGregors!'

'I had not thought of that. I will go now, make inquiries as to what exactly happened at Balquidder!' He found one of Iain's henchmen in the kitchen, sitting at table and chewing on a leg of chicken. He looked up awkwardly as Roderick strode over and stood staring fiercely at him hand on hip and legs apart.

'You there, Donald MacKay—I demand to know exactly what transpired at Balquidder yesterday!' The man stared back at him uneasily.

'Why, we juist burned down a ruined hut where an old MacGregor woman was living and sent her screeching into the hills! It was a comical sight, for first we stripped her and...!' he lowered his head sheepishly at the expression on Roderick's face.

'And what else?' he asked sternly.

'Another of them we shot at, a tall wild looking fellow with black hair and pock marked face. He fell. We started to run forward to finish him, but

240

a woman helped drag him to his feet and the two of them vanished into a gulley. We searched, but de'il a sicht of them did we find, or any other'

'And after that, what happened?'

'Why, we searched thoroughly for more of them, but as soon as they espied us disappeared like will o the wisps! After that, Iain Campbell said we should return home. That was it!' His face expressed his unwillingness to continue.

'But there was more, wasn't there?' pursued his interrogator. 'Tell me of Ewan Dhu? And before you say anything, you should be aware that word came to me this morning by one who witnessed last night's happenings!'

'Since you know of it, why question me, Laird. Perhaps it is Iain Campbell you should be speaking to,' he dropped his gaze uncomfortably.

'You will answer my questions—now tell me what occurred!' he demanded inexorably. His eyes raked the man's face.

'We were on the road juist past the Kingshouse, when a man shouted from the brae above us. It was Ewan Dhu. He called that Lord Mamore was at Glenlarig. To our amazement, your uncle raised his gun and shot Ewan! He fell, tumbled down the brae onto the roadside. We were ordered to ride on. We did so.'

'And none of you thought to see if Ewan had survived the shot?'

'Could we gainsay Sir Iain Campbell's orders? But sad I am for Ewan Dhu who was a guid man and a bonny fighter!' Donald shook his head in regret.

'Do not discuss the matter with any others!'

'It is not a thing to boast of, sir!' He gave a sigh of relief as Roderick walked back into the house. There would be trouble coming over the matter without a doubt!

Mamore and Roderick sat in the study. They had breakfasted together, Lorna outwardly her usual serene self. Mamore had already said he would be leaving at about mid day and Roderick knew he had to speak of Iain's latest wild behaviour, hence their quiet discussion now as Mamore learned of the attempted murder of Ewan Dhu.

'I will speak most strongly to Iain about such conduct! As for your man Ewan Dhu I know him for a good and trustworthy fellow who would give his life for you. But tell me now of this young woman of the MacGregor who is caring for the man—Sheena her name?' And Roderick did so, mentioning her sudden appearance at Glenlarig with a message for Kieran of the dying words of Annie MacGregor who had brought up the Campbell child as her own. He explained about her torn gown, that they had invited her in while it was repaired, instead of which Lorna had supplied her with clothing Kieran had left behind.

'You would not believe the difference in her appearance,' exclaimed Roderick enthusiastically. 'I had not previously noticed that she has an unusual beauty.' He stopped short as he saw the smile about Mamore's lips.

'So your heart has at last been smitten—but by a member of the Gregorach!' he probed in amusement.

'Not so,' replied Roderick hastily. 'I merely remarked on her looks as one would of a fine sunset—or the sun throwing sequins on the loch!'

'Just so—quite poetical, but it must be remembered that she is perhaps related to the family of Rory MacGregor who murdered your own father!'

'Mamore, one of these days, old hatreds must be forgotten so that our country may heal, look to a better future for all!'

'You have been speaking with Sorley Mor, these words such as he would use. I am not saying you are wrong, mind you—merely always to remember that you are a Campbell and we are the strongest clan in Scotland, rule this land under the British government.'

'I will never forget it!' but his tone was enigmatic.

When Iain Campbell presented himself below stairs somewhat later, looking more himself but with a sullen turn to his lips, he was called to a private meeting with Lord Mamore. None others were present at that meeting, but when he emerged from it Iain Campbell bore a chastened appearance. He bowed to Lorna but spoke no word to his wife in excuse of his discourteous behaviour towards her, instead called for his horse and one of his ghillies to accompany him.

Roderick watched him go from the window a troubled expression in his eyes. Mamore came to stand at his side. He clamped a reassuring hand on the younger man's shoulder.

'When Ewan Dhu returns here, none will ever raise hand against him again,' was all he said. 'As for his treatment of Lorna, he knows my opinion on this also. Well, duty calls me!'

Roderick stood at the door and waved salute to Mamore who rode away ahead of his two captains his men in file behind them, and Angus Mac Seumas raised his pipes and played the visitors on their way, the poignancy of the sound echoing between the hills.

'Where do you suppose Iain has gone,' asked Lorna, her face expressing her deep concern. 'He looked strange I thought.'

'Dear Aunt—I do not know. Only that Mamore will have had a stern word with him. Time alone will tell if he heeds what was said.'

None would have found the entrance to that cave on the steep flanks of hill above Loch Voil. It was screened from view by huge boulders and gorse. Within its secret depths a whole family lived their frugal lives, had made it as comfortable as possible, sheepskin rugs on its cold rock surface, wooden couches spread with heather to sleep on, a fire kept burning on which to cook, the smoke disappearing unseen against the grey rocks above. Many others lived in similar caves, their former houses burned to the ground by the militia.

'How are you feeling today, Ewan Dhu,' asked a sweet voice as the man she called to, attempted to sit up. Sheena MacGregor smiled at him encouragingly.

'Why lady—I am well enough,' he replied in quiet voice. 'You have been more than kind to me but I should go.' It was only today that the fever he had experienced since his wounding had broken. The girl bent over him and examined his shoulder with gentle fingers.

'It is healing well! You were lucky indeed. But what will you do now?' she inquired. 'If you return to Glenlarig then surely you risk the man Iain Campbell trying to kill you again. I think he may not miss a second time!' Her dark violet eyes examined him in concern.

'But return I must to my master. Laird Roderick will need me.'

'He knows you are here, and what befell you! I sent message by a child who informed that old piper—called Angus Mac Seumas if I remember?'

'You did that for me? But why take trouble?' he asked in surprise.

'Because you were hurt when trying to keep me safe on the road,' she explained. 'Not that I needed protection. Rather it was you in need of it!' At her words the man chuckled softly.

'I fear you are in the right of it,' he agreed. 'But I needs must leave this place and go back to Glenlarig.' He attempted to swing his legs over his rough couch and winced. She drew her brows together sternly.

'You will stay for at least another day. Besides, there are questions I would ask you of Kieran Stewart!' her violet eyes considered him inquiringly. 'I speak of the wife of Sorley Mor Stewart.'

'What is it you wish to know?' he demanded in surprise.

'How did she appear when she lived among you at Glenlarig? Was she happy there would you say?' She watched his face. He pondered the question.

'How does one person know what goes on in the mind of another? She was kind, gentle with all she came in contact with, seemed content, but there was a look of sadness in her eyes.' His reply did not seem to surprise her.

'How could it be otherwise? She threw in her lot with the enemy. Her conscience must have been pricking her!' she replied sharply. But Ewan Dhu shook his head.

'She was coming to terms with her true parentage that is true. Difficult it must have been for one who considered herself to be of the Gregorach! But it was more. She was grieving for that good man she married, Sorley Mor Stewart.'

'Then why leave him in the first place—if she loved him?'

'That, you must ask her, lady! To me it would appear that she feared his reaction once he knew she was of Campbell blood. But all is now well. I accompanied Laird Roderick when we escorted the couple and their children back to Edinburgh.' As she heard this she drew in her breath and smiled.

'So you know where she lives—could perhaps guide me there?' she asked.

'That, I could! I have visited the doctor's house more than once. A fine enough house, but not of the size of Glenlarig.' he explained. 'Why would you wish to see Kieran Stewart?'

'Because Annie MacGregor who was foster mother to Kieran died recently and with her dying breath asked me to take a message to Kieran!' He nodded at her words. A promise to the dying must always be kept, a solemn matter indeed. He considered the situation.

'When would you wish to go?'

'Soon! It was this matter that brought me to Glenlarig only to find my journey in vain—that she was no longer there.'

'You saved my life. For this I owe you a kindness in return. But first I must speak with Roderick Campbell—and then there is the problem of Sir Iain. I needs must speak with him. Blood lies between us!'

'But surely his action in attempting to murder you should satisfy his anger over the shooting of his son Fingal? I know little of Roderick Campbell, but surely if he values your devotion to him....?'

'It is more than that. My mother was his wet nurse, his own mother the Lady Catriona not able to nurse him. We grew up together! I would give my life for him.' The bond he mentioned was one well understood in the highlands, strong, close as a brother.

'Yet knowing this, Iain Campbell acted as he did?' She raised her eyebrows questioningly. He spread his hands before him.

'He has not been himself of late. A good man, but with problems,' he added loyally. She snorted dismissively at this.

'I will send word when I am ready to go to Edinburgh. But for now my father needs me. He was wounded by Iain Campbell's men when they ventured into our lands here in Balquidder shortly before we arrived back that evening. This Iain would have been making his way back to Glenlarig when he shot you!'

'He is here—your father?' he looked around curiously, realising that he was lying in a small rocky antechamber of the main cave, which explained why he had heard voices whenever he wakened from sleep.

'My whole family live here! A strange dwelling it is after the fine house we once occupied. It lies in ruins now torn down stone from stone by the English and their allies!' Her eyes flashed their anger and he lowered his head in discomfort. 'We lost all—nothing spared to us save our lives, for we fled into the high places.'

'I know lassie,' he muttered. 'In warfare many actions may seem unpardonable when considered in aftermath.'

'The fighting is over. Yet Iain Campbell came into our glen days back and wounded two of our people, killed another—and raped and terrorised an elderly woman who has now lost her mind! He gets away with such action because the MacGregor are proscribed, to be hunted down and killed by any whatsoever!' she added bitterly.

'Sheena—Come! Ye have spent time enough with yon Campbell,' cried a deep voice and a black haired, bearded man limped over to Ewan Dhu and stared down at him with hostile glare.

'My father—Rob Gregory,' the girl in introduced. Ewan Dhu rose to his feet and the two men took measure of each other. It was Ewan who broke the strained silence.

'I am indebted to your daughter for her care—and to you for allowing shelter,' he said quietly. Rob Gregory knit his thick black brows as he considered him sternly.

'If you are here it is merely because my daughter tells me you gave her your protection on her journey back from Glenlarig. Also, I am curious at a situation where a Campbell turns on one of his own following.' Ewan Dhu stared back at him, seeing the bandaged leg and look of a man in pain.

'I return now to Glenlarig,' was all his reply, then glancing at Sheena added, 'Your daughter will explain my situation once I am gone.'

'Then go you shall, but first blindfolded that you may not later identify the position of this cave!' At this Ewan Dhu felt hands placing a cloth over his eyes. He heard Rob Gregory give orders for bread and meat to be given him for his journey and was then hustled out of the cave to stumble blindly down the hillside, prodded by two who accompanied him to the shores of the loch. There he was forced down to lie amongst the undergrowth.

He heard no sound around him now apart from the song of a dozen larks and cautiously removed his blindfold, realised he was alone. Above his head an eagle soared against the rocky buttresses of the hill. He rose to his feet. He picked up the small package of food and set off on the long walk back to the shores of Loch Tay.

It was night and the stars scintillating in a velvet dark sky when Ewan Dhu left the falls of Dochart behind him and wearily commenced the last of his journey back to Glenlarig. The loch came into view stroked by moonlight, rippling to the soft summer wind and his heart was gladdened by sight of it. Before long the house loomed a dark shape against the hillside and a man on duty at the massive gates challenged him—then relaxed as he was recognised.

'Some thought you dead,' the guard exclaimed. Ewan merely grinned.

'Then they were wrong,' was all he said. He went straight to his bed and fell asleep. The morning would be time enough to speak with Laird Roderick. When he arose he fended off the many questions fired at him by members of the household, then drew in his breath as he saw the master who commanded his complete loyalty approaching.

'Ewan Dhu—it rejoices my heart to see you safe!' exclaimed Roderick warmly. 'Come into my study. We must talk together.' And so it was that Roderick learned exactly what had transpired at the roadside at Balquidder.

'She was unhurt—Sheena MacGregor?' he asked anxiously.

'The lassie was in no danger. None saw her with me. But she saved my life, for I would have died at the hand of Iain Campbell had she not sent for others to carry me to her dwelling—a cave on a hillside, where she tended my wound.'

'Then you owe her much,' cried Roderick. 'Tell me, would you remember the position of that cave?' He stared at Ewan Dhu expectantly, for he felt compulsion to seek out the MacGregor girl and to express his gratitude in person. But Ewan shook his head.

'I was blindfolded and led from the cave. I would not know its position again. But even if I did, then honour would not allow me to speak of it!' He looked awkwardly at the laird who nodded in understanding.

'You say that Mistress Sheena asked a kindness of you in return?'

'She wishes to visit Edinburgh to speak with your sister Kieran, sir! I mentioned that I knew where the doctor lives—and she asked that I would accompany her there. She is to send word when she is ready to travel.' He looked at Roderick hopefully. 'Is it that I have your permission for such a journey?' For a few minutes Roderick considered the situation. If he allowed Ewan Dhu to escort the girl, they could be stopped by patrols of militia along the road perhaps with dire consequences to both. No, it was too dangerous so.

'What I am prepared to do for Sheena Gregory as we must refer to the lady, is to offer my own protection. You and I will bring her safe there together.' He smiled at the gratitude in Ewan's eyes. 'Now—as for my Uncle Iain, he will not risk causing you future hurt. The Lord Mamore has spoken with him on the matter. But I would suggest that you keep away from him when possible. He has been in a strange mood of late.'

'He is greatly angered that I killed his son Fingal!'

'You did so unwittingly—and to save Sorley Mor's life. No, it is more than that. I greatly fear that his mind is somewhat disturbed.' Both men looked troubled at the thought. Then Roderick rose to his feet and nodded that the conversation was at an end.

Iain Campbell returned two days later at sunset and said no word as to where he had been for over a week. He smiled pleasantly at Lorna and treated her with every courtesy and made inquiry of Roderick as to the harvesting which was due to begin. It was as though nothing untoward had happened of late. But Lorna looked at him a little uncertainly, for she sensed that he was acting a part, but glad at least that he was not angry or drunk.

Days passed. Then one morning as he was polishing Roderick's saddle, in the stables Ewan Dhu looked up as he heard movement and saw Iain Campbell staring at him from the doorway.

'I have a question for you, Ewan Dhu! I wish to know what brought you to Balquidder on the night we both know of.' The suddenness and unexpectedness of the question surprised the answer before Ewan Dhu had considered his words.

'I was escorting Mistress Gregory back to her home!' he bit his tongue as he uttered the words.

'Just so! It was mentioned that you were in the company of one of the MacGregor women. What possessed you to do so? All know those of that name to be an accursed tribe!' The words were cold as ice.

'The lady was a friend of the Lady Kieran. She brought a message for her, did not know she was no longer at Glenlarig. I escorted her safe back to her glen. That was all of it, Sir Iain!' Ewan Dhu stared back at him steadily.

'Do you tell me that a MacGregor woman was entertained in this house?'

'It is not for me to answer such question, sir—but Laird Roderick!' he waited for more, but Iain Campbell turned on his heel and marched angrily away. Ewan drew a breath of relief. He regretted that he had spoken of the MacGregor lassie, but it was plain that Iain Campbell was already in possession of the facts. He knew of the man's blind hatred for all MacGregors and felt concern for the lovely young woman who had undoubtedly saved his life. If Iain Campbell ever tried to lift his hand against the girl, then he would deal with him. He drew his dirk and kissed the steel as he made the vow.

Iain Campbell coldly ignored all questions as to where he had spent the last week or more. Lorna frowned as she stared out of the window and watching him set off on his horse that morning, with only one of his favourite ghillies, Tam Breac in attendance. Her husband was in strange mood, outwardly polite to both Roderick and to her, but with an air of secretiveness about him.

She thought of their talk earlier that day, when he had questioned her about the visit of Mistress Sheena Gregory—demanding to know how long the girl had been there and whether Roderick had shown any particular interest in the young woman.

'I have told you several times, that Sheena merely came to deliver a message to Kieran, the dying words of Annie MacGregor who as we know had brought Kieran up as her own daughter...!' He cut her words off in mid flow his studied politeness deserting him.

'That devil's spawn should never have set foot in this house! Her father is cousin to Rory MacGregor, the man who murdered your own brother!' His face was contorted with anger as he spoke and he bunched one of his fists.

'This was no fault of Mistress Gregory! Her skirt was torn in a struggle to detain her when first discovered. I gave her an old gown of Kieran's and then she left. Roderick sent Ewan Dhu to see her safe to her own glen. I am not answerable to you for showing common courtesy and kindness!' She spoke back at him with unusual spirit, tired of his constant criticisms. He had bitten back an angry response and forced a smile.

'Of course, my dearest wife, you behaved with perfect correctness!' He bowed and left her standing looking after him uncertainly. Later she spoke of the incident to Roderick.

'I know of his unrelenting hatred for the MacGregors—understand its cause. But I hope that he does not seek to vent his anger on Sheena!' she said. He looked at her startled at the thought.

'I will have words with my uncle. He will certainly not lay a finger on Sheena Gregory,' he replied and his grey eyes hardened.

'Well I for one couldn't help liking the girl despite her parentage.' She placed a hand on his arm as she spoke. 'She is quite beautiful is she not?'

'She looks well enough,' he replied casually, but she surprised a softer expression on his face as he spoke and wondered at it. 'Where is my uncle now?' he inquired urgently.

'He rode off a few minutes since with Tam Breac, just the two of them. So they will not be harrying any MacGregors!' He relaxed at the information.

'Listen Aunt Lorna, I shall be away for a few days. I go to Edinburgh to visit Kieran and Sorley Mor. I also intend to escort Sheena there to deliver her message to Kieran. She asked Ewan Dhu to accompany her, but with the militia still stopping all they see upon the roads, I think for safety's sake it's best that I am with them.'

'Why, but that is very good of you, Roderick!'

'I do not wish any here to learn that Sheena MacGregor travels under my protection. I know I can rely on your discretion, dearest.' He looked at her seriously and she nodded.

'You have my word, Roderick!'

So it was that a few days later, as Angus Mac Seumas was about to set his chanter to his lips he heard a young voice calling to him. He glanced around and saw the same young boy who delivered him word of Ewan Dhu's survival two weeks back.

'Tell Ewan Dhu that the lady will see him at the spot where he fell upon the road. She will be there two hours after dawn tomorrow. Keep the matter secret!' Then without more ado the child sprang back into the heather and disappeared from sight. The old piper inflated the bag and a satisfying screech arose as his fingers then stroked magic into the damp morning air.

Later he found Ewan Dhu and delivered his message which Ewan then related privately to Roderick. Nor realised they were overheard.

'Tomorrow then?' he confirmed. 'We leave an hour before dawn. Have my stallion ready and your own mount and another for the lady.' Having given his instructions he smiled. It would be good to have another adventure and to get away from the sourness of Iain Campbell. He wondered where that man had gone. He felt slightly uneasy at leaving Lorna there without his support, but after Mamore's warning there should be no further trouble.

He slipped early from his bed and found Ewan Dhu waiting for him together with Ivor Mac Dugal and he smiled, for the two men were close friends, rarely apart and whom he trusted implicitly.

'You will be needing me too perhaps, Laird Roderick?' asked Ivor quietly.

'Come,' said Roderick and the horses snorted as they circled to the front of the house and away down the driveway. Lorna heard the sound of them and smiled. She thought of the MacGregor girl, proud, beautiful and spirited and wondered if despite all that stood between them, these two might become more than friends. Then her thoughts went back to the problem of her husband Iain and she sighed and turned over restlessly in bed.

The hatred Iain felt towards all MacGregors was an evil thing. Yes! Rory MacGregor had killed her brother. Nothing could expunge that fact. The man had paid with his life for shedding that blood and for kidnapping Catriona. She shuddered as she remembered it all.

But young Sheena MacGregor—Gregory as she must be called, was innocent of any involvement in matters that had occurred before her infancy and her father merely distant cousin to Rory MacGregor. One day these blood feuds must end—and the blind unforgiving hatred between different clans—but when?

Roderick rode ahead, humming a tune under his breath and peering through the mist that drifted off the loch and would disperse at sunrise. He turned in his saddle as Ewan called softly to him.

'I thought I saw movement above us on the hill,' he said. Roderick glanced around them. With white mist cladding the hillside it was difficult to see more than a few yards ahead.

'Sheep maybe,' replied Roderick. 'But keep your eyes open.'

'There is a hut of sorts up thereabouts if I remember rightly,' put in Ivor Mac Dugal. They reined in the horses and listened, but no sound broke the silence apart from a water fowl calling.

'Come—we must make better time,' said Roderick impatiently, nor knew he was observed as he led his ghillies on along the track that led to the falls of Dochart and the road south.

She was waiting for them on the side of the brae near the track leading to Balquidder. Roderick drew in a slow breath as he saw her. She was wearing the dress in which she had left Glenlarig and which fitted her to perfection. And yes, she was as fair as he had remembered her—and as haughty he thought, as she stood there a frown knitting her brows when she saw not only Ewan Dhu but Roderick and the other ghillie Ivor, as well.

'Give you good morrow, Mistress Gregory!'

'Roderick Campbell—what do you here?'

'I am making a planned visit to Edinburgh to see my sister Kieran Stewart and her husband. Ewan told me of your kindness—and your request to him. He is now keeping it. The added escort will keep you safe from any unfortunate brushes with the militia.' Roderick smiled at her as he saw the storm clouds gather in her eyes. She bit her lip considering the situation.

'I need no Campbell laird to keep me safe!' she exclaimed witheringly as she stared down at him.

'I fear that you do! Either come with us now—or forget Edinburgh! See I have brought a mount for you!' and he pointed to the horse Ivor led.

'I have a pony of my own tethered nearby. I need no Campbell horse!' she declared, hands on hips as the breeze swept her long, dark hair back from her distrustful face..

'Then I suggest you mount your pony now.' He said firmly. She looked as though she would have disappeared up the brae, but as the thought of Annie's last dying words coming into her mind, she merely nodded. Minutes later she was riding at Roderick's side and taking a journey which was to change both their lives.

It was not long before they were accosted by a red coated troop of militia, marching dispiritedly behind their mounted captain. Their forays into the highland areas brought little of excitement these days, most of those they sought either dead or fled into the hills. With so many of their poor dwellings burned down and the houses of the Jacobite lairds left in ruins, there were no rich pickings for these men whose ruthless efforts over the last three years had caused such devastation.

The captain called to them to halt and give account of themselves. Roderick Campbell quietened his stallion which was snorting at the advent of these strangers, as he stared across casually at the man.

'Roderick Campbell of Glenlarig, late a captain in Mamore's militia,' he announced and as the other man relaxed and smiled he added, 'I am travelling to Edinburgh with my cousin and my attendants.'

'Why, well met then, sir! I thought no rebel would ride thus boldly along the road. We have found little of interest so far. Not even any wearing the forbidden tartan or carrying arms, all such offences punishable by imprisonment.' The man scratched the side of his face which was smarting from the constant attack by midges.

'Where are you bound for?' demanded Roderick. The man shrugged.

'We turn off to the west a few miles on and through Glen Orchy and on to Fort William. We have the whole of the highlands under surveillance now sir. We have knocked all thought of resistance out of the natives' minds. There will be no further uprising I promise you!' He glanced at the girl at the Campbell's side and wondered why one so beautiful should treat him to such malevolent stare. No doubt she was annoyed at this delay on their journey. He raised his hand in salute as his men drew aside to allow the small party to proceed.

'How dared you refer to me as cousin,' exclaimed Sheena as they left the militia far behind them, her face flushed with anger.

'Would you have preferred I had given them your name—identified you as one of the proscribed MacGregors?' he asked reasonably. She merely swore an unladylike oath at him and spurred her pony onwards.

They were stopped twice more, routine checks that took little time, Roderick Campbell's name and former rank passport enough. After a night's stay at Stirling's Golden Lion Inn, where Sheena went immediately to her bedchamber, they resumed their journey early the next day and in late afternoon clattered along Edinburgh's cobbled streets, where Sheena's face expressed her disgust at the smells that assaulted her nostrils. She for one would be glad once her mission was accomplished and she could make return to the fresh mountain air and beauty of Balquidder.

'That is the Castle up on the hill!'

'How far is it to the doctor's house?' she asked

'Not far now.' He was weary of trying to make conversation with the girl, who stubbornly rejected all small advances of friendship. But despite his annoyance at her attitude, there was that about her that softened his heart. Also it would seem that she had been close to Kieran during their childhood.

Ewan Dhu held her pony for her as she dismounted stiffly, and glanced up at the tall terraced house above her. This was it then, the home of Sorley Mor and of Kieran Stewart the woman now known as a Campbell! Roderick offered his hand as Sheena swayed slightly from weariness—it was refused. He glanced at Ewan Dhu and Ivor.

'Here is money. Stable the horses as you did on our earlier visit and remain at the Royal Stag Inn until I need you,' he instructed them. They raised their hands to their bonnets in salute and were gone. Sheena had looked anxiously as her pony was led away, but she trusted Ewan Dhu. She felt Roderick's hand on her arm now guiding her up the steep flight of steps, to the regard of an old lady who watched with blatant interest from her own front door.

Roderick knocked vigorously and smiled as Mistress Lindsey opened to him, thinking it must be a patient disturbing the doctor's peace on a Sunday.

'Mercy me, it is Captain Campbell is it not,' she exclaimed in pleasure, then glancing at his companion, 'and this is your wife perhaps,' surmised the housekeeper.

'I would sooner die that be wife to a Campbell,' snapped Sheena ungraciously. She glared at the woman who made such suggestion.

'I can think of no worse fate than to be wed to you, Mistress Gregory,' Roderick retorted tiredly. 'But come let us try to be civil, guests now in the house of Sorley Mor Stewart. Soon you will meet with my sister Kieran and give her that message too precious to be revealed to another.'

They followed the housekeeper into the sitting room so familiar to Roderick, and where Kieran sat with a small child on either side of her, a book on her lap from which she was reading. She looked up as the door opened and gave a cry of delight as she recognised her brother and set the children down and rose to seek his arms.

'Roderick—oh, glad I am to see you!' She released him realising he was not alone and stared uncertainly at Sheena. Could it be? She had not seen the girl for many years. But as cousins—at least understanding such to be her relationship with Sheena at the time, not knowing then of her Campbell blood, they had once been quite close. It was before she was sent to Paris at fourteen years old, where subsequently she had met and married Alan Stewart, beloved father of her twin children. All of it so long ago now!

'Why—it is Sheena MacGregor is it not,' she said and made to embrace Sheena who shrank back from the contact as though stung.

'Yes, Kieran Campbell—it is Sheena MacGregor!' her violet eyes regarded the other darkly.

'My name is Stewart,' replied Kieran with a catch in her voice.

'But you are a Campbell are you not?'

'My parents were of Clan Diarmid, that I know now. But I am the same person who went up into the shielings with you for the milking and butter making! Remember how we swam together in the loch, picked wild flowers on its banks, listened to the pipes calling men together, the dancing and laughter!' Kieran's grey eyes were wide with memories.

'That person is now dead to me,' was the rebuff, 'Dead, as Annie MacGregor who brought you up as her own daughter—then announced to our people that you were dead to the Gregorach—had betrayed all that you once held dear.' Those words were meant to wound and they did. Tears sprang into Kieran's eyes. She seized on one phrase.

'Annie MacGregor—is dead?'

'Some weeks back! I was with her at the last. She went gladly, saying that she joyed she would be with her husband Duncan again. But she also made mention of you, Kieran Campbell! She asked me to deliver a message to you. Were it not so, wild horses would not have dragged me here this day!'

Before she could continue the door opened and Sorley Mor stood there. Immediately recognising his brother-in-law, he held out his hands in welcome. He felt the tension in the room and wondered at its cause,

'Roderick—what good chance brings you here to my door?' he exclaimed warmly. 'And who is your companion? Just tell me you have at last found a lady to bring joy into your heart?' The girl was beautiful he thought.

'Not exactly,' cried Roderick ruefully as they embraced each other. 'Allow me to present Mistress Sheena MacGregor, who has brought a message from the late Annie MacGregor who mothered Kieran. I had intended to visit you in any case, having left you abruptly on your return to Edinburgh for reason you know of.'

'You are welcome Mistress Sheena,' said the doctor, watching the proud and lovely face of the girl who was staring so balefully at Kieran. The twins sensing the tension held onto their mother's skirts, looking nervously up at the strange woman who was confronting her. 'Kieran you obviously know—and these are our twins, Alan and Ishbel,' he continued.

'They are fine children,' replied Sheena as she looked down at the two innocent young faces. It was hard not to like them she thought, the boy with his red hair and blue gaze looking at his mother protectively now and the little girl Ishbel with her fair curls and green eyes. 'A shame they have Campbell blood!' She almost wished she could have bitten the words back, but there was no denying it.

'Their surname is Stewart, Mistress MacGregor and we love them dearly,' replied Sorley Mor. 'One day I hope that we in Scotland will realise it is a person's worth that matters more than the stock from which they sprang.'

'Yet you I believe fought on the right side in the 45?' she questioned.

'I did. My loyalties for our Stuart King James and his son Prince Charles Edward for whom so many laid down their lives. But that is all done with now. We have to heal as a nation, eventually put aside clan hatreds. This land of ours is more important than traditions that only perpetuate hatred and bloodshed!'

'What sort of canting talk is that?' she cried mockingly.

'Sheena, we are guests in this house,' put in Roderick in annoyance at her rudeness. 'I am sure that your parents would not wish you to display such discourtesy.'

'My parents say you? My mother coughing her life up, from the cruel conditions in which we are forced to live,' she exclaimed hotly. 'And my father Robert MacGregor now lame from the wound he received at Campbell hands but two weeks since!'

'Oh Sheena, I am so sorry to hear your mother is unwell,' cried Kieran softly. 'My husband may be able to give you medicines to help her condition.' But the look she received was cold in the extreme. It was then that Sorley Mor looked closely at the girl.

'Your father is that Robert MacGregor who visited my house many months ago to tell me of Kieran's whereabouts?'

'I did not know he had done so,' she replied frowning. 'Why did he not tell me of it?' She stared at them all from troubled eyes. 'Look, I wish to speak my message to Kieran Campbell and then to leave.' At this Kieran whispered to Sorley Mor to take the little ones to Bess. She did not want them caught up in any more unpleasantness and was now as anxious to be free of Sheena's presence as the girl was to be away from here. He nodded.

'Come Roderick, we will go to my study and take a glass of wine together and you shall tell me of how matters are now at Glenlarig,' said the doctor as tucking a child under each arm he called for Bess who came running. The door closed behind them. Kieran looked at Sheena.

'Please sit down,' she said firmly. The girl hesitated, but seated herself grudgingly on the edge of one of the comfortable chairs.

'Now Sheena, whatever your thoughts are of me, I just ask that you reveal Annie's message?' She looked directly into Sheena's violet eyes, her own grey gaze serene. Sheena hesitated. She longed to give further hurt to this woman who had denied her Gregorach relatives to join with the detested Campbells. But Annie's dying wishes had to be observed.

'Annie said to tell you that she still loved you and knew that you had no alternative but to find out the truth of your birth once certain facts had been revealed to you. She said that she should have told you the truth of it long ago.'

'Oh Sheena—bless you for bringing this message,' cried Kieran brokenly. 'The pain of knowing I could never go back to the glen and live among you more has been tearing at me ever since I learned the truth.'

'Do you wish to tell me of it,' asked Sheena now. And Kieran did so. She spoke of her marriage to Alan Stewart, the weary months of waiting for word of his fate during the rising and the joy of his return with his friend Sorley Mor—of his murder and that of his father at the hands of the militia, their defilement of her. At this last Sheena cried out in horror.

'They did that to you?'

She spoke of Sorley Mor's help, without which neither Lachlan nor she would have survived; of his brother an Episcopal priest beaten almost to death by the redcoats, who had lived with them in that cave of the waters as she referred to it. Then told of her knowledge that she was pregnant, the fear that her babe might be the result of that horrific rape.

'Oh Kieran, how you suffered—I knew none of this,' cried Sheena. Kieran glanced at her broodingly, and then spoke of that encounter with Lord Mamore and her brother Roderick, when she learned for the first time of her Campbell ancestry.

'I could not bring myself to tell Sorley Mor of it. David had married us back there in Appin. It was a marriage in name only to protect my reputation. How could I tell the man I had come to love that both of my parents were Campbells? I just could not do it. Roderick suggested I should leave Edinburgh, bring the children to Glenlarig and I did so, left Sorley Mor as I thought forever. We have only been reunited but recently, and he accepts me despite my Campbell blood. Says it matters not a jot— and we are now so happy!'

'What an amazing story,' breathed Sheena. 'And you say that Roderick Campbell and Sorley Mor love each other as brothers?'

'Roderick is a very special person. I feel the richer for having him in our lives. Tell me Sheena—how chanced you to meet with him?' she asked.

Sheena told of her attempt to deliver Annie's last words to Kieran at Glenlarig, her encounter with Ewan Dhu and meeting with Roderick—her torn skirt and Lorna's kindness as it was explained that Kieran had left the house to return to Edinburgh.

'I am wearing one of your gowns—you recognise it I suppose? Lorna insisted I take it, mine not decent to travel in so badly ripped when your brother tried to detain me! That torn skirt had been my one remaining presentable garment since we were forced to flee our home which was destroyed with all our possessions!' her tones were full of bitterness.

'I should have tried to find all of you—wanted to so badly, but how could I knowing myself to be a Campbell?' Kieran's voice was choked by tears.

'I understand your situation now and am sorry for it. But did you not stop to think that Annie was aware of your parentage? She adopted you as one of us. Could you not have trusted to that love?' She shook her head sadly. 'Surely it would have been better so than to have thrown in your lot with the clan which above all others had caused so much distress and cruelty in the highlands?'

'But consider this—I had two small babies to care for,' exclaimed Kieran defensively. 'Also I had found my brother—and I was curious to learn more of the family from which I had been torn by circumstance. I found much love and kindness at Glenlarig. Aunt Lorna is a wonderful woman and Roderick and I have become very close. You will remember I spoke of that terrible day when I was raped—that the redcoat captain had cruel green eyes and a limp? I would see that face in my nightmares!'

'I would that my father had found him! He would have plunged his steel into the villain's heart!' cried Sheena her eyes flashing.

'He came on a visit to Glenlarig—did not recognise me in my fine clothes as the girl he had raped and given to his men to pleasure. But I revealed the matter to Roderick. He rode down to the city where the man was attached to the castle garrison. There was a duel. He killed the rapist, Sheena—was badly wounded himself and came to this house that Sorley Mor might remove the bullet from his shoulder. It was then that they became friends.'

'For a Campbell he behaved as one of the Gregorach in this matter!' exclaimed Sheena. 'Perhaps I will view him with different eyes from now on.' And she knit her brows in thought.

'I hope so! He is a fine and honourable man. His Uncle Iain a more difficult character. He was full of welcome when first I arrived with the children—but coldly angry when my husband came Glenlarig and we were reconciled, more especially so on hearing that I was going to return to Edinburgh with Sorley Mor. He ordered attempt on my husband's life! It was thwarted by Ewan Dhu!'

'Iain Campbell—I spit on that name,' cried Sheena. 'He it was who almost took my father's life but recently and left Robert permanently lamed. How now will he manage to drive the cattle we manage to deprive those despicable landowners of who stood against the Prince!' At these words Kieran hid a smile, for it was by reiving that the MacGregors had survived and to them this manner of life had become one of necessity, nor could Kieran really deplore it.

'Where are you living now Sheena?'

'In a cave like to the one you spoke to me of in Appin. There are many such caves in the hills and gullies of Balquidder where whole families live. Royal our race! We are as you know descended from the third son of Alpin Mac Achai, King of Scotland way back in time. Long years since were proscribed, our name not to be spoken—and it continues so. Yet our men are the bravest in battle, always rise when called. Times were hard enough before Culloden—almost impossible now.' Her eyes were sad, 'so many die each winter from the cold and exist close to starvation.'

'Oh my dear, it is indeed terrible. And not only for the Gregorach but for all who rose for the Prince! I have seen sights so sickening that they haunt my dreams. Women and children naked and dead of starvation—and old people driven helpless from their homes, terrified and trembling, all burned behind them, to wander in the hills until they drop. What the English did to our country will leave indelible stain on their name throughout time.'

'And it was with the help of the Campbells!' flashed Sheena. 'How could they have acted so and turned against their own people?'

'Perhaps for power,' Kieran suggested. 'But there again I have heard it said that they realised that since Scotland lost its sovereignty through the union of the parliaments, that they serve our people best by keeping their own authority intact. Better so than by having English usurpers amongst us here forever more.' Kieran spread her hands out before her helplessly.

'One day we will be free again,' breathed Sheena fiercely. 'I know it may not be in our lifetime—but come about it will! No nation can be subjugated by another without eventually standing up to such injustice and saying enough is enough! One day Scotland again become an independent nation, the Scottish Lion lift its head with pride!'

'I pray you are right,' cried Kieran. 'In this we are sisters, Sheena!' She opened her arms and clasped the other girl to her in mutual embrace. It was at this moment that the door opened and Roderick and Sorley Mor stood looking at the two.

'You have delivered your message to my sister?' asked Roderick quietly. 'Do you desire to leave now? If so I can arrange for you to stay at a hotel if you wish.' He was only too aware of her anger towards Kieran, but curious now to see them in embrace. Was it possible that they had become friends?

'Sheena will be our guest here together with you brother,' Kieran said, nor did the other girl protest the suggestion.'

'Well that is settled then,' cried Sorley Mor in relief. 'Mistress Lindsey is preparing a fine meal for us. Roderick, you have yet to meet the partner I have brought into my growing practice. John Patterson will join us at table as well as Lachlan!'

Kieran smiled at Sheena. 'I will show you to your room Sheena. I know how tiring that journey can be. You will wish to refresh yourself before dinner—come!'

'None of this is what I expected,' replied Sheena plaintively. 'But I thank you—Kieran Stewart!' And all knew that in dropping the name Campbell for that of Stewart was a token of her acceptance of Kieran. And the men watched them walk off together with sighs of relief.

Later as they sat at table and enjoyed a fine roast of lamb and vegetables followed by one of Mistress Lindsay's rich fruit puddings they discussed the ambitious plans being examined to build a new town, an extension of the old city where those who could afford to live there would occupy fine houses set around leafy squares with pleasant walkways.

'And what will happen to the poor,' cried Sheena. 'I saw some of those tall tenement buildings as we rode here, and where I am told great numbers of working folk are squeezed together in deplorable conditions. And as for the smells—how can any put up with such foulness!' They all looked down at her outburst, for what justification could there be for a plan which would satisfy the rich but leave the majority of Edinburgh's impoverished citizens in the same squalid condition in which disease abounded.

'Any start to improve matters is better than none,' suggested John Patterson in his deep voice. 'Yes—much needs to be done to improve the lot of those suffering overcrowding. Some might say that the horses of the rich are stabled better than most citizens are housed! There is also a need to provide new employment—some form of industry. In England there are many factories and mills—not that conditions are particularly good in them. But we need opportunity for people to earn money to better themselves,' he exclaimed hotly.

He had spoken with feeling and Roderick Campbell surveyed Sorley Mor's assistant physician curiously. He had been told very little of John Patterson save that he was a fine doctor—an Edinburgh man. But that scar that ran from the right of his forehead down to his mouth looked result of a sabre cut to him—and his voice held highland lilt. He stared at Patterson. The name meant nothing to him. But had he ever seen the man before?

'You look strangely familiar to me, Doctor Patterson,' said Roderick curiously. 'Have we ever met before today?'

'I meet many in my work as physician. But no, I do not think our paths have crossed previously,' said Patterson easily, but his hazel eyes looked wary.

'Were you at Culloden?' The question shot across the table like a sword thrust. But Patterson kept his composure. A smile crossed his face.

'Perhaps after such tragic event, we should not seek to rummage among old hurts. I am a physician sir. My work is in the healing of men. I would also say that the healing of our country should be the priority of all men of good will.' He had not answered the question directly, but nor could Roderick after these words attempt to pursue the point. But looking at Patterson he was sure he was right in his surmise. The man was a Jacobite and it was more than their love of medicine that bound him to Sorley Mor. But the secret was safe with him.

'Your good health—Doctor John Patterson,' he said and lifted his glass in salute and the tension around the table subsided. Sheena Gregory had listened to every word that passed. She too realised that Patterson was one who had risen for the Prince and liked him the better for it. As for Roderick's interrogation of the man it was stark reminder that Kieran's brother was a Campbell and not to be trusted.

'Tell me Roderick Campbell is Ewan Dhu now safe from your Uncle Iain's attempt to murder him? I understand that Ewan saved Sorley Mor when Iain's base born son Fingal Beag tried to kill him at your uncle's orders—that Ewan Dhu shot Fingal in defence of Sorley Mor?'

She knew that it would embarrass Roderick to discuss the matter, but it would also divert his attention from Patterson. Roderick looked as though he would protest the question, so she continued gleefully to pressure him, violet eyes sparkling with mischief. She leaned forward across the table, fingers toying with her glass of wine as she said, 'Iain Campbell shot Ewan Dhu in my sight and left him for dead at the roadside near Balquidder, in retribution I understand for the killing of Fingal. It would seem that Clan Campbell, despite imposition of English law to regulate the lives of others, solve their own problems by blood!'

'I have spoken with my uncle on the matter. I assure you such will never happen again,' replied Roderick calmly and skilfully changed the subject back to the proposed changes needed in the Capital.

'They are speaking of draining the Nor Loch,' explained Sorley Mor, then looking directly at Roderick said in casual voice, 'The body of a man surfaced in its foul waters but recently—too decayed to identify the man but he died of a bullet.' As his gaze locked with Roderick's he saw expression of relief on the other's face. Neither of them doubted but that the corpse was that of the rapist Bradshaw, all evidence of that duel now obliterated by those evil smelling waters.

Sheena MacGregor also caught the doctor's meaning and remembered Kieran's tale of a duel fought by Roderick in support of his sister's honour. Again she revised her feelings towards this young Campbell with his grave demeanour and who so closely resembled Kieran, the same red gold hair, same grey eyes and fine features. Maybe he was an exception to the generality of this abusive and murderous clan. But memories of the hatred between the Gregorach and Clan Diarmid ran deep, deep!

She turned to Lachlan Stewart who had been sitting quietly, hearing all and but remaining silent. She addressed him directly for the first time.

'Lachlan Stewart, you are brother to Kieran's first husband Alan, are you not—so her brother-in-law? Strange it is that a woman should have a Campbell brother and Stewart brother-in-law!' She stared at the youth curiously, for he had coloured at becoming the focus of general attention.

'My mother who died at my birth was my father's second wife, Alan Stewart and I half brothers. He was very dear to me! As for Kieran, she cared for me as almost both mother and sister during those terrible days following the defeat of all our hopes. Without her help and that of Sorley Mor I would not have survived.' His words were simple.

'Will you ever return to Appin,' asked Sheena quietly.

'Who knows? But I think not. All I knew and loved—people, places destroyed. But I have begun to realise that the past has to remain the past. If our nation is to survive then eventually there has to be forgiveness Mistress Sheena—and that forgiveness has to start with each one of us!' All looked at his earnest young face in silence. Then Sorley Mor spoke.

'You are right in what you say, Lachlan. Sadly it may take several generations before all such bitterness fades. But time is a great healer it is said. Also I fear there is worse to come for our people in the years ahead. I have heard of plans—no more than plans at this stage, to clear the highlands of its inhabitants and replace them with sheep! There will be forced mass emigration to other lands far across the seas, poor crofters and cottars driven from their homes, leaving the land empty. Sheep—only sheep will be seen on our hillsides, our folk banished!'

His words rang across the table and Roderick Campbell lowered his eyes, knowing that this atrocity was feasible, had also heard it spoken of.

'We live at a time of great change in our country,' he said. 'But of one thing I assure you, none of Clan Campbell will ever be party to any on our lands being so used.'

'But you would countenance it for others?' questioned Sorley Mor.

'No, I would not. But consider Sorley that new laws are coming into effect. All is changing.' He looked around earnestly as he continued, 'The chief of the clan was once regarded as father of his people. He gave them the protection of his name and they paid small rents for their crofts and strips of land and rose to fight at his command. But many of those chiefs have been attainted for their part in the rebellion, their lands passing into the hands of others, while they live out their lonely years in exile in France.'

'Yes,' cried Kieran hotly. 'And now strangers take our lands!'

Her husband nodded, saying quietly, 'And those newcomers either from the borders or further south, have no link with the highlands, no sense of responsibility for those whose ancestors have lived on their native hillsides and in their beloved glens, throughout centuries of time.'

'I have heard that many of those who could afford passage have already taken ship voluntarily to distant lands,' said Doctor Patterson. 'This in conjunction with the devastation caused in the cruel aftermath of the rising, where whole areas were systematically cleared of all human habitation, innocent people slaughtered, their cattle driven off and sold to English buyers and now grazing on hillsides not their own thus enforcing starvation, has already denuded the highlands of so many of its people.' He paused for breath. 'But should this new proposed clearance ever take place on the scale suggested—well, the highlands would never recover from it!'

His words fell prophetically on their ears and silence reigned in the room. Then seeking to lighten the mood, Kieran stood up walked to a cabinet and lifted her violin—her original instrument Lorna's gift, remained at Glenlarig, this was a replacement. She started to play a delicate highland air known to all of them and the sound of it brought peace to their troubled hearts. Then Sheena came to stand beside her. The words she sang in the Gaelic were poignant and wildly beautiful, her voice richly soaring around the room. Roderick Campbell leaned forward as he listened to her and his eyes were soft.

Kieran played other songs to them and the men joined with Sheena and the evening ended more happily than it had begun and all went to bed with different thoughts pricking away at the back of their minds. What did the future hold for any of them?

Chapter Thirteen

The following morning having breakfasted Sheena MacGregor spent time with Kieran as the twins cautiously accepted this new person into their lives. At first when she approached they clung to Bess, remembering Sheena's stern face of the previous day. But before long little Alan was showing her his wooden horse and Ishbel held up her doll and laughter rang around the nursery.

'Kieran, they are adorable,' breathed Sheena. 'So different in their colouring, the boy has your red hair!'

'He favours his father in the shape of his face and his blue eyes,' replied Kieran fondly. 'As for Ishbel, she has her grandfather's blond hair and green eyes.'

'You speak of Colin Campbell,' replied Sheena frowning.

'Yes, I saw his portrait when I was at Glenlarig. And I was glad, reassured to see it, Sheena, for the man who raped me had fair hair and green eyes,' and she shuddered. 'You can guess my thoughts when first I saw my daughter.'

'There were other men who abused you on that dreadful day,' said Sheena.

'True. But it was his revolting face that remained in memory to goad me in my night time hours. Rape is a most terrible crime, Sheena. So many of our women folk suffered it at the hands of the English—and of those of our own people who so disgracefully stood with them against the Stuart cause.'

'All this we are to forget according to Lachlan and Sorley Mor,' said Sheena angrily. 'But how can we forget, never mind forgive all that has happened?'

'Perhaps it is not possible in our own strength,' sighed Kieran, 'but with the help of the great God who sent his own Son to lead men into the paths of peace, giving his life in expiation for our sins!'

'You believe in all this,' frowned Sheena sceptically.

'I am not a religious person Sheena, but recently my husband has been talking with me on such matters. His own dear brother was a minister of the Episcopal Church. He also spoke of forgiveness, even of those who so cruelly beat him for not revealing the names of those who arose for the Prince in his village!'

'This was the man David Stewart? He was brave!'

'He went to France with Lachlan after we made our home in Edinburgh. He died there of pneumonia. Lachlan loved him dearly. He returned to us here, brought David's bible with him.'

Sheena was silent for a few minutes.

'I can never forgive,' she said. 'Why should I when my people have suffered so cruelly throughout the years—treated as dogs!'

'As have countless others, Sheena dear, but yes, the Gregorach more than most. All this I realise! I thought I would never be able to forgive Alan's cruel death—his elderly father butchered—my rape and the terrible sights I have seen.' Her grey eyes were full of pain as she spoke.

'And do you tell me that you can now forgive?'

'Sorley Mor whose own young son was blown apart at his side by Cumberland's canon, spoke recently of Christ's crucifixion—that He forgave those who hammered cruel nails into his hands before hoisting him up to die in agony on a cross. Sorley said we also should try to forgive, however difficult—but that it was only recently that he had managed to do so.' She spoke falteringly, her eyes damp with unshed tears as she stared at the younger girl.

'Perhaps it is easier to forgive while living in a fine house with a soft bed to lie on and good food! Try it while scraping existence in a dark, damp cave, freezing in winter, risking life to bring down a deer or any small game to be found to feed your family.' She looked scornfully at Kieran.

'I also lived for some months in a cave in constant fear of my life—have walked long miles through freezing mist on bare hillsides above roads alive with redcoat militia. All of our experiences are different Sheena, but one thing I do know. Allowing the cancer of hatred to eat away at your heart is to destroy all hope of real happiness.'

'On this we shall never agree!' ground out Sheena, although her eyes were thoughtful. The face of Roderick floated before her eyes and then that of Iain Campbell and she swore a passionate oath lifting her gown and snatching a knife strapped to her thigh. 'On this sacred steel, I swear will never forgive!' she cried and the twins looked up at her startled. They clung nervously to Kieran's skirts as Bess spoke soothingly to them. As the anger died from Sheena's eyes she made a gesture of contrition.

'I did not mean to scare the bairns,' she said awkwardly.

'Well, how would you feel if we should take a turn around the shops and market. Take the children with us. Bess, they are ready aren't they?' and the nursemaid nodded.

'What of the men?' Sheena asked.

'My husband and John Patterson together with Lachlan and Nurse Effie, are dealing with patients already. As for my brother, he has matter of business to attend to with his lawyer, which leaves us free of male involvement!' She smiled at Sheena, who hesitated, her purse containing only a few small coins. She did not wish to face embarrassment in having to admit this. But Kieran's smile was difficult to ignore.

'Why yes, I would like to see something of Edinburgh while I am here,' she declared.

The weather was warm, the all pervasive smells of the city causing Sheena to again wrinkle her nose in disgust, but interest took over as she considered the busy throng of people about their business and saw sedan chairs and private carriages bearing the wealthier of Edinburgh's citizens in their fine clothes and holding sweet smelling herbs to their noses. There was much bustle today which had been lacking on Sunday the day of her arrival with Roderick Campbell.

'Most would have been at the Kirk of a Sunday or spending the day quietly,' explained Kieran. She tightened her grip on Alan's little hand as the toddler pulled her toward a sweetie seller's stall. Ishbel gave a cry of delight as she glimpsed the candy and Bess followed her mistress over to the rosy faced woman who smiled encouragingly at these prospective customers.

It was at this moment that a troop of red coated militia came marching along the street towards them, people scattering resignedly from their path.

'Look at them,' cried Sheena eyes smouldering with anger. 'Would that the earth would open and swallow them up!' And Kieran nodded in agreement. ✓

They drew to the side of the pavement amongst the crush of indignant passersby. Suddenly, Kieran felt a quick tug on Alan's hand and he was torn from her grip! At the same time Bess screamed in protest as Ishbel was similarly snatched! The last of the militia passed by as the women fought to grab the children back from the two masked men who held them struggling under their arms. A black carriage without crest drove out from a side street and approached. The men in movement almost too swift to comprehend leapt inside the vehicle as the driver shouted and whipped his horse. The carriage disappeared at speed.

Several on lookers who had watched the event in horror attempted to comfort the distraught young mother, while Sheena set off on foot in attempt to follow the carriage. She was soon back her head lowered in despair.

'It went too fast,' she said, as she put an arm about Kieran's shoulders. 'What black hearted de'ils would steal two wee bairns?'

'I don't know—oh, I don't know,' wept Kieran deep in shock. 'We must tell Sorley Mor. He will know what to do!'

'It could be a kidnap for ransom,' reasoned Sheena.

'But we are not wealthy people,' she faltered. 'Sorley Mor has only what he earns from his practice. Many of his poorer patients pay nothing. He is much loved by all. Why would any steal our children?' And she broke into wild sobs. Bess placed her hand on Kieran's arm.

'Look, Mistress Kieran—is that not your brother?' cried a tearful Bess pointing a shaking finger. 'He has seen us—is crossing the street!' she waved frantically and he waved casually back.

It was Sheena who cried out to him in urgent voice. His greeting smile left his face and he ran the last few steps realising that something was amiss.

'Kieran—what has happened?' he asked, pulling the weeping girl into his arms. She could barely speak, her voice choked with sobs, trembling and incoherent.

'My babies,' she managed. 'They have been stolen—and I don't know where they have been taken or why!' Then she stood there shaking in his embrace. He looked appealingly at Sheena.

'Can you give me details of what has happened,' he asked. She did so, explaining all in a calm but urgent voice.

'The two kidnappers were masked—dressed in black, nothing to distinguish them. Black also the coach into which they bundled the children and away! I gave chase—came to a crossroads. Looked in all directions but the vehicle had disappeared from sight!'

'I will get my men to assist in search for the bairns,' he said in unsteady voice. 'If they have been harmed in any way...!'

'We should get Kieran home. Sorley Mor must be informed,' she said and he inclined his head in agreement. Kieran was calmer now, but her face was white with shock. They had become the focus of an interested and sympathetic crowd who had surrounded them, all expressing opinions as to possible motive for the deed. Roderick addressed them with authority and they parted to allow the small group of people pass on their way.

It was but a ten minute walk back to the house, quicker on foot than to have waited for a hackney carriage. The housekeeper opened the door and put her hand to her mouth in horror as Bess whispered what had happened. She helped Kieran now in a state of near collapse onto a couch in the living room, and ran for the doctor, rushing into his surgery. He looked up in surprise as did Patterson.

'Sorley Mor—Come quickly—your bairns have been kidnapped,' she cried at the physician, who looked at her in disbelief, but seeing the expression on her face, hurriedly handed the bandaging of a young lad's hand wound to Lachlan.

He sat beside Kieran, drew her head onto his shoulder and taking a handkerchief wiped the tears from her red, swollen eyes as he attempted to soothe her.

'Hush, my heart's darling. Be calm I pray you.' He looked at Roderick. 'You were there—can tell me what happened,' he demanded. But his brother-in-law shook his head. In a few coherent words he explained what little he had established. He looked at the MacGregor girl standing silent and distressed.

'You should speak to Sheena. She was there. I am going to get Ewan Dhu and Ivor. We will find the children, bring them back. Better I go now!' His mouth formed a hard angry line and his grey eyes held a look Sorley had never seen there before.

'I will come with you!'

'No. Your wife needs you my friend. Leave this to me for the now.' Then he was gone. The doctor stared after him indecisively. He wanted to be out there searching for the children but knew his immediate duty was to Kieran.

'Help me get her to her bed,' he said quietly to Sheena. 'I will give her a draught to quieten her, help her to sleep.'

Soon afterwards he listened carefully to all Sheena had to relate. Two masked men—a black carriage that had disappeared before any could stop it. But none of it made any sense. Why should anyone wish to kidnap Alan and Ishbel?

Kieran slept in drug induced slumber, as Sorley Mor now strode back and forth below in the sitting room. He thanked Sheena for her attempt to follow the coach. 'Did you overhear anything those devils said,' he asked suddenly. She frowned trying to remember.

'One man addressed the other as Niall—a common enough name! "Hurry, do not drop the brat, Niall!" were his words. He spoke in the Gaelic, so perhaps no Edinburgh man.'

'It may be of help,' he said distractedly. 'Mistress Sheena I am grateful for your help to my wife. I do not know how she will bear it if anything happens to the twins. I can only hope that Roderick has good news by now!'

It was night by the time that Roderick Campbell wearily climbed the steps and knocked. Sorley Mor had seen him coming and opened the door almost immediately, hurrying him into his study. He poured them both a brandy, seeing the tiredness on the other's face. Roderick sank into a chair.

'I am sorry, Sorley Mor! My men and I have searched Edinburgh and found no trace of the bairns. We did find an empty black carriage however abandoned at the entrance to an alley. An old man directed us to it. There on the back seat I found a ribbon. Does this belong to Ishbel,' he asked tendering the stained blue satin.

'It does,' choked out Sorley Mor. 'Where was it that you found the coach?'

'Close to the Netherbow Port! It is my opinion that the kidnappers may have taken the children out of Edinburgh. I asked information of the guards on duty at the city gate there. He reported seeing a couple with two small children aboard a coach bound for Stirling. But he could not describe the wee boy and girl apart from the fact they were asleep and appeared to have been crying.'

'You should have followed!'

'I needed to speak with you first. There are a great many black coaches in Edinburgh you know. I had to be sure that the ribbon was Ishbel's.'

'It is—I have told you that it is!' cried Sorley Mor. Roderick touched his arm in sympathy, trying to calm him.

'However slight the clue of the couple with two small children may seem, Ewan and Ivor are on the road to Stirling now,' he said quietly. 'They will try to catch up with the coach, two hours to make up. Certainly they will check at the coaching inn for that particular couple. It's only a slight chance that those particular small children are yours my friend!'

'You are right. And there are probably many couples with fretful children travelling the roads. But it is good that your men are checking it out,' said Sorley Mor heavily. 'But the twins might well be hidden in a house somewhere here in Edinburgh.'

'We need to establish a cause for their kidnap. Have you any enemies that come to mind?' probed Roderick. Sorley Mor shook his head distractedly.

'Enemies? No—not that I know of! Nor has Kieran. I have given her a sleeping draught, but dread her state of mind when she awakes. But come Roderick, you are tired, must eat.' They both looked up as Sheena knocked and came in, a shawl draped over her night shift.

'What news?' she demanded brusquely, seating herself on the side of the doctor's desk. They explained the little gleaned so far and she frowned.

'If they have been kidnapped for ransom, then you will have a demand for money within the next few days,' she said practically. 'If not for money, then what other cause?' And she drew in her breath suddenly. A thought had come into her mind but she did not dare to frame it in speech. It was a wild notion and she had no wish to cause further hurt to this family until she had thought the matter through.

'Sheena, all is a nightmare at this moment!' said Sorley Mor. 'John Patterson is to care for my patients for the next while until all is resolved—

I have maze of terrible situations swirling through my mind. Have they been taken by those perverts who take their pleasure with little ones—or sold to a wealthy childless couple miles away, perhaps in England? You hear of such stories!'

'Do not torture yourself with such thoughts,' said Roderick firmly. 'I have given all details of the kidnap to the Watch, also left word of it at the Castle Garrison. There will be many looking for little Alan and Ishbel. That I promise you!'

'You should get some sleep,' said Sheena regarding both men in genuine sympathy, 'Better able then to make sound judgements on the morrow.' Roderick smiled at her, this beautiful and fiery offspring of the Clan that had brought such sorrow to his particular family. He realised that she had strength to match that of his sister Kieran, the two young women strangely alike in temperament. He acknowledged a certain fondness for her. But this was no time to be thinking of such matters.

They retired to their beds but none slept well that night. As for Kieran, she was racked by occasional sob in her drug induced slumber.

When Kieran awoke the following morning terrible realisation of what had happened flooded back. But whereas yesterday she had been distraught beyond measure, today she put away her outward grief, knowing that she would need a clear head in whatever lay ahead.

She evaded her husband's arms not daring to expose her raw emotion, splashed her face with cold water, combed her tumbled hair and dressed.

Sorley Mor watched, understood and then communicated what little news Roderick had managed to bring of the twins. She nodded numbly. So Alan and Ishbel could be just anywhere now. Were they crying for her? Had they been hurt by those who snatched them? It took all of her self control not to break down. She looked at Sorley Mor, saw his own face torn by grief and touched his hand.

'We will get them back—I know it in my heart,' she said firmly.

'I will do all in my power to find them—as will Roderick,' he reassured her. 'Remember too that Ewan Dhu and Ivor should be returning from Stirling soon with news of the two children seen leaving the city yesterday in that public coach.' He knew how flimsy the clue was.

'But they could well still be in Edinburgh? That is so is it not?'

'Yes, my darling. But I think we should go below now, speak with your brother and Sheena. Come.'

None ate much that morning as Mistress Lindsay tried to coax them to breakfast on porridge, or eggs and fresh bread at least, while John Patterson and Lachlan offered their sympathy, asking what they could do to help. Sorley Mor merely replied that by caring for the daily influx of patients would be help enough. Of Roderick there was no sign, nor of Sheena, who had seemingly left the house together a little earlier.

Sheena sat opposite Roderick Campbell in a coffee house, face pensive.

'Now tell me why we could not have spoken back at the house,' he demanded, staring impatiently at the girl's imperious face. She reached across the table and placed one slim tanned hand on his.

'What I must ask you of is a delicate matter! If I am wrong in what I suspect—then as well that Sorley and Kieran do not know of my suspicion.' She fixed her dark violet eyes upon his face as she spoke and removing her hand as he stiffened.

'Well, go on then?'

'Kieran told me she believed that your Uncle Iain wanted Sorley Mor dead so that she would remain at Glenlarig with the children. That since you Roderick, had as yet no wife and seemed most unwilling to marry, that Iain knew wee Alan Stewart was the next legitimate heir to the estate after you, wished to keep him close by.' He listened to her intently and nodded slow agreement that such was the case.

'My Uncle Iain is not himself these days,' he replied. 'In fact I fear for his sanity, as does my aunt Lorna!' He shook his head sadly as he thought of Iain's recent erratic behaviour. 'But what has this to do with the kidnap of my small nephew and niece? Surely you do not think....?'

'Has your uncle a man named Niall in his employ?'

'Niall, why yes! There are the MacNicol brothers, Archie and Niall. They are among his most trusted attendants. Rumour has it that he fathered a daughter on their sister many years ago—the family much in his favour! But what of it—you are not suggesting Iain is behind the kidnap?'

'Think Roderick! One of the two villains who stole the children was addressed the other as Niall.'

'But it is a common enough name! What you are proposing is totally ridiculous!' He regarded her in outrage, the expression in his eyes hardening. 'My uncle would never stoop to such infamy!' he declared hotly.

'I pray you are right! But it seems to me the man who attempted to murder Dr Stewart might not flinch at the idea of stealing of your sister's wee son to further his ambitions!' she stared at him. He flinched at the idea, dismissed it. He looked at her reprovingly.

'Since I am very much alive, then I hardly think Iain's main priority is to find a replacement heir,' he said in lighter tones. 'After all, I may decide to marry one day. I simply have found no woman to my taste as yet.'

'And what characteristics would your wife need then that you are having such difficulty in finding one?' She stared at him sudden merriment shining in her eyes. 'Let me see—a Campbell of course, with a rich dowry, fine clothes and jewels at her neck—and biddable!' she teased. He drew in his breath as he met the challenge in her eyes.

'Certainly not a highland wildcat,' he said shortly and rose. 'We must leave, Mistress Sheena. I will see you safe back to the house and then I go to the inn where if they are back I hope to meet with Ewan Dhu and Ivor. Hopefully they may have news of the bairns.'

'May I come with you?'

'No. Kieran though will be glad of any comfort you can give her. I must ask that you make no mention of your unjust suspicions regarding my uncle.' He relaxed as she gave grudging agreement.

The two ghillies were waiting for him as Roderick made his way to the public bar of the inn. They looked tired, despondent and his spirits sank.

'Tell me,' he said, calling for a drink for them. It was Ewan who began the story.

'When we arrived at the coaching inn at Stirling it was but an hour since the coach had arrived there,' said Ewan Dhu. 'We inquired if any who had travelled on the coach were staying at the inn and found several people who were.'

'We questioned all of them very carefully,' put in Ivor, as Ewan Dhu nodded agreement and continued his account.

'They said they had seen the couple with the two small bairns—but that they had left the coach near the village of Dullan a few miles short from Stirling, the children sleeping as they carried them away it appeared in the direction of a farm track. Then the coach went on. The other travellers had seen nothing to make them think anything was amiss.'

'Did they give any description of the children,' asked Roderick keenly.

'That is it, sir,' replied Ewan Dhu. 'They said the boy was red haired, the wee girl fair. Perhaps two years of age. We went to Dullan, the village they mentioned this morning. We inquired at several cottages if any there knew of a couple with children of this description. None were able to help in the matter. I believe they spoke truth too.'

'But at least we know now that those children were almost certainly Alan and Ishbel,' breathed Roderick in satisfaction. 'We must discover the movements of the couple who have them. It's possible that they left the coach where they did in order to travel further by other means.' The ghillies exchanged glances, thinking that he was probably right.

'We did our best, Laird,' said Ivor. 'We would give our lives for those wee bairns.'

'We will find them—I swear it,' added Ewan Dhu.

'I cannot wait to get my hands on whoever is behind the kidnap,' snarled Roderick grimly. 'I must return with this news to my sister and her husband. Be ready to ride should I need you again!' he instructed.

Back at the house, Roderick looked compassionately at his sister and brother-in-law as he related the little he had discovered, answering all anxious questions as best he could. At least they could be fairly sure that the twins were no longer in the city, must seek them at least forty miles away.

Sheena MacGregor, who had been listening intently, watched him interrogatively under her long lashes. Had he given any further thought to her own wild suggestion she wondered? His face gave no clue as to his private thoughts. But as he glanced at the girl, Roderick remembered her suggestion regarding Iain Campbell, considered it for brief moment and then dismissed the idea as before. Whoever had taken the children must have had agents in Edinburgh ready to put such affair into effect. Iain Campbell rarely if ever visited the capital. His behaviour and thoughts too erratic to make such plan!

A week went by on leaden wings. Sorley Mor and Roderick visited the hamlet of Dullan together, speaking at length with the few cottars who lived there. It was as the ghillies had earlier reported. None knew of a couple with children of such age and description, but when they heard of the kidnapped children they were only too anxious to help.

'Did you see any leave the village in other form of transport that day than the stagecoach,' asked Sorley Mor of an old farm labourer who stood at his gate. The man thought slowly and puffed on his evil smelling pipe before answering.

'A cart went past my door maybe half an hour after the coach passed by here. It comes to my mind that it was a hay cart,' he said. 'Not from this farm though!' Sorley Mor looked hopefully at Roderick, and pressed a small coin into the old man's hand. They had already inquired at every dwelling in that village without success. This scrap of information was the first they had gleaned.

Who owned that cart—and where was it bound? Was it possible that two small frightened children had been carried away in it? They widened their search, asked people for help in every one of the villages along the route but to no avail. It was as though the cart like the children had vanished!

It was now two weeks since the children had been snatched, as Kieran and Sorley Mor waited anxiously for a possible ransom demand for their return. When none came, Kieran was plunged into a deeper trough of despair. It was as though a lamp had been extinguished in her heart, her grief colouring every thought. In vain Sorley Mor tried to lighten her spirits, saying that sooner or later they would find the little ones. But he knew that the longer there was no news, the more likely that they would never be heard of again.

'Sorley Mor—I must make return to Glenlarig,' said Roderick one morning as the doctor prepared for his busy day ahead in the surgery. 'It is near to three weeks since I left Lorna there—and I must be sure that all is well with her. My Uncle Iain is of difficult temperament these days!' His grey eyes expressed his anxiety and Sorley nodded understanding.

'You have been more than kind spending so much time helping to search for the twins. Of course you must go! Mistress Sheena too has been worrying about her parent's health. I understand her mother has a lung problem and her father's leg cause for concern. I will give her medication for them.' His thoughts were of the cave Sheena had described as their abode, and he remembered the months that he had spent with Kieran, David and Lachlan in another cave—that cave of the waters.

Kieran clung to Sheena as the two young women said farewell to each other. They had become close as sisters over the last weeks and Kieran knew how much she would miss the fiery MacGregor girl with her directness and bright courage. She pressed a parcel of clothing on her and warm blankets for the family. Now she stood at the door with her husband as they waved to Roderick, Sheena, Ewan Dhu and Ivor and watched as the horses clattered away over the cobbles and were lost to sight.

'Roderick will be back, once he ensures all is well at Glenlarig,' comforted Sorley Mor. 'I am sure too that you will see Sheena again one of these days.'

'Perhaps we may see them together,' she said with a faint smile, the first on her lips for many a day. 'I believe Roderick has a fondness for her!'

'I doubt if his family would ever approve of Sheena MacGregor as possible wife for your brother. Do not forget that her father is cousin to the late Rory MacGregor—the man who killed Colin Campbell, who was Roderick's father and yours—and stole his wife Catriona! I do not have to tell you your own history my darling. It is not merely the traditional blind hatred of one clan for another that we have here—but a blood feud.' He looked down sadly as he spoke.

'But have you yourself not said that one day all must bury such hatred and, make a fresh start? If Roderick should ever ask Sheena to be his wife, I for one would rejoice at it!' He looked at her flushed face, glad to see her concentrating on something other than the loss of the children and he smiled.

'I join with you in that,' he said simply. 'It is merely I know from personal experience how fanatical Iain Campbell can be. But there again, Roderick is his own man!' She nodded agreement at his words, her brother Roderick certainly not one to be intimidated even by his autocratic uncle. Then her thoughts flew back to her missing children and a deep sigh of frustration passed between her lips.

It was approaching night when they arrived. Roderick Campbell gave his stallion to a sleepy groom as Ewan Dhu and Ivor dismounted and prepared to stable their own horses, glad to be back at their native Glenlarig. Then Roderick turned stiffly towards the house to find his aunt Lorna at the door to welcome him.

'Where have you been all this long while,' she cried as she embraced him. 'I began to fear some ill had befallen you!'

'Well my dearest aunt, you see that I am well and the better for seeing you again,' he replied fondly. 'Where is Iain?'

'He stays away for days at a time now and will not say where he goes. Matters of the estate all I get from him.' She sighed. 'But at least he seems less angry—although still not his normal self.' Her eyes were sad as she spoke. She led him to a chair by the fire, for although the August days were warm, the nights chilly. A maid was dispatched to the kitchen, to prepare supper for the laird. He waited until a cold collation was brought and ate it there by the fire, putting off the news which he knew would cause her such pain. So far he had merely said that Kieran and Sorley Mor were well, making no direct mention of the twins.

Lorna poured him a glass of wine, and glancing at him fondly asked curiously about Sheena.

'Sheena—she is safe home by now. We left her at Balquidder. She was determined to go on alone.' She noticed his voice softened at mention of the girl. Then he put the down tray and reached forward where she sat beside him placing a gentle hand on hers.

'Aunt Lorna, I have news for you which you will find distressing.'

'Kieran?' she cried apprehensively. 'Is something wrong with Kieran?'

'Not her—no easy way to tell you this. Little Alan and Ishbel have been kidnapped, snatched from their mother's side in broad daylight by villains who drove off in a coach. It is the reason I have been away so long!'

'What is this you tell me?' Her face turned pale as his words sank in her eyes widening in shock.

'The twins have been kidnapped, taken out of the city,' he continued. 'We had word of them at a village south of Stirling—but there the trail ends! Sorley Mor and I have searched, questioned numerous people. Many are looking for them, the militia alerted. I would have stayed longer, but was also worried about you, aunt.'

'You should have remained there with your sister!'

'Perhaps so!' he said. 'Once sure that all is well here I may well ride south again.' He paused and then said, 'Incidentally, Mistress Sheena did much to help Kieran through the horror of the situation—an amazing young woman. She needed to return to her parents, not could I permit her to travel alone. Her mother is very sick of a lung infection. Her father's wounded leg just starting to heal when she left.'

'The family live in a cave do they not? It does not bear thinking of with the winter short months away.' But Lorna's thoughts were centred on those precious missing children who had brought such happiness to her during their all too short stay.

'Yes, in a cave, like so many others seeking any form of shelter since the Jacobite rising. The country in a sad state,' he said, but his words went unheeded.

'Tell me Roderick, why would anyone, want to kidnap two small children,' she asked in a trembling voice. As she spoke the door opened and Iain Campbell stood there, propping himself up against the doorframe, his face flushed from alcohol.

'Ah, the philander returns,' he jeered at Roderick. 'Oh yes, I have heard of your riding off to who knows where with a girl of the Gregorach! You cannot bring yourself to offer marriage to any decent woman, but associate with a daughter of the sons of dogs!'

'Uncle—you are drunk!' cried Roderick in disgust.

'You befoul our name by consorting with Sheena MacGregor! I would not put it past you to offer marriage to the slut!' He glared scornfully at Roderick who snapped back furiously, his words a challenge.

'I marry whom I please. Nor do I need your approval!'

'You're a fool boy—a weak fool,' jeered Iain drunkenly as Lorna listened horrified at her husband's words. She rose to her feet and brought her hand down heavily on the table. He stared at her in surprise.

'Iain—husband, something terrible has occurred,' cried Lorna. 'Kieran's twin children have been kidnapped and none know where they may be found!' If she looked for sympathy she found none.

'No business of ours,' he said abruptly. 'Kieran decided to remove herself from her rightful home. If she has been unable to care for her children, what is that to me now—or to you, wife!' At these harshly cruel words Lorna flinched back as though he had struck her. Not so Roderick who fronted on the man in outrage.

'What has happened to you of recent months that you treat those about you with such scorn? Have you lost all slightest form of compassion? Kieran is absolutely distraught at the kidnap of little Alan and Ishbel! I have seen you toss them up in your own arms and kiss them in the past— why then this lack of all normal sympathy?'

'The situation is none of my choosing. Kieran has preferred life with that pathetic Stewart rebel doctor, to remaining here with her own family. Whatever has happened is now result of her actions!' His words were calmer, but his eyes were fiercely implacable. He stared at them both for a further minute during which none spoke, then turned on his heel and slammed the door.

'Aunt Lorna, has Iain been behaving so since I left? What of his movements. You say he been much away from home?' Sheena's ridiculous suggestion came back hauntingly into his mind, but not instantly rejected as on other occasions. 'Have you really no idea of where he goes?' He watched her face, saw the honesty in her troubled eyes.

'I believe he attempts to pretend he is still in sole charge of Glenlarig—will not relinquish his authority over the estate and its people which was his during your minority.' She sighed. 'He has often been away for days at a time—now less so, but spends some hours away most days.'

'Do any accompany him?' he inquired casually.

'The MacNicol brothers and Donald MacKay—enough then for his own protection, although it is long since there have been any insurgents to worry about.' She saw his face stiffen as she mentioned those names, but then he smiled and rose from his seat.

'I pray you will not worry about any of this. We will speak again in the morning—I am for my bed, am stiff from riding!'

He glanced around the familiar setting of the great hall, its portraits of Campbell ancestors adorning the walls, interspersed with heads of magnificent antlered stags and an arrangement of swords and spears above the main door—that enormous table—the huge fireplace.

All seemed so normal, all as he remembered it from his childhood. But whereas in the past he had found comfort in the place, now he sensed a chill which was not of the late august night. He restrained a slight shudder before bending to kiss his aunt. She heard the sound of his feet ascending the stairs to his room. Then she too prepared for bed, later pretending sleep when Iain Campbell threw himself heavily beside her. The smell of stale alcohol on his breath was obnoxious to her, but knew she must endure it.

Roderick's dreams were troubled. He tossed and turned restlessly as the faces of his small niece and nephew floated before him and he wakened with a start. Where were they little Alan and Ishbel? He loved them almost as his own. What would it feel like actually to have children of his begetting he wondered? But for that to happen needs he must take a wife. That prospect had always seemed distasteful to him. Now as he lay there memory of Sheena MacGregor came to haunt his thoughts as often she did his dreams. But she was of the Gregorach and worse related however distantly to the man who had murdered his father!

He closed his eyes against the fingers of moonlight invading the room between heavy velvet curtains not properly closed, turned his face into the pillow and eventually drifted into a deep sleep.

He awakened to bird song and the sound of the pipes of Angus Mac Seumas skirling hauntingly on the wind. He dressed, pulled on his boots and opened the window and stared down at the old man, who strode importantly back and forth, his grey hair lifting in the breeze, a brave sight in his tartans. He looked up sensing the laird's presence and bowed to Roderick.

At the sound of that music and the old man's reassuring presence, Roderick found disturbing notions of his uncle's possible involvement with the twins kidnap evaporating as completely nonsensical. He breathed a sigh of relief that such was of course the case, and made his way downstairs. Lorna was already up, wearing a silver grey gown, her thick dark hair touched with white at the temples tucked under a frilled cap, grey blue eyes serene but slightly reddened, and Roderick bit his lip realising she had recently been weeping.

'Ah, Roderick,' came a deep voice and Iain Campbell surveyed him from the table where he had been breakfasting. 'I am glad to see you look well rested after your journey. You must forgive me if I was a trifle brusque last night. It had been a tiring day.' He cast a slight smile at Roderick, one which did not reach his eyes.

'What had you been doing then, uncle?' inquired Roderick evenly.

'Visiting those who hold land from us, seeing that all is well with them. Work which I am sure you will soon wish to take off my shoulders, lad! Later I am off to bring down a deer for the table.'

'I will come with you!'

'No need—no need! Your Aunt will be glad of some company! Oh and bye the bye, I am truly sorry to learn of the children's kidnap.' His expression was inscrutable as he rose from the table. 'My dear,' he said to Lorna, 'I will be back later.' And with that he was gone.

Roderick walked to the outer door and stood watching. Before long he saw his uncle mounted on his favourite horse beckoning to three of his ghillies. They were the MacNicols and Donald MacKay. They set off not taking direction to the right where deer were most likely to be found high on the hill—but left, taking the path bordering the loch towards the falls. He frowned, then as Lorna pressed him sat down as the maid brought in his breakfast.

Lorna invited him into her parlour and seating herself before her harp, played a theme beautiful in its poignancy. He sat watching as her fingers delicately plucked her melancholy theme. Then suddenly she dropped her hands into her lap and stared at him.

'Something is very wrong, is it not?'

'What exactly do you mean?' he said lightly.

'Iain—he was scathing in his comments on you in our bedroom this morning, but all sweetness and concern as he spoke of the twins just now.' She looked at him helplessly. 'He has strange mood swings—can be quite frightening at times!'

'He should control his moods better. It angers me that he should vent his spleen on you, dearest. Now that I am back I will keep a close eye on matters,' he said gently.

'But you will not be here for long, will you? I know you plan to return to Edinburgh to help Kieran and Sorley Mor in their search for the twins. Oh Roderick, my heart grieves for these dear bairns. Who has taken them— and why steal these particular children?' Her eyes watched his face as though she would find the answer there. But he merely sighed.

'My dearest Aunt, I will certainly make return to Edinburgh—but I have the feeling that it's not where we will find the children. That sighting of them was at Dullan, near Stirling. They would have been moved on from there almost at once. The fact is they could be anywhere in Scotland now. Kieran and her husband know this—feel as helpless as I do.' His grey eyes were sombre as he spoke and she bowed her head at his words, her eyes damp.

Roderick sat on a lichened rock, looking down at the loch, nor knew that Ewan Dhu watched over him from behind a bank of gorse. Ling heather bloomed in purple splendour all around him and dragon flies skimmed past, while high above all an eagle soared, returning to its mountain eyrie. The spicy fragrance of heath and wild flowers, of gorse and invasive bracken were such sweet relief after the smells of Edinburgh and he wondered as he stared across the shimmering expanse of sun kissed waters how any could prefer to live in the city.

He thought of his sister. He knew of her own deep love for the country and wondered how she had found the courage to live in Edinburgh. But of course she had followed her heart. It was Sorley Mor Stewart who had drawn her back there. It must be very strong indeed, this bond that bound those who truly loved.

Sheena—what was she doing now? When would he see her again? He tried to imagine her in that cold cave she had described. If only she were not of Clan Gregor! He rose to his feet and scowled his frustration. Then he set his feet for home. He heard the sound of gun shots and a protesting grouse shot up from the heather. That would be Iain he thought. If it was only now, late in the afternoon he had brought down a deer, what had he been about for the rest of the day?

It was early evening before Iain returned and sure enough his men carried carcases of two fine deer behind them. He was in a good mood, whistling under his breath as he came in and smiling as he sat at dinner with them.

'Where were you?' asked Roderick'

'I was not aware that I was accountable to you for my every movement, nephew,' was the casual reply. 'The estate needs careful handling should all not go to rack and ruin!' he added waving a negligent hand.

'Your meaning, uncle!' retorted Roderick

'You have not shown much interest in Glenlarig of recent times.' He gave a mocking smile and glanced disparagingly at Roderick as his teeth tore at a chicken leg running with gravy. Roderick glared in outrage, the criticism so far from the truth.

'Well I assure you it remains my main priority uncle. You may desist from labours obviously onerous to one of your advancing years! No doubt a rest will do you good.' He stared determinedly at the man and added, 'All affairs of the estate now to rest where they should be—in my hands!'

'What's that you say? You would pension me off like some old labourer? I think not, lad!' His face flushed with rising anger. 'Who looked after Glenlarig when you were a child, eh? Who cared for it when you were gallivanting around the countryside in a fancy uniform chasing Jacobite rebels? Look around you! Fine cattle grazing the hills, fat sheep and a respectful tenantry—it did not happen so by chance!'

'No,' exclaimed Roderick hotly, 'But by the husbandry of our people and the valour of those who have defended the land and our values. I thank you for all that you have done in the past. I am not ungrateful. But from this time on all matters regarding Glenlarig mine to decide.' His gaze locked with Iain's and saw the other's fury mount. The eyes of the various attendants seated at the lower end of the table were now fixed on Iain Campbell—and realising this, the man forced a smile.

'Glenlarig is yours. Have I ever said otherwise? But my advice always ready if needed!' By this answer he defused further controversy. But his eyes held an evil glint as he raised a glass to his lips, tossing off the amber fluid as though it were water, then he rose to his feet and signalled to Donald MacKay and the MacNicols to attend him as he stalked out of the hall.

'That needed saying, laird,' said Ewan Dhu exchanging a delighted grin with Ivor. But Lorna looked distressed. She knew her husband's behaviour could be difficult when crossed and for the first time feared for Roderick at his hands.

'Was that wise?' she asked softly.

'Time indeed that I showed Iain who is laird of Glenlarig. Do not worry, aunt. All will be well,' he replied confidently.

For the next few days Iain Campbell kept a low profile, his most charming self at mealtimes and courteous beyond the normal to his wife. It was almost as though the years had slipped away and he had become again the man Roderick had so admired as a child. Roderick and Lorna began to relax. Perhaps the firm tone Roderick had taken with his autocratic uncle had borne fruit.

'Aunt Lorna, as I said last night, I needs must return to Edinburgh, discover if there is any news of the twins—have only waited this long to be sure that Iain is to be trusted in his behaviour of you.' His eyes as he watched her were full of concern. But she smiled at him reassuringly.

'You have only been back a few days—but I understand and approve the need to help your sister and Sorley Mor. You must not worry about me. Do everything you can to find the little ones. Will you take Ewan and Ivor with you?' she asked.

'Ewan Dhu, yes—but Ivor I will leave behind to watch over Iain's comings and goings. There is something amiss here and I am not sure what it is. Where does Iain go when he disappears?'

'Another woman I think! No, do not look concerned. It has always been so and I have had to close my eyes to his philanderings,' she explained sadly.

'A woman, eh?' exclaimed Roderick. 'I had not thought of this.' And although he knew how distressing such situation must be for Lorna, nevertheless it blotted out thought of Iain's involvement in the children's kidnap which sometimes pricked his mind. Yes, this would explain why the man took only two or three with him.

'Have you any idea which woman he favours,' he asked gently.

'I have reason to believe it is again Mourna MacNicol—sister to Archie and Niall. I know that she bore him a daughter Mhairi, long years ago. The women have a small cot on the estate—about two miles from the falls. He does not realise I have knowledge of it. I believe he may go to visit Mourna and his daughter.' She smiled and shrugged. 'A wife has sometimes to pretend to ignorance of such matters.'

'So a daughter, Mhairi—and then there was Fingal! How many others has my uncle fathered I wonder. I am so sorry that you should have had to bear all of this,' he said in compassion. But she merely shook her head.

'I know that Iain loves me in his own way. Human beings can be strange and complex characters. Now stop worrying about me and prepare for your journey. Wee Alan and Ishbel your priority—and you must carry my fondest love to Kieran and tell her she is always in my prayers!'

Lorna watched as Roderick and Ewan Dhu galloped off down the long driveway. A soft rain was falling and the skies looked heavy. Another saw the young man go. Iain Campbell smiled, had already given certain orders.

They kept up a good pace and now were approaching the track that branched off to Balquidder. Roderick pulled back on his reins and stared across at the rolling hills. Somewhere on one of those hillsides was the cave which sheltered Sheena MacGregor. Ewan brought his own snorting garron up short.

'You are thinking of Mistress Sheena,' he ventured.

'Yes. I would I knew exactly where she bides. Perhaps another time I will try to find her. But duty calls me to Edinburgh—although I fear it is not where we will find the children.' He sighed in frustration urging his stallion on again with his knees. As did so Ewan gave a warning cry.

'Behind you, Roderick—beware!' he shouted!

In immediate reaction Roderick swerved. A pistol ball whizzed past his head, missing him by merest fraction as with howl of fury Ewan Dhu whipped his garron up the steep bank to their left. Roderick stared about him in shock, heard Ewan's voice raised in the war cry of their clan. Then came a gurgling scream such as Roderick had heard oft times before as a man died horribly on the battlefield. Then within minutes Ewan Dhu appeared again, as he guided his garron back down onto the road.

'He will not try to murder any other,' he said grimly.

'Who was it,' Roderick demanded as the ghillie wiped blood from his dirk before sheathing it. Ewan did not reply at once, his face grim. 'Well, who was it man?' persisted Roderick.

'Laird, it was a cousin of Donald MacKay—Ronald Og his name!'

'I do not know the fellow!' said Roderick perplexed.

'He used to bide in the village of Killin. Donald was known to be close friends with him.' He urged his garron close to Roderick and proffered a weapon to him. 'This is what he used to shoot at you with, sir!'

'Give it to me.' Roderick examined the pistol. It was ornate of a good quality and inlaid with silver, more the weapon of a gentleman. 'Why should this man attempt to kill me?' he asked.

'I would say that someone ordered him to do so! He had a reputation for acting as a paid assassin.' He met Roderick's eyes, not quite daring to frame his suspicion of the matter—saw from the expression on his face that the same suspicion also occurred.

'I suppose we should bury him,' said Roderick.

'No need! I dragged the body over to a gulley, threw it down into a thicket of gorse. The foxes and birds of the air will dispose of it.'

'Maybe you are right.'

'We should leave this spot I think, sir!' said Ewan Dhu as he looked at Roderick's troubled face. 'Who knows if any other such murdering de'ils are harbouring along the way.'

'I owe my life to you, Ewan Dhu!'

'My duty only—but let any dare raise their hand against one I love as a brother!' exclaimed the man, his dark eyes regarding Roderick with almost fanatical gleam. 'It comes to my mind that perhaps we should have had Ivor ride with us too!'

'I needed one I could trust to watch over Lorna—and to take account of the comings and goings of my Uncle Iain,' explained Roderick. 'Come—let us ride!' They set off again and Ewan Dhu who had been silent for some miles, now called across to Roderick.

'I am wondering if you have given any thoughts as to why Ronald Og should have attempted your life at just that spot?'

'No,' replied Roderick pulling on his reins as he surveyed the ghillie.

'It was in MacGregor country—your death would have been blamed on them! Reprisals possibly brought against Rob MacGregor, Sheena's father!'

'I had not thought of it,' replied Roderick grimly,' but I believe you are right, Ewan! I am going to see if we can trace ownership of this pistol when I have time to spare.'

'There is a fine pistol maker in the village of Doune. Many in this whole area buy from him. If of his workmanship, he may remember to whom he sold it,' suggested Ewan Dhu, watching Roderick as he spoke. 'We will pass through Doune on our way to Stirling!'

'We will break our journey there,' replied Roderick softly. They found the premises of the pistol maker, just off the High Street in the small village of Doune, directed by an old man near the Mercat Cross.

'Oh yes sir, we get many coming to our village for a brace of pistols,' smiled the keen eyed man they now addressed. 'Are you wishful to see some for yourself?' He saw from Roderick's dress and demeanour that he was one of the highland gentry, sensed a new customer.

'At this time I need information. Please examine this pistol,' and he proffered the weapon that had so nearly ended his life that day. 'Is this one of yours?'

'Indeed it is, sir! See, here atop the barrel—this mark. Yes it's one of mine.'

'To whom did you sell it? Can you remember?' asked Roderick quietly.

'Let me see now—that pattern of a boar—yes! It was to Sir Iain Campbell of Glenlarig, a brace mind you not just one. Such is the way we make and sell them.'

'I thought I had seen my uncle with one of this style,' said Roderick offhandedly. 'Having found this I wanted to be sure it was indeed Sir Iain's!' He gave the man a gold coin for his time, saying he might stop by on his return, perhaps give order of his own.

'It is not confirmation that my uncle ordered the shooting—or gave this weapon to Donald MacKay,' reasoned Roderick. 'The man may have stolen or found it,' he said turning to Ewan Dhu as they remounted their horses. But both men knew in their hearts, that Iain Campbell was the mind behind the attempted murder and they continued their journey in silence.

Roderick's dreams as he sought sleep that night at the Stirling inn, were deeply troubled. Why should Iain Campbell who had cared for him as his own son during his earlier years, now seek to take his life? What had he done to so enrage the man? Was it merely frustration at losing past control of Glenlarig? But he must have been aware that when Roderick attained manhood such would be the case—had not seemed to take obvious umbrage until recent months.

'It is his drinking,' murmured Roderick distractedly into his pillow. 'It has affected is brain, destroyed all natural thought.' He tossed and turned. Then his thoughts returned to Sheena MacGregor. Iain had stated his fear that Roderick might take the girl to wife. The idea totally ridiculous of course—or was it?

Chapter Fourteen

Sorley Mor answered the knock on the door himself and welcomed Roderick with a questioning smile, hoping against hope that perhaps Kieran's brother had news of his beloved children.

'I'm sorry, Sorley—I have questioned so many and have found no further clues since that sighting at Dullan,' Roderick admitted ruefully. 'I am sure in my own mind that they are safe, held captive for some unknown reason. Certainly not ransom or you would have heard from the kidnappers by now.' He sank down into an armchair in that well remembered sitting room and accepted a glass of wine.

'But what gain would there be for any in holding them?' Sorley Mor bit his lip in frustration. 'My greatest fear that they have been sold to perverts of some kind—or for adoption by some wealthy childless couple.'

'You may be right about the latter—but there may be yet another reason.'

'Your meaning?' demanded Sorley Mor fixing his dark gaze on the younger man. Roderick did not answer at first, but sat fingering the design on his wine glass. Once his suspicions left his lips if unjustified they could cause much harm.

'Where is my sister—where is Kieran,' he prevaricated glancing around,.

'She has taken Bess with her, as she does every day to question any that might have seen the twins taken.' The doctor shook his head sadly. 'Some time has now passed memories fading from the minds of any onlookers of that deed—but still she persists.'

'I understand. My poor sister needs to feel she is helping in some way,' exclaimed Roderick feelingly.

'You said there might be some other reason for their kidnap. What did you mean?' asked Sorley Mor directing his gaze on Roderick, as though he would explore the other's mind. And still Roderick hesitated. But at last he looked his brother-in-law in the eye.

'Yesterday—as I began my journey to Edinburgh, I was almost murdered upon the road!'

'What is that you say?' Sorley Mor regarded him in shocked surprise.

'Had it not been for Ewan Dhu's vigilance, this weapon would have taken my life,' said Roderick. He removed the pistol's bulge from his coat pocket and held it towards the doctor. Sorley Mor handled the pistol curiously, then raised his eyes to Roderick questioningly as he handed it back.

'Have you any idea of your assailant's identity?'

'Yes—a man related to one of my uncle's closest attendants! Ewan Dhu informs me that this Ronald Og whom he dispatched, was cousin to one of Iain's favoured retainers—Donald MacKay! Perhaps you may remember this man from your stay at Glenlarig?'

'Indeed I do. An uncouth looking fellow,' nodded Sorley Mor. 'But why should kin of this man MacKay seek your life?' He glanced across at the pistol that Roderick still held. 'If I may venture, that pistol is not such as a poor man would normally possess—for it would take several years wages to purchase. Unless taken from a defeated foe on the field!' he added, thinking this to be the answer.

'It belonged to my Uncle Iain, one of a brace he had especially made by that famed pistol maker at Doune! The craftsman confirmed his workmanship and that he made it for Iain Campbell!' Now that he words were out, Roderick lowered his head on his chest, not knowing whether he should continue.

'Is there more I should know?' demanded Sorley Mor. 'Do you suppose that Donald MacKay stole the pistol and either gave or sold it to his cousin?'

'Does no other solution come into your mind? Have you forgotten the attempt on your own life—murder planned by my uncle!' He raised his head and stared levelly at Sorley Mor. And as the other caught his meaning there was a minute's silence. Then the doctor rose to his feet, stared at him.

'I think you need to tell me more—and explain if you think the children's kidnap is in any way connected with all this?'

And blunderingly at first, feeling he was betraying family loyalty to the man who had cared and protected him in his younger years, Roderick went over all point by point, and framing his thoughts in words felt certain that he was right in his suspicions. It was obvious that Sorley Mor concurred with his analysis.

'So you believe Iain stole the children, holding them as future heirs to Glenlarig? With a child as heir, he would have continuing power over the estate. For this reason he attempted your life to clear his path? But to endeavour to kill you Roderick—this is indeed a horror hard to stomach!' and he looked pityingly at the other.

'Sheena placed initial suspicion in my mind. I was angered at her. Would not believe Iain capable of stealing little Alan and Ishbel, although I knew he loved them dearly when Kieran brought them to live at Glenlarig.' Roderick tossed off his wine and rose to face Sorley Mor. 'What action now?'

'We need evidence,' declared Sorley Mor slowly. 'So far all is supposition.' He gathered his thoughts. 'You say that your uncle has taken to heavy drinking of late, been discourteous to Lorna and treated you with scorn. Has anything new occurred to cause his anger?' he probed.

'Nothing happens at Glenlarig that he's unaware of. He heard of Sheena MacGregor's visit when she came seeking my sister. Knew that I spoken with her, admitted her into the house, then sent Ewan Dhu to see her safe back to Balquidder. But it was when he learned that I was to escort her to Edinburgh that he began to fear I had a fondness for the girl. He hates all of the Gregorach and in particular those in any way related to the man who killed my father.'

'And you have told me that Sheena's father is cousin to the late Rory MacGregor. I know Robert MacGregor. He visited this house to tell me of Kieran's whereabouts when she left me to go to Glenlarig! But go on!'

'I think Iain fears I may marry Sheena! I believe it is for this that he raised his hand against me!' said Roderick grimly.

'And would you indeed be prepared to marry Sheena? Do you love her?' asked Sorley Mor with a curious smile.

'I am not sure. What is love—how to define it? She is beautiful, courageous and of a fiery spirit. I enjoy her company, the first woman I can truly say that of. Find myself thinking of her at night, dreaming of her!' explained Roderick awkwardly.

'All are symptoms of a man in love!' nodded the other. 'So Iain Campbell has cause to fear you might marry one of a clan he hates and despises. But is this sufficient reason to seek your life—and to steal Alan and Ishbel?' He stared at Roderick inwardly debating the truth of the matter. Was all fantasy? Ronald Og could have fired on Roderick in mistake for another. But instinct told him that Roderick's suspicions were correct.

'I know him to be of a disturbed mind. It seems of late as though some evil has entered into him,' said Roderick quietly.

'Well if you are right and Iain has the children in his power, hidden away who knows where—how best to make him divulge their whereabouts?' So busy were they talking that they did not notice the sitting room door open. Kieran had overheard their last words and stood there clutching the door frame, staring at them in horror.

'Kieran,' cried her husband as he turned his head and saw her standing there. Had she heard them talking? 'My dear, see here is your brother come to visit us!' but she hardly acknowledged Roderick's presence.

'Is it true? Iain Campbell has our children?' she demanded.

He took her in his arms, then led her to the couch and held her close as with Roderick's help he explained their suspicions. No real proof existed—all perhaps merest supposition. At last she stopped trembling, became calmer. Her thoughts rioted. If Iain had taken Alan and Ishbel where would he have hidden them? Were they safe—being cared for properly?

'Roderick, you know him better than any other. Do you truly believe that Iain has the children? If so how did he manage the kidnap? It would have taken much planning surely? He has not been in Edinburgh of recent weeks, has he?' As she fired the questions, the men looked at each other. How indeed had the affair been managed?

'Aunt Lorna mentioned Iain often disappears from Glenlarig long days at a time—never divulges where he has been!' frowned Roderick.' It is possible he visited Edinburgh, made arrangements to have the children snatched and removed from the city. But it will be difficult to prove,'

'Force him to admit it then,' cried Kieran fiercely. 'The two of you must find a way to make him speak! If necessary go to Lord Mamore!'

'I doubt if any could make Iain speak against his will,' said Roderick. 'No, we will set a watch on his movements! Sooner or later he will wish to visit his small captives—and that will be the moment we recover them!'

'I believe you are right,' said Sorley Mor. 'We must keep him under surveillance. But you also must have a care of your person,' he added meaningly. Roderick brushed aside the last suggestion. Now that he was on his guard, Iain Campbell would find him a more difficult target.

'Suppose your uncle harms the children,' exclaimed Kieran fearfully.

'If he has them you may be assured they will be well looked after. I remember the care he showed me as a child,' replied her brother sadly. 'Once I am out of the way, little Alan Stewart is the next heir!' At his words Kieran looked at her brother protectively.

'It is so hard to believe that the kind, courteous gentleman who welcomed me so graciously into your home, is the same deranged creature who first attempted Sorley's life, then yours—and has stolen Alan and Ishbel! You must watch he offers you no further hurt, brother mine,' she said her grey eyes full of worry, and reached out for his hand.

'Have no fear for me, Kieran, dear heart! But look, we can do no more at this moment—and I am greatly hungered!' he said plaintively. It raised a smile from her and she hurried to call Mistress Lindsey.

They decided to take Lachlan and John Paterson into their confidence and the five of them sat talking together long into the night. Sorley Mor longed to ride north to personally confront the man who had stolen the two small children he loved as his own. Wished to settle account with the one who had brought such grief into his beloved Kieran's life to further his own warped ambition! But Roderick shook his head at the notion.

'If you were to be seen at Glenlarig it would only alert my uncle to our suspicions. No, it is better I return as I left with only Ewan Dhu at my side. Should I need help, have further news for you, I will send a message.'

Roderick spent another two days at the doctor's house, noticing the steady stream of patients who made their way to his door, saw how greatly needed his work was and the esteem in which he was held. And Nurse Effie smiled to see the young Campbell chief there again and Bess asked after Lorna whose kindness she remembered.

They stood on the steps to wave him off. Ewan Dhu held the impatient snorting stallion as Roderick mounted. He turned once to raise his hand in farewell. Then both he and Ewan Dhu clattered off guiding their horses along the busy street and disappeared from view.

'I feel the heavy cloud that has fallen upon our lives has lifted slightly,' said Kieran, as her husband held her close. 'At least now we have hope!'

'You are right, mo chridhe! I feel in my bones that we will soon have our beloved wee Alan and Ishbel back in our arms,' said Sorley Mor and kissed her as he stroked her red gold hair. 'Perhaps too, we will have another wedding in the family—Sheena and Roderick!'

'You say that he loves her?'

'Oh yes, no doubt of it—even though he does not seem to fully realise it yet!' he chuckled.

'I can think of no other I would rather welcome as a sister,' exclaimed Kieran—and as aunt to our baby!'

'What is that you say?' Sorley Mor held her back from him staring at her in amazement. She blushed and laughed as she saw the excitement rising in his eyes. 'Kieran—do you mean it?'

'It is only a few weeks since you made me truly your wife at Glenlarig—but there are signs and having been pregnant before, I know what they betoken.' She smiled at him shyly. 'Say you are pleased at my news!'

'My heart's darling—you make me the happiest man in all Scotland!'

As they took the long road back to the Trossachs, Roderick took Ewan Dhu into his confidence, told him of his certainty that Iain had taken the twins and his reasons for believing it so. The man looked at him in horror, but readily conceded that it made sense of so much that had happened.

'We should choke it out of him,' he exclaimed with an oath. 'But oh desperate sad is the day when one as highly respected as Sir Iain Campbell should turn against his own kin! Woe to his black heart, that it is so!'

'I believe the reason he set Fingal to attempt Sorley Mor Stewart's life was to prevent Kieran leaving Glenlarig with the children—her son Alan the next heir after me.'

'But why not wait until you marry, Roderick brother of my heart! You would then provide children in plenty!' declared Ewan Dhu supportively.

'Because he knows I have a certain fondness for Sheena MacGregor. No more than that just now—but I esteem her highly—and he abhors the idea I might marry a girl of the Gregorach,' sighed Roderick impatiently.

'And one related to that Rory MacGregor who took your father's life! Oh yes, I see now why he acts so.' He looked across at Roderick as they rode and gave a slow smile. 'She is a special young woman, that Sheena MacGregor—and well able to defend herself!' he added, remembering certain hurt to his person. But he for one would be very glad to see Sheena as future lady of Glenlarig. But he also knew many of Iain's retainers, might take an opposite, and sourer view.

As was their custom, Roderick and Ewan Dhu broke their journey overnight at their favourite Stirling inn, leaving the next day at dawn. They were stopped twice along the road north, but merely as routine, the militia who accosted them realising at first glance that this gentleman and his retainer offered no threat. But boredom caused the sergeant of the second troop to attempt civil exchange of pleasantries.

'You say you have been to Edinburgh, sir?' He was a big, bluff fellow with keen eyes and sandy moustaches. 'Perhaps there is some new excitement there?' he asked hopefully.

'Not that I am aware of!' replied Roderick. 'The city is quiet these days. All the talk is of plans for draining the Nor Loch, building a new town with fine houses.'

'No more rebels brought to justice then—hangings?'

'No. All is quiet and orderly, the citizens not such as involve themselves in rebellion!' Roderick was impatient to be on his way, but knew it was politic to be on good terms with those who patrolled the roads. To his surprise the sergeant posed another question.

'Is there any news of the kidnapped children, twins under the age of two and stolen from their mother there? We were told to be on the lookout for them—that they might be found upon the road, but that was a while back.'

'You speak of my nephew and niece, sergeant! And no, there is still no trace of them. Their mother, Kieran Stewart is my sister. But it pleases me that you are keeping watch for them. I thank you for it!' he smiled at the man.

'I have children of my own, sir! I hope that you have good news soon!' He saluted and let Roderick continue his journey.

As they left Callander skirting the river and seeing the mountains soaring up before them, Roderick uttered sigh of content. The miles slipped by and now they rode beside Loch Lubnaig, its waters today still as glass, reflecting the forested heights towering above and already touched with early September's gold. How any could be happy living in the stuffy atmosphere of towns was beyond him. Here in amongst the hills where the air was fresh and pure and the larks sang out their tiny hearts and the heron swooped over the loch a man could breathe freely!

But what if that man was a Jacobite, he pondered? One who had thrown in his lot with Charles Edward Stuart to be hunted down like vermin! Other risings there had been in the Highlands and retribution had followed in their wake, but nothing before had matched the recent savagery that had denuded great areas of the land of its people. Yes, he of Clan Campbell could rejoice as he rode back to his fine home—but what the fate of any who had escaped the sword and the gallows? What future was theirs?

Sorley Mor had said that eventually hatred between clans had to come to an end. That if ever Scotland was to regain its ancient freedom then its peoples must unite—lowlands and highlands alike! But with rumour of the clan system being broken for all time, chiefs becoming landlords and plans broached to abandon their own people driving them from their small plots of land—replacing people with sheep, well, such schemes could not be allowed to become fact!

But it was only rumour—so far. And so Roderick pondered all these things as he rode and Ewan Dhu glancing at him wondered what caused that deep frown between his brows. No doubt he would be thinking of Iain Campbell. Soon they would be back there—at Glenlarig.

'What are your plans,' asked Ewan Dhu as they rode up Glenlarig's long driveway and the house reared solidly before them in the evening light. 'Will you confront Iain—ask him directly about the children?'

'No Ewan. He must not realise my suspicions. But both you and Ivor must keep watch over his every movement. You understand?'

'Aye, that I do,' replied Ewan Dhu grimly. 'I will also keep close guard over you! Woe betide Iain Campbell, should he raise hand against you again!' His hand went to his dirk as he spoke.

Iain Campbell had eaten well and drunk better and now rose from place at the head of the table, nodding drunken approval to Lorna. He was in a jovial mood as he walked to stand at the fireplace glass in his hand.

Days past he had worried when he received no news from the man he had set to kill his nephew—what had happened to Ronald Og? Then he thought of a possible explanation. The assassin had not been in time to waylay Roderick at Balquidder that day according to the arrangement. No, he would therefore await Roderick's return from Edinburgh and dispose of him then, good news to be expected soon! And so he relaxed—and waited.

'Bid you good evening dearest Aunt—and greetings to you also, Uncle!' As his nephew's familiar voice lanced through the air, Iain turned his head in sudden shock, then quickly recovering his composure, forced a reluctant smile onto his face.

'Ah, you are returned Roderick! I hope your journey was fruitful, news received of the whereabouts of the twins?' he said in slurred tones as Roderick walked over to Lorna and kissed her.

'It is so good to see you safe back again, my dear,' cried Lorna appearing unaware of the friction between the two men. 'Tell me, how is Kieran and is there any news of the little ones?' Her eyes swept hopefully over his face, and her mouth drooped as he sadly shook his head.

'Alas, there is no trace of them! Kieran and Sorley Mor are distraught, but never giving up hope. I pray that one day they will be safely back where they should be—in their mother's arms!' He sank down tiredly at the head of the table in the place vacated by Iain, as Lorna cried for another plate to be set and a serving man bent over him attentively.

As he set to, munching on a slice of venison, he watched Iain's face from under his lashes. His uncle looked both troubled and uncertain. And inwardly amused, Roderick guessed at the man's thoughts. But however tempting it would be to challenge Iain Campbell over the children's kidnap, knew that he must be circumspect in all he said. Not by any slightest inflection of the voice must he let Iain know of his suspicions, for that might lead to further hurt to the two small children, innocent victims of the deranged man's pride and arrogance.

'Did you meet any upon the road?' inquired Iain at last.

'Why yes, the usual troops of militia,' said Roderick looking across at him. 'They have orders from command in the castle, to be on constant lookout for wee Alan and Ishbel and are vigilantly obeying this.'

'The children are not thought to be still in Edinburgh?'

'Search continues there, uncle! Meanwhile their mother, my beloved sister grieves!' Roderick turned a searching smile on him. 'But they will be found!'

'Your journey was uneventful then? No doubt now you will have time to spare for matters of the estate,' said Iain. 'Did you by chance see anything of Mistress Sheena MacGregor on your travels?' He cast a mocking glance at Roderick.

'No. Why do you ask, uncle?'

'We harried some of the Gregorach whilst you were away, her family perhaps among them!'

'Iain!' cried Lorna shocked. 'You spoke no word to me of this!'

'I do not necessarily wish to burden your ears with routine attempt to rid the country of a pack of thieves and cattle rustlers, my dearest wife! As a proscribed clan they are fair game to any who wish to cleanse the land of those the law has determined to be treated as vermin—men and women the same!'

So great his fury, Roderick almost rose to his feet, but restrained the urge. He knew Iain was baiting him and he must not respond. He lifted a glass to his lips instead.

'A toast to new times ahead, when men may look on all their neighbours with kindness and common courtesy,' he said. In reply Iain Campbell threw his glass into the fire where the spirit flared.

'The words of a simpleton—or a coward!' he jeered and signalled to his retainers sitting at the end of the table to attend him as he lurched from the room. His men looked at each other uncertainly. They were beginning to realise that Iain was no longer in control of his behaviour, and wanted no outright rift with the young laird to whom all were officially answerable.

'Go—see him to his bed,' instructed Roderick—and they went.

'Now tell me,' said Lorna 'Is there really no news of the twins?'

'As soon as I have any knowledge of their whereabouts you shall know it, that I promise,' replied Roderick. 'Tell me, how has Iain been behaving since I left?'

'Away from dawn to dusk, as before! I did not know of his latest harrying of the MacGregors,' she said sadly. 'I pray that Mistress Sheena was not harmed!'

'For his sake I hope not,' he said grimly.

'You are very fond of the girl?' she probed looking into his smouldering grey eyes and their expression softened.

'I love her,' he replied and realised it was the first time he had admitted the fact even to himself. He glanced down at Lorna's face saw the genuine happiness there at his news. 'Could you ever accept her here, as my wife?'

'Yes—with joy! I liked her when we met—and reminded me of a sweet budding rose with many protective thorns! She has a bright courage and integrity, Roderick. But will her MacGregor pride allow her to accept a Campbell as husband?' and she placed a sympathetic hand on his arm.

'That is to be seen,' he replied huskily. 'Now listen dearest aunt, I wish you to be careful of Iain over these next few days. I think you know he is not to be trusted. It saddens me to speak so of one I have always loved and respected—looked up to as a child.'

'It is the alcohol that changes him, Roderick!'

'He takes it because of that canker in his heart, bolstering up arrogance and blunting all thoughts of normal kindness and behaviour. I need you to very careful of him, my dearest. Tonight you should sleep on the couch in your drawing room.'

'I will.' And he led her to the door of the great hall and watched as she entered the gracious small room she had made so much her own, heard the key turn in the lock. Tonight she should sleep peacefully.

Although tired, his thoughts were disturbed that night as he tossed and turned in bed, and sleep came hard. How best was he to deal with the present situation now positive that his small niece and nephew were in Iain's power? Tomorrow he would speak with Ivor, discover if the man had any news of Iain's movements over the last few days.

He found Ivor in conversation with Ewan Dhu in the courtyard grooming the horses, the stable lads mucking out the stalls and not within earshot. The men's faces were troubled. They looked up as Roderick approached and inclined their heads in greeting.

'Laird, Ewan Dhu has told me of the attack upon you and I am cut to the heart I was not also at your side to protect you!' said Ivor. He turned hurt expression on Roderick, who smiled at this expression of the man's devotion.

'I gave you another task to perform! Have you any news of my uncle's movements when I was away from Glenlarig?' he studied the man's face as he asked the question. Ivor hesitated.

'Laird, beloved chieftain of my heart, I did indeed follow him as you instructed me. He rode on two occasions with the MacNicol brothers Archie and Niall running behind, Donald Mackay also. They took roundabout route up through the hills, but ending up at Mourna MacNicol's cottage where this woman he has favoured much in the past lives with her daughter Mhairi!'

'I know the cottage you mean,' put in Roderick. 'But continue!' he looked at Ivor expectantly. The man did so.

'Iain Campbell knocked and went in, leaving the three men to wait outside in the heather, where they enjoyed a laugh together.'

'They did not observe that you were keeping watch?'

'No—I was like a very ghost!'

'Did Iain stay long in the cottage with the women?' demanded Roderick.

'Not so—on both occasions half an hour perhaps—not more than that! But he fondly embraced Mourna at the door on leaving!' recollected Ivor, as Roderick considered his words thoughtfully. Was his uncle merely enjoying renewed personal relationship with the mother of his young daughter, or was there another reason for his visits there? He stared at Ivor who was anxious to relate more.

'Well, continue Ivor Mac Dugal!'

'Then there was the day he went harrying the MacGregors! I was not invited to join that expedition as were others of our men. But I followed in their wake, saw all that they did at Balquidder!'

'Mistress Sheena—she was not harmed?' cried Roderick urgently.

'I cannot say for sure, laird! But I did not see her. All was confusion, two men shot and a woman raped and others screaming into the hills! It was Iain Campbell who killed the two Gregorach!'

'That I can well believe,' Roderick ground out.

'Most of his followers had no real taste for killing that day, perhaps knowing that you are laird not Iain, this work maybe not of your desire. So they went searching for stolen cattle. Donald MacKay it was who assaulted the woman, middle aged, grey haired besom, trying to protect her cow. I was hiding on top of a ridge, careful not to be observed.'

'But you saw no sight of Sheena MacGregor?'

'No, Laird—I did not see the lassie!'

'Thank the good God for that,' breathed Roderick. 'Mistress Sheena has become very dear to me, you understand, Ivor?'

'From this day on I will care for her as for your own dear self,' declared Ivor stoutly.

'Did Iain go elsewhere?'

'Once he stopped by a deserted shepherd's hut on the heights of Creag Gharbh. Went inside it, then out again and shot a deer before returning home. Always he brought meat back for the table.'

'You say the hut was deserted?'

'Aye, Laird—I took a look myself when they left! Had not been used in years to my knowledge—all dust and dirt and cobwebs!' Roderick thanked the man and turned away.

None had seen the younger stable lad Jack, who had crept close enough to overhear the latter part of their conversation. This boy now made his way to find his father. Niall MacNicol listened to the lad uneasily then went to seek Iain Campbell whom he found alone in the hall. His news was greeted with a scowl as Iain Campbell bit his lip sudden anger.

'Bring your son Jack here to me,' he instructed, then, when the lad stood uncomfortably before him scratching at a pimple on his young face, Iain plied him with questions. Once he was sure that he had extracted every last word the boy had overheard, he dismissed father and son from his presence and stood there at the window.

Why had Roderick set his man Ivor to follow him? What was it that Roderick suspected? Nothing specific it would seem, merely an intrusion into another's affairs. Then he thought of Roderick's reported words regarding his affection for Sheena MacGregor! Well, soon the young laird would lie cold in the earth before ever he had chance to make closer bond with the MacGregor bitch!

But what had happened to Ronald Og? Why had he not sent word of explanation that he had so far failed in his mission? He had promised the man gold when offered proof of Roderick's death, and Ronald Og loved gold! What had gone wrong? One thing he did realise, Roderick was now watching him—even as he shrewdly kept that young man under observation. Knowing this he must exercise caution in all his actions. But Roderick must die as soon as it might be safely arranged.

Later Lorna became even more painfully aware of the growing tension between husband and nephew when two days later Roderick demanded ledgers containing accounts of the running of the estate be brought to him in the library.

'You are not used to such matters, lad,' flashed his uncle, hurrying in as the heavy ledgers always kept in his possession until now were carried in by Ewan Dhu, who had demanded them politely in his master's name, of an irate Iain Campbell

'You will find that I am indeed well able to manage Glenlarig. Besides which I shall be engaging a lawyer to assist me in checking these accounts uncle,' said Roderick a steely look in his grey eyes, as he turned the pages of the first ledger.

'But I have my own man of business in Perth! Nicholas Brodie a fine accountant! I have always used him,' said Iain emphatically as though that was an end of the matter.

'Precisely so, uncle.' returned the younger man. 'I prefer to employ a man of my own choosing for the future. I will not detain you at the present time as I am sure you have more pressing affairs to attend to—visiting old friends, perhaps?'

'You will regret this impudence, sir!' Iain's face had turned a furious dark red, the more startling under his white hair.

'And you uncle should mind your tongue!' said Roderick coldly. The older man looked as though he was bursting to retaliate, but swallowing his fury stalked angrily away. Ewan Dhu noted the evil glint in his eyes as he passed. As for Lorna she drew in her breath anxiously and looked across at Roderick.

'Do you think it was wise to provoke him so, my darling?' she asked quietly. He looked up from the desk on which he was studying the ledger to smile at her reassuringly.

'Have no concern, dearest Aunt! I think it was good time I looked into the financial aspect of running Glenlarig. Come here—see this entry. Thirty prime beef cattle sold at the Doune Fair—but no price entered against the item! I have only glanced through this most recent page and seen much to query.' She half rose from her chair and stared at Roderick in slight bewilderment.

'Surely you do not think that Iain has been deliberately defrauding the estate? Even he would not act so. He loves Glenlarig!' she exclaimed.

'I told him I was going to employ the services of a new man of business and this I am resolved to do. If all is well, then Iain has nothing to fear. Do you not agree?' He smiled at her gently, knowing how difficult all of this must be for one as tender hearted as Lorna. However bad a partner Iain had become, nevertheless he was her husband and once dearly loved, and like all good wives she felt loyalty to her companion of many years.

'Roderick, why have matters become so tense between you—is there something else I should know?' she asked. 'Is it merely that you are making your position as laird plain to him and demonstrating your disapproval of his drinking—or is there a deeper problem?' Her eyes were damp, her concern apparent. He rose and put his arm about her shoulders, wondering how she would cope in the future if her husband were accused of stealing wee Alan and Ishbel. He feared she would be devastated. Better to keep all from her for now.

'No dearest, there is nothing for you to worry about! Why not go and play your harp again—I have not heard your beautiful music in a long while. The sound of it will reach me here as I work!' At his smile she relaxed and left. Minutes later, the sound of her harp echoed sweetly around all of that great building. He nodded and smiled, then bent his head over the ledger once more and the smile left his lips.

Kieran Stewart was feeling nauseous, knew it to be confirmation of that new life within her. But much as she joyed in the knowledge that she was to give Sorley Mor a son or daughter of his own begetting, her heart continued to feel as though it would break from sorrow at the loss of little red haired, blue eyed Alan and his winsome twin sister with her silver blond curls and green gaze. How she missed them! Today she stood in the nursery with Bess, touching their clothes, their favourite toys, as picture of them appeared behind her closed eyes.

'Oh, Bess—how I wish we had not taken them out that morning!' she exclaimed. The young nursemaid nodded. If only there was something she could say to help Kieran in her despair.

'You will have them back one day—I am sure of it,' she said stoutly, but worried in case such should not happen. This had been such a happy household before that frightful day of the kidnap. She hesitated now, wondering if she should reveal the conversation between Lachlan and Dr Patterson she had overheard.

'Mistress Kieran—is it possible that Sir Iain Campbell is involved in all this,' she asked. 'I heard Lachlan and Dr Patterson discussing it.'

'Oh Bess—none else were supposed to know of this suspicion, because it is no more than that at present. Under no circumstance must you speak to anyone of what you may have heard! To do so might endanger the children's lives!'

'No Mistress—not a word will I say. You have my promise!' She looked at Kieran pityingly. 'Why would a great gentleman like Sir Iain want with two wee bairns?'

'Bess dear—it is all too complicated to explain—except to say that little Alan is next in line to my brother Roderick as heir to Glenlarig! Iain Campbell is we believe wishful of having custody of my son for his devious purposes.'

'But what of Roderick, lady?' exclaimed Bess in confusion. 'He will wish to marry one day—have children of his own!'

'But should anything happen to Roderick before this happens...' she bit her lip not wanting to continue, but Bess caught her meaning.

'Are you suggesting someone might mean harm to your brother? Surely you do not think....?' and she too did not finish her thought, too frightful if true. Kieran nodded.

'Not a word now, Bess! I need your promise!'

'Need you ask it? But mistress Kieran, if there is anything I can do to help in all this, you have but to say!' for answer Kieran caught the younger girl to her in embrace.

'One day I may ask for your assistance if we discover exactly where Alan and Ishbel are being held.' And now her thoughts crystallised.

'Would that mean going all that long way back to the highlands again?'

'Perhaps,' replied Kieran thoughtfully.

'Then I would see Ewan Dhu once more,' aid the young maid artlessly.

'Why Bess—have you a liking for that fierce ghillie?' she saw by the girl's blush that such was the case. 'Who knows what the future holds,' she said gently. That night Kieran could not sleep. A plan was forming in the back of her mind and one she could not share with her husband. Dawn was breaking before she closed her eyes as fitful dreams chased behind her eyelids, and when she arose an hour later her mind was made up!

Sorley Mor worked hard that day, a procession of mothers with young children suffering diarrhoea and vomiting, as John Patterson and Lachlan tended many other similar cases. He looked up as he left his consulting room, as Mistress Lindsey approached holding out a sealed letter.

'The mistress gave me this. She said you should have it at the end of the day so as not to interrupt your work, doctor!' and she handed it to him. He looked at her in amusement.

'Why could Kieran not come and say whatever is on her mind to me in person!' he broke the seal and as his eyes skimmed the message there, he went white.

'Where is my wife now, Mistress Lindsey?'

'Why, she left the house this morning with Bess—who was carrying a bag with her. I thought perhaps she was going to visit the families of some of your poorer patients, as has been her custom.' As she looked at the doctor's stricken face, she put a hand to her mouth. Surely the doctor's young wife had not left him again as once she did before? He said nothing, but hurried upstairs to sit on their bed to read Kieran's letter through once more.

'My dearest husband,

I am travelling to Glenlarig, taking Bess with me. Had I asked your permission it would have been refused! Nor could I expect you to accompany me there for Iain Campbell would surely attempt your life once more. But in his own way he has some small affection for me. I do not think he will harm in me.

I shall attempt to discover where the children are. Do not come to me for that would ruin all and inflame the man more. I intend to persuade him to allow me to see the twins, especially if I pretend desire to live at Glenlarig again. He knows I left you once before, and may be persuaded I have done so a second time.

So do not worry about me, dear Sorley Mor. Just leave all to my mother's instinct at this time. Should I be in serious trouble, you may be sure I will send for you. To have any hope of getting the children safely back, I believe my plan must work. I know Roderick will have a care of me. Do not worry. All will be well. Always remember I love you with all my heart. God bless you my own true love,

Kieran

He tossed the letter on the floor with an oath. His first thought was to go in pursuit and bring her home. No doubt there would be tears and frustration, but at least she would be safe. His dark eyes stared restlessly around, looking for his riding coat, found it where it lay over a chair. As he struggled into his long leather boots, paused and suddenly straightened up and sat there on the end of the bed considering matters logically.

What Kieran wrote was true. It was unlikely she would come to harm at Iain's hand if indeed she could make the man believe that she had left her husband and wished to throw in her lot with her Campbell relatives. Even though he might still wish to kill Roderick, he would know that it would be to his advantage to allow wee Alan and Ishbel to live openly at Glenlarig in their mother's care. Her idea might just work!

But what if Iain Campbell was so unstable that he would lift his hand against Kieran? After all, he had tried to murder his own nephew, his niece might fare no better. And so his thoughts rioted back and forth. At last he removed his boots picked up Kieran's crumpled letter and went to seek John Patterson and Lachlan, found them relaxing in the sitting room over a glass of wine. He handed them the letter.

Lachlan Stewart immediate reaction was all for going after Kieran, swearing roundly in the Gaelic of his fierce desire to kill Iain Campbell. John Patterson though studied Kieran's words thoughtfully.

'Sorley my friend, I think that as she says, you have to trust to Kieran's instincts in this. Do not forget she is a mother deprived of her children, and will not behave in any manner that may lessen her chances of getting them back. I know how anguished your own feelings must be, but now is the time for calm decision.' His hazel eyes held the doctor's impatient dark gaze for a long minute. Then Sorley Mor relaxed slightly.

'Pray God you are right in this,' he said simply. 'Kieran is brave as she is beautiful. If Iain Campbell hurts her in anyway, it would be better for him he had not been born!'

Kieran was wearing one of her best gowns in wine velvet, a matching fur trimmed travelling cape over her shoulders, a wide feathered hat over her red gold curls. She took the driver's proffered hand as she stepped down from the coach into the courtyard of the inn. He looked after her impressed at the quality of this particular traveller and her maid.

As ever the inn was crowded and very noisy and smelt strongly of beer and spirits. The landlord glanced at her as she stood there looking around—and recognised her.

'Good day to you, lady,' he said bowing politely. 'It is Mistress Stewart is it not? Your brother the captain was here a week or so back. Do you stay long?' He watched her curiously, wondering why she had no man to protect her, but of course on that first occasion here she had also arrived alone, apart from her maid—and two babies. Would she want word sent for her brother now as on that previous visit?

'I shall stay overnight. Have you a quiet room, landlord and an adjoining one for my maid?'

'Certainly, lady! Are you travelling far?'

'Back to Glenlarig tomorrow I hope. I will need horses. You can supply them?' He glanced at the heavy purse at her belt and nodded.

'Horses are no problem—but travelling alone along these roads and into the wild highlands, well it may not be safe you understand. Would it be best to send for Sir Roderick?'

'I am well able to look after myself,' replied Kieran and he shrugged. No affair of his then if she did not wish to take his advice. The following morning she left shortly after dawn. He watched her go, had supplied one of the best horses from his stable, and a stout pony for her maid. She could leave the horses at the Kingshouse Hotel by Balquidder change them there for fresh mounts.

Kieran's thoughts were troubled as she rode. She knew her husband would be distraught and angry at her action, but hoped he would see the wisdom of her plan. But it was sheer joy to ride through the beauty of the countryside once more and passing out of Callander beneath stately Ben Ledi, she sighed delight to sound of the rushing burn at the left of the road, where it hurled its brown foam tossed waters in falls and rapids.

She glanced around avidly, noting early September had already placed light golden touch upon birch and oak, and clusters of glowing flame red berries festooned the rowans. Now they were skirting Loch Lubnaig where two stately swans dipped into the sparkling silver waters and above all an eagle soared.

On they rode, Bess complaining of soreness from this unaccustomed activity. Kieran looked back at her in sympathy, but was resolved not to stop until they reached the Kingshouse. They passed through the small village of Strathyre, leaving the woods behind and now the scenery became wilder as they rode on amongst the hills.

Suddenly there was a shout as a bare legged man in a ragged tunic leaped out from the side of the track in front of them, Kieran's horse reared in snorting fright and Bess uttered a scream of fear. He snatched at Kieran's reins and as she fought to jerk them free of his great calloused hands, he swore and leered at her.

'Down ye get my fine lady—now don't struggle, de'il tak ye! I will juist relieve you of that purse at your waist—also any jewels you may have upon your person!' He had a brutal pock marked face. 'Obey me at once— else you die, for I will have what I need either way!' he sneered, removing one hand from the reins as he now clutched at her skirt.

'If you release me for a moment I will give you what you ask—only please do not harm me,' exclaimed Kieran in frightened tones as she cowered away from him and with a laugh he stepped back but still with a firm hold on the reins. She made as though to release her purse. But her hand went to a small pistol concealed in pocket of her cape. Suddenly it was in her hand. She levelled it at the man's head.

'Back up onto the bank with you—or I shoot and I promise you I will not miss!' At the sight of the pistol trained on his forehead and sudden authoritative change in her voice he stared back in shock, then raising his hands stepped slowly backwards to the side of the road. Then with a string of oaths he stumbled up the bank, throwing himself into shelter of bracken and scrub birch.

'Come,' cried Kieran urgently to Bess. 'There may be others of his persuasion nearby!' She pulled on her reins and raised her whip to strike at her maid's pony, which leapt forward with such vigour it almost unseated Bess. Just around the next bend they were again accosted, but this time by a militia troop.

Their sergeant stared in surprise to see one who was obviously a lady, riding attended only by a maid. He inquired her destination and when she mentioned Glenlarig and that she was the laird's sister he seemed even more disturbed, for he knew of Roderick Campbell.

'I do not think Captain Campbell would approve of your riding alone in such way! There be many dangers upon road such as this!' he said reprovingly. At his words Bess was about to inform him of their encounter with the highway robber, but Kieran shook her head at the girl.

'Oh, I am sure none would really wish to hurt a woman,' she said artlessly. He stared at her in disbelief.

'You do not really believe that, do you,' he replied loftily. 'You say you are for the Kingshouse. I also intend to stop there for a break, will accompany you.' Realising there was nothing she could reasonably say to dissuade him from his unwanted assistance, Kieran allowed him to ride at her side, Bess following closely, as the red coated militia troop resumed their march behind their mounted Sergeant.

Kieran made arrangements for a change of horses at the inn. It was obviously a hostelry much used of the military and many curious glances were thrown at her as she called for ale and a light meal. She knew the sergeant wanted to share her table but she ignored his hopeful stare. She asked the landlord if there was another door out of the inn and glancing at the many members of the militia watching this unusual traveller, he smiled understandingly and told her to follow him.

They were on the road again, now on fresh horses which it was arranged should be returned from Glenlarig by one of Roderick Campbell's men. But they had ridden but a few miles when they heard a sudden shout behind them. Kieran turned her head and saw an officer of the militia swiftly approaching on his obviously much faster horse, a spirited grey.

'Your pardon, but did I hear aright? You are sister to my friend and cousin Roderick Campbell?' He was level with her now and as she glanced into his face, saw he was regarding her kindly from clear blue eyes, as he removed his hat from his short, curling fair hair and bowed from the saddle.

'Yes sir, I am Kieran Stewart,' she replied.

'Stewart—ah yes! Roderick said you were married to a doctor of that name! May I introduce myself—Major Kenneth Campbell of Kilrannoch?'

'But of course—Roderick mentioned that you had ridden with him to Edinburgh that time—supported him in dealing with Captain Bradshaw!' She forced out the name of the rapist with venom and the major who had never learned for what exact offense against his sister Roderick had held the fellow to account lifted an eyebrow in surprise and curiosity.

'Your brother took his life in his hands when he faced Bradshaw. The man had a reputation as an excellent shot. But I take it that he had much to answer for. Certainly his reputation made him unfit for the company of honest men!'

'Or women,' she replied then bit her lip, not wishing to disclose the hurt Bradshaw had dealt her. Nor did the major inquire further as he read her expression.

'So tell me, where are you bound now? I am guessing it is Glenlarig!' he surmised with a smile. 'If so I am sure your brother will take you to task for riding alone, when you might so easily be assaulted by broken men from the hills made desperate by prevailing conditions.'

'I am well able to take care of myself,' Kieran replied. 'Nor am I alone. My maid Bess accompanies me as you can see.'

'Your ability to take care of yourself is questionable! Nor do I understand why your husband permits you to ride unescorted!' he said with a frown.

'Sorley Mor was unaware of my plans! I left a letter,' she explained awkwardly. 'The last time he was at Glenlarig an attempt was made on his life! He would have been at risk again and I could not bear it if anything happened to him!' Sudden tears gathered in her eyes as she said this. He reached over and caught at her reins, pulling her horse to a halt. He dismounted and invited her to do likewise.

'Let us sit on the bank here and you shall explain your trouble to me,' he said. She stared at him, wondering whether she should trust him. But he was Roderick's good friend and cousin.

Kenneth Campbell tied their horses to a nearby spindly rowan as he then led Kieran to a bank of heather slightly apart from Bess who was only too glad to be off her own horse for a time, sore from her unaccustomed riding. Below them on the floor of the steep glen rushed a burn, swollen by cascades of tiny streams leaping down from neighbouring heights above. Bees homed amongst the purple ling and thyme and small lilac scabious, and spires of tall thrusting purple knapweed, as fragile bluebells danced in the grass to a wind that bore autumn's bite in its breath.

And so it was that the major learned for the first time of the cataclysmic events in which the young woman had been caught up. He swore under his breath as he heard of Roderick's near escape from death, that the attempted murder by the assailant had almost certainly been paid for by Iain Campbell who had also tried to murder Kieran's husband and was suspected of kidnapping her two innocent children—babes of not yet two years.

'I heard speak of two bairns stolen from Edinburgh—had no idea they were kin to Roderick! But what assails your uncle that he behaves so?

Surely it is the behaviour of a madman!' He looked at her in genuine concern.

'When I first met my uncle, he was all courtesy and kindness. Also he seemed to hold Roderick in high esteem at that time.' She paused as she thought back to her arrival at Glenlarig and Iain Campbell's warm welcome.

'So pray continue—what caused such change?' he asked leaning forward and studying her face curiously.

'Over the months his behaviour altered. He began to drink more heavily than usual, and started to show obvious resentment of Roderick's right to manage the estate as laird. During his nephew's minority he had always seen himself in this role did not relinquish it easily,' she explained, impatiently flicking back a tendril of red gold hair that the breeze blew across her cheek. He nodded studying her face thoughtfully.

'This I suppose is understandable to a degree—an older man's umbrage at giving way to a younger one. But the latter actions you mentioned may not so easily be laid to this cause.' His gaze was puzzled. 'It is not normal behaviour to try to murder a son-in-law even though he is a Stewart and I suspect a former Jacobite.'

'He wanted to prevent Sorley Mor carrying me back to Edinburgh with the children! He was passionately fond of the twins and deeply angered at my decision to leave Glenlarig. For this reason he instructed his illegitimate son Fingal to kill my husband. It was a mercy the shot narrowly missed. We left the following morning accompanied on our way by Roderick and Ewan Dhu.'

She continued to explain subsequent events, the kidnap of tiny Alan and Ishbel—the attempt on Roderick's life as he rode on recent visit to see her, the perpetrator cousin to two of Iain's retainers, the pistol recovered from the man's body one of a pair especially made for Iain Campbell.

She then mentioned her brother's growing affection for Sheena Gregory whose true name was MacGregor—Iain's fury that his nephew should keep company with one of the hated Gregorach and Kenneth Campbell chuckled softly.

'Ah, so Roderick has at last given his heart to a lady! I thought it would never happen. I can see the difficulty though with choice of a MacGregor, but in my opinion this clan have been much maligned—are of a good courage and loyal to whatsoever cause they espouse.'

'My uncle would never allow any future heir to be mothered by a MacGregor, their blood mixing with that of his clan.' She paused. 'Of course, I have no way of knowing just how fond Roderick is of Sheena! But I can vouch for her courage and honesty—would be glad to call her sister!' He stared at her musingly as she said this. Then bent forward and took her hand and helped her to rise.

'I will escort you to Glenlarig and will speak there with Roderick! If I can do anything to help, I am yours to command. I am on leave, was going to make my way home. But that can wait.'

It was evening as the gates of Glenlarig loomed out of the white mist drifting off the loch. Now that they were almost there, Kieran felt a sudden fear constrict her heart. Planning this had not troubled her—but having arrived all was now too real. And Iain Campbell might not believe her thin story of leaving her husband for a second time!

There was consternation mixed with delight on Lorna's face as Kieran walked slowly into the great hall. She saw the girl pause to glance around her, and guessed it was because she saw no sign of Iain that she uttered that sigh of relief. Bess followed close behind her mistress trying to look unconcerned and Major Kenneth Campbell strode in on their heels, very elegant in his red coat and tartan and advanced towards Lorna.

'Major Campbell—Kenneth, how good to see you. You are welcome, sir!' She extended her hand and he bowed over it. Then she turned affectionately to Kieran love shining in her eyes.

Kieran my dear, what wonderful surprise,' she cried. And then the two women were in each other's arms. Lorna held the girl back from her and looked towards the door. 'So, where is Sorley Mor,' she asked and looked bewildered at Kieran's reply that he was not with her

'Then how did you come here? Did the major escort you from Edinburgh?'

'No He gave me his protection over just the last few miles—the point where he came across me!'

'Then what was your husband thinking of to allow you to ride alone, so dangerous for a woman!' Lorna stared aghast.

'Sorley did not know I was coming here. He will have learned it by now though, and must be furious!' said his wife unrepentantly.

'Let us go where we will not be interrupted,' said Lorna, then after calling instructions to one of the maids to prepare Kieran's room which was still kept in readiness, and another chamber for their military visitor, she led them through to her own private drawing room where Kieran saw all was as she remembered it, calm and beautiful, a place apart in that noisy tension filled house.

Lorna offered them wine explaining dinner was shortly to be served in the hall, that she was merely awaiting Roderick's return, but for now they could relax and talk here in private.

'Roderick is well, Lady Lorna?' inquired Kenneth Campbell

'Yes, but much troubled as are we all about Kieran's missing children!'

'It must be matter of great concern to you that your husband is thought to have stolen them for his own purposes,' said Kenneth and Kieran bit her lip as she saw the shock on Lorna's face. She had not thought to warn the major that Lorna was totally unaware of their suspicions. He realised his mistake as soon as he saw her shocked expression.

'What can you mean, sir?' she said her face white and rising from her chair stared at him in horror. He held up a conciliatory hand.

'Forgive me, Lady Lorna! When Kieran told me all that had been happening, of Iain's attempt on her husband's life and more recently Roderick's own close escape from death at the hands of a man related to one of Iain's retainers and that it is suspected that your husband is behind the kidnapping of Kieran's bairns—I just assumed that Roderick would have told you!' He ran a hand through his silver hair as he cursed himself for showing such lack of discretion.

'I think you both owe it to me to explain these matters,' said Lorna faintly as she sank back into her chair. Kieran went to her side and placed Lorna's untouched glass of wine to the woman's trembling lips.

'I am so sorry you had to learn all of this in such a way. Roderick wanted you to remain unaware of the recent attack on him''

'When did it occur,' asked Lorna.

'On the road near the track that leads to Balquidder,' Kieran explained.

'One of the MacGregor then no doubt,' exclaimed Lorna in relief. 'But wait—what was it you said Kenneth, that relative of one of Iain's men was involved?'

'It was Ronald Og MacKay,' replied Kieran softly, placing her hand on one of Lorna's. 'The pistol used one of a pair especially made for Iain by pistol maker at Doune!' At her words Lorna opened her mouth as though to cry that it could not be so. But then her lovely face crumpled. She knew it was the truth and that her husband had attempted to kill their nephew, whom they had brought up as though their own son from small bewildered child grieving both the death of his father, and then of a mother torn from his side, who died in childbirth a few months later.

But why? Why would Iain seek Roderick's life?' Surely it cannot be because he has lost control of the estate which is now rightly in the hands of our nephew. Why would he kill the heir? It makes no sense!' she cried wringing her hands.

'To replace Roderick with my small son Alan!' replied Kieran. 'We have no proof that this is so, but the facts point most surely to it. I believe he had the twins kidnapped and brought to this area—that they are perhaps not far from Glenlarig. Roderick said he intended to keep watch over Iain's movements!'

'Why did Roderick not warn me of this?'

'Because he did not want you to be worried,' said Kieran gently 'Listen Lorna, I am going to give it out that I have left Sorley Mor. I hope Iain may believe this as I did so before. Perhaps he may eventually let me see the children, trust me to bring them up here. But in the meanwhile Roderick's own life remains at risk.'

'I know he is greatly angered at Roderick's attachment to Sheena MacGregor!' said Lorna slowly, 'but to raise his hand against my own brother's son, to steal two innocent children—how do I pretend that all is normal when next I see him? Oh Kieran, for the first time in my life I am afraid!'

'But I am here—will stay for at least two weeks if that will help,' said Kenneth who had remained silent as Kieran explained the true danger of the situation to her aunt. He leaned forward. 'You must endeavour to behave as though all is normal! Do not give your husband any cause for suspicion that you are aware of his plans!'

Lorna returned his gaze and nodded her head. She straightened up knowing how much would now rely on her ability to disguise her burgeoning horror of the man to whom she was married.

'Thank you for this kindness, Kenneth,' she said quietly. 'And do not upset yourself for inadvertently revealing this. It was right I should know!'

'You are a very brave woman,' he said compassionately. 'You must keep a cool head—Kieran will need your support in the days ahead.'

Suddenly the door opened. They all three swung around. It was not Iain Campbell who stood there, but Roderick and his face creased to a warm smile as he saw his sister and his cousin.

'Kieran! How came you here?' and he embraced her, then turning to the major. 'And you cousin what kind fate brings you to my door?'

'Roderick, dear brother, the major knows all—and so now does Lorna!' explained Kieran.

'You should have told me,' said Lorna.

'Told you what wife,' said a deep slurred voice. 'Iain Campbell stood there framed in the doorway regarding them curiously. How much had he overheard they wondered?

'Why—that I've left my husband—and for good this time!' said Kieran. 'I have been grieving the loss of my children. He has been worse than useless in trying to find them! Any other man would have been searching the streets, but not Sorley Mor Stewart! No—he spends all his day caring for the sick children of others! I am done with him! Lorna says I may stay here. You I hope are in agreement that I should?' She fixed her dark grey eyes beseechingly upon his face. 'I should have listened to you, uncle,' she said sorrowfully.

'Huh! So at last you have discovered exactly what kind of a man you married!' and he looked at her critically, swaying slightly from the effects of the alcohol he had consumed. 'Once before I explained that the marriage could be put legally to an end. More difficult now that you deliberately went back to him!' He turned his gaze on Lorna.

'You did not tell me our niece was expected,' he said suspiciously.

'That was because I did not know it before she walked in the door with the major,' said Lorna in placatory tones.

'Ah yes—Kenneth Campbell of Kilrannoch. You are welcome, sir!' and he bowed. Then he turned toward Roderick. 'And you, Roderick, were you aware your sister was to arrive here? Perhaps you invited her—had private reason for doing so?' His nephew did not trouble to reply to the autocratic sneering tones in which Iain addressed him, but took Lorna's arm as a maid announced that dinner was served.

The meal was truly excellent. As they ate there in the great hall, beneath the painted gaze of long dead Campbell ancestors, Roderick chatted away companionably with Kenneth Campbell, watched broodingly by his uncle.

'I would have thought you might have preferred to spend your precious leave on your own estate,' he said suddenly to Kenneth. He had just learned the major had been invited by Roderick to stay at Glenlarig for at least two weeks—but why? The man's presence here would be a distraction to his plans and there was an angry glint in his eyes as he probed the matter.

'Why Sir Iain, I have none there to welcome me at home, no immediate family and know that my factor runs all efficiently in my absence.' Kenneth smiled blandly at the older man. 'I was able to offer protection to your niece upon her way here to Glenlarig, which brought all of you into my thoughts.'

'So, you did not accompany her from Edinburgh?'

'I would have welcomed the opportunity, but no. I came across her a few miles north of Kingshouse. I considered it was unsafe for a woman to travel alone apart from her maid as she did, as you will doubtless appreciate—her husband remiss in allowing it!'

'We are agreed upon that,' snarled Iain. 'Well if you are to stay, I will try to see you are offered some good sport. Some fine hinds on the hill!'

'I am sure that Roderick will find time to accompany me. We have many memories to share together regarding our work in putting down the recent rebellion!' He smiled courteously at Iain, but made plain whom he considered his host was and saw Iain's face darken. Without a word, Iain pushed his plate roughly aside and with a contemptuous look at his wife, rose and left the hall, banging the door heavily behind him. Nor did any have appetite after that. The meal now over, Lorna looked shakily at

Kieran, as Roderick and his cousin exchanged glances and went to talk standing by the fireside.

'I am glad you are here,' said Lorna to the girl she loved as a daughter. 'But you must behave with great caution. If you are right and Iain has got the bairns in his power, then we must not let him have the slightest suspicion it is this that has brought you here!'

'Aunt Lorna—you may be sure I will not do or say anything to endanger them! He really is unbalanced now, isn't he! Darling I'm so sorry you have all this worry to bear!' She folded the other in her young arms.

'My worries are as nothing compared with the heartache you are presently enduring, Kieran. But with God's help we will find wee Alan and Ishbel and they will soon be safe back in your arms!' declared Lorna quietly.

'Do you think Iain believed what I said about leaving Sorley Mor?'

'We can only pray that he did. I think your words pricked his vanity. But you must be so very careful, Kieran! Now come, let me show you up to your room which has always been kept in readiness—even though I knew it most unlikely you would return,' she added wistfully.

'We could neither of us have guessed what would have caused this visit! But I am so glad to be with you again—I have missed you, Lorna!' She took the heavy branched candelabra from her aunt's hands carrying it herself to light them up the dark stairs to the bedrooms. In her early days at Glenlarig Kieran had felt safe and content, never worrying about her life there. Now she sensed an atmosphere of evil in that place.

Bess attended her then satisfied that here mistress had all she needed bid her goodnight, and now she was alone in that familiar bedroom. She walked to the window and restrained a shudder as she and stared down into the murky night scene below her, where a thick mist coiled from the loch and motionless trees dripped damp.

'Where are you, my darling children,' she whispered urgently. 'My beloved babes—where are you?' she tossed and turned restlessly in the comfort of that bed and the pillow was moist with her tears when sleep came at last.

Chapter Fifteen

She awoke the following morning to the sound of heavy rain lashing against the window. There was a knock at the door, and Annie the middle aged maid who had previously cared for her on her previous stay there smiled and curtsied as she carried in a ewer of warm water.

'Good morning Lady Kieran,' she said. 'Lady Lorna asked me to wait on you—but if you prefer to have Bess about you, please just say so.'

'It is good to see you again, Annie,'' said Kieran carefully. 'Bess normally cares for wee Alan and Ishbel—will continue to do so once they are found. Until then it will occupy her time to wait on me. But I would be glad of your help in looking after my clothes. I have brought little with me, but such as I have, are crumpled from the journey.'

'Och, it is so sorry I am to learn the babes were stolen from you. What fiend would have done such an evil thing,' exclaimed Annie indignantly and bent to unpack Kieran's travelling bags. Even as she spoke Bess appeared at the door and at a word from Kieran gave grudging smile to Annie, but in a few minutes they were chatting quietly together as Kieran walked across to the window and stared out at the relentless rain streaking down the glass.

She was about to turn away, when she saw a familiar figure below and waved as old Angus Mac Seumas raised his pipes to his lips in salute to the young woman he knew had returned to her home among them. He raised his eyes and saw her standing there at the window as she lifted her hand to her lips in greeting.

The sound of his music touched her heart and brought tears to her eyes. What if Iain Campbell had allowed such evil to invade all their lives, against this was the love of her Aunt Lorna and of her brother Roderick, the devotion of Ewan Dhu and Ivor and the caring of this dear old man standing so proudly in the rain, his music blending hauntingly with the soughing of the wind.

And now her courage returned, the despair of the previous night put firmly aside. She knew that on her efforts depended the future of her children, perhaps their very lives!

She was wearing one of the gowns she had left behind when she had taken hurried departure with her husband following the attempt on his life by Iain's son Fingal. She wanted to look her best before Iain Campbell. He had always admired her in this sapphire blue looped up over a lace trimmed underskirt. She had splashed her face earlier, removing any slight stain of night time's tears, red gold hair dressed high on her head.

She found Roderick and Kenneth Campbell already at table, as was Lorna, but of Iain Campbell there was no sign. The men rose as she entered and smiled welcome. She had eaten little the previous evening and realised that she was hungry as she seated herself and fell to on a breakfast of ham and eggs and freshly baked bread with good appetite.

'I was going to take Kenneth for a ride in the hills, but will wait until this downpour has stopped,' said Roderick casually.

'It seems to be faring up now,' said the major, planting himself before the window. 'See, it is brighter on the horizon!'

'May I ride with you?' asked Kieran quickly.

'Perhaps not this time!' replied her brother gently. 'A rest will do you good after yesterday's long journey here.' There was warning in his voice and she did not pursue her request, realising that the two men were no doubt wishful to speak quietly together, make plans perhaps. So she rose from the table and followed Lorna into her peace of that small drawing room, where her aunt seated herself before her harp.

Kieran listened enthralled to the beauty of the music that filled that small room and penetrated the rest of that great house. Then almost automatically she walked over to the table on which lay her long abandoned violin, tuned it carefully, roisined the bow and then with a smile at Lorna started to accompany her. It was at this moment that the door opened suddenly and Iain Campbell stood there, staring coldly at the two women. Then as his eyes took in the picture the young woman made, her head thrown back as her bow spilt throbbing chords to enhance Lorna's own magical notes, a softer expression came into his dark eyes.

'You have not forgotten how to play then niece,' he said heavily.

'Sometimes music helps to heal the pain of separation—makes interlude of peace from constant heartache for my children,' she replied softly.

'You should never have taken them from this place, where they would have grown up in perfect safety,' he replied reprovingly. 'If ever they should be found, returned to this place, then it would be well to remember that Glenlarig is their real home.' And with that he turned on his heel and walked away. The two women stared at each other.

'I fear you are right—it is indeed my husband who has the children,' breathed Lorna quietly.

'Yes, but how to make him admit to it,' frowned Kieran. 'I have the feeling that I must reach out to him with apparent meekness—appeal to his assumed authority as laird.' She lifted the bow and again the music soared, expressing passion of longing for her beloved husband Sorley Mor and their children. It was as Kieran rose from her chair that Lorna thought she noticed the slightest thickening at the girl's waist and she drew in her breath.

'Tell me, Kieran—am I wrong, or are you carrying a child?'

'I didn't know it showed. I am not yet four months, conceived when Sorley Mor came here, it was I think that special time in the heather overlooking the loch when he truly made me his wife!'She coloured slightly as she spoke and Lorna gave a cry of delight as she went over to the girl and embraced her.

'My darling child, only another woman would have guessed it. You have that special radiance about you all pregnant women show and this despite your sorrow for the little ones,' said Lorna gently.

'Sorley Mor is well pleased—a child to be born of his own seed. He loves Alan and Ishbel as his own—but I delight I am able to give him this gift!' she exclaimed shyly.

'But to have ridden such journey in your condition!' cried Lorna. 'Did you not fear you might miscarry?'

'No, for I knew that I would be given the strength to overcome all obstacles in my search for the twins!' replied Kieran spiritedly. 'But I do realise I have to behave with caution that Iain does not suspect my real motive in returning.'

The rain had stopped. There was still some warmth in the late September sunshine and every wet blade of grass and bush sparkled in its light as a myriad small burns traced lacy passage in furious race down the hillside. The two men who rode along the wet track through fading heather and juniper were accompanied by Ewan Dhu and Ivor. They had proceeded perhaps just over a mile when Ivor called softly to his companion who looked casually around and then nodded.

'Roderick—we are being followed,' hissed Ewan Dhu as he closed the distance between them, 'Behind those rocks above us. Do not let the fellow see you are aware of him!' Taking that advice Roderick did not show any apparent concern as Ewan Dhu now dropped back again. The major however cast a quick glance above him as he bent over his horse's neck, adjusting the rein.

'Your man is right—there are two of them!' said Kenneth and swore. 'Should we challenge them as to their business think you?' He glanced at Roderick's face which remained untroubled.

'No—not yet! If they are on foot then they must have been running hard to have kept pace with us—always supposing they are Iain's men and from Glenlarig.'

'Where else?' wondered Kenneth.

'Let us see whether they continue to watch us once we have passed the cottage where lives Iain's light of love and her daughter—'tis there I guess the bairns are hidden,' said Roderick quietly and Kenneth nodded. They continued to ride leisurely along the track bordering the loch until Roderick spoke softly again. 'There, high on the brae—see that small cot?'

'I do! That is the one? Why do we not ride up to it and demand to see inside?' exclaimed the major enthusiastically, longing for a little excitement to spice the morning.

'Yes, we could do so—but do you not see that the men who were following us are now joined by a party of others? Obviously Iain has his suspicions regarding any knowledge I might have gleaned of the children's whereabouts. If we make attack at this moment, we put at danger those we seek to rescue!'

'I see them! About ten altogether I would judge. But there are four of us if you count your ghillies—all seasoned fighters!' Kenneth sighed as Roderick continued to ride placidly on. 'Do you fear that your uncle would actually harm the bairns?' he studied his cousin's face. Roderick shook his head.

'I am not sure—nor is there any way of knowing whether he is one of those about the cottage! What is certain, he is a badly deranged individual and as such might prefer to kill the children rather than allow them into my care.' He reached out and placed a hand on the other's arm. 'It is that I fear! Nothing would give me greater pleasure than to ride at them now,' and his grey eyes blazed steel hard. 'But better I think that we pretend our plans take us further afield so that Iain is relaxed in his mind.'

'What have you in mind?'

'A visit to Balquidder—my uncle is outraged that I have a fondness for a lady of the MacGregor there!'

'Your sister mentioned this and that the lady in question is very fair. Sheena her name I recollect?' He cast a curious look at the younger man.

'She calls herself Sheena Gregory—but she is MacGregor through and through! Kenneth my friend, she is proud and beautiful and of a fiery spirit! I have not declared my love—but plan to do so,' cried Roderick.

'I am delighted that you have at last found a woman to your liking!'

'The trouble is I do not know where to find her in all that wild area of hills and gullies and hidden caves above Loch Voil. My hope is that should she see me—then she might appear from the cave she presently calls home. Iain recently harried the Gregorach and I am not even sure if she survived the attack, so now you see why I would go there!' and at these plaintive words Kenneth's face expressed his sympathy.

'Come then—let us not waste time.' and they rode on sensing the hostile glances from those above them about the cottage where two small children might possibly be incarcerated.

'I am hopeful that Iain may think I am so besotted with Sheena, that my sister's babes mean little to me and that I have no slightest notion that he has the children in his power. When I am satisfied he has lost suspicion of me, then I will act—and let my uncle beware should he offer any slightest harm to the twins!'

The ride was long, over twenty miles, but at last they had left the road just before the Kingshouse Inn and taken the path forking to Balquidder. Now that they were arrived the problem was where in all that area was Sheena MacGregor? She could be anywhere. They men dismounted on the shores of the gently splashing waters of Loch Voil as Ewan and Ivor allowed the horses to slake their thirst at the loch side. A bottle of wine with bread and slices of cold venison brought from Ewan's pack was shared among them.

'See there—movement in those bushes,' whispered Ivor.

'Now what in the devil's name...!' exclaimed Roderick, rising to his feet. He sprang forward, reached out a hand and pulled a young lad from hiding place behind some straggling gorse! 'Who and what are you boy—and why do you spy on us?' The child struggled ineffectually in his grasp.

'I know this lad,' said Ewan Dhu. 'He stays with the family of Mistress Sheena—his name Grigor!' At his words the boy glanced towards the black haired, black bearded man who spoke and recognised him and smiled relief.

'Ewan Dhu! I meant no harm—keep watch on any strangers to our glen!'

'Then you are well met, young Grigor,' said Roderick, still holding the lad firmly by the wrist. 'My name is Roderick Campbell and I seek Mistress Sheena MacGregor!'

'I know you, Campbell,' said the boy stiffly. 'Why should I bring my cousin to you? It was but recently that your people rode into our glen and caused much distress here! It is as murderers and rapists you are known among us!' His small, thin, tanned face bore expression of hatred and disdain. Roderick loosed his grip.

'Grigor, if that is your name, I was in no way involved in what happened here during my absence. My uncle it was who came here and wreaked havoc. Sheena MacGregor is held in high esteem by me and also by my sister Kieran. I wish to have word with Sheena on matter of importance.' His grey eyes held the boy's cold stare and saw slight uncertainty cross the young face.

'Stay here then. I will see what she says. It may take time.' and he was gone like a flash of lightning.

'Where did he go,' cried Kenneth Campbell his eyes puzzled.

312

'Look,' cried Ewan Dhu and his pointing finger led their eyes to a small boat being rowed across the loch. 'It is Grigor—and it comes to my mind that although blindfolded when I was led away from the cave, it was on the opposite side of the loch that I received shelter and aid when wounded by Sheena MacGregor and her family.'

We should have taken the path along the south side of the loch then,' exclaimed Roderick. 'Better to bide here now and see if Grigor brings her back to us.' An hour passed and the men had almost given up, when Ivor rose from the rock on which he was seated,

'See there—the boat—and two now in it!' he exclaimed. All four men trained their eyes on that small craft and as it drew nearer could hear sound of the dip of the oars as it skimmed towards them.

'Wait here,' said Roderick and clambered down the steep bank to the shore. He waded into the water and caught at the rope thrown to him by the woman who had filled his dreams since first they met.

'Sheena! How grateful I am that you have come to me!' He pulled the boat ashore and held out his hand to her, but she leapt lightly onto the sandy bank, ignoring his courtesy. Then she stood surveying him from frowning eyes, glancing around her and noting the others standing politely aside.

She spoke no word in answer, merely continued to stare at him. Then at last she acknowledged him, 'Greetings to you, Laird Roderick Campbell. What is it that you want with me?'

'That is something we will discuss later!' he blurted, and he drew in his breath, examining the picture of lissom loveliness she presented wearing the blue gown she had accepted those many weeks back on her visit to Glenlarig, legs and feet bare.. Yes, she was indeed as fair as he remembered, eyes dark as newly opened violets, that full lipped mouth above cleft chin, ripe for kissing, and the tangled black curls hanging below her shoulders making dramatic frame to her perfect features.

'Do you perhaps come to inquire after the health of those your thrice damned uncle and his men injured on his raid on our people—or to ask after two grieving widows—or a middle aged woman recovering from brutal rape?' She had placed her hands on her hips as she uttered these scornful words.

'Sheena—you must know none of this was of my doing! When I heard he had been here I was concerned for your safety—and that of your family!'

'My father's leg still prevents his moving far from our cave, my mother still sick. As for me, why should you care?' Then as she realised what hurt the coldness of her words were causing him, she relented. 'Well, I am pleased to see you alive here and not a corpse of your Uncle Iain's making! Tell me—is there any news of the children?' she asked more gently.

'They are still missing, Sheena. But Kieran is at Glenlarig, rode all the way from Edinburgh alone with her maid Bess and pretended to have left Sorley Mor!'

'Why would she do such a thing?' exclaimed the girl worry knitting her brows. Roderick reached forward and took one of her hands.

'Because we are now sure you were right in your suspicions that Iain was behind the kidnap and has the twins—I should have listened to you!' Her face softened at this, but focussing her gaze on Kenneth Campbell where he stood a few paces back with Ewan Dhu and Ivor her stance stiffened.

'I see you have brought another Campbell with you—one of the military?'

'Let me introduce Major Kenneth Campbell, my cousin and valued friend.' He beckoned Kenneth forward, who bowed and would have taken her hand but she snatched it away and glared at him.

'You should not have brought any others of your clan here to spy that they might fall upon our people in the future!' Her words were ice. Kenneth however forced an easy smile to his lips.

'Lady, you are all that my cousin told me and more! He said you were very fair and spoke his admiration of you.' His eyes watched her with slight amusement and meant his words. The girl was indeed beautiful.

'I am no jade for the light conversation of men!' she snapped. Then Roderick made a dismissive motion to Kenneth and the ghillies as he slipped a daring arm about her slim waist and drew her towards the screen of some young, gold sequinned birch, and there pulled her down on the springy grass.

'Listen Sheena—I would have preferred to have spoken to you of this at more appropriate time, not now when burdened with responsibility for rescuing two innocent babes from a demented man's clutches.' He stared at her earnestly and seeing something in his eyes that spoke his intent, she would have pulled away. But he took hold of one slim, tanned wrist and held it firm.

'Sheena MacGregor—I love you with all my heart. Lassie, will you do me the great honour of marrying me?' Her struggles ceased and she stared at him in amazement. Her eyes widened.

'Do you joke, sir?'

'Indeed I do not! Sheena, since first we met vision of you invades my thought, and all my night time dreams are of you. Do you think you could possibly love me, trust me enough to become my beloved wife?' He raised her hand to his lips.

'But you are Campbell—and I of the Gregorach! More than this great barrier is the fact that I am related to that Rory MacGregor who killed your father and stole your mother! You are of the blood of those who hanged my uncle Rory and have harried my people unmercifully not only during the last conflict but over the long years!' She forced the words out dutifully between stiff lips, wishing passionately that they were not true—but they were and they both knew it.

'And do you think it right that this hatred between our people should endure? Is it not far better that our coming together in love may persuade others that there can be change in our land? It was Sorley Mor who told me that one day in the fullness of time all men should brothers be, no matter their clan or history, family disputes put aside, love of country and need of healing for all taking priority in this?' He drew her into his arms and attempted to kiss her. She turned her face aside.

'Your words are those of a dreamer, Roderick! We live in a real world where the strong attack the weak, money and possessions all important to those who have no real love for this land of ours—its beauty and its harshness. And an English king of German origin rules over our people and seeks to destroy our traditions, our language—all that makes us a unique nation!'

'Sheena, all this I know. But unlike the rest of Clan Campbell who enjoy certain privileges for supporting and upholding the Hanoverian dynasty, I do not feel the same way,' he exclaimed.

'How can you say that—you who fought at Mamore's side,' she cried.

'True I fought against Charles Edward, thought his harebrained attempt to regain the throne for the Stuarts doomed to failure when he came to these shores without either money or promised French regiments. The sooner he was sent packing the better. The longer he was here, the more harm to our people—or so I thought at the time.' He stared at her sadly.

'You did not approve the measures taken against all Jacobites then? The cruel murder, and raping of women, mindless slaughter of the elderly and even wee bairns, stealing our beasts, leaving people to starve by the ruins of their burned out crofts?'

'I now believe it was wrong—but such has occurred throughout history! Kieran has told me what happened to her people and I have heard countless stories that have sickened me from others. Scotland has to change, Sheena.'

'Change, say you but how—when?' she demanded through trembling lips.

'Listen my darling one, the change may not come in our own lifetime or even that of our grandchildren, but one day Scotland will regain its ancient independence. Until then, all we can do is to attempt to sink these clan hatreds and start showing care for one another.'

'Do you truly think this is possible?'

'It can start with you and me. I ask you again my dear—will you marry me?' His grey eyes held her wide doubtful gaze for long moments. Then neither knowing quite how it happened, they were in each other's arms and her mouth opened to his kiss. He felt the urgency of her response.

'Yes, I will marry you, Roderick Campbell! Be sure it is what you really want.' Her eyes were damp with sudden tears. 'But how will I ever be able to explain it to my father and mother—or you to your family!'

'Lorna already loves you, mo chridhe—as does Kieran. As for my uncle he hates me because I have taken the running of the estate from his hands and moreover is furious at the prospect of MacGregor blood flowing through the veins of our children. For this reason I believe he has stolen little Alan and Ishbel—that they may inherit Glenlarig once I am dead. And he plans that death I know.' He spoke calmly of the matter.

'Iain Campbell knows of your love for me?' she demanded in surprise.

'He more than suspects it!'

'Then how can I marry you and put you in greater danger,' she cried in alarm.

'Of course you do not know! Awhile back Iain had one of his men attempt my life as I rode past the Balquidder path on my road to Edinburgh! Ewan shouted warning and the pistol ball barely missed my head. Ewan dealt with the fellow. He identified the assailant to me and retrieved the pistol. It was one of my uncles, made to his specification.' He smiled at the look of horror that crossed her face.

'Why do you not accuse him—have him arrested!'

'He is my uncle. More importantly I am sure that he holds the twins in a cottage on the estate. If he thinks I suspect him he will either move them— or worse may harm them.'

'I know of men who would gladly kill him for you!'

'No, Sheena. Blood only begets blood.'

'But what now,' she cried anxiously. 'Am I to wait in fear that he may murder you in your sleep?'

'Ewan Dhu keeps watch outside my room at night. His mother was my wet nurse and he is friend as well as trusted retainer. He also thinks highly of you my darling!' He smoothed the dark glossy curls back from her face.

'Kieran's maid Bess has a liking for Ewan. Did you know this?'

'Bess and Ewan Dhu—two such opposites?' he exclaimed in surprise. 'And yet why not—it would give me great pleasure to see Ewan Dhu happily wed. But first there is our own ceremony to plan!'

'You go too fast!'

'Why should we wait? There is a church nearby is there not—at Balquidder village.' He kissed her again. She stroked his hair as she lay there thinking.

'Yes, there is indeed a church, where my ancestor Rob Roy MacGregor lies buried. Behind the church a path winds between trees to a waterfall where snowdrops and celandine grow in the spring. It is beautiful there and peaceful.'

'Then that is where I will make you my wife!' he held her close and she gasped as she felt the hardness of his rising passion—his exploring hands travelled down, then reluctantly he desisted.

'Forgive me, my dearest heart! Would I could take you here and now— yet respect you too much to do so. But our wedding night will be very special!' Minutes later they rose to their feet as she straightened her gown and smiled shyly at him as he took her hand and led her back to the others.

'Congratulate me,' he said and added hardly believing his own words, 'Sheena MacGregor has agreed to become my wife—and we would wed as soon as is possible!' Now Sheena blushed as they accepted exclamations of delight from Kenneth Campbell and Ewan Dhu and Ivor Mac Dugal and only young Grigor looked askance.

'I will need to meet and speak to your parents,' said Roderick slowly. 'Will they agree to this think you?'

'I cannot say! My father is a reasonable man, but his hatred of your clan runs deep—as does my mother's too. Let me speak with them first, but whatever the outcome I will keep my word to you.' She gave a sudden smile. 'Do you suppose Kieran would attend me at the wedding?' she asked wistfully

'I am sure she would be only too delighted to do so! Kenneth— will you be present at the ceremony?'

'It will be my great pleasure!' said the major then frowned. 'What of your uncle? This will only intensify his hatred of you!'

'He must not know of it! It will be the secret of all here.' Roderick looked considerately at the boy Grigor, sensed that he was far from happy at their plans. 'Grigor, you do not know me yet. I have no doubt that you see me as an enemy, but I am not, would be your friend. Will you trust me—help me perhaps?' he smiled gently at the boy whose eyes held only hard dislike.

'I detest all Campbells,' he replied at length with a dignity beyond his years. 'But I dearly love and respect Sheena. If she is to be your wife, then I will try to ignore all natural hatred of you at least—and these others.'

'And we two are friends,' said Ewan Dhu reaching out a strong hand to the lad. 'We have shared salt together. When men have done this it makes bond between them.'

'I did not choose to share salt with you man—it was only that Sheena had you brought to our cave when you were wounded. Otherwise my dirk would have sought your breast,' he said squaring his slim shoulders. 'But I agree to your words. Disgrace it would be to turn on one with whom one has shared salt—as your clan did when murdering the MacDonalds at Glencoe!' At this barb Ewan Dhu bowed his head, for what could one say to this black deed carried out so many long years ago, but staining his clan's history.

'Perhaps we should remember it was done on the orders of an English king, if Dutch Will could be described as such!' put in Roderick. He reached out and took the lads reluctant hand. 'Tell me Grigor—was it you who brought message from Sheena to my piper Angus Mac Seumas a while back?'

'It was,' the hand was snatched back.

'Would you bring message between us in the future. It might present danger—you would have to beware of my Uncle Iain who has kidnapped Kieran's weans—Alan and Ishbel. I trust you with this secret. We fear for their lives.'

'Where are they then—Kieran's bairns?' He looked at Roderick in curious surprise. 'Why have you not rescued them?'

'I am not entirely sure where he keeps them—perhaps in that small cottage on the side of the brae beside the Bhuidhe burn—roughly two miles along the shore of the loch after leaving the falls. You may have noticed it?' he asked.

'I do not mind it—but would be able to find it without doubt. For Kieran's sake I will keep watch over this cottage—see if the bairns are there,' replied Grigor face set in youthful determination.

'Och no—too dangerous for you to attempt that,' exclaimed Roderick apprehensively. 'It is guarded well as we noticed passing it this morning. No Grigor lad—I ask only that you bring news of Sheena to me when possible. Make sure none see you except Ewan here and Ivor—and Seumas. Trust no others.' He made to offer the boy a gold coin, but was fiercely repulsed.

'If we are to be friends, Campbell—then understand no gentleman pays another for a kindness!' the words coming with such dignity from the child made Roderick blink back sudden tears.

'We should go,' said Sheena suddenly. 'I will send word, make inquiries about the church—let you know my parents' views on all this. I fear their attitude may be of outright refusal—at least at first!' Then as Grigor pushed the boat from the shore she leapt in and the men watched as it skimmed to the far side of the loch, then banked between a screen of trees, nor could any see trace of where girl and boy disappeared to, hard as they looked.

'They call them the children of the mist and with reason,' cried Kenneth. 'Come cousin, we have work to do I think!' and at his words the party mounted and were soon proceeding back along the miles separating them from Glenlarig. As they rode Roderick's heart was singing with new happiness such as he had never experienced before. Sheena loved him—had agreed to become his wife! He could not wait to tell Kieran and Aunt Lorna. He tried to imagine her at table with him—beside him in bed, sharing all their days and nights together, and the prospect was intoxicating.

His spirits dampened as he saw Kieran's anxious face. She was standing at the door to welcome them back. ✒

'Did you find any trace of the children,' she asked plaintively. He shook his head.

'No, sister—I fear I did not. But I have suspicion that they may indeed be in Mourna MacNicol's cottage. When we rode out this morning, we were followed as far as the cottage and glancing up at the place saw around ten men there. Why? What would bring ten men to a lonely middle aged woman's dwelling in such remote spot—unless they keep watch there?'

'Did they realise you had seen them?' Her eyes were troubled.

'No. We were careful. Nor did we mark any movement on our way back this evening—although Ewan Dhu said he saw a man with a musket amongst the heather some few hundred yards away from the cot,' he said grimly.

'So what do we do now? I am fearful for their safety—oh Roderick, my heart is sore for them. Iain is in strange mood today. He knows you were out with the major—is suspicious.' He slipped a reassuring arm about her shoulders.

'Where is he now?'

'No one knows!' she shrugged and attempted a smile to Kenneth Campbell who was standing patiently listening to the exchange. 'You enjoyed your ride, sir?'

'Not as much as that I recently enjoyed with you, Lady Kieran!' he said whimsically then glanced at Roderick. 'I believe your brother has news for you,' he added and bowed, unbuttoning his coat as he entered the great hall and looked around. It was empty apart from Lorna Campbell who was standing alone by the window and looking charming in a gown of soft green wool, a tartan wrap about her shoulders, face wistful. None of Iain's men were in evidence.

'Ah—you are safe back,' she cried to them.

'Where is everyone, Aunt Lorna,' asked Roderick easily as he bent and kissed her.

'Iain went out this morning before you left. Was away for hours—then returned and asked if you were back—when he found you were not here he stormed out in a great temper. I do not know what is wrong with him!'

'He is not a well man. Lorna—you must be very cautious in all you say to him. He must never suspect we guess he has the children! But you realise that!' He slipped his arm about her waist. 'Now listen my dearest—I have news for you.' Then turning to his sister with a smile, 'Come closer Kieran,' he said, 'for you must hear this too'

'Whatever is it,' asked Lorna curiously.

'Sheena—you have expressed your love for her?' cried Kieran expectantly.

'More than that! I have asked her hand in marriage and she has agreed to become my wife!' At this both women embraced him, laughing and tearful all at once, as Kenneth looked on with tolerant smile.

Then Lorna stepped back and her face betrayed alarm. 'What will happen if Iain discovers your plans? I fear he will be furious—has said he would never tolerate MacGregor blood in the family!' and her face was deeply troubled.

'The decision not his to take,' was all the reply. 'Let us first find Kieran's beloved bairns and then I will make my news public. Lucky it is that we have Kenneth with us now as witness to all that is happening.' There was sound of noise in the outer lobby and the heavy hall door suddenly swung open to reveal a flushed Iain Campbell. His eyes went immediately to the small group at the window.

'Ah—you have returned nephew! Did you work hard about the estate today? You must have been busy away for so long!'

'Not as long as you uncle—but perhaps more productively,' replied Roderick calmly.

'And where were you exactly sir?' demanded Iain scornfully, 'Chasing some MacGregor slut no doubt!' At this challenge the blood burned in Roderick's veins, but he managed to retain a tolerant smile on his face.

'You seem to have the Gregorach on your brain these days uncle! An order I now give—there are to be no more raids on Clan MacGregor without my given permission. You understand?' Iain Campbell looked as though he would explode, but turned on his heel and went out without a word slamming the inner door behind him.

'Should you taunt him like that?' asked Lorna quietly. 'He is in evil temper. I fear for all of us.'

'Why not just order dinner brought, dearest aunt—and do not worry! Ah and Kieran, I have a question for you, sister'

'What is it?'

'Will you attend Sheena at our wedding? She asked me to make the request.' He saw Kieran's face brighten with excitement at the prospect

'Oh—joyfully,' she cried warmly. 'Where will the ceremony take place?'

'At Balquidder church!' he replied. 'I once heard tell that an ancient saint blessed the site centuries past. Saint Angus I think.'

'And that the fairies dance there,' added Lorna with a smile.

'Surely you do not believe such things,' asked Kenneth curiously.

'I suppose not. Yet stories of the little people are still told to this day,' she replied lightly. 'I was brought up on such tales and of water kelpies and giants and dark misshapen wee men who live in caves! All fantasy perhaps, but our ancestors believed all this.' And the conversation brightened between them and by the time that dinner was served there was a complete relaxation of tension.

It did not last long. A message had been sent to Iain Campbell that dinner was on the table, but had been ignored and so the meal had already started before the door was flung open and Iain marched in followed by a dozen of his retainers led by the MacNicol brothers. They seated themselves at the end of the table their master at the top next to Lorna. Then Iain roared for his men to be served, more meat brought. Now these men were usually served in room adjoining the kitchen except on special occasions. Iain stared at his wife, daring her to object to his action, but she ignored him.

Ewan Dhu appeared at the door and glanced questioningly towards Roderick who nodded at him. Minutes later another dozen or so men known to be loyal to Roderick appeared and took seats beside the others. Iain rose to his feet—stared, his face apoplectic.

'Who gave you permission to dine here?' he cried to them.

'Who else but the laird?' replied Ewan Dhu politely, 'I refer to Sir Roderick Campbell!' he added pointedly.

'We need more plates in here,' cried Lorna authoritatively. 'See to it, please Maggie and Norah!' and the maids scurried off at her bidding. And the meal proceeded in awkward silence broken only by Iain shouting for more wine as his bloodshot eyes considered his nephew and then the major seated beside him, this unwanted guest whose presence was causing delay to his plans.

'Did you enjoy your ride today, sir?' he said eyeing Kenneth Campbell coldly.

'Yes indeed,' was the reply. 'Roderick is a most pleasant host! He has even suggested I should extend my projected stay as I actually have a whole months leave from the regiment.' The scowl these words brought upon the older man's features told its own tale of suspicion and irritation. With this particular member of the military known to be highly esteemed of Lord Mamore by his side, it would make Roderick a more difficult target. He would have to be patient and was angered such was necessary. He brought his glass down sharply on the table, its contents spilling— pushed back his chair.

'Come,' he cried to his men. 'We are done in here,' and without so much as a glance at his wife, he stalked out of the hall, followed by the MacNicol brothers, Donald MacKay and Tom Breac as the others looked at each other questioningly, unwilling to show open disrespect for the young laird to whom all would be answerable one day.

'Let us have music in here,' cried Roderick. 'Where is my piper,' he demanded. 'Where is Angus Mac Seumas?' He smiled as the old man appeared.

'Some music Angus,' he requested with a smile, 'Something to set our feet adancing!' He indicated the wide space before the fire. 'Come, dearest aunt!' and he took Lorna's hand. 'Kenneth, do you take Kieran!' Within minutes they danced and swung in a spirited reel as the sound of the pipes flooded through the house and beyond.

It was as though the dancing, bringing unusual sense of jollity in the hall produced a welcome camaraderie between those retainers whose loyalty perhaps still to Iain Campbell, and those on whom Roderick knew he could depend. They glanced sheepishly at each other and at a sign from Roderick rose to their feet and joined the dancers on the floor, table and chairs pushed well back.

Then as the original dancers relaxed by the fire, these men with the blood of the highlands in their veins commenced their own wild dances steps passed down through time, leaping and twirling as their shouts and cries blended with the sound of the pipes. There was complete end to tension and Roderick saw from the faces of those whose loyalties had seemed questionable, that there was spirit of healing, and lack of friction between all as in former times.

'Enough,' called Roderick at last. 'Listen, my friends, over the next few weeks I will explain plans for Glenlarig that will be of advantage to all here. I ask your patience in the meanwhile—and your loyalty. Goodnight to you now. And I thank you Angus Mac Seumas for your music which made us remember who and what we are—Clan Campbell!' And applause followed his words.

A week passed, a week in which Roderick and Kenneth spent time in the hills bringing down game for the table. Kenneth suggested taking a boat on the loch, fishing one of his favoured pastimes. But Roderick mindful of what easy target they would present to Iain's animosity on the water did not agree.

'I would that your sister was not married to that physician fellow,' confided Kenneth to his cousin as they clambered onto a flat topped rock and sat staring down at the loch. 'I fear I am losing my heart to her. She is the most beautiful woman I have met in a long while—and the most determined!' he added ruefully.

'I wish for your sake she was free to your advances—but she dearly loves her husband Sorley Mor who is respected friend of mine, and who has twice saved my life! But one day you will find another.' He reached out a consoling hand.

'When my late wife died five long years ago, I swore then I would never love again.' His voice betrayed his emotion.

'How did she die—you have never spoken of it?' probed Roderick.

'She had a canker in her breast—was gone within months! I will never forget Margaret. It was an arranged marriage but one in which we both found love.' There was tenderness in his voice, his eyes sad.

'Five years ago you say—then, a year before the rebellion! Was this why you made the army your life?' Roderick questioned and saw the other clench his fist.

'I think it gave release to my grief and frustration to target those Jacobite rebels on whom I could slake pent up fury at what had happened in my life. Also there is a camaraderie and structure to the military life with its discipline and chain of command.' Roderick nodded understanding at this.

'Now,' continued Kenneth, 'having seen your great content in the freedom of this place, joy in Sheena MacGregor and how love has changed you—well, perhaps I wish I might emulate you in the path you have chosen.'

'I wish you well in this. My sister Kieran is as I say happily married. But you will find another, of this I am sure! Come—let us return. I am hopeful there may be some word from Sheena by hand of young Grigor!' They called to Ewan Dhu and Ivor who had slung the carcases of the two roe deer they had shot onto a garron and the party made return down the hill to the house.

It was the following day that the old Angus, having lowered his pipes after his morning's musical offering in front of the house, was attracted by the sound of a shrill whistle. He glanced questioningly around.

'Why—ye are the lad who came here before from Mistress MacGregor,' he cried softly. 'What do ye here again?' He walked slowly towards the bushes where the boy crouched partially concealed, and stood there appearing to examine the bag of his pipes in case he was observed.

'I need to speak with the young laird—or with Ewan Dhu. It is secret matter. I trust you not to tell any other I am here!' the boy whispered warily.

'I will get Ewan Dhu. It would attract attention should I go directly to Laird Roderick. Wait here—and be careful you are not seen!' He walked casually away his eyes still directed on his pipes. He found Ewan Dhu at the stables, checking that the groom had the horses ready for the day.

'Ewan Dhu—a moment of your time,' he said. Then his eyes rested thoughtfully upon the young stable boy who had drawn closer to them. He did not trust this youngster, nor wanted his words overheard.

'Perhaps you could walk with me—see if you think the laird will approve the tunes I am minded to play on his birthday!' The two men stepped away together companionably, the stable boy no longer bothering about them. As they walked Angus lowered his voice and spoke of their hidden visitor, this lad who wished to talk with Laird Roderick.

'Ah—it must be young Grigor,' whispered Ewan Dhu

'He also wished to speak with you, Ewan Dhu,' added Angus softly. 'Now I am going to play a few notes and you must appear to listen in case we are observed—Iain would have the lad's life should he find him here!'

The message was soon given and Ewan Dhu whistled under his breath at what he heard uttered by the boy's young high pitched voice.

'Well done indeed, Grigor,' he exclaimed, training his eyes upon the old piper as he spoke, that none should see his gaze upon the lad who had taken such risk for them. 'You are sure—the two bairns are wee Alan and Ishbel?'

'I had not seen them before—but the boy has red hair, the wee lassie pale gold—about two years I would think,' he stated thoughtfully.

'Grigor—are you sure none saw you stare into the window at them?'

'No! Think you I am stupid, Ewan Dhu? There were two women there and a great man with a curly brown beard and a red scar on his cheek—all were eating. Two other men were keeping watch a hundred yards away—watching the path below where it skirts the loch.'

'Grigor lad—the laird and Lady Kieran will owe you a great debt of gratitude for this news! Go now and take great care. If the bairns are moved from that place come quickly here to me.' The boy nodded, hesitated.

'There is another message for Roderick Campbell. Sheena says she will wed him in three weeks time—but without permission from her parents. They were much angered at her news. And no wonder,' he added feelingly.

'Wait—have you anything to eat?'

'I have oatmeal in my pouch which I mix with water from the burn—and there are berries too. Do not worry for me, Ewan Dhu!' and he was gone.

Roderick had just risen from his breakfast and was talking with Kenneth Campbell when he noticed Ewan standing at the door patiently trying to attract his attention. He smiled at the major and said he would meet him in the library when he had attended to whatever problem brought the ghillie there. Minutes later he listened to Ewan's triumphant whispered news.

'It is true—the lad was sure it was the twins he saw?' Face tense he waited confirmation from the man.

'He described them accurately enough,' said the Ewan Dhu stroking his thick black beard. 'No doubt in my mind that he spoke truth. What should we do now? Go there with a party of men and bring her bairns safe back to Lady Kieran?' He squared his shoulders in anticipation and looked at Roderick longing for him to agree to this.

'My every instinct is to do so,' replied Roderick passionately then stood quiet for a moment. 'But there is much to be considered,' he added. 'If I leave here with more than both you and Ivor, it is bound to be noted. Iain watches me—and as you know one of his men follow when the major and I ride into the hills. No doubt he has given orders to remove the babes to another spot if any see us approaching—and that cottage has an uninterrupted view of the road and glen.'

'At night then—none likely to suspect it?' suggested Ewan Dhu.

'It might serve. But Iain is increasingly unstable. I know he plans my own death, consider this is why he holds wee Alan as the next legitimate male heir. I cannot risk bringing the twins here—it would be to endanger them. For once he realises he has lost power over them he may turn on the bairns—even kill them. They need to be returned to Sorley Mor in Edinburgh—but the road there is long, they would have to be well protected.'

'But here with their own mother to look after them at Glenlarig—and all love Lady Kieran!' said Ewan Dhu. 'As for Iain's desire for your own death, Roderick, you who are dearer to me than life itself, who suckled at my mother's breast—think you he would survive such attack? No—he would die at my hand and I would glory in his blood!'

'Then we attempt it. I believe that many of those who have taken his orders in the past are now changing allegiance to me—and accept that I am laird, not my uncle who has long behaved as though that position was his.'

'The dancing last night was a good thought, Roderick!'

'A moment's inspiration—good that it worked. But we must show every care! Always remember that a wolf is most dangerous when cornered—and I rate my uncle as one such now.' His grey eyes expressed sadness. 'It should have been so different. Iain could have stepped back, all natural honour extended to him. But when ambition and pride cloud a man's judgement, he is no longer to be reasoned with.'

'Will you tell your sister of your plans?' asked Ewan. Roderick hesitated.

'No—I think not. She might inadvertently betray her joy at such definite news of the children's survival. I hate to keep it from her—but better so for her own dear sake.' He pressed Ewan Dhu's arm. 'Not a word now—except to Ivor and then when you are alone.'

'Trust me for it.'

He found his cousin in the library standing impatiently before the window, while ruffling through the pages of a book on military history.'

'I thought you had forgotten me!' cried Kenneth

'No, cousin—but there is news,' cried Roderick trying to contain his excitement as the major eyed him curiously.

'Good news? Sheena has sent word?'

'Yes—but it is more than that. You remember the lad Grigor? He was here and told Ewan Dhu that he has seen the twins. They are definitely at Mourna MacNicol's cottage! He spied them through the window—was not seen. He noted but one fellow inside with the women and two other men keeping watch over the road.'

'Splendid news indeed—then we go and rescue those puir wee bairns!' exclaimed Kenneth his eyes shining in anticipation of action.

'I am considering the matter. Iain must have no glimmer of suspicion that we know of their whereabouts for he might kill them and dispose of the bodies to cover his tracks,' said Roderick heavily. 'We are so close now to retrieving them—must not imperil their safety in any way.'

'Is he capable of that—killing those innocents?' the major looked appalled.

'I hate to think it—but know it is a possibility.' They looked at each other.' 'He may also have left instruction for their removal should any there see us approaching the cottage. Then it would be hard indeed to find them again!'

'Have you any plan in mind?'

'We will rescue them by night! A few of us break in scoop them up onto our horses and away.......' he broke off at a snort of approval from Kenneth.

'Ah, now you are speaking sense!' interrupted the major in satisfaction.

'I would actually prefer to take them directly back to Edinburgh into the keeping of their father, Sorley Mor Stewart, until all is sorted here. But when news is brought to Iain and he realises we have the twins, he might deal harshly with my aunt and sister in our absence! The alternative to bring them here to Kieran at Glenlarig, and have it out with my uncle face to face—accuse him of his crime!'

His face was torn. The thought of publicly exposing his uncle was repugnant to him. It went against all family loyalty—but else could he do?

'He deserves no less!'

'True—but suppose there is fighting between his own followers and ours and Kieran and the children not to speak of Lorna, are caught up in such violence? Do you see now why I find myself in a quandary?' He spread his hands out indecisively. 'But if I hesitate overlong Iain may move the children far away from this place and we may never find them more.'

'What does your instinct tell you then?' asked Kenneth. 'Do not forget that I am witness to all that is happening. What do you think Mamore would say should it come to his ears? He would I think be mortified that Iain Campbell had so defamed our name as to behave in such despicable matter!' His face expressed his contempt of the man.

'Let us go out on the hill—discuss the plans logically between us,' cried Roderick. 'I long for fresh air to clear my thoughts!'

'Yes, the weather too fine to spend among books,' snorted the major feelingly. 'We should go armed I think.'

Some ten minutes later they had left the house attended by Ewan Dhu and Ivor—and followed inconspicuously or so he thought by Niall MacNicol, who was fleet of foot and managed to keep them in sight.

They had ridden some five hundred yards when Ewan Dhu pointed out the man's dark head to Roderick, who raised his gun and scowled his displeasure.

'Get you back to the house!' he cried training his weapon in the MacNicol's direction—and the man rose sheepishly from behind a heather bank—and trudged disconsolately away. Iain Campbell would be angered at his inefficiency. But at least he could report that the young laird and the high ranking officer his cousin, were bound in opposite direction to a certain cottage.

Satisfied they were no longer in danger of being overheard, the four men dismounted and sat in the fading heather, staring across the loch—and plans were formulated that were to change the lives of many.

Chapter Sixteen

It was a Sunday morning and all of Edinburgh's bells seemed to be ringing at the same time as people, their faces suitably solemn streamed towards the many kirks, women lifting their skirts to avoid the effluent on pavements and overflowing gutters, minding that warning call of 'Gardy Lou' as night jars were emptied from above. The all pervading stink of the city was slightly less offensive now that the weather was becoming colder as October brought early mists to blend with smoke from hundreds of chimneys.

It would be good to be away from the place for a time reflected the man who folded a shirt and collected hose.

Sorley Mor Stewart was packing two capacious saddlebags as he waited for his horse to be brought from the stable. His decision was taken. He was no longer prepared to wait ineffectively here in Edinburgh while his pregnant wife faced danger at the hands of her unstable uncle at Glenlarig. He shook his head firmly now at Lachlan, as the young man pleaded to be allowed to accompany him on his journey.

'I have already said no, Lachlan. Your place is here to help care for the sick in my absence!' he insisted, for he wanted no distraction on his mission. But the young man doggedly persisted.

'John Patterson is well able to care for any patients for a week or two,' exclaimed Lachlan Stewart. 'And you may need me, Sorley Mor! The work ahead fraught with danger—I mind well you told me yon Campbell almost had you murdered when last you were at Glenlarig! With me at your side you will have better chance than alone.'

'I know you speak from your heart,' replied the physician kindly, 'but there may be fighting with those who are seasoned fighting men. Such will be Iain Campbell's retainers,' he added warningly.

'But I can handle a sword as well as any other! When I was in France, an old Stewart exile there taught me how to fence—and I also learned to be a good shot!' he cried defiantly. The physician stared at him in surprise.

'What? And did David approve this,' cried Sorley Mor looking with new eyes at the youth recognising that although merely sixteen, he had reached man's stature in more ways than one. Already his learning of medical matters, under Patterson's guidance and Sorley Mor's own careful instruction, had progressed beyond the normal for a student of his years. But so gradually had the youngster matured that it gone unnoticed, Sorley still regarding him as the lad he had first met in Appin.

'David did not know of it,' replied Lachlan. 'But every man needs learn how to defend himself and those dear to him! I too love Kieran and her babes. You cannot deny me, brother in law!' At this assertion of their kinship Sorley Mor gave a grave smile.

'Then come you shall. But I need your word you will obey me in all things!' His dark blue eyes held the boy's gaze. Lachlan nodded agreement.

'But of course! I swear it on the steel!' He produced a dirk from inner pocket of his leather doublet, unsheathed it and raised it to his lips.

'Lachlan—do you not know it is against the law to carry a weapon? It could bring you into much trouble if discovered!' said Sorley Mor reprovingly.

'I will say it is but a toothpick! May I tell Dr Patterson that I go with you?' Lachlan's eyes shone in anticipation of the adventure.

'I will do so myself,' lad, replied the physician. 'Best collect a few essentials to take—and I will need to hire a mount for you at the stables.' And he watched as Lachlan hurried up the stairs to his room, before he sought John Patterson.

The two doctors sat facing each other in the comfort of the familiar sitting room with its straggling plants at the window, comfortable armchairs and couches where they could relax and with that overflowing bookcase and shelving holding files of medical notes, a much used chessboard, and table bearing glasses and decanter. Here they spent so much of their leisure time together, often interrupted over the course of an evening by urgent knocks at the front door as Mistress Lindsey would apologetically interrupt their discussions over a glass, to report some emergency that had arisen.

'You are determined on this course then,' said Patterson, whose real name was Grant and who was now established as such welcome part of the practice. His hazel eyes regarded Sorley Mor quizzically. 'Are you sure it may not interfere with Kieran's own attempt to discover the whereabouts of the children for you to suddenly arrive on the scene—especially if she has declared to those there that she has left you for good!' His tones were troubled.

'None there will know of my presence. I shall hide out in the heather— like you, I have much experience in that! I shall watch what is going on— find occasion to speak with Roderick away from the house. Damn it all John, my wife is pregnant and has placed herself in danger from a fanatical Campbell who has already shown his own contempt for human life!'

'Then all I can do is to wish you well my friend. I wish you would allow me to accompany you, but I understand the necessity of remaining to care for the surgery.' Patterson lifted his shoulders regretfully but the other merely smiled.

'Listen Patterson—I take Lachlan Stewart with me!'

'But he is over young—perhaps lacks the correct experience and discipline for such venture?' suggested John Patterson his eyes grave.

'I have agreed to it—and he tells me he learned how to shoot and fence whilst in France! It is agreed then? You will care for all in my absence?' He reached out a hand to Patterson who gripped it firmly.

'Need you ask? I owe my whole new life to you, Sorley Mor Stewart. This place will be safe in my care as it was on your last trip to the highlands! But if you need help—send for me!' Sorley nodded assent to this and rose.

'Good—then it is settled! I will see if Lachlan is ready.' But then as he made towards the stairs, there came determined knocking at the front door. He hesitated, looked back.

'I will deal with it,' called Patterson. But a moment later the housekeeper having answered the door, nervously whispered the name of this Sunday visitor to John Patterson, who called up urgently to Sorley Mor.

'What is it then,' asked the other resignedly, turning around his dark gaze impatient.

'You have a visitor—John Campbell of Mamore, or so he announced himself,' said Patterson his face suddenly grave and uncertain.

'Show him into the sitting room—I will speak with him there alone,' stated Sorley Mor decisively. He could only imagine the shock it was to his friend, this former escaped Jacobite prisoner to be brought face to face with the feared Major General John Campbell of Mamore.

The two men looked at each other as Sorley Mor bowed and took the officer's proffered hand and invited his guest to be seated. Mamore did so, smiled and fixed his strong interrogative gaze on the doctor.

'I know that you are reunited with your wife Kieran—and thought I would call on you whilst here in Edinburgh. I am but newly returned from a tour of the islands and the west coast. Where is Kieran, my friend—and those delightful children of yours?' He accepted the glass of fine whisky the physician offered and raised it in toast. 'To you and your family, Sorley Mor,' he said courteously.

'You had not heard then,' cried Sorley Mor.

'Heard what precisely?'

'That the twins were kidnapped a few weeks back. Despite our best efforts, no trace of them yet found. But there is suspicion that they are stolen by Iain Campbell, uncle to Roderick!'

'What's that you say?' cried Mamore in astonishment. 'The children are stolen by Iain? But for what reason—it makes no sense!' Then the younger man explained the series of events that had recently taken place. He spoke of the recent attempt on Roderick's life—of the weapon so used, pistol belonging to Iain Campbell.

'Do you tell me that Iain tried to have his nephew murdered? Has he gone completely mad?' exclaimed the astonished soldier.

'Apparently he is unwilling to relinquish rightful control of Glenlarig and its lands to Roderick. Also, he may perhaps be angered—at a fondness between his nephew and a certain Sheena Gregory,' added Sorley Mor carefully.

'Do you say so—why, yes I remember Roderick spoke of his attraction to this MacGregor woman! Just a passing fancy I thought it.' He sat for a moment in thought, 'Certainly Iain has always shown a deep hatred for this proscribed clan of rogues and cattle thieves!' added Mamore sternly, his face expressing his own disapproval of the Gregorach. But the other man lashed back in protest.

'Perhaps they do no more than the Hanoverian armies who lifted thousands of cattle from whole districts of the highlands and left our people to starve—sold the same cattle for profit to the English!' The words were out before he could bite them back and Mamore regarded him sourly for a moment. Then he smiled slightly.

'I would suggest you watch your tongue when speaking of such matters to others owing rightful allegiance to King George and his government! However, I take your point! Many unfortunate things happen in war, sir! You must realise that the spirit of the highlands had to be broken to prevent further uprising, more death and destruction.'

'And this repeated sufficient times, will throw disguising veil over the cruelties perpetrated.' Sorley Mor uttered a sigh. 'Certainly we look at recent history through different eyes. But one thing I have realised, for our country ever to prosper, all such hatreds must eventually be put aside.'

'On that at least we agree,' replied Mamore smoothly. 'Now let us leave politics aside. I would hear more regarding your suspicion that Iain is holding wee Alan and Ishbel in some secret place?' The two men sat in close discussion for half an hour, as Mamore tried to prise every scrap of relevant information from Sorley Mor.

His face was grim at the close of that examination. He handed Kieran's letter back to the doctor, sent he heard as the young mother took her own way to Glenlarig accompanied it would seem only by her maid.

'Thank you for showing me this. I see now why you did not take horse immediately to bring her home.' He ran his hand through his thick silver curls as he pondered the matter. Sorley Mor restored the precious letter back to his pocket.

'Listen Lord Mamore—Iain has a fondness for Kieran. My hope that he will not offer harm to her, even consider returning the bairns to her care, providing she gives undertaking to remain at Glenlarig. But to further his villainy he needs must proceed with plans to kill Roderick! Only thus can he use wee Alan as next presumptive heir and continue to run Glenlarig during his childhood!' The major general stared at him as he registered the words.

'If you are right in all this, there is a chance that Kieran may persuade him to divulge the twins hiding place. But I imagine any sight of you would inflame the situation!' He frowned indecisively, wondering how he personally could act best to help restore the couple's children.

'I am taking horse this very day for Glenlarig,' explained Sorley Mor,' I was all but ready to depart when you arrived at my door.'

'But we have already decided that your presence might precipitate tragedy of some kind,' objected the soldier brusquely.

'Listen, Lord Mamore—Kieran is pregnant of our child! I fear for her safety in all this!' cried Sorely Mor his face expressing his concern.

'She expects another child—why my congratulations, wonderful news indeed! It is more reason not to rouse Iain's suspicions by your presence at this time—would you not agree?' the other expostulated.

'I do not intend to go openly about my business—but take to the heather. Young Lachlan Stewart accompanies me.' The man's eyes were shining.

'The lad you had about you at Glencoe? Well I cannot stop you in this. But I am determined to take my own part in this affair—Iain Campbell is behaving in such way as to bring discredit on our clan. He must be stopped and I have the necessary power to insist he return her children to Kieran!'

Sorley Mor stared at him uneasily. 'What do you intend?' he inquired.

'I shall take a troop with me as though in routine inspection of that part of the central highlands. What more natural than I should break my journey at Glenlarig? Do you wish to ride with me, at least as far as—shall we say Strathyre?' But the doctor shook his head. The last thing he wanted was to be seen associated with this Campbell, second only in authority to the hated great Argyll himself.

'Better we go separately. Perhaps we may meet in the vicinity of Glenlarig, sir. I thank you for the help you offer—ask only that you tread lightly in the matter. Believe me, Iain Campbell is suffering some severe disorder of the mind and like to be dangerous if obviously crossed!'

'I think I know best how to deal with member of my own family! Now do you have parchment—a pen?' He bent his head down and wrote—a drop of wax now showed impression of his seal. 'At least take this pass with you—it covers both you and young Lachlan Stewart and may ease you past any delays upon the road.'

'I thank you, sir. This was kind,' replied the doctor.

'Not at all—not at all! Fare ye well, Sorley Mor Stewart. Despite your unfortunate Jacobite leanings, I respect your principles!' And he rose to his feet. Minutes later a splendid carriage bearing the Campbell crest was seen departing from the front of the doctor's house.

'That was Lord Mamore?' cried Lachlan. 'I could hardly believe my eyes that he came to visit you!' He stared critically at the doctor. Sorley Mor clamped a reassuring hand down on the youth's shoulder.

'We must remember that he is related to Kieran and bears real affection for all members of his family—is appalled to learn of the kidnap. He intends to provide help in finding the little ones and to deal with Iain Campbell. My only fear is that he may inadvertently provoke Iain into losing all control!'

'But we still go as arranged?'

'Of course—you are ready Lachlan?'

'Yes,' replied the youth steadily. 'Let us away, for I cannot wait!'

It was over an hour before they were finally left Edinburgh behind them. It had taken time to hire a mount for Lachlan and purchase provisions suitable for days spent sleeping rough in the heather. At the bottom of one of Sorley's saddlebags wrapped about in his shirt was a pistol and shot. He wished that he might carry a claymore with him, but knew the law prohibiting any to carry arms apart from the military, was strictly enforced. But with Mamore's pass and carrying his physician's bag strapped behind him, he felt reasonably safe upon the road.

Major General John Campbell of Mamore was making his own preparations. On the afternoon of that same day he left the castle at head of a troop of twenty well armed, mounted members of the militia. The party were but a few hours behind Sorley Mor and Lachlan. They made overnight stop at Stirling. Mamore looked around the dining room of the Golden Lion Inn, wondering if the doctor would be found there—but of Sorley Mor he saw no sign.

Sorley Mor had decided for a smaller hostelry to the north of Stirling. Here they stabled their horses, dined on mutton stew served by a sulky waitress, inspected a room boasting indifferent bedding and planned early start the next day. They were up before dawn, breakfasted and were off on the road, as the Stirling and its garrisoned castle perched on high rocky buttress quickly disappeared into the distance as they made towards Doune and Callander.

'No sign of Mamore! I prefer we do not encounter him as we ride,' called Sorley Mor and Lachlan nodded fervent agreement. They passed through

Doune, and were held up there for ten minutes by a cattle drover until he turned off the road with his bellowing herd. Just as they were on their way again they saw a troop of red coated militia immediately ahead of them.

'Halt,' cried their sergeant, turning his head as he heard the sound of their approach. 'Halt and identify yourselves!'

'Doctor Sorley Mor Stewart and my assistant Lachlan Stewart on our lawful business to visit relatives at Loch Tay,' replied Sorley authoritatively.

'Lawful business—so you say! Let us inquire further into this,' said the sergeant heavily. He was bored. Nothing had happened to brighten his day so far, now these two travellers might supply sport.

'Perhaps if I mention that I go to visit family of Major General Mamore,' said the doctor calmly. 'You might care to glance at this document, Sergeant? The pass bears Lord Mamore's signature and his seal!' The man took the pass and glanced at it and his expression changed from that of bully to one of reluctant politeness.

'Following my orders you understand, doctor! Is it Finlarig Castle you are bound for?' he asked.

'No—Glenlarig House,' replied Sorley Mor. 'It is good to see how carefully you keep watch on the roads! Wish you good day, sergeant!'

'I wish I could have spat in his eye,' cried Lachlan once they were out of earshot. 'What would have happened think you had we not had that pass?'

'Possibly our bags would have been searched and our persons! Come now, I wish to be at Glenlarig before Lord Mamore!' and he looked behind wondering whether the major general was also on the road, keeping his promise to deal with Iain Campbell.

They were stopped on two further occasions, the first of these two encounters with a cheerful young captain who having glanced at Sorley Mor's pass became quite talkative, saying that he and his troop were on their way to Oban by way of Crianlarich. There had been rumour of a French ship said to have landed a Cameron laird there wanted by the authorities.

'What is the man's name' inquired Sorley Mor idly.

'Archie Cameron—a doctor like yourself sir, so it is said,' replied the Captain stroking his moustache and did not notice the worried look in Sorley Mor's eyes, for the wanted man was close friend of his. But he managed a slight shrug of his shoulders.

'I doubt it is indeed but a rumour,' he replied. 'After all, why would a man who had been involved in the rebellion and escaped to France risk return here? It makes no sense. Well, we must be on our way, Captain!' and with a smile urged his horse forward once more.

It was coming on to evening when they drew level with the path turning off the main road to Balquidder that another troop approached them coming from this direction. They were dragging two men with them, hands bound and ropes about their necks to encourage them to keep up with their captors. Again they were stopped, this time by the mounted sergeant in charge of his good humoured, swearing foot soldiers enjoying their power over their quarry. He gave Sorley Mor a suspicious stare.

'What have we here then? State your name and business,' he growled, wiping sweat from his fat, red face, as he peered belligerently at the doctor. Production of Mamore's pass provided grudging acceptance that the travellers had protection by a name known and respected in this area.

'Your prisoners, sergeant—what is their misdemeanour,' asked Lachlan daringly, glancing with pitying eyes at the two men who looked tired unto death.

'Something wrong with your eyes then?' demanded the sergeant scornfully. 'Look at their clothes! Tartan as is banned under the law!' He pointed derisory finger at his prisoners. 'Seems they may have tried to disguise it with mud—but the rain has washed it so that any can see it is tartan! Six months for them—deportation if it turns out to be a second offence!'

'But surely if they have tried to dye their clothing with mud it shows they are trying to comply with the law?' put in Sorley Mor. 'Men such as these probably do not have the money to purchase new apparel!'

'That is their problem—not mine,' snapped the sergeant. 'I would suggest you get on your way doctor, nor try to delay His Majesty's soldiery about their duty!' With a shout to his troop the two prisoners were once more jerked forward by the halters about their necks. Alone on the road again Sorley Mor and Lachlan stared at each other.

'It seems that little has changed since 46,' breathed Lachlan angrily. 'Back there in Edinburgh it would seem as though the Rising had never occurred. People go carelessly about their business. But here in the passage of but one day, we have seen what is still happening. Will there be no end to all this cruelty and suffering?' His young face showed the pain he was experiencing.

'Sadly, it may continue for many years yet,' responded Sorley Mor despondently. 'These patrols are meant to cow people already traumatised, break their spirit! With their homes destroyed, burned to the ground in those first few terrible months and all cattle and livestock stolen—our people are now denied the clothing they have worn for centuries—our language not to be spoken or written down—all weapons forbidden us even a knife—the pipes banned! The future looks bleak indeed.' He

paused. 'But hope must remain eternal for eventual change—God with us.'
And his lips formed firm determined line.

'Perhaps Charles Edward may come again—this time with a French
army to back him!' and Lachlan waved his hand as though brandishing a
sword.

'No, Lachlan!' reproved Sorley Mor. 'Those days are over forever. Now
we strive to survive! Somehow and whatever the cost, keep memory of our
traditions enduring—pass all on to the next generation. It has taken me
long to accept that Scotland is much more than a playground for a Stuart
dynasty passing into history—more too than land to remain forever
crushed by England and her German house of Hanover!'

'What are you saying then, Sorley Mor?'

'That however long it takes, our land must be free again. Perhaps not by
force of arms this time, but by the established will of the Scottish people,
demanding their right to become an independent nation once more!' His
voice echoed on the wind that blew down from the hills, blending with an
eagles cry as its majestic shape circled above.

Lachlan pointed to the bird a faraway look on his earnest young face as
he faced Sorley Mor and spoke passionately through trembling lips

'The lion and the phoenix are symbols of our nation are they not? But to
me Scotland is better represented by the eagle—flying high, proud above
all. Like the eagle our people will rise above their difficulties, however
hard pressed they may be in the future.' The older man glanced back at
him, his dark blue eyes shining approval.

'Keep that hope forever burning in your breast, lad! And yes, you are in
the right of it. Like the eagle Scotland will fly high again, destined once
more in the fullness of time to become proud independent nation' He
raised his head to study the bird's powerful flight. 'Yes indeed—high soars
the eagle!' he said softly. 'But come Lachlan Stewart, we have many miles
ahead.'✐

They had proceeded barely half a mile, when a man leaped down from
the wooded bank to their left and raised his hands to show he had no evil
intent. The riders brought their horses to snorting halt beside him. Sorley
Mor examined him swiftly—and knew him!

'Why, it is Mr Robert MacGregor is it not?' He gave a smile at the man
who confronted him, recognising the strong, arrogant features beneath the
thick dark matted curls and the direct stare in the man's eyes—and
remembered him as the visitor who had called on him at Edinburgh many
months ago with news of Kieran's whereabouts, that she was at Glenlarig,
and for which news he would always owe the man a debt of gratitude.

'Aye, it is Robert MacGregor,' replied the other. He stepped closer and
Sorley Mor noticed the man's limp, recalled Sheena telling him of her

father's injury. 'We saw you in conversation with those who took away two puir fellows setting traps for hares. De'il tak all such bluidy English invaders of our land—and those who support them!' he cried furiously.

'They said they had arrested them for the wearing of tartan—but it was obvious the men had tried to dye their clothes if only with black mud!' The doctor's glance took in the faded kilt worn by MacGregor. 'I see that you do not trouble to disguise your own tartan,' he said quietly.

'If they should come upon me—then die I will dressed as a highland gentleman should be! Experience the kiss of death sooner than have them take me,' he proclaimed grimly tossing back his head. Sorley Mor gestured to the road behind them.

'You are no doubt aware of their troops regularly marching along the roads still?' questioned the doctor warningly.

'We watch them, even as they search for us!'

'Your daughter, Sheena—how is she?'

'I prefer not to discuss her,' growled her father. But Sorley Mor persisted.

'She has become very dear to Kieran. As you know my wife and I are reunited and my gratitude to you sir for bringing me news of her whereabouts that day!' and he inclined his head to the other.

'I hear that she is back again at Glenlarig?' probed MacGregor.

'That is so—but without my permission. She left me a note saying that she hopes to persuade Iain to reveal where our children are concealed— you know of their kidnap I take it?' MacGregor nodded his understanding of the matter.

'You have my sympathy sir. Sheena told me of it—mentioned her suspicion that Iain Campbell is involved, which knowing what I do of the man I can well believe!'

Then Sorley Mor briefly explained all to Robert MacGregor who inclined his head gravely, but most of what he heard he was already aware of.

'You may have heard that Sheena has expressed wish to marry Roderick Campbell who has asked her to become his wife? She demands my blessing on such match! Further dares to say that they will wed either with or without my consent.' The words exploded from the man's lips and the doctor tried to restrain a smile at the news. So, Roderick who never thought to marry had as guessed fallen in love with the fiery young MacGregor girl—and actually proposed to her!

'Mr MacGregor—I can only say that I have found your daughter to be a fine and courageous young woman. As for Roderick—I know him as honourable and decent man and my friend! I can understand your frustration at thought of one of your blood marrying a Campbell. But consider Sir, one of these days all such clan hatreds must be put aside.'

'Put aside, say you?'

'Yes, Rob! For hundreds of years there has been clan struggle in our land. But in the future all must start to pull together in the knowledge that only through our unity may Scotland once again regain her independence!'

'How can MacGregor and Campbell come together?'

'You could consider how I who fought at Culloden in the Jacobite cause, managed to find great love with my wife Kieran, Stewart and Campbell together in us—the child we expect, blend of the best of both!' But his words had little effect on the man who stood fiercely before him.

'If Sheena is determined on this wedding, then she is no longer daughter of mine!' he growled. 'But as for your own wife—she was raised as a MacGregor and that surely must have done much to dilute the shame of her Campbell blood,' he added reflectively.

'To me she is neither Campbell nor MacGregor—but just my own dear wife,' said Sorley Mor quietly. 'She has been away over two weeks now. I could not stand the worry of it more.' His eyes betrayed his inner anguish.

'But you are now going to risk confrontation with Iain Campbell? Is that wise in the circumstances?' demanded MacGregor in surprise.

'Not so. I intend to hide out in the hills, keep watch over Iain Campbell's comings and goings—hope perhaps he may lead me to the children. I only trust that Mamore, now on his own way up here, will not inadvertently push Iain into some wild act before we have the bairns safe! The man is suffering some mental imbalance!' He patted his restless horse soothingly.

'Call it plain evil—devilry,' cried Robert MacGregor. 'You say Mamore is on his way? Then I must go—warn our people!'

'Your leg—how is it these days?'

'The salve sent by Sheena's hand provided healing—my gratitude to you, doctor! My wife also is better of the medicine you gave. If I can do anything to help you against Iain Campbell you have only to say. My men at your disposal if needed—although the presence of that devil Mamore would make such intervention difficult,' he amended cautiously, as the doctor smiled understanding. He gave the man a straight look.

'Think on what I said about Sheena's wedding! I vouch for Roderick as a good and gallant man. Give her my regards, and to your wife,' he added thinking fleetingly of the sick woman he had never met. The MacGregor leapt back up the bank and was gone. Sorley Mor gestured to Lachlan to proceed once more.

It was dusk when they arrived at the falls, where the Dochart swirled noisily over rocks in the gloom, the sound of its rapids echoing about them.

Sorley Mor gestured towards the path that turned to the right and led as he remembered to the shores of the loch and on towards Glenlarig. Lachlan looked about him as they rode, had never been in these parts before. Even in the dim light of evening he could see how beautiful the area was—not exactly like his own beloved Appin, but very fair.

'Up this way—but show care,' and Sorley Mor set his horse up the steep brae the youth following and frowning growing concern.

'If we are to take to the heather now—what of the horses,' asked Lachlan in a low voice.

'What indeed? I had intended stabling them at that small inn we passed a few miles back on the road. But it might have drawn attention to us. After all, why would two men forgo their horses to travel on foot in this wild area?'

'So what do we do?'

'Look for a sheltered spot up there on the hill. Once the moon is up, we will see more clearly!' and he dismounted now and led his mount upwards through heather tussock, gorse and bracken, Lachlan following suit. At last they came upon a small declivity where the dark shapes of birch and alder hovered over a splashing burn and a wild cat shot across their path startling the horses.

'This place should serve us well,' approved Sorley Mor. They allowed the horses to drink at the burn, before unsaddling them, removing their packs, and tethering the beasts to a tree. Both were men were stiff from riding and hungry and Lachlan unpacked the provisions they had brought with them, bread, cheese and some cold meat and a bottle of wine.

'How far away is Glenlarig from here?' the youth inquired, for all he could make out below them by the light of a pale moon not at the full, was the dull shimmer of the loch

'Some two or three miles as I remember,' was the reply. 'Make yourself comfortable Lachlan lad—try to get some sleep! At least we should not be troubled overmuch by midges at this time of year,' he added.

Lachlan was soon relaxed in slumber, as Sorley Mor lay there thinking of his beloved Kieran, hoping she was not in any immediate danger from Iain Campbell and whispering prayer to the Christ for her safety and that of two small frightened children, longing for the comfort of their mother's arms. At last he too slept.

He woke with a start. Dawn was breaking at the eastern end of the loch, spreading in flood of red gold brilliance along the glittering stretch of its waters. But it was a sound that had wakened him. He sprang to his feet and glanced cautiously around. Then he spied him---a young, slim shape moving cautiously between the trees.

'You there—come forward,' cried Sorley Mor and at his words the child, for he was no more than that, slowly approached their campsite and stood poised for flight. 'Who are you,' inquired Sorley Mor in gentler tones.

'Grigor my name,' said the lad stiffly. 'I saw you last night—followed you here! But you are not of Iain Campbell's men?'

'I am glad to say I am not. My name is Sorley Mor Stewart. I am a doctor!' replied the other courteously as though speaking to an adult.

'Ah—it is you who are married to Lady Kieran then,' exclaimed Grigor and ventured a smile. 'I have heard tell of you. That you are a friend of Sheena's!'

'Well Grigor—are you hungry? ' He gestured for the boy to seat himself and handed him a piece of bread, which the youngster ate ravenously, as Lachlan now awake looked on curiously. Sorley Mor introduced him to Grigor, who nodded a greeting to this relative of Kieran's.

'Now can you tell me if all is well with my wife?' asked Sorley Mor.

'She is sad for her children, does not yet know the place where Iain keeps them—safer so for her!' Sorley Mor heard the boy's words in astonishment.

'And you, Grigor—you know where wee Alan and Ishbel are,' he asked trying to keep his voice steady, his eyes shining with hope.

'I do, as does Roderick now—and Ewan Dhu and Ivor as well! Yes and old Angus Mac Seumas—who is a fine piper for a Campbell!' added the boy nonchalantly. 'It was I Grigor MacGregor, who brought word to them of where the bairns are held! They were not sure before—guessing just.'

'Iain Campbell does not know you have discovered them,' cried Sorley Mor urgently. Grigor smiled scornfully and shook his head.

'He does not. Listen doctor and I will tell you where they are—but you must promise not to go there or it will upset the plans the men have to rescue them. They are close guarded. If you are seen it could ruin all!' He looked longingly at the half loaf of bread. Lachlan heeded that look and offered the boy more, some cheese with it.

'Now tell me exactly where the twins are—for I will certainly not do anything to endanger them,' said Sorley quietly. The lad looked into those steady dark blue eyes and nodded.

'Listen then,' said Grigor softly. And Sorley Mor drew in his breath as he realised how close he actually was at this time to those dear children whose kidnap had caused such heartache to Kieran and himself. When he was certain he had understood their exact location he straightened up exultantly.

'Grigor, do you think you could get word to Roderick that I am here,' he began—but at that moment the boy placed a finger to his lips and scrambled nimbly up the silvered trunk of a young birch. He put his hand over his eyes, so bright the sunlight.

'Redcoats down there on the road—led by an elderly man whose coat is all gold braid—and rides a fine white horse,' he exclaimed. 'He wears a plaid—in Campbell tartan!' and he spat.

'It will be Lord Mamore,' exclaimed Sorley Mor. 'He comes to have words with Iain Campbell and I only hope he does not upset all at this time! Grigor, I have no right to ask you to seek out Roderick—but it would help much should he know of my presence here!'

'I will go.'

'Be careful. Take no risks!' But the lad has already disappeared, gone like will-o'-the-wisp. No sound now but the chuckling of the burn and a pheasant's cough and the soft wind stirring the golden leaves on the birches, above their heads.

Roderick Campbell had risen early from his bed that morning but found his aunt Lorna was abroad before him. She had taken to sleeping on her sitting room couch on a regular basis these days, leaving her husband to snore nightly in drunken slumber in their conjugal bed. It had caused further estrangement between the couple, but Lorna had developed an instinctive fear of Iain since she had learned not only of his involvement in the attempted murder of Sorley Mor, and later of Roderick—but also of the twins kidnap.

'Did you sleep well, dearest,' said Roderick solicitously. Lorna looked pale and slightly frail these days and he worried over her health.

'Yes—but it took me time to relax. Someone tried my door in the early hours and I heard cursing—Iain it must have been, but the door was locked. After that sleep came hard.'

'I would I had been there! Have you seen any sign of him this morning yet?' he asked quietly.

'No. Oh—someone is coming!' she said nervously and he turned at the sound of the hall door opening, but it was his cousin Kenneth who came in. The major smiled at them. He pointed to the sunlight shining in from the windows.

'The weather is very fair, perhaps a suitable time for adventuring,' he said and Roderick took his meaning, the recovering of those precious, small bairns—possibly tonight? And he wondered if there was any fresh news from young Grigor. He could not speak privately to the major now, for the maids belatedly bustled in laying the table for breakfast, while a lad appeared carrying fresh logs. Soon fire flared up in the massive fireplace with welcome warmth, for although the thin late September sun shone bright outside, it was cold within that massive stone building.

Roderick smiled as his sister Kieran now joined them. She glanced around, looking for her uncle and was partly relieved not to see him, was purposefully wearing the sapphire blue gown she knew was pleasing to Iain Campbell.

Over the last few days she had attempted to allay the man's suspicions of her return to Glenlarig, outwardly maintaining her expressed contempt for Sorley Mor's feeble attempts to find her missing children. She felt Iain was beginning to warm to her again. His wife's coolness and Roderick's obvious scorn had left him with only the support of his MacNicol henchmen and other of his trusted retainers. It flattered him that Kieran still observed her earlier affection and respect for him.

Then Iain was there amongst them, as a serving man pulled back his chair for him—but no longer at the head of the table, that place was now surrendered to Roderick. He threw himself down with a scowl. The conversation that had flowed before he arrived now dwindled somewhat, but he did not appear to notice. Outside the sound of the pipes was borne towards them, as Angus Mac Seumas made greeting salute to the morning.

Ewan Dhu hovered at the door and caught Roderick's eye. The man stood there for but a minute unnoticed by the others and disappeared. A few moments later Roderick pushed back his plate and with murmured excuse to Lorna, rose from the table. 'An affliction of the bowels, perhaps.' sneered Iain as he passed—then temporarily forgot his nephew, glancing approvingly instead at the picture Kieran presented and relaxed as the girl smiled back at him trustingly.

Roderick made straight for Ewan Dhu who was waiting for him in the passageway.

Well, is there news?' he demanded

'Yes indeed. Much to relate, sir! But too many listening ears nearby!' and he indicated a youth sidling about the kitchen door. Roderick recognised him as one of Niall MacNicol's sons.

'Be about your work, James,' said Roderick sternly and the youth sullenly withdrew. 'Come Ewan Dhu—I feel like a breath of air. Let us go outside!' The sound of the pipes delighted their ears as they walked around the west side of the house. The old piper bowed a greeting, and continued to play, but one hand briefly indicated some nearby bushes.

'Grigor—are you there, lad?' cried Roderick softly.

'I bring news of Sorley Mor Stewart,' whispered the boy urgently. 'He and another named Lachlan are camping half a mile from the woman Mourna's cottage!'

'What—Sorley Mor is here? Does he know where the twins are held?'

'I told him. He will not act until he hears from you, Roderick Campbell! He wished me to let you know he is here.' He watched for Roderick's reaction.

'Tell him not to make a move until I send word! Is he safe hidden from Iain Campbell's men?' he asked with a worried frown.

'Not well enough! But I would say he is a man able fine to look after himself,' approved the lad. 'But I have other news, laird! A troop of militia led by a man the doctor named Mamore, are approaching—almost here. I ran all the way over the hill to get here first—warn you!'

'This could upset our plans,' hissed Roderick in frustration. 'Go lad and be careful you are not seen. If possible keep an eyes on that cottage—any comings and goings. Is there any news from Sheena,' he added wistfully.

'I have not been back to Balquidder. You told me to watch the bairns!'

'Yes of course—quite right! Away with you, Grigor, and my thanks, you are a brave lad!' The child nodded and disappeared just as Ewan Dhu uttered an exclamation of dismay.

'See laird, Grigor was right!' and he pointed. 'Look ye—down there on the road—soldiers!'

'I must warn Lorna—tell Kenneth!' He clamped hand on Ewan's shoulder in gratitude as he turned back to the house.

'Ah Roderick—you join us again,' cried Iain looking at him curiously. 'But I will not have continued pleasure of your company, for I ride on the hill to bring down a deer for the pot!'

'Perhaps you should delay,' said Roderick easily. 'We have visitors arriving!' All looked at him in surprise and Lorna rose to her feet, indicating to the maids that they should clear the table and tidy all.

'Visitors, Roderick?' she said her thoughts already turning to reception of any coming to their door. She looked at her nephew for guidance.

'They will soon announce themselves, dearest aunt,' he replied gently, 'Lord Mamore and his men are apparently only minutes away.' As he spoke he turned from Lorna to her husband who stared back at him darkly, with frustration stamped across his face.

'Now what brings Mamore here,' he growled his face baffled. 'Word had it that he was in the west.'

'It will be good to see him again,' said Roderick quietly. 'Give opportunity to discover what is happening across the highlands at this time. But apart from that, I have great respect for Mamore—matters here on which I may seek his advice!' He saw Iain glare at him suspiciously, but he merely smiled back at the man genially.

Now was not the time for seeking confrontation with his uncle. He wondered how the major general's visit would impact his own tentative plans for rescue of the twins—perhaps it might serve to keep Iain back here at the house and give window of opportunity to return the poor bairns safe to Kieran's arms.

Then of course there was new added complication of Sorley Mor's presence, although this might prove helpful. Somehow he must get word to the man. All these thoughts flashed through his mind as he walked to the window and stared out. He watched as he saw the disciplined mounted troop led by the famous soldier he called uncle, ride up the driveway, saw Lord Mamore dismount and hand his horse over to one of the grooms who had hurried forward from the stables eager to be of assistance.

'I will greet him,' cried Roderick ignoring Iain's cold stare and called for Ewan Dhu to attend him. He walked down the steps, Ewan at his heels as he bowed before the major general, who stiff from riding, stared at him testily for brief moment and then smiled. He gestured to his officers to fall back while he spoke a few words in private.

'Well Roderick, seems perhaps you have encountered problems here at Glenlarig needing attention!' he inquired softly

'You are certainly right, sir!' replied Roderick. 'But how did you come to hear of it?'His face was puzzled. Mamore brushed the dust from his coat as his eyes darted around ensuring that they were indeed private, his men not within earshot, before replying.

'Why after touring the islands and the west coast, I'd barely arrived in Edinburgh, expecting a few weeks peace mind you, when I thought to call on Sorley Mor Stewart hoping to see Kieran and the children there—I heard his account of basest treachery shown by Iain Campbell! And knowing the doctor, I take it he spoke truth?' He fixed analytical glance on Roderick watching his face.

'Yes,' replied Roderick steadily. 'We believe my Uncle Iain is responsible for stealing wee Alan and Ishbel—and further that he has them hidden close guarded in a cottage not far from the falls!'

'The de'il you say! I heard also that Iain made attempt on your own life but recently?'He stared at Roderick in concern.

'Correct. Listen sir, Iain does not know that we have discovered the children's whereabouts, and fear that should he realise it they will either be moved– even killed perhaps. Lorna knows of this, as does Major Kenneth Campbell. But not Kieran so far, for fear the knowledge might be more than she could bear.'

'Just so—I can only imagine her grief at being deprived of her children! But tell me, what does your cousin Kenneth here?' He listened as Roderick hastily explained the situation. Then placing an arm about the young man's shoulders mounted the steps at his side to where Lorna stood waiting to greet him on the threshold. He kissed her hand and glancing down at her fondly. He had a soft spot in his nature for her.

'Lady Lorna—I call without warning and hope you may receive my men at this time—about twenty of us.' He smiled as she called that all should

344

enter and refreshments were being prepared. Then he noted her husband Iain approaching behind her placing himself so as to block access to the lobby. Mamore's face showed its usual courteous stare as he bowed slightly to this man who had caused such grief in his family, wondering at the change in one who had in the past been perfect gentlemen and genial host. The doctor had blamed addiction to alcohol and overriding ambition as having corroded Iain's behaviour.

He noted as he took in Iain's appearance that his linen looked crumpled and that he was unshaven, his silver white hair unkempt.

'Greetings, Iain—how is it with you,' he inquired levelly. 'I hope I see you well, sir!' and noted the man's discomfiture at his arrival.

'Well enough,' replied Iain forcing a smile. 'To what do we owe the pleasure of your visit?' he demanded uncomfortably.

'I had wish to meet with Roderick and Lorna and yourself of course— and also to see how my niece Kieran fares? I called on her husband Sorley Mor Stewart whilst in Edinburgh and found the good doctor much disturbed. He reported that his wife Kieran had left him and a story of deep distress mutually suffered by the couple that their twin children had been kidnapped in broad daylight from an Edinburgh street!'

'They should have remained here in the security of this place,' replied Iain casually. 'Kieran now agrees that my earlier advice on the matter was sound. She has seen the light and left that doctor fellow for good!' Then he stood back allowing Mamore with Roderick at his side to enter unobstructed, as the major general's shrewd eyes swept around the handsome hall he knew so well and lighted on a man he recognised.

'Why, it is Major Kenneth Campbell is it not? I am pleased to see you again, sir!' said Mamore affably as the other soldier bowed to him courteously.

'I am on leave, Lord Mamore! I met with Roderick's sister Kieran travelling alone on the road with but a maid in attendance—saw her safe here and have been invited by my host to spend my leave at Glenlarig!'

'Indeed the major was very kind,' said a musical voice, and Mamore smiled as his eyes lighted on Kieran Stewart walking towards him and as beautiful as he remembered her, and so very like her late mother Catriona whom sadly the girl had never known. She was looking very winsome in her blue gown, red gold hair swept up high on her head, a few curls framing her face, her dark grey eyes steady and inquiring.

'Why niece—I am pleased to see you and looking well despite the heartache you endure for your missing children.' He hesitated and then said quietly, 'My dear, I visited your husband who explained the situation—that you have decided to make your home back here again. I am sorry for Sorley Mor's sake of course, but his loss is Glenlarig's gain!'

'Exactly what I said,' replied Iain Campbell, closing the gap between them and anxious to overhear what was said and watching the girl intently. He relaxed as he heard her slightly scornful reply to Mamore.

'I have left my husband. He failed to do enough to find wee Alan and Ishbel, so taken up with his work as physician. He is a good man I allow, but I was tired of him and of Edinburgh's nauseous smells!' She held his gaze, wondering whether Sorley Mor had indeed told him the truth of the situation, that she merely played a part to disarm Iain's suspicions.

Two of Lord Mamore's officers now entered at his command, the others of his men after attending to the stabling of their horses, were to rest in one of the barns where food would be served to them.

Mamore stretched back in his chair, comfortably replete after enjoying a splendid breakfast, washed down by a good white wine.

'Has there been any disturbance in the district of recent months,' he inquired casually. Roderick shook his head.

'Thankfully not—as you know sir, here in Breadalbane the late rebellion caused little disturbance, this area Campbell controlled. And I believe that within the Campbell stronghold of Argyll there is similar peace, the western highlands alone offering few flash points now?' He looked inquiringly at Mamore.

'Yes, all is agreeably quiet, those who rose against the lawful government of this country all subdued, dead or shipped to the colonies as indentured servants—slaves!' he paused and stared at Roderick. 'I suppose you have had no trouble of late with the Gregorach? His eyes twinkled to see the flush rise on his nephew's face.

'I have always made it my business to make raid into Balquidder from time to time,' put in Iain Campbell suddenly, leaning forward his face aggressive. 'But alas, Roderick has now curtailed my lawful efforts to cleanse the area of those who are worse than rats! It seems he has a fancy for one of the MacGregor wenches!' His eyes travelled scornfully across at Roderick, who now rose to his feet, his dark grey eyes blazing fury.

'My Lord Mamore—I would have chosen quieter time to have made this known to you—but I have asked to wife a lady from Balquidder— Mistress Sheena Gregory, dear friend to my sister Kieran, who knows her family!'

'I see,' replied Mamore, keeping his features well under control. 'The name Gregory replacing the proscribed MacGregor I take it? Well, if you love the lady my boy, then I wish you well in this!' At his words Roderick relaxed while Iain stared at the major general open mouthed. He had thought to throw final discredit on Roderick by his assertion—to have Mamore's approbation of a MacGregor bride entering this place was intolerable.

'You actually applaud the mixing of MacGregor blood with our own,' spluttered Iain Campbell. He drew a deep breath, suddenly realising how cold the expression on Mamore's face, but doggedly continued his complaint. 'This Sheena is related to Rory MacGregor who slew Roderick's father! All common decency precludes such match!' he said loftily. The famous soldier leaned forward eyes snapping in annoyance.

'Enough, sir!' snapped Mamore, 'If I have given my own blessing to Roderick in this, I expect no less of you! Once he has taken her to wife, she will become a Campbell! Yes and a member of this family!' He glared at Iain who stared back at him with smouldering gaze, but bit back further retort.

'Some more wine, John,' smiled Lorna, and poured it with her own hand. She was delighted at Mamore's unexpected approval of the match between her beloved nephew and Sheena.

'You have met her, Lorna?' He viewed her over his glass.

'Yes— I received Mistress Gregory here as a guest, and liked her,' she exclaimed for in truth she had been much taken with the girl at their meeting. Thinking back to the day, she knew instinctively that Sheena would make a good wife to Roderick. Perhaps such marriage might help to heal the hatred between those involved in dark matters of almost twenty years ago. 'Sheena is a fine young woman,' she said, ignoring Iain's furious glance in her direction. 'Having met her I quite understand Roderick's love for her. She is brave and extremely beautiful.'

'And I love her as a sister,' put in Kieran suddenly, despite fearing it would inflame Iain, but wishing to show support for Sheena.

'Then more fool you, Kieran,' ground out Iain, rising to his feet. 'No doubt your own earlier association with the MacGregors has blunted your sensibilities!' He swung about, turning to Mamore who had fixed him with reproving gaze.

'Your pardon sir, but I have matters needing my attention,' he said. 'No doubt my wife and nephew will keep you entertained this day!' Then before any could stop him, he stalked purposefully to the door signalling to his ghillies to attend him. It was rankest discourtesy to their exalted guest to behave in this way, but Iain was past caring about such niceties.

His anger was now rising also against Kieran Stewart, for so he now referred to her in his mind. No true Campbell would have supported Roderick in his association with his MacGregor wench, as she had! He had decisions to make—important decisions and his mind in turmoil as he walked to the stables.

What to do with Kieran's bairns? So far none had any reason to suspect his involvement in their kidnap, or so he thought. But with Mamore now here, those two precious heirs to Glenlarig must be moved to safer place than Mourna's cottage—but where to? And when best to attempt their removal? They had to be kept safely out of sight until he had accomplished his nephew's death—and that would not be possible while the powerful Campbell lord was here.

'With Roderick dead I will then find some way to achieve a miraculous rescue of the bairns, put myself about as their saviour and protector,' he muttered, as the MacNicol brothers stared at their master uneasily, for he was uttering soft disjointed sentences aloud whilst seeming unconscious of their own presence there at the stables.

'What are your orders, sir?' asked Niall respectfully, looking at his master's indecisive, scowling face.

'What's that you say—my orders? When I have my mind made up you will learn my orders! Until then, we ride upon the hill—anywhere away from this company I find little to my taste,' and he glared wild eyed back towards the house. The brothers stared at each other and shrugged and called for Donald MacKay and some others—and minutes later their horses clattered down the driveway and off in opposite direction to that certain cottage! Their departure was watched curiously by Mamore's militia, from the open door of the barn where they had finished their meal and awaited further orders.

Ivor Mac Dugal also watched them go—then mounting his shaggy pony, kicked his heels against its flanks as he followed, keeping them carefully in sight.

Chapter Seventeen

They were now high on the hill. The loch glittered dull silver below them at the foot of the glen, guarded opposite on its northern bank by the stately heights of Ben Lawers. It had been a taxing climb for the horses. Iain Campbell dismounted and pointed to a strangely shaped rock known as Fingal's stone, beneath which a small wee burn gurgled its way down the steep hillside its waters edged by a few solitary wind bent rowans, alder and willow. This was favourite spot of his, a solitary place where he could think and plan.

How to accomplish his nephew's death? It needs must be done in such way that no suspicion could be thrown on him! Yes—and that death occur soon before Roderick could make true his boast that he would wed Sheena MacGregor—perhaps make her pregnant of his child! There was no way on this earth that he Iain could allow this to happen—Campbell blood adulterated by that of the despised MacGregor race.

He picked up a fallen twig, snapped it into small pieces and threw them one after the other into the burn and watched as they were born away on its miniature flood, to be seen no more. In such way must Roderick Campbell also disappear from the sight and memory of men! He came to sudden decision. Tonight! This very night the bairns must be moved from their temporary home in Mourna's cottage and placed in remoter spot.

Within his tortured mind, no recollection remained of the love he had once felt for Roderick, the orphaned boy that he and his wife had taken into their care, had watched grow into fine and independent young man who had brought credit upon himself and his family in the fighting to put down the late rebellion, winning approval of Mamore himself.

All his thoughts were anchored in the fact that Roderick had shown scant respect for the man who had carefully protected him over the years and shaped his loyalty to clan and country. His nephew should have continued to take a back seat in the running of the estate, allowing him Sir Iain Campbell to continue as laird in all but name! That way a fine relationship might have continued between them.

'He has disrespected me,' he hissed into the cold breeze sweeping down between the peaks. 'And this of offering marriage to a MacGregor is not to be born! No—Roderick must die before he brings disgrace upon the family!'

As he sat there he heard sound familiar at this time of year—the bellow of rutting stags, fighting for supremacy over their rivals for the right to impregnate the shy females just coming into season. And the sound resonated through his heart. Power of the strongest, destruction of the weaker—that was what life was all about!

'Hsst! see down there, Laird!' Archie MacNicol pointed below them, where divided by the line of a burn, two stags faced each other, one young and vigorous, shyly surrounded by his hinds, the other a mature giant, greying slightly and of great spread of antlers.

Iain drew in his breath as he watched the age old drama unfold. The younger male threw back his head, opened his mouth and bellowed contempt for the intruder, his rough, red coat stroked by the thin sunlight. His rival, mature, cunning and champion of many successful encounters over the years studied the young male carefully once more, before leaping through the burn, scrambling up the bank and lowering his head in menacing stance.

Both stags measured each other as they bellowed noisy challenge, perhaps each secretly hoping his rival would take the wiser course and depart the scene. Then as though triggered by instinct too powerful to disregard the stags ran at each other, locked antlers and struggled as each fought to overcome his rival. The sound of those clashing antlers rose up to the men lying on their stomachs and staring down at the scene.

'The young one will be the winner,' declared one of the ghillies. 'Look how he forces the intruder's head into the dust!' But then, in unexpected reversal of their roles the older stag broke free, made sideways move and deeply gored the others' flank. It was over. The younger stag limped ignominiously away as the new leader of the herd roared victory.

'An omen,' whispered Iain Campbell blithely, and Niall MacNicol looking at him caught his meaning.

'Have you any plan made yet, Laird Iain,' he inquired.

'Tonight we will move the bairns from Mourna's cottage. It is too risky to leave them there longer with so many about the estate,' said Iain decisively.

'But where will ye move them to?'

'I have been considering the matter,' was the reply, then—'I know of a deserted cottage on the opposite shore of the loch. It will serve. None so comfortable perhaps but 'twill do for the now.'

'But how to get them there from my sister's cottage without being detected?' asked Niall. 'Roderick's men are keeping watch over all our movements. I would not be surprised if one of them has not got us in his sights just now.' His swarthy face expressed his misgivings.

'We will proceed by night! Six of you will meet me by the shore. Have a boat ready and row until parallel with Mourna's place. Once arrived there, we climb up the brae to the cottage, collect the children who should then be sleeping and carry them down to the boat—and so across the loch!' His plan was made.

'But if we are seen, laird?' exclaimed Archie apprehensively. 'With the militia at Glenlarig, is it not a dangerous time to attempt this?'

'Who would expect anything of this sort at such time? No, we will turn Mamore's visit to our own advantage. I will pretend to extreme fatigue, excuse myself to the company after dinner this evening—wait until all have sought their beds and then down to the shore.' He stared at his men exultantly. 'Remember this, the child Alan Campbell is your future chief. His life must be protected by us all—kept ready for the time when my unworthy nephew is no more!'

The men looked at each other uneasily, but Iain Campbell was their leader whom they had obeyed over the last twenty years. If they had lingering doubts about the rightness of his plans, they now put them aside. After all, those two wee bairns were grandchildren of the late Colin Campbell slain by Rory MacGregor! If Colin's son Roderick was now so minded as to marry a woman of the MacGregor related to his father's killer, and as explained by Iain forgetful of all family loyalty—then surely it was only right to remove by death the young man who had so forgotten his duty and replace him with his own young nephew, to be brought up under Iain Campbell's wise guidance.

'The boat will be ready,' said Niall, his dark eyes screwed in thought. 'I'll hide it behind that screen of trees down by the shore.' And Iain nodded satisfaction. He took a brandy flask from his jacket and took a swig. His plans were gradually approaching fruition.

'We will need to take provisions for wee Alan and Ishbel,' said Archie, 'and warm plaids to wrap them in!' he added.

'All of this I will leave to the two of you! Come—let us back to Glenlarig!' Below them, as the men mounted and made their way back, taking track down the steep slope, yet another stag had come to bellow challenge. They did not see that this time the older stag succumbed.

Whilst Iain Campbell was coldly making his nefarious plans that morning, Lord Mamore decided to take advantage of the man's absence to discuss the sad state of affairs that had brought him to the central highlands at time when he had been looking forward to a well deserved rest in Edinburgh. He glanced questioningly at Roderick, who whispered to his aunt asking that Kieran and she should keep Mamore's two officers amused for a while, as he needed time apart with the major general.

She smiled instant understanding, as Roderick now arose, inviting Lord Mamore and Major Kenneth Campbell to accompany him to his library, supposedly to discuss military matters. Ewan Dhu stationed himself outside the closed door to ensure none approached to listen to the men's deliberations.

Mamore glanced thoughtfully at those many overcrowded shelves of books, and then walked over to Roderick's desk and took chair behind it, indicating the two younger men should seat themselves opposite. He leaned forward, brushing aside an open volume on Greek mythology, as he stared fixedly at the young man he styled his nephew.

'So Roderick, now that we are private, tell me exactly what has been transpiring here—put meat on the bones!' He sat back and listened gravely, putting in a question every so often, mentally cross referencing Roderick's account with that he had previously obtained from Sorley Mor. He paid particular attention to description of the pistol that had almost brought death to Roderick on the early part of his most recent trip to Edinburgh.

'I would see this pistol you say belonged to Iain Campbell. Where is it, Roderick?' He leaned forward.

'It is in my bedchamber—hidden under my mattress. I will send for it.' Roderick opened the door and whispered to Ewan Dhu who hurried to do his bidding, was back within minutes with the pistol, which Roderick then duly presented to Lord Mamore, who handled it curiously.

'A fine piece! You say Iain still has the twin to it?' he inquired softly.

'That is so. The pistol maker at Doune recognised his work and remembered for whom this particular pistol was made, that it was one of a pair made for my uncle,' replied Roderick steadily.

'So no possibility of a mistake then!' he murmured. 'Call Ewan Dhu,' he instructed and as the fierce faced ghillie who was also close friend to Roderick came to stand before him, Mamore questioned him.

'I hear Roderick owes his life to you yet again, Ewan Dhu! That he was attacked at that point on the road south, near where path leads off to Balquidder. I take it you remember the incident well?' He studied the face of the man he knew and trusted.

'Indeed and I do, sir,' replied Ewan Dhu. 'I saw a man aiming a pistol at the laird's head, yelled warning and the ball missed Roderick by merest hair's breadth! I then dealt with the fellow,' he added nonchalantly.

'Just so!' replied Mamore. 'What was his name and condition?'

'I recognised him as a cousin of Donald MacKay, one of Iain's men and his name Ronald Og! A man known in the district as ever ready to execute any devilry—should he be paid enough! May the hounds of hell now tear him apart,' he said eloquently.

'You killed him then?' said Mamore trying to restrain a smile.

'But of course, sir! What else would I do with one who sought to murder my master! Furthermore I believe that Roderick's killing was planned to take place in spot where it would be blamed on the MacGregors. I threw the body down into a gulley where it would not be seen and foxes and birds of the air cleanse the land of it.'

'Well done, Ewan Dhu! Now I remember hearing that Iain Campbell previously tried to take your own life—shot you and left you for dead on that same roadside and that you were then aided by Mistress Sheena—er Gregory?' and he gave twinkling sideways glance to Roderick.

'A fine young woman, my lord, brave and bonny!' declared Ewan warmly, rare smile about his lips.

'Indeed, so it would seem—and was witness to that attempt on your own life. Well, Ewan Dhu, matters are like to become difficult over the next day or so. You know of course that the twins are held by Iain in a certain cottage?'

'Yes. We receive word by Grigor—a young boy of the MacGregor! The laddie risks his life to keep watch over the bairnies and gets word to us here. He also reported that Dr Sorley Mor is hiding out on the brae above the cottage'

'I think I mentioned it,' put in Roderick now. 'And it certainly was Grigor who confirmed the children's whereabouts—described their appearance seen dimly through the window'

'The child should be rewarded,' approved Mamore. 'Now major, have you any comments to make on the affair?' and he turned his face towards Kenneth Campbell.

'Just that it is all quite extraordinary—and I am concerned for Kieran's safety in this. She is a wonderful young woman who has already suffered much. If anything was to happen to the twins, should they die I fear it would send her into a decline,' and he shook his head in concern.

He did not know with what affection he spoke of Kieran Stewart, but Mamore noticed it—and thought regretfully that it was shame she had not met the major before committing her life to the Stewart doctor. But there again, he had much respect for Sorley Mor. We cannot arrange events in life to our own liking. All lay in the hands of God. He was startled at his own thought, not being a religious man.

'So, now we have to be practical. First I wish to know the state of Iain's mind. Roderick—would you say that the man is definitely deranged?'

'I believe that he is. The change started slowly, almost imperceptibly. How much is due to his heavy drinking, and how much some severe affliction of the mind I am not sure. It is so hard to recognise the coarse and vicious individual he has become with the wise and courtly man who brought me up with such kindness.' He shook his head in bafflement.

'Even to the most cursory glance he is not himself,' agreed Mamore. 'So, we know he is capable of murder—that of recent time he ordered the death of Doctor Stewart, left Ewan Dhu for dead—and even planned your own murder, Roderick. Added to this we place at his account the kidnap of little Alan and Ishbel, know where he holds them quite dangerously at risk at his hands.'

'The sooner we rescue the bairns the better,' exclaimed Roderick.

'I agree,' put in Kenneth. 'But supposing we manage to get them safe from Iain's control and return them to Kieran—what is to stop the man from snatching them again? And what of the risk to Roderick's life in this—when Iain obviously wants him dead in order to replace him with little Alan Stewart? The stewardship his then until the child is grown man!'

'How many of Glenlarig's men do you suspect owe allegiance to Iain rather than to you as laird,' inquired Mamore of Roderick.

'Less than a dozen,' the young man surmised. 'Originally it was more, but now many are turning from him. His chief supporters are the MacNicol brothers, their sister Mourna one of his mistresses, she it is who cares for the twins in her cottage. Donald MacKay is another and these three men are steadfastly loyal to Iain—Tom Breac perhaps also.' He shrugged and added, 'As to the others, I can only hope their hearts may turn away from a man who behaves so irrationally.'

'Have you a plan of your own prepared,' demanded Mamore.

'Yes. To wait until all are abed tonight and ride for the cottage, take up the bairns and bring them back here. What to do from that point on is difficult to predict.' His grey eyes met Mamore's level gaze. 'How say you?'

'It is best so. Once you have them safe here, I will take it upon myself to deal with Iain. It may be necessary to imprison him for a while until he comes to his senses!' He paused and thought. 'Now I could ride with you to the cottage—take a party of my men with us. But perhaps surprise is the safest method as far as the bairns are concerned—your way the best.'

'Also sir, you will be in place here to confront Iain with his misdeeds. With the children safely restored to Kieran and Sorley Mor, there is nothing he can then say in his defence. But I am sad for my aunt Lorna in this,' and his face was deeply troubled, for he loved Lorna as a mother.

'Lorna is a strong woman. She has your love to sustain her and I believe her marriage to Iain is one in name only these days—or I miss my mark.' He paused, 'Now, what of Sorley Mor Stewart? You have told me he is concealed not far from the cottage—word must be taken to him for he will want to be involved in the rescue,' said Mamore.

'I will go to him,' said Ewan Dhu. 'Better it will be to wait until dusk. They have men watching over the cottage and all that happens around it.'

And so all was arranged—with none guessing that Iain's own plans just made would so impinge on their own!

Iain Campbell strolled casually back into the house. He glanced into the great hall saw no sign of his nephew or Kenneth, nor of Mamore either, but the major general's two officers were engaged in conversation with his wife Lorna and seemingly enjoying this welcome break from their normal taxing regime.

He threw back his silver head, placing his hands swaggeringly on his hips as the officers acknowledged his presence. Then he glanced around for Kieran. She was standing beneath the fine portrait of her late father staring up searchingly at his painted features, nor did Iain guess it was not filial devotion he observed in her, but a desperate longing for little Ishbel whose colouring resembled that of Colin Campbell.

He ignored his wife and walked over to Kieran. She turned as she heard his step, managing to control her revulsion for the man who had not stopped at attempted murder and kidnap to further his plans.

'He was a gallant man, your father,' he said now, smiling at her with evident approval. 'Should your children ever be restored to you, then needs must you fulfil your bounden duty to bring up your son and daughter as heirs to his fine heritage?' At his words her eyes filled with sudden tears.

'Do you think they still live, uncle? Do you think I will ever hold them again in my arms,' she whispered fixing him with despairing, plaintive look.

'If your mind is set in the right direction—well who knows what might happen,' he said lightly. 'Tell me, where is your brother and Lord Mamore?'

'I am not sure. Perhaps they have taken a walk,' she replied glancing around uncertainly. He frowned then approached Lorna to ask the same question. But she also was unable or unwilling to give the desired information. He walked away and as he did so, saw Mamore descending the stairs together with his nephew and the major, Ewan Dhu walking respectfully behind, and as he watched, the party seemed to be making for the door leading to the stables.

'Ah Iain—I hope you enjoyed your ride,' exclaimed Mamore regarding the older man genially, and Iain relaxed under the soldier's casual stare.

'I rode up on the hill. The stags are rutting. I witnessed a splendid encounter with a younger male bellowing his scorn of challenge by an older beast. At first the battle went to the younger stag, a fine looking animal in his prime—but the victory was with the older stag, wisdom and cunning outdoing the other's furious onslaught. You should have seen it Roderick,' said Iain provocatively with meaningfully glance at his nephew.

'I am glad you found amusement, uncle,' replied Roderick evenly. 'I also believe you had the best of the day!' He pointed drawing back from the open door where heavy rain was now beginning to fall in one of those sudden storms often encountered in the highlands. They saw a vivid lightning flash followed soon after by a deep growl of thunder when it started to rain with a vengeance, curtain of water lashing down in furious onslaught.

'I think we will put off our ride around the estate until tomorrow,' opined Mamore. 'I am not displeased at prospect of a quiet day. Shall we make ourselves comfortable within gentlemen?' He was watching Iain's face, saw his obvious satisfaction that they were not to go riding, guessed the man's concerns that they might come across the cottage, perhaps stop at its door for refreshments or to speak with its tenant as would not have been unusual in a normal ride of inspection on the estate.

The day passed on leaden wings for certain individuals concerned with adventure of the oncoming night. But meanwhile Angus Mac Seumas was called upon to entertain on his pipes and also to draw upon his powers as orator, to tell stories of ancient times, fact and legend mixed as he expounded tales of valorous exploits and hard fought victories, speaking of the origins of their clan and its history. Even Kieran listened curiously to the old man's vividly spoken narrations to which Mamore's troop also had been invited from their sojourn in the barn to enjoy such entertainment, and as Lorna was prevailed upon to play upon her harp.

And so time passed pleasantly enough for most, as outside the thunder growled menacingly, lightning zigzagged and every hillside was riven by leaping, rushing burns, seeking the face of the loch where its earlier calm, shining length of waters was now transformed into heaving wave crested fury. Candles were lit early in sconces and candelabras, the sky lowering darkly allowing but little light in the house.

Dinner was about to be served when Ewan Dhu exchanged inquiring glance with Roderick who nodded imperceptibly—time now to slip out quietly, to alert Sorley Mor Stewart of the plan to rescue two small frightened children from their captors. Ewan Dhu did not risk going to the stables, deciding to proceed on foot. He carried a sword under his plaid, was armed with pistols and a flask of whisky.

He slipped between the bushes lining the driveway and plunged his way not down to the path bordering the loch, but some five hundred yards above it, keeping all in sight in case he was followed. His brogues easily encountered the heather tussocks, juniper and gorse with stride of one who can run mile upon mile without tiring as he splashed through sudden unseen hollows of peaty water, then climbing upwards began to make for the heights above where he knew Sorley Mor was concealed—and very faintly below him he saw faint light and knew it to come from Mourna MacNicol's cottage. From a single candle it must have been he thought.

He easily found the ragged cluster of wind stunted trees bordering the burn without trouble, knowing every inch of this place since his childhood—and noting the changed sound of that same small burn, chattering furiously now as it leaped swiftly downwards between its banks swollen by many hours of heavy rain. He plunged through the burn and panted up the bank as he heard the sound of a horse neighing, when of a sudden a hand shot out of the gloom and laid hold of his plaid. 'Identify yourself,' cried a deep voice and Ewan Dhu recognised the familiar tones of Sorley Mor Stewart and smiled

'Why 'tis myself doctor—Ewan Dhu!' he replied and felt that hand relax.

'Ewan man—you are welcome! Come—there is slight shelter from the rain beneath this tree,' exclaimed the doctor. 'Lachlan Stewart and I have been impatiently waiting some word from Roderick!'

'Well met again, Ewan Dhu,' cried a youthful voice as Lachlan extended a slim hand in greeting as the three of them crouched down together under such scant shelter as was offered by the rowan from the driving rain. Ewan Dhu handed his flask to them and as each swallowed a gulp of the fiery liquid, it brought sense of warmth to their limbs.

'Now listen my friends, this is what laird Roderick has in mind,' explained the ghillie. 'Soon he will make his own way to the cottage with Ivor and a few others known to be trustworthy. He wants us to join him there—will give signal, flash a light three times!' As they crouched there together, Ewan Dhu described Iain's erratic behaviour and his fear that the man might attempt Roderick's life soon again. Frowning, Sorley Mor expressed his concern.

'I believe Roderick must show great care, for the man is deranged!'

'Perhaps it is well that Mamore is at Glenlarig at this time,' exclaimed Ewan Dhu and listened as Sorley Mor related fact that it was outcome of his own explanation of events given back in Edinburgh, that had brought the great Campbell major general here.

'He is to wait at the house, keeping watch with his men that Iain Campbell does no harm to Roderick or Lady Kieran—and being ready to take charge of the situation when we bring her rescued bairnies back to their mother.'

'So now we wait,' said Sorley Mor, shaking off the heavy drops of rain that were pouring down his forehead as he screwed up his eyes against the never ending rain, whilst Lachlan equally frustrated at the weather, wrung out his soaking wet plaid before wrapping it about himself once more.

'If only the rain would cease—the clouds clear and some moonlight appear to shed light on the cottage,' grumbled Lachlan.

'This same rain will mask our approach. Be glad of it,' reproved Ewan Dhu, and so they sat all three waiting for the anticipated signal to move. And as they waited there, it came to Sorley Mor's mind, that during the next hour or so the lives of those two precious small children were going to be greatly at risk—as indeed were their own—and Roderick's.

'Lachlan, would you care to join with me in prayer for wee Alan and Ishbel—for their safe rescue, and for the Lord's help in this enterprise.'

'It would indeed be good to pray,' agreed Lachlan quietly and Ewan Dhu bowed his own head as the doctor rested his head on his clasped hands and uttered a few fervent and moving words to the Almighty.

'Great Father of all—we pray to you in the name of your own dearly beloved Son, Jesus Christ, for your protection over the lives of wee Alan and Ishbel, that we may rescue them from the hands of evil men and that you will guide us in all our actions—our own safety in your Almighty hands Father.' His words were echoed in the hearts of his two companions as they whispered their soft amen.

'Your prayers such as David Stewart would have uttered,' said Lachlan softly and Sorley Mor's eyes were damp at this gentle reminder of his brother.

A fine dinner had been served at Glenlarig House, with salmon drizzled with lemon, roasts of venison, joints of beef, stuffed wild duck and pheasant, some few vegetables, followed by fruit dumpling and cream. But it was noticeable that neither Iain, nor Roderick ate over much of the feast. In fact, once a toast had been drunk to Lorna for arranging such delicious repast, Iain Campbell rose to his feet, putting a hand to his mouth as though to hide his yawns and with unusually courteous bow to his wife and Mamore, said he was fatigued and would have an early night.

Ivor caught Roderick's eye shortly afterwards, reporting that Iain had indeed retired to his bedroom—and that no light now showed under his door. Roderick relaxed slightly at the news, but felt suspicious nevertheless. He did not trust his uncle. But if he really was asleep, it should make the next few hours easier.

Two hours passed during which Iain Campbell waited in fever of anxiety for time to become ripe for the company below stairs to disperse to their rooms, providing the quiet he needed to slip unobtrusively from his door and make his way down to the loch shore, where his men should be waiting with the boat. That the loch might be dangerous at this time, its waters driven along its length by strong easterly gale, did not occur to him. His one thought was to remove two small children to safer hiding place.

At long last there was quiet in the house, and he knew that only some few servants would be busy in the kitchen, tidying up all after the feast. He rose from the bed, his eyes dark and feverish from the alcohol he had consumed, as he armed himself and threw a plaid about his shoulders, before quietly descending the stairs. But one saw him as he made his way to the side door. Ivor Mac Dugal had been placed on watch.

The ghillie drew in a hissing breath as he saw Iain Campbell open that door and slip out, closing it behind him. Ivor immediately reopened it, and watched as Iain ran down the full length of the driveway. Why was the man on foot? He followed him, saw Iain ignore the loch path but instead make his way down to the shore. A boat was moored there, men beside it waiting to push it away from the bank into the turbulence of the loch. One of them helped Iain to seat himself, and almost immediately oars were seized as it slid away from the bank.

Ivor took to his heels and rushed back to the house running as though his chest would burst. He found Roderick waiting for him, armed and determined, and quickly imparted this new information to his master.

'He is being borne in the direction of the cottage. I believe he goes to collect the children—remove them by boat,' panted Ivor frantically.

'Then no time to waste—we leave immediately!' He gave a quick order and three men on whom he knew he could depend stepped out of the kitchen from where they had waited. He glanced around for Kenneth Campbell, but saw no sign of his friend—could not wait. Nor knew Kenneth was at the privy relieving himself, and deeply mortified that he had been left behind.

'Let us to the horses,' said Roderick. 'No need for concealment at this stage. Iain will reach the cottage before us if we do not proceed at all speed. Are all prepared?' and he smiled grimly as the men produced their swords and dirks. He himself wore pistols at his belt and a sword he had not carried since leaving the army.

Mamore's men watched curiously from the barn, as the young laird and his men swiftly mounted and clattered into the night. They had been ordered by their officers not to interfere with anything that might transpire that night until so ordered.

The rain had eased somewhat as they rode along the loch path, waves crashing onto the shore a few yards below them, as a few wistful stars shone forth between the dark scudding clouds which were driven along in goblin shapes in the restless sky. And all around them was the sound of running water, as even the smallest burns now in furious spate leapt down from the hill. Of a sudden a small form ran out in front of them and

Roderick was hard put to rein in his horse which reared up. It was the boy Grigor.

'What is it lad? You might have been killed jumping out in such fashion,' cried Roderick in annoyance at this delay.

'Sir—I have seen something happening at Mourna MacNicol's door. She is standing there waiting, holding the twa bairns by the hands.' He looked at Roderick urgently. 'I was running to get word to you!'

'Thank you, Grigor,' approved Roderick hastily. 'We are on our way there now. Up here beside me, you may be of use in this.' Without hesitation, the child took Roderick's hand, to be scooped up behind the rider. 'When we are closer to the cottage, I want you to make your way onto the hill and alert Sorley Mor Stewart. I was going to shine a light for him—but the wind would blow out any such,' explained Roderick.

Some five minutes later, Grigor was scrambling up the hillside, making his way by instinct for all was in darkness. He had found the course of the burn and followed it up—and heard a voice call to him and ran towards the sound.

'Grigor—here!' hissed a voice. It was Ewan Dhu, beside him Sorley Mor and Lachlan, the latter two mounted and ready. The child stared at the three of them in the dim light.

'Laird Roderick sends message he is down below waiting! You needs must go quickly. He told me to say Iain Campbell may already have arrived at the cottage—the man took a boat before any knew what he was at!' He heard Sorley Mor curse—as then Grigor found himself once more on a horse. They were off. But the animals had to pick their way cautiously down the heathered hillside in the near dark.

Roderick was almost at the cottage now and gave whispered order to dismount, as his men quietly surrounded the thatched, white washed building. He glanced upwards waiting for any sign of Sorley Mor and to his relief saw movement in the dark as minutes later the doctor was at his side together with Lachlan Stewart and Ewan Dhu. The lad Grigor slipped quietly away to watch proceeding from behind a bank of gorse.

'Ready,' breathed Roderick, throwing himself against the door which was standing slightly ajar and yielded easily. As he glanced swiftly around him, he saw by the light of a guttering candle, the form of a half naked woman holding a bedcover about her. She was the sole occupant of the cottage. He grabbed her and placed a dirk at her throat.

'Where are the children,' he demanded hoarsely, disappointment at not seeing them almost too much to bear—and it was with shock Mourna MacNicol recognised Roderick Campbell.

'What children would that be, sir,' she whimpered in pretended innocence, eyes wide with fright. She felt the edge of the knife against her skin. Saw another man beside him, his face dark as thunder and she began to tremble.

'You know well what children—Alan and Ishbel Stewart! Where are they? Answer me if you value your life!' At the look in Roderick's eyes together with the furious stare of Sorley Mor and cruel glint in the eyes of the other men who now surrounded her, all courage left Mourna. She pointed to the door.

'Laird Iain has them—took them some minutes before you came! But you will never see them more,' she announced triumphantly and found herself thrown to the ground as the men rushed out into the night and mounted.

'See—there they go,' cried Ewan Dhu urgently, and there some two hundred yards below them were several fleeing shapes, making towards the shore of the loch. The men were on foot, should be easy to catch—but some instinct had made Iain Campbell turn about and he saw the men bearing down upon him! He caught at the shoulders of the MacNicol brothers, each of whom held a struggling child.

'Give the children here,' he gasped and snatched the crying youngsters from the grip of those who carried them, tucking one under each arm. 'Down into the boat with the rest of you—make as though returning to Glenlarig! Beach the boat in the cove you know of some few hundred yards short of the jetty!' He turned away.

'But Laird—what are we to say if they catch us?' they cried.

'Do not be caught! You may fire at will! I will contact you when opportunity occurs. Farewell!'

They were no longer his concern. He bent low behind a screen of gorse and scrub birch while the men obedient as always to his orders, ran their way down to the shore. By now their pursuers were almost upon them. The snorting horses would have closed the distance the sooner had it not been for the difficulty in placing reluctant hooves on the sodden, boggy area near the shore.

'Can you see which of them carries the bairns,' cried Sorley Mor urgently.

'No,' was the shouted reply from Roderick. 'It's too damnably dark! But we will be with them in another minute!' He raised his pistol and fired a shot into the air in the hope of scaring the kidnappers to a standstill before they could board the small craft that would bear the twins out of sight. One of the men turned and fired back at the pursuers and there was a cry as one of Roderick's men sustained a wound to his leg.

It was then that Iain rose from his hiding place to take aim at Roderick. He had recognised his nephew from both his voice and his carriage. He saw the young man recoil from the shot and fall from his horse—and Iain uttered cry of triumph, and again snatched up the frightened children who were now too scared even to cry and lumbered off into the darkness, making towards the distant wooded area that bordered the junction of the loch path and the river.

In the semi darkness it had been impossible to see from whence came that shot that flung Roderick Campbell to the ground. Lachlan Stewart was instantly off his own pony and knelt beside the fallen man seeking to staunch the blood he could feel spreading beneath the young man's shirt.

'You go on, Sorley!' he cried. 'I will attend Roderick!' and watched briefly as the doctor nodded and obeyed, spurring his horse forward—and Ewan Dhu uttered the most bloodcurdling cry Lachlan had ever heard as that man, accompanied by Ivor and the doctor and their two unwounded fellows, charged down upon those trying to scramble into the boat.

The two MacNicols, Donald Beag and Colum Ban discharged their weapons the shots going wild. They then fell beneath the furious onslaught that followed. But two of their fellows escaped, managed to get the boat away from the shore and turned it against the prevailing wind back towards Glenlarig. Sorley Mor watched it go in despair, thinking his children must surely be aboard the small craft.

He was about to fling himself into the water and attempt to swim after the boat, but Ewan Dhu placed a restraining hand on his shoulder.

'Wait doctor! I spoke with Niall MacNicol before he expired, abjured him in the name of Him before whom he will soon have to give account of himself, where the bairns are! They are not in that boat, sir!'

'Then where?'

'He said Iain took them when he caught sight of our approach—told the men to get into the boat without him. A diversion it must have been!' Ewan Dhu shook his head in exasperation as they stared about them in the gloom of that place. For how could they tell in what direction the deranged man who held those innocents would have taken? And the longer they delayed the further away he would get.

'Sorley Mor!' It was Lachlan's voice. Instinctively the doctor heeded that cry and went to the side of his wounded brother-in-law.

'How is it with you, Roderick,' he said gently.

'Lachlan says the bullet went through below my right shoulder—but not life threatening,' was the whispered reply. Sorley Mor stared down into the white blur of the younger man's face as he knelt beside him.

'I have staunched the bleeding,' said Lachlan. 'But where are the twins?'

'Iain Campbell did not try for the boat with the others,' replied Sorley Mor heavily. 'He took the bairns with him. He would not be able to make much speed with a double burden—but we have no idea which way he went!' His tones were despondent.

'Perhaps doctor, we should split up,' said Ivor who had just panted his way up to them, clutching his arm which had sustained a sword thrust and Lachlan immediately went to the man's side to tend him, a flesh wound only.

'I can tell you which way the Campbell laird went,' cried a high pitched young voice and Grigor bounded lightly down the slope towards them. 'I saw him! He it was who fired at Roderick Campbell! He then caught the twa wee bairnies up beneath his arms and awa wi' them. He went that way!' and he pointed in opposite direction to Glenlarig.

'Are you sure of what you say,' demanded Sorley Mor urgently, new hope rising in his breast. Grigor regarded him impatiently. He liked the Stewart doctor, was determined to help him all he could. But the doctor must listen.

'I will lead you to him,' he said. 'You will do better on foot, sir!' but his suggestion was ignored and he shrugged.

'I will come with you, doctor,' cried Ewan Dhu, but his face was turned anxiously towards Roderick all his devotion to his master in that glance. Sorley Mor saw that look.

'Not so, Ewan Dhu—your duty to return Roderick safely to Glenlarig and acquaint Lord Mamore with all that has happened.' He looked down on the wounded man with worried eyes. 'Are you able to ride?' he asked compassionately.

'If I have help in mounting,' replied Roderick, the pain about his mouth portraying his suffering as he spoke. 'But go you quickly—save your bairns.' His voice broke on a groan and instantly Ewan Dhu was down at his side, murmuring endearments and encouragement to the man he loved as brother as well as chieftain. Together with Lachlan's help, they managed to get him into the saddle. The other wounded ghillie was similarly helped to mount as within minutes, the little party turned back towards Glenlarig, leaving only the wounded Ivor Mac Dugal and Sorley Mor to urge their horses to follow the impatient young sprig of clan MacGregor as guide in the search for Iain Campbell and his small captives.

Following few hours lull in the storm that had besieged the district all day, the rain began to fall again in earnest, as great stinging drops lashed into Iain's face driven by a furious buffeting wind, as lighting split the sky in jagged flashing shards of light, and thunder once more reverberated among the hills. The sound of the wind was all about the man, as he stumbled on through wet heather clumps, ploughing between brambles and bracken, using all his strength to carry his precious burden under his arms.

They no longer cried or protested, and when he glimpsed their small faces illumined by lightning flash, he saw that they bore fixed expression of terror.

'Do not fear, wee Alan and Ishbel,' he said in panting breath. 'Soon all will be well and you will rest safely.' They made no answer, too scared to take in his words, which were in any case difficult to hear with the howling of the wind. His eyes tried to penetrate the darkness

Another lightning flash showed him the dark shape of familiar birch woods just in front of him. Once within the slight shelter he would find there, he might be able to rest awhile, whilst trying to work out where best to take the children. He knew his own strength was fading fast. He was after all a man approaching his sixties, at a time when life expectancy was often much shorter than this.

Again lightning lanced the sky this time brightly illuminating the shape of the heavily burdened man, doggedly struggling to carry those two small shapes.

'Look, sir—see there, just ahead!' cried Grigor triumphantly.

'Well done my young friend,' exclaimed Sorley Mor. He turned to Ivor. 'We must take great care now,' he said. 'Iain Campbell is not in his right mind, and should he see us too soon, then he may do harm to the bairns.'

'Ye are in the right of it, doctor,' breathed Ivor softly. 'We will go carefully, but mind once in the woods he may be difficult to find again.' The darkness seemed even more intense after the brilliance of that lightning flash, but Grigor carried on in front of them as though he saw that which was closed to their sight. Uttering prayer to God for His help in whatever lay before them Sorley Mor urged his horse carefully ahead on the flying heels of Grigor.

Panting and gasping Iain pressed forward amongst the dense clustering birches whose slender silver dappled limbs strained to the furious pull of the wind, stinging twigs of their lower branches lashing against his face. At last after proceeding some hundred yards, the man almost fell as his foot caught on looped tree root, and he dropped little Ishbel to the ground. Still holding Alan fast, he bent and groped for her in the darkness, murmuring relief as his fingers encountered the child's wet hair.

'I must rest—yet cannot afford to do so,' he muttered into the noise of the wind, as he managed to get the girl child under his free arm once more. He stared around him uneasily in that torrent of darkness—welcomed the next flash of lightning which illumined the way ahead. But he did not look behind him, did not see the three figures bearing determinedly in his direction.

Back at Glenlarig House, Kieran Stewart was wakened from her bed by noises of shouting and much agitation below stairs. She rose and by light of the guttering candle she ever kept burning at night, groped for her plaid and wrapped it about her night shift and slipped shoes upon bare feet.

She hurried to the great hall from whence the noise seemed to come, entered quietly, then held onto the door frame as she saw her beloved brother Roderick stretched upon the table, face as pale as death, his upper half bare as a youth she recognised as Lachlan Stewart, tended a wound on the wounded man's shoulder under the eagle eye of Ewan Dhu as Lorna stood holding bowl of water. Others also stood around that table, faces grim.

'Lachlan—you here? What has happened to Roderick?' she demanded in trembling voice. 'Oh, tell me he lives!' she added piteously. And Lachlan, raising his head from his work, smiled reassurance at her.

'Aye, he lives, Kieran—has lost much blood, but the wound should heal well!' he returned to his ministrations.

'Do not distress yourself, niece,' said a deep voice and Lord Mamore stepped away from the table to lead her to a seat. 'Your brother sustained his wound at the hand of Iain Campbell who seems to have suffered a brain storm. Your husband is pursuing him now together with Ivor Mac Dugal.'

She stared at him in utter bewilderment. 'Sorley Mor is here—when did he arrive—and why was I not made aware of it?

'He has been hiding out on the hill. It seemed wiser not to burden you with such worry until we had the children safe,' he began and realised his mistake, for of course the young mother knew nothing of the fact that her small twins were held in the MacNicol cottage.

'My children—my little Alan and Ishbel—you know where they are?' she placed frantic fingers on his sleeve, as her deep grey eyes frantically devoured his face for answers. 'I beg you to explain!' He swallowed awkwardly.

'Say rather we knew where they were. Roderick and your husband were to release them tonight from the cottage where they have been close guarded by Iain's men. Ewan Dhu will tell you more exactly of recent events!' And Ewan Dhu was at her side, his devotion to Roderick's sister as deep as his love for his master.

He spoke softly to the girl lapsing into his native Gaelic which fell gently on her ears as her brain seized on the most important fact in all this. The children were still alive—but in imminent danger from Iain Campbell and that her husband was in pursuit of the man, and instinctively she relaxed somewhat in that knowledge. If any could save their children it was Sorley Mor.

'How did my brother come to be shot, Ewan Dhu?' she asked suddenly.

'It was by Iain's hand,' he replied and Lorna who had stepped across to Kieran now Lachlan was fixing the last dressing, her own duty over, overheard that statement and caught onto the back of Kieran's chair, almost fainting from shock at the knowledge.

'Are you alright, Lady Lorna,' asked Mamore, guiding her to an adjacent seat. 'I can only guess how distressing all of this is to you. But your husband is obviously assailed by a sickness of the mind—perhaps not to judged too severely,' he added. But the grim expression in his eyes proclaimed his own true feelings in the matter however compassionately he spoke to Iain's wife.

Now Kieran seemed to throw off her earlier almost despairing attitude, and of a sudden rose from her chair and looked firmly at Ewan Dhu.

'Ewan—do you remember the direction in which Iain was going? Could you guide me there?' As she stood facing him, her tumbled red gold hair about her shoulders, imperative grey eyes so like Roderick's own steely grey, he stared at her perplexed. He caught at his beard.

'Lady—he was making in direction of the small birch wood where it meets up with the road south—and the river! But he may have diverted elsewhere in the meanwhile!' He watched her under his shaggy brows, 'In this night of storm difficult indeed to track down.'

'But you are prepared to try? Who if any, has Sorley Mor got with him?'

'Why, just Ivor Mac Dugal—and a wee laddie who leads the way, by name Grigor! He it was who brought news of the bairnies whereabouts. He is trustworthy and true.' He looked at her expectantly.

'Then let us go. Come Ewan Dhu!' she cried urgently. But Mamore immediately remonstrated. He looked at the girl commandingly one hand on his hip, face stern.

'Not so, Kieran! You would never find them in such night of dark and storm, might yourself come to ill. You should bide here with Lorna until we have news and happily your bairns safely back in your arms.' He laid a restraining hand on her arm—then shook his head as she broke away from him and ran out of the room behind Ewan Dhu.

'You should put more clothes on—you cannot go out like that,' cried Lorna, but the girl disappeared and they heard the sound of doors banging. Lorna Campbell looked at Mamore imploringly. 'Surely you could send some of your men to attend her?' she cried fiercely.

'I dispatched ten of them off immediately when Roderick was brought back here! Major Kenneth Campbell elected to lead them—he had planned to accompany Roderick, who left in haste without him. But in this storm it is doubtful whether they will manage to find either the good doctor or your husband, Lorna!' He drew her gently to the window. 'See for yourself! It is as black as pitch out there and blowing a severe gale.' But even as he spoke lightning again flashed across the sky and showed the girl astride her favourite mare, bare legged, hair streaming in the wind and already disappearing down the driveway in the wake of Ewan Dhu,

'I could not bear it if anything were to happen to her,' whispered Lorna, as thunder clapped its fury almost overhead.

'Short of laying hands on her person, it would have been impossible to stop her! She is her father's daughter,' he replied with grudging approval. 'Ewan Dhu will keep her safe, never fear!' He turned back to the table, where Lachlan was assisting Roderick to painfully sit up as two of his retainers sprang forward to help.

'Carry him through to my room—lay him on the couch there,' instructed Lorna, her thoughts returning to her beloved nephew as she hurried to his side. 'Take heart, my darling boy.' She took his hand and he forced a faint smile. And as she gazed at him it was hard for Lorna Campbell to deal with the fact that it was her own husband Iain who had so nearly taken Roderick's life. She made mental prayer for the safety of the two helpless little children whom the mentally tormented man now had in his power.

Chapter Eighteen

The party of rain drenched militia had heard faint shouts from the shore of the loch as they rode, and dismounting drew their horses down the bank to see what was occurring there. They came upon a boat with two of Iain's men attempting to tie it up to a large rock, as the wind driven waters obstinately fought to jerk the rope free. One of the men was wounded for he limped.

'Stand and account for yourselves!' cried Major Kenneth Campbell authoritatively, as the men turned to flee into the darkness. Nothing loth at the prospect of action, his men laid hands on the two, who now stood surly and uncertain in their captor's grip!

'You are Iain Campbell's men?' continued the officer.

'Aye—and if we are?' replied one with an oath.

'Where is your master?'

'Ask that of the night owl,' was the contemptuous reply. At this one of the militia struck the man across the face. The fellow spat back at him.

'Listen to me,' said the major harshly. 'The lives of two small children are at stake here. If you refuse to cooperate with us, then you will be responsible for any ill that attends them. Do you want their deaths set to your account?' The men looked at each other and shrugged insolently at the major.

'Bind them,' ordered Kenneth brusquely, for there was no time to spare if they were to find Iain Campbell. He gave brief command to a couple of his men to escort their captives back to Glenlarig that Mamore should deal with them.

'It will be the rope for the two of you,' added the sergeant watching them disappear into the turbulent black void of the night. He glanced at Major Kenneth Campbell for approval and merely received order for all to remount and continue to follow the loch path, the officer taking up place of leadership once more. Shortly afterwards his horse neighed and almost stumbled.

'What the devil! Hold that lantern still a bit.' He dismounted and examined the corpse that lay in his path. As best he could see by the flicking light, the man had died of a sword thrust to his breast. 'Look around. See if there are more of them,' cried the major urgently. He had recognised the dead face as belonging to one of Iain Campbell's retainers he had noticed about that man.

'Here, sir! This one is dead too!' came a cried one of the soldiers.

'And here another—this one stirs, so thankfully alive!' announced the sergeant. 'Bring that light nearer.' He pulled the man up into a sitting position. 'What is your name,' he asked sternly.

'I am called Donald Beag MacKay,' the man replied faintly.

'Where is your master? Where is Iain Campbell?' He jerked the man by his shoulders causing scream of pain.

'I do not know where he is, sir! We were told to take the boat and row back home—whilst he then went away off with the bairns.' All the man wanted was to be left in peace and for the pain to cease, would have told the redcoats anything to achieve it.

'In which direction did your master go?' inquired Major Kenneth Campbell now fixing the man with imperative stare.

'I did not see! Men were attacking us with sword and dirk—and we were firing back at them. One of them fell. So did three other of our party, Colum lying there and the MacNicol brothers! Laird Iain called that he was taking the bairns. But where he went after this I do not know.' There was the note of truth in the man's voice and the major considered it of little use to question him further. They bound the man's hands, slung him on the back of one of the horses, its rider instructed to deliver him to Mamore to join their two earlier captives.

'It was at this moment in lull of the wind, they heard the sound of horse hooves splashing approach along the track and spread themselves out across the path to stop whoever ventured there.

'Lady Kieran Stewart—can that be you?' exclaimed Kenneth Campbell, as their lantern's struggling light described the bare limbs of the girl who rode astride, the rain making her thin shift cling to her form revealing its shapeliness. Beside her he made out Ewan Dhu, recognising him at once as one of Laird Roderick's favoured retainers. But what did these two do here at this time of peril?

'Kenneth, have you seen any sight of Iain Campbell yet,' Kieran demanded in panting breath. 'We came upon two of his men you're sending back under guard—I see you have another here also—oh!' She had just seen the corpses. Ewan Dhu leaned over and stared down.

'Tis Niall and Archie MacNicol,' he said. 'Praise be that they are no more! And who is it ye have there—Colum Ban maybe?' and he peered closer, 'Aye it is!'

'But none of it of our doing, unfortunately,' replied the major and turned reprovingly to Ewan. 'But why have you brought Lady Kieran into this mess, putting her own life in danger? Have you no sense man!' he said frowningly.

'I would have gone on my own had Ewan not agreed to accompany me! So have you no idea where Iain is—or my husband?' She raised impatient hand to drag her windswept wet tresses back from her face, watching his face anxiously. 'Yes, I've heard Sorley Mor and Ivor Mac Dugal are searching for the children. You of course know that Iain Campbell has the twins—and is like to harm them if he feels himself trapped? Ewan Dhu is to take me onto the hill to a place where he thinks we may find Iain.'

'Ah—then we will come with you,' cried the major immediately. But the girl shook her head. The sight of these armed men might make Iain even more desperate than he probably was right now.

'I suggest you continue along the loch path with your men, Kenneth,' she said firmly. 'It will bring you out upon the south road, banking as you will remember onto the Dochart! Ewan and I will take path over the hill and through the wood which will bring us out to much the same destination. This way we watch for him both ways.'

'Then at least allow me to send some of my men with you to your protection!' But she shook her head in impatient refusal.

'We will attract less attention just the two of us! Besides which Iain may very well be just ahead of you along the loch path—you may come across him before we do!' He knew her words made sense, but feared for her safety. But there was no time to waste on discussion, He nodded grudging agreement but was uncomfortable in letting her go with only a ghillie for guard but knew enough of her character not to spend time in argument.

Without waiting for more she nodded to Ewan Dhu who turned his garron off the path and up the brae. Kieran whipped her mare lightly, encouraging it to follow up amongst the soaking heather and bushes on that wild hillside. Then as though the heavens were aware of the need for such benison, the rain suddenly ceased and minutes later the clouds parted to allow of a faint beam of wistful moonlight to filter down.

'Look—juist ahead of us, lassie! There lies the birchwood where there's chance Iain may lie concealed!' cried Ewan Dhu. 'Possibly we may also come upon your husband thereabouts!' At thought of this last, Kieran's spirits lightened. If only she could feel Sorley Mor's arms about her for but an instant, it would lessen her silent terror for the safety of her children. She could only imagine their fear at being dragged through the night by their demented uncle—doubtless having also seen the horror of the fighting down by the loch side, heard the shots, the cries!

'Oh Alan—Ishbel! Hold fast my darlings, we come for you,' she whispered into the wind, nor knew that some two hundred yards ahead Sorley Mor and Ivor rode keeping Iain in sight, as that man panting and stumbling, struggled with failing strength, to carry his precious burden blindly onwards, the children feeling dead weight, and not even knowing for certain where he would look for shelter or succour.

'We should perhaps dismount here, sir,' said Ivor. 'Perhaps Grigor could hold the horses for us—we will follow more easily on foot.'

'Yes—not so likely to be observed.' Dismounting both gave their reins to the lad, who was disappointed not to be included in the confrontation so soon to come and watched regretfully as thin shaft of shifting moonlight illuminated their disappearing figures under the wind tossed birches.

And so it was that Kieran and Ivor came upon the boy who was patiently restraining two restless horses.

'Why, 'tis young Grigor,' announced Ewan Dhu and Kieran stared curiously at the lad of whom she had heard much but not seen until now. He looked very young, perhaps some nine or ten years she thought vaguely and gave him a greeting smile.

'You are Grigor—a friend of Mistress Sheena MacGregor,' she said. The boy beamed a smile back at this young woman who spoke Sheena's name with respect, nor named her Gregory.

'Yes, lady—and you will be Mistress Kieran Stewart I doubt not,' he replied with youthful dignity. 'Your husband is but a hundred yards ahead of you, following close upon Iain Campbell's heels. But you should show care that Iain does not see you! The man is possessed of an evil spirit I would say!' and the lad made sign of the cross.

'You may well be right,' she whispered fearfully. 'Did you see if he has my children, Grigor?' she tried hard to focus on the boy's face by the thin pencils of moonlight filtering down between the swaying trees. He nodded.

'Aye, lady, Iain Campbell has the bairns—one of them beneath each arm! But he is tiring and Sorley Mor and Ivor close behind him. They are on foot as he is. Horses would attract his attention crashing through the trees. Better so you dismount—and do not go too near!' he admonished.

'Will you care for our beasts too, Grigor,' asked Ewan Dhu as he helped Kieran to dismount, thinking she looked like pale wraith as she sped off before him, feet sinking into the sodden mud of the forest floor, stumbling and catching at barks of the slender birches to steady herself. Ewan caught up with her and put out a steadying hand.

'Careful, lady—time now to proceed with caution,' he said softly, his voice barely discernible in the sound of the wind. She quietened under his touch paused, looking wildly around her in near desperation.

'Are we going in the right direction?' she asked with trembling lips. 'It feels as though the whole wood is in motion, branches like the sails of a great ship swaying to every gust of the wind!' But Ewan Dhu squeezed her arm encouragingly. She had to keep that bright spirit of hers going now as never before.

'Have faith in Him, daughter,' he said. 'Pray that God will have the bairnies in His tender loving care—that you will soon hold them safe again.' And his words strengthened her, as they fought their way onwards between the wind whipped trees.

Iain Campbell was glad of that moonlight filtering between the dancing branches of the birches, their once golden tresses stripped bare of leaf by the violence of the wind. He now had vague plan in his mind. There was a small inn not far from the falls where he would seek shelter for the night. He ever wore a money belt of gold, and a coin or two should secure the silence of the innkeeper about his belated guest and persuade him to deny any knowledge of seeing two small bairns if asked.

He never thought to look behind him, for how would any have been able to follow him through that storm which was perhaps the worst in living memory. Certainly he could never recall one that had lifted the waters of the loch into such fury—impossible it would have been to row the children across in such turbulence of wind and wave. Even crossing the hill had been feat taxing him to the limits of his strength and this last part of his flight through these trees that lashed and clutched at him like intrusive angry ghosts, their breath soughing and whining about him was terrifying experience enough.

And now another sound came to his ears—a roaring that was the more deafening as he drew nearer and knew it for the Dochart in spate! A sudden superstitious thought entered his mind, the screaming sound of the wind pouring through the trees blending with malevolent roar of the falls like voice of the legendary giant Fingal, striding ever nearer to take hold of him and dash out his brains. He gave moan of terror now, as all the goblins and monsters of early childhood nightmare seemed to assail him together.

He must go on—must go on! It was not much further, he assured himself. The din of the waters was growing ever louder as encouraging thought struck him—knowledge that his nephew was dead! Throwing his head back into the wind, a string of oaths left his lips as he uttered fiendishly triumphant chuckle, rejoicing that the first part of his plan had succeeded—Roderick Campbell now no more!

The man gloated thinking of how his nephew fell of his unerring pistol shot, never now to bring disgrace of MacGregor bride across Glenlarig's threshold. He felt strengthened by the knowledge, reflecting that under his tutelage little Alan Stewart Campbell would become laird who would bring honour to his house. He must keep the boy safe—and the delightful wee Ishbel who so favoured the late Sir Colin Campbell in her colouring. His tired arms sought to press the children closer to him.

Ewan Dhu's eyes were adjusting to the faint glimmering of ever shifting moonlight as he glimpsed movement of dark shapes ahead. He laid restraining hand on Kieran's arm.

'Be still, lassie. Bide here whilst I take look yonder—something moves!' She hesitated wishing to keep him at her side, but obeyed his hissed command. He stole carefully forward from tree to tree, until he realised a more open area of bush and heather lay immediately ahead. The roar of the river was now almost deafening in its power. He recognised the spot and that it was but yards from the road that bordered the Dochart. The man he followed was just before him now. He strained to focus his eyes upon him—then relaxed.

'Why, it is not Iain, but the doctor!' he muttered between compressed lips. There was that about the walk and stature of the man who strode before him that had pricked memory. He drew nearer and found himself suddenly set upon by one he had not noticed, but had been watching his own careful approach and now leapt out on him!

'Ewan Dhu—is that you?' came soft joyful cry of recognition as Ivor released him with smile of relief. Sorley Mor swung about to see what delayed the ghillie, his eyes straining through the darkness. 'It is Ewan Dhu who comes, sir!' explained Ivor gladly. Sorley Mor relaxed the hand that had gone to his dirk. He beckoned Ewan to his side.

'What are you doing here, man—I thought you would have stayed with Roderick? How fares he—his wound?' he asked, but his attention focussed ahead of him as his eyes strained to pierce the dark for a cloud was passing over the moon.

'Lachlan has tended him, says all should heal well, but painful just,' replied Ewan Dhu, his own eyes fixed on movement he observed some twenty feet before them. Sorley Mor forced impatient reply.

'You are welcome, but no time now to talk. See, down there!' and he pointed, 'Iain Campbell—with the children! I fear for their safety, extreme care is needed. When we close the gap he'll see us—and the river is so close, the man out of his mind!'

Ewan Dhu had almost forgotten Kieran who now stole silently forward, wondering frantically why the man had not returned to her side. Then she too saw her husband, knew him from the set of his head and profile as he turned. But he had not noticed her where she stood hidden by bole of an ancient oak, his attention firmly fixed on situation on the road immediately below them. And seeing him staring so rigidly ahead, intuition told her that it was Iain Campbell he saw. She uttered a desperate prayer for help, crying out to the God she had long neglected to think of, reaching cupped hands up to the restless heavens.

'Father—I pray you save my little ones and keep my husband safe. In Jesus sweet name,' she cried and moving forward looked frantically ahead, her eyes fiercely seeking the man who had stolen her babes.

Once free of the trees and bushes that had impeded his progress, Iain set his feet thankfully upon the road. The noise of the river was almost deafening now, its waters dimly seen, but rushing it seemed into eternity and producing great surging roar as it hurled itself over massive rocks encountered in its bed, dramatically leaping onwards, the force of the current sweeping all before it, swirling with tremendous speed into the falls.

Iain paused, turned and faced the river and still clutching his precious burdens stepped curiously onto a rocky shelf immediately above it and stared in fascination as the moon briefly escaping its cloud cover pooled silver sheen on the darkness of the waters mighty flow. On any other occasion he would have delighted in the wildness of the scene, the sheer drama before his eyes. But he had other things on his mind, for sudden thought of Mamore smote him, and he frowned. Damn Mamore for coming when he did!

What reaction could he expect of the great Campbell chief when presented with the corpse of the young man for whom he had shown such undeserved regard as both soldier and relative? This uneasy thought provoked new rising anger in him as he stepped down from the rocks onto safety of the road. He drew a deep breath. No time now to worry on such problems he told himself, as his arms sent pain messages to his brain resulting from the unaccustomed strain of carrying the children this long time.

As he prepared to follow the road parallel with the river, he gave cry of sudden shock as a form leapt down before him from the opposite bank. He uttered an expletive as he found himself staring into the ice cold stare of Sorley Mor Stewart. The man held a pistol levelled at his head. Behind him he saw two others also armed, knew he had little chance against them.

'Put the bairns down—or I fire!' cried Sorley Mor incisively and there was no doubt in Iain Campbell's mind that their father meant his words. But he laughed aloud in scorn and with almost superhuman strength, seized an arm of each child, lifting them suspended high above his head, as he made reckless way back towards that rocky shelf over the river. Sorley Mor watched in horror as Iain clambered boldly onto slippery surface of that small rocky promontory, to swing around and face him.

'Fire away then, doctor!' he cried mockingly, his words just discernible above the noise of the flood. Both he and Sorley Mor knew that to fire would be to send little Alan and Ishbel, as well as Iain himself, to their deaths. Each watched the other. There was stalemate. But Iain's arms flamed with pain at his load thus uplifted. He realised that sooner or later he would have to drop the bairns. But still his demented mind gave him extraordinary staying power.

'You do not shoot, doctor,' he challenged. Then his jaw dropped and his eyes widened in shock, and a look of terror spread across his face. He abruptly lowered the two inert small forms to lie at his feet, heads almost hanging over the greedy river as he pointed terrified finger at one who walked slowly towards him, arms stretched open wide before her. Kieran did indeed appear wraith like, her white shift floating about her in the wind, eyes set in unwinking stare she approached the man in relentless advance.

'A ghost,' he cried as he put hand to his mouth to repress a scream. Then as the moon shone brighter, he stared harder and thought he knew her.

'Will that be you, niece Kieran—or is it your death shadow?' he cried, fear still upon him. 'But be you flesh and blood or bogle, you shall not have your hands on these!' he called malevolently, and stooped to retrieve the children. But in so doing, he was caught by violent gust of wind that spun him about, causing him to lose precarious balance. With shout of helpless fear he fell backwards into the relentless maw of the river.

Instantly Sorley Mor and Kieran exchanged one agonised glance, and ran forward to retrieve the two small forms where they lay bare inches above the waters flow looking like sad bundles of wet rags, even as Ewan Dhu and Ivor now raced to stare down into the flood looking for any trace of Iain Campbell. Saw there was none. And as they turned to be of help to the distraught parents a shout was heard, and Kenneth Campbell together with his small troop galloped towards them.

The major had just been in time to see Iain fall into the swollen river and alerted a couple of his men to seek along its bank for any sign of the man. But the doctor and his wife barely looked up at sound of his arrival as they knelt there side by side—all their attention on the two seemingly lifeless children.

'Are they dead, husband,' whispered Kieran frantically, as she held her daughter's small form against her breast, kissing the pale shape of the little face in that uncertain light, noting in desperation the closed eyelids. 'I am not sure if she breathes! Help me!'

'Alan lives. Oh, thank God—but is not conscious, needs warmth if he is to survive!' he wrapped his wet plaid about the boy and handed him into Ewan Dhu's strong grasp as he took Ishbel gently from her mother's arms, set his ear to the child's chest and smiled relief. 'Ishbel is not dead either, my dearest, but unconscious like her brother. We must get them to Glenlarig as soon as possible.' Ivor tore off his own wet plaid and proffered it.

'Use this for the wee lassie,' he said.'

'What can I do to be of service?' asked a quiet voice and Kenneth Campbell came to stand next to the little party. Kieran glanced up at him and made quick introduction to her husband.

'Sorley Mor—this is Major Kenneth Campbell, a good friend and cousin,' she said, her eyes still on those two still small forms. The doctor looked across at the major and gave considering, slightly weary smile.

'Ewan Dhu mentioned you, sir,' he said. 'I am glad to make your acquaintance. But it is of importance these children should be brought into the warm soon, or I fear they may die. I left my horse and that of Ivor with young Grigor back in the wood....'

'Mine also,' cried Kieran, 'We must get word to him.'

'No need. For it would seem that he has come to you,' replied Kenneth glancing up as he heard the sound of horses other than his own, snorting nearby and there on the brae at the edge of the wood they discerned the slim outline of the child.

Ewan Dhu gave cry of welcome and beckoned to the lad and scrambled up to help him in care of the four restive animals that were obviously fearful at the sound of the river, and soon had them down on the road.

Minutes later Sorley Mor and Kieran were each mounted, the doctor clasping Alan protectively to his breast, as Ewan took the small girl child into his own careful charge and Ivor set young Grigor before him on his rough pony. Then with Kenneth Campbell leading the party, the militia in the rear, they set forth along the loch path taking their way back to Glenlarig. They had not gone far, the wind now in their faces and making the going slow, when they heard faint cry behind them, turned to see the two soldiers set to search the bank for Iain Campbell, riding towards them and waving, saw something slung awkwardly to bounce behind one of them.

'We found the man Iain Campbell, major,' they cried as they caught up with the party. 'Caught between two rocks, near the bank he was—far downstream!'

'Quite dead, sir,' called his companion.

'Even the river did not want him.' pronounced Ewan Dhu. 'It cast him up from its waters for the evil being he had become!'

Kieran lifted her head as she heard his words, her heart experiencing glad relief, rejoicing that her uncle was dead, could cause no further harm to his family. But at least Lorna would be able to give him Christian burial she thought, as she tried in difficulty of the dim light to make out her small daughter's features, where she was clasped close to Ewan Dhu's chest, as her gaze then swung to her equally precious son safe in his father's care.

She was beginning to tire now, the shock of all that had happened catching up with her. Kieran was also very cold, her thin, soaking wet nightshift no barrier to the cold easterly wind that continued to buffet them tearing fiercely towards them between the dark soaring shapes of the mountains, funnelling its fury along the loch. But at least the rain had stopped, the clouds starting to disperse, allowing of the moon's pale, ghostly brilliance to light their way. Kenneth, who had dropped back and had been watching her, pulled off his own jacket, and drawing his horse alongside and handed it to the girl. She smiled back at him and letting go the reins for a moment, pulled it about her. Her husband saw the incident and chided himself for not having given thought to her comfort himself. But for both parents the children had been chief concern.

He fixed the young major with a curious stare as they rode. From what he could make of his features, the man was handsome and of a good carriage. For the first time he wondered how his wife had fared at Glenlarig since she had taken leave of their home with only a note left in explanation. But such matters could wait until later. The children's wellbeing of immediate importance and he could only applaud the courage she had shown in helping to discover their whereabouts.

At last they passed between Glenlarig's tall gates and proceeded the last short distance up the driveway to the house, where every window seemed lit by blaze of candles. The door burst open and several figures ran down the steps to greet them. It was Lord Mamore who lifted an exhausted Kieran from her mare, handing her to Lorna who folded the girl in her arms. The older woman's eyes then swept over the other riders and gave great cry of relief as she saw that Sorley Mor and Ewan Dhu each carried a small child.

'They are safe,' she cried, tears of relief springing to her eyes. Then as she glanced around those others now dismounting and who looked at her awkwardly, she took a deep breath—for she guessed. 'My husband,' she asked calmly now. 'Where is Iain Campbell?'

'Sadly he is dead, Lady Lorna,' said a quiet voice and Kenneth Campbell approached her. He bowed before her, his face full of sympathy and she loosed Kieran in the shock of his words. 'We have brought him home to you,' he added.

'He did not die at anyone's hands, God be thankit, but fell into the Dochart,' explained Ewan Dhu. 'Laird Iain was not himself, lady. At least the bairns are safe—but needing care!' Then he offered Ishbel into her mother's eager arms, as Sorley Mor dismounted carefully bearing the inert form of little Alan Stewart and minutes later the welcome warmth of the house enveloped them all.

Bess who had been standing watching all with delight, smiled at Ewan Dhu, then hurried to the doctor's side as both he and the children's mother leaned over the twins where they had been placed on a settle near the fire, the couple now drawing off the torn, soaking wet muddied garments, sponging away the dirt and chafing their small limbs and towelling their hair dry, before wrapping them in the comfort of shawls provided by Lorna.

Alan was the first to open his eyes and stare about him with strange, fearful blue gaze. He started to tremble as Kieran gave choking cry and held him to her, stroking his hair back from his forehead.

'Alan frighted,' he whispered. 'Bad man hurt me!'

'Oh Alan, my darling one, no one shall ever frighten you again,' said Kieran soothingly, as she cradled him. How thin he felt. Terror had stamped its ugly imprint on the little face, which only time and gentleness would cure.

'I'm sorry. Not let them take me away more,' he whispered, fixing his frightened blue eyes apprehensively on her face. Did he blame her for what had happened to him? She felt a fierce anger towards Iain Campbell who could so have used two small children for his own warped purposes. At least he was dead, could do no further hurt.

She felt a gentle hand on her arm and lifting her face saw it as Sorley Mor who smiled down at her. He bent and kissed her, but she barely responded.

'Ishbel has also recovered,' he said. 'Look, mo chridhe! See she has opened her eyes—needs you.' And with a cry Kieran turned to her other child, the little girl also not seen for so many weary months. Ishbel looked up at her mother with scared, puzzled glance—then raising her head looked nervously around

'I'll be good,' she whispered softly. 'Please—not hurt me.' And tears appeared in her green eyes, spilling down her pale cheeks. There were tears furrowing down Sorley Mor's face at this as Kieran started to weep out loud. And now he took his wife into his arms, kissing her tears as they blended with his own and in that moment their love for each other reawakened as never before and Kieran relaxed, her head against his breast.

'I have made their cots ready,' said a quiet voice and there stood Bess smiling at them both. 'What the bairns need now is sleep I think!'

'Look at the two of you, absolutely soaking! Time now to change out of your wet clothes—but here, drink this first,' said Lorna. She gave them glasses of whisky beaten with cream and spices and the drink sent invigorating warmth through their bodies. Then she looked at them firmly. 'Bed is the best place for you now also. Account of what happened can wait until the morning. Bess will watch over the little ones—and I must return to Roderick!'

'Roderick—how is it with him?' demanded the doctor in dismay, 'I will go to him!' But Lorna shook her head at him.

'Lachlan has done all that is needful. My nephew is sleeping and I will sit with him for the next few hours. Now goodnight—go!' She spoke with authority and the couple trembling with weariness needed no further bidding, leaving Kenneth Campbell to give report to Lord Mamore and Ewan Dhu and Ivor to seek their own beds.

Kieran slept in Sorley Mor's arms that night, her red gold hair spread across the pillow. Both had been too exhausted for lovemaking, but their joy and relief at recovering the twins almost unimaginable. Sometimes a repressed sob shook Kieran's body, as her nervous system started slowly to relax from all she had endured. At last she slept quietly at peace.

Two older women of the household were instructed to prepare Iain Campbell's body in way needful for burial. Message was brought to Lorna when all was done. She knew she should go and look her last on the man she had been married to for so many long years and rose reluctantly from Roderick's bedside where he lay in restless sleep.

'I cannot face the sight of him.' She whispered to herself, then just before daybreak, duty stronger than emotion took her to that small room where Iain lay. They had washed him, combed the tangled silver white hair, and dressed him in full highland regalia where he lay on a table, hands clasped before him as though in prayer. All the anger and pride had drained from his features with loss of the life force. The face bruised and cut from the violence of the river, stern in its last repose bore unlooked for expression of peace.

Lorna took a deep breath. She stooped over him and placed a kiss on that ice cold pale forehead.

'Farewell, Iain Campbell, whom once I loved. I will try to hold only memory of our earlier life together. May you rest in peace!' she murmured. Then hardly glancing at the two women who had drawn discreetly aside, she walked quietly away. They curtsied, their faces full of sympathy.

So Lorna went, glancing down at the crumpled green gown she wore and had not changed since yesterday, for she had she slept all that long night in keeping watch over Roderick. She must change—go into the formal black of mourning, was now a widow. The knowledge felt strange to her. Yet in it was release and comfort that no longer would she have to endure Iain's drunken sneers and rages. There was the funeral to be attended to. Normally she would have called upon her nephew as her nearest male relative to put all in motion—this out of the question for he lay abed of his wound. But first she wanted to speak with Kieran and Sorley Mor—questions she must ask.

As she climbed the stairs on slow feet, holding a candle for the staircase was always dark even by daylight, she saw Bess on the landing looking down at her anxiously, and her thoughts flew to the twins.

'Beth—how fare the children?' she cried in sudden new worry.

'Oh Lady Lorna, they are well indeed, in body at least,' exclaimed the young maid soothingly 'But I fear their little minds remain disturbed from all they have been through—for they slept fretfully!' She put an arm about Lorna as the older woman wearily took the last stair. 'It is you I am concerned for, mistress. I know the strain you have been under,' said the young girl with innocent perception.

'I am well enough, Bess. Is my niece abroad yet—and her husband?'

'Both are with the bairns now. Were up before dawn,' replied Bess. 'Lady Kieran asked me to see how it is with her brother? I was on the point of going below to inquire.'

'Roderick sleeps! Lachlan is keeping watch over him as is Ewan Dhu,' said Lorna, then both women looked up as they heard voices and saw Lord Mamore approaching along the corridor together with Major Kenneth Campbell. Greetings were exchanged as Mamore expressed sympathy over Iain's death, but all there knew it to be mere formality—for death had brought closure to a situation that would have brought discredit on Glenlarig and Clan Campbell should the facts have been bruited abroad.

On hearing sound of those voices, Kieran rose uncertainly from her chair set between cots of her two small sleeping children in the nursery that adjoined her bedroom. On hearing her movement Sorley Mor turned from the window where he had been observing sunrise in the sullen sky, and came to her side.

'Such state of devastation to be seen all around from the storm,' he exclaimed. 'Several great trees uprooted and branches littering the driveway and water from the hill is running down it like a river! It must have continued to blow long after we fell asleep, my darling.' He bent and kissed her as he looked down tenderly at the twins who were sucking their thumbs in sleep. 'They look peaceful enough now!' he said softly.

'It was absolute miracle that we were able to save them,' she replied in a low voice. 'I should have been told that they were being kept in that cottage! Had I but known, I would have gone to them instantly—demanded them of Iain!' and her grey eyes flashed as she spoke. But he shook his head.

'And do you think he would have heeded you, Kieran my love? No, the man was of disturbed mind. If he had known you were aware of where he kept them, he might well have injured you—and them! I believe Roderick was right to keep it from you.' He drew her into his arms, but she resisted slightly and posed a question.

'And why was I not informed that you were on the hill?'

'For similar reason Roderick thought it better so. What good to have burdened your heart to no purpose! Good it was that you were able to behave absolutely naturally before Iain Campbell while plans were secretly ongoing for rescue of wee Alan and Ishbel!' She stared back at him soberly, knew he was right but hated to admit it.

'Well—it was sight of me at the last that caused Iain Campbell to fall to his death in the Dochart!' she exclaimed. That could not be denied she thought.

'I believe he thought you a ghost in your white shift!' and he repressed a smile. 'I almost took you for one myself, suddenly appearing on the scene from nowhere! You took unbelievable chance you know!' At this she gave answering smile

'But in holding the man in fear of your pistol when you did, this prevented his escape with the bairns! Yes and I realise Ewan Dhu and Ivor were involved, and owe much to them—and I remember a laddie— Grigor?' Having established her own position in the rescue she was prepared to be generous to all others.

'We all owe much to that boy, my dearest. I am told it was Grigor who at risk to his young life crept up to that guarded cottage and peered through its window and saw the children. He is a brave boy—seemingly is an orphan who lives with Sheena MacGregor and her family.' He raised one of her hands to his lips.

There was a knock at the door and Bess appeared. She was accompanied by a woman whom Kieran knew well. It was Morag Burns who had been wet nurse to the children when their mother's milk was less than enough. The woman uttered a cry of delight, as she ran to the cots and fell on her knees beside them, murmuring quiet endearments in the Gaelic tongue.

'Morag will watch over the bairns while you and the doctor take breakfast, Lady Kieran!' exclaimed Bess as she curtsied to Sorley Mor.

'That is well thought of,' replied Kieran and gave Morag welcoming smile. 'I hear voices outside Bess?' she added inquiringly.

'Why it is Lady Lorna asking after you and the doctor. Lord Mamore is with her—and the Major.' She gave a tired smile to Kieran, who now realised with dismay that the girl had been up all night looking after the twins.

'Thank you Bess my dear. Now, off to your own bed,' she said firmly and with final glance at Morag, allowed Sorley Mor to escort her reluctantly out of the nursery and downstairs to the great hall. It was a solemn party who breakfasted that morning after events that would take much time to recover from by all involved. The servants went about their duties on quiet feet. Much as Iain's recent behaviour had been abhorred by some and approved only by his own faithful retainers, there was a feeling of shock and bewilderment at his death.

Chapter Nineteen

It was later that morning when Lady Lorna now wearing a full skirted black gown, her hair drawn severely back beneath a black lace cap, her eyes darkly shadowed by all that she had so recently endured, called a meeting of all house staff and ghillies. They crowded respectfully into the great hall and stood looking compassionately at the woman all loved for her kindness over the long years.

'Greetings to you all,' she said quietly, one hand holding onto back of dining chair to support her. 'This is day of both joy and sadness—and much regret. As all will know by now, my husband Iain Campbell lies dead. He had not been well in his mind for many long months. Therefore I pray you that we remember happier times, when all were able to hold him in high esteem!' she spoke the words through stiff lips and a ripple of assenting voices came towards her.

'Iain's body will be carried to our own graveyard on the hill, where he will lie with his ancestors. Major Kenneth Campbell will take place of my nephew in the ceremony as Laird Roderick is recovering from bullet wound to his shoulder! Lady Kieran's dear husband, respected physician Sorley Mor Stewart says that Roderick should make good recovery.' At this there was cry of relief from the assembly—even those few who had followed Iain now joining in the murmured applause.

'Now to wondrous note of joy in all this—as some of you will know, Lady Kieran Stewart went through months of grief when her beloved twins, wee Alan and Ishbel, known and loved by you all, were stolen from her side, kidnapped in Edinburgh by evil men, as both she and her loving husband then devoted themselves to finding their missing children. Sadly the parents began to realise the twins had been taken by one to whom they should have looked to for love and protection. I refer to my husband and those about him who lent themselves to this horror.' She choked back a sob and Lord Mamore put steadying hand on her arm.

She recovered and now a slight smile reached her lips as she spoke.

'The joy which I referred to is that wee Alan and Ishbel now sleep safely in their cots above stairs, recovering from all that they have endured. The exact sequence of last night's events will doubtless be given you by others.

But for now, I commend my dear nephew Roderick Campbell to those of you who already love him and hold him in respect as Laird of Glenlarig—and also to those who from ill considered disloyalty to him gave greater obedience to my late husband. Let there be peace among us now—as all strive together for a good future!'

It had been a speech such as she had never thought herself able to make, having always kept a quiet profile in her husband's shadow, a speech that none who heard it that day would ever forget.

Iain Campbell had been placed in his coffin, a minister of the nearest church brought to say prayer over him, as the body was carried shoulder high, through the sodden grass and heather, high onto the bleak hillside where Iain had loved to bring down deer, pheasant or brace of grouse for the table and where but short time since he had listened to sound of those rutting stags and rejoiced to watch the many antlered monarch overcome the younger animal—nor stayed to see situation soon reversed.

It was hard, difficult going for the mourners on ground spongy and full of water neath their brogues from a storm such as none had ever witnessed before, as countless urgent, wee burns chortled music in swift restless flow down the hillside. The patient elderly minister, followed by Major Campbell, walked before all, intoning prayers for the soul of the departed, of whom he had heard such conflicting reports. But he was in God's hands now. All that man could do, was to show fitting respect of his internment.

It was not until the last sod had been put firmly in place, that a thin dazzle of sunlight lifted the pall of mist that had overshadowed the scene, and men shared a dram together in final salute, to sound of the wild lament on the pipes of old Duncan Mac Seumas borne hauntingly on the wind, before making their way back down to Glenlarig, where funeral feast was to be held, to which none of the neighbouring gentry had been invited, because of unprecedented events preceding Iain Campbell's death, the ill manner of it.

None of the women of the household had attended the funeral, it being the custom for men only to deal with such. But preparations were underway for a quiet funeral reception.

Under Sorley Mor's supervision, Roderick had been lifted from the couch where he had spent the night on the couch in Lorna's private sitting room, and carefully carried to his own chamber above stairs—and now at last Lorna was able to relax. She felt she could never bear to reoccupy the chamber that she had shared with Iain since their marriage. Eventually she would have one of the spare rooms appointed to her taste. Now she was too tired emotionally to even contemplate such matters.

As for Kieran, as soon as breakfast was over and Lorna had addressed the household, and she had assured herself that her aunt was coping as well as possible in such difficult situation, she took her anxious way back to the nursery. Here she found Morag and Bess holding a child each, the children's little faces pale and solemn, but they turned their heads as she came into the room and looked at her longingly.

'Mama,' cried Alan. 'Why bad men take us—why Uncle Iain say we not see you again?' His troubled blue eyes searched her face and saw the tears spring into her eyes. She knelt down bedside him, sought for words his little mind could comprehend.

'Your Uncle Iain was not a well man, Alan dear! He had an illness of the mind. Just as we can get a cough or cold—or hurt ourselves in some way, so also that part of us in which our thoughts are born, can become ill. Uncle Iain loved you both. But his mind was sick.'

'You mean—he could not help what he did?' asked the little boy, trying hard to understand. She stroked his hair as he looked at her with the same inquiring gaze she remembered observing on the face of the father he had never known. And she thought of Alan Stewart now, and whispered softly under her breath, 'Oh, Alan eudail, help me to explain in way he can accept.' It was his small sister who came to the rescue.

'Mama, Mama—Uncle Iain was very bad! But he gave me a doll and Alan a wooden sword. So he was a bit good too.' She smiled up at her mother. 'I expect he is sorry for what he did!' And in this way the child dismissed the months of fear and distress of separation from her mother. Alan looked from sister to mother. He frowned in thought and then gave a small smile.

'Uncle Iain said he loved us. Must not be cross with him anymore,' he proclaimed. For him the matter was settled. He screwed his little face in thought. 'So, when do we go home?' he asked, sliding off Morag's lap and throwing his arms about Kieran.

'When, Mama?' said Ishbel wistfully, straining vaguely to remember her old nursery full of toys and the noise of Edinburgh, as she too came to embrace her mother. Kieran smiled through her tears as she wondered at the forgiving nature of those two small individuals and hugged them tight..

'Oh my darling ones, I promise we will return home as soon as possible— and it will be in just a few day's time if all goes well!' she held them to her breast and so it was that her husband found them when he quietly entered the room. The children smiled at him excitedly.

'Father,' cried Alan looking up at him. 'Mama says we may go home!'

'Home, home—home!' cried Ishbel in delighted chorus.

The man stooped over them as Kieran rose to her feet, and took them up in his strong arms. He kissed one small face after the other, his joy not only that they were they so well recovered physically and in so short a time— but seemingly putting their terrifying experiences behind them already. He could not know that it would be many difficult months before Alan and Ishbel would be free of nightmare repeatedly disturbing their sleep, bringing worried parents to their sides to comfort and constantly reassure them.

But now there was only the most intense happiness that the family was reunited once more. And Sorley Mor bethought him of that other child, as yet small mystery beneath his wife's heart and showing as barely perceptible fullness at her waistline. He returned the twins to Bess and Morag's arms, as breathing deep sigh of relief, he caught Kieran close, kissing her brow, her lips, stroking her red gold hair and reflecting how easily she could have lost their babe when exposed to the fear and trauma of recent events—her endurance altogether remarkable. His sole desire was to make safe return to Edinburgh, there to keep his dear ones safe.

'Kieran sweetheart, I am going to see how Roderick fares,' he said gently. She glanced at him in dismay, uncomfortable that so far she had not been to see her brother this morning.

'I will come too!' she declared as they closed the nursery door. 'It is almost unbelievable it was Iain's gun that almost took his life! How hard is that going to be for Roderick to live with?' and she shuddered. He placed soothing arm about her shoulders.

'He lives—is young with a whole good life ahead of him! And I must say that Lachlan has made an excellent job of tending your brother's wound. He will make a fine physician one day. Luckily the bullet passed just below the right shoulder, causing much pain but no serious damage. And so far there is no sign of infection,' he added approvingly.

They found Roderick propped up on pillows. Ewan Dhu sat beside his bed, filling him in on all that had happened from the time when he had reluctantly left Roderick in Lachlan's care, in order to keep Kieran safe from all harm, escorting her on that wild expedition into the night in search of her children. And Roderick listened spellbound to the account, visualising the scene when Kieran had stepped wraith like before the demented man who was holding her babes aloft over the river's fury.

'It was Sorley Mor who first came upon Iain,' said Kieran. 'I watched as he raised his pistol and held Iain in its sight—Ewan and Ivor at his side. The man looked at them, knew escape was impossible—but I think his mind was blind to all reason. It was then that he raised the children each by an arm, dangling them over the water. My feet bore me towards him— holding my hands out to him.' She paused her lips faltering as she re-enacted all in memory.

'He thought Kieran a ghost at first,' said Sorley Mor, taking one of her hands in his. 'He was still not quite sure even when he recognised her face.

In that white shift blowing about her, hair wild and her eyes strangely staring—well they were,' he said to her with a smile.

'It was obvious that Iain Campbell was of a mind to kill those bairns if he could not have them for himself,' said Ewan Dhu. 'It was the Lord God himself who kept them safe from death that night—blessed be His name,' and he crossed himself, for Ewan was of the old religion.

'We also owe much to that wee laddie Grigor,' put in Ivor, who stood listening. At his words, Kieran looked at her husband uncomfortably. It seemed boy Grigor had been the first to establish the children's whereabouts and led Sorley Mor in search for the wretch who had stolen them—and sadly until now no one had thought of him. Where was he? They must make their gratitude known to this brave child. She remembered his slim form, those dark eyes in determined thin face.

'Lady, he slept in my bed last night—but was gone before I opened my eyes the morn,' said Ivor watching her face. 'No doubt he will have taken his own way back to the Gregorach!' he added reassuringly.

'And to Sheena,' exclaimed Roderick softly. 'Tell me Sorley Mor, how long before I can ride a horse again. I needs must speak with the minister of the Balquidder church, a marriage to be arranged.' And at his words Kieran stooped and kissed his cheek, a soft light in dark grey eyes so like to his own.

'Oh Roderick, such wedding I long to see!' she turned to her husband. 'We needs must delay our return to Edinburgh until after such happy event!' And looking down at the pale determined face of his brother-in-law, he could only agree.

The boy who made difficult return amongst wide spread debris following fury of such storm as had not been witnessed in living memory, felt young arms and legs sorely scratched from brambles clutch, knees bruised in process of clambering over fallen trees in his path, feet caked with wet mud as he walked relentlessly on, squelching through boggy, sodden heather moorland. At last he had left the birchwood behind him and stood facing the roaring Dochart its waters mightily swollen still in spate as every furious wee burn raced down the hillside to empty into its roaring advance.

'It was a water kelpie took that de'il Iain Campbell to his doom,' stated Grigor to himself. He perched on a rock and stared at the scene, reconstructing all in memory. Often would he relate the story in the future around many a fireside—and the part he had played in all, small though it had been! On he walked again, meeting none upon the road, but his eyes alert for any sign of the militia who regularly patrolled the road. Once he paused, heard the detested sound of orders shouted on the wind, marching feet and he scrambled up the brae lying flat until the small troop had passed.

At long last his weary feet took the path that branched off from the road to the Braes of Balquidder and home. As he reached the shores of Loch Voil a voice called to him softly and a man he knew well, helped him down into his small boat, and rowed the tired child across the width of the loch. He asked no questions, saw from Grigor's face the child was beyond words. Once across, he set the lad's feet in the right direction. When at last Grigor almost fell into the welcome warmth of the cave, he was at the point of exhaustion. But he raised his head triumphantly as Sheena bent over him her features tense with anxiety.

'Iain Campbell is dead!' he announced grandly. 'Roderick Campbell was shot—but lives! Do not fear,' he said as he saw the girls face blench at his words. 'The young Campbell laird is strong a bullet wound nothing to one such as he!' And having proclaimed this, he put his head down on a bed of dried grass and heather and fell into a deep sleep. Sheena sat looking down on him, longing to question him further. Her father watched her there, saw the distress in her eyes and knew she worried for the man she loved and was willing to risk estrangement from her family to marry.

He rose to his feet and stepped outside the cave and glanced soberly around. The sun was low in the heavens, but still casting sufficient light to show the devastation caused by last night's storm. Rowan and birch had been uprooted in the fury of its passing, a great boulder some hundred feet below, split asunder by lightning's sword. But the brackens russet and gold was undimmed and some slight, faint pink still marked the massed browning heather on that battered hillside and all around was the voice of myriad tiny burns, their racing peat brown waters touched with foam, as they leaped ever downwards, making white lace against the dark of the hill.

How would his daughter manage without these fine views to sustain her spirit, he wondered? This place was the cradle of her race. Was she to exchange all this for a home however splendid in the heart of Campbell country? The fact that the views Sheena would look on there were equally beautiful was of no account to the man.

She came to stand at his side, the wind blowing her hair across the strong planes of her lovely face.

'Campbell and MacGregor have ever been enemies, daughter,' he said without preamble. But even as he spoke, memory of conversation with Sorley Mor Stewart came to mind—he tried to recall the substance of the doctor's words—in effect the clan struggles that had existed over the long centuries had to be put aside if ever Scotland was once again to become a strong, independent nation! Deep in his heart he knew this to be true.

'And what has such enmity ever brought us,' said the girl in poignant tones.

'Why, honour and right to hold our heads high, despite them all!' But perhaps the words held slightly hollow ring he thought. He breathed a deep sigh. Was the doctor right? He glanced behind him at the cave he called home. Was it right that any man's wife and children should have to live like this without walls to call their own? Their clan proscribed—any who killed them to be applauded! No, too much had happened over the long years to let go of hatred born of his mother's milk and too deeply ingrained in his soul for removal. But Sheena now, she was proud and passionate—had mind of her own. What indeed if his daughter and the young Campbell laird might make new start for the future?

Rob MacGregor drew his heavy brows together in thought. He would speak with her mother Flora, although the poor woman showed little interest in anything but her own failing health these days and would in any case be entirely guided by him in the matter. But if Sheena remained determined on this match, then even if not approving of it, at least he would not cast her off as would be proper in such case.

He turned and faced her, placing his hands on her shoulders.

'I do not approve of this wedding with one of our clan's bitter enemies. But Sheena lassie, if this Roderick is the one you would cleave to in life, then although it goes against the grain, I give you my blessing!' and he kissed her. At this she burst into storm of tears and buried her head against her father's breast.

'Och, father—these words mean the world to me,' she said softly between her sobs. 'The morrow's morn I will take myself over to Glenlarig and see how he fares. Grigor said he had been shot and....'

'Aye, I heard the laddie—but that he said this Roderick would be fine. But if you must go, then take great care upon the road!' he said anxiously. 'Those damned redcoats ever ready to arrest any they come upon and have slightest suspicion of.'

'I have been there before on my lane, know the way well—and will keep clear of the redcoats, father!' She smiled up at him, dashing tears of relief from her eyes. 'Come, I left the broth bubbling and ready to be served!' and with final glance at the stormy sunset where clouds of bruised violet and magenta outlined in flame cast dappled shadow on the loch, she slipped her arm about her father's waist, his hand on her shoulder as they re-entered the cave together.

The following morning, Sheena extracted all possible information from young Grigor, who had awakened from his long sleep looking his usual determined self. He ate a great bowlful of porridge washed down with water from the spring and smiled up at Sheena, who was wearing the blue gown that had once been Kieran's. The girl had washed her hair and brushed it to fall as shining cape on her shoulders and her green eyes shone with anticipation.

'I am ready,' he said to her.

'Ready for what, Grigor?' she asked.

'Why, to accompany you back to Glenlarig!' he replied simply. She stared at him then smiled approval. It would be good to be able to speak with him along the way. Her mother looked up at her, a weary smile about her worn face. She tried to restrain the cough that was getting worse.

'May the good God keep you safe, daughter,' she said and watched with brooding sadness as the girl walked away.

It was her father who rowed them across the loch, sweeping the area with his spyglass before setting them safe on the shore. He watched them go, his fine young daughter with her proud swinging stride and the child he had taken into his family as his own since Annie MacGregor's death. He raised hand in farewell and lifted the oars once more.

It was late afternoon before the couple stood high on the hillside looking down on Glenlarig. Grigor pointed to the courtyard, where small red coated figures could be seen moving about.

'I had almost forgotten you said that General Mamore was there with his soldiers,' said Sheena with a frown. She was not happy about encountering the hated Campbell chieftain.

'I tell you what we will do,' said Grigor. 'You will hide here behind these bushes, whilst I go and find Ewan Dhu who will ask advice of Laird Roderick.' Before she could protest he had left her, and was running down the hillside like a hare. The boy slipped through the hedge bordering the drive about the side of the house and almost ran into one of the redcoat militia. He stared up casually at the man, as nonchalantly whistling a tune he turned toward the kitchen entrance.

He looked inquiringly at the cook and his mouth watered at the smell of the roast venison being prepared and his eyes widened at sight of so much delicious food upon the scrubbed kitchen table.

'Where is Ewan Dhu,' he demanded. The woman glanced at him, remembered seeing him in company with Ewan Dhu and Ivor. She sent one of the maids to find Ewan and cut the hungry youngster a slice of meat to chew upon while he waited.

Roderick Campbell turned his head as Ewan escorted Grigor to his bedside. He was already looking better and making good recovery from the severity of his wound, even laughing with Sorley Mor and joking that now he would have scar on this shoulder to match with that received from his duel with the rapist Bradshaw.

'To say nothing of the dirk wound that I treated when first we met,' added Sorley Mor. 'The body can take just so much punishment, Roderick. You should strive to treat yours with more concern now.' Then as the boy approached the invalid's side, Roderick recognised him and gave a smile.

'Grigor! I am glad to see you again! I wish to thank you for the courage you displayed when helping to find the bairns—for guiding Sorley Mor and Ivor, your help to my sister Kieran. You are a brave boy!' The boy looked at him seriously.

'It was my pleasure Laird Roderick,' he replied graciously with all the dignity of a man grown as he gazed on the man who lay back against his pillows smiling at him. 'How are you now,' he asked. 'Sad I was that night to see your uncle fire at you. The world is well rid of such a one!' At his words Roderick paled. None had informed him that the shot had come from Iain's pistol. Yet should he be surprised when Iain had previously set a man to kill him on the road a few weeks since?

'Is this so,' he asked, glancing at Ewan Dhu. 'I was not informed of it!'

'Aye, Laird it is,' replied the ghillie heavily. 'But he was not himself as you know and death heals all quarrels.' And sighing, Roderick nodded his head.

'You asked to see me, Grigor,' said Roderick now, studying the boy with attempted smile, trying to dismiss knowledge of his uncle's blind hatred from his memory. A sudden hope sprang to his mind. Was it possible Grigor had come bearing a message from Sheena?

'Sheena MacGregor waits on the hill and is wishful to see you. But we spied redcoats about the place and she was uneasy at thought of meeting with any of them. What shall I tell her?' He looked inquiringly at Roderick who gave exclamation of joy.

'Grigor, here is wonderful news indeed! Sheena here—she is at Glenlarig?' He turned to his brother-in-law. 'Sorley Mor, I ask you do me the greatest favour and go with Grigor and escort Sheena safe to my arms!'

She came to him barefooted, mud spattered from her journey, carrying shoes and stockings in a small bundle, not given time to refresh herself by the doctor, who on seeing her sweet face as she stood up from concealment behind clump of gorse bushes, gave her greeting kiss and hurried her down the brae and into the house past interested maid servants, and straight up to Roderick's room. It was the medicine above all to bring greatest healing to the mental as well as physical hurt he had suffered.

Ewan Dhu followed Grigor and Sorley Mor out of the room, leaving the couple to embrace in private with the tenderness of those who truly love. Here it was that Lorna found them some half an hour later, hearing with delight of the girl's presence. She knocked and entered, to find Sheena perched on the side of her nephew's bed, as he held one slim tanned hand to his lips, new look of gentleness on his face.

'Aunt Lorna! Come take a chair and sit with us! Sheena and I are discussing our marriage. We want it to take place as soon as possible—after so much that has been difficult to contend with.' He looked expectantly at this woman who had taken the place of the mother he could barely remember and whom he had loved since his childhood. Her response was all he could have desired. She kissed first one and then the other of them.

'You told me before of your love for Sheena and although knowing her only from our first brief meeting—seeing the two of you together now, I can see how right it looks! My dear, I welcome you into our family and know you will make good and loving wife to Roderick!' She folded the girl in her arms and Sheena felt all nervous tension leave her. She looked at Lorna compassionately.

'I thank you, Lady Lorna,' she said shyly. 'Allow me to express my regret at your husband's death,' she added as in duty bound.

'Perhaps it was for the best,' was the quiet reply. 'But come my dear, you will surely wish to wash and tidy yourself after such long journey on foot!'

'Oh—yes, I see what you mean,' replied Sheena glancing down ruefully at her muddied gown and bare feet. 'One thing I must mention though—there are redcoats about the place—and the great Campbell Major General, Mamore. I would not wish to meet with any of them!' She relaxed slightly as Lorna assured her this would be of her own choosing and led her away.

Lorna ushered her guest into the small chamber she had hastily arranged for her use. Here was water for the girl to wash, soft towels, and lying on the bed was a deep rose coloured velvet gown and petticoat, bodice trimmed with lace. Sheena had never seen anything so lovely. But would it not be better to brush the mud from her poor blue skirts and appear in her normal apparel. But almost in a dream, she dressed and stood before a long gilt framed mirror, staring at the transformation in amazement.

She turned her head at a light tap at the door and Kieran came in. The two girls looked at each other in delight and fell into each other's arms—and as they kissed, Kieran was glad of the gesture she had made in gift of this one of her favourite gowns. For it suited Sheena's dark beauty to perfection!

'You look beautiful,' exclaimed Kieran fondly. 'Just time now before dinner for you to come and see wee Alan and Ishbel!' and taking her hand took her to the nursery, where Morag Burns and Annie were tending the children. Sheena uttered cry of delight as she saw them. They looked round as they heard her voice and vaguely recognised Sheena whom they had met in Edinburgh before the horror of their kidnap.

'Oh what sweet relief you have them safe home again,' cried Sheena, leaning down and placing soft kiss on their cheeks. 'Grigor told me of what happened—of your own bravery in confronting Iain Campbell—bad cess to his name!'

'He was threatening to drown them,' whispered Kieran as they left and closed the nursery door quietly behind them.

'I think the man was possessed of a devil!' cried Sheena fiercely

'Certainly he was of a sick mind,' replied Kieran. 'But I shall try to remember only the original kindness with which he received me, when first I came to Glenlarig.' She looked at Sheena.

'How he must have changed then!' said Sheena deep in thought.

'Sorley Mor says that an illness of the mind can be as harmful as that of the body. My husband has a deep belief in God—and in His son, the Christ who came into the world to teach us of the Father's love. If only Iain had possessed such faith, perhaps he would not have acted as he did. But there again, maybe when our minds are taken up with pride and hatred we block admittance of Christ's healing grace.' Kieran was remembering recent conversation with her husband

'That all sounds rather difficult for me to understand,' said Sheena slowly. 'When you and I have seen so much of man's cruelty during our lives, it is almost impossible to think of a loving God. If he is all powerful, why would he not see that the wicked get their just deserts? Why not intervene?'

'Men have asked themselves that down the centuries,' said a deep voice and startled they looked around. Sheena almost recoiled from the tall well set man in his gold braided scarlet jacket, plaid fastened with silver mounted cairngorm and trews of the Campbell tartan, who stood viewing her by the flickering light of the wall sconces lighting the passageway. 'Will you not introduce me, Kieran?' he asked looking with interest at the young woman who to his surprise was glaring at him in unexpected disdain.

'Sheena, this is our guest, Major General John Campbell, Lord Mamore,' replied Kieran and placing restraining hand on Sheena's arm and glancing at the soldier, 'Pray meet my future sister-in-law Mistress Sheena—Gregory.'

'Say rather Sheena MacGregor,' almost spat out the girl, lightning in her eyes. The man heard her in astonishment and raised a lazy eyebrow as he examined the furious young woman who stood so defiantly before him.

'MacGregor—hmm! No doubt my nephew will remedy this misfortune when he makes a Campbell of you,' he retorted. 'Yes my dear, Roderick has spoken of his love for you, extolled your beauty and courage—and now I see his words well warranted.' He glanced with approval from one young woman to the other, Kieran with her wealth of red gold hair and storm grey eyes, her fine figure beneath black, silver laced gown now showing sign of the new life she carried, and Sheena with her imperious dark loveliness.

'Shall we go down to dinner,' he suggested as sound of the pipes was heard. Before Sheena could object, he had taken one of her unresponsive hands tucking it firmly under an arm, offering the other to Kieran. And so the three of them walked down the wide staircase, the girls looking straight before them, nor glancing at the portraits of Campbell ancestors that stared down at them.

To her delight and no small relief, Sheena's eyes fell on the figure of Roderick sitting to the right of the empty chair at the head of the table, seat which Mamore took as of right after first courteously seating the two young women.

'It is good to see you up and about again so soon, nephew,' he said to Roderick, noting however that the man was pale and obviously still in some discomfort. 'You should take care however, early days yet after your wound!' he added, and could only guess at how his nephew had managed the stairs even with help from Ewan Dhu and Ivor.

But the young man barely heard his words, rising to his feet, his eyes on Sheena in her rose coloured gown. He reached a hand out to her.

'Oh, my darling—welcome,' he said, his heart in his eyes, 'And how very beautiful you look!' He glanced around those at the table, at Lorna outwardly serene in black velvet gown and severe black lace cap, at Sorley Mor his dark blue eyes fondly caressing Kieran, at Kenneth Campbell regarding all with musing smile, and at the two officers of the militia who had joined them—his glance then returning to Mamore, as he lifted a glass.

'Ladies and gentlemen—before we eat, I would ask you to raise your glasses to Mistress Sheena MacGregor, who has done me the very great honour of consenting to be my wife!'

At announcement of this very public secret, there were cries of congratulation from around the table, Sheena's dusky cheeks flushing deeper rose than her gown. Roderick withdrew something from his pocket. It was a curiously wrought gold and amethyst ring, two clasped hands embracing the jewels rich glowing heart surrounded by tiny pearls. He took Sheena's hand and gently slid it on her finger, formal sign of their betrothal.

So many conflicting thoughts swirled through the girl's head as she looked down on the heavy gold ring. Was she dishonouring her people by accepting this Campbell laird as her future husband? True her father had given his reluctant approval, but she knew she risked being ostracised by all other members of the Gregorach. But as she glanced around the table at the faces of those it would have been inherent as her duty to hate she realised that they were in fact just ordinary human beings as she was. That hatred passed down through the generations is an evil weed that needs uprooting, to be stamped upon.

'Music,' called Roderick and old Angus Mac Seumas who stood behind Roderick's chair, gave deep bow to the couple, raised his pipes and as they listened to the grace notes with which he embroidered his joyful salute, there was instant applause. And so the evening went on.

'I leave soon after daybreak tomorrow,' announced Lord Mamore at the conclusion of dinner. He looked keenly at Roderick. 'Earlier in the day I took opportunity to speak with your retainers, laid down in no uncertain terms what any could expect if they showed the slightest disobedience to you, Roderick. It is to their credit that I realised my words were not needed, all spoke of deepest loyalty to you, their abhorrence of the deeds done by Iain Campbell.'

'That was good of you, sir,' replied Roderick politely but secretly wishing Mamore had left all such matters in his hands.

'Now as to the fellow Donald MacKay I take him with us, and two others involved in Iain's misdeeds. I could put them on trial for their offences, but knowing these men ill advisably followed orders of Iain Campbell I have given them option of joining the army as recruits as preferable to possible hanging. This way, we keep quiet as possible all that has recently transpired, do so in respect of Lady Lorna!'

All knew that stories would inevitably circulate, but hopefully such rumours concerning the late Iain Campbell would soon be put to rest.

As Sheena MacGregor watched the red column disappearing along the loch path early the next day, her heart felt lighter. Now with her future husband's love to sustain her and with Kieran and Sorley Mor for company as well as the joy of playing with wee Alan and Ishbel, and also beginning to know Lorna better, her mind felt more at rest.

Lorna took her on a tour of the house, opening each room by turn. The girl looked around at the busy kitchen, in amazement, what she saw so far removed from any cooking she had seen before. There was clatter and steam and noise as Jessie MacNab raised red cheeked face from the dough she was pounding to call instructions to the kitchen maids. Lorna saw the girl's surprise.

'You see Sheena apart from the immediate family many workers on the estate have their meals here. Others who have cottages nearby dine there if they so prefer. We are blessed in having an excellent cook in Jessie and several maids to help her in the kitchen—then there are housemaids and a boy who brings logs for the fires—and of course gardeners—and stablemen!'

'There are so many folk?' asked Sheena.

'Oh yes!' Lorna smiled, paused and continued, 'The ghillies provide meat for the table and at times Roderick also will go up on the hill to bring down a deer. You will soon be mistress of this place, Sheena! There is much you must learn of your future duties, but I know you will manage well!' She placed an affectionate arm about the girl's slender waist.

'But you are mistress here!' Sheena was not at all sure she wished for duty of overseeing so many, would willingly leave all such to Lady Lorna. But the older woman was gently insistent, understanding the girl's lack of confidence.

'I have managed all while Roderick was yet unmarried. But as soon as you are wed all this will change. But never fear, I will be here to offer help and advice when needed. Now, let us find Roderick!'

The next few weeks passed pleasantly, as the days grew shorter and colder the mountain peaks already white with snow as November waited in the wings. The day on which Roderick Campbell took Sheena to wife at Balquidder, was one with bright sunshine warming the old stones of the little church and softening the harsh message of the gravestone speaking of journeys end, and striking copper into the dying bracken and few leaves left on the trees after the great storm.

Robert MacGregor had been persuaded to give his daughter away and defiantly appeared in kilt of his clan's tartan accompanied by young Grigor who had returned to Balquidder, as with Sorley Mor acting as best man and Kieran as attendant to the girl who had long been childhood friend and now was sister-in-law the service began. As the minister gravely officiated and spoke touching benison at the conclusion of the ceremony he noted there was tremendous joy in the small congregation.

Only Kenneth Campbell although face bearing a smile, seemed slightly withdrawn, knowing that the cobweb of daydreams concerning Kieran had been swept to naught by the obvious love she shared with her husband. After the ceremony he was to return to Edinburgh, his leave over.

Lorna was not present. She thought the long ride on horseback would have been too much for her and so she remained at Glenlarig to welcome the wedding party home and also making sure that all was well with wee Alan and Ishbel. Physically the twins seemed almost completely recovered from their ordeal, little faces so thin and pale when rescued from Iain's clutches now held the healthy bloom of childhood. And it was a joy to watch their innocent play. But already it was noticeable that their sleep had fallen into disturbed pattern.

It was late indeed when the wedding party returned to Glenlarig. Then at last in the early hours Roderick Campbell drew his wife into his arms and laid her across the bed, and smiled lovingly down. Lorna had provided

Sheena with a nightdress of white lawn trimmed with froth of exquisite lace and the flickering candlelight revealed her shapeliness.

Roderick unbuckled his kilt, stepped out of its folds, she gasped as she saw his need of her and soon that sheer nightdress also lay on the floor as he tenderly roused her to passion to match with his own. There was quick pain and she cried out as he penetrated her, then they became one indeed as they consummated their love for each other and both knew it was one that would endure for all time.

The next morning she awoke before he did, and sat looking down at him, her long lashed, deep violet eyes full of love, her dark glossy tresses framing the beauty of her face. She stared at the scars on his body—one below each shoulder and one over his breast and whispered prayer of thanks to God that he had survived three such appointments with death.

'Roderick—husband,' she called softly and he woke and stared at her almost uncomprehendingly for split second before memory explained the joy of her presence—that Sheena was now his dear wife. And with gasp of delight he pulled her down on him as his mouth explored hers and his hands caressed her body as once again they gave themselves to each other in throbbing ecstasy.

'I love you, Sheena, heart of my heart,' he whispered as they relaxed together murmuring endearments. Neither guessed then that it was of those first hours of their love that their son was conceived.

It was late before they came downstairs, and Sheena blushed as she felt the eyes of all upon them both. Their joy in each other was obvious. It turned to some sadness though when Sorley Mor explained that he had to get back to his practice in Edinburgh.

'Kieran has asked that we stay longer, but I have those who depend on me and our home awaits us there.' And he added in further explanation, 'Patterson has been managing all on his own, since Lachlan came here with me!' There was a moment of dismayed silence.

'Could you not stay here and become physician in this area?' exclaimed Roderick hopefully, knowing how he would miss the man who had taught him so much of caring and humanity. Also he hated to think he would have to do without the sister whose presence meant so much both to him and to Lorna—and knew how much his aunt would also miss the children.

'We will return on visits—this I promise,' replied Sorley Mor.

'We are just so happy to have taken part in your wedding, brother mine and joy to see Sheena your dear wife!' said Kieran and she hugged Sheena and gave her a kiss. 'But needs must I return to my own home,' she explained softly.

'When do you plan to travel,' asked Lorna putting on a brave face. She was still not recovered from shock of all she had recently endured, combined with the realisation that news of her late husband's villainy would doubtless spread about the neighbourhood. But the happiness and content she had in her nephew's marriage had brought much needed solace.

'Sorley suggests we set forth tomorrow! But I believe I must leave my maid Annie behind,' said Kieran with a smile. 'It seems that Ewan Dhu has asked her to wife! The twins will miss her greatly.'

'Perhaps I had some slight idea of this,' exclaimed Roderick. 'I had often thought the man would be well of a wife, but none here have ever taken his fancy! He is much more than ghillie to me—almost a brother. I will make a good cottage available to them!' He smiled, 'But I am sorry for your loss, sister!'

'Annie is very good with little ones—you may have need of her services in the future,' added Sorley Mor with a smile and Sheena blushed at his implication and Lorna's eyes brightened at thought of possible new young life to come.

Old Angus Mac Seumas settled the bag of his pipes, inflated his lungs, took deep breath of the cold slightly misty air of early November and the notes that floated hauntingly on the air in farewell lament touched the hearts of those leaving, as Sorley Mor, Kieran and Lachlan, accompanied by Ewan Dhu and Ivor, the ghillies each carrying precious burden before them, set forth on long journey to Edinburgh.

Behind them, waving from the steps of Glenlarig house they left a sad faced Roderick Campbell, his arm about Sheena's waist. By their side stood Lorna Campbell vainly trying to stem tears that rose unbidden to her gentle eyes. When sound of clattering horse hooves disappeared on the cold breeze blowing down from Ben Lawers and his fellow peaks, they turned back into the house. It was Lorna who noticed the forlorn girl, apron over her eyes, sobbing as though her heart would break.

'Annie child, be comforted,' said Lorna kindly. 'Ewan Dhu will soon return and then you shall be married!' She thought the young maid's sorrow was at temporary separation from the fierce eyed, black bearded ghillie who had stolen the girl's heart.

'Oh, I know this is so, Lady Lorna,' sobbed Annie. 'But I have had to say goodbye to Kieran and those darling bairns. I will miss them so!'

'We all will, Annie. But take heart, Sorley Mor has promised they will make return visit when this is possible. You will see them all again!' And she took comfort from her own words. In the meanwhile there was Sheena, this beautiful, tempestuous young woman now Roderick's dear wife. She would need Lorna's help in running Glenlarig, and she smiled now, for like many in this world knew the need to be needed.

Back in that special room she had made so much her own, Lorna fell quietly on her knees and uttered prayer to Almighty God. Again she gave Him thanks for the safe return of little Alan and Ishbel and prayed relief from their childish nightmares, prayed his lovely Son the Christ would have his hand over all her dear family—and then the most difficult of all, she prayed for the soul of Iain Campbell. And as that prayer left her lips, she felt as though a soothing hand was placed on her shoulder as of a sudden she experienced sensation like to cool spring water flowing throughout her veins, refreshing mind and body.

The beautiful chords that stole upon the air as she plucked strings of her beloved harp drew Roderick and Sheena to open the door and stand listening in delight.

'Will you teach me to play one day?' asked Sheena softly, fixing respectful gaze on Lorna from curious violet eyes. She had been listening intently to the music, had never before heard such sweetness of sound.

'My child, it would give me greatest pleasure,' replied Lorna rising from her instrument. 'I have longed for someone who would come to love this old instrument as I do!' At this the couple put their arms about her. Despite lingering sadness on the departure of Kieran and Sorley Mor and the children, they all knew the future that lay before them would be good.

Sorley Mor was called upon to show the return pass issued to him for his party by Lord Mamore before the General's departure from Glenlarig some weeks back, and was glad of the thoughtfulness shown by the soldier in preventing unnecessary delays. Once more they broke their journey at the Golden Lion Inn at Stirling, where Kieran soothed her fretful bairns tired from their jolting ride. Already Kieran was missing Annie's help with the twins, but Lachlan who seemed to have a special way with little ones, came to her rescue.

It was late afternoon of the following day that the familiar castle high on its ancient rock came into view, with Edinburgh crouched around it. As they drew nearer, Kieran glimpsed the smoke haze that hung over the city as every tall chimney exhaled minute dark particles and buildings that once would have enchanted with their bright stone, now wore witches garment of soot.

But tired though she was the girl sensed the energy of this place, a vibrancy born of the indomitable spirit of those who lived here and despite difficulties of sanitation and cramped, dark accommodation and often meagre diet, amazed in the bright courage with which they seemed endued, as they went about their daily grind.

When at last the horses came to snorting halt outside the doctor's house, the young mother almost fell off her horse with tiredness, would have done so had it not been for Sorley Mor's strong arm about her. He helped her up the steps and as he did so the door was opened to them and there was Mistress Lindsey smiling welcome and relief at their return. And the housekeeper's expression turned to joy as she saw the small twins carried in by the fierce faced highland ghillies, with Lachlan struggling behind with the luggage.

'Oh welcome home, doctor! And Mistress Stewart—and mercy me, you have your bairnies safe back—and how they have grown! Wait Lachlan, I will give you a hand with those bags!' Then on hearing the noise, John Patterson excused himself to his elderly arthritic patient, as together with Nurse Effie he hurried to the hall to join in the welcome.

That evening Mistress Lindsay prepared a tender joint of roasted lamb and vegetables, followed by an apple pie the pastry almost melting in the mouth and served with cream. And there was a fine white wine from the cellar. At the conclusion of the meal, Kieran excused herself to the men and sought her bed. But first she checked wee Alan and Ishbel were lying fast asleep in their own beds once more, and smiled to see them resting so peacefully on their pillows. It was now that Mistress Lindsey came to her.

'I hope I am not taking too great a liberty, Mistress Stewart—but knowing now that Annie has decided to marry that great hairy highlander, I have bethought me of a girl whom I know to be of good and honest character and much used to the care of children.'

'Really? Pray tell me about her,' cried Kieran in quick interest. The housekeeper smiled and sought in her mind how best to describe this possible new nursemaid.

'Her name is Kathie Blair. She was only twelve when her mother died and of necessity she took over the care of her three small siblings, and was a second mother to them. Her father recently remarried and Kathie has found the new wife—well difficult,' and the housekeeper snorted.

'That is a shame,' said Kieran.

'The upshot of it is that the wife wants Kathie out of the house, saying that at sixteen years the lass is woman grown and should make her own way in the world.' She watched Kieran's face hopefully. 'I can vouch for her,' she said quietly. 'She is of a kind and gentle nature!

'Bring her to see me tomorrow,' smiled Kieran tiredly, 'and thank you for your helpfulness! Perhaps I should tell you that Sorley Mor and I are to be blessed with a baby come the spring!'

'Why, congratulations Mistress Stewart,' cried the housekeeper with a smile, for she had already detected the fullness at Kieran's waist. 'All the more need then for another dependable pair of hands!'

'That is very true,' agreed the girl softly.

When her husband came to bed, he found Kieran already fast asleep. He stared down at her by the light of his bedside candle, realising that her face was thinner than it had been and, despite the outward signs of her pregnancy, she had lost weight. He could only guess at the fear and frustration she had undergone at Glenlarig, coping with the incontrovertible fact that her uncle had her children in his power and lacking knowledge of where he had hidden them.

She was brave as she was beautiful this woman he had taken to wife in marriage initially mere formality to protect her name, as he had then fallen deeply in love with her, and despite all the storms of life they had endured, separations and heartache, now at last they would be able to face the future together united in a love that would last as long as life itself. He slid down in the bed beside her, blew out the candle and eased her head onto his shoulder. She stirred slightly and then his lips sought hers—and she responded.

'Oh, my love—my dearest love,' he whispered as she came to his arms. They settled down to sleep at last, but after a few hours were disturbed by urgent cries from the nursery. They hurried through to peer anxiously into the two cots, to find little Ishbel writhing feverishly in nightmare. Her screams had wakened Alan who now raised his indignant voice with hers.

'Oh, my darlings—hush now, do not cry! You are safe home in your own beds—and nothing can harm you,' soothed Kieran as she lifted the frightened little girl in her arms and Sorley Mor cradled Alan's small head against his breast.

They sat long with the children, Kieran softly intoning a song her MacGregor foster mother had sung to her when small. And the sound of that sweet Gaelic lullaby seemed to possess magic in its words and melody. For the little ones closed their eyes and as the weary parents placed them back in their cots, knew their children's minds were at peace—at least for now.

The following morning, not long after breakfast, when Sorley Mor and Lachlan had already joined John Patterson in dealing with patients come early to the door, Mistress Lindsey knocked and entered the sitting room, bringing the young girl she had suggested as nursemaid for the twins, who were presently in the care of Nurse Effie.

'Mistress Stewart this is Kathie Blair,' she said, and turning to the slightly built newcomer wearing worn faded blue skirt and striped blouse, fair hair tied tightly behind her neck, 'Come then—make your curtsey lass!'

Kieran looked at the girl curiously, knowing how important it was to find just the right person to help with the twins and smiled at Kathie encouragingly.

'Mistress Lindsey has already told me a little about you, Kathie—that you have been looking after your small brother and sisters since your mother died and you were all so sadly orphaned. So I know you have good experience in the care of children—but I am looking for someone who will not only care for their physical needs, but genuinely love them.'

'Lady, if you will but give me the chance, I will do my very best. I love all children. May I see them?' Kieran glanced into the girl's forget-me-not blue eyes and saw the honesty there—and the integrity.

'Come with me then,' she replied with a smile and led her upstairs to the nursery. She watched carefully, saw the girl glance in delight at the blue eyed little boy, his red gold hair so like his mother's—and at his twin sister, whose silken curls were like pale moonlight.

'Why, but they are just so beautiful,' the young girl whispered. She knelt down and opened her arms to them. Effie stepped back, encouraging them to approach. It was Ishbel who made the first move, holding her doll out to Kathie.

'My new doll,' she said.

'What is her name, wee Ishbel?'

'She not have name,' replied the child, staring curiously at Kathie. 'You give her name!' and she pushed the doll into Kathie's hands.

'Mary is a good name,' said Kathie. 'Will that do for her?

'Yes,' replied the little girl thoughtfully as her brother Alan now decided to join in the conversation.

'How you are called,' asked the small boy guardedly, memories of Mourna MacNicol's harsh treatment still fresh in his mind.

'My name is Kathie—and I hope your mother will allow me to help in looking after you both—if you agree,' she said quietly, looking directly into eyes as blue as her own. He cocked his head on one side and considered her, then nodded, as he glanced at Ishbel.

'You will be like Bess,' he said then. 'I will be your friend!' Then the two of them allowed themselves to be taken into their new nursemaid's arms and Kieran glancing in relief at Mistress Lindsey, relaxed.

Kathie Blair was to become part of the family treasured for her kindness and good humour, and that special gift some few have of being able to enter into the world of the child.

Over the next few months Kieran learned something of the girl's own history. That her father and mother had fled the highlands during the atrocities meted out on all by the victorious Hanoverian army, whether they had been involved in support of Charles Edward or no. Hearing what was already happening to those in neighbouring villages, the couple had taken their children and hidden in a cave above their small farm, watched in despair as their house burned, smelt the acrid smoke rising as the poor home they had built up over the years was destroyed by the red coated vandals, livestock slaughtered apart from their few cows which were driven away to be sold for English profit.

Her parents had taken the dangerous choice of running the gauntlet of the rash of redcoat patrols spreading relentlessly across the land and shooting any they saw on sight, and by sheer good fortune made their way safely to Edinburgh. Here Kathie's father had taken any job however menial or badly paid to put food into his family's mouths. It was soon after this that his wife died of a lung disease—but also he was sure of a broken heart.

Hearing all this, Kieran's heart went out to Kathie, realised how difficult life had been for her. It brought Kieran's own experiences flooding back into memory. She knew that many Highlanders had made their way to Edinburgh and Glasgow and other cities. But their hearts like her own must ever grieve the loss of their own dearly loved glens, the heathered hillsides where deer roamed and lochs lay deep dreaming, mirroring their guardian snow clad mountain peaks—and where eagles flew.

Would she ever be truly happy here in this city of foul smells and tall tenement buildings, where people were squeezed tighter together than shoal of herrings and smoke rose like a pall over all? But there was a good side to all this too, she acknowledged. Her husband was able to practice the medicine he truly loved, Lachlan was proving apt and eager student and would one day become a fine physician in his own right. And this city was also the seat of learning, of literature and the arts—and the new sciences. If as Sorley Mor told her the plans in progress to build a new town on the outskirts of the city should come into fruition, then surely life would improve?

But oh to hear the melody of the larks once more, small fragile feathered throats spilling enchantment into the crystal clear air! How she missed it all, the bleat of sheep, peat smoke rising in the glen, the hares dancing and antlered stags booming challenge, and above all the eagle soaring high! Even though the Trossachs was not as fair as her own beloved Appin, nevertheless she had found it extremely beautiful—and while there it had filled the sore spot in her heart. In a way she envied Sheena who would now enjoy all of this at Glenlarig.

But even if in days to come they should be able to make return to the land of her long love, of high mountain peaks swathed in cloud silk and hills fading blue in the distance, of rushing burns and wild waterfalls, where dainty bluebells danced and bog cotton streamed in the wind—even with all this something would not be the same. Scotland had lost its independence, sold many years back by unscrupulous lords for bribe of handful of gold, and now was overrun by English troops with their clipped accents and complete lack of understanding of the hearts of those in whom the lamp of freedom burned ever bright.

Sorley Mor came upon his wife as she brooded thus. With the intuition of one who loved her more than his own life, he held her to him and for a while neither of them spoke.

'You are thinking on all that has gone,' he asked gently.

'Yes, husband of my heart—I am—grieving for all we have lost,' she cried brokenly. He stroked her hair, kissed her brow.

'My darling one, I share in your grief. But consider now the good things that God has given us to compensate. We have the joy of wee Alan and Ishbel, the happiness of knowing that at last their nightmares have ceased and they laugh and play—and surely best of all, the wonder of that lovely babe you have given me, young Colin Sorley Stewart, lying there in his cradle!'

'Kind it was you allowed me to name him after the father I never knew—even though Campbell!' she said thoughtfully and smiled through the tears she had been shedding.

'What is it that is still troubling you, mo chridhe?' and his dark eyes regarded her searchingly.

'That our country has lost its ancient freedom! I walk down the street and see red coated militia marching as though they owned the place. On memory's page I still smell the smoke of the burnings, hear the cries of those lying in their blood, see phantoms of starving women and children dead of hunger and despair. I know you have helped me to believe in God again, restored my faith in the Christ who came to teach all men how to live and behave to each other. Why then does He allow our land to suffer so? Will it never change—tell me, Sorley Mor?'

'The truth is I fear that it may not change in our lifetime—or even that of our children. But I truly believe in time to come our people may arise up and not by the force of arms, but by common consent and in all legal requirement demand that freedom back—by an act of parliament!'

'But we no longer have our own parliament, husband,' she cried, 'So how can this be?' Her grey gaze burned with the question.

He stared at her broodingly half closing his eyes as though he glimpsed certain events to come through curtain of time. And what he saw brought warm smile to his lips.

'It will not be now—presently subject to Westminster. But in the fullness of time we will have our own parliament once more!' His dark blue eyes held the mystic light of the seer as his lips formed the words he spoke.

'Kieran, dear wife—I foresee a time when by the stroke of a pen Scotland will again become an Independent country! It will indeed be the end of an old song and start of a new!' And he raised his eyes exultantly.

He held her in his arms, and as she felt the beat of his heart Kieran accepted his words. Knew that like all their people she must endeavour to do her best in sure knowledge that his prophecy would come true!

Scotland this dear land they loved, like unto the proud, noble bird whose flight Kieran sorely missed, become once more truly free! Scotland's folk, proud and independent and at peace with their neighbours, heads held high—high! Just as forevermore—High Soars the Eagle!

Printed in Great Britain
by Amazon

23010456R00225